ANDRÉE DE TAVERNEY:

OR, THE

DOWNFALL OF FRENCH MONARCHY.

ANDRÉE DE TAVERNEY:

OR, THE

DOWNFALL OF FRENCH MONARCHY.

BEING THE FINAL CONCLUSION OF

"THE MEMOIRS OF A PHYSICIAN," "THE QUEEN'S NECKLACE," "SIX YEARS LATER," AND "COUNTESS OF CHARNY."

BY ALEXANDER DUMAS.

AUTHOR OF "THE COUNT OF MONTE CRISTO," "THREE GUARDSMEN," "TWENTY YEARS AFTER," "BRAGELONNE," "THE IRON MASK," "LOUISE LA VALLIERE," ETC., ETC.

TRANSLATED FROM THE ORIGINAL FRENCH EXPRESSLY FOR THIS EDITION,

BY HENRY L. WILLIAMS, ESQ.

VOLUME ONE.

Translator's Notice of the Work.

"Andrée de Taverney" is the fit conclusion of the great series to which it belongs. Not a few other writers have taken incidents from the reign of the Sixteenth Louis, and wrought books upon them, but this work of Alexander Dumas alone has comprised the whole drama of the downfall of French monarchy, whose last scene beheld the fogs of passion roll away from before it to reveal the unknown form of the guillotine!

All is wonder how the throne of the beautiful Marie Antoinette could ever have crumbled, till one here sees the motive thoughts of the revolutionists When some of them acted through love of liberty, many, like Billot, by a thirst of revenge for injury, a still greater number from hate, poverty and evil instincts—how could royalists—though every one a Charny or an Andrée de Taverney—hope to maintain it?

We form the acquaintance of how many in this book? The King, the Queen; Oliver de Charny, dying beneath the axes and pikes of the sans-culottes, gasping: "For the Queen I'm dying, as fell my brothers!" Then, Andrée, his wife, who would not save her life with silence, when that silence might cast doubt on her opinions; the repentant Gilbert; Catherine Billot, "widow without having been wife," the good, simple Pitou, whom all must like, and Billot, the inflexible patriot. Then, the country scenes form that repose for the mind, which may be over-excited by the bloody scenes of city riots One turns gladly from the storming of the Tuileries, by the mob, to the quiet, natural pictures of provincial life; from the gory, streaming locks of heads borne amid yells on pikes, to the seas of verdure of the forest, where a sweet-smelling breeze murmurs sleepily; from the spirited speeches from the rostrum—through which winds Robespierre's "hush!" like a serpent's hiss—to the revolution in miniature at Villers Cotterets. Andrée de Taverney will prove to be Dumas' greatest book, and must have a sale unparalleled in the annals of literature.

Fredonia Books
Amsterdam, The Netherlands

Andrée de Taverney:
The Downfall of French Monarchy

by
Alexander Dumas

ISBN: 1-4101-0060-X

Reprinted from the 1862 edition

Fredonia Books
Amsterdam, The Netherlands
http://www.fredoniabooks.com

In order to make original editions of historical works available to scholars at an economical price, this facsimile of the original edition of 1862 is reproduced from the best available copy and has been digitally enhanced to improve legibility, but the text remains unaltered to retain historical authenticity.

CONTENTS

CONTENTS.

ANDRÉE DE TAVERNEY.

BY ALEXANDRE DUMAS.

AUTHOR OF "MONTE CRISTO," "THE THREE GUARDSMEN," "BRAGELONNE," "THE COUNTESS DE CHARNY," "MOHICANS OF PARIS," &c.

TRANSLATED FROM THE FRENCH,

BY HENRY L. WILLIAMS, Jr.

CHAPTER I.

THE BATTLE FIELD.

WE have, in a previous work (The Countess de Charny) endeavored to relate the terrible events which transpired on the Champ de Mars on the afternoon of the seventeenth of July, seventeen hundred and ninety-one; let us now try to give an idea of the spectacle which the stage presents—after having set before the eyes of our readers the tableau of the drama just enacted, the two leading performers in which were Bailly and La Fayette.

This spectacle was the sight which struck a young man wearing the uniform of an officer in the National Guard, who, coming out through the Rue Saint Honore, had crossed the Pont Louis Quinzieme, and skirted the Champ de Mars by the Rue de Grenelle.

This view—which was illumined by a moon at two-thirds of its waxing period, rolling between heavy black clouds in which it was every now and anon lost—was lugubrious to look upon!

The Champ de Mars had the aspect of a field of battle strewn with the dead and dying, among whom roved, like shadows, the men charged to throw the dead bodies into the Seine River, and carry the wounded to the Military Hospital of Gros Caillou.

The young officer, whom we follow from the Rue Saint Honore, stopped for an instant at the border of the Champ de Mars, and, clasping his hands with a gesture of unaffected terror, muttered:

"Lord Jesus! has the affair been still worse than they have told me?"

Then, after having watched for several minutes the strange work in operation, approaching two men who were carrying a corpse towards the Seine, he inquired of them:

"Citizens, will you be so kind as to inform me what you are going to do with this man?"

"Follow us," responded the couple, "and you will see."

The young officer walked on after them.

On reaching the wooden bridge, the two men swung the body, counting:

"One, two, three, and away!" and, at the third word, hurled their burden into the Seine.

The young man uttered an exclamation of terror.

"Why, what *are* you doing, citizens?" demanded he.

"You can see well enough, officer," answered the pair; "we are clearing the ground."

"Have you orders to act thus?"

"So it seems."

"From whom?"

"The municipality."

"Oh!" ejaculated the young man, stupefied.

(21)

After a moment's silence, and after having returned with them upon the Champ de Mars, he asked :

"And have you already thrown many bodies into the river ?"

" Five or six," replied one of the two men.

"I beg your pardon, citizens," resumed the young man, " but I have a great interest in the question I am about to put to you : among those five or six bodies, have you remarked one, a man of from forty-six to eight-and-forty years of age ; short and thickset, vigorous, half countryman, half townsman ?"

" The fact is," returned one of the two men, " we have only one remark to make : which is, whether the persons here lying are dead or alive ; if dead, we throw them into the river ; if they are not dead, we carry them to the Hospital of Gros Caillou."

"Ah," said the young man, "one of my best friends has failed to return home, and, as they told me he was here, that he had been seen here part of the day, I greatly fear he may be among the dead or the wounded."

" In truth," said one of the two bearers, shaking a body while the other flooded it with light from his lantern, " if he is here, it is very likely he is here still ; if he has not gone home, it is extremely probable he will not go home at all."

Redoubling the shake he had given to the form stretched out at his feet, the man employed by the municipality shouted :

" Ha ! are you dead or alive ? If you are not dead, make haste and answer."

"Oh, this fellow is really gone !" said the second ; " he has received a bullet fair in the middle of the chest."

" Then to the river !" said the first.

With that, the two raised the corpse and took up again the road to the wooden bridge.

" Citizens," said the officer, "you have no need of your lantern to throw that into the water ; be so obliging as to lend me it for an instant ; while you are going your way, I will look for my friend."

The corpse-bearers consented to the request, and the light was transferred into the hands of the young officer, who commenced his search with a carefulness and an expression of his countenance betokening that he had given to the dead or wounded person he sought for a title which came not only from his lips, but from his heart, as well.

Ten or a dozen men, furnished like him with lanterns, were, like him, busied in the funereal task.

From time to time, amidst the stillness—for the terrible solemnity of the scene seemed, by the aspect of the dead, to smother the voice of the living—from time to time, amid the silence, a name uttered in a high voice traversed the space.

At times a wail, a groan, a scream, responded to the call ; but much oftener it obtained in reply merely a lugubrious silence !

The young officer, after having hesitated, as though his tongue was chained up by a certain terror, followed the example that was shown him, and three times shouted :

" Monsieur Billot ! Monsieur Billot ! Monsieur Billot !"

But not a sound made answer to him.

" Oh, I am quite sure he is dead, " muttered he, wiping away with his sleeve the tears streaming from his eyes. " Poor Monsieur Billot !"

At this juncture, a pair of men passed near him, carrying a body towards the Seine.

" Halloa !" exclaimed the one who was supporting the breast and was, consequently, the nearer to the head, " I fancy our corpse has just given a sigh !"

" Pshaw !" said the other laughing, " if we had to listen to all these fellows, we wouldn't have any dead men at all."

" Citizens," broke in the young officer, " for mercy's sake, let me see the man you are carrying !"

" Oh, willingly, officer," rejoined both.

So saying, they placed the body in a sitting posture to give the officer more facility in illumining the face.

The young man held the lantern up close, and uttered a cry.

In spite of the frightful wound which disfigured him, he believed he recognized the individual he was seeking.

Only, was he dead or was he alive?

This sufferer, who had already traveled half the road to his wet grave, had his head laid open by a sabre cut: the wound, as we have before mentioned, was frightful! it had glanced off all the hairy covering of the left parietal bone, the flap hanging down on the cheek, and leaving uncovered the skull bone; the temporal artery had been cut; so that the whole body of the dead or living man was inundated with blood.

On the side of the gash, the wounded man was past recognition.

The young man tremblingly turned the lantern to survey the other side.

"Oh! citizens!" cried he, "it is he! it is he I am looking for—it is Monsieur Billot!"

"The deuce it is!" said one of the two men. "Well, your Monsieur Billot is a little damaged!"

"Did you not say he had uttered a sigh?"

"I think I heard it, at any rate."

"Then do me the favor——"

The officer produced a crown-piece from his pocket.

"What?" asked the corpse-carrier, full of willingness at sight of the piece of money.

"Do me the favor of running to the river, and bringing some water in your hat."

"Willingly."

The man hurried to the bank of the Seine.

The young man took his place, and sustained the wounded man.

At the end of about five minutes, the messenger returned.

"Dash the water on his face," said the young man.

The other obeyed; he dipped his hand into his hat and, shaking it like a holy-water sprinkler, bedewed the wounded man's face.

"He stirred!" exclaimed the young man, who held the moribund in his arms; "he is not dead. Oh, dear Monsieur Billot, how fortunate that I should have arrived as I did!"

"Yes, indeed, it is lucky!" said the two men; "twenty steps further, and your friend would have come to himself in the fishermen's nets at Saint Cloud."

"Throw more water on him."

The body-bearer renewed the operation.

The wounded man shivered and gave vent to a sigh.

"Come, come," said the second carrier, "decidedly he is not dead."

"Well, what shall we do?" inquired the first.

"Help me to carry him to the Rue Saint Honore, to Doctor Gilbert's house, and you shall have ample recompense," said the young man.

"We cannot."

"Why not?"

"We are ordered to throw the dead into the Seine and carry the wounded to the Hospital of Gros Caillou. Since this one shows he is not dead, and as, consequently, we cannot throw him into the Seine, we must carry him off to the hospital."

"Well, let us carry him to the hospital," said the young man, "and as soon as possible."

He looked around him.

"Where is the hospital?"

"Pretty near three hundred paces, by the Ecole Militaire."

"So, that's where it is?"

"Yes."

"We have the whole Champ de Mars to cross?"

"We have to pass over its whole length."

"Good heavens! have you no litter?"

"Why, the truth to say, one can be found," rejoined the second bearer; "it's just like the water. With a crown——"

"That is but just," said the young man; "you receive nothing. There, there's another crown; find a litter of some sort."

Ten minutes afterwards, a handbarrow was brought.

The wounded man was placed on a mattress; the two men took up the burden, and the funereal cortege moved on towards the Hospital of Gros Caillou, escorted by the young man, who, lantern in hand, walked by the wounded man's head.

A fearful thing was that nocturnal march over ground reddened with blood, among stiffened, unmoving corpses that they stumbled over at every step, or wounded who half rose to fall back again gasping for aid.

At the end of a quarter of an hour, they stepped across the threshold of the Hospital of Gros Caillou.

CHAPTER II.

THE HOSPITAL OF GROS CAILLOU.

AT this period, hospitals, and especially military ones, were very far from being organized as they are at the present day.

Hence, one should not be astonished at the confusion which reigned over the Hospital of Gros Caillou, and at the immense lack of order which opposed the accomplishment of the surgeons' desires.

The first thing which they stood in need of was beds. They had therefore levied on the mattresses of the dwellers in the neighboring streets.

These mattresses were spread out on the floor, and some even were laid in the courtyard; on each of them was a wounded man, appealing for relief; but surgeons were deficient as well as beds, and were more difficult to obtain.

The officer (in whom those of our readers who formerly made his acquaintance must certainly have recognized our old friend Ange Pitou) by disbursing a couple of crowns more, managed to have the mattress on the handbarrow left; so that Billot was quite gently deposited in the yard of the hospital.

Pitou, wishing at least to take up that position which had some advantage, had had his friend set down as near as possible to the door, in order to stop, as he passed, the first surgeon who might come out or go in.

He was strongly desirous to run into the halls and bring one, cost what it might; but he did not dare quit the patient; he dreaded that, under the pretext that his friend was dead—they might easily deceive themselves on that point without malice—some one would walk off with the mattress, after rolling the supposed lifeless corpse on the pavement of the courtyard.

Pitou had stayed where he was stationed for all of an hour, calling loudly to two or three chirurgeons whom he had seen going by, without any one replying to his calls, when he caught sight of a man clothed in black, lighted by two sick nurses, who were visiting one after another all those couches of agony.

The closer the man in black advanced in Pitou's direction, the more the latter believed he recognized him; ere long all his doubts ceased, and Pitou, venturing to move a few steps from his friend to so much the nearer approach the surgeon, shouted with all the power of his lungs:

"Ho! this way, Monsieur Gilbert—this way!"

The surgeon, who was, indeed, Gilbert, ran to him on hearing his voice.

"Ah, is it you, Pitou?" said he.

"Yes, M. Gilbert."

"Have you seen Billot?"

"Why, monsieur, he is here," answered Pitou, disclosing the still motionless form.

"Is he dead?" asked the doctor.

"Alas, dear Monsieur Gilbert, I trust not; but I will not hide from you he is on the high road to the grave."

Gilbert stepped up to the mattress, and the two nurses who followed him lit up the face of the wounded man.

"It is on the head, Monsieur Gilbert," said Pitou, "on the head! Poor dear Monsieur Billot, his skull is cloven to the jawbone."

Gilbert examined the wound attentively.

"The fact is, the wound is serious," muttered he.

Then, turning to his two attendants, he added:

"I must have a private room for this man, who is one of my friends."

The two nurses consulted.

"There is no room vacant," returned they, "but there is the laundry."

"It will suit first-rate," said Gilbert; "let us carry him into the laundry."

They took up the wounded man as tenderly as could be; but, whatever the caution they used, there escaped from him a groan.

"Ah!" said Gilbert, "never has exclamation of joy given me pleasure equal to that sound of pain. He is living—that is the principal thing."

Billot was transported to the laundry, and there transferred to a bed of one of the hospital servants; whereupon, Gilbert proceeded instantly to examine him.

The temporal artery had been severed, and from thence had come the immense loss of blood; but this waste of the life fluid had brought on syncope, and the swoon, by checking the throbbing of the heart, had stopped the hamorrhage.

Nature had immediately curdled the blood, of which a clot had closed the artery.

Gilbert, with admirable skill, first tied up the artery by means of a silken thread; then he washed the flesh and re-applied the skin to the skull. The freshness of the water, or it might as well have been some acute pains caused during the washing, made Billot open his eyes and utter several unintelligible words.

"There is concussion of the brain," muttered Gilbert.

"But," said Pitou, "inasmuch as he is not dead, will you not save him, Monsieur Gilbert?"

The latter smiled sadly.

"I will try," answered he; "but you have seen already, my dear Pitou, that nature is a much more skilful surgeon than any of us."

Thereupon, Gilbert finished the operation. The hair being cut off as much as was possible, he brought the two edges of the cut together, bound them there by strips of diachylon plaster, and ordered heed to be taken that the wounded man should be placed almost in a sitting posture, his back—not his head—leaning against the pillow.

It was only then—all this having been accomplished—that he asked Pitou how, being in the city, he had chanced upon there arriving just in the juncture to help Billot.

The reasons were very simple: since the disappearance of Catherine Billot, and the departure of her husband, Farmer Billot, Mother Billot (whom we have never held up to our readers as of very vigorous mind) had fallen into a sort of idiocy which had been continually augmenting. She lived, but in a quite mechanical manner, and, every day, some new spring in that poor human machine either stretched or snapped; little by little, her words had been less frequently spoken; then she had concluded by not speaking at all, and even grew bedridden, and Doctor Raynal had declared that there was only one thing in the world that could draw Mother Billot from that mortal torpor: to wit, the sight of her daughter.

Pitou had instantly offered himself to go to Paris, or better to say had set out for Paris without offering himself.

Thanks to the long legs of the captain of the National Guard of Haramont, the eighteen leagues which separated the country of Demoustier from the capital were to him merely a pleasant trip.

Truth to say, Pitou had started at four o'clock in the morning and, between half past seven and eight o'clock in the evening, was at Paris.

Pitou seemed predestined to come to Paris to see great events.

The first time, he had come to witness the Taking of the Bastile, and play a part in it; the second time, to see the Confederation of 1790; the third time, he arrived on the day of the Massacre at the Champ de Mars.

So he had found Paris all in animation: which was, however, just as he was in the habit of seeing Paris.

From the first groups which he came across, he learnt what had taken place on the Champ de Mars.

Bailly and La Fayette had caused the people to be fired on; hence the people were cursing with all the breath of their lungs Bailly and La Fayette.

Pitou had left them being made gods and worshipped! He found them overturned from their altars, and cursed : he could make absolutely nothing out of it.

What he only could understand was that there had been, at the Champ de Mars, a struggle, a massacre, slaughter, all about a patriotic petition, and that Gilbert and Billot had been in all likelihood there.

Though Pitou had, as is vulgarly said, his eighteen leagues on his stomach, he doubled his pace, and went to Rue Saint Honore, to Doctor Gilbert's apartments.

The doctor had returned home, but nothing had been seen of Billot.

"The Champ de Mars, however," said the servant who gave Pitou this information, " is covered with dead and wounded : likely enough Billot was among one or the other."

The Champ de Mars strewn with dead and wounded ! this intelligence no less astonished Pitou than had that about Bailly and La Fayette, those idols of the people, firing on the populace.

The Champ de Mars strewn with the dead and wounded ! Pitou could not imagine it. That Champ de Mars which he had aided, as one of the ten thousand, to level, which his memory recalled so full of illuminations, joyful songs and gay amusement ! strewn with the dead and dying ! because people had wished to celebrate, as on the preceding year, the anniversary of the Taking of the Bastile and of the Confederation !

Impossible !

How, in one twelve-month, could there have been a motive of joy and triumph converted into a cause of rebellion and massacre ?

What wild spirit had during this year, passed into the heads of the Parisians ?

We have not omitted to state that the court, during this year,—thanks to Mirabeau's influence and to the creation of the Club of the Feuillants, and to the support of Bailly and La Fayette, and, lastly, to the reaction which took place following the Return from Varennes—the court, we say, had recovered its lost power : which power was manifested by massacre and mourning.

The seventeenth of July avenged the fifth and sixth of October.

So, as Gilbert had said, royalty and the people were neck and tie—the puzzle was to say which would win in the long run.

We have seen how, preoccupied by all these ideas, none of which however, had the influence of slackening his pace— our friend Ange Pitou, still wearing his uniform of captain of the National Guard of Haramont, had arrived at the Champ de Mars along the Pont Louis Quinzieme and the Rue de Grenelle, just in season to prevent Billot from being flung as dead into the River Seine.

On the other hand it will remembered how Gilbert, being with King Louis XVI., had received a note with no signature, but which he had recognized to be in Cagliostro's handwriting, the following paragraph in which had struck him :

"Leave those two condemned persons still called in derision the King and Queen, and hasten, without losing an instant, to the Hospital of Gros Caillou, where you will find one, though dying, less hopelessly lost than they ; forasmuch as you can save this dying one, while they—besides being beyond your power to save—will drag you down with them in their fall."

Instantly, as we have mentioned (having learnt from Madame Campan that the Queen, who on leaving him had begged him to wait for her return, was still detained and now gave him leave to depart) Gilbert had quitted the Tuileries and, taking nearly the same road as used by Pitou, had skirted the Champ de Mars, had entered the Hospital of Gros Caillou, and had already, lighted on his way by two sick nurses, visited—from bed to bed, from mattress to mattress—the halls, corridors, vestibules, and even the courtyard, when a voice had summoned him to the bedside of a dying man.

The voice, we know, was Pitou's ; the dying man was Billot.

We have stated in what a condition Gilbert had found the worthy farmer, and the chances which his situation presented, chances both good and bad, but, among which the latter would certainly have carried the day over the former, if the wounded man had fallen into the hands of a man less skilful than Doctor Gilbert.

CHAPTER III.

CATHERINE.

Out of the two persons whom Doctor Raynal had believed it to be his duty to forewarn of Madame Billot's state, one, as we have seen, was kept to his bed, in a similar condition bordering on death: this was her husband; the other person alone could come, therefore, to be with the dying woman in her last moments: this was her daughter.

It was necessary that Catherine Billot should learn the state in which was her mother, and even her father; but where was Catherine ?

The only possible way of finding this out was to address the Count de Charny.

Pitou had been so pleasantly, so gratefully received by the Countess Andrée on that day when, on account of Gilbert he had restored her son to her, that he did not hesitate to offer to go and ask for Catherine's address at the mansion in the Rue Coq Heron, however late indeed was the hour of the night.

In fact, the half after eleven had sounded from the clock of the Ecole Militaire when, the bandaging being completed, Gilbert and Pitou were free to leave Billot's bed.

Gilbert left the wounded man to the care of the nurses : there was nothing more to be done, than let nature work out the cure.

Besides, he meant to return the following day.

Pitou and Gilbert jumped into the doctor's carriage, which was waiting at the hospital doors : the doctor ordered the driver to stop at the Rue Coq Heron.

The houses were all shut up and without lights in that district.

After having pulled the bell for a quarter of an hour, Pitou, who was going to give up the bell knob for the knocker, heard at last grating on its hinges—not the street door—but the door of the porter's lodge, and a voice roughly and ill humoredly challenged with a tone of annoyance which there were no attempts made to disguise:

" Who is there ?"

" I," answered Pitou.

" Who are you ?"

" Oh, I forgot——Ange Pitou, captain in the National Guard."

" Ange Pitou ? I never heard the name."

" Captain in the National Guard."

" Captain," repeated the porter, " captain ?"

" Captain," reiterated Pitou, laying a stress on the title, the influence of which he was aware of.

In fact the porter was led to believe, this being the moment when the National Guard at least balanced the former preponderancy of the army, that he had to do with some aid-de-camp of La Fayette.

In consequence, in a much smoother tone, but without opening the door, which, however, he came a little nearer to, the porter asked :

" Well, Monsieur le Capitaine, what do you require ?"

" I wish to speak with his lordship the Count de Charny."

" He is not here."

" With my lady the countess, then."

" She is not here, either."

" Where are they ?"

" They went away this morning."

" Where to ?"

" For their estate of Boursonnes."

" The deuce they did !" said Pitou speaking to himself; " it must have been they whom I encountered at Dammartin ; they were doubtless in that post-carriage. Oh, if I had known it !"

But Pitou had not known it; and he accordingly had let the count and countess pass on.

" My friend," said the doctor's voice intervening at this point in the conversation, " can you, in the absence of your master, give us some information?"

"I beg your pardon, sir," said the porter who, from his aristocratic habit, had recognized a superior's voice in that which had just spoken with so much gentleness and politeness.

And, opening the door, the speaker came, with his cotton nightcap in his hand, to take his orders, as they say in domestic parlance, at the door of the doctor's carriage.

"What information does the gentleman desire?" inquired the porter.

"Do you know, my friend, a girl in whom my lord the count and my lady the countess must have shown some interest?"

"Mademoiselle Catharine?" counterqueried the porter.

"Precisely," answered Gilbert.

"Yes, sir. His lordship the count and my lady the countess have been twice to see her, and they often sent me to inquire if she stood in need of anything; but, poor girl! though I do not believe her rich, neither her nor her dear child, she always answered that she had everything she wanted."

On the word "Her dear child," Pitou could not prevent heaving a deep sigh.

"Well, my friend," said Gilbert, "poor Catharine's father has been wounded to-day on the Champ de Mars, and her mother, Madame Billot, is dying at Villers Cotterets: we wish to impart this sad news to her. Will you be so kind as to give us her address?"

"Oh! poor girl, heaven assist you! she is unfortunate enough as it is! she lives in Ville d'Avray, sir, on the high road—I cannot tell you the number, but it is in front of a fountain."

"That will do," said Pitou; "I will find it."

"Thank you, my friend," said Gilbert, slipping a six livre crown piece into the porter's hand.

"I have done nothing to earn this, sir," returned the latter, "Christians, heaven knows, should help one another."

And, making his reverence to the doctor, he went back into the house.

"Well?" inquired Gilbert.

"Well," responded Pitou, "I start for Ville d'Avray."

Pitou was all ready.

"Do you know the way?" asked the doctor.

"No; but you will point it out to me."

"You have a heart of gold and muscles of steel!" said Gilbert laughing. "But you must rest: you can go to-morrow morning."

"Still, if time presses——"

"On neither side is there urgency," said the doctor: "Billot's state is a serious one; but, unless there is some unforeseen accident, it is not mortal. As for Mother Billot, she may still live ten or twelve days."

"Oh, Monsieur le Docteur, when she was put to bed day before yesterday, she could not speak, nor move; her eyes alone seemed to be still living."

"No matter, I know what I say, Pitou, and answer for her living, as I have told you, ten or twelve days yet."

"Of course, Monsieur Gilbert, you know better than I about it."

"So it is just as well to let poor Catharine have another night of ignorance and repose: one night of sleep the more for the unfortunate is important, Pitou."

Pitou yielded to the latter reasoning.

"Well, then," inquired he, "where shall we go, Monsieur Gilbert?"

"To my house, of course. You will find your own room there."

"It will much please me to see it again," said Pitou smiling.

"And, to-morrow," continued Doctor Gilbert, "at six o'clock in the morning, the horses shall be put to the carriage."

"What do we want of the horses to the carriage?" asked Pitou, who absolutely looked upon horses as an article of luxury.

"Why, to take us to Ville d'Avray."

"Is it fifty leagues from here to Ville d'Avray?" went on Pitou.

"No, it is only two or three," rejoined Gilbert, before whose eyes passed, as a vision of his youth, the walks he had taken with his master Jean Jacques Rousseau in the woods of Louveciennes, Meudon, and Ville d'Avray.

"Why, then," said Pitou, "it is an

hour's tramp—three leagues, Monsieur Gilbert; I could get over that space before a moderate eater could finish an egg!"

"But, Catharine," said Gilbert, "do you fancy she has the same power to travel the three leagues from Ville d'Avray to Paris, and the eighteen leagues from Paris to Villers Cotterets?"

"True! you're right," exclaimed Pitou, "excuse me, Monsieur Gilbert; I am a goose. By the bye, how does Sebastian get along?"

"My son? wonderfully! you can see him to-morrow."

"Is he still at Abbe Berardier's?"

"Still."

"Ah, I would like to see him."

"And he will be glad to see you, too, Pitou; for, as I do, he loves you with all his heart."

And, as this assurance was given, the doctor and Ange Pitou stopped before the door of the former's house in the Rue Saint Honore.

Pitou slept as he walked, ate and fought, that is to say, earnestly: only, thanks to the habit contracted in the country of rising with the lark, he was up at five o'clock.

At six, the carriage was ready.

At seven, he was knocking at Catharine's door.

It was agreed, between him and Doctor Gilbert, that, at eight o'clock, Pitou and the daughter should be at Billot's bedside.

Catharine came to open the door, and uttered a scream when she perceived Pitou.

"Ah," exclaimed she, "my mother is dead!"

She turned pale, and leaned against the wall.

"Not so," said Pitou; "only, if you want to see her before she does die, you will have to hurry, Mademoiselle Catherine."

This interchange of words, which in a few syllables spoke so many things, did away with all beating about the bush and set, at the very first, Catherine face to face with her misfortune.

"And then," continued Pitou, "there is still another sad thing."

"What?" demanded Catherine in that curt and almost indifferent tone of a creature who, having been made to drain her fill of human griefs, no longer has any fear of her sorrow augmenting.

"Monsieur Billot was dangerously wounded yesterday on the Champ de Mars."

"Ah!" ejaculated Catherine.

Evidently, the girl was much less affected by this intelligence than by the first.

"Here is what I said to myself," resumed Pitou, "and it is also Doctor Gilbert's way of thinking:—Mademoiselle Catherine will make a visit as she passes, to Monsieur Billot, who has been carried to the Hospital of Gros Caillou, and, from thence, she will take the diligence to Villers Cotterets."

"But you, Monsieur Pitou?" inquired Catherine.

"I thought," Pitou then made answer, "that inasmuch as you are going to smoothe Madame Billot's road to death, it was my duty to stay here to try to help Monsieur Billot back to life. I will remain by him who has no one to care for him, do you see, Mademoiselle Catherine?"

Pitou delivered the above words with his angelic simplicity, without being aware that he was also telling in a few words the entire story of his devotion.

Catherine held out her hand to him.

"You have a good heart, Pitou!" said she, "come and see my poor little Isidore." She walked on before, for the short scene we have just related had taken place in the alley of the house, at the street gate. She was handsomer than ever, was poor Catherine! in mourning though she was dressed; which made Pitou utter a second sigh.

Catherine preceded the young man into a small room overlooking a garden: in this chamber, which, with a kitchen and dressing-room, composed all of Catherine's establishment, there was a bed and a cradle.

The mother's bed, the child's cradle.

The infant was sleeping.

Catherine pulled aside a gauze curtain, and stepped out of Pitou's way to let his eyes look into the cradle.

"Oh, the lovely little angel!" said Pitou clasping his hands.

And, as if he were really before an angel, he knelt down and kissed the babe's hand.

Pitou was speedily repaid for what he did : he felt floating over his face Catherine's tresses, and lips touching his forehead.

She returned the kiss given to her son.

"Thank you, good Pitou," said she. "Since the last kiss it had received from its father, no one but myself has caressed the poor little one."

"Oh, Mademoiselle Catherine !" murmured Pitou, bewildered by the girl's kiss, as if by an electrical shock.

Yet this kiss was simply composed of all that there was holy and grateful in a mother's love.

CHAPTER IV.

DAUGHTER AND FATHER.

TEN minutes afterwards, Catherine, Pitou and little Isidore were rolling away in Doctor Gilbert's carriage over the road to Paris.

The vehicle stopped before the Hospital of Gros Caillou.

Catherine alighted, took her child in her arms and followed Pitou.

On reaching the door of the laundry, she stopped.

"You told me that we would find Doctor Gilbert at my father's bed?"

"Yes."

Pitou half opened the door.

"And he is there indeed," said he.

"See if I may enter without fear of causing him too much excitement."

Pitou went into the chamber, questioned the doctor, and almost instantly returned to Catherine.

"The concussion caused by the blow is such that he is not yet able to recognize any one, so Monsieur Gilbert says."

Catherine was about to enter with little Isidore in her arms.

"Give me your child, Mademoiselle Catherine." said Pitou.

Catherine had a moment's hesitation.

"Oh, give it me," repeated Pitou, "it is the same as if you had not left it."

"You are right," said Catherine.

And, as she would have done towards a brother—with more confidence, it may be—she handed her child to Ange Pitou, and advanced with steady step into the room, walking straight to her father's bed.

As we have before mentioned, Doctor Gilbert was at the wounded man's bedside.

Very little change had taken place in his patient's state ; he was placed, as he had been the evening previous, his back propped by the pillows, and the doctor was moistening, by the aid of a sponge dampened in water, and the pressure of his hand, the bandages which made fast and kept down the dressing of the wound. In spite of the commencement of a very characteristic inflammatory fever, Billot's face—seeing the quantity of blood he had lost—was of deathly pallor ; the swelling had spread to the eye and part of the left cheek.

On the first impression of coolness, he had stammered several disconnected words, and opened his eyes : but that overpowering tendency towards sleep which physicians term *coma* had again chained up his tongue, and closed his eyes.

Catherine, on reaching the bed, there fell upon her knees, and, raising her hands heavenward, said :

"O my God ! Thou art my witness that I pray of Thee from the very depths of my heart, for the life of my father !"

This was all that could be asked by this daughter for the parent who had tried to kill her lover.

On her voice, however, a tremor agitated the wounded man's frame ; his breathing grew more hurried : he opened his eyes once more and his gaze, after having wandered for an instant around him as if to discover whence came the voice, was riveted on Catherine. His hand made a movement, as though to wave away the girl, whom the sufferer took, no doubt, for a vision in his fever.

The girl's look met her father's, and Gilbert saw, with a sort of terror, crossing one another two flames that much more resembled as many flashes of hate than beams of love.

After which, the girl rose and, with the same step wherewith she had entered, went to return to Pitou.

Pitou was down on his hands and knees, playing with the child.

Catherine caught up her child with a violence closer allied to the love of a lioness than that of a woman, and pressed him against her breast, exclaiming : " My child ! oh, my child !"

There was in that outburst all the anguish of the mother, all the complaints of the widow, all the sorrows of the woman.

Pitou wished to accompany Catherine to the office of the diligence, which was to start at ten o'clock in the morning. But she refused.

" No," said she, " as you have said, your place is beside him who is alone ; remain, Pitou."

And with her hand, she pushed Pitou into the chamber.

Pitou only knew to obey when Catherine commanded.

While the young man approached Billot's bed, the latter, at the sound made by the rather heavy tread of the captain of the National Guard, opened his eyes, and a soothed, pleased expression succeeded on his face the hateful imprint which had swept over it, like a cloud of the tempest, on the sight of his daughter—Catherine descended the stairs and, with her child in her arms, gained the Hotel of the Plat d'Etain (Pewter Plate), in the Rue Saint Denis, from which house started the stage-coach for Villers Cotterets.

The horses were ready harnessed, the postillion was in his saddle ; there was one place inside : Catherine had it booked for her.

Eight hours afterwards, the vehicle stopped in the Rue des Soissons.

At six o'clock in the afternoon, that is to say, it was yet quite light.

A maid and coming, Isidore still living, to see her mother in health, Catherine would have had the diligence stopped at the end of the Rue de Largny, would have gone around the town, and might have arrived at Pisseleu without being seen, for she would have been ashamed.

A widow and a mother, she never even thought of the broad country jokes ; she got down from the coach without forwardness, but without fear ; her mourning and her infant seemed to her angels—one a gloomy angel, the other a smiling one—which would repel from her insult and scorn.

Firstly, Catharine was hardly to be recognised ; she was so changed and pale, that she no longer appeared to be the same woman ; then what still better led looks astray from her true identity, was that air of distinction which she had won from her connection with the elegant young de Charny.

However, one person did recognise her, and at some distance off.

This was Pitou's Aunt Angelica.

Aunt Angelica was at the door of the town-hall, where she was conversing with two or three gossips about the oath the priests were required to take, declaring that she had heard the Abbé Fortier say that he would not take an oath for the Jacobins and the Revolution, and that he would rather suffer martyrdom than bend his neck beneath the revolutionary oath.

" Oh !" exclaimed she, all of a sudden, breaking off in the climax of her discourse, " Heavenly Father ! there's Billot's girl and her ch ld getting out of the coach !"

" Catharine ? Catharine ?" repeated several voices.

" Why, yes ; stay a bit, yonder she is running down the lane."

Aunt Angelica was in error.

Catharine was not running away. She was in haste to reach her mother, and therefore walked briskly. She took the lane, because it was the shortest way.

Many children, on Aunt Angelica's outcry of " There's Billot's girl !" and the exclamation of her neighbors of " Catharine !" many children, we repeat, began running after the girl and, having caught up to her, they said :

" Ah ! oh ! why, yes, it is true ; it is mademoiselle——"

"Yes, my children, it is I," returned Catharine softly.

As she was very much beloved by the children especially, for to them she had always something to give, a kiss or a pat on the head if nothing better, the little things wished her :

"Good day, Mademoiselle Catharine !"

"Good day, my little dears," responded Catharine. "Is my mother still alive ?"

"Oh, yes, mademoiselle."

One boy added :

" Doctor Raynal says she has a week or ten days yet before her."

"Thank you, my children," said Catharine.

She continued on her way, after having distributed some pieces of money among them.

The children returned.

"Well ?" inquired the gossips.

"Well, it is her," answered the children, "and if you won't believe us, we tell you she asked us news of her mother, and here's some money she gave us."

With that, the merry band displayed the coin they had received from Catharine.

"It appears that what she has sold fetches a good price in Paris," sneered Aunt Angelica, "for her to be able to give silver to the brats running after her."

Aunt Angelica had never liked Catharine Billot.

Catharine Billot was young and beautiful—Aunt Angelica was old and homely ; Catharine Billot was tall and graceful—Aunt Angelica was short and limped.

Moreover, it was in Billot's house that Ange Pitou, driven out of hers by Aunt Angelica, had found shelter.

Then, lastly, it was Billot, who, on the day of the Declaration of the Rights of Man, had gone to force the Abbe Fortier to say mass on the altar of the Country.

All sufficient reasons, joined above all to the natural acerbity of her character, for Aunt Angelica hated the Billots in general and Catharine in particular.

And, when Aunt Angelica hated, she hated earnestly, like a devotee.

She hastened, therefore, to the Abbe Fortier's house, and announced to Mademoiselle Adelaide, the niece of the abbe, the news.

The Abbe Fortier was supping on a carp caught in the ponds of Wallue, flanked by a plate of buttered eggs and a dish of spinach.

It was a fast day.

The Abbe Fortier had taken upon himself the rigid and ascetic bearing of a man who expects at any moment martyrdom.

"What is that ?" inquired he as he heard the two women chattering away in the corridor ; "do they come to seek me to deny the name of God ?"

"No! not yet, my dear uncle," replied Mademoiselle Adelaide ; "no, it is only Aunt Angelica (everybody, after Pitou, gave his name to the old maid), it is only Aunt Angelica come to bring me some fresh scandal."

"We live in times when scandal runs through the streets," returned the Abbe Fortier. "What is the new scandal you have to tell, Aunt Angelica ?"

Mademoiselle Adelaide introduced the letter-out of chairs to the abbe.

"Your servitor, Monsieur the Abbe," said the old maid.

"It is 'servant,' you ought to say, Aunt Angelica," corrected the abbe, unable to renounce his pedagogical habits.

"I have always heard 'servitor' used," returned the other, "and I repeat what I hear others say : excuse me if I have offended you, Monsieur the Abbe."

"You have not offended me, Aunt Angelica, but syntax."

"I shall make my excuses to him the first time that I meet him," humbly responded Aunt Angelica.

"Very well, Aunt Angelica, very well! Will you take a glass of wine ?"

"Thank you, Monsieur the Abbe," answered Aunt Angelica, "I never drink wine."

"You are wrong: wine is not forbidden by the canons of the church."

"Oh, it is not because wine is or is not forbidden that I do not drink, but because it costs nine sous a bottle."

"So, you are rather saving, Aunt Angelica?" queried the Abbe Fortier, falling back into his armchair.

"Alas! goodness! Monsieur the Abbe, saving! a body must be saving when one is poor."

"Poor? is the letting out of chairs which I give you for nothing, Aunt Angelique, good for nothing? Why, I could let it out for a hundred crowns to the very first person one might meet."

"Nay, Monsieur the Abbe, it would be pretty hard to meet with such a person. Why, it is nothing, Monsieur the Abbe! one can only drink water on it."

"That's the very reason I offer you wine, Aunt Angelica."

"Accept it," interpolated Mademoiselle Adelaide; "my uncle will be displeased, if you do not take it."

"Do you think it will displease your uncle?" inquired Aunt Angelica, who was ready to die with her eagerness to jump at the gift.

"I am quite sure."

"Then, Monsieur the Abbe, I will take two fingers of wine, if you please, so as not to disoblige you."

"Very well," said the Abbe Fortier, pouring a glass full of rich Burgundy pure as a ruby; "toss that off, Aunt Angelica and, when you get reckoning over your crown-pieces, you will see them doubled."

Aunt Angelica had just brought the glass to her lips.

"My crowns?" said she. "Ah, Monsieur the Abbe, don't be saying such things; you are a truth-telling man, and folks will believe you."

"Drink, Aunt Angelica, drink."

Aunt Angelica, to please the Abbe Fortier, dipped her lips in the glass, and, while closing her eyes, a third or thereabouts of its contents slipped down her throat.

"Oh, it is too strong!" said she; "I don't know how it is people can drink wine pure!"

"And I," said the abbe, "I do not know how it is anybody can put water in with their wine. But, never mind, that does not prevent me wagering that you, Aunt Angelica, have a good-sized hoard of money."

"Oh, oh, Monsieur the Abbe, don't be speaking in that way. I cannot even pay my contributions, which amount to three livres ten sous a year."

Aunt Angelica swallowed another third of the wine in her glass.

"Yes, I know very well what you say; but I will answer for it that, on the day when you give up the ghost, if your nephew Ange Pitou seeks well, he will find, in some bundle of old linen, the wherewithal to buy out the Rue du Pleu."

"Monsieur the Abbe! Monsieur the Abbe!" exclaimed Aunt Angelica, "if you speak such things, you will get me murdered by the brigands who burn down houses and destroy the crops; for, on the word of so holy a man as you, they will believe I am rich. Oh, goodness me! what a misfortune!"

With her eyes moist—perhaps with a tear—she gulped down the rest of the wine.

"Well," went on the abbe, still in his jesting vein, "now, you see, you have made the acquaintance of that wine, Aunt Angelica."

"It's very strong," said the old maid.

The abbe had nearly finished his supper.

"Well," inquired he, "let us hear what is the fresh scandal troubling Israel?"

"Monsieur the Abbe, Billot's girl has just come in the diligence with her child!"

"Aha!" said the abbe, "I thought she had got rid of it by putting it in the Foundling Hospital."

"She would have done better if she had done so," remarked Aunt Angelica; "at all events, then, the little brat would not have had to blush for its mother."

"Indeed, Aunt Angelica," observed the abbe, "that is looking at the institution from a new point of view. And what brings her here?"

"It appears she wants to see her mother; for she asked the children whether her mother was still alive."

"You know, Aunt Angelica," said the abbe with an evil smile, "that Mother Billot has forgotten to be confessed?"

"Oh, Monsieur the Abbe," returned

3

Aunt Angelica, "that is not her fault; the poor woman, since these three or four months, seems out of her head; but she was, in the days when her daughter had not given her so much trouble, a very devout woman, fearing God, who, when she went to church, always hired two chairs, one to sit down on, the other to put her feet upon."

"But her husband?" ejaculated the abbe, his eyes glistening with rage; "Citizen Billot, the conqueror of the Bastile, how many chairs did he hire?"

"Why, forsooth, I do not know," answered Aunt Angelica simply; "he never comes to church, but as for Mother Billot——"

"It is well, very well," interrupted the abbe; "it is an account we will settle on the day of her burial."

Making the sign of the cross, he added :

"Say grace with me, my sisters."

The old maids repeated the sign of the cross which the abbe had just made, and devoutly said grace with him.

CHAPTER V.

DAUGHTER AND MOTHER.

DURING this time, Catherine was pursuing her road. On coming out of the lane, she turned to the left, followed the Rue de Lormet, and, at the end of that street, had, by a path made across the fields, reached the Road to Pisseleu.

All along the way painful recollections had crowded upon Catherine.

First, yonder was that little bridge, where Isidore de Charny had bidden her farewell, and where she had remained in a fainting fit until the moment when Pitou had found her, cold as if turned to ice.

Then, while approaching the farm, rose the hollow willow-tree in which Isidore had hidden his letters.

Still nearer, that little window was the one through which Isidore had entered her room ; and the same as that where the young man had been fired at by Billot in the night-time, when, for-tunately, the farmer's gun had hung fire.

Lastly, facing the main gateway of the farm, ran the Boursonnes Road which Catherine had so frequently traveled over, and which she knew better from its being the route to come to her which Isidore used to take.

How many times, in the evening, leaning on that window's sill, her eyes fastened on the highway, had she breathlessly awaited and on perceiving her lover in the shades, always punctual and faithful, and felt her bosom relieved, as she opened both her arms to receive him !

Now he was dead; but, at all events, her arms folded over her bosom pressed to it his son.

What were people saying of her dishonor, her shame ?

Could so lovely a child ever be to a mother a shame or a dishonor ?

Therefore, she rapidly and fearlessly walked into the farm.

A large dog barked as she came, but suddenly recognizing his young mistress, he drew his chain tight to get as close to her as possible and reared up, his paws in the air, while he emitted sharp joyful yelps.

On the barking of the watchdog a man appeared on the threshold, coming to see what had caused it.

"Mademoiselle Catherine?" exclaimed he.

"Pere Clovis !" cried Catherine.

"You are welcome, my dear young lady," said the old huntsman; "the house has need of your presence—come in !"

"My poor mother ?" inquired Catherine.

"Alas ! neither better nor worse, or if anything, worse than better ; she is gradually going, poor dear woman !"

"Where is she ?"

"In her room ?"

"Quite alone ?"

"No, no. Why, I would never have allowed that. You must excuse me, Mademoiselle Catherine, in your absence, I have made myself some little the master here : it is as if to pay up for the times which you spent in my humble hut, and made it seem as if I had a little family of my own : I loved you so much, you and poor Monsieur Isidore !"

" So you know ?" began Catherine, wiping away her tears.

" Yes, yes, killed fighting for the Queen, like Monsieur George, his brother. But, mademoiselle, there is left to you this pretty child—weep for the father, but you must smile on his son."

" Thank you, Pere Clovis," said Catherine, holding out her hand to the ancient huntsman ; " but my mother ?"

" She is in her room, as I have told you, along with Madame Clement, the same sick-nurse who took care of you."

" And," asked Catherine hesitating, " has—my poor mother still got her consciousness ?"

" There are times when one may believe so," returned Pere Clovis ; "that is when your name is spoken. Yes, that's the great means, which lasted until day before yesterday ; since then she has shown no signs of being in her senses, even when your name is spoken."

" Let us enter, Pere Clovis," said Catherine, " Let us enter."

" Pass in, mademoiselle," said the old huntsman opening the door of Madame Billot's chamber.

Catherine gazed into the apartment.

Her mother, couched on her bed with green serge curtains, lit up by one of those three wicked lamps to be seen at the present day in French country cottages was watched, as Pere Clovis had truly stated, by Madame Clement.

This latter woman, seated in an ample armchair, was nodding in that state of dozing peculiar to sick-nurses, which is a somnambulic medium between wakefulness and sleep.

Poor Mother Billot did not seem altered, with the exception that her complexion had become of the pallor of ivory.

She seemed to be in slumber.

" Mother, mother !" broken forth from Catherine as she rushed to the bed.

The patient opened her eyes, turning her head in the direction of Catherine : a light of intelligence enkindled her look ; her lips stammered unintelligible sounds, not even attaining the level of disconnected words, her hand was lifted, endeavoring to complete, by touching her, the nearly extinguished senses of hearing and sight ; but the effort failed, the movement died away, the eyes closed, and the arm fell like a lifeless limb upon the head of Catherine, who knelt by her mother's bed side, and the dying woman fell back anew into the immobility from which she had been momentarily drawn by the galvanic shock given to her by her daughter's voice.

The two lethargies of the father and the mother had, like two lightning flashes darting from opposite quarters of the horizon, flashed out two feelings quite contrary.

Father Billot had started from his swoon to repulse Catherine from him.

Mother Billot had shaken off her torpor to draw Catherine to her.

Catherine's arrival had produced a revolution in the farm.

They expected Billot, and not his daughter.

Catherine related the accident happened to Billot, and told how, at Paris, the husband was as near to death as the wife was at Pisseleu.

Yet it was evident that each of the two so near to death were traveling a different road.

Billot went from life to death.

Catherine went into her room of other days.

There were many tears shed by her over the recollections that little chamber called up before her, where she had passed over her childhood's bright dreams, her maidenhood's burning passions—and to which she returned with the rent heart of the widow.

From that moment, Catherine reassumed over the house in disorder all the authority her father had one day conceded to her, to the detriment of her mother.

Pere Clovis, thanked and rewarded, went back to his " burrow," as he called his abode by the Clovis Stone.

The ensuing day, Doctor Raynal came to the farmhouse.

He came to it every second day, through a sentiment of conscience rather than by a feeling of hope : he very well knew that he could do nothing, and that the life, which was dying out like a lamp burning its few last drops of oil could not be saved by any human effort.

He was rejoiced to find the girl arrived.

He hinted on the momentous question which he had not dared to argue with Billot: that of receiving the sacrament.

Billot, our readers are aware, was an outrageous Voltairian.

Not that Doctor Raynal was of exemplary devotion: quite the contrary; to the spirit of the times he joined the mind of science.

Now, granting the times to be only as yet at the point of doubting, science was already over the bounds of denial.

Nevertheless, Doctor Raynal, in circumstances analagous to that in the present instance, looked upon it as a duty to warn the relations.

Such, if pious, would take heed by the warning and send for the priest.

Impious parents or kindred ordered, if the priest should present himself, that the door should be slammed in his face.

Catherine was pious.

She was ignorant of the differences which had sprang up betwixt Billot and the Abbe Fortier, or rather she did know of them, but attached no importance to them.

She charged Madame Clement to proceed to the house of the Abbe Fortier, and ask him to come and bring the last sacrament to her mother.

Pisseleu, being too small a hamlet to have its own church and curate, was dependent on Villers Cotterets. And it was even in the burying-ground of the latter place the dead of Pisseleu were interred.

An hour afterwards, the bell of the viaticum tinkled at the farmhouse door.

The holy sacrament was received by Catherine on her knees.

But, hardly had the Abbe Fortier entered into the sick chamber, hardly had he discovered that she for whom he had been summoned was speechless, voiceless, and with glazed look, than he declared that he would only give abso-lution to persons who were able to confess; and, in spite of all the dissuading used, he had the viaticum borne away.

Abbe Fortier was a priest of the gloomy and terrible school.

He would have been a Saint Dominique in Spain, and a Valverde in Mexico.

There was no applying to anybody besides him; Pisseleu, as before mentioned, belonged to his parish, and no priest in the neighborhood would have ventured to entrench on his rights.

Catherine had an affectionate as well as pious heart, but at the same time it was full of reason; she only regarded Abbe Fortier's refusal as something which she ought to bear, trusting that God would be more indulgent in favor of the dying woman than was His minister.

Thereupon, she continued to fulfil her duties as a daughter towards her mother, her duties as a maternal parent to her child, sharing herself entirely between that young soul entering upon life and that fading spirit fleeing along to the Vale of Shadows.

During eight days and as many nights, she never left the bedside of her mother save to step to her infant's cradle.

In the night between the eighth and ninth day, while the girl watched by the pillow of her dying mother's bed—whose occupant, like a vessel deeper and deeper sinking in the sea, was lower and lower submerged in eternity—the bedroom door opened, and Pitou appeared on the threshold.

He arrived from Paris, from which he had started in the morning, according to his habit.

On seeing him, Catherine started.

For an instant, she feared that her father was dead.

But Pitou's countenance, without being exactly cheerful, was nevertheless not at all that of a man bearer of such mournful tidings.

Indeed, Billot was going from better to best; since four or five days before, the doctor had answered for him, and, on the morning of Pitou's departure, the patient had been transported from the Hospital of Gros Caillou to the doctor's house.

From the moment when Billot was out of danger, Pitou had declared his formal resolution to return to Pisseleu.

He feared no longer for Billot, but for Catherine.

Pitou had foreseen the moment when would be announced to Billot what they had not been willing to impart to him before ; that is, the state in which was his wife.

His conviction was that at that moment, however weak he might be, Billot would set off for Villers Cotterets. And what would happen were he to find Catherine at the farm ?

Doctor Gilbert had not concealed from Pitou the effect exerted over the wounded man by the entrance of Catherine and her being for an instant near his patient's bed.

It was clear that his reason had returned ; the wounded man flung about him looks which had gradually passed from uneasiness to hate.

No doubt he expected to see at any moment the fatal vision appear anew.

However, he spoke not a word; not once did he pronounce the name of Catherine ; but Doctor Gilbert was too acute an observer not to have divined and read everything.

Consequently, on Billot's convalescence, he had despatched Pitou to the farm.

The purpose was for him to remove Catherine.

Pitou requiring, for that design, two or three days before him, the doctor would not, before three or four days also, risk informing the convalescent of the bad news which Pitou had brought.

The latter imparted his fears to Catherine with all the earnestness which Billot's character inspired in him ; but Catherine declared that were her father to kill her at the bed-side of her dying mother, she would not move from it before she had closed her eyes.

Pitou deeply bewailed this determination ; but he could find no word to combat it.

Hence he kept himself ready to interpose, in case of necessity, between the father and the daughter.

Two days and two nights passed over;

during that series of hours Mother Billot's life seemed to leave her with each breath.

For more than a week the sick woman had not been able to eat ; she was nourished by a few spoonsful of broth now and then.

One could hardly believe that a body could have life from such sustenance. Though it is true that that poor body had very little life !

During the night of the tenth day, as it faded into the morning of the eleventh day, at a moment when even perspiration seemed to have ceased within her, the sick woman appeared to become reanimated, her arms made some movement, her lips quivered, and her eyes opened widely and fixedly.

" Mother, Mother !" exclaimed Catherine.

She hurried towards the door to go for her child.

One beholding this would have fancied Catherine drew her mother's mind with her ; when she returned, holding little Isidore in her arms, the dying woman made an effort to turn towards her.

Her eyes remained continually open and fixed.

On the reappearance of her daughter, her eyes threw out a flash, as she uttered a cry, and as her arms were extended.

Catherine dropped on her knees by her mother's bed.

Then a strange phenomenon took place.

Mother Billot rose up on her pillow, slowly stretched out her arms over the head of Catherine and her son, and, after an effort, like to that of Crœsus' dumb son, she said :

" My children, I bless you !"

With that, she fell back on her couch, her arms dropped, and her voice was hushed.

She was dead.

Her eyes alone remained open, as if the poor woman, not having seen enough of her living, still wished to watch her daughter from the other verge of the grave.

———

CHAPTER VI.

IN WHICH THE ABBE FORTIER CARRIES
OUT, WITH RESPECT TO THE WIFE OF
BILLOT, THE THREAT HE MADE
TO AUNT ANGELICA.

CATHERINE piously closed her mother's eyes, with her hands first, next with her lips.

Madame Clement had since long before foreseen this hour, and had purchased in advance two candles.

While Catherine, her tears profusely flowing, carried back into her room her crying child, and rocked it to sleep in her arms, Madame Clement lit the two tapers, placed one on each side of the bed, clasped the dead woman's hands over her breast, put a crucifix between her fingers, and set upon a chair a bowl full of holy water, with a box-wood twig of the last Palm Sunday.

When Catherine returned, she had only to kneel beside her mother's bed, her prayer-book in her hand.

Meanwhile Pitou took upon himself the other funeral arrangements: to wit—not venturing to go to the Abbe Fortier, with whom, it will be remembered, he was on delicate ground—he went to the sacristan to order the mass for the dead, to the bearers to let them know the hour at which they were to come for the coffin, and to the grave-digger to tell him to dig the grave.

Then he went to Haramont to inform his first and second lieutenants and his thirty-one men of the National Guard that Madame Billot's burial was to take place at eleven o'clock the next morning.

Inasmuch as Mother Billot had not filled during her life any public office, or any rank in the National Guard or the army, Pitou's communication to his men was officious, and not official, of course; it was an invitation for them to join in the funeral, and not an order.

But, very well known was what Billot had done for this Revolution which turned every head and enflamed all hearts; well known too was the danger that at this very moment Billot ran stretched on his couch of pain, wounded as he had been whilst defend-ing the sacred cause—this was all too well known for the invitation not to be looked upon as an order; the whole National Guard of Haramont therefore promised their leader to voluntarily and punctually be under arms at eleven o'clock at the house.

In the evening, Pitou was on the return to the farm; at the door, he found the coffinmaker, who carried the coffin on his shoulder.

Pitou had instinctively all the delicateness, so seldom found in country-people, and even among people of the world.

He hid the coffinmaker in the stable, and, to spare Catherine the sight of the funereal box, and the fearful sound of the hammer, he entered the house alone.

Catharine was praying at the foot of her mother's bed; the corpse, by the cares of the two women, had been sewn up in a shroud.

Pitou gave Catharine an account of his day's doings, and begged her to come out to take a little air.

But Catharine wished to perform her duties to the bitter end, and refused.

"It will hurt your little Isidore to confine him thus," remarked Pitou.

"Take him out, then, Monsieur Pitou."

Catharine must have had great confidence in Pitou to entrust her child with him, were it for only five minutes.

Pitou went out, as if to obey: but he returned in about five minutes.

"He does not want to go out with me," said he; "he cries!"

Indeed, through the open doors, Catharine heard her child's cries.

She kissed the forehead of the dead woman, whose form and almost the features could be distinguished through the sheet, and, wavering between her promptings as mother and as daughter, she left her parent to go to her son.

Little Isidore was crying in truth: Catherine took him up in her arms and, following Pitou, left the house.

The coffinmaker and his burden entered it behind her.

Pitou's intention was to keep Catharine away for about half an hour.

As if by chance, he led her over the Boursonnes Road.

This way was so full of recollections for Catharine that she walked half a league without speaking one word to Pitou, listening to the various voices in her heart, and answering them as they spoke.

When Pitou thought the funereal work was over he said:

"Mademoiselle Catharine, how about returning to the house!"

Catharine threw off her thoughts like a dream.

"Oh, yes," responded she. "How good you are, Monsieur Pitou."

Whereupon, she turned back on the road to Pisseleu.

On their return, Madame Clement gave a nod of the head to Pitou which indicated that the work was completed.

Catherine went into her own room to put little Isidore to bed.

This done, she went to resume her place at the deathbed.

But, on the threshold of the chamber she found Pitou.

"Useless, Mademoiselle Catherine," said he, "all is ended."

"How?"

"Yes. While we were away, mademoiselle—"

Pitou hesitated.

"While we were away, the undertaker——"

He checked himself again.

"Ah, and that is why you insisted on my going out. I understand, good Pitou!"

For his recompense, the young man received from Catherine a grateful look.

"One last prayer," said she, "and I will return."

Catherine entered her mother's room; Pitou following her on tiptoe, but halting on the threshold.

The coffin lay on a couple of chairs in the middle of the room.

On seeing this Catherine stopped with a start, and fresh tears streamed from her eyes.

Then she knelt down by the coffin, pressing against the oaken plank her brow, pale with weariness and grief.

On the dolorous way that leads the dead from their bed to the grave, the everlasting resting-place, the living following them stumble at every instant over something new which destined to unclose the fount of tears and let it flow to the last salt drop from the parting hearts.

The prayer was a long one.

Catherine could not tear herself from the coffin: she, poor girl, deeply felt how she had in the world, since Isidore's death, two friends only: her mother and Pitou.

Her mother had just blessed her and bidden her adieu: her mother, shrouded now, would be in the grave next day.

Pitou alone remained with her.

It is hard to part with your last friend but one, how much harder when it is a mother!

Pitou felt that he should go to Catherine's aid; he entered, and seeing words would be useless, tried to remove the mourning daughter by taking her by the arm.

"Another prayer more, Monsieur Pitou! only one!"

"You will make yourself ill, Mademoiselle Catherine," remonstrated Pitou.

"What of that?" said Catherine.

"Then I would have to seek out a nurse for Master Isidore."

"You are right, right, Pitou," said the girl. "How good you are, Pitou! how I do love you!"

Pitou reeled and nearly fell backwards. He receded to the door, leaning against the wall, while tears silently, almost of joy, coursed down his cheeks.

Had not Catherine just said that she loved him?

Pitou did not deceive himself as to the way in which Catherine loved him: but, whatever her affection, it was a great deal to him.

Her prayers terminated, Catherine, as she had promised Pitou, rose and walked away slowly, leaning on the young man's shoulder.

Pitou passed his arm around Catherine's waist to support her, without her resisting it.

Before crossing the threshold, turning her head over Pitou's shoulder and casting a last look on the coffin, sadly lit by the two candles, she said:

"Farewell, mother! a last time, farewell!"

She went out.

At the door of Catherine's chamber, as she was about to go in, Pitou stopped her.

Catherine began so well to know Pitou that she comprehended he had something to tell her.

"Well?" inquired she.

"Do you not think," faltered Pitou a little embarrassed, "do you not think, Mademoiselle Catherine, that the time has come for leaving the farm."

"I shall not leave it until my mother herself shall have quitted it," responded the girl.

Catherine spoke the words with such firmness that Pitou plainly saw it to be an irrevocable resolve.

"When you do leave the farm," went on Pitou, "you know there is, within a league of this, two places where you are sure to be well received: the cabin of Pere Clovis and Pitou's little house."

Pitou called his one room and his closet a "house."

"Thank you, Pitou," returned Catherine, indicating by a sign of the head that she at the same time accepted both shelters.

Catherine entered her room without in the least minding Pitou, who was himself always sure of finding a roof.

At ten o'clock on the following day, the friends called together for the funeral assembled on the farm.

All the farmers in the neighborhood, from Boursonnes, Noue, Ivors, Coyolles, Largny, Haramont, and Vivieres, were at the farm.

The Mayor of Villers Cotterets, the good Monsieur de Longpre, was one of the first to come.

At half past ten, the National Guard of Haramont, with ruffling drum and draped flag, marched up without a man being absent.

Catherine, all in black, holding in her arms her child, in mourning too like herself, received every arrival, and, it must be acknowledged, there was no other feeling than that of respect for the mother and her child.

At eleven o'clock, more than three hundred persons were collected at the farm.

The priest, churchmen, and the pall-bearers were alone absent.

They waited a quarter of an hour.

Nothing came.

Pitou went up into the barn, the highest building on the farm.

From its window could be overlooked the plain stretching out from Villers Cotterets to the little village of Pisseleu.

In spite of Pitou's good eyes, he saw nothing.

He descended and communicated to Monsieur de Longpre, not only his observations, but his reflections besides.

His "observations" were that nothing was certainly coming; his "reflections" that nothing would probably come.

He had been informed of Abbe Fortier's visit, and his refusal to administer the sacrament to Mother Billot.

Pitou knew the Abbe Fortier: he saw through it all: the abbe was not willing to lend the concurrence of his holy ministry to Madame Billot's interment, and the pretext, not the cause, was the absence of confession.

These reflections, imparted by their author to M. de Longpre, and by the latter to the gathering, produced a painful impression.

Each regarded the other in silence.

"What of it?" said one voice; "if the Abbe Fortier is not willing to say the mass, we can get along without it."

This voice was Desire Maniquet's.

He was well known for his anti-religious opinions.

There was an instant's pause.

It was clear that Maniquet's hearers thought it would seem very bold to do without the mass.

Nevertheless, Voltaire and Rousseau were very popular.

"Gentlemen," said the mayor, "let us go to Villers Cotterets. There, all will be explained."

"On to Villers Cotterets!" cried every voice.

Pitou made a sign to four of his men, who slipped the barrels of two muskets under the coffin, and thus lifted the body.

At the door, the procession passed before Catherine kneeling, and little Isidore, whom she had made to kneel beside her.

The coffin having passed, Catherine rose, and having crossed the threshold of that door through which she never again calculated going, said to Pitou: "You will find me in the cabin of Pere Clovis."

By way of the farmyard and the gardens on the banks of the Noue, she hurried rapidly away.

CHAPTER VII.

IN WHICH ABBE FORTIER SEES THAT IT IS NOT ALWAYS EASY AS SOME BE-LIEVE TO KEEP A PLEDGED WORD.

THE funeral procession was advancing slowly, forming a long line on the road, when suddenly those closing the line heard behind them a call.

They turned.

A man on horseback was riding at a gallop, coming from Ivors, along the Paris highway.

Part of his face was barred by two black bands: he held his hat in his hand and waved it for them to stop.

Pitou turned as well as the rest.

"Monsieur Billot!" cried he. "I would not like to be in the Abbe Fortier's skin."

On the name of Billot, everybody stopped.

The horseman came up rapidly and, proportionably to his nearing them, as Pitou had recognized the farmer, so did the others recognize him in their turn.

On reaching the head of the train, Billot jumped down off his horse, flung the bridle on its neck, and, after having said in a voice so clear that everybody heard it: "Good morning. Thank you, citizens!" he took behind the coffin, Pitou's place, the latter having in his absence headed the mourners.

A boy took charge of the horse, and led it back to the farm.

Everybody glanced curiously at Billot.

He had grown thinner a little, and was much paler.

Part of his forehead and around his left eye had kept the violet colors of extravasated blood.

His serried teeth, his frowning brows, denoted anger which only waited for the proper time to burst forth.

"Do you know what has happened?" Pitou asked him.

"I know everything," returned Billot.

As soon as Doctor Gilbert had confessed to the farmer the condition in which was his wife, the farmer had taken a cab which had carried him to Nanteuil.

As the horse could not be driven any farther, Billot, weak though he was, had taken a post-horse; at Levignan he had relayed, and had reached his farm as the funeral train left it.

In a couple of words, Madame Clement had let him know everything.

Billot had remounted his horse: at the turn of the fence, he had caught sight of the procession, which, spread along the road, had been stopped by his shouts.

Now as we have said, it was he who, with frowning brows, mouth curled threateningly, his arms folded over his breast, led the mourners.

Silent and gloomy previously, the escort became still more so.

On the entry into Villers Cotterets they met a group of people waiting for them; this party took a place in the train.

As the body proceeded through the streets, men, women and children left the houses, saluting Billot, who returned it with nods and they became incorporated with the ranks.

When the gathering reached the village square, it numbered more than five hundred persons.

From the square the church could be perceived.

What Pitou had foreseen was really so: the place of worship was shut up.

They halted at the door.

Billot had become livid: the expression of his countenance had grown more and more menacing.

The church and the mayor's house touched. The old woman—who was at the same time as keeper of the church-keys, house-keeper to the mayor, consequently depending on both the mayor and the Abbe Fortier—was called, questioned by M. de Longpre.

The Abbe Fortier had forbidden any one connected with the church from having anything to do with the interment.

The mayor asked where the keys were.

At the beadle's house.

"Go get the keys," said Billot to Pitou.

The latter opened his compass-like legs and returned five minutes afterward, saying:

"The Abbe Fortier had the keys taken to his house, to be sure the church was not opened."

"We'll go after the keys at the abbe," said Desire Maniquet, a prominent promoter of extreme measures.

"Yes, yes, let us go after the keys at the abbe's!" shouted two hundred voices.

"It would take up too long a time," interposed Billot, "and, when death knocks at the door, it is not usual for it to wait."

Thereupon, he looked around him: in front of the church, a house was being built.

The carpenters were shaping a beam.

Billot walked up to them, making them a sign that he needed the timber they were at work on.

The workmen stepped aside.

The beam was laid on blocks.

Billot ran his arm in under the beam, above the middle of the piece; with a single effort, he lifted it.

But he had calculated on absent strength.

Beneath the enormous weight, the colossus struggled, and for an instant it was thought he would fall.

This was only an instant, though.

Billot recovered his balance, smiling a frightful smile; then he strode forward, the beam under his arm, with a step slow but steady.

He might have been likened to one of those ancient battering-rams with which the Alexanders, Hannibals, Cæsars breached walls.

He stationed himself, with legs apart,

before the church door, and set his beam in motion.

The door was of oak, the bolts, bars, locks and hinges were of iron.

At the third blow the bolts and locks were bent out of their sockets, the hinges were loosened: the oaken door opened.

Billot dropped his beam.

Four men picked it up and carried it with difficulty back to the place from which Billot had taken it.

"Now, Monsieur le Maire," said Billot, "have the coffin of my poor wife, who never did a single soul wrong, placed in the choir, and you, Pitou, get together the beadles, the chanters and chorister boys: I will see to the priest."

The mayor, conducting Madame Billot's remains, entered the church; Pitou went after the persons detailed to him, taking along with him his lieutenants, Desire Maniquet, and four men, in case they met any obstreperous. Billot proceeded towards the Abbe Fortier's house.

Many of the men were desirous of following Billot.

"Leave me alone," said he; "perhaps what I am going to do may be serious: let each be responsible for what is his own act."

He descended the Rue de l'Eglise (Church Street), and took the Rue de Soissons.

This made the second time, a year apart, that the revolutionary farmer had gone to meet the royalist priest.

Our readers will recal what had happened on that former occasion: probably they will be witness of a similar scene.

Therefore, as they watched him walking briskly towards the abbe's dwelling, everybody remained motionless wherever they were, following him with their eyes and shaking their heads, but without making a step.

"He has forbidden us to follow him," said the spectators to one another.

The door of the abbe's house was shut and locked as the churchdoor had been.

Billot looked about him to see if

there was not near by some erection being put up from which he might take another beam; there was only a kind of stone post loosened by the playing of children, which trembled in its orbit like a loose tooth in its socket.

The farmer caught hold off this post, shook it violently, enlarged the hole it was inserted in, and tore it out from the earth.

Then, brandishing it over his head, like another Ajax or Diomede, he drew back three steps, and rushing forward, hurled the granite block with the same force as a catapult might have done.

The shattered door fell in splinters.

At the same time as Billot dashed in the door, the window on the first floor flew open, and the Abbe Fortier appeared, calling with all his lungs for help from his parishioners.

But the pastor's appeal was not hearkened to by the flock, which was fully determined to let the wolf and the shepherd fight it out between themselves.

It took Billot a certain time to break through the two or three doors still separating him from the Abbe Fortier, as he had broken in the outer entrance. This took about ten minutes.

At the end of that space, by the more and more violent outcries and the more and more expressive gesticulations of the abbe, the outsiders could see how the increasing agitation arose from the danger closer and closer approaching the churchman.

Indeed, all at once, behind the latter appeared Billot's pale face, then a hand was stretched out and laid on his shoulder.

The priest clung to the wooden sill of the window: he was of proverbial strength, also, and it would have been no easy matter for Hercules himself to have made him let go.

Billot passed his arm, like a girdle, around the priest's waist: he slowly rose on his legs and, with a pull capable of uprooting an oak-tree, he tore away the Abbe Fortier, with the wooden crosspiece broken in his hands.

The farmer and the priest disappeared within the room, and nothing more was to be heard beyond the abbe's outcries which died away like the bellowing of a bull borne, by a lion of Mount Atlas, to his lair.

During this time, Pitou had brought the trembling chanters, chorister boys, and the beadle; every one of them, on the example of the mayor's housekeeper, had hastened to don their capes and gowns, and afterwards light the tapers and get ready everything required for the mass for the dead.

All was prepared when they saw the re-appearance, by the little doorway opening on the Place du Chateau, of Billot, whom they had expected to see coming through the great door on the Rue de Soissons.

He dragged after him the priest, and, in spite of his resistance, moved with as rapid a pace as if he were alone.

He was more than a man he was one of nature's forces, like a torrent or an avalanche: nothing human seemed capable of withstanding him: it needed an element to struggle against him!

The poor abbe, when a hundred paces from the church, ceased to resist.

He was completely subdued.

Everybody stepped aside to let the two men pass.

The abbe flung a frightened look on the door shivered like a pane of glass, and, seeing in their places—with their instruments, staff or book in hand— all the men whom he had forbidden to set foot within the church, he shook his head as if he acknowledged something powerful and irresistible weighed, not on religion, but on its ministers.

He entered the sacristy, and came out an instant afterwards in his officiating attire, the holy sacrament in his hands.

But, at the moment when, after having mounted the altar steps and deposited the pyx on the table, he turned to speak the opening words of the service, Billot stretched out his hand.

"Enough, evil servant of God!" said he; "I have meant to curb your pride, that is all; but I do wish it to be known that a pure woman like my wife can do without the prayers of a hateful, fanatical priest like you."

Then, as a loud murmur ran under the vaulted ceiling of the church at his speech, he subjoined :

"If this be sacrilege, let the crime fall upon me."

Turning to the immense gathering which not only filled the church but the sides, he said :

"Citizens, to the burying-ground !"

Every voice repeated :

"To the burying-ground."

The four bearers then thrust the barrels of their guns again under the coffin, lifted their burden and, in the same way as they had come—without priest, chants of the church, or any of the funeral pomp with which religion is accustomed to form as escort to man's mourning—they went away. Billot led the mourners ; six hundred persons followed the train towards the cemetery, situated, it will be recollected, at the end of Pleux Lane, about five-and-twenty paces from Aunt Angelica's house.

The gates of the graveyard were fastened as had been that of the Abbe Fortier's house, and that of the church.

There. strange fact ! before this weak obstacle, Billot stopped.

The dead respected the dead.

On a signal from the farmer, Pitou ran to the grave-digger.

He had the key of the place, of course.

Five minutes afterwards, Pitou brought not only the key but a couple of spades besides.

The Abbe Fortier had proscribed the poor dead woman from both church and holy ground : the gravedigger had received an order not to break the earth for a grave.

Upon this final manifestation of the priest's hate against the farmer, something like a thrill of menace ran through the assemblage. Had there been in Billot the fourth part of the gall indispensable to the devout (which had the semblance of astonishing Boileau), Billot had but one word to say, and the Abbe Fortier would have had at last the satisfaction of that martyrdom which he had loudly cried for on the day when he had refused to say mass on the altar of the Country.

But Billot had the wrath of the people and the lion : he rent, tore, crushed as he moved, but never retraced his steps.

He thanked Pitou with a nod, in which the recipient comprehended the intention, took the key from his hands, opened the gate, had the coffin carried in first, followed it himself and was followed by the funeral train which had recruited all who could walk.

The royalists and the devout remained alone at home.

It is needless to say that Aunt Angelica, who was one of the latter, had fastened up her door with terror, screaming out abomination and calling down heavenly lightnings on her nephew's head.

But all who owned a good heart or had sense and loved their family, were revolted by hatred being substituted for mercifulness, vengeance for forgiveness ; three quarters of the town were there, protesting—not against God or religion—but against priests and their fanaticism.

Arrived at the spot where the grave was to be made, which the grave-digger, ignorant that he would receive a countermand, had marked out, Billot held out his hand to Pitou, who gave him one of his two spades.

Thereupon, Billot and Pitou, with bared heads, amid a circle of country people whose heads were uncovered like theirs under the devouring sun of the last days of July, set to work digging the grave of the unfortunate creature who, pious and resigned throughout life, would have been greatly astonished had she, while living, been assured of the scandal she would cause after her death.

The labor lasted an hour, yet neither of the delvers had the idea of rising before it was finished.

Meanwhile, ropes had been sought for, and when the pit was made, the ropes were ready.

It was Billot and Pitou who lowered the coffin into the grave.

These two men so naturally and simply rendered this last duty to the dead, that not one among the beholders entertained the thought of offering his aid to them.

All thought it wrong not to let them proceed to the end.

When the first shovelfuls of earth sounded on the oaken board, Billot passed his hand across his eyes, and Pitou his sleeve.

Then they resolutely proceeded to throw in the earth.

When the pit was filled up, Billot cast his spade far from him, and opened his arms to Pitou.

The young man fell upon the farmer's breast.

"God bear me witness," said Billot, "that I embrace in you all the great and simple virtues that are on earth, charity, devotion, self-denial, brotherly feelings with fellow man,—and I devote my life to the triumph of those virtues !"

Stretching out his hand over the grave, he continued :

"God bear me witness that I swear everlasting war to the King who had me assassinated ; to the nobles, who have dishonored my daughter ; to the priests, who have refused burial to my wife !"

And turning to the lookers-on, who were full of sympathy for this triple adjuration, Billot concluded :

"Brothers, a new Assembly is about to be called together in place of the traitors who sway the Feuillants : select me for representative to that assembly, and you shall see whether I do not know how to keep my oaths."

A shout of universal adhesion greeted Farmer Billot's proposal and, at that very hour, over his wife's grave—a terrible altar, worthy of the oath he had sworn—the nomination of Billot to the Legislative Assembly was performed : after which, Billot having thanked his fellow citizens for the sympathy which they had shown to him in his love and in his hate, each, townsman or peasant, retired to his own dwelling, bearing with him in his heart that spirit of propagating revolution to which, in their blindness, kings, noblemen and priests furnished the most deathly weapons—the very ones which destroyed them !

CHAPTER VIII.

THE events which we have just related had produced a deep impression, not only over the inhabitants of Villers Cotterets, but moreover on the farmers of the villages surrounding.

Now farmers have great power in election matters ; they each have under them ten, twenty or thirty farm-hands, and though popular suffrage was, at that period, in two classes, election depended completely on what was styled the "country."

Every man on leaving Billot, as they came to shake his hand, said to him merely the two following words :

"Rest easy."

Whereupon, Billot had returned to his farm, easy, indeed ; for, for the first time, he saw a mighty method of repaying to the nobility and royalty the evil which they had done him.

Billot felt, he did not reason, and his thirst for vengeance was as blindly directed as the blows he had received.

He entered his dwelling without speaking a word to Catharine ; no one knew whether he was aware of her momentous presence in the farmhouse. In no period during a year had he uttered his daughter's name : she was the same to him as though she no more existed.

It was not thus with Pitou, that heart of gold ! he had regretted from the bottom of his heart that Catharine could not love him ; but, on seeing Isidore de Charny, and comparing himself to that elegant young man, he had clearly comprehended how it was that Catharine should love him.

He had envied Isidore, but had wished nothing evil against Catharine ; quite otherwise, he had always loved her with profound and absolute devotion.

To say that this devotion was completely exempt from pain would not be saying the truth ; but the very pangs that wrung Pitou's heart, at each fresh proof of love which Catharine gave to her lover, showed the boundless goodness of that heart.

When Isidore de Charny had been killed at Varennes, Pitou had only felt deep commiseration for Catharine; then it was that, rendering perfect justice to the young nobleman, quite the contrary from Billot, he had remembered all that was handsome, good and generous in him who, without suspecting it, had been his rival.

The result was what we have seen: that not only had Pitou perhaps loved Catharine, sad and in mourning, as much as he had loved the joyous coquettish Catharine of other days, but besides—a thing which may be believed impossible—he had come to love the poor little orphan as much almost as herself.

Hence, no wonder should be expressed that, after having taken leave of Billot like the rest, Pitou, instead of proceeding in the direction of the farm, should have taken the road towards Haramont.

So accustomed were the people to the disappearances and unexpected returns of Pitou that, despite the high position which he filled in the village as captain, not a soul any longer minded his absence. Pitou would depart, and they would whisper:

"General La Fayette has called Pitou!"

And all was settled.

When Pitou returned, news from the capital was inquired for, and as Pitou, thanks to Gilbert, gave the freshest and truest; and as, several days after his information was given, Pitou's predictions were realized, they continued to have in him the blindest confidence, as well for the captain as for the prophet.

On his part, Gilbert knew all that there was good and devoted in Pitou; he felt that, at a given moment, he was a man to whom he could confide his life, or the life of his son Sebastian, a treasure, a mission, everything, in short, that one may entrust to loyalty and strength. Each time that Pitou went to Paris, Gilbert, without making Pitou heighten his color the least in the world, had asked him if he stood in need of anything; almost always Pitou had answered: "No, Monsieur Gilbert," which did not prevent the latter personage from handing Pitou a few louis which Pitou would drop into his pocket.

Half a dozen louis, for Pitou, along with his private income from his toll established over game in the Duke of Orleans' forest, was a fortune; so Pitou had never seen the end of his louis by the time he next saw Doctor Gilbert, and a shake of the latter's hand renewed in his pockets the source of the Pactolus.

No one will, therefore, be astonished that Pitou, being in the secret of the whereabouts of Catharine and Isidore, should separate himself from Billot to learn what had become of mother and child.

His road in going to Haramont, went by Pere Clovis's hut; a hundred paces from his hut he met Pere Clovis who was returning with a hare in his game-pouch.

It was his day for hare.

In a brace of words, Pere Clovis announced to Pitou that Catharine had come to ask of him his old habitation, which he had hastened to give up to her; she had wept a great deal, had the poor girl, as she entered that chamber where she had become a mother, and where Isidore had given her such clear proofs of his love.

But all her sorrows were not without a kind of charm; whoever has felt a great grief knows that the most cruel hours are those when the salt tears refuse to flow, that the sweetest, happiest hours are those when tears pour forth plenteously.

Hence, when Pitou showed himself on the threshold of the cabin, he found Catharine seated on her bed, with her cheeks wet, and her child in her arms.

On seeing Pitou, Catharine sat her child down on her lap, and held out her hands and presented her forehead to the young man.

Pitou joyfully took both her hands, kissed her on the brow, and the child found itself for an instant shadowed over by the arch made above him by the clasped hands, and Pitou's lips pressed on his mother's forehead.

Falling on his knees before Catharine, and kissing the infant's tiny hands, Pitou said:

"You may rest easy. Mademoiselle Catharine, I am rich. Monsieur Isidore shall want nothing."

Pitou owned fifteen louis : he called that being rich.

Catharine, good herself in mind and heart, appreciated all that was praiseworthy.

"I thank you, Monsieur Pitou," she returned, "I believe you, and am happy in believing you, for you are my only friend, and, were you to abandon me, we would be alone in the world ; but you will not abandon me, will you ?"

"Oh, mademoiselle," said Pitou sobbing, "do not speak of such things ! you make me weep all the tears I have in me !"

"I was wrong," said Catharine, "I was wrong. Excuse me."

"Nay, nay," said Pitou, "you were right, on the contrary : I am stupid to be crying this way,"

"Monsieur Pitou," said Catharine, "I have need of breathing the fresh air ; give me your arm, and we will take a walk under the tall trees. I think it will do me good."

"So it will me, mademoiselle," said Pitou, "for I feel myself stifled."

The child, though, had no need of air ; he stood in greater want of sleep.

Catharine laid him on her bed, and gave her arm to Pitou.

Five minutes afterwards, they were strolling under the lofty trees of the forest, the magnificent temple erected by God's hands to nature, His divine and ever-during daughter.

In spite of himself, this walk, during which Catharine leaned upon his arm, recalled to Pitou the one he had taken, two years and a half before, on Whitsuntide, escorting Catharine to the ballroom where, to his great sorrow, Isidore de Charny had danced with her.

How many events had accumulated during those two years and a half, and how well did Pitou—without being a philosopher on a level with Voltaire or Jean Jacques Rousseau–understand that he and Catharine were but atoms swept away by the general whirlwind.

But such atoms, in their infinity, have none the less, like great lords, princes and monarchs, and their queens, their joys and their pains ; that mill which, turned by Fatality's hands, shattered crowns and queen's thrones to dust, had broken and beat to powder the happiness of Catherine, neither more nor less than if she had been seated on a throne and had worn a crown on her head.

To sum up, at the end of two years and a half, the following is the difference which the Revolution, to which he had contributed so powerfully without being fully aware of what he was doing, had worked over Pitou's situation.

Two years and a half previously, Pitou was a poor little peasant boy, driven from home by his Aunt Angelica, received by Billot, protected by Catherine, cast off by her for Isidore.

To-day, Pitou was a power : he wore a sword by his side, and epaulets on his shoulders ; he was called a captain ; Isidore de Charny was dead, and he, Pitou, protected Catherine and her offspring.

The reply of Danton to the person who asked him "His design in inciting a revolution ?" "To set up that which is below, and trample down that which is above !" was, therefore, relatively to Pitou, of perfect correctness.

But, it has been seen, albeit all these ideas did travel through his head, the good, modest Pitou took no advantage, and he it was who on his knees entreated Catherine to allow him to aid her and her child.

Catherine, on her side, like every sufferer, had a much sharper appreciation in sorrow than in gladness. Pitou, who in the days of her happiness, was to her a good sort of a lad, without any consequence whatever, became the creature he really was : to wit, a man fraught with goodness, candor and devotion. Hence, being unfortunate, and wanting a friend, she felt that Pitou was just the friend she lacked ; and always greeted by Catherine with one hand held out to him, with a charming smile on her lips, Pitou commenced to lead a life of which he had never dreamed, even in his visions of Paradise.

During this time, Billot, always mute with respect to his daughter, pursued while he was harvesting his idea of being appointed deputy to the Legislature. One man alone might have been elected over him, had he had the same ambition; but wholly absorbed in his love and bliss, the Count de Charny, living with Andrée in his Chateau of Boursonnes, revelled in the delights of an unexpected felicity. The Count de Charny, oblivious of the world, fancied himself forgotten by it: he thought no more.

Hence, nothing opposing in the district of Villers Cotterets to Billot's election, the farmer was elected deputy by an immense majority.

Once elected, Billot began realizing as much money as he could. The year had been a good one; he settled accounts with his tenants, laid aside the seed meant for sowing, stored up the straw, hay and oats for the fodder of his horses, put away the money required for paying his farm hands, and one morning he sent for Pitou.

Pitou, as we have said, went from time to time to pay a visit to Billot.

The latter always received the young man with open heart, inviting him to dinner if it happened to be dinner time, to breakfast if it was the breakfast hour, offering him a glass of wine or cider, according to which it was the hour for drinking.

But never had Billot sent for Pitou. So it was not without uneasiness that Pitou went to the farm.

Billot was always grave; no one could say he had ever seen a smile flit over the farmer's countenance since the moment when his daughter had quitted the old homestead.

Billot was this day graver than commonly.

Nevertheless he held out as usual his hand to Pitou, squeezed with even more than customary vigor that Pitou tendered him, and held it in his own.

Pitou gazed at the farmer in astonishment.

"Pitou," said the latter, "you are an honest man!"

"I hope so, monsieur," returned Pitou.

"I am sure of it!"

"You are very kind, Monsieur Billot," said Pitou.

"Therefore, I have decided that, I having to go, you, Pitou, shall be head of the farm."

"I, sir?" queried the astonished Pitou. "Impossible!"

"Why is it impossible?"

"Why, Monsieur Billot, because there are a quantity of details for which a woman's eye is indispensable."

"I know it," responded Billot; "you will yourself select the woman who will share with you the duties of overseer. I will not ask you her name; it's no business of mine to know it, and, when I shall be coming back to the farm, I will give you a week's notice beforehand, in order that, if I should not see this woman, or if she ought not to see me, she will have time to go."

"Very well, Monsieur Billot," said Pitou.

"Now," continued Billot, "there is in the barn the necessary seed for sowing, in the granaries, hay, straw and oats required by the horses, and, in this drawer, the money necessary for the wages and expenditure of the men."

Billot opened a drawer full of money.

"Stop a moment, stop a moment, Monsieur Billot!" interposed Pitou; "how much is there in this drawer?"

"I don't know," answered Billot, pushing it shut.

Then, locking it up, and handing Pitou the key, he added:

"When you are out of money apply to me."

Pitou saw how much confidence in him lay in this reply; he held out both his arms to embrace Billot; but suddenly seeing how bold what he was about to do would be, he said:

"I beg your pardon, Monsieur Billot, a thousand times pardon."

"Pardon for what, my friend?" asked Billot, affected by such humility; "pardon for one honest man having opened his arms to embrace another honest man? Come come, Pitou, come to my arms!"

Pitou threw himself into Billot's arms.

"And if, as it may be, you need me in town?" said he.

"Rest easy, Pitou, I shall not forget you."

Then he added:

"It is two o'clock in the afternoon now: I set out for Paris at five. At six, you can come here with the woman you will have chosen to help you."

"It is well. I have no time to lose," said Pitou. "God be with you, dear Monsieur Billot, till we meet again."

"Till we meet again, Pitou!"

Whereupon, Pitou darted out of the house.

Billot watched him as long as he was in sight, and, when he had disappeared, said:

"Oh, why did not my daughter Catherine yield to the suit of a brave lad like this one, rather than to that rascally nobleman who leaves her widowed without being married, a mother without being a wife?"

It is useless to say that at five o'clock, Billot left in the diligence from Villers Gotterets for Paris, and that at six o'clock, Pitou, Catherine and little Isidore entered his farmhouse.

CHAPTER IX.

THE ASPECT OF THE NEW ASSEMBLY.

It was on the first day of October, seventeen hundred and ninety-one, that the inauguration of the Legislative was to take place.

Billot, like the rest of the deputies, reached Paris about the close of September.

The new assembly was composed of seven hundred and forty-five members; among their number might be counted four hundred lawyers and rulers of the state: seventy-two literary men, editors of papers, or poets; seventy constitutional priests: in other words, they had taken the oath to the Constitution. The two hundred and three others were landholders and farmers like Billot, who was farmer and landholder at once, or else men exercising the liberal or even manual professions.

The particular characteristic under which appeared the new deputies, was youth; the greater portion of them was not over six and-twenty years of age; one would have declared a new and unknown generation was sent by France to violently sever itself from the past; dashing, tempestuous, revolutionary, she was bent on dethroning tradition: almost every one a cultivated mind, some poets, as we have said, some lawyers, others doctors; full of energy and grace, of extraordinary spirit, of boundless devotion to their idea, very ignorant in State affairs, inexperienced speechifiers, active, eager to enter upon a contest—they clearly appertained to that great but terrible mass termed *the unknown*.

Now, what is unknown in politics excites always uneasiness. Condorcet and Brissot excepted, almost any one of these men could be asked: "Who are you?"

In truth, where were the firebrands, or even the lights of the Constituency? where were the Mirabeaus, the Sieyes, the Duponts, the Baillys, the Robespierres, the Barnaves, the Cazales?

All these had disappeared.

From spot to spot, as if lost among this ardent youth, a few white heads were to be seen.

The remainder represented young or virile France—France with black hair.

Fine heads to cut off in a revolution—and they were nearly all cut off!

Inasmuch as civil war was foreboded in the interior, as battles abroad were foreshadowed, all these young men were not simple deputies—but were combatants. The Gironde—which in event of war, had offered itself entire, all its people from twenty years to fifty, to march to the frontier—sent a vanguard.

This vanguard were the Vergniauds, Guadets, Gensonnes, Fonfredes, Ducos: it was that nucleus, in brief, which was to be called the Gironde, and give its name to a famous party which, despite its faults, has ever been sympathized with in its misfortunes.

Scenting the breath of battle, they sprang in with a single leap, like the athletes, respiring the combat, upon the bloody arena of political life.

By the mere seeing them tumultuously take their places in the Chamber, any one might have divined in them those puffs of the tempest which heralded the storms of the 20th of June, the 10th of August, and the 21st of January.

No more right side; that was suppressed: consequently there were no more aristocrats.

The entire Assembly was in arms against two enemies; the nobles and the priests.

If they resisted, the mandate had gone forth for them to be crushed.

As for the King, it was left for the conscience of the deputies to be judge over the course to be pursued with respect to him; he was sorrowed for, and it was hoped that he would escape the three-fold power of the Queen, the aristocracy and the clergy; if he upheld them he was to be destroyed with them.

Poor monarch, he was no longer styled the King, or Louis the Sixteenth, or his Majesty: they called him "the executive power."

The first action of the deputies, on entering this hall which was completely unknown to them, was to look around them.

On either side was a reserved tribune.

"For whom are those two?" demanded many voices.

"They are for the going-out deputies," answered the architect.

"Oho!" muttered Vergniaud, "what does this mean? a censorial committee! Is the Legislature a chamber of representatives of a nation, or a class of scholars?"

"Wait," said Herault de Sechelles: "we will see how our masters teach us."

"Usher," broke in Thuriot, "you will tell them as they enter that there is in the Assembly a man who had the governor of the Bastile flung from the top to the bottom of its walls, and that this man is named Thuriot."

A year and a half after this very speaker was called *Tue-Roi* (the King-Killer).

The first act of the new assembly was to send a deputation to the Palace of the Tuileries.

The King had had the imprudence to transact his business with it by a minister.

"Gentlemen," this latter had said: "the King cannot receive you just at present: return in three hours."

The deputies retired.

"Well?" inquired their fellow members on seeing them appear again so soon.

"Citizens," replied one of the envoys, "the King is not ready, and we have three hours before us."

"Very well," cried out from his place Couthon the cripple, "let us make use of the three hours. I propose to suppress the title of 'majesty.'"

An universal hurrah made answer.

The title was struck off by acclamation.

"What shall we call the executive power?" then asked a voice.

"Let it be called the King of the French," responded another voice. "That is a good enough title for Monsieur Capet to be contented with."

Every eye turned to the speaker who had called the King of France, "Monsieur Capet."

It was Billot.

"Agreed for the King of the French!" shouted they almost unanimously.

"Stay," interposed Couthon, "two hours are still left to us. I have a new proposition to make."

"Let us hear it!" cried all the voices.

"I propose that on the King's entrance, we rise, but, once that the King has entered, we take our seats and keep on our hats."

There uprose for an instant a terrible tumult: the shouts of adhesion were so boisterous that they might have been mistaken for those of opposition.

At length, when the sound was calmed, it was seen that all agreed.

The proposition was adopted.

Couthon glanced at the clock.

"We have an hour before us yet," he said. "I have a third proposition to make."

"Make it, make it!" broke out every voice.

"I propose," resumed Couthon, in that insinuating voice which, on occasion, can vibrate in so terrifying a manner, "I propose that there shall be no more a throne for the King, but a simple armchair."

The orator was interrupted by applause.

"Stay, stay," said he, lifting his hand; "I have not finished."

Silence was instantly re-established.

"I propose that this chair of the King shall be on the left hand of the president."

"Take heed!" warned one voice, "this is not only suppressing the throne, but subordinating the King."

"I propose," retorted Couthon, "not only to suppress the throne, but, besides, to make the King subordinate."

There were deafening acclamations.

The 20th of June and the 10th of August were all in those thundering clapping of hands.

"It is well, citizens," said Couthon; "the three hours have elapsed. I thank the King of the French for having made us wait; we have not lost our time in the meanwhile."

The deputation returned to the Tuileries.

This time the King did receive them, but what was done could not be undone.

"Gentlemen," said he, "I cannot before three days go to the Assembly."

The deputies looked at one another.

"Then, sire," said they, "it will be for the fourth?"

"Yes, gentlemen," answered the King, "for the fourth."

Upon which, he turned his back on them.

On the fourth day of October, the King sent word that he was ill, and could not join the session until the 7th.

This did not prevent, on the fourth, during the King's absence, the Constitution of 1791—that is, the most important work of the former Assembly—making its entry into the new Assembly.

It was surrounded and guarded by the twelve oldest representatives of the Constituency.

"There's the twelve old men of the Apocalypse!" cried out a voice.

Camus, the keeper of the rolls, car-ried it; he mounted with it on the tribune, and showing it to the people, said like another Moses:

"People, here are the tablets of the law!"

Then commenced the ceremony of taking the oath.

The whole Assembly defiled, gravely and coldly; many knew beforehand that this powerless constitution would not outlast a year; they swore to swear, because it was a ceremony imposed upon them.

The three-quarters of those who swore were decided not to keep their oath.

Meanwhile, the rumor of the three decrees had spread over Paris.

No more majesty!

No throne!

A simple armchair to the left of the president!

This was very nearly saying:

"No more a king!"

Moneyed men were the first who, as always they are, were frightened; the funds fell fearfully; the bankers commenced to break.

On the 9th of October, a great change took place.

By the terms of the new law, there was to be no longer a commanding general of the National Guard.

On the 9th of October, La Fayette gave in his resignation, and each of the six heads of legions commanded in turn.

The day fixed for the royal session arrived; it will be recollected it was the seventh.

The King entered.

Quite otherwise from what might have been expected, so great was the privilege then, that at the entry of the King, not only did they rise and uncover their heads, but moreover unanimous plaudits arose.

The Assembly cried:

"Long live the King!"

But on that very instant, as though the royalists were bent on hurling defiance at the new representatives, the tribunes cried:

"Long live his Majesty!"

A prolonged murmur ran along the benches of the representatives of the nation ; all the eyes were directed on the tribunes, and it was then perceived that especially in the tribunes reserved for the former constituents these cries had arisen.

"It is well, gentlemen," said Couthon; "to-morrow, we will attend to you."

The King made a sign that he desired to speak.

All were hushed.

The speech that he delivered, composed by Dupont du Tertre, was written with the utmost artfulness, and produced a great effect ; it dwelt entirely on the necessity of maintaining order, and of rallying everything to the love of country.

Pastoret presided over the Assembly. He was a royalist.

The King had said, in his discourse, that " he had need of being loved."

" So have we, sire," said the president, " we have need of being loved by you !"

Upon these words, the whole hall broke forth into applause.

The King, in his discourse, supposed the Revolution ended.

For an instant, the entire Assembly thought as he did.

" For that, sire, you cannot be the voluntary King of the priests, or the involuntary King of the *emigres !*"

The impression exerted over the Assembly immediately spread over Paris.

In the evening, the King went to the theatre with his family.

He was hailed with a thunder of applause.

Many wept, and he himself, so seldom yielding to such weakness, shed tears.

During the night, the King wrote to all the powers of Europe to announce to them his acceptance of the Constitution of 1791.

It was well known that one day, in a moment of enthusiasm, he had sworn to this Constitution, even before it was finished.

The following day, Couthon remembered what he had promised the evening before to his constituents.

He announced that he had a motion to make. Couthon's motions were tolerably well known

All were silent.

" Citizens," said Couthon, " I demand that all traces of privilege shall be removed from this Assembly, and that, consequently, all the tribunes shall be open to the people."

The motion passed unanimously.

The day following, the people crowded into the tribunes of the former deputies, and, before their rush, the shadow of the Constitutionalists faded away.

CHAPTER X.

FRANCE AND ABROAD.

As we have mentioned, the new Assembly was particularly sent against the nobility and the priesthood.

It was a real crusade ; with the exception that the banners—in lieu of bearing the scroll : " Heaven wills it !" —were inscribed with the legend : " The people will it !"

On the 9th of October, the day of La Fayette's resignation, Gallois and Gensonne read their report on the religious disturbances in La Vendee.

It was sagacious, moderate, and, on that very account, made a deep impression.

Who had inspired it, if not written it ?

A very skilful politician, whom we will soon see make his entrance on the scene and into our book.

The Assembly was tolerant.

One of its members (Fauchet) only asked that the state should cease to pay such priests as declared their unwillingness to obey the voice of the state, though giving, meanwhile, pensions to those of the refractory who were aged and infirm.

Ducos went still farther : he invoked tolerance, and asked that full liberty should be left for the priests to take the oath or not.

Much farther went the constitutional Bishop Torne. He declared that the very refusal of the priests was allied to great virtues.

We shall presently see how the devotees of Avignon replied to this toler-ance.

After the discussion—not terminated yet, however—on the constitutional priests, they passed on to the emigres.

It was going from war interior to war exterior—that is, touching the two wounds of France.

Fauchet had treated the question of the clergy.

Brissot spoke upon that of the emigration.

He took the elevated, humane side; he took it up where Mirabeau a twelve-month before had let it drop from his dying hands.

He asked for a difference to be made between leaving the country through fear and leaving it through hate; he requested indulgence for the former, severity for the latter.

In his opinion, citizens should not be restricted to their country; on the contrary, every door should be left open to them.

He did not even ask confiscation against the emigration through hate.

He only required a cessation of payment to those who were armed against France.

A wonderful fact, indeed!

France continued to pay to foreigners the entertainment of the Condes, the Lambescs, the Charles de Lorraines!

We shall presently see how the emigres replied to this mildness.

As Fauchet finished his discourse, there arrived intelligence from Avignon.

Brissot had just closed his speech when news from Europe came.

Then a bright light shone up in the west like an immense conflagration; this was tidings from America.

Let us commence with Avignon.

Let us tell in a few words the history of this second Rome.

Benedict the Eleventh had died (in 1304) in a scandalously sudden manner.

Hence it had been said that he died from some poisonous figs.

Philip the Fair, who had struck the face of Boniface the Eighth by Colonna's hand, had his eyes fixed on Perouse, where the conclave was held.

Since a long time previously, he had had the idea of laying hands on the papacy and bringing it to France, when—once that he had it in his jail—he might make it labor for his profit, and, as says our great master Michelet, "to dictate to it lucrative bulls, to translate its infallibility, and constitute the Holy Ghost scribe and preceptor to the house of France."

One day there came to him a messenger powdered with dust, ready to drop with weariness, barely able to speak.

The news he brought was as follows:

The French party and the party opposed to the French were so evenly balanced in the conclave, that no pope's name would have a majority of the scrutinies, and that they spoke of assembling in another city, in a new conclave.

This resolve was not agreed to by the people of Perouse, who clung to the honor of having a pope made in their city.

So they put into use an ingenious method.

They formed an enclosure around the cardinals to prevent the cardinals having anything to eat or drink.

The cardinals remonstrated loudly.

"Appoint a pope!" cried the people, "and then you shall have whatever you want."

The cardinals held out for twenty-four hours.

At the end of that time, they had decided.

The Anti-French party were allowed to select three cardinals, and the French party, out of those three candidates was to choose a pope.

The Anti-French party set their choice upon three declared enemies to Philip the Fair.

But, in the number of this trio of enemies to Philip the Fair was the Archbishop of Bordeaux, Bertrand de Got, who was known to be a better friend to his own interest than enemy to Philip the Fair.

A messenger was dispatched with this intelligence.

This was the horseman who had sped over the road in four days and four nights, and arrived nearly dead with fatigue.

There was no time to be lost.

Philip sent an express to Bertrand de Got—who was still completely ignorant of the high mission he was to be charged with—to give him a rendezvous in a forest near St. Jean d'Angeley.

Bertrand de Got failed not to keep the rendezvous.

It was a gloomy night, which resembled those chosen by magicians to invoke spirits. The place was a cross-road where three roads met; similar spots and times are used by those who, wishing to obtain superhuman powers, call up the devil, and, swearing to be his liege man, kiss Satan's cloven hoof.

However—doubtlessly to encourage the archbishop—the King and the priest heard mass; and at the moment the host was elevated, they swore on the altar, by the God they both adored, to maintain an inviolable secrecy ; then the wax tapers were extinguished, the church was vacated, the assistants, followed by the chorister boys, hastened away, bearing the cross and the sacred vessels, as if they feared they would be profaned if left to be mute witnesses of the scene about to occur.

The archbishop and the monarch were left to themselves.

Bertrand de Got was yet ignorant as to the nature of the secret he had sworn to keep.

Who informed Villani of what we are about to tell ? Satan, perhaps, for he must have made the third in the interview.

From Villani we read:

"Archbishop," said Philip the Fair, "I have it in my power to make thee pope; for that purpose I have met thee."

"The proof?" inquired Bertrand.

"It is here," answered the King.

With that he showed him a letter from his cardinals, who, instead of stating their choice was made, asked whom he wished them to select.

"What must I do to attain this?" inquired the Gascon, wild with joy, and he threw himself at the monarch's feet.

"Grant me six favors I shall beg of thee," asked Philip the Fair.

"It is for thee to command, and for me to obey," said the future pope. "Speak out, O my King!"

The oath of servitude was taken.

The King raised the priest from the ground, kissed him on the mouth, and said :

"The six favors I shall ask of thee are the following——"

Bertrand listened with all his attention ; for he dreaded, not that the King would require things endangering his soul's salvation, but that he would ask something impossible.

Philip said:

"Firstly, thou shalt completely reconcile me to the church, procuring pardon for the evil deed I perpetrated on Pope Boniface VIII., by arresting him at Amagni."

"Granted !" Bertrand de Got hastened to respond.

"Secondly, thou shalt administer to me and mine the communion of which Rome has deprived me."

(Philip the Fair had been excommunicated).

"Granted !" said Bertrand de Got, astounded that so little should be asked of him for being made so great.

Yet there were four more requests for him to hear.

"Thirdly, thou shalt, as a contribution towards the expenses of the war in Flanders, grant me the tithes of the clergy throughout my kingdom for a space of five years."

"Granted !"

"Fourthly, thou shalt destroy and annul the memory of Pope Boniface ;—*Ausculta fili.*"

"Agreed, agreed !"

"Fiithly, thou shalt restore Messires Jacobo and Pietro Colonna to the dignity of cardinal; and with them make certain other friends of mine cardinals."

"Agreed, agreed."

Then, as Philip was silent, the archbishop inquired in some uneasiness :

"And the sixth, my lord ?"

"Concerning the sixth favor thou art to grant me," returned Philip the Fair, "I reserve to myself the right to speak to thee thereon, at a fitting place and season ; for it is a weighty and secret thing."

"Weighty and secret ?" echoed Bertrand de Got.

"So weighty and secret," responded the monarch, "that I desire you beforehand, to swear it me on the cross."

Whereupon drawing a crucifix from his bosom, he presented it to the archbishop.

The latter did not for an instant hesitate ; it was the last ditch to cross— that done, he was a pope.

He stretched out his hand on the image of our Saviour, and, in a steady voice, said :

"I swear."

Thus Bertrand de Got took the oath for the known favors, and for the one that was yet unknown.

"It is well," said the King. "In what place in my realm do you wish to be crowned ?"

"Lyons."

"Come with me ! you are pope, under the name of Clement V."

Clement the Fifth followed King Philip, but he was rather ill at ease as to the sixth condition, which his suzerain had reserved.

When this was revealed, he looked upon it as a very little thing ; hence he made no opposition ; it was—what the King had not dared to breathe as a sequel to the others—the destruction of the Templars.

In addition to the promise and the oath he had taken on the Corpus Domini, Bertrand de Got gave his brother and two of his nephews as hostages. The King for his part, swore to make Bertrand pope, as we know.

This was not right in the eyes of Heaven, for it showed its wrath in a manifest way.

The coronation of the pope, shortly afterwards celebrated at Lyons, and which commenced the era of the church's captivity, seemed displeasing in the sight of heaven. At the moment when the papal cortege, coming out of the church where Clement the Fifth was crowned, was passing a wall crowded with spectators, it gave way, wounding the King and killing the Duke of Brittany.

The pope was cast to the earth, and the triple crown rolled in the dust.

A week afterwards, during a banquet given by the new pope, the people of

his Holiness and the servingmen of some cardinals got into a brawl.

The pope's brother tried to part them and was slain.

These were evil foreshadowings.

To such presages was linked bad examples.

The Pope was an extortioner from the church, but a woman extorted money from the pope. This woman was the beautiful Brunissande, who—if we credit the chroniclers of that day—cost Christianity dearer than the Holy Land.

Meanwhile Clement the Fifth fulfilled all the promises of Bertrand de Got.

Philip was reconciled to the church, and admitted to the communion ; the purple once more adorned the shoulders of Colonna, and the church was constrained to pay for the wars in Flanders and Philip de Valois' crusade against the Greek empire.

If not destroyed and annulled, the memory of Boniface VIII. was at least made to wither ; the walls of the Temple were thrown down, and the Templars perished by fire in front of the Pont Neuf.

This pope whom Philip created was his special pope, a kind of goose with the golden eggs which he made to lay night and morning, and which he threatened to cut up if it stopped laying.

Every day, as the Merchant of Venice thirsted to do, he cut away a pound of flesh from his debtor off the limb suiting him.

In short, Pope Boniface the Eighth declared a false, heretical pope, the King relieved from excommunication, the church tithes given for five years, twelve cardinals appointed at the royal behest, the bull of Boniface the Eighth which shut Philip the Fair out of meddling with the purse of the clergy revoked, the Order of the Temple abolished and the Templars arrested—it came to pass on the 1st day of May, 1308, that the Emperor Albert of Austria died.

Clement the Fifth had worked to bring about this result.

The slavery of this man in bondage continued : the poor soul of Bertrand de Got, saddled and bridled, was to be ridden by the King of France to hell.

It had, however, the spirit to throw its terrible rider.

Clement the Fifth wrote ostensibly in favor of Charles de Valois, secretly against him.

From that moment forward he had to think of leaving the kingdom ; the pope's life was all the less in safety within the royal territory from the fact of the nomination of the twelve cardinals placing the future pontifical elections in the hands of the King of France.

Clement the Fifth remembered the figs of Benedict the Eleventh.

He was at Poitiers.

He managed to flee during the night and reach Avignon.

It is rather difficult to explain what Avignon was.

It was France, and it was not France.

It was a frontier, a land of sanctuary, a fragment of an empire, an old municipality, a republic like Saint Marin. Only it was governed by two kings.

The King of Naples, as Count of Provence, the King of France, as Count of Toulouse.

Each of the two had as lordship a half of Avignon.

Neither could arrest a fugitive on the other's territory.

Clement the Fifth naturally took refuge in that portion of Avignon which belonged to the King of Naples.

But, albeit he might escape the power of King Philip the Fair, he did not escape the summons of the Grand Master of the Templars.

From the stake at which he perished (on the Isle of the Cite, Paris) Jacques de Molay, had cited both king and priest, his two executioners, to appear in a year's time before God.

Dying men have prophetic spirits, says Aristophanes.

Clement V. obeyed the summons first. He had already, in a dream, seen his palace in flames. "From this moment," says Baluze, "he became melancholy, and he did not last long."

Seven months afterwards came Philip's time.

How did he die?

There are two versions of his death.

Both seem to be a vengeance from heaven.

The chronicle translated by Sauvage makes him die at a hunt.

" He saw the stag coming at him, he drew his sword, spurred his steed and, while charging to cut down the deer, he was by his horse carried against a tree, so violently, that the good king fell to the ground severely wounded in the heart, and was carried to Corbeil."

There, the chronicle continues, the wound grew worse and he died.

But according to the account given by William de Nangis, Providence had reserved a very different death for the victor at Mons en Puelle.

"Philip, King of France, was long suffering from a malady of which the cause, unknown to the physicians, was for them and others the subject of great surprise and stupor : all the more from neither his pulse nor his habits showing that he was ill or in danger of death. Finally, he ordered that he should be transported to Fontainebleau, his birthplace. There, after having in presence and view of a great number of people received the sacrament with admirable fervor and devotion, he surrendered his soul to his Creator in the confession of the true and Catholic faith, in the thirtieth year of his reign, on Friday, the eve of the Apostle Saint Andrew's Day."

It was Dante who could find a death for a man he hated.

He makes him die ripped up by a wild boar.

" The man who had been seen coining false money on the banks of the Seine died by the wild boar's tusk."

The popes who dwelt in Avignon after Clement the Fifth—who were John the Twenty-Second, Benedict the Twelfth, Clement the Sixth—only waited for a chance to buy Avignon.

It came for the last named.

A young woman still a minor, Joanna of Naples, we will not say sold it, but gave it for the absolution of an assassination committed by her lovers. When she reached her majority, she claimed back the cession ; but Clement the Sixth had hold of it, and kept his hold.

And so firmly that when Gregory the Eleventh (in 1377) carried back the seat of the papacy to Rome, Avignon, administered by a legate, remained submissive to the Holy See.

It was so still in 1791, when occurred the events which are the cause of this lengthy digression.

As in the days when Avignon was shared between the King of Naples as Count of Provence, and the King of France as Count of Toulouse, there were two Avignons within Avignon: the clerical or Roman, the commercial or French town.

The priests' town had its popish palace, its hundred churches, its two hundred cloisters, its innumerable bells—always ready to sound for rebellion or conflagration; to give the alarm for murder.

The commercial town had its Rhone, its workmen in the silk manufacture, and its main roads; the one running north and south, the other east and west—from Lyons to Marseilles, from Nimes to Turin.

There was in some sort, in this hapless town, the King's Frenchmen, the Pope's Frenchmen.

The former were really French.

The others were Italians.

The Frenchmen of France—the commercial men—had much to do to make out a living for themselves, their wives and children, they hardly succeeded in so doing.

The Italian Frenchmen—the priesthood—had everything, wealth and power; they were abbes, bishops, archbishops, cardinals—idle, immoral, elegant, bold; cicisbeos of the titled ladies, kings of fashion and autocrats of the drawing-room, kissing the hands of ladies whose admirers they constituted themselves; extending their own hands graciously to women of a lower grade, whom they led astray alike by their doctrine and their practice.

Do you, reader, wish for a type of this race of abbes?

Take the Abbe Maury, who was a Franco-Italian of the Comtat Venaissin, if ever there was one; son of a shoemaker, he was as aristocratic as the Duke de Lauzan, as proud as a Clement Tonnerre, as insolent as a lackey!

Everywhere, before being men, and, consequently, having passions, children love.

At Avignon they are born hating.

On the fourteenth day of September, 1791—in the days of the National Assembly—a royal decree had joined to France Avignon and the Comtat Venaissin.

During a year, Avignon had been, now in the hands of the French party, now in the hands of its opponents.

The storm broke out in 1790.

One night the papists amused themselves by hanging a puppet decorated with the red, white, and blue.

The Rhone has been turned from its course; the Durance has been made navigable; barriers have been constructed to restrain the torrents which rush from the tall summit of Mount Ventoux when the snows of winter melt.

But no mortal man has ever succeeded in arresting the terrible, the living tide of the population of Avignon, when once that rushing stream had burst its bounds.

At sight of the puppet swinging from a cord, and sporting the national colors, the French town of Avignon emerged from its homes with a growl of rage.

Four papists, suspected of having perpetrated this sacrilege—two marquises, one citizen and a workman—were torn from their houses and hung up instead of the puppet.

This took place on the 11th of June, 1790.

The French party had as leaders two young men, Duprat and Mainvielle, and one man named Lescuyer.

He was a Frenchman in every sense of the word.

He was not a young man; on the contrary, he might almost be called an old man, and was not even a native of that region.

He was a Picardian, at once an ardent and a reflective man; a notary by profession, he had been long established at Avignon. He was secretary of the municipality.

These three chiefs had got together

some soldiers, two or three thousand, perhaps, and had attempted with them an expedition against Carpentras, which had not succeeded.

The rain—a cold, freezing shower, mingled with hail—one of those falls which come down from Mount Ventoux, had dispersed the army of Mainvielle, Duprat, and Lescuyer, as the tempest shattered Philip's Invincible Armada.

Who had caused to fall this miraculous rain which had the power of breaking up the revolutionary army?

The Virgin!

Avignon, dear reader, is like a portion of Italy. Miracles are necessities there; and if no real miracles take place, somebody is sure to invent a few false ones. Then again the miracle must bear reference to the Virgin : for in Italy, that poetic country, the Virgin, *La Madonna* is everything. The mind, the heart, the language of every Italian is alive with these two words.

But Duprat, Mainvielle and Lescuyer suspected a Catalan named the Chevalier Patus, whom they had appointed general, of having so efficaciously seconded the Virgin in the miracle that they attributed all the honor to him.

At Avignon, justice makes short work of treachery ; they kill the traitor.

Patus was killed.

Now, of what was composed the army representing the French party?

Peasants, porters, deserters.

A man of the people was sought to command these men of the people.

They believed they had found the right man in one named Mathieu Jouve, who had made himself be called Jourdan.

He was born at Sainte Just, near the town of Puy in Velay. He had first been a muleteer on the steep heights which surround his native city, then a soldier without war—war might, perhaps, have humanised him—then he had kept a cabaret in Paris.

At Avignon, he sold madder.

He was a boaster of murders, a self-glorifier of crime.

He used to show a large sword and say that with it he had cut the throat of the governor of the Bastile, and two of the royal body guard on the sixth of October.

Half in jest, half in fear, to the surname of Jourdan which he had assumed himself, people added the nickname of " the Cut-throat."

Duprat, Mainvielle, Lescuyer, and their General Jourdan the Cut-throat, had been long enough masters of the town for them to have become less feared.

A secret, wide-spread conspiracy was organized against them, well-managed and well-concealed as plots of priests always are.

Religious passion was stirred up against them.

The wife of a French patriot gave birth to an armless child.

Rumor wafted it around that the husband, while removing a silver angel out of a church during the night, had broken its arms.

Hence the incomplete infant was nothing else than a judgment of heaven.

The father was forced to hide himself. He would have been cut to pieces, before one would have thought whether any angel had been stolen from a church.

Everywhere the Virgin protected the royalists, whether they were chouans in Brittany or papists in Avignon.

In 1789, the Virgin shed tears in a church in the Rue du Bac.

In 1790, she appeared in the Vendean Bocage, behind an old oak tree.

In 1791, she dispersed the army of Duprat and Mainvielle, by blowing hail and sleet into their faces.

Lastly, in the Church of the Cordeliers, she had blushed, with shame doubtless, on the indifference of the people of Avignon.

This last miracle, vouched for by the women, especially—men did not have such faith—had already elevated minds to a great height, when a report of another nature quickly spread which raised the excitement to the highest pitch.

A great chest was reported to have been conveyed through the town. This raised the curiosity of the inhabitants of Avignon.

What might this chest contain?

The next day it was no longer one chest, but six.

The day after that, it was eighteen large chests that had been carried towards the Rhone.

What was the contents of them?

A porter had revealed the secret. The French party had resolved to exile itself from Avignon, and was carrying away pledges left at the mont-de-piete (government pawnbroker's).

Upon this news, a gust of a storm swept over the town: this wind was the famous *zou, zou,* the peculiar cry of the Avignon people; a sound which seems composed of the serpent's hiss and the tiger's growl; which in riots is to be heard.

To carry away the pledges left at the mont-de-piete, was synonymous with despoiling the poor, for, so great was poverty at Avignon, that everybody had something pledged.

However little the pledge of the poorest, its total loss was ruin to him.

The rich are ruined for a million, the poor for a petty coin: all is relative.

This was the sixteenth of October, a Sunday morning.

All the peasants of the neighborhood had come into the city to hear the mass.

Everybody moved armed at this period: consequently none were without weapons.

The moment was a well chosen one: the whole game, in fact, was cunningly played.

Then there was no longer parties for nor against the French: thieves had committed a robbery, an infamous robbery, the poor had been plundered!

The crowd rushed into the Church of the Cordeliers. Peasants, citizens, workmen, white, red, tri-color, shouted out on the same instant that the municipality should show its accounts through the organ of its secretary Lescuyer.

Why was the popular wrath bent on Lescuyer?

It is unknown.

When life is required to be torn from a man, there seems a fate about the selection.

Suddenly, in the very midst of the church, Lescuyer was dragged.

He was on the way to the council house, when he had been recognised, arrested—no, not arrested—forced by fists, kicks, and clubs into the church.

Once within the holy edifice, the unfortunate man, pale, but cool and calm, nevertheless, stood upon a seat, and undertook to clear himself.

This was easy, he had but to say:

"Go ye and look at the monte-de-piete, and it will be seen that the plate we are accused of having removed is still there."

But he commenced:

"My friends, I considered the Revolution necessary, and therefore put forth all my strength——"

The fanatics saw that if Lescuyer succeeded in explaining himself he was saved.

This was not their design.

The terrible *zou zou,* piercing as the mistral, interrupted him.

A porter jumped up into the pulpit and threw him on the crowd.

The bugle-call of "In-at-the-death!" was sounded.

The hounds sprang on their prey.

He was dragged to the foot of the altar.

It was there they meant to finish the revolutionist—to make a sacrifice worthy of the Virgin, in whose name all this went on.

Still living, he escaped in the choir from the hands of the assassins, and took refuge in a stall.

Charitable hands passed to him writing materials.

He had not time to write what he wanted to write.

An unlooked for success gave him a moment's respite.

A Breton gentleman who was, by chance, passing on his way to Marseilles, entered the church, and was affected by pity for the poor victim. With the courage and obstinacy of a true Breton, he tried to save him; two or three times he pushed aside clubs or knives ready to strike him, crying out:

"Gentlemen, in the name of the law, in the name of honor, in the name of humanity!"

Knives and clubs were turned on him, then ; but he, threatened by the sticks and blades, none the less earnestly covered poor Lescuyer with his body, repeating :

"Gentlemen, in the name of humanity !"

At last, the rioters got tired of being so long kept back from their game ; they seized this gentleman and dragged him away to hang him.

But three men released the stranger, saying :

"Let us finish with Lescuyer first ; we can take care of this meddler afterwards."

The mob acknowledged the soundness of this reasoning, and let the Breton go.

He was forced to escape.

He was named M. de Rosely.

Lescuyer had not had time to write ; had he had it, his note would not have been read ; there was too great an uproar.

Amid all the tumult, Lescuyer had noted a small door behind the altar : could he reach that, perhaps he would be saved !

He rushed out for it at a moment when he was believed to be overcome with terror.

Lescuyer managed to touch the door.

The murderers were taken by surprise.

But, at the foot of the altar, a mattress-worker, armed with a cudgel, gave him such a terrible blow on the head, that the stout weapon was broken in two pieces.

Then the crowd rushed on the poor prostrate form ; and with that mixture of ferocity and sinister humor for which the people of the south are remarkable, the men began to dance on his body, and crush him with stones, like Saint Stephen, howling out songs the while ;— women proceeded to cut and mangle his lips with their scissors, in order, they said, that he might expiate the revolutionary blasphemy of "Liberty forever !"

From the midst of this horrible group there arose a cry or rather a moan from those bleeding lips ; this moaning cry said :

"In the name of Heaven, brothers ! —in the name of the Virgin, sisters ! —in the name of humanity !—kill me at once !"

This was too much to ask.

He was condemned to live on in his agony.

This was till evening.

For five hours did that agony last ; and during all that time did that poor crushed form lay gasping on the steps of the altar, amid brutal insults and roars of ferocious laughter from the crowd.

Such was the news that arrived at the Legislative Assembly in reply to Fauchet's philanthropic speech.

It is true that, the day but one after, fresh tidings came.

Duprat and Jourdan had been warned of what had happened.

Where could they find their scattered men ?

Duprat had an idea.

To ring as a rallying signal the famous silver bell which only rang on two occasions : the consecration of popes, their death.

It sent forth a strange and mysterious peal, rarely heard.

This sound produced two widely-opposite effects.

It chilled the heart of the papists.

It restored courage to the revolutionists.

At the toll of the bell ringing an unknown alarm, the countrymen hurried from the city, and took to flight, each in the direction of his dwelling.

Jourdan, on the appeal of the silver bell, got together about three hundred of his soldiers.

He locked the city gates, and left a hundred and fifty of his men to guard them.

With the remainder, he marched on the Church of the Cordeliers.

He had two cannon. He would plant them in the street, aim at a crowd, and fire at random.

He reached the church.

It was deserted.

Lescuyer was writhing at the feet of the Virgin, who has done so many miracles, but did not stretch forth her divine hand to relieve the unfortunate.

It seemed that he could not die; the bleeding mass, which was one whole wound, clung yet to life.

In this condition he was carried through the streets.

Everywhere, at the passing of the procession, people closed up their houses, and shouted :

" I was not at the Cordeliers !"

Jourdan and his hundred and fifty men might do whatever they liked with Avignon, and its thirty thousand inhabitants, so great was the terror.

They did in miniature what Marat and Panis did in Paris on the 2nd of September.

(It will hereafter be seen why we say " Marat and Panis," and not Danton.)

They pushed seventy or eighty unfortunates into the pontifical dungeons in the Tour de la Glaciere.

The Tour Trouillas, as they say in those parts.

Such was the news that arrived and made Lescuyer's death be forgotten by these terrible reprisals.

As for the emigres whom Brissot defended, and wished to throw open the gates of France, what they were doing abroad was as follows.

They reconciled Austria with Prussia, and made bosom friends of those two enemies born.

They brought Russia to forbid the French Ambassador showing himself in the streets of St. Petersburgh, and send a minister to the refuges at Coblentz.

They caused Berne to punish a Swiss town which had sung the revolutionary " Ca ira."

They made Geneva,—the country of Rousseau, who had done so much for the revolution France was now at work on—direct the muzzles of its cannon at France.

They led the Bishop of Liege to refuse to receive a French Ambassador.

It is true, that of themselves, the sovereigns did something else.

Russia and Sweden sent back to Louis the Sixteenth, unopened, the despatches by which they were officially informed of his adhesion to the Constitution.

Spain refused to receive them, and handed over to the Inquisition a French-

man, who only escaped the San Benito by killing himself.

Venice flung upon the Square of Saint Mark the corpse of a man strangled during the night, by order of the Council of Ten, with this simple scroll.

" Strangled because a Free Mason."

Lastly, the Emperor and King of Prussia answered by a menace.

" We desire," said they, " this to be a warning of the necessity of taking serious precautions against the return of things which gave rise to such sad auguries."

Therefore, there was civil war in La Vendee, civil war in the South of France, foreign war all around.

Moreover, from the other shores of the Atlantic, rolled the groans of the entire population of an island, whose throats were being cut.

What was going on over there, in the west ?

Who were those black men—those slaves who were butchering ?

The negroes of Saint Domingo were taking a bloody revenge !

How came such an event to arise ?

In a few words—in a less prolix manner than we treated Avignon (for we let ourselves be led away by Avignon)—in a few words, we will endeavor to explain.

The Constitutionalists had promised the negroes freedom.

Oge, a young mulatto (one of the bravest, most ardent and devoted hearts I ever knew), had crossed the ocean, bearing the liberating decrees which he had caught up on the very instant of their being issued.

Though nothing official had yet arrived concerning these decrees, in his haste for liberty, he summoned the governor of the province to proclaim them.

The governor gave an order for him to be arrested.

Oge took refuge in the Spanish part of the island.

The Spanish authorities—it is very well known how Spain looked upon the Revolution—gave him over to the French.

Oge was broken alive !

Terror overcame the whites upon his death. He was supposed to have had accomplices throughout Hayti.

The planters created themselves judges, and executions multiplied.

One night, sixty thousand blacks rose.

The whites were aroused by the conflagrations sweeping over their plantations.

A week afterwards the fire was quenched in blood.

What would France, poor salamander encircled in a ring of fire, do ?

We are about to see.

CHAPTER XI.

WAR.

IN his brilliant, energetical speech on the emigres, Brissot had clearly shown the intentions of the crowned heads, and the species of death they reserved for the Revolution.

Would they dash at it sword in hand ?

No, they would smother it.

After having drawn the picture of the European league, after having disclosed the circle of sovereigns, some with drawn blades with the standards of hate waving over them, others still covering their features with the mask of hypocrisy until they might cast it off, Brissot lifted up his voice :

" Well, then, so be it ! not only do we accept the challenge of aristocratic Europe, but we will forestall it ; do not let us wait till we are attacked— let us attack ourselves !"

Upon this outburst, immense applause greeted the orator.

Brissot, rather a man of instinct than a man of genius, had just answered to the main thought of devotion which had prescribed over the elections of 1791 : War !

Not that the selfish war declared by a despot to avenge an insult made to his throne, his name, his ally's name, or to add a subjected province to his kingdom or empire ; but the war which carries with it the breath of life ; the war whose brazen clangor speaks wherever it is heard :

" Arise, ye who would be free ! we bring ye liberty !"

Indeed, the world had began to hear a deep murmur rising and increasing, like the beat of the sea on a rocky coast.

This sound was the mutterings of thirty millions of voices not yet speaking aloud, but growling already.

This growl had been translated by Brissot when he said :

" Do not let us wait till we are attacked—let us attack ourselves !"

From the moment when to these threatening words universal applause had responded, France was strong : not only could she attack, but she could win, besides.

There remains matters of detail.

Our readers must have perceived that this is an historical work, and not a romance, that we are writing ; we shall in all likelihood, never return to this great period on which we have already founded " Blanche of Beaulieu," " the Chevalier of Maison Rouge," and a book written several years ago, not yet printed, but which will be published : we take this opportunity of explaining what it will contain.

We will, nevertheless pass rapidly over the minutiæ to arrive as speedily as possible at the events left for us to narrate, those with which the characters of our book are more particularly related.

The recital of the occurrences in La Vendee, the massacres of Avignon, the insults from Europe, broke like a thunderbolt on the Legislative Assembly.

On the twentieth of October, Brissot, as we have seen, was content to impose a restriction on the property of emigres : on the twenty-fifth of the same month, Condorcet condemned their possessions to sequestrations, and exacted from them the civic oath.

Such an oath to men living out of France and armed against her !

Two representatives, thereupon disclosed, became, one the Barnave, the other the Mirabeau of the new Assembly.

Vergniaud, Isnard.

Vergniaud, one of those poetical, tender and sympathetic figures revolutions always drag along after them, was a son of fertile Limoges, gentle, slow, affectionate rather than passionate, well-born, noticed by Turgot, the intendant of the Limousin and sent by him to school at Bordeaux : his speech was not so biting nor so powerful as Mirabeau's, but although inspired by the Greeks and a little overcharged with mythology, less prolix and less of a lawyer's than Barnave's.

What constituted the inspiring and influential portion of his eloquence was the manly tone which constantly vibrated in it ; at the Assembly, in the very midst of the burning, elevated anger of the tribunes, from his breast was ever to be heard flowing the accents of nature or of pity : a leader of an eager, violent, disputing party, he soared ever calm and dignified above the scene, even when it was a mortal situation : his enemies said he was indecisive, easily moved, at times indolent ; they asked where was his spirit, which seemed absent.

They were right.

His spirit was only his when he made an effort and enchained it in his breast; his whole soul was a woman's ; it wandered over the lips, mingled its light with the clearness flowing from the eyes, it vibrated on the harp of the beautiful as good and charming Candeille.

Isnard—quite the opposite of Vergniaud, who was in some sort the calm —was the wrath of the Assembly.

Born at Grasse, in that land of perfumes and the storm-wind, he owned the sudden, violent outbursts of that giant of the air which, with the same breath, unearth's rocks and plays over roses : his strange voice broke out of a sudden in the Assembly like one of those unexpected thunder claps of the first summer-showers. At the first accent of that voice, the entire Assembly started, the ones whose minds were farthest away lifted their heads, and every one, shuddering like Cain at the voice of the Lord, was ready to say :

" Speakest thou to me ?"

Somebody interupted him.

" I ask," cried he, " of the Assembly, of France, the world,—of you, sir !—"

He pointed to the interrupter.

" I ask if there be one who—in good faith, approved by the secret demands of his conscience—is willing to uphold that the self-exiled princes are not conspiring against the country. I ask, in the second place, if there be one in this assembly who durst maintain that any conspirator ought not to be, as soon as can be, accused, pursued and punished. If such a one there be, let him rise !

* * * * * *

" They tell you that indulgence is the duty of strength ; that certain powers are disarming—but I tell you that we must be on the watch ; that despotism and the aristocracy are neither dead nor asleep, and that, if nations slumber one instant, they will awake enchained. The least pardonable of crimes is that whose design is to return man to slavery. If heavenly fire were at man's disposal, it should strike those aiming at the people's liberty !"

This was the first time such words had been there heard : this wild eloquence carried away everybody with it, as the avalanche rushing down from the Alpine peaks sweeps before it trees, herds, men and houses.

The session terminated, it was decreed:

" That, if Louis Stanilaus Xavier, French prince, does not return in two months he abdicates his claims to the regency."

On the 8th of November :

" That, if the emigres do not return by the 1st of January, they will be declared guilty of conspiracy, will be pursued and punished with death."

On the 29th of October, was the turn of the priesthood :

" The civic oath will be required," within eight days.

" Those refusing to take it will be looked upon as suspected of revolt and the eye of authority will be kept upon them.

" If such are in a district where religious disturbances are going on, the head of the department may remove them from their ordinary dwelling.

" If they disobey this they shall be imprisoned for a year or more ; if they resist, for two years.

" The district which obliges an armed force to be there mantained, must furnish their support.

" Churches will only use the stated service ; those of them not needed may be purchased to be used for any worship but that of those refusing to take the oath.

" Townships will send in to the departments, which will transmit them to the Assembly, the list of the priests who have sworn and those who have not, with remarks on the connection between them and with emigres, in order that the Assembly may organize means of rooting out rebellion.

" The Assembly regards as a benefit the good works which may enlighten the country on the pretended religious questions : it will have them printed and will reward the authors."

We have mentioned what became of the Constituents, otherwise the Constitutionalists.

We have shown what was the design in founding the Club of the Feuillants.

Their mind was perfectly in harmony with the department of Paris.

It was the mind of Barnave, La Fayette, Lameth, Duport, Bailly—who was still a mayor, but who was presently to cease to be so.

They saw in the decree to the priests —" a decree," they said, " rendered against the public conscience"—and in the decree on the emigres—" a decree rendered against family ties"—a means of testing the royal power.

The Club of the Feuillants prepared and the Directory of Paris signed a protest against both the decrees, in which they entreated Louis the Sixteenth to put his veto on the decree concerning the priesthood.

(It will be borne in mind that the Constitution reserved to King Louis this right of veto.)

Who signed this protest ?

The man who had been the very first to assail the clergy, the Mephistophiles who, with his clubfoot, had broken the ice.

Talleyrand !

The man who has, since then, made diplomacy see less clearly in revolutions.

The rumor of the veto spread around beforehand.

The Cordeliers pushed forward Camille Desmoulins, that lancer of the Revolution to be found ever ready to couch his spear.

He also sent in his petition.

But, unintelligible stutterer, when he undertook to speak, he charged Fauchet to read it.

Fauchet did so.

It was applauded from one end to the other.

It would have been difficult to manage the question with more irony and yet go as deep to the bottom.

"We do not complain," said the college comrade of Robespierre and the friend of Danton, " we do not complain either of the Constitution, which has granted the vetoing power, or of the King, who uses it ; we call to mind the maxim of a great politician, Machiavel : 'If the prince ought to renounce sovereignty, the nation would be too cruel and unjust if it thought him wrong in constantly opposing himself to the general will, because it is hard and against nature for one to willingly fall from such a height.'

"Penetrated with this truth, we shall never exact of the former ruler an impossible love for the national sovereignty, and we do not think ill of him from his putting his veto to the best decrees."

The Assembly, as we have recorded, applauded and adopted the petition, resolved its insertion should be in the minutes, and resolved to send copies to the departments of the country.

That evening, the Feuillants were in excitement.

Many members of the club, representatives to the Legislative Assembly, had not been at the session.

The absentees of the previous night made an invasion on the following day into the Assembly.

They numbered two hundred and sixty.

The decrees of the previous meeting they annulled, amidst the hootings and hisses of the audience.

This was war between the Assembly and the Club, which rested then on the Jacobins, represented by Robespierre, and on the Cordeliers, represented by Danton.

In fact, Danton was gaining in popularity; his monstrous head began to appear above the crowd : a giant Adamastor, he rose up before royalty, saying to it :

" Beware ! the waters over which you sail is called the Sea of Tempests !"

Then, most unexpectedly, the Queen came to the aid of the Jacobins against the Feuillants.

The hatreds of Marie Antoinette were to the Revolution what to the Atlantic are squalls and whirlwinds.

Marie Antoinette hated La Fayette ; the same La Fayette who had saved her on the sixth of October, and who had lost his popularity for her on the seventeenth of July.

La Fayette aspired to replace Bailly as the Mayor of Paris.

The Queen, instead of helping La Fayette, led the royalists to vote for Petion.

Strange blindness !

In favor of Petion, her brutal traveling companion on the return from Varennes !

On the 19th of December, the King presented himself to the Assembly, bringing his veto to the decree against the priests.

On that evening, at the Club of the Jacobins, there had taken place a serious demonstration.

A Swiss from Neufchatel, Virchaux, the same who, on the Champ de Mars, drew up the petition for the Republic, had offered to the society a Damascus sword, intended for the first general who should vanquish the enemies of liberty.

Isnard was there.

He snatched the blade from the young republican, drew it from its scabbard, and rushed into the tribunal, shouting :

" Behold ! the sword of the exterminating angel ! It shall be victorious ! France will give vent to a mighty call, and people will reply ; then will the earth be covered with combatants, and the foemen of freedom shall be wiped off from the list of mankind !"

Ezekiel could not spoken more to the purpose.

The sword drawn was not to be restored to its sheath.

Two-fold war was declared against the interior and exterior.

The sword of the Swiss republican was to first strike the King of France ; then, after that monarch, foreign sovereigns.

CHAPTER XII.

A MINISTER IN THE FASHION OF MADAME DE STAEL.

GILBERT had not seen the Queen since that day when the latter, having asked him to wait an instant in her cabinet, had left him to hear the political plan which Monsieur de Bruteuil brought from Vienna, and which was conceived in the following terms.

" Act with Barnave as was done with Mirabeau ; gain time ; swear to the Constitution ; execute it literally to show that it cannot be carried out. France will cool down and change. The French are light-headed ; some new crotchet will arise, and that of liberty will pass away.

" If it does not pass away, a year will have been gained ; and by a twelvemonth, we shall be ready for war."

Six months had elapsed since that period ; liberty had not vanished, and it was clear that foreign rulers were on the road of accomplishing their promise, and were prepared for war.

Gilbert was astonished one morning to see enter into his room the King's valet-de-chambre.

He thought at first that the King was sick, and had sent for him.

But the valet banished that fear.

He told him he was wanted at the chateau.

Gilbert insisted that he should know what he was wanted for ; but the messenger, who had doubtless received his orders, would not go beyond the formula :

"You are asked for at the chateau."

Gilbert was deeply attached to the King ; he sorrowed for Marie Antoinette more as a woman than as a Queen ;

she inspired in him neither love nor devotion, he felt for her only profound pity.

He hastened to obey.

He was introduced into the "great cabinet" room, where Barnave had been received.

A woman was waiting there in an arm chair, and she rose on seeing Gilbert appear.

The latter recognized her as Madame Elizabeth.

For her he had a deep respect, knowing all the angelic goodness that was in her heart.

He bowed before her, and on the very instant understood the situation of affairs.

Neither the King nor the Queen had dared to send for him in their own name; they put forward Madame Elizabeth.

The latter's opening words proved to the doctor that he had fallen into no error through his surmises.

"Monsieur Gilbert," said she, "I do not know whether or no others have forgotten the marks of interest which you showed to my brother in our return to Versailles, and those you gave my sister during our arrival from Varennes,—but I remember them."

Gilbert bowed.

"Madame," said he, "God has decided in His wisdom that you should have every virtue, even to that of memory; a rare virtue in our days, and especially among royal persons."

"Do you not mean that for my brother, Monsieur Gilbert? My brother speaks often of you, and thinks highly of your experience."

"As a physician?" inquired Gilbert, smiling.

"As a physician, yes, sir; only, he believes your experience may be applied at the same time to the health of the ruler and of the realm."

"The King is very kind, madame," remarked Gilbert. "For which patient does he call me this time?"

"It was not the King who called you, sir," returned Madame Elizabeth, reddening slightly, for her chaste heart did not know how to tell a falsehood unblushingly. "It was I."

"You, madame?" inquired Gilbert.

"Oh, you cannot be fearful of your health, at least; your paleness is that of fatigue and uneasiness, but not that of sickness."

"You are right, sir; it is not for myself that I am troubled, but for my brother; he causes my disquietude."

"So does he mine," replied Gilbert.

"Oh, our disquietude does not probably flow from the same source," said Madame Elizabeth. "I mean to say that his health makes me fearful."

"Is the King ill?"

"No, not precisely," responded Madame Elizabeth; "but the King is prostrated, disheartened. For ten days from this present one—I count day by day, you notice—he has not spoken a single word, except to me, and in his part in the customary game of backgammon, when he is obliged to speak the words indispensable to the play."

"It is to-day, eleven days ago," said Gilbert, "that he presented himself to the Assembly to give his veto. Why was he not mute on that morning, instead of losing speech the following day?"

"So your opinion is," cried Madame Elizabeth, "that my brother should have sanctioned that impious decree?"

"My opinion is, madame, that to set the King before the priests in the coming torrent, against the rising flood and the growling storm, is to wish to have King and priests crushed by the same blow!"

"But in my brother's stead, what would you have done?"

"Madame, there is at this moment a party growing like the genii in the Arabian Nights' Entertainments who, enclosed in a flask, an hour after their receptacle was broken became a hundred cubits in height."

"Do you mean the Jacobins, sir?"

Gilbert shook his head.

"No, I speak of the Girondists. The Jacobins do not wish war; but the Girondists do—the war is national."

"But war—war to whom? To our brother the emperor? to our nephew the King of Spain? Our enemies, Monsieur Gilbert, are in France, and not out of it; and the proof of that is ——"

Madame Elizabeth hesitated.

"Say on, madame," said Gilbert.

"I do not really know if I can tell you it, doctor, though it is for that I have sent for you."

"You may tell me everything, madame, as to a man devoted to the King, to whom he is ready to give his life."

"Sir, do you believe any counter-poison exists?" inquired Madame Elizabeth.

Gilbert smiled.

"Universal? No, madame; yet every venomous substance has, generally, its antidote, which is, it must be said, almost always powerless."

"Oh, good heavens!"

"It must first be known whether the poison is mineral or vegetable. Usually, mineral poisons act on the stomach: vegetable poisons on the nervous system, which some inflame and others deaden; of which species of poison would you speak, madame?"

"I will impart to you a great secret, sir."

"I am listening, madame."

"Well, I fear that the King is to be poisoned."

"Who do you think of in connection with such a crime?"

"Here is what has happened: Monsieur Laporte—the intendant on the civil lists, you know?"

"Yes, madame."

"Monsieur Laporte has cautioned us that a man of the royal establishment, who is a pastrycook at the Palais Royal, is performing the duties of his charge, which becomes his from the death of his predecessor. Well, this man, who is a rabid Jacobin, has said out aloud that the poisoner of the King would be of great benefit to France."

"In general, madame, men who would commit such a crime never vaunt of it beforehand."

"Oh, sir, it would be so easy to poison the King. Fortunately, he whom we distrust furnishes nothing more to the palace than pastry."

"Then, you have taken precautions, madame?"

"Yes, it has been decided that the King should not touch them; that the bread should be brought by Monsieur Thierry de Ville d'Avray, steward, who is at the same time to attend to the wine. As for the pastry, as the King is fond of it, Madame Campan has received the order to purchase it as for herself, sometimes from one, sometimes from another pastrycook. We have been advised to especially avoid powdered sugar."

"In which arsenic may be mixed without suspicion?"

"Precisely. It was the Queen's habit to use that kind of sweetening in her water-drink: we have completely done away with it. The King, the Queen and myself eat together, dispensing with any servants: if we need anything, it is rung for. Madame Campan, when the King is at table, brings in through a private entrance, pastry, bread and wine: this is hidden under the table, and we pretend to drink the wine from the cellar, and to eat the bread and pastry served up. That is how we live, sir! and yet every instant, the Queen and I tremble to see the King suddenly turn pale, and hear him utter the three fearful words: 'I am suffering!'"

"Let me affirm to you, firstly, madame," said the doctor, "that I place no credence in these threats of poisoning: but, still, I none the less place myself wholly at the service of their Majesties. What does the King desire! Does he wish to give me a room in the chateau? I will remain so as to be found at any moment, until his fears——"

"Oh, my brother fears nothing," quickly interrupted Madame Elizabeth.

"I was wrong, madame, until your fears shall have passed. I have some skill in poisons and their antidotes: I will hold myself in readiness to counteract them, of whatever nature they may be; but allow me to add, madame, that, the King willing, soon there would be nothing to fear for him."

"Oh, what must be done to ensure that!" asked a voice which was not Madame Elizabeth's, and which, from its thrilling tone, made Gilbert turn.

The doctor was not wrong,

The voice was the Queen's.

"Madame," said he, "have I need of

renewing to the Queen the protestations of devotion which, I just now made to Madame Elizabeth?"

"No, sir, no; I have heard everything —I merely wish to know your sentiments with respect to us?"

"Does the Queen doubt the firmness of my feelings?"

"Oh, so many heads and hearts have been turned by this wind of the tempest, that one really no longer knows to whom to trust?"

"Is that why the Queen is going to receive, from the hand of the Feuillants, a minister shaped out by Madame de Stael?"

The Queen started.

"Do you know that?" queried she.

"I know that your Majesty is engaged with Monsieur de Narbonne."

"No doubt you blame me?"

"Nay, madame, it is as good an attempt as any other. When the King shall have tried everything, perchance he may end with what he commenced with."

"Do you know Madame de Stael, sir?" inquired the Queen.

"I have that honor, madame. On my leaving the Bastile, I presented myself at her house, where, through Monsieur Neckar, I learned that it was on the Queen's recommendation that I had been arrested."

The Queen blushed visibly, saying, with a smile:

"We promised never to refer to that error."

"I did not return to it, madame; I answered a question which your Majesty did me the favor of asking."

"What do you think of Monsieur Neckar?"

"He is a brave German, composed of heterogenous elements, who, passing from commonplace, rises to emphasis."

"But were you not one of those who urged the King to restore him?"

"Monsieur Neckar was, wrongly or rightly, the most popular man in the kingdom: I told the King: "Sire, rely on his popularity.""

"And Madame de Stael?"

"Your Majesty, I think, does me the honor of asking my opinion on Madame de Stael?"

"Yes."

"Why, as to personal appearance, she had a nose not delicate, coarse features, stout form—"

The Queen smiled : being a woman, it was not disagreeable for her to hear it said of a woman who occupied much attention that she was not handsome.

"Continue," said she.

"Her skin is but of slightly attractive quality, her gestures are rather energetic than graceful, her voice is rough, becoming so much so at times as to lead one to doubt its being feminine. With all this, she is twenty-four or five years of age, with a neck like a goddess, magnificent black hair, superb teeth, and a flaming eye : her look is a world?"

"But her mental qualities? her talent —merit?" the Queen hastened to interpose.

"She is good and generous, madame : not one of her enemies would remain her enemy after having heard her speak for a quarter of an hour."

"Speak of her genius, sir—politics are not carried on by simply the heart."

"Madame, the heart never does one harm even in politics ; as for the term 'genius', which your Majesty has used, be chary of the word, madame ; Madame de Stael has a great and immense talent ; but it never rises to the height of genius ; something heavy, yet strong, dense though powerful, weighs on her feet when she would leave the earth ; the difference between her and her master, Jean Jacques Rousseau, is that between iron and steel."

"You are discoursing on her talent as a writer, sir ; speak to me a little of the female politician."

"Under that heading, in my opinion, madame," returned Gilbert, "much more importance has been given to Madame de Stael than she merits. Since the departure from France of Mounier and Lally, her saloon is the tribune of the English party, semi-aristocratic along with the two Chambers. As she is one of the citizen class, and very humble, she has the weakness of worshipping great noblemen : she admires the English because she believes the British people a race eminently aristocratic: she does not know the history of England, and is ignorant of the workings of its government: so that she mistakes for gentlemen of the times of the crusades, noblemen created yesterday pushed incessantly down. Other nations, out of the old, make the new. England, with the new, constantly makes the old."

" Do you think that it is on account of that feeling that Madame de Stael proposes Narbonne to us?"

"This time, madame, two likings are combined: that of aristocracy and that of the aristocrat."

" Do you believe Madame de Stael likes Monsieur de Narbonne on account of his aristocracy?"

"I should not think it was for his merits!"

" But no one is less lofty of birth than Monsieur de Narbonne: his father is not even known."

" Ah! that is because nobody dares look at the sun——"

"Come, Monsieur Gilbert, I am a woman and, hence, inquisitive. What do they say of Monsieur de Narbonne?"

"They say he is profligate, brave, and witty."

"I speak of his birth."

"They say that, when the Jesuit party hunted Voltaire, Machault, d'Argenson—those styled philosophers, in brief—there was struggling against Madame de Pompadour: now, the traditions of the Regency bear upon this: all are aware what paternal love can do doubled by another love; therefore, they chose—the Jesuits have a lucky hand in such choices, madame!—they chose a daughter of the King, and induced her to sacrifice herself: whence this charming gentleman whose father is not known, as your Majesty says, not because his birth is lost in darkness, but because it is dazzling with light."

" So you believe, as do the Jacobins, like Monsieur de Robespierre, for instance, Monsieur de Narbonne springs from the Swiss Ambassador?"

"I do, madame, with the exception that he came from the wife's boudoir, not from the husband's closet. To suppose that Monsieur de Stael be connected with it would be doubting him to be husband of his wife. Nay, it is not an ambassador's treachery, but a lover's weakness. Nothing less than love, the great and eternal fascinator, could push a wife into giving to the hands of that frivolous rake the gigantic sword of the Revolution."

" Do you speak of him who has abased Monsieur Isnard in the Club of the Jacobins?"

" Alas, madame, I speak of him who is suspended over your head."

" Then you think, Monsieur Gilbert, that we have done wrong to accept Narbonne as Minister of War?"

" You would have done better, madame, had you taken first him who will succeed him."   " Who?"

" Dumouriez."

" Dumouriez, a soldier of fortune?"

" Madame, that is a bad word, and, morever, to him you apply it, it is unjust."

" Has not Monsieur Dumouriez been a private soldier?"

" Monsieur Dumouriez, I well know it, madame, has not that court nobility, to which everything is sacrificed. Monsieur Dumouriez, a country noble, unable to obtain or purchase a regiment, enlisted as a common huzzar. At the age of twenty, he fought five or six men rather than surrender, and despite such a proof of courage and real intelligence, he has languished in the lower grades."

" His intelligence, yes; it was displayed in his spy-service to Louis the Fifteenth."

" Why call spy-service in him what is termed diplomacy in others? I well know that without the knowledge of the royal ministers, he entered into correspondence with the King. What noble of the court has not done likewise?"

" But, sir," exclaimed the Queen, betraying her deep study of politics by the details which she let herself expose, " he is a man essentially immoral, this one you recommend! he has no principles, no sentiment of honor! Monsieur de Choiseul told me that Dumouriez had presented to him two plans relative to the Corsicans, one to enslave them, the other to free them."

"True, madame, but Monsieur de Choiseul forgot to tell you that the first was his preference, and that Dumouriez fought bravely to have it succeed."

"The day on which we should accept Dumouriez for minister, would be the same as if we made a declaration of war to Europe."

"Why, madame," said Gilbert, "the declaration is made in every heart! Do you know how many the registers of this department give as the number of citizens whose names are down for starting voluntarily? Six hundred thousand. The women have declared that all the men may go, and that if pikes are given them, they will be enough to keep the country."

"You have spoken a word that makes me tremble, sir," said the Queen.

"Excuse me, madame," said Gilbert, "tell me which word it is, so that I may not utter it again."

"It was the word 'pikes!' Oh, the pikes of '89, sir! I still see the heads of my two poor body guards on the points of the pikes!"

"Yet, madame, it is a woman and a mother who proposes to open a subscription to have pikes made."

"Is it also a woman and a mother who has made your Jacobins adopt the red cap—of the hue of blood?"

"Your Majesty is in error as to this," responded Gilbert. "They wished to consecrate equality by a symbol; it could not be decreed that every native of France should wear a similar dress; for more facility, a part of a costume was adopted; the headdress of the humble peasants; only, the red color was preferred, not because it was of the gloomy hue of blood, but, on the contrary, because red is gay, attractive and agreeable to the mass of the people."

"It is well, doctor," said the Queen. "I do not lose all hope, so greatly are you the partisan of new inventions, of seeing you some day coming to feel the King's pulse with a pike in one hand and the red cap on your head."

Half-jesting, half-bitter, seeing that she could find no weak spot in the man

she would have liked to conquer, the Queen retired.

Madame Elizabeth was about to follow her.

But Gilbert, in an almost suppliant voice, said:

"Madame, you love your brother, do you not?"

"It is adoration, not love that I feel for him," rejoined Madame Elizabeth.

"Are you disposed to give him some good advice, advice coming from a friend?"

"Oh, say it, and if it is really good——"

"In my point of view, it is excellent."

"Then, speak, speak!"

"Well, it is when this Feuillant minister shall have fallen—and that time will not be long coming—it will be best to take a minister wholly wearing this red cap, which so greatly frightens the Queen."

Bowing low to Madame Elizabeth, he went out.

————

CHAPTER XIII.

THE ROLANDS.

WE have brought in the preceding conversation of the Queen and Doctor Gilbert to interrupt the current, always a little monotonous, of a historical romance, and to show, in a chronological table somewhat less dryly the succession of events and the situation of parties.

The Narbonne Ministry lasted three months.

A speech of Vergniaud's killed it.

The same as Mirabeau had said, "I see, from here, the window"—Vergniaud, on the intelligence that the Empress of Russia had treated with Turkey, and that Austria and Prussia had signed (on the 7th of February at Berlin) a treaty of alliance offensive and defensive, mounting the rostrum, cried:

"And I, too, may say that from this tribune, I behold the place wherein is growing the counter-revolution, wherein is being prepared the plotting that is to surrender us to Austria. The day is dawned when you can fix a bound to so much audacity, and confound the conspirators; dread and awe often in aforetimes came from this palace, in the name of despotism ; let awe and dread now enter it in the name of the law !"

By a powerful wave of the hand, the splendid orator seemed to drive away from before him the two dishevelled daughters, Awe and Dread.

They did indeed creep into the Tuileries, and Narbonne, lifted up by a breath of love, was cast down by a gust of the tempest.

This fall took place about the commencement of March, 1792.

Hardly three months after the Queen's interview with Doctor Gilbert, a man of small stature, active and well-built, with intelligent head in which sparkled eyes full of flame, aged in the neighborhood of fifty and sixty, although he appeared to be ten years less, with a face darkened by embrowned tints of bivouac, was introduced into the King's Chamber.

He wore the uniform of lieutenant colonel.

He did not have to stay an instant alone in the room into which he had been ushered, the door presently opened, and the King entered.

This was the first time that these two persons had ever faced each other.

The King cast upon the short man a dull, heavy look which was not, however, exempt from observation : the short man fixed on the other a scrutinizing gaze, fraught with fire and defiance.

No one was there to announce the stranger ; which proved that he had been announced in advance.

" M. Dumouriez ?" questioned the King.

Dumouriez bowed.

" How long have you been at Paris ?"

" Since the first of February, sire."

" Did not Monsieur de Narbonne send for you ?"

" To announce that I was employed on the Italian army under Marshal Luckner, and that I was to command the Besancon division."

" Yet you have not gone ?"

" Sire, I accepted ; but I deemed it my duty to make the observation to Monsieur de Narbonne that, the war being near at hand——"

Louis XVI. started visibly

" That the war being near at hand and threatening to become general," went on Dumouriez, without showing he had or had not remarked the start, " I thought that it would be well to keep strict watch in the South of France, where at any moment we might be suddenly attacked ; that, consequently, it seemed to me urgent that a plan of defence for the South should be drawn up, and a general-in-chief and an army sent there."

" Yes, and you gave your plans to Monsieur de Narbonne, after having communicated it to Monsieur de Gensonne and several members of the Gironde ?"

" Monsieur de Gensonne is my friend, sire, and I believe him to be like myself a friend of your Majesty."

" Therefore," said the King smiling, " I am conversing with a Girondist ?"

" With a patriot and a faithful subject of his King."

Louis the Sixteenth bit his thick lips.

" Was it to more effectually serve the King and the country that you refused the place of Minister of Foreign Affairs for the interim."

" Sire, I first answered that I preferred, to a minister's post with or without having it only by an interim, the command which had been offered to me. I am a soldier, not a diplomatist."

" I have been assured on the contrary, that you were both, sir," said the King.

" Too much honor is done me, sire."

" And I insisted, on that assurance."

" Yes, sire, and I continued to refuse, in spite of my own great regret, to obey you."

" And why refuse ?"

" Because the situation is serious, sire ; it has overturned Monsieur de Narbonne and compromised Monsieur de Lessart ; every man believing himself possessor of something has the right to employ it or not, or ask that he shall be employed according to his estimate of his worth. Now, sire, I am worth something or I am good for nothing; if the latter, leave me in my obscurity: who knows from what destiny you would draw me? If I am worth something, do not make me a minister for a day, do not give power for an instant: but let me have the wherewithal for me to rest upon, in order that you may rely upon me. Our affairs—I beg your Majesty's pardon, sire, you see I make his affairs mine—our affairs are in too great a disfavor abroad for courts to treat with a minister for an interim—excuse the outspokenness of a soldier (no one was less outspoken than Dumouriez; but, in certain circumstances, he could pretend what he was not)—this interim would be an unskilful move against which the Assembly would rise and strip me of popularity; more I will say: this interim would compromise the King, who would have the semblance of retaining his former ministry, and appear to be only waiting for an opportunity to call it back."

"Were such my intention do you fancy such an act possible, sir?"

"I believe, sire, that it is time your Majesty breaks off fully with the past."

"Yes, and make myself a Jacobin? Have you spoken thus to Laporte?"

"If your Majesty does this, you will be harrassed on all sides, and perhaps by the Jacobins more than by others."

"Why do you not counsel me at once to put on the red cap?"

"Why, sire, if there were a way—" began Dumouriez.

The King for an instant eyed with marked distrust the man who was going to give him such an unusual reply; then he asked:

"Is it not a minister without interim that you wish to be, sir?"

"I wish nothing, sire; I am ready to receive the King's orders: with the exception that I would like the royal behest to send me to the frontier rather than to retain me in Paris."

"And, if I, on the contrary, give you an order to stay at Paris, and definitely take the Ministry of Foreign Affairs, what would you say?"

Dumouriez smiled,

"I should say, sire, that your Majesty is returning to the favorable aspect in which you have viewed me."

"Well, yes, entirely, Monsieur Dumouriez. You are my minister."

"Sire, I devote myself to your service; but——"

"Restrictions?"

"Explanations, sire."

"Speak; I am listening."

"The position of minister is not what it was in former days; without ceasing to be the faithful servant of your Majesty on entering upon my duties, I would become a servant of the nation. Hence, do not ask of me, from that time forth, the language you are accustomed to hear from my predecessors: I shall only know how to speak according to liberty and the Constitution: enclosed in my functions, I shall not be paying court to you: I would only work with you or at the council, and I forewarn you in advance, sire, this work will be a conflict."

"A conflict, sir? wherefore?"

"Oh, it is quite simple, sire: nearly all your diplomatic body is openly against the Revolution: I pledge myself to you that I will change it, go contrary to your tastes in selections, proposing to your Majesty some subjects of which he does not even know the name, and others which will displease him."

"In that event, sir?" quickly interrupted Louis XVI.

"In that event, sire, when your Majesty's repugnance would be too strong, inasmuch as you are the master, I should obey; but if the choice should be suggested by you out of your train, and seem clearly made to compromise you, I would entreat your Majesty to appoint my successor. Sire, reflect on the terrible dangers that beset your throne; it must be upheld by public confidence. Sire, it depends on you!"

"Allow me to stop you, sir."

"Sire—"

Dumouriez checked himself, bowing.

"I have thought over these dangers a long time."

Extending his hand towards a por

trait of Charles the First of England, Louis the Sixteenth continued, wiping his forehead with his handkerchief:

" And could I have forgotten them, yonder picture would have been a reminder."

"Sire—"

" Stay, I have not concluded, sir. The state of things is the same ; the dangers are similar ; the scaffold of Whitehall may rise on the Place de Greve."

" This is looking too far, sire."

" It is seeing the horizon, sir. In this case, I move towards the scaffold the same as went the first Charles, not, it may be, as like a knight as he, but at least as much of a Christian. Proceed, sir."

Dumouriez was greatly astonished at this firmness which he had not expected.

"Sire," said he, " permit me to lead the conversation to another subject."

"As you like, sir," responded the King, " but I tried to prove to you that I do not fear the future which some have endeavored to appal me with, or, granting I do fear it, at least I am prepared."

" Sire," said Dumouriez, "despite what I have had the honor to tell you, am I still to regard myself as your Minister of Foreign Affairs ?"

" Yes, sir."

"Then at the first council I shall bring four despatches ; I forewarn the King that they will in no respects resemble those of my predecessors, neither in principles nor style. They will beseem circumstances. If this first work suits your Majesty, I will continue, if otherwise, sire, I shall always have myself ready to go to serve France and my King on the frontier; and whatever may have been said to your Majesty of my talents in diplomacy," added Dumouriez, " that is my strong point, the object of all my labors for six-and-thirty years."

Upon which he bowed, previous to going.

"Stay," said the King, " we agree on one point ; but there are six others to be settled."

" My colleagues ?"

" Yes; I do not want you to come

and say that you were hampered by so and so. Choose your ministry yourself, sir."

" Sire, you lay serious responsibility upon me !"

" I think in so doing I am helping your desires."

" Sire," said Dumouriez, "I know not a soul in Paris saving one named Lacoste whom I recommend to your Majesty for the Navy."

" Lacoste ?" said the King; " is he not a simple intendant commissary ?"

" Yes, sire, who sent in his resignation to Monsieur de Boynes rather than participate in an unjust act."

" That is a good recommendation. Now for the others. What do you say ?"

" I will consult, sire."

" May I know whom you will consult with ?"

" Brissot, Condorcet, Petion, Rœderer, Gensonne—"

" The whole of the Gironde, in other words ?"

" Yes, sire."

" Let it be the Gironde, then ; we shall see if it can manage better than the Constitutionalists and the Feuillants."

" There's another thing yet, sire."

" What ?"

" Whether the four letters I intend to write will suit you ?'

"Can we not see about that this evening, sir ?'

" To-night, sire ?"

" Yes, events press; we will have an extraordinary council composed of you, and Messieurs de Grave and Cahier de Gerville."

" But, Dupont du Tertre ?"

" He has resigned."

" I shall be this evening at your Majesty's orders."

And Dumouriez bowed preparatory to taking leave.

" Nay," said the King, " stop an instant : I wish to compromise you."

He had hardly finished before the Queen and Madame Elizabeth appeared, holding their prayer books in their hands.

" Madame," said the King to Marie Antoinette, " here is Monsieur Dumouriez, who promises to serve us well, and who is going to confer with us this evening upon a new ministry."

Dumouriez bowed, while the Queen in curiosity surveyed the little man who was to have so much influence over the affairs of France.

"Are you acquainted with Doctor Gilbert?" inquired she.

"No, madame," rejoined Dumouriez.

"Well, you should make his acquaintance, sir."

"May I know under what heading your Majesty advises this?"

"As an excellent prophet; three months ago he foretold that you would be Monsieur de Narbonne's successor."

At this moment, the doors of the royal cabinet were thrown open for the King to go to hear mass.

Dumouriez went out among his retinue.

The courtiers avoided him as though he were a leper, or plague-stricken.

"Did I not tell you," whispered the King to him, laughing, "that I would compromise you?"

"With the aristocracy, sire," returned Dumouriez. "It is a further favor your Majesty deigns to grant me."

He withdrew.

CHAPTER XIV.

BEHIND THE HANGINGS.

At the appointed hour that evening, Dumouriez entered with his four dispatches; Grave and Cahier de Gerville were already in attendance and awaiting the King.

As if the latter had only waited the entry of Dumouriez to make his own, the minister had hardly appeared through one door than the King came in by another.

The two ministers quickly rose.

Dumouriez was still standing and merely bowed.

The King saluted them with a nod.

Taking a chair and placing it in the centre of the table, he said:

"Gentlemen, be seated."

Dumouriez fancied that the door by which had entered the King, had remained open, and that the hangings were shaking.

Was it the wind? or was it from the contact of somebody listening on the other side of the tapestry, which interrupted sight but let sound pass?

The three ministers took seats.

"Have you your dispatches, sir?" the King asked Dumouriez.

"Yes, sire."

The general drew four letters from his pocket.

"To what powers are they addressed?" inquired the King.

"To Spain, Austria, Prussia, and England."

"Read them."

Dumouriez flung a second glance at the tapestry, and, by its tremor was convinced that there was an eavesdropper there.

He began his reading in a steady voice.

The minister spoke in the King's voice, but in the feeling of the Constitution—without threatening but without weakness.

He discussed the true interests of each power, relatively to the French Revolution.

As every power complained of the Jacobin pamphlets, he laid the paltry slurs to that freedom of the press on which the sun had made so many rank weeds grow, but from which would be reaped so rich a harvest.

In the close he demanded peace in the name of a free nation, of which a king was an hereditary representative.

The King listened, and at every fresh dispatch, lent deeper attention.

"Ah," said he, when Dumouriez had concluded, "I have never heard the like of this, general."

"It is how ministers should always write and speak in the names of rulers," said Cahier de Gerville.

"Well," said the King, "let me have the dispatches; they shall go to-morrow."

"Sire, the couriers are ready, waiting in the court-yard of the Tuileries," interposed Dumouriez.

"I would like to keep duplicates to show them to the Queen," observed the King, with some embarrassment.

"I foresaw your Majesty's desire," returned Dumouriez, "and here are four copies certified by me to be perfect."

"Let your letters be sent," said the King.

Dumouriez went to the door by which he had entered, an aide-de-camp was there waiting; he handed the missives to him.

An instant afterwards was to be heard the gallop of several horses together, dashing out of the Court of the Tuileries.

"It is well," said the King, replying to his thoughts, when this significant sound had died away; "and now let us see your ministry."

"Sire," said Dumouriez, "I first of all wish your Majesty to request Monsieur Cahier de Gerville to be so kind as to stay at his post."

"I have already entreated him so to do," returned the King.

"And I have had the regret of persisting in my refusal, sire; my health is wearing away day by day, and I require rest."

"You hear him, sir," said the King, turning to Dumouriez.

"Yes, sire."

"Well, your ministry, sir," persisted the King.

"We have Monsieur de Grave, who will remain."

De Grave put out his hand.

"Sire," said he, "the language of Dumouriez astonished you a while ago from its frankness; mine will now surprise you with its humility."

"Speak, sir," said the King.

"Here, sire," went on de Grave, drawing from his pocket a paper, "here is an appreciation of me, somewhat severe but quite just, formed by a woman possessing much merit; have the goodness to read it."

The King took the paper and read:

"De Grave is a small man in every respect; nature made him gentle and fearful; his prejudices command pride of him, while his heart bids him be amiable. The result from this is, that, in his earnestness to please everybody, he is really nothing. Methinks that seeing him walk mincingly like a courtier behind the King, his high head over his weak body, showing the whites of his blue eyes (which he can only keep open after meals by aid of three or four cups of coffee,) speaking but little, as though from reserve, but, in fact, because he is backward in ideas, and loses his wits amidst business—seeing him, methinks he will some day beg his withdrawal!"

"Indeed," said Louis the Sixteenth, who had hesitated to read the paper to the end, and had only done so on the insisting of M. de Grave himself, "this is a woman's estimate. Can it be Madame de Stael's?"

"No, it is stronger than hers; this comes from Madame Roland."

"And do you say, Monsieur de Grave, that such is your own opinion of yourself?"

"In many points, sire, it is. Therefore I will remain in the ministry until I may have seen my successor posted; after which I will entreat your Majesty to grant me my dismissal."

"You are right, sir; this is language much more astonishing than that of Monsieur Dumouriez. I would like, if you absolutely will retire, to receive your successor from your own hand."

"I would beg your Majesty to allow me to present to him Monsieur Servan, an honest man in every sense of the word, of a firm stamp, pure manners, all the austerity of a philosopher, and the goodness of heart of a woman; over and above that, sire, an enlightened patriot, a courageous soldier, a vigilant minister."

"Let it be Monsieur Servan, then. We have three ministers agreed on. Monsieur Dumouriez for Foreign Affairs, Monsieur Servan for the War, Monsieur Lacoste for the Navy. Who shall we have for the Treasury?"

"Monsieur Clavieres, sire, if you are willing. He is a man who has deep financial knowledge, and superior skill in handling money."

"Yes," coincided the King, "he is called active and laborious, but irascible, tenacious of opinion, punctilious, and hard to manage in discussions."

" They are faults common to all men of cabinets, sire."

" Then, let us pass over the failings of Monsieur Clavieres ; he is the Minister of Finances. Now for the Minister of Justice. To whom shall we give the appointment ?"

" A lawyer of Bordeaux, sire, Monsieur Duranthon, has been recommended to me."

" By the Gironde, of course ?"

" Yes, sire ; he is a very enlightened man, upright, a good citizen, but slow and weak ; we will incite him, and shall be strong for him."

" The Minister for Home Affairs still remains."

" The unanimous advice is that Monsieur Roland suits this the best, sire."

" Madame Roland, you mean to say ?"

" Monsieur and Madame Roland."

" Do you know them ?"

" No, sire, but I have been assured, one resembles a man out of Plutarch, the other a woman from Livy."

" Do you know what they will call your ministry, Monsieur Dumouriez, or rather what they already do call it ?"

" No, sire."

" The Sans-culotte Ministry ?"

" I accept the title, sire."

" Are all your colleagues ready ?"

" Hardly half of them are aware of their honors."

" Will they accept ?"

" I am sure of it."

" Well, you may go, sir ; the day after to-morrow, we will meet at the first council."

" The day after to-morrow, sire."

The King turned to Cahier de Gerville and de Grave.

" You will have till then to conclude your reflections, gentlemen."

" Sire, our minds are made up, and we shall only come on the day after to-morrow to instal our successors."

The three ministers retired.

But before they reached the main staircase, a servant caught up to them, and, addressing Dumouriez, said :

" Sir General, the King asks you to follow me ; he has something to tell you."

Dumouriez bowed to his companions and inquired, as he fell behind them :

" The King, or the Queen ?"

" The Queen, sir ; but she thought it useless for those two gentlemen to know that it was she who asked for you."

Dumouriez shook his head.

" This is what I feared," muttered he.

" Are you not coming ?" asked the servant, who was no less a person than Weber, the Queen's foster-brother.

" I follow you."

" Come."

The valet, through dimly lighted corridors, conducted Dumouriez to the Queen's apartments.

Without announcing the general by name, the guide said :

" Here is the person your Majesty asked for."

Dumouriez entered.

Never, when dashing on the foe in a charge or mounting a breach, had his heart leaped so violently.

This came—he well understood it— from his never having incurred the same danger.

The road spread open before him was strewn with bodies of the dead or living, and he might at any moment stumble over the corpses of Calonne, Neckar, Mirabeau Barnave and La Fayette.

The Queen was pacing the room : she was very high in color.

Dumouriez stopped on the threshold by the door, which had been closed behind him.

The Queen advanced to meet him with an irritated, though majestic air.

" Sir," said she, entering upon the conversation with her usual vivacity, " you are almighty at this moment ; but this comes from favor of the people, and the people soon break their idols. I have been told you possess many talents ; have first that one of understanding that neither the King nor myself can suffer all these innovations. Your Constitution is a pneumatic machine ; royalty is stifling for want of air ; I have, therefore, sent for you to tell you, before going further, to take your course, and choose between us and the Jacobins."

" Madame," responded Dumouriez,

"I am grieved at the painful confidence your Majesty places in me; but, having divined that the Queen was hidden behind the curtain, I expected what would take place."

"Consequently, you have an answer ready?" inquired the Queen.

"Here it is, madame: I stand between the King and the nation; but, before either, I belong to the country."

"The country! the country!" echoed the Queen. "Is the King no longer anything? does everybody now belong to the country, and none to the King?"

"Excuse me, madame, the King is always the King; but he has taken an oath to the Constitution, and, from that day when he swore, the King should be one of the foremost slaves of the Constitution."

"A forced oath, sir! void!"

Dumouriez paused a moment mute, and—a cunning actor—during that instant, he gazed on the Queen with profound commiseration.

"Madame," at last he said, "allow me to say to you that your salvation, the King's, that of your august offspring, is bound to that Constitution which you spurn, but which will save you—if you consent to be saved by it. I should poorly serve you, madame, and poorly serve the King, were I to otherwise speak to you."

But the royal lady, interrupting him with an imperious wave of the hand, said:

"Oh, sir, sir! you are going along a wrong road, I assure you!"

With an inexpressible tone of menace, she added:

"Take heed to yourself!"

"Madame," said Dumouriez in a perfectly unmoved tone, "I am more than fifty years of age; my life has been traversed by many perils, and, in accepting the ministry, I have not failed to tell myself that the ministerial responsibility is not the least of the danger I have run."

"Oh," exclaimed the Queen, clapping her hands, "there only remained to you that one thing—calumniating me, sir!"

"Who has done so, madame."

"You. Do you ask me to explain to you the words you have just uttered?"

"I would like you to do so, madame."

"Well, you said I was capable of having you assassinated, oh, oh!"

Tears fell from the Queen's eyes.

Dumouriez had gone as far as was possible: he had learned what he had wanted to know; to wit, whether there remained feeling in that heart.

"Heaven forbid," said he, "my casting such a reproach at my queen! Your Majesty's character is too lofty and too noble, to impose in her most cruel enemy such a suspicion; she has given heroic proofs which I admire, and which attach me to her."

"Do you speak true?" said the Queen in a voice in which was emotion.

"On my honor, madame, I swear to you."

"Then, excuse me," said she, "and give me your arm, I am so weak that at times I can hardly stand."

Indeed, turning pale, she dropped her head.

Was this real?

Was it one of those terrible wiles in which that seducing Medea was so cunning?

Dumouriez—cunning as he was himself—let himself be ensnared, or else—craftier still than the Queen—he, perhaps, feigned to have let himself be caught.

"Believe me, madame," he said, "I have no interest in deceiving you, I abhor as much as you anarchy and its crimes; believe me, I have experience, I am better placed than your Majesty to judge on events: what has happened is no intrigue of the Duke of Orleans, as you have been informed; nor is it the effect of Pitt's hatred, as you have supposed it to be; nor is it even a momentary popular movement; it is almost unanimous uprising of a great nation against inveterate abuses! There blaze up through it all, I well know, certain hates which feed the conflagration. Lay on one side the fools and rascals; simply look on the revolution as regards the King and the nation; everything tending to separate them is allied to their mutual ruin. I, madame, have come to work with all my power to re-unite them : lend me aid instead of endeavoring to thwart me. Do you mistrust me? Am I an obstacle to your counter-revolutionary designs? Tell me, madame; I will instantly bear my resignation to the King, and will go to bewail in obscurity the fate of my country and yours."

" Nay, nay," broke out the Queen, " remain. Excuse me."

" I excuse you, madame. Oh, I entreat you not to thus humble yourself."

" Why should I not humiliate myself? Am I still a queen? am I still a woman?"

She went to the window and opened it, notwithstanding the coolness of the evening; the moon was silvering the leafless tree-tops of the Tuileries.

"Has not everybody a right to air and the sun? To me, they are both refused: I dare not show myself at a window, neither on the side of the courtyard, nor on that of the garden; the other day, I was looking on the court; a gunner of the National Guard flung a coarse insult at me, and added : ' Oh, how I would like to carry your head on my bayonet point !' Yesterday, I opened a window looking on the garden; on one side, I saw a man standing up on a chair, reading horrible things against us; on another, a priest was being dragged away to a fountain basin, overwhelmed with insults and blows; and, during this time, as if such doings were everyday occurrences, people were playing football, or tranquilly strolling about. What times, sir! what a people ! Do you yet wish me to believe myself a queen, when I hardly believe myself a woman?"

The Queen fell upon a sofa, hiding her head in her hands.

Dumouriez knelt with one knee on the floor, respectfully lifted the hem of her dress, and kissed it.

" Madame," said he, " from the moment when I take upon myself the sustaining the brunt of the charge, you will become again the happy woman and the powerful queen—else I shall leave my life where the struggle raged most furiously !"

Rising, he bowed to the Queen, and went out precipitately.

The Queen watched him go with a hopeless look.

" The powerful queen !" repeated she. " Perchance, thanks to your sword, it may be still possible ; but ' the happy woman,' never ! never ! never !"

She let her head fall on the cushions of the ottoman, while murmuring a name which, every day, became dearer and more sorrowful to her.

It was the name of Charny !

CHAPTER XV.

THE RED CAP.

DUMOURIEZ had retired so rapidly as we have seen, firstly, because the Queen's despair was painful to him, (Dumouriez, rarely affected in his ideas, was much affected by persons ; he had no sentiment of political conscience, but he was very yielding to human pity); next, because Brissot was waiting for him to take him to the Jacobins, and Dumouriez did not wish to be tardy in paying his submission to the terrible club.

As for the Assembly, he little cared for it, since he was the chosen man of Petion, Gensonne, Brissot and the Gironde.

But he was not the man for Robespierre, Collot d'Herbois and Couthon : and they were the leaders of the Jacobins.

His presence had not been foreseen ; it was too audacious a move, this going to the Jacobin Club; hence, hardly had his name been uttered, than every eye was turned towards him.

What would Robespierre do ?

Robespierre turned and, like the others, listened to the name wafted from mouth to mouth ; then, frowning, he fell back into silence and coldness.

A chilling stillness immediately spread over the hall.

Dumouriez saw that he had better burn his fleet.

The Jacobins had just adopted, in token of equality, the red cap; three or four members alone had doubtlessly deemed their patriotism to be well enough known for them to be beyond the need of giving this proof.

Robespierre was one of this number.

Dumouriez did not hesitate: he flung his hat from him, took off the head of the patriot near whom he had sat down the red cap he wore, put it on, pulled it down to his ears, and mounted the tribune under the token of equality.

The entire hall burst into applause.

Something like the hiss of a viper wound through the plaudits, and they died instantly away.

It was the "hush!" coming from Robespierre's thin lips.

Dumouriez more than once acknowledged, since then, that never had the hurtling bullets, flying within an ace of his head, made him start as did the hissing "hush!" from the ex-deputy of Arras.

But a sturdy jouster was Dumouriez, both a general and an orator, difficult to unhorse on the battle-field or in the rostrum.

With a calm smile he waited until the freezing silence was well restored, when he said in a vibrating voice:

"Friends and brothers, every moment, my life through, shall be henceforward devoted to carry out the will of the people, and justify the confidence of the Constitutional King; I shall bring to bear upon my negociations with foreigners, all the powers of a free people, and these negotiations will produce either a secure peace, or a decisive war!"

Here, in spite of Robespierre's "hush!" applause broke forth anew.

"If we have this war," continued the orator, "I will break my diplomatic pen and take my rank in the army, to triumph or to die free with my brothers! A heavy fardel weighs upon my shoulders; brothers, aid me to bear it; I stand in need of advice: let me hear it through your journals; tell me the truth, the purest truth, but drive away calumny, and not repulse a citizen whom you know to be sincere and fearless, as well as devoted to the cause of the Revolution."

Dumouriez had finished. He descended amid approbation: these plaudits irritated Collot d'Herbois, that speaker so often hissed, so rarely acclaimed.

"Why this applause?" cried he from his place. "If Dumouriez comes here as a minister there should be no reply to him; if he comes as one affiliated and as a brother, he merely does his duty and comes up to the level of our opinions; we have, therefore, but one response to make to him: 'Let him act as he speaks!'"

Dumouriez made with his hand a sign which meant:

"So I intend to do."

Thereupon, Robespierre rose with his stern smile; it was seen that he was going to the rostrum, and everybody moved aside: that he was going to speak, and all were silenced.

This silence, however, compared to that which had received Dumouriez, was soft and velvety.

He mounted the speaker's stand and, with a solemnity to him habitual, said:

"I am not one of those who believe it absolutely impossible that a minister can be a patriot, and I accept with pleasure the presages Monsieur Dumouriez gives us. When he shall have fulfilled these presages, when he shall have overcome the enemies armed against us by his predecessors and by the conspirators to this day directing the government, notwithstanding the expulsion of several ministers—then, only then, will I be disposed to accord him eulogies, but, even then, I will not think that any good citizen of this association will not be his equal; the people alone are great and worthy of respect in my eyes; the hobbies of ministerial power vanish before them. It is from respect for the people, and for the minister himself, that I demand that his entrance here shall not be signalized by homage attesting the loss of the public mind. He asks of us counsel; I, for my part, promise to give him those which will be useful to him and the public welfare. As long as Monsieur Dumouriez, by striking proofs of patriotism, and especially by real services rendered to the country, makes it clear he is the brother of good citizens and the people's defender, he will have here supports alone. I do not fear for this society the presence of any minister whatever, but I declare that at the moment when a minister has more ascendency than a citizen, I shall demand his ostracism. He shall never go on so."

Amid applause, the bitter orator came down from the tribune; but a plot awaited him on the last step.

Dumouriez, feigning enthusiasm, was there with his arms unfolded.

"Virtuous Robespierre!" said he, "incorruptible citizen, permit me to embrace you!"

In spite of the efforts of the former constitutionalist, he pressed him to his heart.

The lookers-on only saw this act performed, not the repugnance Robespierre showed as it was accomplished.

The entire hall once more burst out in acclamation.

"Come," whispered Dumouriez to Brissot, "the comedy is played. I have put on the red cap and embraced Robespierre; I am a sacred saint."

In fact, it was amid cheers from the hall and tribunes that he reached the door.

At the door, a young man, enwrapped in the dignity of usher, exchanged with the minister a rapid glance and a still more rapid shake of the hand.

This young man was the Duke de Chartres.

Eleven o'clock in the night was ringing.

Brissot guided Dumouriez.

Both with quickened pace, went to the Rolands' residence.

This was still in the Rue Guenegaud.

The Rolands had been advised the previous evening, by Brissot, that Dumouriez—on the instigation of Gensonne and himself—would present to the King Roland as Minister of the Interior. Brissot had, therefore, asked Roland whether he felt strong enough for such a burden, and Roland, simple this time as always, had answered that he believed so.

Dumouriez came to announce to him that the thing was done.

Roland and Dumouriez only knew each other by name, they had never seen one another.

The reader may understand with what curiosity the future colleagues looked at each other.

After the usual compliments, in which Dumouriez evinced to Roland his private satisfaction at seeing called to the government an enlightened, righteous patriot, like him, the conversation fell naturally on the King.

"From thence comes the obstacle," remarked Roland, with a smile.

"Well, that is where you show a simplicity for which I certainly shall not gain honor," said Dumouriez; "I believe the King to be an honest man, and a sincere lover of the country."

Seeing that Madame Roland did not make any observation, merely smiling, Dumouriez inquired:

"Was not that Madame Roland's opinion?"

"Have you seen the King?" she asked.

"Yes."

"Have you seen the Queen?"

Dumouriez, in his turn, did not reply, otherwise than by a smile.

They made an appointment between them for eleven o'clock next day morning, in order to be sworn in.

On leaving the Assembly, they would go to the royal apartments.

It was now half after eleven.

Dumouriez would have remained longer, but it was a late hour for humble folks like the Rolands.

Why would Dumouriez have remained?

That's the question!

In the rapid glance, on entering, Dumouriez gave over wife and husband, he had first of all noted the age of the latter (Roland was ten years older than Dumouriez, and Dumouriez appeared twenty years younger than Roland), and the wife's richly-formed figure.

Madame Roland, the daughter of an engraver, had, in her childhood, worked in her father's workshop, and when she became a wife, in her husband's study; labor, that harsh protector, had safe-guarded the virgin, as it ought to have shielded the wife.

Dumouriez was one of that class of men, who cannot look at an old husband without laughing, and on a young wife without coveting.

Hence he at once displeased the husband and the wife.

This was why both made Brissot and the general remark that it was late.

Brissot and Dumouriez went out.

" Well," Roland asked his wife, when the door was closed, "what do you think of our future co-laborer ?"

Madame Roland smiled.

"He belongs," responded she, "to those men whom one has need of twice seeing to form an opinion upon them. He has a crafty mind, a supple character, a false look ; he has expressed great satisfaction upon the patriotic choice which he was charged to announce to us ; nevertheless, I should not be astonished if he dismissed you one day or other."

"That is, point for point, my own way of thinking," coincided Roland.

And both retired with their habitual calmness, neither of them suspecting that Destiny's iron hand was writing their names in letters of blood in the book of the Revolution.

The following day, the new minister took the oath at the National Assembly, and then proceeded to the Tuileries.

Roland wore bows in his shoes, in every likelihood because he had not money to buy buckles ; he wore a round hat, never having worn any other.

He went to the Tuileries in this everyday attire of his.

He was the last in the train of his colleagues. The Master of Ceremonies, Monsieur de Breze, let the five first pass, but stopped Roland.

The latter was ignorant why he should be refused entrance.

" But I, also," remonstrated he, " am a minister like those other gentlemen ; Minister of the Interior, even."

The Master of Ceremonies did not appear to be in the least affected.

Dumouriez heard the wrangle, and intervened.

" Why," he asked, " do you refuse Monsieur Roland's entering ?"

" Why, sir," cried the Master of Ceremonies, lifting his hands, " a round hat and no buckles !"

" All is lost !" said Dumouriez, with the utmost coolness.

With that he pushed Roland into the King's cabinet.

CHAPTER XVI.

WITHOUT AND WITHIN.

THIS ministry which had had so much trouble to enter the royal cabinet might have been styled the ministry of war.

On the first of March had died the Emperor Leopold, in the midst of his Italian harem, slain by the aphrodisiacs which he composed himself.

The Queen, who had read one day in some Jacobin pamphlet that a pie-crust would be the death of the Emperor of Austria ; the Queen, who had summoned Gilbert to ask him whether there existed a universal antidote, had loudly cried that her brother had been poisoned.

With Leopold had perished the temporizing policy of Austria.

The next mounter on the throne, Francis Second—whom we have known, as, after having been our fathers' cotemporary, he was ours—was of mixed German and Italian blood. An Austrian King born at Florence, he was weak, violent and cunning ; an honest man in the eyes of the clergy : of bigoted, harsh spirit, concealing his duplicity beneath a placid physiognomy, under a rosy mask of frightful fixedness, walking as if by springs like an automaton, like the statue of the Commander or the spectre of Hamlet's Father ; giving his daughter to his conqueror rather than part with his territory, then stabbing him from behind at the first retreating step which the chill northern blast made him take; Francis the Second, in short, the man of the Venetian lead mines and the dungeons of Spitsberg, the executioner of Andryano and Silvio Pellico !

Such was the protector of the fugitive nobles, the ally of Prussia, the enemy of France.

M. de Noailles, the French ambassador at Vienna, was, so to say, a prisoner in his palace.

The French ambassador at Berlin, M. de Segur, was preceded thither by the rumor that he came to obtain the King of Prussia's secrets by becoming the lover of one of his mistresses!

Monsieur de Segur presented himself at the public audience at the same time as the envoy from Coblentz.

The sovereign turned his back upon the ambassador of France, and asked aloud of the man from the princes of the health of the Count d'Artois.

Prussia believed at this period what it believes down to this day: that it was at the head of German progress; it lived in those strange philosophical traditions of King Frederick, who encouraged the Turkish resistance and the Polish revolutions, while strangling the liberties of Holland, a government with hooked hands, which unceasingly fishes out of the troubled waters of Revolutions, now Neufchatel, now a part of Pomerania, then a portion of Poland.

These were the two visible enemies of France, Francis the Second and Frederick William: the enemies still unseen were England, Spain and Russia.

The head of all this coalition was to be the bellicose monarch of Sweden, that dwarf armed as a giant, Gustavus Third, whom Catherine Second held in her hand.

The ascension of Francis Second to the throne of Austria was manifested by the following diplomatic note.

"Firstly. Satisfy the German princes having possessions in the realm—otherwise have the imperial sovereignty recognised in our territory.

"Secondly. Render up Avignon, in order that, as before, Provence should be dismembered.

"Thirdly. Re-establish the monarchy on the basis of the 23rd of June, 1789." *

---

* Michelet. If I were obliged to quote our great historian every time I borrowed something from him, our readers would find his name at the foot of every page.

It was clear that this note corresponded with the secret desires of the King and Queen.

Dumouriez shrugged his shoulders.

One would have thought that Austria had fallen to sleep on the 23rd of June, and, after a year's slumber, believed it woke up on the 24th.

On the 16th of March, 1792, Gustavus was assassinated in the midst of a ball.

Two days after this regicide, still unknown in France, the Austrian note came to Dumouriez.

He instantly carried it to Louis Sixteenth.

As much as Marie Antoinette, the woman for extreme courses, desired a war which she fancied to be for her a war of deliverance—so much did the King, the man of mild means, of slowness, tergiversations and bias, fear it.

Indeed, the war being declared, suppose a victory: he would be at the mercy of the conquering general; suppose a defeat, and the people would make him responsible, cry treachery, and rush upon the Tuileries.

In short, if the enemy did penetrate to Paris, what would it bring?

The King's brother, in other words, the regent of the realm.

Louis Sixteenth being overthrown, Marie Antoinette accused as an unfaithful spouse, the royal offspring perhaps pronounced adulterous issue—such were the results of the return of the emigration party to Paris.

The King might confide in Austrians, Germans or Prussians, but he distrusted the emigres.

On the perusal of the note, he, nevertheless, understood that the hour of drawing the sword of France had come, and that there was no receding.

On the twentieth of April, the King and Dumouriez entered the National Assembly, bringing the declaration of war with Austria.

This was enthusiastically received.

At this solemn juncture, when romance has not the courage to proceed, leaving that to history, there existed in France four very distinct parties:

The absolute royalists: to these belonged the Queen;

The constitutional royalists : to these the King pretended to belong;

The republicans ;

The anarchists.

The first, apart from the Queen, had no potent leaders in France.

They were represented abroad by the King's brother, the Count d'Artois, the Prince de Conde and Duke Charles de Lorraine.

M. de Breteu'l at Vienna, M. Merci d'Argenteau at Brussels, were the representatives of the Queen in this party.

The heads of the constitutional party were La Fayette, Bailly, Barnave, Lameth, Duport, all the Feuillants, in brief.

The King asked nothing better than to abandon the absolute royalty, and march with the latter ; nevertheless, he would rather hang back than lead it.

The chiefs of the republican party were Brissot, Petion, Roland, Isnard, Ducos, Condorcet and Couthon.

The foremost of the anarchists were Marat, Danton, Santerre, Gonchon, Camille Desmoulins, Hebert, Legendre, Fabre d'Eglantine and Collot d'Herbois.

Dumouriez would be anything that he might be wanted to be, provided that he gained interest and renown.

Robespierre had fallen back into the shade ; he waited.

Now, whom should be given the flag of the Revolution, which Dumouriez, that vague patriot, had flaunted from the tribunes of the Assembly ?

To La Fayette, the man of the Champ de Mars !

To Luckner !

France only knew him from the evil which he had done it when a partisan during the seven years' war.

To Rochambeau, who only wished defensive war, and who was mortified to see Dumouriez address his orders directly to his lieutenants, without making them undergo the censure of his experience.

These were the three men commanding the three armies ready to enter upon the campaign.

La Fayette held the centre ; he ought to dash down the River Meuse, pushing Givet to Namur.

Luckner guarded Franche Comte.

Rochambeau, Flanders.

La Fayette, resting on a corps which Rochambeau would send from Flanders under command of Biron, would take Namur and march on Brussels, where the outbreak of Brabant awaited him with open arms.

La Fayette had the brightest part ; he was in the vanguard, and to him Dumouriez reserved the first victory.

This victory would make him commander in-chief.

La Fayette victorious and general over all, Dumouriez Minister of War, they might toss the red cap to the winds ; they would crush under one hand the Girondists ; with the other, the Jacobins.

The counter-revolution was begun.

But Robespierre ?

We have said he had entered into the background, and many asserted that there was an underground passage between Duplay the joiner's shop and the royal abode of Louis XVI.

Was it not from this that came the pension hereafter paid by the Duchess d'Angouleme to Mademoiselle de Robespierre ?

But this time, as always, La Fayette failed.

Then war was waged against the partisans of peace; the contractors especially were the friends of the enemies of France; they would have willingly left the troops without food or munitions, doing so to ensure bread and powder to the Prussians and Austrians.

Besides, remark how the man of dim mines and dark saps, Dumouriez, did not neglect his connections with the Orleanists—relations that were his ruin.

Biron was an Orleanist general.

Thus Orleanists and Feuillants, La Fayette and Biron, were to deal the first swordthrusts, sound the first trumpeting of victory.

On the morning of the twenty-eighth of April, Biron took Kevrain and marched upon Mons.

On the next day, the twenty-ninth, Theobald Dillon swept from Lille on Tournay.

Biron and Dillon were two aristocrats : two handsome and brave young profligates, of the school of Richelieu, one frank in his patriotic opinions, the other not having had time to know his own mind before he was assassinated.

We have said somewhere before that the dragoons were the aristocratic arm of the army: two regiments of dragoons marched at the head of Biron's three thousand men.

Suddenly, the dragoons, without even having seen the foe, shouted:

"Each for himself! we are betrayed!"

They wheeled round, riding, still shouting, over the infantry, which they trampled under hoof.

The infantry believed them to be pursued and took to flight.

The panic was complete.

The same thing happened to Dillon. He encountered a body of nine hundred Austrians; the dragoons of his vanguard took fright, galloped off drawing the footsoldiers with them, leaving wagons, guns, equipage, and did not stop ere reaching Lille.

There, the fugitives laid their cowardice on the commanders, killing Theobald Dillon and Lieutenant Colonel Bertois; after which they gave their bodies to the mob of Lille, which hung them and danced around them.

By whom had this defeat been organized, which had, for design, making hesitation enter the hearts of patriots, and confidence enter those of their enemies?

The Girondists—who had wished the war, bleeding now on each side with the double wound it had received, and who, it must be acknowledged, had right by all appearances—accused the court, the Queen in other words.

Their first idea was to repay Marie Antoinette blow for blow.

But they had left royalty have time to gird on a breastplate more secure than the shirt of mail which the Queen had obtained for the King and had tested it to be ball-proof, with the Countess de Charny.

The Queen had gradually re-organized that famous constitutional guard authorized by the constitution: amounted to no less than six thousand men.

And what men!

Hectors and fencing-masters who went to insult the patriot representatives even on the benches of the Assembly; Breton and Vendean gentlemen, Provencals from Nimes and Arles, robust priests who, under pretext of refusing the oath, had flung off their frock and taken up, in place of rosary, sword, dagger and pistol; besides, a multitude of Knights of Saint Louis who came from no one knew where, who were decorated with the order for what no one could tell.

(Dumouriez himself complains of this in his Memoirs: "Whatever be the government succeeding this, it cannot restore this order, of the crosses of which it has been so lavish." He had bestowed six thousand in two years!)

This went to such a point that the Minister of Foreign Affairs refused for him the *grand cordon*, and made him give it to M. de Watteville, Major of the Swiss regiment of Ernest.

The commencement was to find a weak point in the cuirass; then they could strike the King and the Queen.

All at once, rumor had it that, at the ancient Ecole Militaire, there was a white flag; that this flag had been given to it by the King.

This reminded people of the black cockades of the fifth and sixth of October.

They were so astonished—with the counter-revolutionary opinions which the King and the Queen were known to entertain—not to see the white flag on the Tuileries, that they expected to behold it floating on some other building some fine morning.

The people, on the intelligence of the existence of this flag, rushed on the barracks.

The officers wished to resist; the soldiers left them.

There was found a white flag about as broad as one's palm, which had been planted in a cake given by the dauphin.

But, beyond this unimportant fact, were found a number of hymns in honor of the King, a number of songs insulting to the Assembly, and thousands of counter-revolutionary sheets.

Bazire, on the very instant, sent in a report to the Assembly: the royal guard had burst into cheers of joy on learning the defeat of Tournay and Kevrain ; it had expressed the hope that in three days, Valenciennes would be taken and that, in a fortnight, foreigners would be in Paris.

More than that.

A trooper in this guard, a sound Frenchman by the name of Joachim Murat, who had believed he had enlisted in a really constitutional body, as its title denoted, gave in his discharge : a price was set upon him so that he might be sent off to Coblentz.

This guard was a terrible weapon in the hands of royalty ; might it not, on the King's order, march upon the Assembly, surround the place, make prisoners of all the representatives of the nation, or shoot them down from the first to the last ?

Less than that : might they not take the King, escort him out of Paris, conduct him to the border, make a second Flight to Varennes, which would this time succeed ?

Therefore, on the twenty-second of May—three weeks after the double check at Tournay and Kevrain—Petion, the new Mayor of Paris,(the man appointed through the Queen's influence, though the man who had brought her back from Varennes, and whom she helped through hatred for him who had let her flee), Petion, we repeat, had written to the Commander of the National Guard, expressing out-spokenly his fears over the King's possible departure, asking him " to observe, watch and multiply the patrols in the suburbs—"

To watch and observe whom—what ? Petion did not state.

To multiply the patrols—why ? The same silence.

But what was the use of naming the Tuileries and the King ?

Observe whom ?

The enemy !

Multiply the patrols around what ? The enemy's camp !

What was the enemy's camp ? The Tuileries.

Who the enemy ? The King.

Thus is the great question answered.

It was Petion (the petty lawyer of Chartres, the son of a proctor) who put this great question to the descendant of Saint Louis, the grandson of Louis the Fourteenth, the King of France !

And the King of France complained —for he felt that this voice spoke louder than his own—in a letter that the directory of the department had posted him on the dead-walls of Paris.

But Petion did not feel one jot uneasy : he did not reply ; he kept up his order.

Hence, Petion was the real monarch.

If the reader doubts this he shall presently see the proof.

Bazire's report demanded that the King's constitutional guard should be suppressed and that a decree should be issued to arrest its leader, M. de Brissac.

The iron was hot ; the Girondists hammered at it like the sturdy smiths they were.

They were working for their being.

The decree was granted that same day : the constitutional guard was disbanded, the Duke de Brissac decreed arrested, and the post at the Tuileries given in charge to the National Guard.

Oh, Charny, Charny, where were you ?

What would you—who, at Varennes, had undertaken to rescue the Queen with your three hundred troopers — have done at the Tuileries, with six thousand men ?

Charny was happily living, forgetting everything in Andrée's arms.

CHAPTER XVII.

THE RUE GUENEGAUD AND THE TUILERIES.

OUR readers will remember the resignation given by de Grave; it had been almost refused by the King, entirely refused by Dumouriez.

Dumouriez was bent on keeping de Grave, who was his man; he did retain him, indeed; but on the tidings of the two-fold check we have aforementioned, he was obliged to sacrifice his Minister of War.

He threw him over, a cake tossed to the Cerberus of the Jacobins to quiet its barking.

He took, in his stead, Colonel Servan, an ex-tutor of the pages, who had been at first proposed to him by the King.

Doubtless he was ignorant what kind of man was becoming his fellow-laborer, and what a shock this man was going to give to royalty!

While the Queen watched in the upper floors of the Tuileries, scanning the horizon to see if she did not descry the so-long expected Austrians, another woman was watching in her little saloon in the Rue Guenegaud.

One was against the revolution, the other was revolution.

Our readers will have guessed we speak of Madame Roland.

It was she who had urged Servan for the ministry, as Madame de Stael had pushed forward Narbonne.

Woman's hand is everywhere in those three fearful years—'91, '92, '93.

Servan was continually in Madame Roland's saloon, like all the Girondists whose breath and light, whose Egeria she was—he was inspired by that valiant soul, which burnt incessantly without ever being consumed.

Some said she was Servan's mistress; she let them say on, and, encouraged by her conscience, smiled at calumny.

Every day, she saw her husband come home crushed by his struggle; he felt himself being drawn into the abyss with his colleague Clavieres, and yet nothing was visible, and everything might be denied.

On the evening when Dumouriez had come to offer him the Ministry of the Interior, he had made his conditions.

"I have no other fortune than my honor," he had said; "I wish to have my honor come out intact from my post. A secretary shall be at all the deliberations of the council and report each one's opinions; thus it may be referred to if ever I fail in patriotism and liberty."

Dumouriez had agreed to this; he felt the need of covering the unpopularity of his name with the Girondist cloak. Dumouriez was one of those men who will promise anything, being ready to keep the pledges as it suits them.

Dumouriez had not kept it, and Roland vainly sought for the secretary.

Thereupon, Roland, unable to procure this secret archive, called for publicity.

He had founded the paper, "The Thermometer," but he very well comprehended it himself, there would come some council, of whose proceedings the immediate revelation would be treason in favor of the enemy.

Servan's nomination came to aid him.

But it was not enough; neutralized by Dumouriez, the council advanced in nothing.

The Assembly struck a blow; it disbanded the Constitutional guard, and arrested Brissac.

Roland, on returning home with Servan in the evening of the twenty-ninth of May, brought the news to the house.

"What have they done with the disbanded guardsmen?" inquired Madame Roland.

"Nothing."

"Are they free, then?"

"Yes, only they will be obliged to cast off the blue uniform."

"To-morrow they will assume the red uniform, and go about as Swiss."

On the ensuing day, in truth, the streets of Paris were reddened with Swiss uniforms.

The disbanded guards had changed their coats, that was all.

There they were, in Paris, holding out their hands to the foreigner, ready to open the gates to him.

The two men, Roland and Servan, could find no remedy for this.

But the woman, Madame Roland, took a sheet of paper, put a pen in Servan's hand and said :

"Write : Proposition to establish at Paris, for the holiday of the fourteenth July, a camp of twenty thousand volunteers—"

Servan dropped the pen before he had finished the sentence.

"The King will never consent!" said he.

"Hence this measure is not to be proposed to the King, but to the Assembly ; hence it is not to be claimed as a minister, but as a citizen."

Servan and Roland, by the flash, had seen a boundless horizon.

"You are right," exclaimed Servan, "with that and a decree over the priesthood, we shall hold the King."

"You understand ? the priests are counter-revolution in families and societies ; the priests have added this phrase to the Creed : 'And those who pay the tax imposed shall be damned!' Fifty sworn priests have been slaughtered, their houses pillaged, their fields destroyed, since six months. Let the Assembly issue a decree of urgency against the rebellious priests. Finish your motion, Servan. Roland will draw up the decree."

Servan completed his sentence.

Roland had been writing in the meantime.

"The transportation out of the country of a rebellious priest shall take place within a month, if it is demanded by twenty active citizens, approved by the district and the government ; the transported person will receive three francs a day, as travelling expenses, as far as the frontier."

Servan read his proposition concerning the volunteer camp.

Roland read his plan of a decree for banishing the priests.

The whole question, in fact, lay in this :

Would the King act frankly ?

Would the King betray?

If the King was truly constitutional, he would sanction both decrees.

If not, he would veto them.

"I will sign the motion for the camps as a citizen," said Servan.

"And Vergniaud will bring forward the decree on the priests," said together the husband and the wife.

On the ensuing day, Servan sent in his request to the Assembly.

Vergniaud pocketed the decree and promised to produce it when the time should come.

On the evening of the sending of the motion to the National Assembly, Servan went to the council as usual.

His action was known : Roland, and Clavieres supported him ; against him were Dumouriez, Lacoste and Duranthon.

"Oh, come, sir," cried Dumouriez, "and give us an account of your conduct."

"To whom, if you please?" asked Servan.

"Why, to the King, the nation, and to me !"

Servan smiled.

"Sir," resumed Dumouriez, "you have taken an important step."

"Yes," responded Servan, "I know it is of the utmost importance !"

"Did you have the King's order to act thus ?"

"No, sir, I confess it."

"Did you take the opinions of your colleagues ?"

"No more than I did the King's orders, I must acknowledge."

"Then, why did you act thus ?"

"Because such was my right as a private citizen."

"Then, it was as a private citizen that you presented that incendiary motion ?"

"Yes."

"Why, then, did you join to your signature the title of Minister of War?"

"Because I desire to prove to the Assembly that I was ready to support, as a minister, what I demanded as a citizen."

"Sir," said Dumouriez, "what you have done is an act both of a bad citizen and a bad minister !"

"Sir," returned Servan, "allow me to have only myself as judge of the promptings of my conscience; if I took a judge over so delicate a question I will find one not named Dumouriez."

Dumouriez turned pale, and made one step towards Servan.

The latter clapped his hand to his sword-hilt.

Dumouriez did the same.

At this moment, the King entered. He was still unaware of Servan's motion.

All were hushed.

On the next day, the decree requesting the collection of twenty thousand federalists at Paris was debated at the Assembly.

The King was in consternation at the news.

He summoned Dumouriez.

"You are a faithful servitor, sir," he said to him, "and I have learnt in what manner you defended the interests of royalty, with respect to that wretch Servan."

"I thank your Majesty," said Dumouriez. "Is the King aware of the passing of the decree?" he inquired, after a pause.

"No," answered the King; "but that little matters; I am decided, in this circumstance, to use my right of veto."

Dumouriez shook his head.

"Do you not think I should, sir?" asked the King.

"Sire," responded Dumouriez, "without any resisting force, a butt as you are to the suspicions of the greater portion of the nation, to the rage of the Jacobins, to the deep policy of the republican party,— such a resolution on your part would be a declaration of war."

"Well, let the war come! I have waged it on my friends; I can wage it against my enemies."

"Sire, in one case you have ten chances of victory, in the other, ten chances of defeat."

"But do you not know what is the design of their demanding these twenty thou and men?"

"Let your Majesty grant me five minutes' free speech, and I hope to prove to him that not only do I know what is designed, but that, furthermore, I can foresee what will happen."

"Speak, sir," said the King, "I will listen."

And, indeed, with elbow on the arm of his chair, his head on the hollow of his hand, Louis Sixteenth listened.

"Sire," began Dumouriez, "those who solicit this decree are as much enemies of the country as of the King."

"You see," interrupted Louis, "you confess it yourself."

"I will say more; its accomplishment can only produce great misfortunes."

"Well, then?"

"Allow me, sire—"

"Yes, go on."

"The Minister of War is very culpable to have solicited the assembling of twenty thousand men near Paris, while our armies are weak, our frontier ungarrisoned, our treasury exhausted."

"Oh, culpable, I believe you!" said the King.

"Not only culpable, sire, but imprudent, besides, which is worse ? imprudent to propose near the Assembly the uniting of an undisciplined troop, called under a name which exaggerates its patriotism, and of which the first ambitious man may take advantage."

"It is the Gironde speaking through Servan."

"It is," Dumouriez agreed; "but it is not the Gironde that will profit by this, sire."

"Perhaps the Feuillants?"

"Neither one nor the other, but it will be the Jacobins! the Jacobins whose brotherhoods extend all over the kingdom, and who, out of twenty thousand federalists, will find perhaps nineteen thousand adepts. So, rely on it, sire, the promoters of this decree will be overturned by the instrument itself."

"Could I believe so, I would be almost consoled!" exclaimed the King.

"I therefore think, sire, that this decree is dangerous for the nation, the King, the National Assembly, and especially for its authors, whose scourge it will be; and still my advice is that you should not do otherwise than sanction it; it has been provoked by malice so deep, that I say, sire, there is a woman underlying it all."

"Madame Roland? Why do not these women knit or sew instead of dabbling in politics?"

"Who can help it, sire? Madame de Maintenon, Madame de Pompadour and Madame du Barry have made them lose the habit of it. The decree, I say, has been provoked by deep malice, debated eagerly, adopted enthusiastically; everybody is blind with respect to this unlucky decree; if you apply your veto to it, it will be none the less carried out. Instead of the twenty thousand men called out by the law, who consequently will submit to ordinances, there will arrive from the provinces, on the approaching day of the federation, forty thousand unregulated men, who can, at the same blow, overturn the Constitution, the Assembly and the throne! If we had been victors instead of being vanquished," added Dumouriez, lowering his voice, "if I had had a pretext of making La Fayette General in-chief and to place under his hand, sire, one hundred thousand men, then I would have told you : 'Do not accept!' We are beaten without and within, so I say, sire : 'Accept!'"

At this moment there was tapping at the door.

"Come in," said Louis.

It was Thierry, the King's valet-de-chambre.

"Sire," said he, "Monsieur Duranthon, the Minister of Justice, asks speech of your Majesty."

"What does he want? See about it, Monsieur Dumouriez."

Dumouriez went out.

At the same instant, the tapestry, which fell over the door of communication between the royal closet and the Queen's apartments, was lifted, and Marie Antoinette appeared.

"Sire, sire!" she said, "hold out firmly! this Dumouriez is a Jacobin like the others! Has he not put on the red cap? As for La Fayette, you know, I would rather be ruined without him than be saved by him!"

As they heard the steps of Dumouriez approaching the door, the hangings fell, and the vision vanished.

CHAPTER XVIII.

THE VETO.

JUST as the tapestry ceased to rustle, the door opened.

"Sire," said Dumouriez, "on Monsieur Vergniaud's motion, the decree upon the priests has passed."

"This is a conspiracy," said the King rising. "How is the decree conceived?"

"There it is, sire; Monsieur Duranthon has brought it. I thought that your Majesty would do me the honor of privately imparting to me your opinion before speaking in the council."

"You are right. Give me that paper."

In a voice tremlous with agitation, the King read the decree the substance of which our readers are informed upon.

After having perused the paper, he rolled it up between his hands and cast it far from him.

"I shall never sanction such a decree!" exclaimed he.

"Excuse me, sire," said Dumouriez, "for being, this time again, of opposite mode of thinking from your Majesty."

"Sir," said the King, "I may waver in political matters; in religious matters, never! In the former, I judge with my mind and the mind is fallible; in the matters of religion, I judge with my conscience, and that is infallible."

"Sire," resumed Dumouriez, "a year ago you sanctioned the decree to make the priesthood take the oath."

"I was forced to do so, sir," returned the King.

"Sire, it was to that that you should have put your veto; this second decree is but the consequence of the former. The first decree has produced all the evils of France; this will be a remedy to them : it is harsh but not cruel. The first was a religious law, attacking the liberty of thought in its cultivation this one is a political regulation which only concerns the safety and tranquility of the realm : it is the shield of the unsworn priests against persecution. Far from saving them by your veto, you will deprive them of the help of a law, you will expose them to be massacred, and urge the French to become their butchers. Hence my advice, sire —excuse the frankness of a soldier— my opinion is that having, I dare to say it, committed the fault of sanctioning the decree of the oath of the clergy, your veto applied to this second decree, which may stop the deluge of blood about to pour out, will charge your Majesty's conscience with all the crimes the people should bear."

" But what crimes, sir ? what crimes are greater than those already accomplished ?" broke in a voice coming from the background of the apartment.

Dumouriez started at the vibrating voice ; he had recognized the Queen's ringing tone.

" Ah, madame," said he ; "I would have preferred ending it all with the King."

" Sir," said the Queen, with a bitter smile for Dumouriez and an almost scornful glance on the King. "I have but one question to put to you."

" What is it, madame?"

" Do you believe that the King should any longer support Roland's menaces, the insolence of Clavieres and Servan's malice ?"

"No, madame," responded Dumouriez, " I am indignant as you are ; I admire the King's patience and, if we reach that point, I venture to supplicate the King to entirely change his inmistry."

" Entirely ?" echoed the King.

" Yes ; let your Majesty dismiss all six of us, and choose, if they can be found, men who are of another way of thinking."

" Nay, nay," remonstrated the King ; " Nay, I wish you to remain, you and the good Lacoste, and Duranthon also ; but render me the service of disembarrassing me of those three insolent and contentious men ; for I avow to you, sir, my patience is at an end."

" The thing is dangerous, sire."

" Do you recoil from the dangers ?" inquired the Queen.

" No, madame," returned Dumouriez ; "only I make my conditions."

" Conditions ?" queried the Queen haughtily.

Dumouriez bowed.

" Speak, sir," went on the King.

" Sire," resumed Dumouriez, " I am target for the blows of the three factions dividing Paris. Girondists, Feuillants, Jacobins have all their darts to hurl at me in emulation ; I am completely shorn of popularity, and, as it is only by popular opinion that a few threads of the government may be held. I am really useless to you save on one condition."

" Which is ?"

" Let it be spoken openly, sire—it is that I remain, with my two coleagues, only to sanction the two decrees that have just been passed."

" This cannot be!" broke out the King.

" Impossible !" exclaimed the Queen.

" Do you refuse ?"

" My most cruel enemy, sir," said the King, " would not impose on me harsher terms than those you have just stated."

" Sire," responded Dumouriez, " on my gentleman's faith, on my soldier's honor, I believe them necessary to your salvation."

Then turning to the Queen, he continued.

" Madame, it is not for yourself; if the fearless daughter of Maria Theresa not only scorns danger, but, with her mother's example, is ready to march upon it, let her think, madame, she is not alone; think of your royal consort, of your children; instead of pushing them into the abyss, join with me to hold his Majesty on the brink of the chasm whereon totters his throne !

" If I had believed the sanction of both decrees necessary before his Majesty had expressed his desire of being rid of the two weighing upon him," added he, addressing the King, "judge how much when he speaks of dismissing them, I think this sanction indispensable; if you send away the ministers without approving these decrees, the people will have two motives to think as urging you : they will look upon you as enemy of the Constitution, and the dismissed ministers will pass before their eyes as martyrs, and I will not answer for, a few days from this, the greatest events not putting in peril your crown and your life. As for me, I forewarn your Majesty that I cannot, even to serve him, go on—I shall not say contrary to my principles —but against my convictions. Duranthon and Lacoste think as I do; nevertheless, I did not undertake to speak for them. In what concerns me, therefore, I have told you, sire, and I repeat it, I will not remain in the cabinet without your Majesty signs both the decrees."

The King made an impatient start.

Dumouriez bowed and proceeded towards the door.

The King exchanged a rapid glance with his royal partner.

"Sir," said the latter.

Dumouriez stopped.

"Think how hard it is for the King to ratify a decree which will bring to Paris twenty thousand rascals who may massacre us !"

"Madame," returned Dumouriez, "I am aware that the danger is great; that is why it must be surveyed, but not exaggerated. The decree says that the executive power will indicate the gathering point of these twenty thousand men, who are not all rascals; it also says that the Minister of War will take upon himself the giving them officers and a plan of organization."

"But, sir, the Minister of War is Servan !"

"Nay, sire, the Minister of War—Servan having retired—will now be myself."

"Ah, yes, you ?" said the King.

"Will you assume the Ministry of War ?" asked the Queen.

"Yes, madame, and I will turn, I hope, against your enemies, the sword hanging over your heads."

The King and the Queen glanced at one another again to consult.

"Suppose," proceeded Dumouriez, "that I settle upon Soissons as the site of a camp, that I appoint as commander a firm, wise lieutenant general, with two safe officers next under him ; they will form these men in battalions, so that there will be four or five breaks, each part being diversified by bearing different weapons ; the ministry will profit by the calls of the generals to send them to the frontier, and then you will see well enough, sire, that this decree, originated with evil intention, far from being noxious, will become useful."

"But," objected the King, "are you sure of obtaining permission to make this assembling at Soissons ?"

"I will answer for it."

"In that case, take the Ministry of War," said the King.

"Sire," said Dumouriez, "in the Ministry of Foreign Affairs, I have but a light and indirect responsibility ; it is quite otherwise with the Ministry of War ; your generals are my enemies ; you have just seen their weakness ; I will have to answer for their faults ; but as it is for the life of your Majesty, the safety of the Queen, and of her august children, and the maintenance of the Constitution, I accept ! We are, therefore, in agreement on that point, sire, of the sanction of the decree for twenty thousand men ?"

" Were you Minister of War, sir, I would entirely confide in you," said the King.

"Now as to the decree concerning the priesthood ?"

"That, sir, as I have told you, I can never approve."

"Sire, you have put yourself under the necessity of approving the second by having ratified the first"

"I have committed one fault for which I reproach myself; that is no reason for my committing a second."

"Sire, if you veto this decree, the second fault will be far worse than the first !"

"Sire !" exclaimed the Queen.

The King turned to the speaker.

"Do you too, madame, desire this ?"

"Sire, I must acknowledge that on this point, after the explanations which he has given us, I am of the opinion of Monsieur Dumouriez."

" Well, then—" began the King.

"Then, sire," repeated Dumouriez

"I consent, but on the condition that as speedily as it may be, you will rid me of this factious trio."

"Believe me, sire," returned Dumouriez, "that I will seize upon the first occasion and, I am sure of it, that occasion will not keep us waiting for its coming."

With that, bowing to the King and Queen, Dumouriez retired.

Both their Majesties followed with their eyes the new Minister of War, until the door was closed behind him.

"You made me a sign to consent," said the King; "now, what have you to say?"

"Accept firstly the decree for the twenty thousand men," responded the Queen; "let him make his camp at Soissons; let him disperse his men, and then—well, then, we will see what we will do about the decree over the priests."

"But he will remind me of my pledged word, madame!"

"He will be entangled, and you can hold him."

"On the contrary, it will be he who will hold me, madame; he will have my word."

"Pshaw!" returned the Queen, "there's a remedy for that when one has been Monsieur de la Vauguyon's pupil!"

Taking the King's arm, she led him into the adjoining apartment.

CHAPTER XIX.

THE OCCASION.

As we have not omitted to state, the real war of the present moment was between the Rue Guenegaud and the Tuileries, between the Queen and Madame Roland.

Strange thing!

Both women had over their husbands an influence which dragged them all four to death.

Each, however, went by an opposite road.

The events we have just related took place on the tenth of June; on the evening of the eleventh, Servan entered Roland's house quite joyful.

"Congratulate me, dear friend!" cried he to Madame Roland; "I have the honor of having been driven from the cabinet."

"How is that!" asked Madame Roland.

"Here are the facts: this morning, I went to the royal apartments to confer with the King upon some business of my department, and, those matters being terminated, I warmly attacked the question of the camp for the twenty thousand men; but——"

"But? go on."

"At the first word I uttered, the King turned his back on me in very bad humor; and, this evening, in his Majesty's name, Monsieur Dumouriez came to take from me my portfolio of war."

"Dumouriez?"

"Yes."

"He has played a villainous part in this, but it does not surprise me. Ask Roland what I said to him of this man on the day when I saw him for the first time. Besides, we were informed that he is daily in conference with the Queen."

"He is a traitor!"

"Nay, he is an ambitious man. Go seek Roland and Clavieres."

"Where is Roland?"

"He is giving audiences at the ministry of the interior."

"What are you going to do meanwhile?"

"Draw up a letter which I shall show to you on your return. Go."

"You are verily the famous goddess, Reason, whom philosophers have been so long invoking."

"And whom men of conscience have found. Do not come back without Clavieres."

"That will probably cause some delay."

"I want an hour."

"Proceed! may the Spirit of France inspire you!"

Servan went out.

Hardly had the door closed than Madame Roland was at her desk, writing the following letter:

"Sire: The present state of France cannot longer exist; it is a state of crisis the violence of which has attained its highest degree; it must terminate by an outbreak in which your Majesty has as much interest as the whole empire.

"Honored by your confidence, and placed in a post where I owe you all the truth, I venture to say it; it is an obligation which is imposed upon me by yourself.

"The French have been given a Constitution; it has made some discontented and rebellious; the majority of the nation wish to maintain it; they have sworn to defend it at the price of their blood, and they have seen with joy the civil war which offers them a great means of ensuring it. Nevertheless, the minority, sustained by their hopes, have combined all their efforts to bear away the advantage; hence this intestine conflict against the laws, this anarchy of which good citizens complain, and by which the ill-contented have taken care to calumniate the new rule; thence this division everywhere incited, for nowhere does indifference exist; the triumph or the change of the Constitution is wished; it must be upheld or altered.

"I abstain from examining what it is in itself, to alone consider what circumstances require, and, estranging myself from the thing as much as possible, I try to discover what it is that is expected.

"Your Majesty enjoys great prerogatives which you believe appanages of royalty; reserved in the idea of preserving them, you cannot see them removed with pleasure; the thought of having them restored was as natural as the regret at seeing them annihilated.

"Such sentiments, which are akin to the nature of the human heart, must have entered into the calculation of the enemies of the Revolution; they have counted on a favor secret until circumstances admit of open protection. These facts cannot escape the nation itself, and they have given it distrust.

"Your Majesty has therefore been constantly in the alternative of yielding to your former habits and private tendencies, or to make sacrifices dictated by philosophy, as well as exacted by necessity; consequently, to embolden rebels in disturbing the nation, or to appease it by uniting yourself with it.

"Everything has an end, and that of uncertainty has at last arrived.

"Your Majesty can, at the present day, openly ally yourself with those who pretend to reform the Constitution, or will you generously devote yourself unreservedly to making it triumph? Such is the real question the solution of which the actual state of affairs renders unavoidable.

"As for the problem of whether the French are ripe for freedom, its discussion has no place in this; for the question is not to judge what we may become a hundred years hence, but to see of what the present generation is capable.

"The Declaration of the Rights of Man has become a political gospel, and the French Constitution a religion for which the people are ready to perish. This enthusiasm has gone already so far as to supplant the law, but— when that was not strong enough to constrain the perturbators—citizens themselves have been allowed to punish. Thus comes it that the property of emigres or persons acknowledged to be of that party has been exposed to the ravages inspired by revenge; that is why so many departments have been obliged to remove their shields from the priests whom opinion had proscribed and made its victims.

"In this shock of interests all sentiments have assumed the pitch of passion. 'Country' is not a word which fancy can embellish; it is a being to which sacrifices have been made, to which every day henceforward all are more and more attached by the solicitudes it awakens, which has been created by mighty efforts, which arises in the midst of inquietudes, and which is loved by what it costs as much as by what is hoped. Every blow dealt at it is the means of enflaming enthusiasm for it.

"To what point will this enthusiasm mount at the instant when the enemy's forces, assembled around, concert with internal intrigues to strike the most fatal blows !

" Excitement is extreme in all parts of the empire ; it will burst in a fearful manner, unless a reason-grounded confidence in your Majesty can at length quiet it ; but such confidence cannot be established on mere protestations ; it must have for basis nothing less than facts.

" It is evident for the French nation that its Constitution can keep erect, that the government will have all the power necessary to it from the moment when your Majesty (absolutely wishing the triumph of that Constitution) sustains the legislative body in all its power of execution, thus depriving the uneasiness of the people of all pretexts, and the discontented of all hope.

" For instance, two important resolutions have been passed : both essentially of interest to the public tranquility and the safety of the State. The delaying of their confirmation inspires mistrust ; if it be prolonged, it will cause discontent, and, I must say it, in the present commotion of minds, discontent may lead to anything !

" There is no time any longer to draw back ; there is no means of gaining time.

" Revolution is made in minds ; it will be worked out at the cost of blood, and will be cemented with it, if wisdom does not foresee and fore-settle the misfortunes it is yet possible to avoid.

" I know that it may be imagined that anything can be done or constrained by extreme measures ; but—let force be displayed to awe the Assembly, let fear be spread over Paris, division and stupor in the suburbs—the whole of France would rise in indignation and, albeit lacerated itself in the horrors of civil war, will develop that unwavering energy—mother of crimes and virtues—ever fatal to those who may provoke it.

" The welfare of the State and your Majesty's happiness are intimately bound together ; no power is able to disconnect them ; cruel pangs and woes will flock around your throne, if it be not supported by yourself on the basis of the Constitution, and well encompass-

ed by the peace which its maintenance must finally procure us.

" Therefore, the state of minds, the course of things, political reasons, your Majesty's interest, render indispensable the obligation of joining with the legislative body and responding to the wishes of the nation ; they make a necessity of what principles set forth as a duty ; but natural sensibility to this affectionate people is ready to find a means of acknowledgment.

" You were cruelly deceived, sire, when it was sought to inspire in you distrust or estrangement for this people so easy to affect ; it is by perpetually working for this object that you have been led into a line of conduct which now alarms the people themselves. Let them see that you are determined to help on the furtherance of this Constitution, to which is linked their weal, and before long you will become the object of their fervent prayers.

" The conduct of the priesthood in many places, the pretexts which fanaticism furnishes to the discontented have given rise to a well-made law against such perturbators.

" Let your Majesty approve it !

" Public tranquility claims it and the safety of the priesthood solicits it; if this law is not confirmed, the departments will be compelled to substitute for it, violent measures, which proceedings the people will outdo by excesses.

" The attempts of our enemies, the agitation which is maifested in the capital, the extreme chafing to which the conduct of your guard has given rise, still more increased by the evidences of satisfaction of which your Majesty has given witness in a really impolitic proclamation for the circumstances ; the situation of Paris, its proximity to the borders, have formed the need of a camp in its vicinity ; this measure (the wisdom and urgency of which have struck all sound minds) only wants for your Majesty's signature.

" Why will you allow delays to give you the semblance of regretfulness, when speed would win all hearts ?

" Already the actions of the staff of the Parisian National Guard against this measure have led to suspicions that it acts under superior inspiration; already the declarations of several extravagant demagogues have awakened the suspicions of their connection with those interested in the overturning of the Constitution; already opinion compromises every one of your Majesty's intentions. Further delay, and the grieved people will see in their ruler the friend and accomplice of conspirators!

"Just heaven! do you smite with blindness the mighty of earth and will they never heed but such advice as drags them to their ruin?

"I know that the stern language of truth is rarely nourished near the throne; I also know that it is because it is never heard that revolutions become necessary; I am especially aware what I owe to your Majesty, not only as a citizen submissive to the laws, but moreover as a minister honored by his trust or clothed with functions that suppose that, and I know of nothing which can prevent my fulfilling a duty which I have on my conscience.

"It is in the same spirit that I reiterate my representations to your Majesty, on the obligation and utility of executing the law which prescribes the having a secretary at the council: the sole existence of this law speaks so powerfully that the execution seems a duty not to be delayed; but it is of moment to employ all means to preserve to deliberations gravity, wisdom and the necessary maturity, and, for responsible ministers, there must be a means of recording their opinions; had such means existed, I would not at this moment be addressing your Majesty in writing.

"Life is nothing to the man who values his duties above everything else; but, after the happiness of having fulfilled them, the single pleasure to him then sensible is that of proving that he has done so with faithfulness, and it is even an obligation for the public man.

"June 10, 1792, Year IV. of Liberty."

The letter was just being finished; she had just lifted off her pen, when Servan, Clavieres and Roland entered. In a couple of words, Madame Roland ventilated her plan to the three friends.

The letter, which was read among them all, would be re-perused on the ensuing day to the three absent ministers, Dumouriez, Lacoste and Duranthon.

Either they would approve of it, and join their signatures to Roland's; or they would reject it, and Servan, Clavieres and Roland would collectively hand in their resignations, the motive of which would be the refusal given by their colleagues to sign a document which appeared to them to express the real opinion of France.

Then they would deposit the letter before the National Assembly, and there would remain to France no doubt on the cause of the going out of the three patriot ministers.

The letter was read, as we have stated, to the three friends, who found not one word to be altered.

Madame Roland was a soul in common from which all might receive the elixir of patriotism.

But this was not so on the morrow, after the reading by Roland to Dumouriez and the other two ministers.

All three approved the idea, but differed on the mode of expressing it; in short, they finally refused, saying that it would be better to personally confer with the King.

This was a way of eluding the question.

Roland, on that same evening, sent to the King the letter signed by himself alone.

Almost immediately, Lacoste handed Roland and Clavieres their dismissals.

As Dumouriez had foretold, the occasion had not kept them waiting.

It is true that the King had not avoided it.

On the day after, as the event had been arranged, Roland's letter was read to the tribunes at the same time as was announced his dismissal and that of his colleagues Clavieres and Servan.

The Assembly declared by an immense majority that the three dismissed ministers had "deserved well of their country."

Thus was war declared to the interior as to the exterior.

The Assembly, ere dealing the opening blows, only waited to learn what the King was going to do with respect to the two decrees.

CHAPTER XX.

THE PUPIL OF THE DUKE DE LA VAUGUYON.

At the moment when the Assembly voted by acclamation thanks to the three out-going ministers, and decreed the printing and sending to the departments of Roland's letter, Dumouriez appeared at the door of the Assembly.

He was known to be brave; they did not know he was audacious.

He had learnt what was transpiring, and had come boldly to take the bull by the horns.

The pretext of his presence at the Assembly was a remarkable memorandum on the state of the military forces of France; Minister of War from the evening previous, he had himself helped compile and had compiled this document in the night; it was an accusation against Servan, which, in reality, should have fallen back upon de Grave, and especially upon Narbonne, his predecessor.

Servan had only been minister some ten or twelve days.

Dumouriez came very highly fortified; he had parted from the King, whom he had conjured to be faithful to the double pledge given with respect to the sanction of the two decrees, and the King had answered, not only by renewing his promise, but further by affirming that the ecclesiastics whom he had consulted so as to quiet his conscience had all been of the same mind as Dumouriez.

Therefore, the Minister of War strode directly to the speaker's stand, which he ascended amidst confused hoots and ferocious yells.

Having mounted it, he coolly asked the floor.

Speech was accorded him in the midst of a frightful tumult.

At last, the curiosity all had to hear what Dumouriez had to say calmed things somewhat.

"Gentlemen," began Dumouriez, "General Gouvion has been killed; heaven has rewarded him for his courage; he died fighting the enemies of France; he is very fortunate! He is not witness of our dreadful discord. I envy his fate."

These few words, spoken loftily with deep melancholy, made an impression on the Assembly; besides, this death made a diversion on the former feelings.

There were deliberations on what the Assembly should do to mark their regret to the general's family, and it was resolved that the president should write a letter.

Thereupon, Dumouriez asked the floor a second time.

It was granted.

He drew his paper from his pocket; but hardly had he read the title: "Memorandum on the Ministry of War," than Girondists and Jacobins began to hoot in order to prevent the reading.

But, in the height of the uproar, the minister read the exordium in so high an accent, with so clear a voice, that all heard that the preface was directed on factions and revolved on the respect due a minister.

Such coolness was calculated to exasperate the auditors of Dumouriez, even had they been in a less irritable state of mind.

"Do you hear him?" exclaimed Gaudet. "He already believes himself so sure of power, that he ventures to give us advice!"

"Why not?" tranquilly retorted Dumouriez, turning on his interruptor.

The most prudent quality in France is what we have so long said it was; to wit, courage.

The courage of Dumouriez imposed upon his adversaries.

They were silenced, or at least they wanted to hear and, hence, listened.

The paper was cleverly written, luminous, skilfully worked; prejudiced as they were against the minister, at two places he was applauded.

Lacuee, who was member of the military committee, mounted the rostrum to reply to Dumouriez ; whereupon the latter, rolled up his paper and quietly returned it to his pocket.

The Girondists saw the movement.

" See the traitor !" shouted out one of them. " He puts his paper in his pocket ; he means to fly with his memorandum—let us prevent it ! that paper will serve to confound him."

But upon these cries, Dumouriez, who had not taken a single step towards the door, drew the document from his pocket and handed it to an usher.

A secretary instantly held out his hand for it and, having received it, looked for the signature.

" Gentlemen, the statement is not signed !" said the recorder.

" Let him sign !" broke forth from all sides.

" Such was my intention," said Dumouriez, " and it is drawn up so faithfully that I should not hesitate to put my name to it. Give me pen and ink."

A pen full of ink was passed to him.

He put one foot on the steps of the tribune, and signed the memoir on his knees.

The usher was then going to take it again ; but Dumouriez thrust aside his hand, and went himself to lay the paper on the table ; then, with short steps, and stopping every instant, he crossed the hall, and went out by the door situated under the benches on the left side.

Quite the contrary from his entrance, which had been so noisy, this exit was accompanied with the utmost stillness ; the spectators in the lobby rushed into the corridor to see this man who had confronted a whole Assembly.

At the door of the meeting-place of the Feuillant Club, he was surrounded by three or four hundred persons who pressed around him with more curiosity than hate, as if they had foreseen that, three months afterwards, he would save France at Valmy.

Several royalist deputies left the chamber one after another, and ran to Dumouriez ; they had no longer any doubts, the general was on their side.

This was precisely what Dumouriez had foreseen, and why he had got the King to give his sanction to the two decrees.

" Why, general, they are raising the deuce in there," said one of them.

" They may be raising the deuce," returned Dumouriez, " but I do not know what the devil has to do with them."

" Don't you know ?" said another, " there is question in the house of sending you to Orleans."

" Good !" replied Dumouriez, " I have need of vacation. I will take baths and drink country milk, and take some rest."

" General," cried a third, " they are just revoking the printing of your memorial."

" So much the better ! It is a foolish step, which will win me over all the impartial."

It was in the middle of this escort and amid these speeches that he reached the chateau.

The King received him heartily ; he was so deeply compromised.

The new council was now called together.

On sending away Servan, Roland and Clavieres, Dumouriez had believed he had the power to replace them.

As Minister of Home Affairs, he had proposed Mourgues of Montpellier, a Protestant member of several academies, formerly a Feuillant who had withdrawn from the club.

The King had accepted him.

As Minister of Foreign Affairs, he had proposed Maulde, Semonville or Naillac.

The King had fixed his option on the last-named.

As Minister of Finances, he had proposed Vergennes, nephew of the former Minister.

Vergennes was perfectly well known to the King, who had him sent for instantly, but he, while showing deep attachment to the King, had utterly refused.

It was therefore decided that the Ministry of the Home Department should be filled, for the interim, by the Minister of Finances, and that Dumouriez, for an interim, also,—while waiting for Naillac, who was absent from Paris,—should take charge of the Ministry of Foreign Affairs.

However, the four ministers, who did not deceive themselves as to the gravity of the situation, had agreed that —if the King, after having obtained the dismissal of Servan, Roland and Clavieres, did not keep his promise at the price of what had been the cause of the dismissal—they would send in their resignations.

The new council, we have said, had met.

The King already knew what had transpired at the Assembly; he felicitated Dumouriez on the attitude he had assumed, immediately confirmed the decree on the camp for the twenty thousand volunteers, but put off till the morrow the ratification of that upon the priests.

He objected on a scruple of conscience, which, he said, his confessor would probably remove.

The ministers glanced at one another; a first doubt had glided into their hearts.

But, taking everything into account, the King's timorous conscience might have need of this delay to become steadfast.

The following day, the ministers returned to the previous evening's question.

But night had done its work; the will, if not the conscience, of the King, had become steadfast; he declared that he would put his veto on the decree.

The four ministers; one after another—Dumouriez the first, to whom speech had been transferred—spoke to the King with respect, but with firmness.

The King listened to them, closing his eyes, in the attitude of a man whose mind was made up.

Indeed, when they had concluded, the King said:

"Gentlemen, I have written a letter to the President of the Assembly to inform him of my resolve; one of you will countersign it, and all four will carry it together to the Assembly."

This was a command couched entirely in the spirit of the former rule but sounded ill to the ears of constitutional, and consequently responsible, ministers.

"Sire," said Dumouriez, after having consulted with a look his colleagues, "have you nothing more to order us?"

"No," said the King.

He retired.

The ministers had a conference and, having finished, determined to ask an audience for the morrow.

They had agreed to enter into no explanation, but to give in an unanimous resignation.

Dumouriez went home.

The King had almost succeeded in making a catspaw of him, the acute politician, the skilled diplomatist, the general whose courage was doubled by intrigue!

He found three notes from different persons which announced to him gatherings in the Faubourg Saint Antoine, and conciliables at Santerre's dwelling.

He instantly wrote to the King to warn him of what he had been informed.

An hour afterwards, he received the following billet, not signed by the royal hand, but written by it:

"Do not think, sir, that I can be frightened by threats; my mind is made up.

Dumouriez caught up a pen and wrote back:

"Sire:

"You judge me wrongfully if you believe me capable of employing such a means. My colleagues and myself have had the honor of addressing your majesty to beg of him the favor of receiving us at ten o'clock to-morrow morning; I now beseech your Majesty to be so kind as to select a successor to me who can replace me within four-and twenty hours on account of the demands of the business of the department of war, and to accept my resignation."

He had this letter carried by his

ANDREE DE TAVERNEY.

The secretary waited until midnight, and, at half after twelve, returned with this note :

" I will see my ministers to-morrow at ten o'clock, and we will speak of what you have written to me."

It was evident that counter-revolution was at work at the palace.

The royalists in truth had forces on which they might rely.

A constitutional guard of six thousand men, disbanded, but ready to come together at the first call :

Seven or eight thousand chevaliers of the order of Saint Louis whose red ribbon was the token of rallying :

Three Swiss battalions of sixteen thousand men each ; they were troops of unshaken discipline, like old Helvetian rocks.

Then, better than all, a letter from La Fayette, in which the following paragraph had been found :

" Persist, sire ! strong in the authority which the National Assembly has delegated to you, you will find every good Frenchman ranked around your throne !"

What was proposed and intended to be done was as follows :

At the signal, assemble the constitutional guard, chevaliers of Saint Louis, and Swiss :

Seize, at the same hour of the same day, the cannon of the sections, shut up the Jacobin clubhouse and the Assembly, rally all the royalists in the National Guard (who formed a contingency of fifteen thousand men or thereabouts), and wait for La Fayette, who, by three days' forced marches, might come from the Ardennes.

Unfortunately, the Queen would not hear La Fayette spoken of.

La Fayette was moderate revolution, and, in the Queen's opinion, such revolution might establish itself, gain a footing and maintain it; the revolution of the Jacobins, on the other hand, would soon push the people to the end of endurance, and could have no consistency.

Oh, if Charny were there !

But it was not even known where Charny was, and had his whereabouts been known, it was too great a stooping —if not for the Queen, at least for the woman—to have him sought for.

The night passed in the chateau in tumult and deliberation; they had the means of offence and defence, but not a hand strong enough to manage them.

At ten in the morning, the ministers came to the royal chamber.

This was the sixteenth of June.

The King received them.

Duranthon spoke.

In the name of all, with deep and affectionate respectfulness, he tendered the resignations of his colleagues and himself.

" Yes, I understand—the responsibility !" said the King.

" Sire," cried Lacoste, " the royal responsibility, yes ; as for ourselves, you may believe it, we are ready to die for your Majesty ; but, in dying for the priesthood, we would but hasten the downfall of the realm !"

Louis the Sixteenth turned to Dumouriez.

" Sir," said he, " are you still in the feelings which your yesternight's letter expressed ?"

" I am, sire," responded the general, " if your Majesty has not let himself be vanquished by our fidelity and attachment."

" Well," said the King moodily, " since your part is taken, I accept your resignation ; I will provide for it."

The four bowed.

Mourgues had his resignation written out ; he handed it to the King.

The others gave theirs verbally.

Courtiers were in attendance in the ante-chamber ; they saw the four ministers come forth, and saw by their bearing that all was over.

Some were rejoiced : others were alarmed.

The atmosphere thickened as on hot summer days ; one felt the storm was coming.

At the gates of the Tuileries, Dumouriez met the Commandant of the National Guard, M. de Romainvilliers.

He was coming through hastily.

"M. le Ministre, I run to take your orders," said he.

"I am a minister no longer," replied Dumouriez.

"But there are gatherings in the faubourgs."

"Go for the royal orders."

"Time presses."

"Hasten, then! The King has just accepted my resignation."

M. de Romainvilliers sprang up the steps.

On the morning of the seventeenth, Dumouriez saw enter his house to him Messieurs Chambonnas and Lajard; both came on part of the King; Chambonnas to receive the portfolio of Foreign Affairs, and Lajard for that of War.

The King expected Dumouriez on the day ensuing (the eighteenth) to conclude with him his last labors of casting up accounts and settling the secret expenses.

On seeing him reappear at the chateau, it was believed he was returning to his post, and many flocked around him to congratulate him.

"Gentlemen," said Dumouriez, "take heed! I am not a man entering, but going out; I merely come to settle my accounts."

A space was quickly made around him.

At this moment, an usher announced the King was waiting for Monsieur Dumouriez in his apartments.

The King had recovered all his serenity.

Was it through strength of mind? Was it deceitful security?

Dumouriez finished his labors, and, having completed the work, rose.

"So you go to join Luckner's army?" said the King, leaning back in his arm-chair.

"Yes, sire; I with gladness leave this frightful city; I have only a single regret—that of leaving you in danger."

"Indeed, I know danger does menace me," returned the King, with apparent indifference.

"Sire," added Dumouriez, "you must comprehend that, now, I speak no longer to you through personal interest;

once out of the council, I am forever separated from you; it is, therefore, from fidelity, in the name of the purest attachment, for my love of my country, for your safety, for that of your crown, of the Queen, of your children; it is in the name of all dear and sacred to the heart of man that I supplicate your Majesty not to persist in putting his veto; this obstinacy will be good for nothing, and will ruin you, sire."

"Do not speak to me any more—my course is taken!" broke out the King, impatiently.

"Sire, sire! you told me the same thing here, in this very chamber, before the Queen, when you promised me you would ratify the decrees."

"I did wrong to have promised you, sir, and I repent it."

"Sire, I repeat to you—being the last time I will have the honor to see you, pray pardon my frankness; I am fifty-three years of age and have some experience—that you were not wrong at the time when you promised to confirm the decrees; it is to-day when you refuse to keep your promise. Your conscience is being abused, sire; you are being led into civil war; you are without strength, you will fall, and history, while pitying you, will reproach you for having caused the woes of France!"

"The woes of France!" echoed Louis Sixteenth; "do you assert, sir, that I will be reproached with them?"

"Yes, sire."

"Heaven is my witness that I only wish its happiness."

"I do not doubt it, sire; but you will have to render account to heaven of not only the purity, but still of the enlightened execution of your intentions. You believe you will save religion; you will destroy it; your shivered crown will roll in your blood, in the Queen's, in that of your children, perhaps, oh, my King!"

Dumouriez pressed his lips to the hand Louis held out to him.

The latter, then, with perfect serenity and with a majesty of which he might have been believed incapable, said:

"You are right, sir, I do expect

death, and I pardon my murderers for it in advance. You have well served me; I esteem you, and know you to be true in your sensibility. Farewell, sir!"

Rising quickly, the speaker retired into the recess of a window.

Dumouriez slowly picked up his papers to have time to compose his features, and give the King that of recalling him; then, with slow steps, he moved towards the door, ready to return at the first word spoken by Louis; but his first was at the same time the last.

"Farewell, sir, be happy!" said he.

After these words, there was no means of remaining an instant longer.

Dumouriez went out.

Royalty had broken with its last sustenance; the King had snatched away his mask.

He found himself with uncovered face before the people.

Let us see what the people were doing on their side.

———

CHAPTER XXI.

A CONCILIABLE AT CHARENTON.

A man had been riding about all day in the Faubourg Saint Antoine, who was dressed in a general's uniform, and mounted on a sturdy Flemish horse, giving shakes of the hand right and left, embracing the pretty girls, giving young fellows money for drinks.

This was one of the six heirs to M. de La Fayette, a commander of the National Guard; the chef-de-batallion Santerre.

Near him, as an aid-de-camp trots by his general, rode, on a vigorous horse, a man who might be recognized by his attire for a country patriot.

A scar had left its mark on his forehead, and—as much as his superior had frank smile and open face—he had gloomy eye and threatening countenance.

"Hold yourselves ready, my good friends! watch over the nation! traitors conspire against it; but we are for it," said Santerre.

"What must be done, Monsieur Santerre?" asked the people of the faubourg. "You know we are your men! Where are the traitors? Lead us to them."

"Wait! when the hour comes," responded Santerre.

"Is the moment coming?"

Santerre knew nothing at all; but, at hazard, answered:

"Yes, yes, take it easy; you will be informed."

The man who followed Santerre, bending over his horse's neck, spoke in the ear of certain men whose acquaintance he gained by certain signs, and whispered to them:

"The twentieth of June! The twentieth!"

These men went away, muttering this date; at every ten, twenty or thirty paces, a group would be formed around them, and the date would circulate.

What was going to be done on the twentieth of June?

No one knew anything yet; but they did know something was to be done on that day.

Among the number of such men as this date had been communicated, might be recognized several who were no strangers to the events we have already recorded.

Saint Huruge, whom we saw set out on the morning of the fifth of October from the garden of the Palais Royal, heading a first troop for Versailles; Saint Huruge, that husband deceived by his wife before 1789, clapped into the Bastile, delivered on July the fourteenth, and avenging on the nobility and royalty his conjugal misfortunes and illegal incarceration.

Verrieres—does not the reader know him already? he has twice appeared to us, that hunchback of the Apocalypse; once, in the wineshop at Sevres with Marat and the Duke d'Aiguillon, disguised as a woman; another time, on the Champ de Mars, an instant before the firing commenced.

Fournier the American, who shot at La Fayette through the spokes of a carriage wheel, but whose gun flashed in the pan; he pledged himself, this time, to strike higher at the ex-commander of the National Guard, and, to prevent his gun missing fire, to strike with a sword.

Monsieur de Beausire—who has not profited by the time during which we have left him in the shade to amend; who had retaken Olivia from the hands of dying Mirabeau, as the Chevalier des Grieux retook Manon Lescaut from the hands which, after having lifted her for an instant from the mire, had let her drop again into it.

Mouchy, a short misshapen man, limping, bandy-legged, ridiculously wrapped up in an enormous tricolored scarf which swathed half his body, a municipal officer, a judge — heaven knows what.

Gonchon — the Mirabeau of the people, whom Pitou thought still uglier than the Mirabeau of the nobility—who vanished with riots as, in a fairy or spectacular piece, the demon of whom the author has need, disappears to reappear hereafter, always more frightful, ardent and more envenomed.

Amongst all this congregation, assembled around the ruins of the Bastile, as on another Mount Aventine, there went and came a thin, pale young man with straight hair, eyes full of lightnings, solitary as the eagle which he was later to take as an emblem, knowing not a soul, and with whom none was acquainted.

This was Bonaparte, lieutenant of artillery, by chance on furlough at Paris; it will be recollected how, on the day when he had appeared at the Jacobin club-house, Cagliostro had made so strange a prediction to Gilbert upon him.

By whom was all this concourse swayed, affected and excited?

By a man with powerful chest, mane like a lion, roaring voice, whom Santerre had found when he went home in the room behind his shop, waiting for him.

It was Danton!

This is the hour when the terrible revolutionist—who was as yet merely known by the tumult he had occasioned in the pit of the Theatre Francais during the performance of Chenier's "Charles IX.," and by his fearful eloquence on the speaker's stand of the Cordelier Club—makes his real appearance on the political stage, over which he unfolds his giant arms.

From whence comes the might of this man, who was to be so fatal to royalty?

From the Queen herself!

The hateful Austrian had not been willing to let La Fayette have the mayorship of Paris; she had preferred to him Petion, her traveling companion from Varennes, who hardly having attained the post, set himself against the King by ordering the environs of the Tuileries to be watched.

Petion had two friends who were at his right and left hands when he took possession of the city hall: Manuel on his right hand, Danton on his left.

He had made the former proctor of the commonalty; Danton his deputy.

Vergniaud had said from the stand, pointing to the Tuileries:

"Dread and awe often in aforetimes came from this palace, in the name of despotism, let awe and dread now enter it, in the name of the law!"

Well, the time was come to translate by a material act the fine, fearful picture of the Girondist orator; dread was to hunted up in the Faubourg Saint Antoine, and urged, with her discordant shrieks and tossing arms, into the palace of Catherine de Medicis.

Who could better up summon her than that terrible revolutionary conjurer, Danton?

Danton was broad-shouldered, had powerful hands, and an athletic chest within which beat a sturdy heart, Danton was the gong of the revolution; the blow he received was instantly answered with a mighty vibration which was communicated to the mob, which it fired; Danton was linked on one side to the mob by Hebert; on the other, to the throne by the Duke d'Orleans; Danton, between the pieman at the street corner and the royal prince at the edge of the throne; Danton had before him an intermediary key each touch on which corresponded with a social fibre.

Throw your eyes on this scale; it comprises two octaves, and is in harmony with his powerful voice:

Hebert, Legendre, Gonchon, Rossignol, Momoro, Brune, Huguenin, Rotondo, Santerre, Fabre d'Eglantine, Camille Desmoulins, Dugazon, Lazouski, Sillery, Genlis, the Duke d'Orleans.

Remark that we do not carry it out here but to the visible limits; now, who will tell us to where rose and fell that power beyond the bounds of our eyesight?

It was this power that swayed the Faubourg Saint Antoine.

On the sixteenth, one of Danton's men, Lazouski the Pole, member of the council of the commonalty, set the ball in motion

He announced at the meeting that, on the twentieth of June, the two faubourgs of Saint Antoine and Saint Marceau would present petitions to the National Assembly and the King on the subject of the veto laid on the decree relating to the priesthood, and, at the same time, would plant on the grounds of the Feuillant Club a liberty-tree, to commemorate " the tennis court meeting " on the twentieth of June, 1789.

The council refused its authorization.

" They must be skipped over," whispered Danton in Lazouski's ear.

The latter repeated aloud:

" This refusal will be skipped over."

Therefore, this date of June the twentieth had a visible and an unseen signification.

One was the pretext: to present a petition to the King and rear a liberty-tree.

The other was the intention known to a few alone: to save France from La Fayette and the Feuillants, and warn the incorrigible monarch who clung to the former rule, that there are such political tempests that a ruler may be submerged in them with his throne, crown and family, as, in the abysses of the ocean, a vessel is engulfed masts, hulk and crew.

Danton, as we have before mentioned,

was waiting for Santerre in his house.

In the evening previous, he had had him informed, through Legendre, that there was going to be next day the commencement of an uprising in the Faubourg Saint Antoine.

Then, in the morning, Billot had come to the patriot brewer, had given the sign of recognition, and had announced that, all day, the committee attached to him to his person.

This was how Billot, while having the semblance of being Santerre's aid de-camp, knew more than the brewer himself.

Danton came to make with Santerre an appointment for the morrow's night in a little house at Charenton, situated on the right bank of the Marne, at the end of the bridge.

There should be found all such men with strange, unknown existences as are ever to be found directing the current of insurrections.

Every man was punctual at the meeting-place.

The passions of all these men were diverse.

It would be a gloomy history to pen.

Some acted through love of freedom; many, like Billot, for vengeance of insults and injuries; a greater number still from hatred, wretchedness, or evil instincts.

On the first floor was a close-shut chamber wherein none but the leaders had right of entrance; they came out from it with clear, precise, well-formed instructions; one would have fancied it a tabernacle where some god wrote out his decrees.

A very large map of Paris was spread out on the table.

Danton's finger traced out on it the springs, feeders, courses, and points of meeting of those brooks, rivers, floods of men which were presently to overflow Paris.

The open space of the Bastile, to be reached by the streets of the Faubourg Saint Antoine, by those of the quartier of the Arsenal, by the Faubourg Saint Marceau, was denoted as rallying-spot; the National Assembly as blind; the Tuileries as the design.

The boulevard was the broad. safe

road along which was to stream all that roaring sea.

After posts had been assigned to each, and each having sworn to be there, they broke up for the night.

The general cry was:

"Let's finish with the chateau!"

In what manner did they speak of finishing?

That remains under clouds.

During the whole day of the nineteenth, groups were stationed on the square by the Bastile, in the neighborhood of the Arsenal, in the Faubourg St. Antoine.

Suddenly, in the midst of this latter crowd, appeared a bold, fear-inspiring amazon, attired in red, with a belt in which were stuck pistols, and, by her side, that blade which was, through eighteen other wounds, to go piercing to find the heart of Suleau.

This was Theroigne de Mericourt, the beauty of Liege.

We have seen her on the Versailles Road on the fifth of October.

What has she been doing since?

Liege had revolted; Theroigne tried to go help her native-place, she had been arrested on the road by the agents of Leopold, and kept eighteen months in Austrian durance.

Did she flee?

Was she released?

Did she file her bars through, or corrupt the jailor?

All this is as beclouded as the opening of her life was mysterious, or as the end of her life was terrible.

However it was, she had returned.

Behold her!

From a courtisan in opulence, she had become the people's prostitute; the nobility had given her that gold with which she had bought the fine tempered blades and damascened pistols with which she struck down her enemies.

Therefore the people recognizing her hailed her with loud outcry.

How seasonably came the beautiful Theroigne, arrayed in red as she was, for the morrow's bloody work!

On the same evening, the Queen saw her gallop along the turf by the Feuillant club-house; she was riding from the square of the Bastile to the Champs Elysees, from the popular gathering to the patriotic banquet.

From the attics of the Tuileries, where the Queen had gone upon the shouts she had heard, she descried spread tables, wine was passed around, patriotic songs rang forth, and, at every toast to the Assembly, the Girondists or to liberty, the feasters shook their fists at the Tuileries.

Dugazon the actor sang verses against the royal couple and, at the chateau, the latter could hear the applause following each chorus.

Who were these revellers?

Federalists from Marseilles, led by Barbaroux: they had just arrived at dark.

On June the eighteenth, the tenth of August made its entry into Paris!

CHAPTER XXII.

JUNE THE TWENTIETH.

DAY dawns early in the month of June.

At five o'clock, the sections were gathered.

This time riot was regulated, it had assumed the aspect of an invasion.

The mob knew its leaders, yielded to discipline; each had his place marked out, his rank, his flag to follow.

Santerre was on horseback, with his staff of men of the faubourg.

Billot had not quitted him; it seemed as though he was charged by some occult power to watch over him.

The assembled multitude was divided into three bodies:

Santerre commanded the first:

Saint Huruge, the second; Theroigne de Mericourt, the third.

At about eleven o'clock in the morning, upon an order brought by an unknown man, the immense mass started on the march.

On its departure from the Bastile, it was composed of men in the neighborhood of twenty thousand.

This troop presented a wild, strange, terrifying aspect!

The battalion headed by Santerre

was the most regular; there were quite a quantity of uniforms in it, and, as to weapons, a good number of guns and bayonets.

But the two others were the army of the people; clothed in rags, haggard, thinned; four years of want and dearness of bread, and, out of those four twelvemonths, three of revolutions!

That was the gulf from which was vomited this band.

Therefore, no uniforms or guns were to be expected here; tattered vests, torn frocks, quaint weapons snatched up in an angry moment; pikes, spits, rusty spears, hiltless swords, knives tied to the end of long poles, carpenters' adzes and axes, masons' hammers, shoemakers' knives.

Then, for standards, they had a gallows, with a puppet dangling at a rope's end, representing the Queen; a bull's head with some obscene device; a calf's heart stuck on the point of a spit with these words: "Heart of an aristocrat!"

Next were flags with such legends as:

"Confirm it or death!"

"Recal the patriot ministers!"

"Tremble, tyrant, thy hour has come!"

The throng split on the corner of the Rue Saint Antoine.

Santerre and his National Guard had followed the boulevard.

Saint Huruge, on a perfectly equipped horse which had been put into his hands by an unknown groom, and Theroigne de Mericourt, reclining on a cannon drawn by bare-armed men, kept on by the Rue Saint Antoine.

They were, by the Place Vendome, to come together at the Feuillant club-house.

During three hours, the army marched past, drawing in its march the population of the districts it traversed.

It was like those torrents which increase as they rush foaming along.

At each crossroad it was swollen; at every street corner it was fed.

The mass of this concourse was silent; however, at intervals, in an unexpected manner, it would break out from its stillness and send up deafening clamor, or there would be sung the famous *Ca ira* of 1790, which, in its modification by degrees, had become, from a song of encouragement, an outburst of menace; finally, they would make the street ring with shouts of:

"The nation forever! Long live the sans-culottes! Down with Monsieur and Madame Veto!"

Long, long before one could catch sight of the foremost of the column, was to be heard the tramp of the multitude, as one may hear the surging beat of the rising tide; next, from moment to moment would resound the thunder of songs, shouts, cheers, as the tempest comes roaring through the air.

On the arrival at the Place Vendome, Santerre's body, which carried the poplar tree to be reared on the green of the Feuillant club-house, found a post of the National Guard barring up the way; nothing would have been easier to that mass than to crush the force at this post in its thousand coils; but no, the people had promised themselves a holiday, and wanted to laugh, be amused and scare "Monsieur and Madame Veto;" they did not care about killing.

The bearers of the pole thereupon gave over the plan of raising it on the fore-arranged spot, and went to plant it in the Courtyard of the Capuchins near by.

The Assembly had been hearing this tumult for close upon an hour, when commissioners from the assemblage came to claim of it, for those they represented, the favor of marching in procession before it.

Vergniaud supported the resolution for the people to be admitted; but, at the same time, he proposed to send sixty deputies to protect the chateau.

The Girondists, also, were bent on frightening the King and the Queen, but they did not wish any harm to be done them.

A Feuillant, arguing against Vergniaud's resolution, said that this precaution would be insulting to the people of Paris.

Did he have the hope of a crime beneath this apparent confidence?

The admission was granted.

The people of the faubourgs might defile in arms through the hall.

Almost immediately the doors were opened and gave passage to the thirty thousand petitioners. The marching past began at noon and was not over until three o'clock.

The mob had obtained the first part of what it wanted ; it had paraded before the assembly, which had read its petition ; there still remained the project of going to ask the King for his confirmation.

As the Assembly had received the deputation, why should not the King receive it ?

The King was not, assuredly, a greater lord than the president of the Assembly, forasmuch as when the King came to see the president, he had only an armchair like his own, and even then it was on his left hand !

The King sent back word that he would receive the petition presented by twenty persons.

The people had never believed they might enter the Tuileries ; they calculated that, while their deputies went in they would march past the windows.

All their flags with threatening mottoes, all their gloomy standards, they would display to the King and the Queen through the windows.

All the doors and gates opening on the chateau were closed ; there was, either in the courtyard or the garden of the Tuileries, three regular regiments, two squadrons of gendarmerie, several battalions of the National Guard, and four pieces of artillery.

The royal family, seeing, through the windows, this apparent protection, showed themselves tolerably at ease.

Meanwhile the throng, without any evil intention however, demanded that, the grating should be opened which allowed admittance to the grounds of the Feuillants.

The officers guarding it refused to open it without a royal order.

Thereupon, three city officers requested leave to pass and go and get this order.

They were permitted to do so.

Montjoye, the author of the " Story of Marie Antoinette," has preserved their names.

They were Boucher Rene, Boucher Saint Sauveur and Mouchet, the little judge of the Marais, the contorted, crippled, misshapen dwarf in the immense tricolored scarf.

They were admitted into the chateau and conducted to the royal presence.

Mouchet was the spokesman.

" Sire," began he, " a procession marches lawfully under the ægis of the law, there should be no uneasiness ; peaceable citizens have united to carry a petition to the National Assembly, and to celebrate by a civic banquet the occasion of the oath sworn to at the Tennis-court, in 1789. These citizens request passage to the green of the Feuillants, of which not only are the gates closed, but there is, besides, an unlimbered gun forbidding access. We come to ask of you, sire, that the grating should be unfastened, and free admittance given to all."

" Sir," rejoined the King, " I see, by your scarf, that you are a municipal officer ; your duty, therefore, is to execute the law. If you deem it necessary to the clearing of the Assembly, have the gate opened of the grounds of the Feuillants ; let the citizens defile over that place and leave by the stable-yard gates. To that effect arrange with commanding general of the guard, and above all have it done so that the public peace may not be disturbed."

The three deputies bowed and went out, accompanied by an officer charged to prove that the order to open the gate had come from the royal mouth.

The grating was opened.

This done, everybody wanted to enter.

There was suffocation from the crushing ; everybody knows what is a close-packed crowd.

The grating gave way like a net-work of reeds.

The crowd took breath and joyfully spread over the garden.

The proper persons had neglected to open the stableyard gates.

Finding this exit barred, the throng streamed past the National Guard lined like a hedge against the front of the chateau.

Then the people poured out by the gate and, as they were desirous of going home to the faubourg, they wanted to enter by the wickets of the Carrousel.

These were locked and guarded.

But the squeezed, bruised, packed mob began to get irritated.

Before their growls, the wickets were opened, and the whole gathering spread over the immense space.

There, it was recalled that the principal affair of the day was the petition to the King to have his veto removed.

The result was that, instead of continuing their road, the concourse waited in the Carrousel.

An hour was thus spent, and they waxed impatient.

They might just as well have gone on their way, but that was not the idea of their leaders.

There were men who went about from group to group, saying :

" Stay, are you not going to stay ? The King will have to give his confirmation ; do not let us enter our houses but with royal sanction, or then we will have to go to work all over again."

Their hearers were of the opinion that these men were perfectly in the right ; but, at the same time, they reflected that this sanction so much talked about was keeping them waiting.

" We are hungry !" was the general cry.

The high price of bread had ceased ; but there was no work, no money ; and, however cheap bread may be, one cannot get it for nothing.

All these people had arisen at five o'clock in the morning, had left their beds, on which many had lain fasting the night before, they all, workmen with their wives, mothers with their children, had started on the way with the vague hope that the King would ratify the decree, and things would then go on well.

The King did not appear the least in the world disposed to sanction the decree.

It was hot weather, and this caused thirst.

Hunger, thirst and heat make dogs mad.

This poor congregation waited, and took patience.

In the meanwhile, they began pounding and shaking the gratings of the chateau.

A municipal appeared in the courtyard of the Tuileries, and commenced to speechify the multitude.

" Citizens," he said, " this is the royal abode, and to enter it armed would be violating it. The King is quite willing to receive your petition, but only when presented by twenty deputies."

So, the deputies—whom the multitude had been an hour waiting for, in the belief that they were in the royal presence—had not been introduced !

All of a sudden, loud cheers arose from the direction of the quais.

It was Santerre and Saint Huruge on their horses ; and Theroigne on her cannon.

" Well what are you doing before this gate ? why don't you go in !" shouted Saint Huruge.

" Indeed, why don't we go in ?" repeated the people.

" But you see well enough that the gate is fastened," objected many voices.

Theroigne leaped down from the gun.

" It's loaded," said she ; " let us blow the gate open with its ball."

The cannon was rolled up against the bars.

" Wait, wait !" cried two city officers; " no violence ; it shall be opened to you."

In fact, they bore their weight on the drawbolt of the gate ; it turned, and the gate flew open.

Everybody rushed through.

Would the reader like to know what a mob is—what a terrible torrent it is ?

The mass poured in ; the cannon, rolled on among its foremost waves, crossed with it the courtyard, mounted with it the steps, and, with it, presently was on the top of the staircase !

On the landing-place were municipal officers in their scarfs.

" What are you going to do with a gun ?" they asked. " A piece of cannon in the royal apartments ! do you fancy to obtain anything by such an act of violence ?"

"True," answered the men, quite in bewilderment themselves that their piece of artillery should have come there.

They turned the gun round and tried to wheel it downstairs.

The axle-tree got jammed in a door-way, and thus the brazen muzzle gaped on the multitude.

"Ho, ho! they had artillery in the royal apartments!" shouted those coming up, who, unaware of how the gun came to be there in that position and not recognizing it to be Theroigne' gun, fancied it to have been already there and turned on them.

During this time, on an order from Mouchet, a couple of men with axes chopped, cut, hewed away the jamb of the door-frame, and disengaged the piece, which was lowered down into the vestibule.

This operation, whose design was merely to remove the gun, led to the belief that doors were being beaten in with axes.

Two hundred gentlemen, or nearly as many, had ran to the chateau, not in the hope of defending it, but they believed the King's life to be in jeopardy, and came to die with him.

There was the old Marshal de Mouchy; M. d'Hervilly, commander of the disbanded constitutional guard; Acloque, commander of the battalion of the National Guard from the Faubourg St. Marceau; three grenadiers of the battalion from the Faubourg Saint Martin, who had alone remained at their posts, Messieurs Lecrosnier, Bridaud and Gosse; a man dressed in black, who already had once before hastened to offer his breast to the assassin's bullet, whose advice was constantly rejected, yet who, in this hour of danger which he had endeavored to conjure away, came, as a last bulwark, to put himself between this peril and the King.

This was Gilbert.

The royal couple, very much agitated by the fearful turbulence of the multitude, were gradually growing accustomed to the noise.

It was half past three in the afternoon; they hoped that the day would end as it had dawned.

The royal family were united in the King's chambers.

All at once, the splintering of wood under the axes came to this room, overcoming the gusts of clamor which seemed the distant warning of the tempest.

At this moment, a man rushed into the royal sleeping-chamber, crying:

"Sire, do not quit me; I answer for everything!"

CHAPTER XXIII.

IN WHICH THE KING SEES THAT THERE ARE CERTAIN TIMES WHEN A RED CAP MAY BE WORN ALTHOUGH ONE IS NOT A JACOBIN.

This man was Doctor Gilbert.

Our readers see him at spaces almost periodical, and in all the peripetia of the grand drama unrolled before them.

"Ah, doctor, is it you? What is going on?" exclaimed the Queen and the King together.

"Sire," answered the doctor, "the chateau is full of people, and the noise you hear is made by the people asking to see you."

"Oh, do not let us leave you, sire!" cried the Queen and Madame Elizabeth at once.

"Will the King," said Gilbert, "kindly give me for an hour the power which a captain of a ship has over his vessel in a storm?"

"I give you it," replied the King.

At this instant, Acloque, the commander of the National Guard, appeared at the door, pale, but determined to defend the King to the last gasp.

"Sir, here is his Majesty," cried Gilbert; "he is ready to follow you; take charge of him."

Then, to the King, he added:

"Go, sire, go!"

"But I want to follow my husband!" cried the Queen.

"And I, my brother!" cried Madame Elizabeth.

"Follow your brother, madame," said Gilbert to Madame Elizabeth; "but, you, madame, remain!" subjoined he, addressing the Queen.

"Sir !" said Marie Antoinette.

"Sire, sire !" cried Gilbert, "in heaven's name, entreat the Queen to rely upon me, or I can answer for nothing."

"Madame," said the King, "hearken to Monsieur Gilbert's counsels, and, if needs must, obey his orders."

Then, to Gilbert, he went on :

"Sir, do you answer for the Queen and the Dauphin ?"

"Sire, I will save them, or die with them ! that is all a pilot can say during the tempest."

The Queen would have made a further effort, but Gilbert held out his arms to bar her path.

"Madame," said he, "you, not your husband, run the true danger. Wrongly or rightfully, it is you whom they accuse of the King's resistance ; your presence will therefore expose him without defending him. Perform the office of a lightning-rod ; turn aside the bolt, if you can !"

"Then, sir, let the stroke fall upon me alone, and spare my children !"

"I have answered to the King for you and them, madame. Follow me !"

Turning to the Princess de Lamballe (who had arrived from a month before from England, and from Vernon by three days), and the other royal waiting-women, Gilbert concluded :

"Follow us !"

These other ladies were the Princess de Tarente and de la Tremouille, Mesdames de Tourzel, de Mackau and de la Roche-aymon.

Gilbert knew the interior of the chateau.

What he sought for was a capacious hall where everybody might see and hear ; this was the first rampart to cross ; he would put the royal lady, her children and the other ladies behind this rampart, and himself before it.

He thought of the council chamber. Fortunately, it was still free.

He pushed the Queen, her children, with the Princess de Lamballe, into the recess of a window. Minutes were so precious that they had no time to speak : already there was a hammering on the doors.

He drew up the heavy council table before the window ; this was the breast work.

Madame Royale stood on the table, beside her seated brother.

The Queen was behind them : innocence defending unpopularity.

Marie Antoinette wished on the contrary, to put herself before her children.

"All is well this way," cried Gilbert in the tone of a general commanding a decisive evolution ; "do not stir !"

As there was a frightful din at the door, and as he could tell there was a great admixture of females in the bellowing sea, he said, as he shot back the bolts :

"Enter, citizenesses ; the Queen and her children await you !"

The door being open, the stream forced through as by the gap of a burst dam.

"Where is the Austrian ? Where's Madame Veto ?" roared five hundred voices.

This was the critical period.

Gilbert well understood that at this momentous juncture, all power leaves man's hand and passes into that of heaven.

"Be calm, madame !" said he to the Queen ; "I have no need to advise gentleness to you."

One woman preceded the rest, with dishevelled hair, brandishing a sword, highly colored with rage, perhaps by the fever of hunger.

"Where is the Austrian ?" she screamed. "She shall die by my hand only !"

Gilbert took her by the arm and, leading her to the Queen, said :

"This is she ?"

"Have I ever done you any personal wrong, my child ?" inquired the Queen in her sweetest voice.

"None, madame," replied the girl of the faubourg, quite astonished by Marie Antoinette's being both gentle and majestic.

"Well, then, why would you kill me ?"

"I was told it was you who ruined the nation," faltered the girl, lowering to the floor her sword point.

"You have been deceived. I married the King of France; I am the mother of the Dauphin, this boy you see here. I am a Frenchwoman, and will never again see my country; I may be happy or unhappy in France alone. Alas! I was happy when you loved me!"

The speaker sighed.

The girl dropped her sword, and began weeping.

"Ah, madame," sobbed she, "I did not know you; forgive me—I see you are good!"

"Continue thus, madame!" whispered Gilbert, "and not only you will be saved, but, moreover, all these people will be in a quarter of an hour at your feet."

Thereupon entrusting the Queen to two or three National Guardsmen who had run up, and to Lajard, the Minister of War, who had entered with the crowd, he hastened to the King.

The latter had undergone a very similar scene.

Louis Sixteenth had hurried to the place of the uproar; as he entered the saloon of Œil-de-bœuf, the panels of the door fell through in splinters, and points of bayonets and lance-heads, with the edges of axes, came through the openings.

"Open, open!" ordered Louis.

"Citizens," said in a loud voice Monsieur d'Hervilly; "it is useless to break in the door; his Majesty is quite willing for it to be opened."

At the same time, he pulled back the bolts and turned the key; the half shattered door creaked on its hinges.

Acloque and the Duke de Mouchy had just time to push the King into the embrasure of a casement, while several grenadiers who were at hand hastened to upset and overturn seats and benches before him.

On seeing the throng surge into the hall with shouts, imprecations, hoots and yells, the King could not help crying:

"To me, gentlemen!"

Four grenadiers instantly whipped out their sabres, and took stations beside him.

"Sheathe your blades, gentlemen," said the King; "stay beside me, that is all I ask."

Indeed, very little more, and it would have been too late.

The flash from a sword blade would have seemed a provocation.

A man in tatters, with naked arms, foam on his lips, stepped up to the King.

"So this is you, Veto?" said he, trying to stab him with a knife blade which was bound to the end of a stick.

One of the grenadiers—who, notwithstanding the royal order, had not yet returned his weapon to his scabbard—pushed away the rude spear with his sword.

But then, the King himself, fully returned to himself, pushed away the grenadier with his hand, saying:

"Allow me, sir! what have I to fear amongst my people?"

Taking a forward step, Louis the Sixteenth—with a majesty of which he might have been believed incapable, and a courage which had appeared till then foreign to him—presented his breast to the various weapons directed on him from all sides.

"Silence! I wish to speak!" said a stentorian voice amid the uproar.

Cannon might have vainly attempted to make itself heard amid the clamor and vociferations and still, at this voice, all the tumult was hushed.

It was the voice of Legendre the butcher.

He came forward so close as almost to touch the King.

There was a circle formed around them.

At this moment, a man appeared on the extreme round of this circle and, behind Danton's terrible "double-ganger," the King observed Doctor Gilbert's pale but serene countenance.

A questioning look asked him:

"What have you done with the Queen, sir."

A smile from the doctor answered:

"She is in safety, sire."

The King thanked Gilbert with a sign.

"Monsieur!" began Legendre to the King.

Upon this word, "monsieur!" which seemed to indicate something unexpected, the person addressed turned as if a serpent had stung him.

"Yes, monsieur—Monsieur Veto, I am speaking to you," proceeded Legendre. "Hear us, then, for you are made to listen to us. You are a perfidious fellow; you have always tricked us, and you're still at your games—but beware! the measure is overflowing, and the people are tired of being your plaything and your victim."

"Well, I listen to you," said Louis XVI.

"I'm glad to hear it! Don't you know what we have come to do here? We are after the confirmation of the decrees and the recall of the ministers. Here's our petition."

Legendre, producing from his pocket a paper which he unfolded, read the same threatening petition which had been already read aloud before the Assembly.

The royal auditor listened to it, his eyes riveted on the reader; when it was finished, without the faintest emotion, apparent at least, he said:

"I shall do, sir, what the laws and the Constitution order me to do."

"Oh, yes!" broke in a voice, "the Constitution is your big war-charger! the Constitution of '91, which allows you to block up the whole machine, to bind France to the stake, there to wait till the Austrians come up to cut her throat!"

The King turned towards this new voice, for he felt that from thither was coming a most furious attack.

Gilbert also gave a start, and laid his hand on the shoulder of the speaker.

"I have seen you before, my friend," observed the King. "Who are you?"

He regarded him with much more curiosity than fear, albeit this man's visage wore a mould of great resolution.

"Yes, you have seen me before. You have seen me three times; once, on the sixteenth of July, on the Return from Versailles; again, at Varennes; the other time, here. Sire, remember my name; I have one of evil augury: I am named *Billot* (the block)!"

At this moment, shouts arose afresh; a man with a pike thrust at the King.

But Billot caught hold of the lance, tore it from the would-be murderer's hand, and, snapping it across his knee, said:

"No assassination! There is but one steel which has the right of touching this man—that of the law! They say there was a King of England whose head was struck off by the sentence of the people whom he had betrayed—you, Louis, ought to know his name. Do not forget him!"

"Billot!" muttered Gilbert.

"This man shall be tried as a traitor, and shall be condemned!" said Billot, shaking his head.

"Aye, traitor! traitor!" cried a hundred voices.

Gilbert threw himself between the King and the people.

"Fear nothing, sire," said he; "try, by some material demonstration, to give satisfaction to these furious men."

The King took Gilbert's hand and laid it on his heart.

"You see I fear nothing, sir," said he; "I have received the sacrament this morning; let whatever they like be done with me. As for the material sign under which you desire me to harbor myself, there—are you satisfied?"

So saying, the speaker, taking a red cap from a sans-culotte, put it upon his own head.

Instantly, the multitude burst out into cheers.

"Long live the King! the nation forever!" cried every voice.

A man pushed through the crowd and approached the King; he held a bottle in his hand.

"If you love the people as you say, fat Veto, prove it by tossing this off to the health of the people!"

He held out the bottle.

"Don't drink, sire!" cautioned a voice; "the wine may be poisoned."

"Drink, sire; I answer for everything," said Gilbert.

The King took the bottle.

"To the health of the people!" said he.

He drank.

Renewed shouts of "Long live the King!" resounded.

"Sire," said Gilbert, "you have nothing more to fear ; allow me to return to the Queen."

"Go," said Louis Sixteenth, pressing his hand.

At the moment when Gilbert went out, Isnard and Vergniaud came in.

They had quitted the Assembly and came of themselves to make for the King a rampart of their popularity and, at need, of their bodies.

"The King?" asked they.

Gilbert waved them to him, and the two deputies hastened towards him.

To reach the Queen, Gilbert had to cross several rooms, and among others, go through the royal bedchamber.

The people had penetrated everywhere.

"Fat Veto has a better bed than ours!" said men, sitting down on the royal couch.

All this, however, was not a whit disquieting ; the first moment of turbulence was past.

Gilbert went back to the Queen more tranquilly.

On entering the hall where he had left her, he flung a hasty glance towards her and breathed again.

She was still in the same place ; the little Dauphin, like his father, wore a red cap.

There was in the adjoining room a great confusion which attracted Gilbert's eyes to the door.

This sound was made by the approach of Santerre.

The colossus entered the hall.

"Oh ! this is where the Austrian is, is it ?" said he.

Giblert walked straight to him, cutting the hall diagonally.

"M. Santerre," said he.

Santerre turned.

"Why, it's Doctor Gilbert !" exclaimed he delighted.

"Who has not forgotten," said the physician, "that you are one of those who opened the gates of the Bastile to him. Let me present you to the Queen, Monsieur Santerre."

"To the Queen? present me to her ?" growled the brewer.

"Yes. Do you refuse?"

"No, I do not," said Santerre ; "I was going to do so alone, but, since you are here——"

"I know Monsieur Santerre," broke in the Queen ; "I know how, during the famine, he alone nourished half the Faubourg Saint Antoine."

Santerre stopped, astonished ; then, his look falling a little troubled on the Dauphin, down whose cheeks ran sweat in large drops, he said to the people standing round :

"Here, take off this cap from the boy ; you're roasting him, can't you see ?"

The royal mother thanked him with a look.

"You have very awkward friends, madame," whispered the Fleming, bending over to her and leaning on the table ; "I know who would have served you better !"

An hour after this, the whole concourse had left the palace, and the King, accompanied by his sister, entered the hall where the Queen and their children were waiting for him.

Marie Antoinette ran to him and knelt at his feet ; his two children grasped his hands ; they embraced him as if they were rescued from a shipwreck.

It was only then that Louis perceived that he still had the red cap on his head.

"Ah, I had forgotten !" exclaimed he.

Snatching it off, he flung it far from him in disgust.

A young officer of artillery, hardly in his twenty-second year, had witnessed the whole scene, leaning against a tree by the water's edge ; he had seen through the windows all the dangers the King had incurred, all the humiliations he had received ; but, at the incident of the red cap, he had not been able to restrain himself longer.

"Oh !" muttered he, "if I only had twelve hundred men and two pieces of artillery, I would soon rid this poor sovereign of all this rascally crew !"

But—inasmuch as he had no twelve hundred men and no pieces of cannon, and as he could no longer support the view of the distasteful spectacle—he retired.

This young officer was Napoleon Bonaparte.

CHAPTER XXIV.

REACTION.

THE evacuation of the Tuileries had been as sad and as speechless as the taking possession of it had been stormy and noisy.

The crowd said, astonished itself at the scanty result of the day's work :

" We have obtained nothing ; we will have to go back again."

It was, truth to say, too much for a threat, too little for an attempt.

Those who had looked ahead of what was to transpire had judged Louis the Sixteenth from his past reputation; they called to mind Varennes, how he had taken to flight under a footman's livery, and they said :

" At the first sound Louis hears, he will hide himself under some table, in side-board or closet, behind some curtain ; a sword thrust may be given him as if by mere random blow, and one will be acquitted by saying like Hamlet, on believing he slew the tyrant of Denmark ' A rat !' "

Things had turned out quite otherwise ; never had the King been so self-possessed ; let us rather say, never had he been so great.

The insult had been immense ; but it had not risen to the level of his resignation.

His timid firmness—if one may thus speak—had had need of being goaded and, in the inciting, had taken the rigidness of steel ; lifted by the extreme circumstances amongst which he had found himself for five hours, he had seen without turning pale, axes gleam over his head, lances, swords and bayonets drawn back before his confronting breast; no general had ever run in ten battles —however deadly they may have been —a danger like to that which he had braved in that slow review of riot !

The Theroignes, Saint Huruges, Lazourkis, Fourniers, Verrieres, all those familiars of assassination, had set out with the very positive intention of killing him, and this unexpected majesty which was revealed in the height of the tempest had made the dagger drop from their hands.

Louis Sixteenth had just had his passion ; the royal Ecce Homo had had the red cap set upon his brows ; among the insults and outrages, Louis had never ceased saying :

" I am your sovereign !"

This is what had occurred.

The revolutionary idea had believed, on forcing in the doors of the Tuileries, to merely find the lifeless, palsy-shaking shadow of royalty, and, to its high astonishment, it had encountered erect and full of vitality, the faith of the Middle Ages !

For an instant two principles were to have been seen face to face—one in its decline, its setting ; the other in its rise, the eastern sky ; something terrific as though there was to be seen in the heavens one sun rising ere the other king of day had set !

There was, however, as much of splendor and of dazzlement in one as in the other, as much faith in the requirement of the people as in the refusal of royalty.

The royalists were overjoyed ; taking all in all, the victory had fallen to them.

Bidden so rudely to obey the Assembly, the King—in lieu of confirming one of the two decrees, as he had been ready to do—knowing that he ran no more risk from rejecting both than in rejecting one, had laid his veto on both.

Royalty, in that fatal day of June the twentieth, had been bent so low, that it seemed to have touched the bottom of the abyss and could do nothing else than mount.

In fact, things seemed taking this turn.

On the twenty-first, the Assembly declared that any gathering of armed citizens should never more be admitted in their presence.

This was disavowing—more than that, it was condemning the evening's proceedings.

On the evening of the twentieth, Petion had arrived at the Tuileries as all was over.

" Sire," he said to the King, " I have only just learnt the situation of your Majesty."

" That's surprising," answered the King. " Nevertheless it has long endured."

On the ensuing day, the Constitutionalists, royalists, and the Feuillants asked of the Assembly the proclamation of martial law.

It will be remembered what the former proclamation of this law had brought on, at the Champ de Mars, on the foregoing seventeenth of July.

Petion hastened to the Assembly.

This request was based upon new gatherings which, they said, existed.

Petion affirmed that these new assemblages had never existed; he answered for the peace of Paris.

The proclamation of martial law was rejected.

On going out from the session at about eight o'clock of the evening, Petion went to the Tuileries to reassure the King on the state of his capital.

He was accompanied by Sergent; Sergent, the etcher, and brother-in-law of Marceau, was member of the city council and one of the administrators of police.

Two or three other members of the municipality were joined with them.

While crossing the court of the Carroussel, they were insulted by the Chevaliers of Saint Louis, the Constitutional Guards and the National Guards.

Petion was personally assaulted.

Sergent, notwithstanding the scarf he wore, was struck on the breast and in the face, even knocked down by a blow of the fist.

Hardly was he introduced, than Petion comprehended that it was a contest he had come to enter upon.

Marie Antoinette darted on him one of those looks which only the eyes of Maria Theresa could flash out besides; two beams of hate and scorn, a double stream of terrible lightning.

The King knew already what had happened at the Assembly.

" Well, sir," said he to Petion, "do you pretend that quiet is restored in the capitol ?"

" Yes, sire," responded Petion, " the people have made their representations to you ; and they are tranquil and satisfied."

" Confess, sir," resumed the King, entering into the struggle, " confess that yesterday's deeds were a great scandal, and that the municipality did neither what it could nor what it should have done."

" Sire," returned Petion, "the public officers have performed their duty ;— public opinion is the judge."

" Say the entire nation."

" The city does not fear the judgment of the nation."

" And at present, in what state is Paris ?"

" Calm, sire."

" That is not true !"

" Sire—"

" Be silent, sir."

" The magistrate of the people cannot be silent, sire, when he does his duty and speaks the truth."

" Very well. You may retire."

Petion bowed and withdrew.

The King had been so violent and his features had displayed an expression of such deep anger, that the Queen— the excited woman, the ardent amazon —was frightened.

" Do you not think his Majesty has been too hasty ?" she asked Rœderer when Petion had disappeared ; " do you not fear that this hastiness will injure him with regard to the Parisians ?"

" Madame," Rœderer made answer, " no one will think it astonishing that a sovereign should impose silence on one of his subjects who showed want of respect for him."

On the following day, the King wrote to the Assembly to complain of the profanation of the chateau, of royalty and the King.

Then he issued a proclamation to the people.

It appears there were two classes of the people ; that which had made the twentieth of June, and that to which the King made his appeal.

On the twenty-fourth, their Majesties

reviewed the National Guard, and were hailed with enthusiasm.

On the same day, the directory of Paris suspended the mayor.

Whence came such audacity?

Three days afterwards, light was shed on the event.

La Fayette, starting from his camp with a single officer, arrived at Paris on the twenty-seventh, dismounting at the residence of his friend, M. de la Rochefaucald.

During the night, the intelligence was communicated to the Constitutionalists, Feuillants and royalists, and preparations were made "to pack" the galleries for the next day.

The general presented himself at the Assembly.

Three rounds of applause hailed him; but each died away under the murmur of the Girondists.

It was plain the session was to be an eventful one.

General La Fayette was one of the most undeniably brave men that ever existed; but fearlessness is not boldness; it is even very unseldom for a really brave man to be at the same time audacious.

La Fayette felt the danger that he ran; alone against all, he came to stake the remnant of his popularity; if he lost it, he would be ruined with it; if he won, he might save the King.

This was so much the handsomer proceeding on his part, from his knowing the royal repugnance for him, and the Queen's hatred.

"I would rather perish through Petion than be saved by La Fayette!"

Perchance he only came to fulfil some lieutenant's bravado, to answer some defiance.

A fortnight previously, he had written to both the King and the Assembly; to the former to encourage him in his resistance; to the latter, to threaten it if it continued to assail.

"He was very insolent in the midst of his army; we shall see if he speaks in the same style, alone amongst us," said a voice.

This speech had been transported to La Fayette in his camp at Maubeuge.

These words may have been the true cause of his trip to Paris.

He ascended the speaker's stand amid the plaudits of some, but also amongst the hoots and threats of others.

"Gentlemen," said he, "I have been reproached for having written my letter of the sixteenth instant from the midst of my camp. It was my duty to protest against this insinuation of fearfulness, to leave that honorable rampart which the affection of my troops formed around me, and present myself alone before you. A more powerful motive still called me. The violent acts of the twentieth instant have excited the indignation of every good citizen, and especially of all in the army; officers, non-commissioned officers and privates form but one; I have received from all bodies addresses full of devotion to the Constitution, and hatred to factions; I have stopped such manifestations; I have taken upon myself the singly expressing of the sentiments of everybody; it is as a citizen I speak to you. It is time to guarantee the Constitution, to ensure the liberty of the National Assembly, and that of the King, as well as his dignity. I entreat the Assembly to order that the excesses of the twentieth June shall be proceeded against as crimes of high treason; to take efficacious measures to make respected all constitutional authorities, and particularly yours and the King's, and to give the army the assurance that the Constitution will receive no hurt from the interior, while brave Frenchmen are so prodigal of their blood in the defense of the frontier."

Guadet had slowly risen proportionably to his calculation of how near La Fayette approached to the conclusion of his speech; amid the applause that greeted it, the bitter orator of the Girondists stretched out his hand in token of his asking permission to reply.

When the Gironde wished to shoot the arrow of irony, it was to Guadet that it handed the bow, and Guadet had but to take at random an arrow from his quiver.

Barely had the sound of the last plaudit been extinguished, than his vibrating voice succeeded it.

"At the moment when I saw Monsieur La Fayette," he began, "a very consoling idea came to my mind. I said to myself, 'We have no longer foreign foes—the Austrians are vanquished—behold Monsieur La Fayette who comes to announce to us the tidings of his victory, and their destruction !' My illusion did not endure long ; our enemies are still the same ; our outer dangers are not changed ; and yet, Monsieur La Fayette is in Paris ; he constitutes himself the organ of honorable men and the army ! Where are these honorable men ? How can this army deliberate ? But, first of all, let Monsieur La Fayette show us his leave of absence."

Upon these words, the Girondists felt the wind shifting towards their quarter ; and indeed, hardly were they uttered than a thunder of acclamation followed them.

A deputy rose and, from his seat, said :

"Gentlemen, you forget to whom and of whom you speak ; you forget who La Fayette is, the elder son of French liberty ; La Fayette has sacrificed to the Revolution his fortune, his title, his life !"

"Are you delivering his funeral eulogy ?" broke in a voice.

"Gentlemen," said Ducos, "freedom of discussion is repressed by the presence within this hall of a general foreign to this Assembly."

"That is not all !" exclaimed Vergniaud ; "this general has quitted his post in face of the enemy ; it is to him, and not to the colonel to whom he may have left this place, that the army he commands has been confided. Let us learn whether he can quit his camp without leave, and, if he has done so, let him be arrested and tried as a deserter !"

"This was the aim of my question, and I support Vergniaud's proposition," said Guadet.

"We support it !" broke forth from the whole Gironde.

"The call by name !" said Gensonne.

The nominal appeal gave a majority of ten votes to the friends of La Fayette.

Like the people on the twentieth of June, La Fayette had dared too much or too little ; it was one of those victories of the kind of that over which bewailed Pyrrhus, bereft of half his army :

"Another such a victory, and I am lost !"

The same way as Petion, La Fayette, coming from the Assembly, went to the palace.

He was received there with a gentler smile, but with a no less embittered heart.

La Fayette had just sacrificed for the royal pair more than his life ; his popularity was gone.

This was the third time that he had given this boon, more precious than a monarch's gift ; the first time at Versailles, October the sixth, the second time at the Champ de Mars, July the seventeenth, the third time, on this day.

La Fayette had one final hope ; it was this hope that he came to commu nicate to his sovereigns.

The next day he would review the National Guard with the King ; there could be no doubt of the enthusiasm which would be inspired in it by the King and its former commanding general ; La Fayette would take advantage of this influence, march upon the Assembly, crush the Gironde ; during the confusion, the King could set out and reach the camp at Mauberge.

This was a bold stroke, but in the present state of minds, it was very nearly sure to succeed.

Unfortunately, Danton, at three o'clock of the morning, entered Petion's house to warn him of the plot.

At daybreak, Petion countermanded the review.

Who had betrayed the King and La Fayette ?

The Queen !

Had she not declared she preferred to perish by another rather than be saved by La Fayette ?

She was helping fate ; she was to perish through Danton.

At the hour when the review would have taken place, La Fayette turned his back on Paris, returning to his army.

Nevertheless, he had not yet lost all hope of saving the King.

———

CHAPTER XXV.

VERGNIAUD WILL SPEAK.

LA FAYETTE'S victory, a doubtful one followed by a defeat, had had a singular result.

It had prostrated the royalists, while the asserted defeat of the Girondists had lifted them up ; it had aided them by disclosing to them the abyss into which they would have infallibly fallen.

Suppose less hatred in the heart of Marie Antoinette, and, perhaps, at this hour, the Gironde would have been destroyed.

It would not do to let the court have time to repair the fault it had just committed.

It might recover strength, and, after for an instant blocking up the revolutionary stream, drive it back to its source.

Everybody was seeking a means to prevent this—everybody fancied he had found one; but when this plan was exposed, its inefficiency was seen and it was given up.

Madame Roland, the spirit of the party, wished to arrive at it through a great commotion in the Assembly.

Who could produce such a commotion ?

Who could deal the blow ?

Vergniaud.

But what was this Achilles doing in his tent, or rather, this Rinaldo lost in Armida's gardens ?

He was loving.

It is so difficult to hate when one loves.

He loved the beautiful lady, Madame Simon Candeille, actress, poetess, musician ; his friends would at times be two or three days in search of him, and would, at length, find him reclining at the feet of this charming woman, one hand linked with hers, the others straying distractedly over the strings of her harp.

And every evening in the orchestra of the theatre, he would applaud her whom he worshipped the day through.

One night, two deputies came out of the Assembly in despair ; Vergniaud's inaction frightened them for France.

They were Grangeneuve and Chabot.

Grangeneuve, the Bordeaux lawyer, the friend and rival of Vergniaud, like him, deputy from the Gironde.

Chabot, the unfrocked Capuchin, the author—or one of the authors—of the " Catechism for Sans-culottes," which poured over royalty and religion the gall collected in the cloister.

Grangeneuve, gloomy and moody, walked on beside Chabot.

The latter eyed him, and it seemed to him that he saw something sweep across his colleague's forehead like a shadow of his thoughts.

" What are you thinking ?" inquired Chabot.

"I am thinking how all this dragging delay will enervate the country and slay the Revolution," answered his companion.

" You think so," queried Chabot, with the bitter laugh that was habitual to him.

" I think," continued Grangeneuve, " that if the people give time to royalty, the people will be lost !"

Chabot laughed again.

" I think," concluded Grangeneuve, " that revolutions have but one hour ; that those who let that escape them, will nevermore find it again, and must render an account for their procrastination to heaven and posterity."

" Do you think heaven and posterity will demand of us an account for sluggishness and inaction ?"

" I fear so !"

After a silence, Grangeneuve spoke again.

" Chabot, I am of the conviction that the people are downcast by their last check ; that they will not again be upraised save by some powerful lever, some bloody motor ; they must have a fit of rage or of terror, or they must quaff a fresh draught of energy."

"How can this fit of rage or terror be given them?" inquired Chabot.

"That is what I am pondering over," returned Grangeneuve, "and I think I have found the secret."

Chabot drew nearer to him; by the intonation of his companion's voice, he had understood that the latter was going to propose something unwonted to him.

"But," continued Grangeneuve, "where could I find a man capable of the requisite resolution for such an act?"

"Speak," broke in Chabot, with an accent of firmness which could leave his hearer no further doubt, "I am capable of anything to destroy those I hate, and I hate monarchs and priests!"

"Well," said Grangeneuve, surveying the street, "I have seen that there is pure blood at the birth of all revolutions, from Lucretia's to Sidney's. For statesmen, revolutions are a theory; for the lower class, revolutions are a vengeance; now if one would urge the multitude on to vengeance, a victim must be shown; this victim the court refuses to give us; well, let us give ourselves to the cause!"

"I do not understand you," remarked Chabot.

"Well, one of us—one of the foremost, widest known, most earnest, purest—must fall under the blows of aristocrats."

"Continue."

"He who falls must be one forming part of the National Assembly, in order that the Assembly may have to take the avenging of him in hand; in brief, this victim must be I, myself!"

"But the aristocrats will not harm you, Grangeneuve—they will take good care not to do so."

"I know it; that is why I say a man of resolution must be found—"

"To do what?"

"To stab me."

Chabot drew back a step, but the speaker caught him by the arm.

"Chabot," said he to him, "a while ago you asserted you were capable of anything to destroy those whom you hated; are you capable of assassinating me?"

The monk remained speechless. Grangeneuve continued.

"My tongue is naught—my life is useless to liberty, while, on the other hand, my death will be to its advantage. My corpse will be the standard of insurrection, and, I tell you—"

Grangeneuve, with a vehement gesture, stretched out his hand towards the Tuileries.

"I tell you yonder palace and those it encloses will vanish as in a whirlwind!"

Chabot looked at the speaker, whilst tremulous with admiration.

"Well?" inquired Grangeneuve.

"Well, thou mighty Diogenes," said Chabot, "put out your lantern—the man is found!"

"Then, let us arrange all," said Grangeneuve, "let us terminate everything this very evening. To-night I will be walking alone here (this was spoken fronting the wickets of the Louvre) in the most lonely and darkest spot. If you fear your hand will fail you, let two other patriots know of it; I will make this sign for them to recognize me."

Grangeneuve raised both arms in the air.

"They will stab me, and, I answer for it, I shall fall without uttering a groan."

Chabot passed his handkerchief over his brow.

"When day comes," went on Grangeneuve, "my body will be found; you will accuse the court; the people's revenge will perform the rest."

"'Tis well; to-night?" said Chabot.

The two strange conspirators shook one another's hand, and parted.

Grangeneuve went home and made his will, which he antedated at Bordeaux a year back.

Chabot went to dine at the Palais Royal.

After dinner, he went into a cutler's shop, and bought a knife.

On going out with his purchase, his eyes fell upon a play bill.

Mademoiselle Candeille performed; the monk knew where to find Vergniaud.

He went to the theatre of the Comedie Francaise, went into the room of the fair comedienne and found in there her usual court : Vergniaud, Talma, Chenier, Dugazon.

She performed in two pieces.

Chabot remained till the end of all.

Then, when the last curtain had fallen, the beautiful actress had changed her dress, and as Vergniaud got ready to ascort her to the Rue de Richelieu, where she dwelt, he followed his colleague into the coach.

"Have you anything to say to me, Chabot ?" asked Vergniaud plainly seeing that the Capuchin had business with him.

"Yes, but rest easy, it will not take long."

"Say it now, then."

Chabot drew out his watch.

"It is not the hour," observed he.

"When will be the hour ?"

"Midnight."

The beautiful Candeille shuddered at this mysterious dialogue.

"Oh !" murmured she.

"Do not be alarmed," said Chabot. "Vergniaud has nothing to fear; the country, however, has need of him."

The coach rolled on to the actress's dwelling.

The woman and the two men remained silent.

When at the door of Mademoiselle Candeille's house, Vergniaud asked :

"Do you come up stairs ?"

"No, you are to go with me."

"Good heavens, where are you going to take him ?" inquired the actress.

"A few yards from here; in a quarter of an hour, he will be free, I promise you."

Vergniaud squeezed the hand of his fair mistress, made her a sign to encourage her, and walked away with Chabot by the Rue Traversiere.

They crossed the Rue Saint Honore, and took the Rue de l' Echelle.

At the corner of this latter street, the monk weighed with one hand on Vergniaud's shoulder, and, with the other, pointed out to him a man who was walking up and down along the deserted walls of the Louvre.

"Do you see ?" he asked Vergniaud.

"Who—what ?"

"That man."

"Yes," answered the Girondist.

"It is our colleague Grangeneuve."

"What is he doing there ?"

"Waiting."

"Waiting for what ?"

"Waiting for him to be killed."

"Killed ?"

"Yes."

"Who is going to do such an act ?"

"I !"

Vergniaud stared at Chabot as one regards a maniac.

"Remember Sparta, remember Rome," said Chabot, "and lend me your ear."

Whereupon, he related everything to him.

Proportionately to the monk's recital, Vergniaud bowed his head.

He felt how far he—the effeminate tribune, the lion in love—was below that fearful republican who, like Decius, asked but a gulf into which to leap for his death to save his country.

"'Tis well, I ask three days to get my speech ready," said he.

"In three days—"

"Be easy," returned Vergniaud, "in three days, I shall be crushed against the idol, or I will have overturned it."

"I have your word, Vergniaud ?"

"You have."

"'Tis a man's ?"

"'Tis a republican's !"

"I have no more need of you ; go reassure your mistress."

Vergniaud turned back on his way through the Rue de Richelieu.

Chabot advanced towards Grangeneuve.

The latter, seeing a man come upon him, retired into the gloomiest place.

Chabot followed him.

Grangeneuve stopped at the foot of the wall, being unable to fall back further.

Chabot approached him.

Grangeneuve made the agreed-on signal, by uplifting his arms.

"Well," said he, seeing that his friend remained unmoving, "what withholds you ? Strike !"

"It is useless, Vergniaud will speak," said Chabot.

"So be it," remarked Grangeneuve, with a sigh, "but I believe the other means would be better!"

What could royalty be expected to do against such men?

CHAPTER XXVI.

VERGNIAUD SPEAKS.

IT was high time for Vergniaud to decide.

Danger was increasing without and within.

Without, at Ratisbon, the council of ambassadors had unanimously refused to receive the minister from France.

England, while entitling itself a friend, was making ready an immense armament.

The princes of the Empire, who vaunted loudly their neutrality, were secretly introducing enemies of France into their strongholds.

The Duke of Baden had let the Austrians into Kehl, a league from Strasburg.

In Flanders things were worse still.

Luckner, an old, deaf, witless man, who miscarried all of the plans of Dumouriez, the only man, if not of genius, at least of mind, the French had in face of the enemy.

La Fayette was at court, and his last step had clearly proved that the Assembly—France in other words—could not depend upon him.

Lastly, Biron, brave and faithful, discouraged by the first reverses, only thought of a defensive war.

Thus far for the exterior.

Within, Alsace had been loudly crying for arms, but the Minister of War, entirely the court's, had taken care not to let it have a weapon.

In the South of France, a lieutenant general of the princes, the governor of Lower Languedoc and the Cevennes, had his powers verified by the nobility.

In the West a simple countryman, Allan Redeler, announced on the going out after mass, that an armed meeting would be given to the King's friends in a neighboring chapel.

Five hundred peasants there assembled at the first word.

Thus was insurrection sown in Vendee and Brittany; it only needed time to grow up.

Finally, from nearly all the department directories arrived counter-revolutionary addresses.

The danger was great, imminent, dread-inspiring; so great that it no longer was men that it impended over, —but the country.

Without having been uttered aloud, the following words circulated in undertones:

"The country is in danger!"

The Assembly waited.

Chabot and Grangeneuve had said: "In three days, Vergniaud will speak."

The passing hours were counted.

On neither the first nor the second day, did Vergniaud appear at the Assembly.

On the third day, every one came, shuddering with expectancy.

Not one deputy was missing from his place; the galleries were packed.

Last of all, Vergniaud entered.

A murmur of satisfaction ran over the Assembly; the galleries applauded like the pit on the entrance of a favorite actor.

Vergniaud lifted his head to seek out who was being clapped.

The redoubling of the applause told him it was he.

Vergniaud was then hardly thirty-three years of age; his character was meditative and sluggish; his indolent genius was pleased with the slightest things; ardent only for pleasure, one would have said that he hastened to pluck the blossoms of a youth which was to have so short a springtime.

He went to sleep late, and did not rise before noon; when he intended to speak, three or four days beforehand, he prepared his discourse, polished it, sharpened it, pointed it, as a soldier, on the eve of a battle, furbishes his weapons, and puts on their keen edge.

He was, as an orator, what they call in fencing-schools a "swordsman fine to look upon;" the stroke he dealt did not appear well to him unless he had brilliantly delivered it, and had been loudly applauded; he reserved his words for moments of peril and danger-fraught junctures.

"He was not the man for all hours, but the man for great days," has said a poet.

As for bodily qualities, Vergniaud was rather short than tall; however he had a robust figure, which betokened the athlete. His hair was long and wavy; in his declamatory gesticulations, he tossed his locks like a lion its mane; below his broad forehead, shaded by thick brows, shone black eyes full of sweetness or of flame; his nose was short, somewhat large, with open, proudly expanded nostrils; his lips were heavy, and, like to the opening of a spring from which gushed sparkling water in abundance, words fell from his mouth in powerful cascades, throwing out spray, foam and sound. Although pitted with the small pox, his skin seemed like marble smoothed only by the stone-cutter's chisel, not polished by the sculptor's graver; his complexion, pale, or empurpled, or livid, according to whether the blood flushed his countenance or flowed back to his heart.

In repose and amid a throng, he was an ordinary man on whom the historian's eye, however piercing, would have seen no reason to stop; but, when the fire of passion made his blood boil, when the muscles of his face twitched in life, when his extended arm commanded silence and lorded over the congress, the man became a god, the orator was transfigured, the rostrum became his Mount Tabor!

Such was the man who came, with hand yet closed, but full of thunderbolts.

By the approbation which had arisen on his appearance, he knew what was expected of him.

He did not ask the floor; he strode straight to the speaker's stand, mounted it and, in the midst of a stillness full of tremulousness, opened his harangue.

His first words were spoken with the deep, saddened, concentrated tone of a prostrated man; he seemed as worn out at the beginning as others are commonly at the end; this came from his having wrestled for three days with the spirit of eloquence; it was because he knew, like Samson, that, in the mighty effort he was come to attempt, he would without fail pull down the temple, and that having gone up to the rostrum among the still erect pillars, from his still suspended vault, he might descend by clambering down over the ruins of royalty.

As Vergniaud's genius is perfect in this discourse, we quote it entire; we believe that the reader of it will feel the same curiosity one experiences, while visiting an arsenal, before one of those historical engines of war which may have breached the wall of Sagonta, Rome or of Carthage.

"Citizens," began Vergniaud, in a voice barely intelligible at first, but which presently grew grave, sonorous, blasting, "citizens, I come to you and I ask:

"Wherefore this strange situation wherein one finds the National Assembly?

"What fatality pursues us and marks each day with events which, carrying disorder into our works, throws us back unceasingly into the yeasty agitation of inquietude, hopes, passions?

"What destiny had in store, for France, this dreadful frothing within whose midst one is tempted to doubt whether Revolution retrogrades or takes a forward stride towards its aim?

"At the moment when our northern armies appeared to make some progress in Belgium, we see them all at once recoil from the enemy, bringing back battle on our own territory. The unfortunate Belgians have only left of us the remembrance of the conflagrations which illumined our retreat!

"On the Rhenish line, the Prussians are incessantly accumulating on our naked border. How comes it that, precisely at the apex of a crisis so decisive for the nation's existence, the movement of our armies should be suspended? how, through a sudden disorganization of the ministry, the bonds of confidence to be snapped, and the safety of the empire to be given to inexperienced hands?

"Is it true that doubt is cast upon our triumphs?

"Is the blood of the army of Coblentz, or that of our own, to be most spared?

"If the fanaticism of the priesthood threatens to deliver us to both the pangs of civil war and invasion, what can be the intention of those who reject, with unswerving obstinacy, the sanction of our decrees? Would they reign over unpeopled cities; over ravaged fields? What is the quantity of tears, misery, blood, the dead, that will glut their vengeance? To what have we come?

"You, gentlemen, whose courage enemies of the Constitution flatter themselves they have shaken; you, whose consciences and probity, every day, it has been attempted to alarm, by intermingling your love of free minds with faction—as if you had forgotten that despotic court and cowardly heroes of the aristocracy had given the name of factious to the representatives who went to take an oath at the Tennis-court, to the takers of the Bastile, to all who have made and upheld the Revolution! You who are calumniated because you are foreign to the caste which the Constitution has thrown down in the dust, and in which degraded men hoped to find accomplices; you who are wished to be alienated from the people, because they know the people are your support, and that—if, by a guilty desertion of their cause, you earn yourself a right of being cast off by it—it would be easy to dissolve you; you whom it is endeavored to divide, but who will adjourn till after the war your divisions and bickerings, and who will not think hating one another so sweet as for you to prefer such infernal delight to the safety of the country; you whom it has been attempted to awe by armed petitioners— as though you did not know that at the commencement of the Revolution, the sanctuary of liberty was encompassed by the satellites of despotism, Paris was besieged by the army of the court,

and those days of danger were glorious ones for our first Assembly; I now call your attention on the crisis at which we are.

"These internal troubles have two causes; aristocratic, sacerdotal intrigues —both tending to the same design: counter-revolution.

"The King has refused his ratification to your decree on religious disturbances.

"I know not whether the dark spirits of Medicis and Cardinal de Lorraine still wander beneath the vaults of the Palace of the Tuileries, and whether Louis the Sixteenth's heart is troubled by the fantastic ideas which they suggest; but it is not allowable to believe (without wronging him, and without accusing him of being the Revolution's most hurtful foe) that he wishes to encourage the criminal attempts of priestly ambition by letting them go unpunished, and return to the proud supporters of the tiara the power by which they equally oppressed king and people; it is not allowable to believe— without wronging him and declaring him the State's most cruel enemy— that he is willing to foster sedition, and make everduring the disorders which hurl it by civil war to its ruin.

"I conclude that, if he resists your decrees, it is because he deems himself, without the means you offer him, powerful enough to maintain the public peace. If, therefore, it comes to pass that public peace is not maintained, that fanaticism's torch threatens still to fire the realm, that yet religious violence desolates the country, the agents of the royal authority are themselves the cause of all our woes.

"Let them answer with their heads for all the trouble of which religion will be the pretext! In this fearful responsibility, display the end of your patience and the nation's disquietudes.

"Your solicitude over the empire's external safety has caused you to decree a camp around Paris; all the federalists of France were to come hither on the fourteenth of July to repeat the oath to live free or to die. Calumny's poisoned breath has blasted this project; the King has refused his sanction. I respect too well the exercise of a constitutional right to propose for you to make the ministers responsible for this refusal; but, if it happens that, before the battalions are assembled, the free soil is profaned, you must treat them as traitors; they must be hurled them-selves into the abyss which their heed-lessness or their malevolence will have dug under the steps of liberty! In short, the bandage which intrigue and adulation have bound over the royal eyes must be snatched away, that he may be shown the end of the path along which deceitful friends conducted him.

"It is in the name of Louis Sixteenth that French princes labor against us in the European courts; it was to avenge his dignity that the Treaty of Pilnitz was concluded; it was to defend him that were to be seen hastening to Ger-many, under the flag of rebellion, the former companies of the body-guard; it was to fly to his help that the emigres enrolled themselves in the Austrian armies, sharpening their weapons to wound the bosom of their country; it was to join these stainless knights couch-ing their lances for the royal preroga-tive that others left their posts in face of the enemy, betraying their oaths, stealing money, corrupting soldiers, and thus trailing their honor in cowardice, perjury, insubordination, theft and mur-der. In short, the royal name is in all these disasters!

"Now, I read in the Constitution:

"'If the King places himself at the head of an army, or if he does not op-pose, by some formal act, any such en-terprise executed in his name, he shall be looked upon as having abdicated the kingdom.'

"It is in vain that the King will an-swer:

"'It is true that the enemies of the nation assert they only act to advance my power; but I have proved that I am not their accomplice; I have obeyed the Constitution; I have put troops in the field. It is true that these armies were too weak; but the Constitution did not state the degree of strength I should have given them. It is true that I marshalled them too late; but the Constitution does not designate the time when I should have raised them. It is true that camps in reserve might have been ready to reinforce them; but the Constitution does not oblige me to form camps in reserve. It is true that when generals advanced without meet-ing resistance on the hostile territory, I ordered them to fall back; but the Constitution does not command me to win victories. It is true that my minis-ters have deceived the National Assem-bly as to the number, arrangement and provisioning of the troops; but the Constitution gives me the right to select my own ministers, and orders me no-where to give my confidence to patriots and shun the counter-revolutionists. It is true that the National Assembly has issued the required decrees for the country's defence, and that I have re-fused to confirm them; but the Consti-tution guarantees me that faculty. Lastly, true it is that counter-revolu-tion is at work, that despotism will put into my grasp its iron sceptre, that I will crush you, that you must grovel, that I will punish you for having had the insolence to be free; but all this shall be done constitutionally. No act has emanated from me that the Consti-tution condemns; it is not therefore al-lowable to doubt my faithfulness to-wards it, and my zeal in its defence.'

"If it were, possible, gentlemen, in the calamities of a fatal war, amid the disorders of a counter-revolutionary move, for the King of the French to hold such derisive language: if it were possible for him to speak of his love for the Constitution with such insulting irony, would we not have the right to reply to him:

"'Oh, King! you doubtlessly think, with Lysander the tyrant, that truth is no better than a lie, and that men may be amused with oaths like a child with playthings; you have feigned to respect the laws only to preserve the power which you make use of to brave them; you have only preserved the Constitu-tion for it not to hurl you from the throne, whereon you have need to remain to destroy it; the nation, but to ensure the success of your perfidy, by inspiring it with confidence; do you dream still of abusing it to this day by hypocritical protests?

"Do you think to change the cause of our misfortunes by the artfulness of your excuses and the audacity of your sophisms?

"Was it to defend us, that to the foreign soldiers forces were opposed whose inferiority left no uncertainty as to defeat? Was it to defend us, that a general who violated the Constitution was not censured even, thus fettering the courage of those serving under him? Was it to defend us that the government was incessantly paralyzed by the continual disorganization of the ministry?

"Did the Constitution leave you the choice of ministers for our welfare or our ruin? Did it make you head of the army for our glory or our shame? Did it in short give you the right of sanction, a civil list, and so many great prerogatives, for the Constitutional destruction of the empire and the Constitution?

"No, no, man whom the generosity of the French has not been able to move! man whom the love of despotism alone can render you sensible! you have not kept your oath to the Constitution! It may be overturned, but you will not reap the fruit of your perjury; you may not oppose by a formal act the victories which may be won in your name over liberty, but never will you reap the product of such unworthy triumphs! You are no longer aught to this Constitution which you have so shamefully violated, or to this people whom you have so cowardly betrayed!

"As the facts which I cite are not free from statements clashing with the royal good faith; as it is certain that the false friends surrounding the King are sold to the conspirators of Coblentz, and are burning to ruin the King in order to transfer the crown to the head of some one of their leaders in the plot; as it is important to his personal safety, as well as to that of the state, that his conduct should no longer be bristling with suspicions, I will propose an ad-

dress which will remind him of the truths I have just declared, and in which he will learn that the neutrality he keeps between this land and Coblentz is a betrayal of France.

"I, over and above this, ask that you shall declare the country to be in danger. You will see, upon that cry of alarm, all the citizens rally, the land vomit forth soldiers, and see renewed those prodigies which covered with glory the people of antiquity.

"Are the regenerated Frenchmen of '89 deficient in patriotism?

"Is not the day come for those to be gathered who are in Rome and on Mount Aventine?

"Do you expect that—weary of the toils of the Revolution, or corrupted by habits of parading around a palace—men have grown weak and accustomed to speak of freedom without enthusiasm and of slavery without horror?

"Is a military rule to be established? The court is suspected of perfidious designs; it speaks of military movements, martial law; its fancy is familiarized with the blood of the people. The palace of the King of the French is turned into a fortalice. Where are its enemies? Against whom are pointed those guns and bayonets?

"The friends of the Constitution have been repulsed from the ministry; the reins of empire are fluttering at random at the moment when, to sustain it, they should be grasped with as much vigor as patriotism. Everywhere is discord fomented, fanaticism triumphant; the connivance of the government increases the audacity of foreign powers, which belch against us steel and bronze, and a chill has settled upon the sympathy of those people who were swearing secret oaths for the triumph of freedom. The enemy's cohorts grow more serried, intrigue and perfidy plan treason; the legislative body opposes to these plots decrees rigorous but necessary; the royal hand tears their parchment!

"Call, while yet time, call on Frenchmen to save the country! Show them the gulf in all its immensity!

"It is only by an extraordinary effort that it can be crossed. It is for you to prepare them for it by an electrical shock that will send a glow throughout the State. Imitate, you of the Assembly, the Spartans of Thermopylæ, or those venerable men of the Roman Senate who waited on their thresholds the death which the ferocious vanquishers brought to their land. No, you will have no need to make such vows to see avengers spring up from your hearthstones; on the day when your blood sprinkles the ground, tyranny, its pride, its palaces, its protectors, will be swept away forever before national omnipotence and the people's wrath."

There was in this speech an ascending force, an increasing gradation, a crescendo of tempests, which beat the air like an immense pair of wings.

The effect was like that of a trumpet-blast.

The whole Assembly, Feuillants, royalists, Constitutionalists, republicans, deputies, spectators, in seats or on the gallery, were all enveloped, overpowered, borne away by the mighty whirlwind.

All uttered shouts of enthusiasm.

On the same night, Barbaroux wrote to his friend Rebecqui at Marseilles:

"Send me five hundred men who know how to die."

CHAPTER XXVII.

THE THIRD ANNIVERSARY OF THE TAKING OF THE BASTILE.

ON the eleventh of July, the Assembly declared the country to be in danger.

But, to promulgate the declaration, it needed the royal authorization.

The King gave it only on the evening of the twenty-first.

Indeed, to proclaim that the country was in danger was an avowal by authority of its powerlessness; it was an appeal to the nation for it to save itself, inasmuch as the King either could not, or would not, do anything.

In the interval between the eleventh and the twenty-first of July, a great terror had agitated the palace.

The court expected for the fourteenth of July an attempt against the King's life.

An address of the Jacobins had strengthened it in that belief; it had been drawn up by Robespierre, as it was easy to recognize by its double edge.

It was addressed to the Federals who came to Paris for the holiday of the fourteenth, so cruelly dabbled in blood the preceding year.

"Hail to the French of the eighty-three departments!" said the Incorruptible; "greeting to Marseilles! hail to the mighty, unconquerable country, who gathers her sons around her on her days of danger and of feasting! Let us open our houses to our brothers!

"Citizens, have you hastened for merely a vain ceremony of confederation and for superfluous oaths?

"Not so, you hasten at the call of the nation appealing to you, threatened from abroad, betrayed within! Our perfidious leaders have led our armies into snares; our generals respect the territory of the Austrian tyrant, and burn down the towns of our Belgian brothers; a monster—La Fayette—has come to insult the National Assembly; insulted, threatened, outraged, does it still exist? So many attempts have at last aroused the nation, and you flock hither. Those who lull the people to sleep will try to seduce you; flee their endearments, their tables where is imbibed moderation and the forgetfulness of duty; keep your suspicions in your hearts; the fatal hour will sound!

"Behold the altar of our native land!

"Will you suffer *base idols* to be thrust between liberty and you, to usurp the worship due to it? Swear only to the country in the immortal name of the King of Nature. Everything on the Champ de Mars reminds us of our enemy's perjury; we cannot turn a rod at a single spot where we will not find it stained with the innocent blood that was spilt upon it! Let us purify this soil, avenge this blood, and not go beyond its enclosure before having decided the salvation of the country !"

It would be difficult to explain things more categorically ; never was advice to assassinate given in more positive terms ; never were bloody reprisals preached in a clearer and more urgent voice.

And it was Robespierre, remark it well, the caustic tribune, the careful orator, who, in his sweetest voice, told the deputies of the eighty-three departments :

" My friends, if you will believe me, you had better kill the King !"

There was great fright at the Tuileries, the King especially.

All were convinced that the twentieth June had had no other end than the murder of Louis Sixteenth during a riot, and that, if the crime had not been committed, that simply came from the King's courage which had imposed upon his assassinators.

There was something true in all this.

Now, all that remained of courtiers to those two condemned persons, the King and the Queen, said that the crime which had been checked on the twentieth of June had been put off to the fourteenth of July.

They were so persuaded that the King was entreated to put on a shirt of mail in order that the first stab or pistol shot would glance from his breast, and give his friends time to come to his succor.

Alas ! Marie Antoinette had no longer Andrée at hand to aid her, as at the former time, in her nocturnal task, and to go at midnight to test with unsteady hand, in an out-of-the-way nook of the Tuileries, as she had done at Versailles, the strength of the silk-like cuirass.

Happily, the breastplate had been kept which Louis, on his first trip to Paris, had tried on to please his wife, but which he had refused to keep on.

The King, however, was so watched over, that not an instant could be found for him to put it on again, and correct the defect it might have.

Madame Campan carried it three days under her dress.

At length. one morning, when she was in the Queen's chamber, whose occupant was still in bed, the King entered, quickly pulled off his coat, while Madame Campan fastened the doors, and tried on the mailed shirt.

When it was buckled and fitted, the King drew Madame Campan to him and whispered to her :

" It is to content the Queen that I do what I do ; they will not assassinate me, Campan, you may be at ease as to that ; their plan is changed, and I must expect another kind of death. At all events, come to my room when you leave the Queen's apartment ; I have something to entrust to you."

The speaker went out.

Marie Antoinette had seen the two have their aside but had heard nothing ; she watched her husband with an uneasy look and, when the door had swung to behind him, asked :

" Campan, what was his Majesty saying to you ?"

Madame Campan knelt down by the Queen's bed, held out her hands to her, and repeated aloud what Louis the Sixteenth had whispered to her.

Her hearer mournfully shook her head.

" Yes," said she, " such is Louis's opinion, and I begin to think like him ; he asserts that all this going on in France is an imitation of what passed in England during the last century ; he unceasingly reads the story of the unfortunate Charles, to bear himself better than did the monarch of Great Britain. Yes, yes, I am growing to suspect a trial of the King, my dear Campan ! As for me, I am a foreigner, and I will be assassinated—alas ! what will become of my poor children ?"

The speaker could go on no farther ; her strength failed her, she burst into sobs.

Thereupon, Madame Campan rose, and hastened to prepare a glass of water, sweetened, and with ether in it ; but her royal mistress waved it away with her hand.

" Nervous attacks, my poor Campan," said she, " are the ailments for happy women ; but all the medicaments of the world can do naught against a mind diseased! Since my misfortunes, I feel my body no longer; I only am aware of my destiny. Say nothing of this to the King; go and find him."

Madame Campan hesitated to obey.

"Well, what ails you?" asked the Queen.

"Oh, madame," cried Madame Campan, "I have to tell you that I have made for your Majesty a corset of similar material to the King's defensive armor, and that on my knees I implore your Majesty to wear it."

"I thank you, my dear Campan," said her mistress.

"Ah, your Majesty accepts it!" exclaimed the lady-in-waiting joyfully.

"I accept it as a token of your devoted attention; but I shall take good heed not to put it on."

Then taking her hand, and speaking in a low voice, Marie Antoinette added:

"I would be too happy did they take away my life! Good heavens, they would do me more joy than you by giving me life; they would be delivering me—Go, Campan, go."

The lady-in-waiting went out.

It was time, she was choking.

In the corridor, she met the King, who was coming towards her; on seeing her he stopped and held out his hand. Madame Campan seized the royal hand and would have kissed it; but the sovereign, drawing her to him, bade her:

"Come!"

Whereupon, he walked on before her, and, stopping in the inner entry which led from his room to the Dauphin's, he felt with his hand for a spring and opened a press completely concealed in the wall, the opening in which was entirely lost among the brown streaks which formed the shadowy portion of the painted stone.

This was the iron, built-in safe which he had walled up and wrought with the aid of Gamain.

A large portfolio full of papers was in this armory, one of the shelves of which bore several thousands of louis.

"There, Campan," said the royal locksmith, "take this portfolio, and carry it into your room."

Madame Campan tried to lift the designated object, but it was too heavy.

"Sire, I cannot stir it," she said.

"Wait," said Louis.

Having closed the secret closet whose opening, once the spring had snapped, became again invisible, he took up the portfolio, and carried it into Madame Campan's closet.

"There," said he wiping his forehead.

"What am I to do with this, sire!" inquired the lady.

"The Queen will tell you, at the same time as she informs you what it contains."

Whereupon, he left the room.

To prevent anybody seeing the portfolio, Madame Campan, with an effort, pushed it between two mattresses of her bed and, entering Marie Antoinette's rooms, said:

"Madame, I have in my room a portfolio which the King has just brought thither; he told me that your Majesty would tell me what it contains and what is to be done with it."

The Queen laid her hand on the arm of her tiring-woman who, standing by her bedside, waited for her reply.

"Campan," said she, "its contents are some documents mortal to his Majesty if—which heaven forbid! they mean to try him; but, at the same time, and that is doubtlessly why he wishes me to acquaint you, there is in that portfolio the report of a session of the council in which his Majesty gave his opinion against war; he made all his ministers sign it, and, in the very event of that trial, he calculates that, in the same proposition as the other papers will be hurtful to him, this one will be useful."

"But, madame, what must be done?" inquired the tire-woman.

"Whatever you like, Campan, provided it be in safety; you are alone responsible; only, you are not to go away from me, even when you are not on service; such are circumstances that, at any moment, I may have need of you. In that case, Campan, as you are one of those friends on whom reliance may be placed, I wish to have you at hand."

The holiday of the fourteenth of July arrived.

The Revolution did not mean to assassinate Louis the Sixteenth on that day—it is likely that no one had even the idea—but to proclaim Petion's triumph over the King.

We have recorded that, following the twentieth of June, Petion had been suspended by the directory of Paris.

This would have been a mere nothing without the royal adhesion, but this suspension had been confirmed by a royal proclamation sent to the Assembly.

On the thirteenth—the eve of the anniversary celebration of the Taking of the Bastile—the Assembly of its own private authority, had removed the injunction.

At eleven o'clock on the morning of the fourteenth, Louis XVI. descended the grand staircase with his wife and children.

Three or four thousand men, indecisive troops, escorted the royal family.

Marie Antoinette fruitlessly sought on the faces of the soldiers and National Guardsmen for some mark of sympathy; the most devoted turned away their heads and avoided her look.

As for the people, there could be no deceiving one's self on their sentiments; shouts of " Long live Petion !" broke out from all sides ; moreover, as though to give this ovation something more durable than momentary enthusiasm, on every hat and cap could be read the two following words, which bore witness at the same time to the defeat of the royalists and the triumph of their enemies:

" Petion forever !"

Marie Antoinette was pale and trembling ; convinced, notwithstanding what she had said to Madame Campan, that a plot was afoot against her consort's life, she started every instant, fancying she saw a hand uplifted with a knife, or an arm stretched out armed with a pistol.

On arriving at the Champ de Mars, Louis the Sixteenth alighted from the coach, took a place on the left hand of the president of the Assembly, and walked on with him towards the altar of the country.

There, the Queen had to part with the King to mount with her children to the raised seats reserved for her.

She stopped, refusing to go up till her husband was safe at his post, and watched him.

At the foot of the altar of his country, there occurred one of those sudden rushes so common to great throngs.

The King disappeared as if swallowed up in it.

The Queen uttered an exclamation, and would have hurried to him.

But he appeared again, ascending the steps of the altar of the country.

Amongst the usual symbols that figure in solemn celebrations, such as Justice, Power, Liberty, there was one which was to be seen shining mysteriously and fear inspiring through a crape veil, carried by a man clad in black and crowned with cypress.

This fearful symbol particularly attracted the eyes of Maria Antoinette.

She stood as if rooted to her place, and, nearly encouraged as to her husband, who had reached the summit of the altar of the country, she could not take her eyes off from the gloomy sight.

At last, making an effort to break the chains fettering her tongue, she gasped, without addressing any one in particular :

" Who is yonder man in black, crowned with cypress ?"

A voice which made her start, replied :

" The executioner."

" What holds he in his hand, under that crape ?" continued Marie Antoinette.

" The axe of Charles the First."

The Queen turned round, bloodless ; it seemed to her she had heard the sound of that voice before.

She was not wrong ; the speaker was the man of the Chateau de Taverney, the Bridge of Sevres, the return from Varennes ; Cagliostro, in short.

She uttered a scream, and fell fainting into the arms of Madame Elizabeth.

CHAPTER XXVIII.

THE COUNTRY IS IN DANGER.

At six o'clock on the morning of July the twenty-second, a week and a day after the celebration on the Champ de Mars, Paris started at the report of a heavy gun fired on the Pont Neuf.

A cannon at the Arsenal made answer to it like its echo.

From hour to hour, throughout the entire day, this dread detonation broke out anew.

The six legions of the National Guard, headed by their six commanders, were assembled, from daybreak, at the city hall.

Two processions were organized to carry through the streets of Paris and its faubourgs, the proclamation of the danger of the country.

It was Danton who had had the idea of the terrible holiday, and he had handed over the getting up of the programme to Sergent.

Sergent, a but middling artist as an engraver, was an unequalled man for making effective scenes; his hate had been augmented by the outrages which had assailed him at the Tuileries, and Sergent had displayed in the whole programme of the day that grand skill of managing, of which he showed the last evidence after the tenth of August.

Each of the two trains, one of which was to go one way, the other another, started from the city hall at six o'clock in the morning.

First rode a detachment of cavalry, with music at the head; the air played by the band was composed for the occasion; it was gloomy and nearly allied to a funeral march.

Behind the cavalry rumbled six pieces of artillery, drawn all abreast when the streets or quais were broad enough to allow it, two by two when the streets were narrow.

Next, four mounted men, bearing as many banners, on each of which was printed one of the four following words:

" Liberty."
" Equality."
" Constitution."
" Country."

Then twelve city officers with their scarfs on, and swords by their sides.

Next rode, alone and isolated, like France, a National Guardsman on horseback, bearing a broad tri-colored standard on a scroll on which were inscribed these words:

" Citizens, the Country is in Danger!"

Sixthly, in the same order as the first, followed six cannon, the heavy wheels of which resounded deeply with hollow rumbling.

A detachment of the National Guard.

A second troop of cavalry closed the line.

At every square, bridge and crossing, the train stopped.

Silence was commanded by roll of the drum.

Then, the banners were waved and, when all sound had been hushed, when the breath of ten thousand spectators was enchained captive in their breasts, there rose the grave voice of the municipal officer reading the resolution of the legislative body and adding:

" THE COUNTRY IS IN DANGER!"

This last phrase was thrilling; it vibrated in every heart.

It was the outburst of the nation, country, France!

It was a mother in her last gasp, screaming:

" Come to my help, my sons!"

And all this while, every hour, thundered the cannon shot from the Pont Neuf with its counterpart at the Arsenal.

On all the open plazas of Paris—the square before Notre Dame was the centre—had been erected amphitheatres for voluntary enrolments.

In the centre of these amphitheatres was a long plank laid on two drums, serving as the table for enlisting, and, at every movement that took place around them, the drums ruffled like a breath of distant storm.

Tents surmounted with red-white-and-blue flags were reared around the amphitheatre; these tents were capped with oak-leaf crowns and tricolored streamers.

City officers, in their scarfs, sat around the table and, proportionately to the enlistments, delivered certificates to the enrolled.

On either side of the enclosure were two pieces of cannon; at the foot of the double flight of steps by which the ascent was made was unceasing music; beyond the tents, following the same curved line, was a circle of armed citizens.

This was both grand and exciting!

It was the intoxication of patriotism. The ranks were broken through every instant by the many who rushed to put down their names, for the sentinels could not repulse those who meant to enlist.

The two stairways of the amphitheatre—one for descent, the other for ascent—were not sufficient, large though they were.

People mounted as they could, aided by those who had already been up; then, having put down his name and having received his certificate, he would leap down to the ground with a proud cheer, waving his parchment, singing the " Ca ira," and would go to kiss the cannon, mouth of flesh and blood to muzzle of brass.

They were the bridegrooms of the French people to be wedded to that twenty-two years' war which, if it had no such result in the past, will have as result in the future the freedom of the world !

Among the volunteers, there were some too old who disguised their age; there were others too young who, pious tellers of untruth, rose on tiptoe and answered " Sixteen years!" when they were but fourteen.

In this way, from Brittany, came old La Tour d'Auvergne; from the South, young Viala.

Those who were retained by indissoluble ties wept that they could not go; they in shame hid their faces in their hands, while the chosen ones cried out to them:

" Sing, you others ! why don't you shout : ' The nation forever !" '

Abrupt, deafening outcries of " The nation forever !" would mount into the air, while thundered the hour-guns of the Pont Neuf and its echo of the Arsenal.

So overpowering was the excitement, so deeply affected were minds, that the Assembly itself was frightened at its work.

It appointed four members to visit every quarter of Paris.

Their mission was to say :

" Brothers, in the name of the country, no rioting! The court wish a riot to obtain the removal of the King; give the court no pretext—the King must remain with us."

Then they added, those sowers of words :

" He must not escape his punishment !"

There was loud clapping of hands everywhere when these men passed by, and there was to be heard running over the multitude, like the gust of a tempest soughing in the branches of a forest:

" He must remain for his punishment !"

They did not say who, but everybody knew well enough the object of that punishment.

This lasted till midnight.

Till the hour of twelve, the cannon bellowed, until that time the amphitheatre was thronged.

Many recruits remained there, dating their first camping-out from the foot of the altar of the country.

Every cannon report had its wave of sound extending to the heart of the Tuileries.

The heart of that palace was the royal chamber, where Louis the Sixteenth, Marie Antoinette, the royal children and the Princess de Lamballe were collected.

They had not gone out the whole day, they clearly felt that it was their fate which was being settled on that solemn, noteworthy day.

The royal family did not separate until midnight; in other words, not until they were sure the last roar had left the brazen throats.

Since the gatherings in the faubourgs, the Queen no longer slept on the lower floor.

Her friends had begged her, until she assented, to go up to a room on the first floor, situated between the apartments of her husband and her son.

Awaking usually at dawn, she exacted that no shutters or blinds should be closed, in order that her sleeplessness might be less painful.

Madame Campan slept in the same room as the Queen.

Let us give the reason for her having consented that one of her women should sleep with her.

One night as the Queen had just retired for the night—although it was one o'clock of the morning or thereabouts —Madame Campan standing before her bed and conversing with her, they heard steps all of a sudden in the corridor, then a sound like a scuffle between two men.

Madame Campan wanted to go see what was happening; but her royal mistress, clinging to her lady-in-waiting, or rather her friend, said :

" Do not leave me, Campan."

During this time, a voice called out from the passage-way :

" Fear nothing, madame ; it is a rascal who came to kill you, but I have hold of him !"

It was a servant's voice.

" Good heavens !" exclaimed the Queen, lifting up her hands, " what an existence ! Outrages in the daytime, assassins in the night !'

Then to the servant, the speaker added :

" Release the man, and open the doors to him."

" But, madame," remonstrated Madame Campan.

" Why, my dear, if he was arrested, he would be carried around in triumph by the Jacobins !"

The man was let go ; he was a serving-man of the King's wardrobe.

Since that day, the King had wished somebody to sleep in the Queen's bed chamber.

Marie Antoinette had selected Madame Campan.

On the night following the proclamation of the danger of the country, Madame Campan awoke about two o'clock in the morning ; a moonbeam, like the dim torch of a friend who had come to peep into the room, struggled through the window panes, and shot upon the Queen's bed, the curtains of which it dyed with a bluish hue.

Madame Campan heard a sigh ; the Queen was restless.

" Is your Majesty ailing ?" asked she, in an undertone.

" I suffer always, Campan," responded Marie Antoinette ; " however, I hope that this suffering will soon finish !"

" Madame !" exclaimed her companion, "has your Majesty some ominous thought ?"

" No, quite the contrary, Campan."

Stretching out her pale hand and arm, made whiter yet by the moonbeam, she said with profound melancholy :

" In a month, the rays of yonder moon will see us free and rid of our chains."

" Ah !" ejaculated her hearer, in delight, " have you accepted Monsieur de La Fayette's help, and are we to flee ?"

" The help of Monsieur de La Fayette ? Oh, no, thank heaven !" returned Marie Antoinette, with an accent of repugnance about which there could be no mistake ; " no, but in a month, my nephew Francis will be in Paris."

" Are you quite sure, your Majesty ?" cried Madame Campan.

" Yes," returned her mistress, " all is decided ; there is an alliance between Austria and Prussia ; the two powers combined will march upon Paris ; we have the line of route of the princes and the allied armies, and we can surely say : ' On such a day, our deliverers will be at Valenciennes—on such a day, at Verdun — on such a day at Paris !' "

" And you do not fear——"

Madame Campan stopped.

" Being assassinated ?" said the Queen, completing the sentence. " That may be ; I know it ; but what can you expect, Campan ? Those who risk nothing, gain nothing."

" On what day are the allied sovereigns hoped to be in Paris ?" inquired Madame Campan.

" Between the fifteenth and twentieth of August," answered the Queen.

" Heaven hear you !" said Madame Campan.

Heaven, fortunately, did not hear, or rather, hearing, it sent to France help of which it did not dream :
THE MARSEILLAISE !

CHAPTER XXIX.

THE MARSEILLAISE.

WHAT encouraged Marie Antoinette was precisely that which should have alarmed her : the manifesto of the Duke of Brunswick.

This manifesto, which ought not to have returned to Paris till July twenty-sixth, being drawn up at the Tuileries, was issued in the first days of that month.

But, at very nearly the same time as that at which the court was composing at Paris that mad production, (the effect of which we have seen), let us tell what was transpiring at Strasburg.

This city, one of the most French that could be, precisely because it had just come from being Austrian, one of the most solid bulwarks we had, as we have stated, now had the enemy at its gates.

Hence, it was at Strasburg that, since six months before—that is to say, since there had been likelihood of war—had gathered those youthful battalions of volunteers with ardent, patriotic spirit.

Strasburg, whose peerless spire is reflected in the Rhine, which alone divided us from the enemy, was a boiling caldron of war, youth, joy, pleasure, balls, reviews, where the clash of instruments of combat incessantly mingles with the music of revelry.

From Strasburg, through one gate of which the volunteers entered, there went out, by another gate, the soldiers who were deemed in fighting condition ; there, friends met, shook hands, bid farewell ; there, sisters wept, mothers prayed, fathers said :
" Go and die for France !"

All this, to the ringing of bells and the reverberations of cannon, those two bronze voices speaking to heaven, one to invoke its mercifulness, the other its justice.

On one of these departures, a more solemn than the others because the most considerable, the Mayor of Strasburg, Dietrich, a worthy and excellent patriot, invited the brave young men to come to his house to fraternize in a banquet with the officers of the garrison.

The mayor's two daughters, with twelve or fifteen of their companions—fair, noble daughters of Alsace, who might have been taken, by their golden tresses, for nymphs of Ceres—were, if not to preside, at least, like so many bouquets of flowers, to embellish the feast.

Among the number of the guests, an habitual visitor to Dietrich's house, a friend of the family, was a young, high-spirited native of Franc Comtois, named Rouget de l'Isle.

(We knew him in after years, and he himself, while we recorded it with our hand from his mouth, related to us the birth of that noble flower of war, at the springing up of which the reader is to be a witness).

Rouget de l'Isle was then of the age of twenty and, as an engineer officer, was in garrison at Strasburg.

A poet and a musician, his piano was one of the instruments to be heard in immense concerts, his voice, one of those which resound above the strongest and most patriotic.

Never was banquet more French, more national, illumined by a more ardent June sun.

No one spoke of himself—all spoke of France.

Death was there, it is true, as in antique festivals ; but smiling death, not grasping in his hand the hideous scythe and mournful hourglass, but a sword in one hand, in the other a palm branch !

They were puzzled what they should sing ; the old " Ca ira " was a song of wrath and civil war ; they wanted a patriotic, brotherly outburst and yet menacing to the foreigners.

Who was to be the modern Tyrtæus who would hurl, amid cannon smoke, the whistling of bullets and balls, the hymn of France to the enemy ?

To this demand, Rouget de l'Isle, enthusiastic, amorous, patriotic, answered :

"It is I !"

He left the saloon.

In half an hour, while his absence was hardly causing any uneasiness, all was formed, words and music; all was cast at the one gush of metal, fashioned in the mould like a god's statue.

Rouget de l'Isle entered, his hair tossed back, his forehead beaded with sweat, breathless with the contest he had wrestled with the two sisters, Music and Poetry.

"Listen—hearken to me all of you !"

He was sure of his muse, the noble young man.

At his voice, everybody turned, some holding their glasses in their hand, others holding a hand in theirs.

Rouget de l'Isle commenced :

"Awake, sons of dear France, awake !
  The day of glory dawns full fair.
Against you now doth tyranny
  Its bloody standard high uprear.
Do you not hear how, in our fields,
  Its ruthless soldiers fiercely cheer ?
They're come to slay, e'en in our arms,
  Our children, all we love so dear !
To arms, citizens ! your battalions form !
      March on, march on !
Until the beams of peace succeed the storm !"

On this opening verse, an electrical shudder overran the entire audience.

Two or three shouts of enthusiasm burst forth ; but the greedy voices of the rest cried instantly :

"Hush, hush ! let us hear !"

Rouget continued, with a gesture of deep indignation :

"What do they want, this horde of slaves
  Of trait'rous monarchs, plotting kings ?
For whom have they had fetters wrought—
  For whom are meant these iron rings ?
For Frenchmen—us ? oh, such outrage !
  All sons of France this must upraise !
Do they dare dream of binding us
  In slavery of other days ?
To arms, citizens !——"

This time, Rouget de l'Isle did not have to sing the chorus himself; a single cry came from every bosom :

"Your battalions form !
  March on, march on !
Until the beams of peace succeed the storm !"

Then, he proceeded amid growing enthusiasm :

"What, shall we to foreign cohorts,
  Without a blow struck, trembling bow—
Shall we confess that our soldiers
  Cannot base hirelings overthrow ?
Great God ! is it on hands enchained
  We are, yoke-weighed, to rest our brow ?
Shall we be serfs of despots ever,
  To tug, like cattle, at the plough ?"

A hundred heaving breasts were waiting, and when the last line was uttered, the final question put, they cried

"No, no, no !"

Then, with the peal of a trumpet, the mighty chorus resounded :

"To arms, citizens ! your battalions form !
      March on, march on !
Until the beams of peace succeed the storm !"

This time, there was such a commotion among all the auditors that Rouget de l'Isle, before singing a fourth verse, was obliged to beg silence.

He was listened to feverishly.

The indignant voice became menacing :

"Tremble, tyrants ! with your allies,
  Whom all hate with one accord.
Tremble ! for your murd'rous projects
  Are fated soon to gain reward.
If our heroes should fall battling—
  Fate has many sad things in store !—
All are soldiers to fight 'gainst ye !
  Our country shall have more, and more !"

"Ay, ay !" cried all the voices.

And fathers pushed forward their sons who could walk, while mothers held up in their arms those who still had to be carried.

This made the bard perceive that there was one verse missing ; the song of the children ; the hymn of the forthcoming harvest, the germinating grain ; and, while the guests frenziedly repeated the chorus, he let his head sink on his hand ; amid the confusion, excitement, bravoes, he improvised the subjoining :

"To march forward we are ready,
  When our elders shall be no more ;
We will follow in their footsteps
  Glorious paths they trod before.
Should we fall while them avenging,
  Should like water our blood outpour :
Pierced by the ball or blade, our hearts
  Had the same feeling our brothers' bore."

Through the stifled sobs of mothers,

the enthusiastic tones of sires, was to be heard the pure voices of childhood singing :

"To arms, citizens ! your battalions form !
        March on, march on !
Until the beams of peace succeed the storm !"

"Ah, but," muttered one of the guests, " is there to be no pardon for those who are misled ?"

"Stay, stay !" said Rouget de l'Isle ; "you will see that my heart does not deserve such a reproach."

In a voice fraught with emotion, he sang this holy strophe, in which is the entire soul of France ; humane, grand, generous and, in her wrath, soaring on the pinions of mercy, above anger itself :

"Frenchmen, when your steel is lifted,
  Take good heed whose blood you're spilling.
Spare all those, the hapless victims,
  Who, 'gainst you, are ranked unwilling—''

Applause interrupted the poet.

"Yes, yes !" came from every side ; "mercy, forgiveness for our misguided brothers, our enslaved brothers, who are pushed against us with whip and bayonet !"

"Yes," resumed Rouget de l'Isle ; "mercy and forgiveness for them !

"But the followers of Bouille,
  Our hands 'gainst them shall know no rest !
Against such tigers pitiless—
  Who thirst to rend their mother's breast—
To arms, citizens ! your battalions form !"

"Ay," cried every voice, "against such let us

      "March on, march on !
Until the beams of peace succeed the storm !"

"Now," cried Rouget de l'Isle, " down on your knees, whoever you be !"

All obeyed.

Rouget de l'Isle alone remained standing ; he set one foot on the chair of one of the guests, as if on the first step to the temple of Liberty, and, uplifting both arms to the heavens, he sang the last verse, the invocation to the spirit of France :

"O, sacred love of native land,
  Strengthen, guide our avenging hands ;
O, Liberty, dear Liberty !
  Strike thou with thy defending bands !
May thy sweet tones call to our flags
  Victory to gild our story ;
May our expiring foemen see
  Thee triumphant and us glory !"

"France is saved !" said a voice.

And from every mouth, in an universal outburst, pealed the *De profundus* of despotism, the *Magnificat* of liberty :

"To arms, citizens ! your battalions form !
        March on, march on !
Until the beams of peace succeed the storm !"

It was now a wild, intoxicated, unrestrained joy ; every one threw himself into his neighbor's arms ; the girls collected flowers in nosegays and chaplets which they strewed at the poet's feet.

Thirty-eight years after this, while of this great day telling me, a young man who had just for the first time heard, in 1830, this holy hymn sung by the people's mighty voice—the poet's brow still shone with the halo of 1792.

And this was justice !

Else how comes it that I myself, while penning these last lines, am thus affected ?

From whence comes it that, while my trembling right hand traces the chorus of the children, the invocation to the spirit of France, my left hand dashes away a tear ready to drop on the paper ?

It is because the holy Marseillaise is not only a battle-cry, but an outburst of fraternity ; because the powerful hand of France is outstretched over all her people ; because it will ever be the last sigh of dying freedom, the first cry of liberty born again !

Now how did the hymn springing into life at Strasburg under the name of the Song of the Rhine, burst suddenly in the heart of France under the title of the Marseillaise ?

That is what we are going to show our readers.

CHAPTER XXX.

BARBAROUX'S FIVE HUNDRED MEN.

On the twenty-eight of July, as if to give a basis to the proclamation of the danger of the country, there arrived at Paris the Coblentz manifesto.

We have said it was a senseless work, a menace, consequently, an insult to France.

The Duke of Brunswick, a man of mind, knew the manifesto to be absurd; but above the duke, were the sovereigns of the coalition; they received the document already drawn up by the King of France and imposed it on their general.

According to the manifesto, every French man was guilty; any town or village might be demolished or burnt. As for the modern Jerusalem condemned to thistles and briars, Paris, not a stone was to be left upon another!

Such was the tenor of this declaration which arrived from Coblentz on the twenty-sixth.

What eagle had brought it in its talons, for it to have traveled two hundred leagues in thirty-six hours?

The reader may imagine the explosion produced by such an act—it was like that made by a spark firing a powder train.

Every heart leaped, all were alarmed and girded themselves for the struggle.

Let us choose, among all such men, one—among all these types, one only.

We have named this man on another page: it is Barbaroux.

We will undertake to paint our type.

Barbaroux, we have mentioned, had written in the commencement of July, to Rebecqui:

"Send me five hundred men who know how to die!"

Who was the man who could pen such a phrase, and what influence must he, therefore, have over his countrymen?

He had the influence of youth, patriotism, and of being handsome.

This man was Charles Barbaroux, of gentle, prepossessing face which troubled Madame Roland in the conjugal chamber, and made Charlotte Corday think even at the scaffold's foot.

Madame Roland began to distrust him.

Why should she?

He was too handsome!

Such was the reproach cast at two men of the Revolution whose heads—fair to look upon as they were—appeared, some fourteen months apart, one in the hand of the headsman of Bordeaux, the other in that of the Paris executioner.

The first was Barbaroux; the second, Herault de Sechelles.

Listen to what Madame Roland said of them:

"Barbaroux is flighty; the worship which he receives from unmannered females has destroyed what there was serious in his sentiments. When I see such handsome young men as Barbaroux and Herault de Sechelles too much elevated by the impressions which they produce, I cannot help thinking that they too deeply adore themselves to love their country enough."

She was in error, that stern Pallas.

The country was, if not the only, the first mistress of Barbaroux; it was she, at all events, whom he loved the best, for he died for her.

Barbaroux was hardly twenty-five years of age.

He was born at Marseilles of a family of those hardy mariners who have made of commerce poetry. In form, grace, ideality, from his Grecian profile especially, he seemed to have descended in direct line from some of those Phœnicians who carried their goods from the shores of the Permessus to the banks of the Rhone.

While young, he had exercised himself in the great art of oratory—that art of which the men of Southern France know how to make at the same time a weapon and an ornament,—then, in poetry, that blossom of Mount Parnassus which the founders of Marseilles transported with them from Corinth Bay to the Gulf of Lion.

He had, besides, occupied himself in the healing art, and was in correspondence with Saussure and Marat.

He was unexpectedly seen to appear during the ferments of his natal city, in consequence of Mirabeau's election.

He was then appointed secretary of the city government of Marseilles.

Later, there were troubles at Arles. In the height of this agitation leaped forward Barbaroux, like Antinous armed.

Paris claimed him; the capacious furnace had need of that immense crucible, that pure metal.

He was sent thither to give an account of the troubles at Avignon; he was said to be of no party, that his heart, like that of Justice, bore neither hatred nor friendship; he spoke truth simple and appaling though it was, and, in saying it, he appeared great like it.

The Girondists had just arrived.

What distinguished them from the other parties, what perhaps ruined them, was their being real artists; they held out their hands warmly to Barbaroux; and, proud of their handsome recruit, they led the son of Marseilles to Madame Roland.

Our readers know what Madame Roland at first sight had thought of Barbaroux.

What had especially astonished her was that her husband, for quite a long period, had been in correspondence with Barbaroux, and that the young man's letters arrived regularly, precise, full of sense.

She had neither asked about the age or aspect of this grave epistolizer; for her he was a man of forty, with head bald with thought, and brow wrinkled by evening studies.

She came to see the object of her vision, and found a handsome young man of twenty-five, gay, laughing, light-hearted, fond of women, one of that rich, burning generation which flourished in '92 to be cut down in '93.

It was in this head, which appeared so frivolous, and which Madame Roland thought too handsome, that perhaps was formed the first thought of the tenth of August.

Storm was in the air; the wild clouds swept from north to south, from east to west.

Barbaroux gave them a direction, massing them over the slated roof of the Tuileries.

When not a soul had any plan drawn up, he wrote to Rebecqui:

"Send me five hundred men who know how to die!"

Alas! the true monarch of France was this King of the Revolution who wrote for half a thousand men of the above description who, as simply as he had asked for them, were sent.

Rebecqui picked them out himself, recruiting from the French party of Avignon.

They had been two years fighting, hating for ten generations.

They had fought at Toulouse, Nimes and at Arles; they were inured to blood, and weariness—they never spoke of that.

On the appointed day, they had undertaken, as it it was the usual allowance of distance for a soldier's march, this journey of two hundred and twenty leagues.

Why not?

They were hardy seamen, sturdy peasants, with faces browned by the African sirocco, or the wind from Mount Ventoux, with hands blackened by tar or callous with labor.

Everywhere they passed, they were called "brigands."

In one halt they made on the other side of Orgon, they received the words and music of Rouget de l'Isle's hymn, under the name of the Song of the Rhine.

It was Barbaroux who had sent them this good cheer to make the road shorter to them.

One of them studied the music and sang the words; then all, with the one immense cry, repeated the great work, much more terrible than ever Rouget de l'Isle had dreamed.

By going through the mouths of the Marseillaise, his song had changed its character, as its words had altered in accent.

It was no longer a lay of brotherhood, but a chant of death and extermination —the Marseillaise, now, the resounding hymn which made us shiver with dread on our mother's bosom.

This little band from Marseilles went through towns and villages, frightening France by its ardor in singing this new song, till then unknown.

When he learnt that they were at Montereau, Barbaroux hastened to inform Santerre.

The latter promised to go and receive the men of Marseilles at Charenton with forty thousand men.

What Barbaroux calculated to do with Santerre's forty thousand men and his own five hundred was as follows:

To put the latter at the head, capture at a sweep the city hall and that of the National Assembly, level the Tuileries, as on the fourteenth of July in 1789, the Bastile had been demolished, and, on the ruins of the Florentine palace, proclaim a republic.

Barbaroux and Rebecqui went to wait at Charenton for Santerre and forty thousand men of the faubourgs.

The brewer came up with two hundred men!

Perhaps he did not fancy giving the men of Marseilles—in other words, strangers—the glory of such a deed.

The little band with flaming eyes, embrowned faces, thrilling tones, went through Paris, from the royal gardens to the Champs Elysees, singing the Marseillaise.

(Why should we call it otherwise from its general acceptation?)

The five hundred were to camp on the Champs Elysees, where a banquet was to be given them on the morrow.

The banquet did take place, indeed; but, between the Champs Elysees and the Pont Tournant, a few steps from the feasters were lined the battalions of grenadiers from the section of the Filles Saint Thomas.

This was a royalist guard which the palace had posted there as a rampart between the new comers and him.

The feasters and the grenadiers of Filles Saint Thomas felt they were enemies. They began by bandying insults, next, exchanging blows; at the first blood drawn, the Marseillais shouted, "To arms!" leaped to their stacked guns, and charged with the bayonet.

The Parisian grenadiers were over-powered by this first attack; luckily, they had behind them the Tuileries and its gates; the Pont Tournant protected their flight as they receded before their enemies.

The fugitives found an asylum in the royal apartments.

Tradition asserts that a wounded man was cared for by the Queen's own hand.

The federals, Marseillais, Bretons and Dauphinois were five thousand men; they were a power, not from number, but through faith.

The spirit of the Revolution was in them.

On July the seventeenth, they had sent an address to the Assembly.

"You have declared the country to be in danger," they said; "but do you not yourselves put it in danger by prolonging the impunity of traitors? Prosecute La Fayette, *suspend the executive power*, remove the directories over departments, renew the judicial power."

On the third of August, Petion himself reproduced the same demand. Petion, with his icy voice, in the name of the commonwealth, claimed a call to arms.

It is true there were behind him two dogs snapping at his legs: Danton and Sergent.

"The commune," said Petion, "denounces the executive power to you. To heal the evils of France, their root must be attacked, without loss of a moment. We would have desired merely the temporary suspension of Louis the Sixteenth; the Constitution opposes this; he unceasingly invokes the Constitution; we will appeal to it in our turn, and *demand* forfeiture."

Thus did the King of Paris denounce the King of France—thus did the monarch of the city hall declare war against the sovereign in the Tuileries.

The Assembly hung back from the fearful measure proposed to it.

The question of forfeiture was adjourned to the ninth of August.

On the eighth, the Assembly resolved there was no grounds for accusation against La Fayette.

The Assembly was recoiling.

What was it going to do on the morrow concerning the forfeiture question?

Was it, too, about to set itself in opposition to the people?

Let it beware!

Did it not know what was to pass, in its imprudence?

On the third of August—the very day on which Petion had come to demand forfeiture—the Faubourg Saint Marceau grew weary of dying of hunger in that struggle which was neither peace nor war; it sent deputies to the section of the Quinze Vingts, and asked their brothers of the Faubourg Saint Antoine:

"If we march on the Tuileries, will you go with us?"

"We will!" the others had replied.

On August the fourth, the Assembly condemned the insurrectionary proclamation of the Mauconseil section.

On the fifth, the Commonalty refused to publish the decree.

It was not enough for the King of Paris to have declared war to the King of France; here was the city government in opposition with the Assembly.

All these rumors of opposition to the movement came to the men of Marseilles; they had muskets, but no cartridges.

They cried loudly for ammunition; none was given them.

On the evening of the fourth, an hour after rumor had gone forth that the Assembly condemned the insurrectionary act of the Mauconseil section, two young men out of the five hundred entered the mayor's office.

There were only two municipal officers at the desks: Sergent, Danton's man; Panis, Robespierre's man.

"What do you want?" inquired the two magistrates.

"Cartridges!" answered the young men.

"It is expressly forbidden to deliver any," said Panis.

"Forbidden?" resumed one of the couple. "But the hour for the combat is approaching, and we have nothing with which to fight!"

"Were we brought to Paris to be butchered?" cried the other.

The first drew a pistol from his pocket.

Sergent smiled.

"Threats, young man?" said he. "With threats you cannot intimidate two members of the commonalty!"

"Who spoke of threats or intimidation?" said the young man; "this pistol is not for you, but for myself!"

Pressing the weapon to his forehead, he added:

"Some powder—cartridges! or, on the faith of a son of Marseilles, I will blow out my brains!"

Sergent had an artist's imagination, a Frenchman's heart; he felt that the words of the young man were those of France.

"Beware, Panis," said he, "if this young man kill himself, his blood will fall on us!"

"But, if we give up the cartridges in spite of the order, we would stake our heads on the throw!"

"Never mind! I believe that the hour is come to stake our heads," returned Sergent. "In any event, let every one take care of his own; I will stake mine, leaving upon you to follow or not my example."

Taking a sheet of paper, he dashed off the order to deliver cartridges to the two young men, and signed it.

"Give it to me," said Panis when Sergent had finished.

And his name was put down after Sergent's.

Minds might be easy after this; from the moment when the five hundred had cartridges, they would not let their throats be cut without resisting.

Therefore, when they were armed, the Assembly received, on the eighth, a thundering petition from them; not only was it received, but the petitioners were admitted to the honors of the session.

The Assembly was very timid; so much so that there was debating whether it should not retire to the provinces.

Vergniaud alone held it back.

Why?

Who could tell if it was not so that he might remain near the beautiful Candeille that Vergniaud wished to stay in Paris?

It little matters, however.

"It is at Paris," said Vergniaud, " that we must ensure the triumph of liberty or perish with her! If we have to leave Paris, let it be like Themistocles, with all the citizens, leaving only ashes and not leaving the enemy a single moment save to dig a grave!"

Thus was everybody in doubt and hesitation, while they felt the ground quake under them and feared it would yawn under a step.

On the fourth of August—the day on which the Assembly had censured the insurrectionary proceedings of the Mauconseil section, the day on which the two Marseillais, through Panis and Sergent, obtained cartridges for distribution among their five hundred companions—there was a meeting at the Cadran Bleu on the Boulevard du Temple.

Camille Desmoulins was there on his own and Danton's business.

Carra was secretary, and drew up the plan of the outbreak.

The plan having been drawn out, the party went to the abode of the ex-constituent Antoine, who lived in the Rue Saint Honore, before the Church of the Assumption, in the house of Duplay the joiner, the same as Robespierre.

Robespierre was not exactly sound on the question; for, when Madame Duplay saw the uproarious band pour into the house and Antoine's room, she quickly ran up to the room with which they had flocked, screaming in her fright: "Oh, Monsieur Antoine, are you going to kill Monsieur de Robespierre?"

"Robespierre is all right," returned the ex-constituent. "Nobody cares a fig for him; if he is afraid, let him hide!"

At midnight the plan, written by Carra, was sent to Santerre and Alexandre, the two commanders of the faubourgs.

Alexandre would have marched but Santerre answered that his faubourg was not ready.

Santerre was thinking of his speech to Marie Antoinette on the twentieth of June.

On the tenth of August, he only marched when he could not otherwise. The insurrection was therefore put off.

Antoine had said that nobody cared for Robespierre; he was wrong.

Minds were so agitated that the idea was entertained of making the motor of a movement him, that centre of immobility!

Who had such an idea?

Barbaroux!

This man was almost despairing; he was on the point of quitting Paris, to return to Marseilles.

Hear Madame Roland.

"We counted little on the defence of the North; we were examining with Servan and Barbaroux, the chances of saving liberty in the South, and founding a republic there; we were tracing boundary lines on maps. 'If our men of Marseilles,' said Barboroux, 'do not succeed, that will be our course.'"

Well, Barbaroux believed he had found another resource: Robespierre's genius.

Or it may have been Robespierre who wanted to know Barbaroux.

The latter's five hundred had left their barracks, too far off, to come to the Cordeliers, which was within eyeshot of the Pont Neuf.

At the Cordeliers, they were with Danton.

These terrible men, in case of insurrectionary uprising, would start off under Danton, and if the attempt succeeded, to Danton would go all the honors.

Barbaroux had asked to see Robespierre.

The latter had the air of condescending to his desire; he had Barbaroux and Rebecqui informed that he waited for them at his house, or rather Duplay the joiner's.

Chance, it will be recollected, had conducted him thither on the evening of the excitement on the Champ de Mars.

Robespierre looked upon this chance as a heavenly blessing, not only because that hospitality for the moment shielded him from imminent danger, but, moreover, because it was naturally the suitable resting-place of his future.

For a man who wanted to deserve the title of Incorruptible, it was just the lodging he needed.

He had, nevertheless, not entered it immediately; he had taken a trip to Arras; he had brought back his sister, Charlotte de Robespierre, and resided in the Rue Saint Florentin with that thin, dry person to whom, eight-and-thirty years afterwards, we had the honor of being presented.

He fell sick.

Madame Duplay, who was a Robespierrean fanatic, heard of this illness, came to reproach Mademoiselle Charlotte for her not having informed her of her brother's malady, and would not allow anything less than the transportation of the patient to her house.

Robespierre yielded to it; his vow, on leaving Duplay's house as a temporary guest, had been to enter it some day as a tenant.

Madame Duplay, therefore, chimed in capitally with his resolves.

She also had dreamed of the honor of lodging the Incorruptible, and had prepared an attic, rather cramped but passable, where she had had brought the best and finest furniture in the house, to match a charming blue and white bed, such as would suit a man who, at the age of seventeen, had had his portrait taken, he holding a rose in his hand.

In this room, Madame Duplay, by her husband's journeyman, had new shelves put up for books and papers.

The books were far from numerous; the works of Racine and Jean Jacques Rousseau formed the whole library of the austere Jacobin; beyond those two authors, Robespierre read only Robespierre.

Hence, all the other shelves were loaded with his briefs as a lawyer, his speeches as an orator.

As for the walls, they were covered with all the portraits which the fanatical Madame Duplay could manage to find of the great man; the same as Robespierre had but to stretch out his hand to read Robespierre, so, whatever way he turned, Robespierre saw only Robespierre.

It was into this sanctum, this tabernacle, this holy of holies, that were ushered Barbaroux and Rebecqui.

Except the actors themselves in this scene, no one can tell with what spider-like care Robespierre wove the web of conversation.

He spoke of the men from Marseilles firstly, of their love of country, of the fear he had of seeing the best sentiments exaggerated; then he spoke of himself, of the services he had rendered to the Revolution, of the wise slowness with which he had regulated its course.

But was it not time this Revolution stopped?

Was it not the hour when all parties ought to unite, choose the most popular man among them, put this Revolution in his hands, charging him to direct the movement?

Rebecqui let him go no farther.

"Ah, I felt you were coming, Robespierre!" said he.

Robespierre pushed back his chair as if a snake had risen up before him.

Rebecqui said, rising:

"We will have no more of a dictator than a king. Come, Barbaroux."

Whereupon, both instantly left the Incorruptible's attic.

Panis, who had brought them there, followed them into the street.

"Ah," said he, "you did not see the thing in the true light; you ill caught Robespierre's thought; it was only concerning a little momentary authority, and, if you had reflected on the idea, no one—certainly not Robespierre——"

But Barbaroux interrupted him, and said, repeating his companion's words:

"No more of a dictator than a king!"

And he went away with Rebecqui.

CHAPTER XXXI.

WHY THE QUEEN DID NOT WISH TO FLEE.

ONE thing encouraged the Tuileries; exactly what disheartened the revolutionists:

The Tuileries, put into a state of defence, had become a fortress with a powerful garrison.

In that famous day of the fourth of August, on which so many things had been done, royalty on its side had not been inactive.

During the night of the fourth and the morning of the fifth, the Swiss companies had been silently brought from Courbevoie to the Tuileries.

A few companies only had been detached and sent to Gaillon, where the King might take refuge.

Three sure men, three proved leaders, were near the Queen:

Maillardot, with his Swiss;

D'Hervilly, with his Chevaliers of Saint Louis and constitutional guard;

Mandat, general commanding of the National Guard, who promised twenty thousand resolute and devoted fighting men.

On the evening of the eighth, a man penetrated to the interior of the chateau.

Everybody knew this man, and he, therefore, reached without hindrance the Queen's apartments.

Doctor Gilbert was announced.

"Bid him enter," said Marie Antoinette in a feverish voice.

Gilbert entered.

"Ah, come, come, doctor! I am glad to see you."

Gilbert lifted his eyes on her; there was glowing over the speaker's features something of delight and satisfaction which startled him.

He would rather have seen her pale and dispirited than flushed and animated as she was.

"Madame," said he, "I fear I have arrived too late and have chanced upon an unseasonable moment."

"Quite otherwise, doctor," returned the Queen with a smile—an expression of which her mouth seemed to have lost the habit; "you are come quite seasonably and are welcome! You shall see something I have been wishing to show you for a long time—a king really a king!"

"I fear me, madame," responded Gilbert, "that you are deceiving yourself, and that you will show me a commander of a stronghold, rather than a monarch!"

"Monsieur Gilbert, it may be that we can no more agree on the symbolical character of royalty than on many other things. For me, a king is not merely a man who can say: 'I do not wish!' It is especially one who says: 'I will!'"

The speaker made allusion to that famous veto which had led the situation of affairs to their present extreme situation.

"Yes, madame," rejoined Gilbert, "and, for your Majesty, a king is, above all, a man who revenges."

"Who defends, Monsieur Gilbert! for, you are aware of it, we are publicly threatened, and are to be attacked with force. There are, I am assured, five hundred Marseillais, led by a certain Barbaroux, who have sworn, on the ruins of the Bastile, not to return to Marseilles until they shall have camped also on those of the Tuileries."

"I have, indeed, heard this," answered Gilbert.

"And did it make you laugh, sir?"

"It frightened me for the King and for yourself, madame."

"So that you come to propose our abdicating and putting ourselves at discretion in the hands of Monsieur Barbaroux and his five hundred?"

"Ah, madame, if the King could abdicate, and guarantee, by the sacrifice of his crown, his life, yours, and your children's!"

"Would you give him this advice, M. Gilbert?"

"Yes, madame, and I would throw myself at his feet to implore him to follow it!"

"Monsieur Gilbert, allow me to tell you that you are not steadfast in your opinions."

"Why, madame," said Gilbert, "my opinion is always the same. Devoted to my sovereign and my country, I have wished to see the King and the

Constitution in accord; from this desire and my successive deceptions come
the different counsels which I have had
the honor to give to your Majesty."

"And what is that which you give
at present, Monsieur Gilbert?"

"Never have you been more able to
follow it than at this moment, madame."

"Let us hear it then."

"I give you the advice to flee."

"Flight?"

"You well know it is possible, madame, and that never has such facility
been offered you."

"Let us hear how that is."

"You have nearly three thousand
men at the chateau."

"Nearer five thousand. sir," said
Marie Antoinette, with a smile of satisfaction, "and double that at the first
sign we make."

"You have no need to make a sign
which may be intercepted, madame ;
your five thousand men will suffice."

"Well, Monsieur Gilbert, what do
you think ought to be done with our
five thousand men?"

"You will place yourself in their
midst, madame, with your husband
and august children; will leave the
Tuileries at the moment most unexpected ; at a couple of leagues from
here, will take horse, and reach Gaillon
or Normandy, where you are expected."

"In other words, place myself in the
hands of Monsieur de La Fayette."

"He, at least, madame, has proved
he is devoted."

"No, sir, no! with my five thousand
men and the five thousand more who
will run up at the first signal we make,
I will rather try something else."

"What would you attempt?"

"To crush this revolt once for all."

"Ah, madame, madame! how right
he was to tell me you were doomed!"

"Who, sir?"

"A man whose name I dare not say
to you, madame ; a man who thrice
has spoken to you."

"Hush!" said his hearer, turning
pale ; "the evil prophet shall be made
false !"

"Madame, I fear you are blind !"

"Are you, hence, of the opinion they
will dare attack us?"

"The public mind tends that way."

"And is it thought that this palace
can be entered as it was on June the
twentieth?"

"The Tuileries is not a strong
palace."

"Nevertheless, if you will come
with me, Monsieur Gilbert, I will show
you that it can hold out some time."

"My duty is to follow you, madame,"
said Gilbert, bowing.

"Then, come," said the Queen, leading Gilbert to the central window, that
one which overlooked the Square of the
Carrousel, and from which one could
survey, not the immense courtyard
which at present extends along the
palace front, but the three little open
spaces enclosed by walls which then existed under the titles : that of the Pavilion of Flora, the "Court of the Princes ;"
that in the middle, the "Court of the
Tuileries," and that which in our days
is ended by the Rue de Rivoli, the
"Swiss Court."

"See," said she.

Indeed, Gilbert remarked that the
walls had been pierced with narrow
loopholes, and would lend the garrison
a rampart through the slits in which
could be repelled the people.

This first outwork being carried, the
garrison could retire not only into the
Tuileries, each door of which opened
on a courtyard, but also into the side
buildings ; so that the patriots who
ventured into the yards would be
caught between three fires.

"What do you say to that, sir?" inquired the Queen. "Do you still advise Monsieur Barbaroux and his five
hundred to attempt their enterprise?"

"If my advice would be listened to
by men such fanatics as they are, I
would make to them, madame, an appeal similar to that I make to you. I
came to ask you not to await the
attack ; I would ask them not to
attack."

"And would not they go on despite
it, on their side?"

"As you on yours, madame. Alas, it
is the misfortune of humankind that it
incessantly craves advice not to follow
it."

"Monsieur Gilbert," said the Queen

smiling, "you forget that the advice you are so kind as to give is not asked for——"

"It is true, madame," said Gilbert taking a backward step.

"Which does not make us any the less grateful to you," added the Queen, holding out her hand to the doctor.

A faint smile of doubt ruffled the latter's lips.

At this moment, carts laden with heavy oaken beams publicly entered the courtyards of the Tuileries, where were waiting for them men who, under their citizen's dress, were to be recognized as soldiers.

These men set to work sawing the beams into lengths of six feet, three inches thick.

"Do you know what those men are ?" asked the Queen.

"Engineers, it seems to me," replied Gilbert.

"Yes, sir, who are, as you see, making the windows *blind*, only reserving slits through which to fire."

Gilbert sadly regarded the speaker.

"What is it, sir ?" inquired Marie Antoinette.

"I am sincerely grieved to have forced your memory, madame, to retain those words, and your lips to speak them."

"There are circumstances, sir," responded the Queen, "when women must be men ; it is when men——"

She stopped.

"But, this time, the King is decided," resumed the Queen, finishing—not her phrase—but her thought.

"Madame," said Gilbert, "from the moment you are decided on the fearful extreme of which I see you are making your gate to safety, I trust that on all sides you have defended the approaches to the chateau ; for instance, the gallery of the Louvre——"

"Indeed, you make me think. Come with me, sir ; I wish to make sure that the orders I gave are being carried out."

She led away Gilbert through rooms as far as that door of the Pavilion of Flora which opens on the picture gallery.

Through the open door, Gilbert saw workmen engaged in cutting up the gallery into spaces of twenty feet.

"You see," said the Queen.

Then, turning to and addressing the officer overseeing the work, she said :

"Well, M. d'Hervilly ?"

"Well, madame, let the rebels leave us twenty-four hours, and we will be ready."

"Do you believe we will be left twenty-four hours, Monsieur Gilbert ?" the Queen asked the doctor.

"If anything is to be done, madame, it will be on the tenth of August."

"The tenth ? a Friday ? A bad day for riots, sir. I should think the rebels would have the sense to choose a Sunday."

She walked on before Gilbert, who followed her.

On leaving the gallery, they met a man in general's uniform.

"Well, Monsieur Mandat," inquired the Queen, "are all your arrangements made ?"

"Yes, madame," answered the commanding general, regarding Gilbert uneasily.

"Oh, you may speak out before this gentleman," said the Queen, "he is a friend."

Turning to Gilbert, she said :

"Are you not a friend, doctor ?"

"Yes, madame, and one of your most devoted," returned Gilbert.

"In that case." said Mandat, "it alters things. A body of the National Guard are placed at the city hall, another by the Pont Neuf, who will let the rioters pass them, and—while Monsieur d'Hervilly and his gentlemen, with Monsieur Maillardot and his Swiss, receive them in the front—they will cut off their retreat and crush their rear."

"You see, sir, that your tenth of August will not be a twentieth of June !" said Marie Antoinette.

"Alas, Madame, I am afraid it will not," said Gilbert.

"For us ?" queried the Queen.

"Madame," evaded Gilbert, "you know what I have told you of Majesty. As much as I deplored Varennes——"

"Yes, so much do you advise Gaillon ! Have you time to descend to the lower floors with me, Monsieur Gilbert ?"

"Certainly, madame."

"Well, come !"

They descended a small flight of winding stairs, which led to the ground-floor of the chateau.

This floor was a real camp, fortified and defended by the Swiss; all the windows had been *blinded,* as the Queen had said.

Marie Antoinette stepped up to the colonel.

"Well, M. Maillardot," she asked, "what have you to say of your men ?"

"That they are ready, like myself, to die for your Majesty."

"They will hold out to the last extremity ?"

"Once the firing commences, madame, it will not cease but on an order written by the King."

"You hear, sir ? Beyond the chateau's bounds, all may be hostile to us; but, inside, all are faithful."

"It is a consolation, madame ; but it is not security."

"Do you know you are dreadfully dispiriting, doctor ?"

"Your Majesty has led me wherever she liked ; will she allow me to conduct her back ?"

"Willingly, doctor ; but I am fatigued ; give me your arm."

Gilbert bowed at this great favor, so rarely granted by the Queen, even to her most intimate friends, since her misfortunes especially.

He escorted her to her sleeping-chamber.

Having arrived there, Marie Antoinette let herself sink upon a chair.

Gilbert knelt down on one knee before her.

"Madame," said he, "in the name of your august husband, in the name of your dear children, in the name of your own safety, a last time, I conjure you to make use of the forces you have about you, not to combat, but to flee !"

"Sir," returned she, "since the fourteenth of July, I have been wishing for the King to take his revenge ; the moment has come, at least we believe so ;

we will save royalty, or be buried beneath the ruins of the Tuileries !"

"Can nothing make you forego this fatal resolution, madame ?"

"Nothing."

At the same time, the royal lady held out her hand to Gilbert, half to make him a sign to rise, half to give him it to kiss.

Gilbert respectfully kissed the royal hand, and, rising, said :

"Madame, will your Majesty allow me to write a few lines which I regard as so urgent that I do not wish to delay them a single minute ?"

"Do so, sir," returned Marie Antoinette, waving her hand to a table.

Gilbert sat down at it, and dashed off the following lines :

"SIR :

"Come ! the Queen is in danger of death if a friend cannot prevail on her to flee, and I believe you to be the only friend who can have such influence over her."

This he signed and directed.

"Without being too curious, sir," inquired the Queen, "may I know to whom you are writing ?"

"To Monsieur de Charny, madame," replied Doctor Gilbert.

"To Monsieur de Charny !" echoed Marie Antoinette, losing her color and shuddering. "Why do you write to him ?"

"For him to obtain of your Majesty what I have failed in."

"Monsieur de Charny is too happy to think of his unfortunate friends ; he will not come," remarked the Queen.

The door opened.

An usher entered.

"His Lordship the Count de Charny, who has arrived this instant," said the usher, " begs to know if he may pay his homage to your Majesty."

From pale that she had been, the Queen became livid ; she stammered some unintelligible words.

"Let him enter !" said Gilbert, "'tis heaven that sends him !"

Charny appeared on the threshold in the uniform of an officer of the navy.

"Oh, come, sir," said Gilbert; "I was just writing to you."

He handed him the letter.

"I was informed of the peril which your Majesty ran, and I am come," said Charny bowing.

"Madame, madame," broke in Gilbert, "in heaven's name, hearken unto what Monsieur de Charny says; his voice will be that of France."

And with this, bowing respectfully to the Queen and the count, Gilbert departed, bearing away with him an unuttered sigh.

CHAPTER XXXII.

THE NIGHT OF THE NINTH TO THE TENTH OF AUGUST.

LET our readers permit us to transport them to a house in the Rue de l'Ancienne Comedie, near the Rue Dauphine.

In its first story resided Freron.

We will pass by his door; it would be useless to knock or ring at it, for he is on the second floor, in the room of his friend Camille Desmoulins.

While we mount the seventeen steps which separate one story from the other, we will rapidly tell who Freron was.

Louis Stanilas Freron was the son of the famous Elie Catherine Freron, so unjustly and so cruelly attacked by Voltaire.

(When at the present day are read the criticizing articles penned by the journalist against the author of "La Pucelle," the Philosophical Dictionary and "Mahomet," the reader will be astonished to see how the journalists of 1754 spoke just what we at 1854 think —one hundred years afterwards.

Freron (the son we speak of), who was then five-and-thirty years of age, irritated by injustice which he had seen overwhelm his parent—who died, in 1776, of grief at the suppression by Miromesnil the Keeper of Seals of his paper "l'Annee litteraire—" Freron had embraced with ardor the revolutionary principles, and published, or was about to publish, at this period the Orator of the People.

In the evening of the ninth of August, he was, as we have mentioned, in the room of Camille Desmoulins where he was supping with Brune (the future Marshal of France and, meanwhile, the) foreman of a printing-office.

Barbaroux and Rebecqui were the two other guests.

One woman alone took part in this repast, which had some resemblance with that meal which martyrs ate before going into the circus, called the "free feast."

This woman was Lucile.

Sweet name!

She has left a sorrowful remembrance in the annals of the Revolution.

We cannot in this work accompany her, at least to the scaffold where she mounted, the lovely, poetical creature! because that was the shortest road for her to rejoin her husband; but we will, as we proceed, sketch her likeness in one or two dashes of the pen.

A single portrait remains of you, poor girl!

You died so young, that the painter has been forced, so to say, to paint you as you flew past.

(This is a miniature which we have seen in Colonel Morin's admirable collection, which was permitted to be broken up, precious as it was, on the death of that excellent man who with so much kindness put his treasures at our disposal.)

In this portrait, Lucile appears small, pretty, rather roguish; there is something commonplace about her charming countenance.

In truth, daughter of a clerk in the treasury and of a notably handsome creature who was asserted to have been the mistress of Terray, the Minister of Finances, Lucile—as her name of Lucile Duplessis Laridon proves—was, like madame Roland, of vulgar extraction.

A love-marriage had (in 1791) united to this young girl, relatively rich to him, that fearful youth, that boy of genius, Camille Desmoulins.

Camille, poor, uncomely, speaking with difficulty, on account of that stammering which prevented him being an orator and perhaps made him the writer we know him to be, Camille had attracted and won her by the fineness of his mind and the goodness of his heart.

Camille—albeit he was of Mirabeau's opinion, which was : " You can never make anything of the Revolution if you do not *unchristianize* it—Camille, we repeat, was married in Saint Sulpice Church pursuant to the Catholic ritual ; but (in 1792) a son being born to him, he carried the child to the city hall and claimed for him the republican baptism.

It was there, in an apartment on the second floor of this house in the Rue de l'Ancienne Comedie that, was to be unfolded—to the high alarm and, yet, at the same time to the great pride of Lucile—all that plan of insurrection which Barbaroux simply confessed to have sent, three days previously, in a pair of nankin breeches to his washerwoman.

Barbaroux, who had no great confidence in the success of the bold stroke which he was himself preparing, and who feared he would fall into the power of the victorious court, showed, with ancient unaffectedness, a poison prepared (like Condorcet's) by Cabanis.

At the opening of the supper, Camille —who had no more hopefulness than Barbaroux—had said, as he lifted his glass, in Latin so that Lucile might not understand :

" *Edamus et bibamus ; cras enim moriemur* (Let us eat and drink ; for we die to-morrow) !"

But Lucile had comprehended.

" Why do you speak a language which I do not understand ?" said she. "I can guess what you said, Camille ; and it is not I—you may be easy as to that —who would prevent you fulfilling your mission."

Upon this assurance, the party had spoken freely and aloud.

Freron was the most resolute of all ; it was known that he hopelessly loved a woman, but it was not known who that loved object was.

His despair, on the death of Lucile, revealed that secret.

" Have you poison, Freron ? "inquired Camille.

" Oh, I," answered he, " if we do not succeed to-morow, I shall get myself killed ! I am so weary of life, that I seek but an excuse to shuffle off the coil."

Rebecqui was he who had the best hope of the result of the struggle.

" I know my men of Marseilles," said he ; " for it was I who selected them ; I am sure of them, from the the first to the last—not one will fall back an inch !"

After supper, they proposed to go see Danton.

Barbaroux and Rebecqui refused ; saying they were expected at the barracks of the five hundred.

This was near by, hardly twenty steps from the the house of Camille Desmoulins.

Freron had an appointment.

Brune spent the night with Santerre.

Each of them was attached to events by a thread.

They parted.

Camille and Lucile went alone to Danton.

These two households were linked, not only by the men, but still by the women.

Our readers know Danton.

We ourselves more than once, after the great masters who have painted him at full length, have been called upon to reproduce him.

His wife is less known.

Let us give her a few words.

It is again in Colonel Morin's cabinet that was to be found a souvenir of this remarkable woman, who was an object of such deep adoration from her husband; however, this was not a miniature remaining of her as in the case of Lucile, but a plaster cast.

Michelet believes this cast was moulded after her death.

The characteristic is kindness, calmness and strength.

Without being as yet ill of that malady which was her death in 1793, she was already sad and restless, as though, being near to death, she had had foreshadowings of the future.

Tradition adds that she was timid and pious.

She had, one day, in spite of this

piety and timidity, vigorously spoken her mind, though it was opposed to her parents'; this was on the day when she declared that she would marry Danton.

Like Lucile in Camille Desmoulins, she had—behind that gloomy face of the ignored man, sans fortune and reputation—seen the god, who, like Jove to Semele, was to devour her by revealing himself to her.

A fearful, tempest fraught fortune was that this poor creature joined herself with; but, perhaps, there was in her decision as much piety as love for this angel of shadow and light who was to have the fatal honor of winding up that great year of 1792, as Mirabeau wound up 1791, as Robespierre was to wind up 1793.

When Camille and his wife arrived at Danton's house—the two dwellings were door to door, Lucile and Camille, as we have stated, in the Rue de l'Ancienne Comedie; Danton, in the Rue du Paon Saint André—Madame Danton was weeping, and, in a resolute way, her husband was endeavoring to console her.

The wife went to the wife, the man to the man.

The two former embraced, the other pair shook hands.

"Do you think it is going to be anything?" inquired Camille.

"I hope so," answered Danton. "Nevertheless, Santerre is lukewarm. Luckily, in my opinion, to-morrow's doings will not be an affair of personal interest to individual benefit; we must rely on the irritation of a long misery, public indignation, the feeling at the approach of foreigners, the conviction that France is betrayed. Forty-seven sections out of forty-eight have voted for the King's forfeiture; they have each appointed three commissioners to meet at the commune, and save the country."

"'Save the country' is very vague," observed Camille.

"Yes; but, at the same, it is very expressive."

"And Marat? Robespierre?"

"Naturally, neither of them is to be seen: one is hid in his attic, the other

in his cellar. When the affair is finished, they will be seen coming out, one like a ram, the other like an owl."

"And Petion?"

"He is very clever who can tell his whereabouts! On the fourth, he dedeclared war on the palace, on the eighth, he warned the department that he could no longer answer for the King's safety; this morning, he proposed establishment of National Guards on the Square of the Carrousel; to night, he asked the department for twenty thousand francs so he could send away the men of Marseilles."

"He wants to lull the court," remarked Camille.

"I shouldn't wonder," agreed Danton.

At this moment, a new couple entered: the Roberts.

It will be recollected that Madame Robert (Mademoiselle de Keralio) dictated, on the seventeenth of July, 1791, on the altar of the country, the famous petition which her husband wrote down.

Quite the contrary from the two other couples, in which the men were superior to the wives, here the wife was superior to the husband.

Robert was a stout man of between thirty-five and forty, a member of the Cordelier Club, with more patriotism than talent, having no facility whatever in composing, a great enemy of La Fayette, and very ambitious, if the Memoirs of Madame Roland are to be credited.

Madame Robert was then in her thirty-fourth year; she was short, skilful, witty and spirited; educated by her father (Guinement de Keralio, Chevalier de Saint Louis, member of the Academy of Inscriptions, who had among his scholars a young Corsican whose gigantic future he was far from foreseeing), Mademoiselle de Keralio had gradually turned into the blue-stocking; at seventeen years of age, she wrote, translated and compiled; at eighteen, she wrote a novel: "Adelaide."

As the finances of her father were hardly enough for his own subsistence, he had to write for the "Mercury" and "Journal des Savants," and more than once he signed his daughter's articles, which were much beyond his in ability.

It was thus she came by that able, rapid, ardent mind which made her one of the most indefatigable journalists of the times.

The Roberts were just come through the Quartier Saint Antoine.

Things looked queer there, they said.

The night was fine, faintly illumined, peaceful in appearance; there was not a soul in the streets; only, the windows were all lighted, and these lights illuminated the streets.

This was ominous!

It was not a holiday illumination; it was like the taper by the bedside of the dying; the faubourg seemed to be in some feverish slumber.

At the moment when Madame Robert finished this intelligence, the toll of a bell made them all start.

This was the first stroke of the alarum sounded from the Cordeliers.

"Good!" said Danton, "I recognize our Marseilles men! I suspected they would be the ones to give the signal."

The women glanced at one another in affright.

Madame Danton especially wore upon her visage all the features of fear.

"The signal?" said Madame Robert. "Is the palace going to be attacked in the night?"

No one answered.

Camille Desmoulins, who, at the first tap of the bell, had passed into the neighboring chamber, returned, a gun in his hand.

Lucile uttered a scream; but—feeling that, at such an hour, she had not the right to weaken the man she loved—she withdrew into the alcove, fell upon her knees, buried her head in the bed of Madame Danton, and began weeping.

Camille came to her.

"Rest easy; I will not leave Danton," said he.

The men went out.

Madame Danton seemed ready to die.

Madame Robert, clinging to her husband's neck, wished to accompany him.

The three wives remained alone.

Madame Danton was seated, as if crushed.

Lucile was on her knees, praying.

Madame Robert strode up and down the room, saying, without being aware that each of her words struck Madame Danton to the heart:

"All this is Danton's fault! If my husband is killed, I will die with him; but, before I die, I will have Danton's life."

Nearly an hour elapsed thus.

They heard the outer door opened.

Madame Robert sprang forward.

Lucile raised her head, while Madame Danton remained immobile.

It was Danton who entered.

"Alone!" exclaimed Madame Robert.

"Take courage; nothing will be done before to-morrow," said Danton.

"But Camille?" asked Lucile.

"Robert?" cried Mademoiselle de Keralio.

"They are all at the Cordelier clubhouse, where they are drawing up the call to arms. I come to give you news of them, to tell you there would be nothing to-night, and, to prove you it, I am going to sleep."

Whereupon, he threw himself, dressed as he was, on the bed and, in five minutes, was sleeping as if there was not being decided at this moment, between royalty and the people, a question of life and death.

At one o'clock in the morning, Camille came in.

"I bring you tidings of Robert," said he; "he has gone to the commune to carry our proclamations. Don't be uneasy; it is only for to-morrow, and yet, yet!"

Camille shook his head like a doubting man, and then laid his head on Lucile's shoulder, and in his turn fell into sleep.

He had been asleep about half an hour when there was a ring at the doorbell.

Madame Robert went down and opened the door.

It was her husband.

He came to seek Danton in behalf of the commonalty.

He awoke Danton.

"Let them make shift without me; I want to sleep," said the latter. "It will be daylight to-morrow."

Robert and his wife went out and went home.

Presently, there was ringing again at the front door.

Madame Danton had to go down and open.

She let in a tall young man of about twenty, dressed as a captain in the National Guard; he carried a musket.

"M. Danton?" asked he.

Madame Danton aroused her husband.

"Well, what is it now?" asked the latter.

"Monsieur Danton," said the young man, "you are expected over there."

"Over where?"

"At the commune."

"Who expects me?"

"The commissioners of sections, and especially M. Billot."

"The—very well; tell Billot I will go over," said Danton.

Then, looking at the young man, whose face was unknown to him and who, though so young, bore the insignia of a quite high rank, he said:

"I beg your pardon, officer, but who are you?"

"I am Ange Pitou, sir, captain of the National Guard of Haramont——"

"Ah!"

"One of the takers of the Bastile."

"Good!"

"I got a letter from Monsieur Billot yesterday, which said there was likely to be some rough work here, and that they had need of all good patriots."

"Then?"

"Then, I started with those of my men who were willing to follow me; but, as they were not such good walkers as me, they are at Dammartin. They will be here early to-morrow morning."

"Dammartin?"

"Yes, sir."

"Why, that's eight leagues from here!" exclaimed Danton.

"Yes. M. Danton."

"And how many leagues is Haramont from Paris?"

"Nineteen. We set out at five o'clock this morning."

"Ah! And did you go your nineteen leagues in one day?"

"Yes, M. Danton."

"And you arrived?"

"At ten o'clock at night. I asked for Billot, and was told that he was doubtlessly in the Faubourg Saint Antoine, at Monsieur Santerre's house. I went there, but was told that I would probably find him at the Jacobins, in the Rue Saint Honore; nobody had seen him there, and I was sent to the Cordeliers, and from thence to the city hall——"

"Where you found him?"

"Yes, Monsieur Danton. Then, he gave me your address, and asked me: 'You are not tired, are you, Pitou?' 'No, Monsieur Billot,' says I. 'Well, go tell Danton he is a sluggard, and that we are waiting for him.'"

"Here's a lad makes me ashamed!" cried Danton, jumping off the bed. "Come my friend, come."

He kissed his wife, and went out with Pitou.

His wife uttered a low sigh, and droped her head on the back of her chair.

Lucile thought she was weeping and respected her sorrow.

But, in a few instants' time, seeing that she did not stir, she awoke Camille; then, she went to Madame Danton.

The poor woman had fainted.

The first lines of the dawn struggled through the windows; the day promised to be fine; but, as if it were a forbidding augury, the sky was streaked red as with blood.

CHAPTER XXXIII.

THE NIGHT CONTINUED.

WE have described what occurred in the dwelling of tribunes; let us now tell what was happening some five hundred yards from there, in the abode of kings.

There also were women weeping and praying.

Chateaubriand says, the eyes of princes are formed to contain a great quantity of tears.

Nevertheless, let us render justice to all.

Madame Elizabeth and the Princess de Lamballe wept and prayed; Marie Antoinette prayed, but did not weep.

They had had supper at the usual hour; nothing could deprive Louis the Sixteenth of his meals.

On rising from the table—while Madame Elizabeth and the Princess de Lamballe retired to the room known under the name of the council chamber, where it was arranged that the royal family should pass the night to receive reports, the Queen took the King aside, and tried to lead him away.

" Where would you take me, madame ?" inquired the King.

" To my chamber. Are you not going to put on that shirt of mail which you wore on the 20th of last July, sire ?"

" Madame," returned Louis XVI, " it was well for me to shield myself from the bullet or dagger of an assassin on a day of excitement or conspiracy; but on a day of battle, when my friends expose themselves for me, it would be cowardice for me not to expose myself like them."

Upon which, the speaker left the Queen to go to his apartments, there to shut himself up with his confessor.

The Queen went to join in the council chamber Madame Elizabeth and the Princess de Lamballe.

" What is the King doing ?" inquired the latter lady.

" Confessing," returned Marie Antoinette with an accent beyond description.

At this moment, the door opened and the Count de Charny appeared.

He was pale, but perfectly calm.

" May I have speech of his Majesty ?" he asked, bowing to the Queen.

" For the present, sir, I am the King," responded Marie Antoinette.

Charny knew this better than anybody ; nevertheless, he insisted.

" You may go up to the King's apartments, sir," said the Queen, "but I tell you, you will greatly disturb him."

" I understand ; his Majesty is with Monsieur Petion, who has just arrived ?"

" The King is with his confessor, sir."

" It is, then, to you, Madame," said Charny, " that I am to make my report, as major general of the chateau."

" Yes sir, if you will be so kind," returned the Queen.

" I have the honor to inform your Majesty of the efficiency of our forces. The horse-gendarmes, commanded by Messieurs Rulhieres and de Verdiere, to the number of six hundred, are placed in line of battle on the great square of the Louvre ; the foot-gendarmes of Paris, within the walls, *intra muros*, are in the stables ; a post of one hundred and fifty men have been detached to form, at the Toulouse Mansion, a guard to protect, at need, the extraordinary, accounts and treasury chests ; the foot-gendarmee of Paris, beyond the walls, *extra muros*, composed of thirty men only, are posted by the lesser royal staircase, in the Court of the Princes ; two hundred officers and privates of the former footguards or horseguards, two hundred young royalists, three hundred and fifty or four hundred combatants are gathered in the Œil-de-bœuf and the adjoining halls ; two hundred or three hundred National Guards are scattered in the courtyards or gardens ; lastly, one thousand five hundred Swiss, who are the real strength of the Chateau, are about taking their different posts, being charged to defend the main vestibule and foot of the stairs."

" Well, sir, do not all these measures reassure you ?" inquired the Queen.

" Nothing can set me at ease, madame," replied Charny, " when your Majesty's safety is imperilled."

" Hence, sir, your voice is still for flight ?"

" My advice is, madame, that you should put yourself, the King and your Majesty's august children, in the midst of us."

His hearer started.

" Your Majesty is repugnant to La Fayette—so be it ! But she has confidence in his Highness the Duke de Liancourt, who is at Rouen, madame ; he has there hired the house of an English gentleman named Mr. Channing; the commander of the province has made his men swear fidelity to the King; the Swiss regiment of Salis Samade, on which we may depend, is stationed along the road. All is still quiet; let us leave by the Pont Tournant, reach the Barriere de l'Etoile; three hundred men either of cavalry or the constitutional guard are there awaiting us? five hundred gentlemen can be easily called together at Versailles. With four thousand men I answer for conducting you wherever you like."

"I thank you, Monsieur de Charny," said the Queen; "I appreciate the devotion which has made you part from the persons who are dear to you to come to offer your services to a stranger——"

"Your Majesty is unjust to me," said Charny; "my sovereign's existence will be ever in my eyes the most valuable of all lives, as duty will be always to me the dearest of all virtues."

"Duty, yes, monsieur," murmured the Queen; "but I also, inasmuch as every one is bent on doing his duty, think I understand mine; it is to maintain royalty great and noble, and to ensure that, if it be struck, it be struck erect, and falls worthily, like those ancient gladiators who studied to die gracefully."

"Is this your Majesty's last word?"

"It is my last desire."

The count bowed and, meeting at the door Madame Campan, who was coming to join the princesses, he bade her: "Beg their Highnesses, madame, to put all their valuables they can in their pockets; we may be compelled to quit the palace."

While Madame Campan went to transmit this warning to the Princess de Lamballe and Madame Elizabeth, Charny, approaching the Queen, said:

"Madame, it is impossible that you have not some other hope beyond the support of our material force; if there be such an one, confide it to me; remember that at any hour to-morrow I may have to render an account to God or men of what will have passed."

"Well, sir," rejoined the Queen, "two hundred thousand francs are to have been transmitted to Petion, and fifty thousand to Danton; by means of these two hundred and fifty thousand francs, Danton will be prevailed upon to remain at home, and Petion to come to the palace."

"But, is your Majesty quite sure of your intermediaries?"

"Were you not saying that Petion had arrived a while ago?"

"Yes, madame."

"That is something, as you see."

"It is not enough. I was told that he had been sent for three times before he would come."

"If he is for us," went on the Queen, "he should, while speaking with the King, lay his forefinger on his right eye."

"But, if otherwise, madame?"

"If he is not for us, he will be our prisoner, and I have issued most positive orders that he shall not be let go out of the chateau."

At this moment, there was heard the toll of a bell.

"What's that?" exclaimed the Queen.

"The tocsin," answered Charny.

The princesses rose in alarm.

"Well," said the Queen, "what is the matter? The tocsin is the trumpet of rebels."

"Madame," said Charny, who appeared to be more affected than the Queen by the sinister sound, "I will go and discover whether that alarum denotes anything serious."

"We will see you again?" queried the Queen.

"I will come to put myself under your Majesty's orders, and will not leave her while there is the least shade of danger."

Charny bowed and withdrew.

The Queen was thoughtful for an instant.

"Let us go see if the King has confessed," muttered she.

And she went out.

During this time, Madame Elizabeth was removing some articles of her apparel that she might recline more at her ease on a sofa.

She took off a cornelian pin and showed it to Madame Campan.

It was engraved; the engraving was a bunch of lilies with a motto.

"Read," said Madame Elizabeth.

Madame Campan drew nearer a candlestick, and read:

"Forget offences, and forgive injuries."

"I greatly fear," said the princess, "that this maxim will have little weight over our enemies; but it should be none the less dear to us."

As she concluded these words, a shot rang in the court.

The ladies uttered a scream.

"That is the first shot," said Madame Elizabeth; "alas! it will not be the last!"

The arrival of Petion at the Tuileries had been announced to the Queen. We will describe under what circumstances the Mayor of Paris made his entry.

He had arrived about half past ten.

He was not made to wait this time in an ante-chamber, but was told that the King was waiting for him; only, to reach the King, he had to go through the ranks of the Swiss first, then of the National Guard, next, of those gentlemen styled the Knights of the Dagger.

Nevertheless, as it was known that Louis the Sixteenth had sent for Petion, and that he might have remained in the city hall, his palace, and not have come to that lion's den, the Tuileries, he was let pass with the names of "traitor" and Judas only being flung in his face as he went up the stairs.

Louis the Sixteenth was expecting Petion in the same chamber as that where he had been so rudely treated on the 21st of June.

Petion smiled as he thought of the retribution fortune gave him.

At the door, Mandat, commander of the National Guard, stopped him.

"Is this you, Monsieur le Maire!" said he.

"Yes, sir," returned Petion with his habitual phlegm.

"What are you come to do here?"

"I might dispense with replying to your question, Monsieur Mandat, not acknowledging in you any right to interrogate me; but, as I am hurried, I cannot stop to speak with inferiors——"

"Inferiors!"

"You interrupt me, when I tell you I am in a hurry, Monsieur Mandat. I come because the King has sent for me three times. Of my own will, I would not have come at all."

"Well, since I have the honor to see you, Monsieur le Maire, I ask you wherefore the police administrators of the city have distributed an abundance of cartridges to the five hundred Marsellais, and why I, Mandat, have only had three rounds of ammunition for each of my men?"

"Firstly," said Petion, without losing a jot of his calmness, "no more was asked for at the Tuileries. Three rounds per National Guardsman, forty per Swiss; they have been distributed as the King requested."

"Why this variation in the number?"

"It is for the King, not me, to tell you that, sir; probably, he distrusts the National Guard."

"But I, sir," said Mandat, "have asked powder of you."

"True; unfortunately, you are not allowed to have any."

"A pretty answer!" exclaimed Mandat; "you, then, will not allow it, for you are the one who issued the order."

The discussion was on a subject which it would be difficult for Petion to defend; luckily, the door opened and Rœderer, the syndic of the commune, coming to the aid of the Mayor of Paris, said:

"M. Petion, the King is waiting for you."

Petion entered.

The King, in fact, was impatiently expecting him.

"Ah, you are here, Monsieur Petion," said he. "How is the city of Paris?"

Petion gave him a pretty fair account of the state of things.

"Have you nothing more to tell me, sir?" queried the King.

Petion opened his eyes to their full extent. "No, sir."

Louis regarded Petion steadily.

"Nothing more—absolutely nothing?"

Petion still stared, not understanding the King's persistence.

On his part the latter was waiting for Petion to carry his hand to his eye; this was, it will be borne in mind, the token by which the Mayor of Paris was to indicate that, by the receipt of the two hundred thousand francs, the the King might rely upon him.

Petion pinched his ear, but his finger did not go a line nearer his eye.

Louis had been deceived.

Some swindler had pocketed the two hundred thousand francs.

The Queen entered.

She just came at the juncture when her husband was at a loss as to what question to put to Petion, and when Petion was expecting some new question.

" Well," whispered the Queen, " is he our friend ?"

" No," responded the King, " he has made no sign whatever."

" Let him be our prisoner in that case !"

" May I retire, sire ?" Petion asked.

" For heaven's sake, let him not go !" exclaimed Marie Antoinette.

" No, sir ; in a moment, you shall be free; but I have something more to say to you," added the King, raising his voice. " Withdraw into this cabinet."

This was telling those within the retreat :

" I entrust M. Petion to you, watch over him and do not let him go."

Those thus addressed understood the intimation well enough ; they surrounded Petion.

Happily, Mandat was not there: he was resisting an order which came to him for him to go to the city hall.

The two blades clashed.

Mandat was wanted at the city hall, as Petion at the Tuileries.

Mandat was very repugnant to obey this order and could not decide at the first blush.

As for Petion, he was the thirtieth man in a small box that would not have been roomy for four.

" Gentlemen," said he in an instant, " it is impossible to stay here—we will be suffocated !"

So they all thought, and hence none opposed Petion's departure.

Every one followed him, that was all.

Besides, they did not dare to lay hands on him.

He went down the first flight of stairs he came to.

This led to a room on the ground floor which opened on the garden.

For an instant, he feared that the door to the garden would be fastened ; it was open.

Petion found himself in a more capacious and more airy prison, but one no less enclosed than the former.

Nevertheless, it was an improvement.

A man had followed him who, once they were in the garden, gave him his arm.

This was Rœderer, the procureur syndic of the department.

The two began promenading along the green stretching by the palace ; this lawn was lighted by a line of lamps ; some National Guardsmen came and put out such of them as were in the neighborhood of the mayor and syndic.

What was their intention ?

Petion did not think it a good one.

" Sir," said he to a Swiss officer by name of Salis Lizers who had followed him, " is there anything evil meant against me ?"

" Be easy, Monsieur Petion," returned the officer with a strongly marked German accent ; " de King has bade me watch over you, and 1 will guarantee that whoever kills you will die an instant after by my hand !"

In a similar case, Triboulet the jester had answered Francis the First :

" Wouldn't it be the same to you if he would die an instant before, sire ?"

Petion replied not a word, and walked on to the lawn of the Feuillants, brightly silvered by the moon.

It was not, as at the present day, ended by a grating, but was closed by a wall eight feet high, and with three gates, two small and one large.

These gates were not only locked, but barred ; they were, besides, guarded by the grenadiers of the Butte des Moulins and the Filles Saint Thomas, well known for their loyalty.

Nothing could be hoped from them.

Petion stooped down every now and anon, picked up a pebble, and tossed it over the wall.

While Petion was strolling and throwing these stones, he was twice told that the King wished speech of him.

"Are you not going?" asked Rœderer.

"No," answered Petion, "it is too warm there! I remember the closet, and have not the faintest wish to enter it again; besides, I have got an appointment with somebody."

And he continued to pick up stones and fling them to the other side of the wall.

"Who have you got an appointment with?" inquired Rœderer.

At this moment, the gate of the Assembly which opened on the lawn of the Feuillants was thrown back.

"I think here comes just what I was expecting," said Petion.

"Order to let M. Petion pass!" cried a voice; "the Assembly calls him to its bar for him to render an account of the state of Paris."

"Of course," muttered Petion; adding aloud:

"Here I am, ready to answer the accusations of my enemies."

The National Guards, fancying things were going against Petion, let him pass.

This was close upon three o'clock of the morning; the day was breaking; only — singular fact! — the sky was streaked red as with blood.

––––––

CHAPTER XXXIV.

THE NIGHT CONCLUDED.

PETION, when sent for by the King, was fully aware that he would not be able to leave the palace as easily as he entered; he had stepped up to a man, whose rugged features were seamed by a long scar that ran across his forehead.

"Monsieur Billot," said he, "what was the news you just now brought from the Assembly?"

"That it was going to have a night session."

"Very well. What did you say you saw by the Pont Neuf?"

"Cannon, and National Guards, posted there by order of Mandat."

"And did you not say, also, that, under the Saint Jean arcade, at the opening of the Rue Saint Antoine, a considerable force had assembled?"

"Yes, sir, still by Mandat's order."

"Well, listen, M. Billot."

"I am listening."

"Here is an order for Messieurs Manuel and Danton to dismiss the National Guards at the Saint Jean arcade, and disarm the Pont Neuf; cost what it may, this order must be carried out, do you hear?"

"I will give it to M. Danton from my own hands."

"'Tis well. Now, you dwell in the Rue Saint Honore?"

"Yes, sir."

"When you have given the order to Monsieur Danton, go home and take some rest; then, about two o'clock, rise and walk up and down by the outside of the wall to the lawn of the Feuillants; if you see or hear stones thrown from the Tuileries, it will show I am a prisoner, and that I am threatened with violence."

"I understand."

"Then go you to the bar of the Assembly, and tell my colleagues to claim me. You understand, Monsieur Billot? I place my life in your hands?"

"I will answer for it, sir," said Billot; "go at ease."

Petion then started off, relying on the well known patriotism of Billot.

The latter had promised this all the more boldly from Pitou being at hand.

He despatched Pitou to Danton, telling him not to return without him.

Notwithstanding Danton's sleepiness, Pitou had brought him.

Danton had seen the guns at the Pont Neuf, and the National Guards at the Saint Jean arcade; he felt the urgency of not leaving such forces in the rear of the popular arm.

With Petion's order in his hand, Manuel and he made the National

Guards retire to their barracks and sent away the gunners at the Pont Neuf.

Thus was the high road of insurrection cleared of hindrances.

During this time, Billot and Pitou returned to the Rue Saint Honore, to Billot's former lodging ; Pitou nodded his head to it as to a friend.

Billot sat down, making Pitou a sign to do likewise.

"Thank you, M. Billot," said Pitou, "I am not tired."

But Billot insisted.

Pitou sat down.

"Pitou, I sent for you," began Billot.

"And, you see, Monsieur Billot, that I have not kept you waiting," returned Pitou with that open smile peculiar to him and which showed his thirty-two teeth.

"No. Have you not guessed that something serious was going to happen ?"

"I suspected so," replied Pitou ; "but tell me, Monsieur Billot——"

"What ?"

"I don't see any M. Bailly or M. La Fayette."

"Bailly is a traitor who had us murdered on the Champ de Mars."

"Yes, I know, for it was I who, so to say, picked you up there, bathed in blood."

"La Fayette is a traitor who tries to steal away the King."

"I did not know that. M. de La-Fayette a traitor ! who would have thought it ? And the King ?"

"He is the greatest traitor of all, Pitou."

"Well, that does not astonish me a bit," observed Pitou.

"The King conspires with foreigners, and wants to give up France to the enemy ; the Tuileries is a hot bed of conspiracy, and it has been determined to take the Tuileries. You understand, don't you, Pitou ?"

"Of course, I understand ! We will take it, M. Billot, as we took the Bastile ?"

"Yes."

"Only it won't be so hard."

"That's where you are wrong, Pitou."

"What—is it going to be a tougher job ?"

"Yes."

"Yet it seems to me the walls are not so high."

"Yes ; but they are better guarded. The Bastile had for garrison only about a hundred invalids, while there are three or four thousand men at the chateau."

"The deuce there is ! three or four thousand men !"

"Without reckoning that the Bastile was surprised, while, from the first of the month, the Tuileries suspected that it was going to be attacked, and has been putting itself on its defence."

"So they are going to defend it ?" queried Pitou.

"Yes," answered Billot, "and all the more likely from its being said M. de Charny has been entrusted with the defence."

"Indeed," Pitou resumed, " he traveled yesterday by the post from Boursonnes with his wife. And is M. de Charny also a traitor ?"

"No, he is an aristocrat, that is all ; he has always been for the court and, consequently, has not betrayed the people. inasmuch as he never wheedled the people into trusting him."

"So we are going to fight against M. de Charny ?"

"It is likely, Pitou."

"Ain't it singular ? neighbors ?"

"Yes, it is what is called civil war, Pitou ; but you are not compelled to fight if it does not suit you."

"Excuse me, M. Billot," said Pitou ; " from the moment when it suits you, it suits me too."

"I would much rather that you would not fight, Pitou."

"Why then did you call me to you, M. Billot ?"

The farmer's countenance darkened with a cloud.

"I called you, Pitou, to give you this."

"This paper ?"

"Yes."

"What is it ?"

"A copy of my will."

"Copy of your will ? why, M. Billot," continued Pitou, laughing, " you have not the appearance of a man going to die."

"No," said Billot pointing to his gun and bullet-bag hanging on the wall; "but I have of a man who may be killed."

"The fact is we are all mortal," observed Pitou sententiously.

"Well, Pitou," said Billot, "I have called you to hand you a copy of my will."

"Me, M. Billot?"

"You, Pitou, for, as I make you my whole heir——"

"I, your heir?" echoed Pitou. "No, I thank you, Monsieur Billot! But you tell me this for a laugh."

"I tell you what is, my friend."

"It cannot be, M. Billot"

"How! cannot?"

"Why, no! when a man has heirs, he cannot give away his property to strangers."

"You are wrong, Pitou, he can."

"Then, he should not, M. Billot."

Another cloud swept over Billot's brow.

"I have no heirs," said he.

"You have none?" repeated Pitou. "What do you call Mademoiselle Catherine?"

"I know no person of that name, Pitou."

"Oh, Monsieur Billot, do not say such things—they make me feel bad!"

"Pitou," said Billot, "from the moment when a thing belongs to me, I can give it to whoever I please; in the same way as, if I die, in your turn, as the property will belong to you, Pitou, you can give it to whoever you please."

"Aha! good! yes," said Pitou, who began to understand; "so, if anything should happen—but how stupid I am! nothing evil will happen to you!"

"You just now said, Pitou, we are all mortal."

"Yes, the fact is you are right; I will take the will, M. Billot; but you are sure, supposing I have the misfortune to become your heir, I will have the right to do whatever I like with your property?"

"Of course, for it will be yours. And they won't try to cheat you, a sound patriot, you understand, Pitou?

as they would such persons who have had connection with aristocrats."

Pitou understood clearer and clearer.

"Well, as things stand thus, M. Billot," said he, "I accept."

"Then, as that is all I have got say to you, put this paper in your pocket, and rest yourself."

"Why, M. Billot?"

"Because, according to every likelihood, we will have work to morrow, or rather this day for it is nearly two o'clock in the morning".

"Are you going out of doors, Monsieur Billot?"

"Yes."

"May I know——"

"Certainly, I have some business at the Feuillants."

"You've no need of me?"

"No, you would rather be in my way."

"In that case, Monsieur Billot, I will eat a bit."

"It is true," exclaimed Billot, "I forgot to ask you if you were hungry."

"Oh!" said Pitou, laughing, "that's because you know I am always hungry."

"I need not tell you where is the larder—"

"No, no, Monsieur Billot, don't trouble yourself about me. You are coming back, ain't you?"

"I shall return."

"Otherwise, you would have to tell me where I should meet you."

"Useless; in an hour, I shall be here."

"Well, go!"

Whereupon, Pitou began his search for food with that appetite which, in him as in Louis Sixteenth, was never affected by events, however serious they might be, while Billot went on his way to the lawn of the Feuillants.

We know what he did there.

Hardly had he reached the spot, when a stone rolling to his feet was followed by a second, that by a third; all telling him that what Petion feared had occurred, and that the mayor was prisoner at the Tuileries.

He had immediately, pursuant to instructions, presented himself at the Assembly, which as we have seen, had claimed Petion.

Petion freed had merely to cross the Assembly hall, and to return on foot to the city hall, leaving, to represent him, his coach in the Courtyard of the Tuileries.

On his part, Billot went home, where he found Pitou finishing his supper.

" Well, Monsieur Billot, is there anything new ?" inquired Pitou.

"Nothing," returned Billot, " save that day is breaking, and the sky is red as blood."

CHAPTER XXXV.

FROM THREE TO SIX O'CLOCK IN THE MORNING.

OUR readers have seen what aspect presented the dawning day.

Its first beams fell upon two horsemen who were riding along the deserted quai of the Tuileries.

These two men were Mandat, the commanding general of the National Guard, and his aid-de-camp.

Mandat — summoned at about one o'clock of the morning to the city hall —had at first refused to obey.

At two o'clock, the order was renewed and more imperatively.

Mandat still resisted, but the syndic Rœderer had approached him and said :

"Sir, pay attention that by the terms of the law the commander of the National Guard is at the orders of the city government."

Mandat had thereupon made up his mind.

Besides, the commanding general was ignorant of two things.

Firstly, that forty-seven sections out of forty-eight had joined to the municipality each three commissioners whose mission was to meet at the commune, and " save the country."

Mandat thought he would there find the old government composed of the same as it had formerly had, and did in no respect dream of meeting a hundred and forty-one new faces.

Next, Mandat was unaware of the order issued by this same municipality to disarm the Pont Neuf and have the Saint Jean arcade evacuated ; an order of the execution of which, on account of its importance, Manuel and Danton themselves had been personally overseers.

Hence, on arriving at the Pont Neuf, Mandat was stupefied to see it completely deserted. He stopped and sent his aid-de-camp on a reconnoissance.

At the end of ten minutes' time the officer returned, he had seen neither National Guards nor cannon ; the Place Dauphin, the Rue Dauphin and the Quay des Augustins were as untenanted as the Pont Neuf.

Mandat continued his road.

Perhaps he would rather have returned to the chateau ; but men go whither destiny urges them.

In proportion to his advance towards the city hall, he seemed to proceed into life ; in like manner as in certain organic cataclysms, the blood, retiring towards the heart, leaves the extremities, which become white and chilled, so was motion, heat, revolution in a word, on the Quai Pelletier, the Place de Greve, in the city hall, the real seat of popular life, the heart of the great body, Paris.

Mandat stopped at the corner of the Quai Pelletier, and sent his aid de-camp to the Saint Jean arcade.

Through this arcade went and came freely the popular stream.

The National Guards had disappeared.

Mandat wanted now to retrace his steps.

But the crowd had massed behind him, and pushed him, like the tide a boat, to the steps of the city hall.

"Stay here," he said to his attendant, " and, if anything evil befal me, go give the chateau warning."

Mandat yielded to the press which bore him away.

The aid-de-camp, whose uniform denoted him to be but of secondary importance, remained at the corner of the Quai Pelletier, where nobody interested himself in him ; all eyes were fastened on the commanding general.

On arriving at the main hall of the city hall, Mandat found himself confronting stern, unknown countenances.

It was the whole insurrection ready to demand an account of this conduct of the man who had not only wished to fight it in its developement, but, moreover, to strangle it in its birth.

At the Tuileries, he had questioned; the reader will recollect his scene with Petion.

Here, he was going to be questioned.

One of the members of the new commune—which was the terrible one which overcame the Legislative Assembly and coped with the Convention—stepped forward, and, in the name of all, asked :

" By order of whom did you double the guard at the chateau ?"

" By order of the Mayor of Paris," was Mandat's reply.

" Where is this order ?"

" At the Tuileries, where I left it, in order that it might be executed during my absence."

" Why did you order out the batteries ?"

" Because I paraded the battalions and, when they march, the cannon go with them."

" Where is Petion ?"

" He was at the chateau when I left that place."

" A prisoner ?"

" No, free, and walking in the garden."

At this juncture, the interrogation was interrupted.

A member of the new commune brought in a broken-sealed letter, and demanded that it should be read aloud.

Mandat had only need to fling his eyes on the letter to tell that he was lost.

He had recognized his own handwriting.

This letter was his order sent, at one o'clock in the morning, to the commander of the battalion posted at the Saint Jean arcade, and enjoining on him to attack in the rear the mob marching on the palace, while the Pont Neuf battalion charged them by the flank.

This order had fallen into the hands of the commune after the withdrawal of the force.

The interrogation was over.

What avowal could they gain from the accused, that would be more damning than this letter ?

The council decided that Mandat should be conducted to the Abbaye prison. Then the sentence was read to Mandat.

Here commenced the interpretation.

While reading the sentence, the president, we are assured, made with his hand one of those gestures which the people unfortunately know too well how to interpret—a horizontal wave or drawing of the hand.

" The president," says Peltier, author of the " Revolution of the 10th of August, 1792," "made a very expressive horizontal gesture while saying :

" ' Let him be taken away ! ' "

This gesture would have been, indeed, a very expressive one a year later ; but such a motion, which had great signification in 1793, could not have meant much in 1792, when the guillotine was not as yet at work ; it was on the 21st of August that fell the head of the first royalist on the Square of the Carrousel ; how, eleven days previously, could a horizontal gesture (unless it was a sign agreed upon beforehand) mean :

" Kill this gentleman ?"

Unfortunately the result seems to justify the accusation.

Hardly had Mandat descended three steps of the stairs of the city hall, than at the moment when his son ran to meet him, a pistol shot fractured the prisoner's skull.

(The same event happened, three years before, to Fesselles.)

Mandat was only wounded, he rose, but fell the next moment pierced by twenty pike thrusts.

The boy threw up his arms and called :

" Father ! father !"

Not the least attention was paid to the boy :

Presently, in that circle where were to be seen arms lifted among the gleaming swords and spears, rose a blood-dripping head severed from the trunk.

It was Mandat's.

His son swooned.

The aid-de camp set off at a gallop

to announce at the Tuileries what he had seen.

The assassins parted into two bands.

One went to fling the body into the river; the other to parade, at the point of a pike, Mandat's head through the streets of Paris.

This was at about four o'clock in the morning.

Let us precede at the Tuileries the aid-de-camp who rode with this fatal intelligence, and let us see what is going on there.

The King having confessed—and, from the moment when his conscience was at ease, he was nearly re-assured as to anything happening—he had gone to bed, for he knew not how to withstand the demands of nature. It is true he went to sleep dressed.

On a doubling of the alarum bells and the rattling thunder of drums beginning to beat, the royal sleeper was aroused.

The person who awoke the King—de la Chesnaye, to whom Mandat on departing, had handed his powers—did so to show the King to the National Guard, and by his presence and by a few seasonable words, to revive their enthusiasm.

Louis rose, with heavy head, staggering, hardly awake; his powdered head, on one side of which he had lain, had lost the powder on that side.

The hair-dresser was sent for—he was not at hand.

The King left his room just as he was.

The Queen, informed, in the council chamber where she was staying, ran to meet her husband.

Quite the opposite from the poor monarch, with his dull look resting on no one, with the muscles of his mouth distended and twitching with involuntary movements, in his violet suit which gave him the air of wearing the mourning of royalty—the Queen was colorless, but burning with fever; her eyes were red, but dry.

She was attached to that species of monarchical phantom which, instead of appearing at midnight, showed itself in broad day-light with its fat, heavy, blinking eyes.

She hoped to give him the superabundance she had of courage, strength, and life.

All went well, indeed, when the royal exhibition remained in the apartments, although the National Guards, mingled with the noblemen, seeing the King so closely—that heavy, awkward man who had so poorly succeeded on a similar situation, on the balcony of Sauce's house at Varennes—began to ask whether this was the hero of the twentieth of June, the King whose poetical legend priests and women were beginning to embroider on funereal crape.

It must be acknowledged that this was not the King whom the National Guard expected to see.

Just at this moment, the old Duke de Mailly—with one of those good intentions destined to form a fresh paving stone for hell—drew his sword, and, coming to kneel at the King's feet, swore in a tremulous voice to die, he and the *nobility* of France, which he represented, for the *descendant of Henry IV.*

Here were two mistakes instead of one.

The National Guard had no great sympathy for this "nobility of France" which the Duke de Mailly represented; and it was no "descendant of Henry IV." that they came to defend, but "the constitutional King."

Therefore, in reply to several cries of "Long live the King!" shouts burst forth on all sides of:

"The nation forever!"

They had to take their revenge for this.

They urged the King to go down into the Cour Royale.

Alas, this poor monarch, disturbed in his meals, having slept one hour instead of seven, a nature wholly material, had no longer any will in him: he was an automaton receiving its impulsion from an external power.

Who gave him this impulse?

The Queen, nervous nature, who had neither eaten not slept.

There are beings wretchedly constituted who, once circumstances are above them, fail or at least poorly succeed in what they undertake.

Instead of drawing to him the dissenters, Louis XVI., on approaching them, seemed coming expressly to exhibit to them how little royalty can lend to a man, when that man has neither genius nor power in him.

Here, as in the rooms, when the royalists uttered a few cries of " Long live the King !" the answer was an immense shout of :

" The nation forever !"

As the royalists had the foolishness to insist, the patriots said :

" No, no ! no other King than the nation !"

The King, almost suppliant, replied to them :

" Yes, my children, the nation and your sovereign make and are but one !"

" Bring the Dauphin here," whispered Marie Antoinette to Madame Elizabeth; " perhaps the sight of a child will touch them."

Search was made for the prince.

During this time, Louis the Sixteenth continued the sad review ; he had the idea of going to the artillerymen.

This was a fault ; they were nearly all republicans.

If he had known how to speak, how to make men listen to him whose convictions were against him, it would have been a courageous act which might have succeeded ; but there was nothing winning in either Louis the Sixteenth's speech or gestures. He stammered.

The royalists tried to cover his hesitation by trying again that silly shout of " Long live the King !" which had twice already failed ; this cry nearly caused a collision.

Some cannoneers left their places and, rushing up to Louis at whom they shook their fists, they said :

" Do you think that, to defend a traitor like you, we are going to fire on our brothers ?"

The Queen drew her husband back.

" The Dauphin !" cried many voices ; " Long live the Dauphin !"

No one repeated the cry.

The poor boy had arrived out of season ; had missed his entry, as they say in theatrical terms.

The King returned towards the chateau.

It was a real retreat, almost a flight.

On reaching his room the King fell out of breath into an armchair.

The Queen, remaining by the door, was sweeping her eyes around her, looking for support from some one.

She perceived Charny standing, leaning against the jamb of the door of her apartment ; she went to him.

" Ah, sir, all is lost !" she exclaimed.

" I fear so, madame," returned the count.

" May we not still flee ?"

" It is too late, madame,"

" What is there left for us to do, then ?"

" To die !" responded the Count de Charny, bowing.

Marie Antoinette uttered a sigh, and entered her room.

END OF VOLUME ONE.

ANDRÉE DE TAVERNEY:

OR, THE

DOWNFALL OF FRENCH MONARCHY.

ANDRÉE DE TAVERNEY:

OR, THE

DOWNFALL OF FRENCH MONARCHY.

BEING THE FINAL CONCLUSION OF

"THE MEMOIRS OF A PHYSICIAN," "THE QUEEN'S NECKLACE," "SIX YEARS LATER," AND "COUNTESS OF CHARNY."

BY ALEXANDER DUMAS.

AUTHOR OF "THE COUNT OF MONTE CRISTO," "THREE GUARDSMEN," "TWENTY YEARS AFTER," "BRAGELONNE," "THE IRON MASK," "LOUISE LA VALLIERE," ETC., ETC.

TRANSLATED FROM THE ORIGINAL FRENCH EXPRESSLY FOR THIS EDITION,

BY HENRY L. WILLIAMS, ESQ.

VOLUME TWO.

Translator's Notice of the Work.

"Andrée de Taverney" is the fit conclusion of the great series to which it belongs. Not a few other writers have taken incidents from the reign of the Sixteenth Louis, and wrought books upon them, but this work of Alexander Dumas alone has comprised the whole drama of the downfall of French monarchy, whose last scene beheld the fogs of passion roll away from before it to reveal the unknown form of the guillotine!

All is wonder how the throne of the beautiful Marie Antoinette could ever have crumbled, till one here sees the motive thoughts of the revolutionists When some of them acted through love of liberty, many, like Billot, by a thirst of revenge for injury, a still greater number from hate, poverty and evil instincts—how could royalists—though every one a Charny or an Andrée de Taverney—hope to maintain it?

We form the acquaintance of how many in this book? The King, the Queen; Oliver de Charny, dying beneath the axes and pikes of the sans-culottes, gasping: "For the Queen I'm dying, as fell my brothers!" Then, Andrée, his wife, who would not save her life with silence, when that silence might cast doubt on her opinions; the repentant Gilbert; Catherine Billot, "widow without having been wife," the good, simple Pitou, whom all must like, and Billot, the inflexible patriot. Then, the country scenes form that repose for the mind, which may be over-excited by the bloody scenes of city riots One turns gladly from the storming of the Tuileries, by the mob, to the quiet, natural pictures of provincial life; from the gory, streaming locks of heads borne amid yells on pikes, to the seas of verdure of the forest, where a sweet-smelling breeze murmurs sleepily; from the spirited speeches from the rostrum—through which winds Robespierre's "hush!" like a serpent's hiss—to the revolution in miniature at Villers Cotterets. Andrée de Taverney will prove to be Dumas' greatest book, and must have a sale unparalleled in the annals of literature.

Fredonia Books
Amsterdam, The Netherlands

Andrée de Taverney:
The Downfall of French Monarchy
(Volume Two)

by
Alexander Dumas

ISBN: 1-4101-0060-X

CONTENTS

CONTENTS.

(17)

EPILOGUE.

ANDRÉE DE TAVERNEY.

BY ALEXANDRE DUMAS.

AUTHOR OF "MONTE CRISTO," "THE THREE GUARDSMEN," "BRAGELONNE," "THE COUNTESS DE CHARNY," "MOHICANS OF PARIS," &c.

TRANSLATED FROM THE FRENCH,

BY HENRY L. WILLIAMS, Jr.

CHAPTER I.

FROM SIX TO NINE O'CLOCK IN THE MORNING.

HARDLY had Mandat been slain than the commune nominated Santerre in his stead, and Santerre had instantly had drums beaten in all the streets, and had issued an order for the alarum to be loudly rung in all the churches; then, he had organized patriot patrols with orders to push forward to the Tuileries, and especially to watch around the Assembly.

The patriots, however, had all night been scouring the environs of the Assembly.

At about ten o'clock in the evening, they had arrested on the Champs Elysees a gathering of eleven armed persons, ten with daggers and pistols, the eleventh with a gun.

These eleven let themselves be taken without resistance, and were shut up in the Feuillants.

During the rest of the night, eleven other prisoners were made.

They were put in separate rooms.

At daybreak, the first eleven had found means to escape by jumping out of their window into the garden, and by breaking through the gates of this garden.

Eleven, therefore, remained, more securely confined.

At seven o'clock of the morning, there was led into the courtyard of the Feuillants a young man of from twenty-nine to thirty years, in the uniform and with the cap of a National Guardsman. The newness of this uniform, the fineness of his weapons, and the elegance of his bearing made it be suspected that he was an aristocrat, and this had brought on his arrest. However, he was very self-possessed.

One named Bonjour, formerly a clerk at the Navy Department, on this day presided at the section of the Feuillants.

He examined the National Guardsman.

"Where were you arrested?" he began.

"On the lawn of the Feuillants," replied the prisoner.

"What were you doing there?"

"I was going to the palace of the Tuileries."

"What for?"

"In order to obey an order of the municipality."

"What said the order?"

"I was ordered to ascertain the true state of affairs, and make my report to the general procureur syndic of the department."

"Have you this order?"

"I have."

"Where is it?"

"Here."

The young man pulled a paper from his pocket.

The president unfolded the paper and read :

"The National Guard bearer of the present order will go to the chateau to ascertain the true state of affairs, and will make his report to M. le procureur general syndic du department.

    "BOIRE,   } *city officers.*"
    "LE ROULX, }

The order was positive ; nevertheless, as it was feared that the signatures were counterfeit, a man was sent to the city hall to discover whether all was right.

This last accusation had collected quite a throng in the court of the Feuillants, and, amongst the multitude, several voices—there are always such voices in popular concourses—began to cry out for the death of the prisoners.

A commissary of the municipality who happened to be there, felt that it would not do to let such voices gain the upper hand.

He mounted a trestle to harangue the crowd and urge it to break up.

At the moment when his hearers were perhaps going to yield to the influence of his merciful speech, the man despatched to the city hall for the verification of the signatures of the two municipals returned, saying the order was real and that the bearer, Suleau, might be set at liberty.

This Suleau was the same man whom we saw during that evening at the mansion of the Princess de Lamballe, when Gilbert made for King Louis the Sixteenth a sketch of the guillotine, and when Marie Antoinette recognized, in that strange instrument, the unknown machine which Cagliostro had shown to her in a glass at the Chateau of Taverney.

At this name, a woman in the crowd raised her head and uttered an angry scream.

"Suleau !" cried she ; "Suleau, the chief editor of the 'Acts of the Apostles ?' Suleau, one of the murderers of the independence of Liege ? I ask for Suleau's death !"

The assemblage parted to give way to this woman, dressed as an amazon in the colors of the National Guard ; armed with a sword which was slung by a shoulder-belt ; she advanced towards the commissary of the municipality, forced him to descend from his elevation, and mounted it in his place.

Hardly was her head above the throng, than from it burst a single cry :

"Theroigne !"

Indeed, Theroigne was the most popular woman of the day ; her cooperation on the fifth and sixth of October, her arrest at Brussels, her stay in Austrian prisons, her aggression of the twentieth of June, had earned her so great a popularity that Suleau, in his sarcastic paper, had given her as lover the citizen *Populus,* in other words, the whole people.

There was in this a double allusion to Theroigne's popularity and the ease of her manners which were asserted to be very excessive.

Besides, Suleau had edited, at Brussels, the Tocsin of Kings, and had thus aided in crushing out the revolt of Liege, and putting under the Austrian sceptre and a priestly mitre a people striving to be free and French.

At this period, Theroigne was writing an account of her arrest, and had already read several chapters to the Jacobins.

She demanded not only Suleau's death, but the death of the eleven other captives with him.

Suleau heard this voice which, amid applause, clamored for his death and his companions ; he called through the door to the commander of the post guarding him.

This force was composed of two hundred men of the National Guard.

"Let me go out," said he, " I will call out my name—I will be killed, and all will be over ; my death will save eleven lives."

They refused to open the door to him.

He tried to jump out of the window.

His companions pulled him back and held him.

They could not believe that they

would be coldly handed over to butchers.

They were in error.

President Bonjour, intimidated by the shouts of the mob, granted Theroigne's claim and forbade the National Guards resisting the people's will.

The National Guards obeyed, and, stepping aside opened the door.

The mob pressed into the prison, and took at random the first comer.

This was a priest named Bouyon, a dramatic author equally known by the epigrams of "Cousin Jacques" and by the failures which three quarters of his pieces had experienced at the Montansier Theatre. He was a colossal man; torn from the arms of the municipal commissary, who tried to save him, he was dragged into the yard, where he began against his murderers a desperate struggle; although he had no other weapon than his fists, two or three of the cut-throats were disabled by him.

A bayonet thrust pinned him to the wall; he died thus without being able to reach his enemies with his last blows.

During this struggle two of the prisoners made out to escape.

The one who succeeded Abbe Bouyon was a former royal guardsman, Solminiac; his defence was no less vigorous than his predecessor's; his death no more cruel.

A third one was slaughtered whose name remains unknown.

Suleau came fourth.

"There, there's your Suleau for you!" called out a woman to Theroigne.

Theroigne did not know Suleau by sight; she also thought him to be a priest, and called him Abbe Suleau.

Like a tiger cat, she flew at him and took him by the throat.

Suleau was young, brave, and active; with a blow of his fist, he dashed Theroigne ten paces from him, shook off, by a violent effort, the three or four men who had grasped him, tore a sabre from the grip of one of his assassins and, with the first two cuts of it, brought a couple of the foremost to the ground.

Then began a dreadful contest.

All the while gaining ground, continually nearing the door, Suleau three times swept a clear space around him; he reached the door; but, obliged to stop to open it, he was for an instant defenceless against the cut-throats.

That instant sufficed for a score of blades to be run through his body.

He fell at the feet of Theroigne, who had the cruel delight of making his last wound.

While Suleau thus fought against the mob, a third prisoner had found means of flight.

The fifth, who appeared dragged out of the guardhouse by the murderers, made the throng utter a cry of admiration.

He was formerly one of the royal bodyguard, by the name of Vigier, who was styled the "handsome Vigier."

As he was as stouthearted as handsome, as active as brave, he held out for more than a quarter of an hour, fell thrice, rose each time, and sprinkled every paving stone with his or his assailants' blood.

Like Suleau, at last he was crushed by numbers.

The death of the four others was a mere butchery; their names are unknown.

The nine bodies were dragged to the Place Vendome, where their heads were struck off; then these heads, stuck on pikes, were paraded through Paris.

In the evening, a servant of Suleau bought his master's head and managed, by dint of search, to recover his body.

Poor Suleau had married, only two months before, a charming woman, the daughter of a celebrated painter, Adele Hal.

It was this good wife, who sought these precious remains to render them the last duties.

Thus, before the actual contest had broken out, blood was spilt at two places: on the steps of the city hall; in the yard of the Feuillants.

We are going to see it flow at the Tuileries presently.

After the drop, the brook; after the brook, the river!

As this slaughter was being perpetrated, between eight and nine o'clock in the morning, ten or eleven thousand

National Guards, called together by the alarum of Barbaroux and Santerre's drums, descended the Rue Saint Antoine, went through the Saint Jean arcade, so well guarded the preceding night, and marched on the Place de Greve.

These ten thousand men came to get the order to march on the Tuileries.

For an hour they were made to wait.

Two versions circulated in the assemblage:

The first, that concessions were hoped for from the chateau.

The second, that the Faubourg Saint Marceau was not ready, and that no march should be made without it.

A thousand men with pikes waxed impatient; as it always is, the worst armed were the most eager.

They forced through the ranks of the National Guard, saying they were going to be the first, and would take the chateau single-handed.

Some federals from Marseilles and ten or a dozen French Guardsmen—the same French Guards who, three years before, had taken the Bastile—put themselves at their head and were hailed as leaders.

This was the vanguard of the insurrection.

Meanwhile, the aid-de-camp who had seen Mandat murdered, had galloped to the Tuileries with slackened rein; but it was not until the moment when, after that damaging walk in the courts, the King went back to his room and the Queen to hers, that he was enabled to see them and imparted to them the mournful intelligence.

The Queen felt what everybody would feel to whom would be announced the news of the death of a man with whom one had just parted; she could not believe it; she had the scene repeated over again, and yet a third time in all its details.

During this time, the noise of a brawl ascended to the first floor and came in at the open windows.

The gendarmes, National Guards and patriotic gunners—such as had cried: "The nation forever!" in short —began to banter the royalists by styling them "those gentlemen, the royal grenadiers," saying that the grenadiers of Filles Saint Thomas and the Butte des Moulins were men sold to the court and, as they were still ignorant below of the death of the commanding general, already known on the first floor, a grenadier shouted out:

"Decidedly, that rascally Mandat has sent nobody to the chateau but aristocrats!"

Mandat's elder son was in the ranks of the National Guard.

We have seen where was the younger; who had uselessly endeavored to defend his father on the steps of the city hall.

On this insult made to his absent father the elder brother rushed out of the ranks, with uplifted sword.

Three or four cannoneers rushed to him.

Weber, the Queen's valet, was, as a National Guard, among the grenadiers of Saint Roche. He flew to the young man's help.

The swords clashed; the quarrel was spreading between the two parties.

The Queen, attracted to the window by the uproar, saw Weber.

She called Thierry, the King's valet-de-chambre, and ordered him to go for her foster brother, Weber.

He came up and told her the whole story.

The Queen told him of Mandat's death.

The noise still continued under the windows.

"See what is going on, Weber," said the Queen.

"The gunners are leaving their pieces! they have rammed home a ball, and, as the guns are not loaded, they are now disabled!"

"What do you think of all this, my poor Weber?"

"I think," replied the good Austrian, "that your Majesty ought to consult Monsieur Rœderer, who appears to me to be one of the most devoted followers you have in the chateau."

"Yes, but where can I speak to him without being overheard, spied over, interrupted?"

"In my apartment, if your Majesty deigns," said Thierry.

"Very well," said the Queen.

"Go find Monsieur Rœderer," said she, turning to her foster brother, "and bring him to M. Thierry's room."

While Weber went out alone by one door, the Queen left by another, following Thierry.

Nine o'clock rang from the chateau clock.

CHAPTER II.

FROM NINE O'CLOCK TO NOON.

WHEN one is treating of a point of history as important as that at which we have now arrived, no detail should be omitted, as long as they are bound to one another, and as the exact joining of all such minutiæ forms the breadth and length of the canvas unrolled before the eyes of the Future, under the eyes of the Past.

At the moment when Weber was going to inform the syndic of the commune that the Queen wished speech of him, the Swiss Captain Durler went up to the King to ask him or the major general for the last orders.

Charny saw the captain looking for some usher or valet-de-chambre who would introduce him to the King.

"What do you wish, captain?" he asked him.

"Are you not the major general?" counter-queried Captain Durler.

"Yes, captain."

"I come to receive the final orders, sir, inasmuch as the head of the insurrectionary column is in sight on the Carrousel."

"You have been told not to give way, sir, the King being decided to die among us."

"Rest easy, sir major," replied Captain Durler.

He went to carry this order to his comrades; it was their death warrant.

In truth, as Captain Durler had said, the vanguard of the insurrection began to appear.

They were those thousand men, armed with pikes, at the head of whom marched a score of Marseillais and a dozen or fifteen French Guardsmen; in the ranks of these latter shone the golden epaulets of a young captain.

This young captain was Pitou, who, recommended by Billot, had been charged with a mission which we shall know all about presently.

Behind this vanguard came, at the distance of an eighth of a league, a considerable body of National Guards and federals, preceded by a battery of twelve guns.

The Swiss, when the major general's order was communicated to them, silently and resolutely took each his place, preserving a cold, gloomy silence.

The National Guards, less strictly disciplined, made ready with more noise and disorder but with equal resolution.

The gentlemen, without any organization, having only weapons of short reach, such as swords or pistols, knowing well that a duel to the death was imminent, beheld, with a kind of feverish intoxication, the moment draw nigh when they were to be in contact with the people—that eternal athlete, that ever-vanquished wrestler, and yet increasing in power during eight centuries!

While the besieged, or those who were going to be besieged, were taking their posts, there was knocking at the door of the Cour Royale, and, while a white handkerchief on the point of a pike was waved above the wall, several voices cried:

"Parley!"

Rœderer was sought for.

He was met, coming that way.

"There is knocking on the Cour Royale gate, sir," said some.

"I have heard it, and come."

"What must be done?"

"Open."

The order was transmitted to the doorkeeper, who unfastened the gate and took to his heels.

Rœderer found himself face to face with the vanguard of pikemen.

"My friends," said he, "you have asked that this gate should be opened to one man for a parley, and not to an army. Where is your speaker?"

"Here he is, sir," said Pitou with his gentle voice and kind smile.

" Who are you ?"

" I am Captain Ange Pitou, of the federals of Haramont."

Rœderer did not know who the " federals of Haramont " were ; but, as time was valuable, he did not deem it necessary for him to inquire.

' What do you want ?" he demanded.

" I want passage for myself and my friends."

Pitou's friends in tatters brandished their pikes, and by other actions appeared to be very dangerous enemies.

" Passage ? why ?"

" We must go and blockade the Assembly. We have twelve cannon ; not one shall be fired if what we want is done."

" What's that ?"

" We want the forfeiture of the King."

" Sir, this is serious," said Rœderer.

" Very serious, yes, sir," responded Pitou with his accustomed politeness.

" It deserves deliberation over it."

" So it does," chimed in Pitou.

Looking up at the chateau clock, he said :

" It wants a quarter of ten ; we will give you to ten ; if, when ten o'clock strikes, we get no answer from you, we will attack."

" Meanwhile, will you not allow the gate to be closed ?"

" Of course."

Addressing his acolytes, Pitou said :

" My friends, let this gate be closed."

And he signed the foremost of the pikemen to fall back.

They obeyed.

The gate was closed without difficulty.

But, thanks to its having been open for an instant, the besiegers had been enabled to view the formidable preparation made to receive them.

When the gate was closed, Pitou's men were greatly of a mind to keep on parleying.

Some of them climbed upon their comrades' shoulders, from thence mounted the wall, which they bestrode, and began talking with the National Guard.

The National Guard shook hands with them and conversed.

Thus was spent tne quarter of an hour.

Then, a man came from the chateau, and gave an order for the gate to be opened.

This time, as the porter had shut himself up in his lodge, the National Guards lifted the bars.

The besiegers fancied that their request had been granted ; the instant the gate was flung open, they pressed in like men who had been kept waiting a long while and were now pushed forward by powerful hands, that is to say, like a crowd, calling loudly to the Swiss, putting hats on the ends of sabres and bayonets and shouting :

" The nation forever ! the National Guard forever ! Long live the Swiss !"

The National Guards answered to the shouts of :

" The nation forever !"

The Swiss presented a profound, sombre silence.

At the cannon's mouth only did the assailants stop and look before and around them.

The main vestibule was full of Swiss, ranked in three lines ; one row, moreover, was on each step of the stairs, which allowed six ranks to fire at the same time.

Some of the insurgents began to reflect, and in the number of these was Pitou.

It was a little late for reflection.

However, this always happens thus in similar circumstances with the mob, whose principal characteristic is being like a child, now good, now cruel.

On seeing the danger, it had not for a moment the idea of fleeing ; but it tried to work around and joke with the Swiss and National Guards.

The National Guards were not far from joking with them themselves, but the Swiss kept their gravity ; for, five minutes before the appearance of the insurrectionary vanguard, the following happened :

As we have related in the foregoing chapter, the patriot National Guard, in the sequel of the quarrel arising about Mandat, had separated from the royalist National Guards, and, on parting with their fellow citizens, they had, at the same time, bidden farewell to the Swiss, whose courage they esteemed and pitied.

They had added that they would receive in their houses, as brothers, such of the Swiss as would follow them.

Thereupon, two Vaudois, replying to this appeal made in their own language, had quitted their ranks, and had come to throw themselves into the arms of the French, their real companions.

But, at the same instant, two shots had been fired from the chateau windows and the bullets had struck the deserters in the very arms of their new friends.

The Swiss officers, excellent marksmen, hunters of izards and chamois, had found this means of cutting short desertion.

This act, as may well be thought, had made the other Swiss serious even to muteness.

As for the men who had been introduced into the courtyard, armed with old pistols, rusty guns and new pikes, in other words, worse armed than if they had had no arms at all, they were the strange forerunners of revolution who are to be seen at the head of all great outbreaks, and who run, laughs on their lips, to open the abyss wherein is to be engulfed a throne—more than a throne at times: a monarchy !

The gunners had come over to them, the National Gnards were ready to do so ; they tried to make the Swiss do likewise.

They did not notice that time was passing, that their leader Pitou had given Rœderer until ten o'clock, and that it was quarter after ten already.

They were amusing themselves ; why should they count the minutes?

One of them had, not a pike, gun or sword, but a hooked pole like the crook gardeners use to pull branches to them which they want to cut.

Said he to his neighbor :

"Suppose I fish for a Swiss !"

"Fish away," said his neighbor.

The pole-man hooked a Swiss by his belt and drew him towards him.

The Swiss resisted just so that he might say he did not go willingly.

"I've a bite !" said the fisher.

"Then haul him in slowly," said his neighbor.

The fisherman pulled gently, and the Swiss was brought through the vestibule to the court, like a fish landed from the river to the bank.

This took place amid loud clamor and bursts of merriment.

"Another, another !" was the cry from all sides.

The man with the hook fastened on another Swiss and out he came like the other.

After this second, came a third, a fourth, and a fifth.

The whole regiment might have thus passed, if it had not been given the order :

"Take aim !"

On seeing the guns being levelled with the regular clank and mechanical precision accompanying this movement in regular troops, one of the mob—there is always in such circumstances, some madman who gives the signal of massacre—one of the mob, we repeat, fired a pistol shot at one of the chateau windows.

During the short interval which, in the manœuvres, separates the words : "Take aim !" from the word : "Fire !" Pitou guessed all that was to transpire.

"Down on the ground !" cried he to his men ; "down on the ground, or you are all dead men."

With that, suiting the action to the word, he flung himself flat on his face.

But, before his advice had had time to be followed, the word "Fire !" rang through the vestibule, which was filled with a blaze and smoke, spitting out, like a giant's blunderbuss, a hail of bullets.

Half the column, perhaps, had entered the courtyard.

The compact mass swayed like the wheat of a field bent by the blast, then like the grain compassed by a sweep of the scythe, then it heaved, and sank.

Hardly a third had been left alive !

This portion fled, passing through the fires of both sides and under the one in their rear.

The soldiers would have killed one another if they had not had so thick a screen of men between them.

This screen fell away in broad patches.

Four hundred men lay stretched on the pavement.

Three hundred had been slain outright!

The other hundred, more or less severely wounded, were groaning, trying to rise, falling back, giving to certain parts of that field of corpses a motion like that of a calming sea, horrible to look upon!

Gradually, all was quieted and, apart from some obstinate revolutionists who persisted in living, all fell back into immobility.

The fugitives spread over the Carrousel, rushing one way over the quais, on the other into the Rue Saint Honoré, shouting:

" Murder !"

When near the Pont Neuf, they met the main body of the army.

This was commanded by two mounted men followed by one on foot who seemed, although without a horse, to share in the command.

" Monsieur Santerre !" cried the fugitive, recognizing in one of the two men on horseback, the brewer of the Faubourg Saint Antoine, remarkable from his colossal stature, to which his enormous Flemish horse served as fit pedestal, " Help, Monsieur Santerre ! they are killing our brothers !"

" Who ?" queried Santerre.

" The Swiss ! they shot at us, while *we were kissing their cheeks* !"

Santerre turned to the second rider.

" What do you think of this, sir ?" he asked him.

" I think," returned, with a very strong German accent, this second rider, who was a short, fair featured man, wearing his hair cut short like a brush, " I think of a military proverb that says : ' The soldier ought to go where is the musketry or cannonading.' Let us go where the fighting is !"

" You had a young officer with you," said the man on foot to one of the fugitives, " I do not see him ?"

" He fell the first, citizen representative; more's the pity, for he was a really brave young man !"

" He was a brave young man !" an-

swered, while slightly losing color, he to whom had been given the title of citizen representative, " so he was a brave young man — and he shall be bravely avenged ! Forward, M. Santerre !"

" I think, my dear Billot," said the brewer, " that, in affairs so serious, not only should courage be called to our aid, but experience."

" Well ?"

" Consequently, I propose to hand over the general command to Citizen Westermann—who is a real general, and a friend of Citizen Danton—offering myself to obey him as a simple soldier."

" Anything you please," coincided Billot, " provided we march without losing a minute."

" Will you accept the command, Citizen Westermann ?" inquired Santerre.

" I will," returned the Prussian laconically.

" In that case, give your orders."

" Forward !" cried Westermann.

The immense column, checked an instant, started once more.

At the moment when its vanguard penetrated the Carrousel by both the wickets of the Rue de l'Échelle and those on the quais, eleven o'clock rang out from the clock of the Tuileries.

CHAPTER III.

THE PRECEDING CONTINUED.

ON returning to the chateau, Rœderer found the valet-de-chambre, who was searching for him on account of the Queen.

He himself was seeking the Queen, knowing that, at this moment, she was the real strength of the chateau.

He was therefore, rejoiced to hear that she was awaiting him in an out-of-the-way place where he might speak to her alone and without being interrupted.

Consequently, he went up stairs behind Weber.

The Queen was seated near the chim

ney-place, her back turned to the window.

At the sound made by the opening door, she turned quickly.

"Well, sir?" queried she, without giving any positive turn to her question.

"Has not your Majesty done me the honor of calling me?" rejoined Rœderer.

"Yes, sir; you are one of the first magistrates of the city; your presence at the chateau is a buckler to royalty; I wish, therefore, to ask you what we have to hope or to fear."

"Very little to hope, madame; everything to fear!"

"Are the people really marching against the chateau?"

"The vanguard is on the Carrousel, and parleying with the Swiss."

"Parleying, sir? But I had the Swiss given the order to repel force by force. Are they ready to disobey me?"

"No, madame; the Swiss will die at their posts."

"And we at ours, sir; the same as the Swiss are soldiers in the services of kings, kings are soldiers in the service of monarchy."

Rœderer was silent.

"Have I the misfortune to be of an opinion not agreeing with yours?" demanded the Queen.

"Madame," said Rœderer, "I would have no opinion if your Majesty had not done me the favor to ask me for one."

"Sir, I do ask yours."

"Well, madame, I am going to tell you mine with the frankness of a convinced man. My opinion is that the King is lost if he remains at the Tuileries."

"But, if we are not to remain here, where should we go?" exclaimed the terrified Queen.

"There is, at the present hour," Rœderer made answer, "but one sanctuary that can protect the royal family."

"What is that, sir?"

"The National Assembly."

"What say you, sir?" inquired his hearer, snapping her eyes and asking the question like a woman persuaded that she had not heard aright.

"The National Assembly," repeated Rœderer.

"Do you believe, sir, I would ask aught of such men?"

Rœderer said nothing.

"Enemies for enemies, sir, I prefer those who attack us in broad daylight and in the front to those who wish to destroy us by striking us in the back in darkness!"

"Well, madame, make up your mind; go out to the people, or beat a retreat to the Assembly."

"Beat a retreat? Are we so much at a loss for defenders as to be forced to retreat before even having opened fire?"

"Would you, before taking some resolve, madame, listen to the report of a competent man, and hear of the forces you can dispose of?"

"Weber, go fetch for me one of the officers of the chateau, either Monsieur Maillardoz, or Monsieur de la Chesnaye, or——"

She stopped herself; she was about to say:

"Or the Count de Charny."

Weber went out.

"If your Majesty would approach the window, she may judge for herself."

The Queen, notwithstanding visible repugnance, made a few steps towards the window, parted the curtains, and looked out on the Carrousel and even the Cour Royale, full of men with pikes.

"Good heavens! but what are those men doing?"

"I have told your Majesty; they are parleying."

"But they have entered into the chateau court!"

"I thought it my duty to gain time to give your Majesty leisure to take some course."

At this point, the door opened.

"Come, come," cried the Queen, without knowing whom she addressed.

Charny entered.

"I am here, madame," said he.

"Ah, it is you! Then, I have nothing to ask of you; for, but a short time ago, you told me what was left for us to do."

"And, in this gentleman's opinion," said Rœderer, "what is that ?"

"To die !" said the Queen.

"You see that what I propose is preferable, madame."

"Oh, on my soul, I know nothing of it," said Marie Antoinette.

"What does the gentleman propose ?" inquired Charny.

"To conduct the King to the National Assembly."

"That is not death, but shame !" ejaculated Charny.

"You hear, sir," said the Queen.

"Can there not be some intermediate means ?" thought Rœderer aloud.

Weber stepped forward.

"I am well aware," said he, "that it is very presumptuous of me to speak in such company ; but, perhaps, my devotion inspires me. Suppose a request is simply sent to the Assembly for it to send a deputation to watch over the King's safety ?"

"Well, so be it," said the Queen, "to that I consent. Monsieur de Charny, if you approve of this proposition, go, I beg you, and submit it to his Majesty."

Charny bowed and went out.

"Follow the count, Weber, and bring me the King's reply."

Weber went out behind the count.

The presence of the cold, grave, devoted Charny was, if not for the queen, at least to the woman, so cruel a reproach that she could not gaze on him without a shudder.

Moreover, perhaps she had some fearful foreshadowing of what was going to happen.

Weber returned.

"The King accepts, madame," said he, "and Messieurs Champion and Dejoly have gone this moment to the Assembly to carry his Majesty's request."

"But, look !" exclaimed the Queen.

"What, madame ?" inquired Rœderer.

"What are they doing ?"

The besiegers were engaged in fishing for the Swiss.

Rœderer looked.

Before he had time to have an idea of what was going on, a pistol shot rang out, followed by the formidable discharge.

The chateau shook, as if quaking to its foundations.

The Queen uttered an exclamation, fell back a step, but, attracted by curiosity, returned to the window.

"Oh, see, see !" cried she with brightened eyes ; "they are flying ! they are routed ! What were you saying, Monsieur Rœderer, about our having no other resource than the Assembly ?"

"Will your Majesty do me the favor of following me ?" replied Rœderer.

"See, see !" continued Marie Antoinette, "there are the Swiss making a sally and pursuing them ! Oh, the Carrousel is free ! Victory, victory !"

"For mercy of yourself, madame, follow me," said Rœderer.

The Queen returned to herself, and followed the syndic.

"Where is the King ?" Rœderer inquired of the first servant he met.

"In the gallery of the Louvre," answered the latter.

"That is precisely where I wish to conduct your Majesty," observed Rœderer.

The Queen followed, without forming an idea of her guide's intention.

The gallery was cut up into three parts and half way was a barricade ; two or three hundred men defended it and could return to the Tuileries by means of a kind of hanging staircase which, pushed off by the last comer's foot, would fall from the first story to the ground floor.

The King was at a window with la Chesnaye, Maillardoz and five or six other gentlemen.

He held a telescope in his hand.

The Queen ran to the balcony, where she had no need of glass to see what was going on.

The insurrectionary army was approaching, lengthy and broad, covering the whole width of the quai and stretching out of eye-shot.

By the Pont Neuf, the Faubourg Saint Marceau was making its junction with the Faubourg Saint Antoine.

All the bells of Paris were ringing

the alarum, the big bell of Notre Dame was overpowering with its heavy voice all the other vibrations of bronze.

A burning sun poured its myriads of beams on the barrels of guns and heads of lances.

Like the distant thunder of the storm, resounded the dull reports of artillery.

"Well, madame?" said Rœderer.

Some fifty persons were collected behind the King.

The Queen flung a lingering look over all the throng surrounding her; this look seemed to go to the depths of hearts to seek out how much remained of devotion there.

Then, poor woman! without knowing whom to address or make an entreaty, she took up her boy, showing him to the officers of the Swiss and the National Guard, and the noblemen.

It was more than the Queen asking a throne for her heir; it was the mother in distress amid a conflagration, screaming:

"My child, who will save my child?"

In the mean time, Louis the Sixteenth was conversing in an undertone with the syndic of the commune, or rather Rœderer was repeating to him all that he had already spoken to the Queen.

Two quite distinct groups were formed around the two august personages.

The crowd around the King was cold, grave, being composed of counselors who seemed to approve of Rœderer's advice.

The Queen's gathering was ardent, enthusiastic, numerous, composed of young soldiers, waving their hats, drawing their swords, raising their hands to the Dauphin, kneeling to kiss the hem of the Queen's robe, swearing to die for mother and son.

From this enthusiasm, Marie Antoinette recovered a little hope.

At this moment, the King's retinue was united with the Queen's, and the King, with his usual impassibility, found himself the centre of the two blended groups.

This impassibility was, perhaps, courage.

The Queen snatched a pair of pistols from Maillardoz' belt.

"Come, sire," said she, "this is the moment to win or die among your friends!"

This action of the Queen had brought enthusiasm to its height.

The King's answer was awaited with suspended breath.

A young, brave king who, with flashing eye and quivering lip, would have thrown himself, a pistol in each hand, into the struggle, might have perchance won back fortune!

All were hoping and expecting.

The King took the firearms from the Queen's hands and gave them back to Maillardoz.

Then turning to the syndic of the commune, he inquired:

"Were you not saying I ought to go to the Assembly?"

"Sire, such is my opinion," returned Rœderer.

"Let us go, gentlemen," said the King, "there is nothing more to be done here."

The Queen uttered a sigh, took up the Dauphin in her arms, and said, addressing the Princess de Lamballe and Madame de Tourzel:

"Come, ladies, since the King is going."

This was telling all:

"I must leave you!"

Madame Campan was waiting for the Queen in the corridor through which she had to pass.

The Queen saw her.

"Wait for me in my apartment," said she; "I will return to you, or send somebody for you to go—heaven knows where!"

Then, bending over to Madame Campan, she murmured:

"Oh, that I were sunk to the bottom of the sea!"

The noblemen were looking at one another, seeming to say:

"Was it for this King that we came hither to meet death?"

La Chesnaye understood this unspoken question.

"No, gentlemen," said he, "it was for royalty! Man is mortal! principles imperishable!"

As for the unfortunate ladies—there were many of them, and some, who were absent from the chateau, had made indescribable efforts to enter it—they were petrified with terror.

They might have been likened to as many marble statues erected in the recesses of corridors and along staircases.

At last, the King condescended to think of those whom he abandoned.

At the foot of the staircase, he stopped.

"What is going to become of those I leave above?" he said.

"Sir," replied Rœderer, "nothing will be easier than for them to follow you; they are in ordinary dress and can pass through the garden."

"True," said the King, "come."

"Ah, Monsieur de Charny," said the Queen, perceiving the count, who was waiting at the garden gate, with unsheathed sword, "if I had listened to you when you advised me to flee!"

The count replied nothing to her; but, approaching the King, said:

"Sire, will not your Majesty take my hat and give me his, which may lead to his recognition?"

"Ah, you are right," observed the King, "on account of the white plume. Thank you, sir."

He took Charny's hat and gave him his own.

"Sir," inquired Marie Antoinette, "does the King incur any danger during this walk?"

"You see, madame, that, if any danger does exist, I have done all I could to turn it aside from him it threatened."

"Sire," said the Swiss captain charged to protect the passing of the King through the garden, "is your Majesty ready?"

"Yes," rejoined the King, pulling Charny's hat on more firmly.

"Then, let us go out," said the captain.

The King advanced in the middle of two rows of Swiss who marched at the same pace as he.

Suddenly, loud shouts arose on the right.

The gate opening on the Tuileries, near the Cafe de Flore, was forced in; a mass of people, hearing that the King was going to the Assembly, rushed into the garden.

A man who appeared to lead the band carried as a standard a head on a pike.

The captain commanded a halt, and the arms to be made ready.

"Monsieur de Charny," said the Queen, "if you see me going to fall into the hands of those wretches, will you not kill me?"

"I cannot promise you that, madame," responded Charny.

"Why not?" cried the Queen.

"Because, before a single hand shall have touched you, I would be dead!"

"Why, that is the head of poor Monsieur Mandat," said the King; "I recognize it."

This crew of assassins dared not approach, but it overwhelmed the royal couple with insults.

Five or six shots were fired.

One Swiss fell dead, another wounded.

The captain ordered his men to level their pieces.

"Do not fire, sir," cried Charny, "or not one of us will reach the Assembly alive!'

"You are right, sir," said the captain. "Shoulder arms."

The soldiers shouldered their guns, and continued to advance, cutting the garden diagonally.

The first heats of the year had yellowed the chestnut leaves; though it was only the commencement of August, the already dry leaves strewed the ground.

The little Dauphin amused himself by kicking the leaves upon his sister's feet.

"The leaves fall early this year," observed the King.

"Was there not one of these men who has written: 'Royalty will not last after fall?'" inquired the Queen.

"Yes, madame," replied Charny.

"And what was the name of this cunning prophet?"

"Manuel."

A new obstacle arose before the steps of the royal family.

This was a rather numerous collection of men and women who waited, with menacing gesticulations, whilst brandishing their weapons, on the steps and lawn which had to be ascended and crossed to proceed from the garden of the Tuileries to the Manege.

The danger was all the more from there no longer being a means of the Swiss keeping their order.

Their captain nevertheless undertook to push them through the crowd ; but he manifested so much rage, that Rœderer cried :

"Sir, take heed ! you are about to have the King killed !"

A halt was made.

A messenger was sent to inform the Assembly that the King was coming to ask sanctuary of it.

The Assembly sent a deputation ; but the sight of this deputation doubled the fury of the multitude.

There was nothing to be heard but roars and yells like the following :

"Down with Veto !"

"Down with the Austrian !"

"Forfeiture or death !"

The two children, understanding that it was their mother especially who was threatened, pressed closer to her.

The little Dauphin asked :

"Monsieur de Charny, why do all these people want to kill mamma ?"

A man of gigantic build, armed with a pike, was trying, by darting this weapon, to strike, now the Queen, now the King, while shouting louder than the rest :

"Down with Veto, and the Austrian !"

The Swiss escort had been gradually beaten apart.

The royal family had around it only the six gentlemen who had left with it the Tuileries, Charny and the deputation from the Assembly that had come to seek it.

There was sixty yards to go through a compact mass.

It was evident that the King's life, and the Queen's above all, was aimed at.

At the foot of the steps, the struggle was renewed.

"Sir," said Rœderer to Charny, "sheathe your sword, or I can answer for nothing."

Charny obeyed without uttering a word.

The royal group was upheaved by the throng as, in a storm at sea, a boat is tossed by the waves, and was swept away from the Assembly.

The King was obliged to push away a man who had thrust his fist into his face.

The little Dauphin, almost smothered by the press, was crying and holding out his arms to ask for help.

A man pushed up to it, grasped it and tore it from its mother's hands.

"Monsieur de Charny, my son !" screamed she, "in heaven's name, save my son !"

Charny took a couple of strides towards the bearer of the Dauphin ; but hardly had he uncovered the Queen, than several pairs of arms were held out to her, and one hand caught her by her breastpin.

The Queen gave a shriek.

Charny forgot Rœderer's caution, and his sword was buried its whole length in the body of the man who had dared to lay hand on the Queen.

The mob yelled with rage to see one of their men drop, and rushed more violently on the little knot.

The women cried :

"Kill the Austrian ! give her to us, till we cut her throat ! death, death !"

A score of naked arms stretched out to seize her.

But she, wild with grief, not thinking of her own self, never ceased crying :

"My son, my son !"

They almost touched the threshold of the Assembly.

The mob made a final effort, feeling that its prey was going to escape.

Charny was so closely beset that he could only strike with the pommel of his sword.

He saw, among the threatening clenched hands one which was armed with a pistol and being directed at the Queen.

He dropped his sword, grasped with both hands the pistol, tore it away from him holding it, and discharged it into the breast of his nearest assailant.

The latter, killed outright, fell.

Charny stooped to pick up his sword.
It was already in the grasp of one of the rioters who was trying to cut at the Queen.

Charny sprang at the assassin.

At this moment, the Queen entered after the King the vestibule of the Assembly.

She was saved!

It is true that the door was pushed to behind her, and that, on the door-step, Charny fell, struck at the same time by an iron bar on the head and a pike in the breast.

"As fell my brothers!" gasped he sinking. "Poor Andrée!"

Charny's destiny was fulfilled, like Isidore's and George's.

The Queen's fate was yet to be accomplished.

At this same moment, a deafening discharge of artillery announced that the insurgents and the defenders of the chateau were at work.

CHAPTER IV.

FROM TWELVE TO THREE O'CLOCK.

FOR an instant—as the Queen believed on seeing the flight of the vanguard—the Swiss might think they had encountered the army itself, and had routed it.

They had killed nearly four hundred men in the Cour Royale, a hundred and fifty or two hundred in the Carrousel; they had taken seven cannon.

As far as eye could reach, not a single man to resist could be found.

A small isolated battery, established on the lawn of a house facing the Swiss guardhouse, alone continued its fire without their being able to silence it.

As they fancied they had mastered the outbreak, they were going to take measures to finish with this battery, come what may, when they heard in the direction of the river line, the roll of drums and deep rumbling of artillery.

This was that force which the King had been watching with his glass, from the gallery of the Louvre.

At the same time, the rumor began to spread that the King had quitted the chateau, and had gone to ask shelter of the Assembly.

It is difficult to say what was the effect produced by this intelligence, even on the most steadfast royalists.

The King, who had promised to die at his royal post, deserting that post and passing over to the enemy, or, at least, yielding himself up as a prisoner without fighting!

The National Guards regarded themselves as discharged of their oath, and almost all retired.

Several gentlemen followed them, deeming it useless to be killed for a cause which confessed itself lost.

The Swiss alone remained, moody and silent, but slaves to discipline.

From the upper part of the lawn of the Pavilion of Flora, and through the windows of the Louvre gallery, could be seen coming those heroic faubourgs which no army has ever withstood, which one day overthrew the Bastile, that fortress of which the base had been taking root for four centuries.

The assailants had their plan; they believed the King to be at the chateau; they surrounded the chateau on all sides in order to capture him.

The column following the left bank received, consequently, the order to force in the gratings on the water's edge; that arriving by the Rue Saint Honore, to break down the door of the Feuillants, while the column of the right bank, commanded by Westerman, with Santerre and Billot under his orders, would attack in front.

This latter body suddenly entered by all the wickets of the Carrousel, singing the "Ça ira."

The five hundred Marseillais led the column, drawing in their midst two small four-pounders loaded with grape-shot.

Two hundred Swiss, or nearly that number, were in line of battle on the Carrousel.

The insurgents marched straight upon them and, at the moment when the Swiss lowered their guns to fire, they unmasked their two pieces and fired them.

The soldiers discharged their guns, but immediately fell back on the chateau, leaving thirty dead and wounded men on the pavement of the Carrousel.

Instantly, the insurgents, having at their head the Breton and Marseillais federals, rushed on the Tuileries, sweeping from the two court-yards; from the Cour Royale, placed in the centre (that on which lay so many dead); and the Court of the Princes, adjoining the Pavilion of Flora and the quai.

Billot had wished to fight where Pitou had been slain; and, it must be said, he had a hope remaining; that the poor boy had been only wounded, and that he might render him, in the Cour Royale, the same service which Pitou had rendered him on the Champ de Mars.

He, therefore, was one of the headmost to enter the central court.

The odor of blood was such that one might have believed he was in a slaughter-house; it exhaled from that heap of corpses, in some sort visible as a steam.

This sight and smell exasperated the assailants; they hurled themselves on the chateau.

Besides, had there been a thought of returning, it would have been impossible; the masses incessantly flowing through the wickets of the Carrousel—much narrower then than in our days—pushed them onwards.

But, let us hasten to state, although the front of the chateau seemed one sheet of fire, not one had even the idea of making a step back.

Once having entered the central courtyard, the insurgents, like those whose blood they marched in ancle-deep, found themselves caught between two fires: the one from the clock vestibule, and that from the double row of barracks.

This latter fire should be the first silenced.

The Marseillais rushed upon the buildings like dogs on a brazier; but they could not demolish them with hands alone; they called for levers, crows, picks.

Billot called for cartridges.

Westermann saw into his lieutenant's plan.

Cannon cartridges were brought, with matches.

At the risk of having the powder burst in their faces, the Marseillais set fire to the fuses, and flung the rude petards into the barracks.

The buildings were soon in flames.

Those defending them were compelled to evacuate them and take refuge in the vestibule.

There, they gave lead for lead, fire for fire.

Suddenly, Billot felt himself touched from behind; he turned, thinking it an enemy; but, on seeing who it was, he uttered an exclamation of joy.

It was Pitou!

Pitou, hardly to be recognized, dripping with blood from head to foot, but Pitou safe and sound, without a single scratch.

At the moment when he had seen the muskets of the Swiss levelled, he had, giving an example, as we have said, cried:

"Down on the ground!"

But his companions had had no time to follow his example.

The musketry, like an immense scythe, had swept along breast high, and had mowed down three-fourths of that field of human grain, which takes twenty-five years to grow, and which in a second was bent and broken in a bloody swath.

Pitou was literally buried under bodies, and bathed with a lukewarm liquid.

Notwithstanding the pressure—profoundly disagreeable—which Pitou felt, stifled by the weight of the dead, steeped in their blood, he resolved not to breathe a word, and to wait, before showing any token of life, for a favorable instant.

This favorable instant he had been more than an hour waiting for.

It is true that each minute of that hour had appeared to be of an hour's duration.

At length, he judged the moment propitious, when he heard his comrades' shouts of victory, and, among them, Billot's voice, calling him.

Thereupon, like Encelades entombed beneath Mount Etna, he had shaken off the layer of corpses covering him, had managed to regain his feet, and, having recognized Billot in the first rank, had hastened to shake his hand, without thinking from what side he approached him.

A volley from the Swiss, which stretched a dozen men on the ground, recalled Billot and Pitou to the gravity of the situation.

Nearly six hundred feet of buildings was burning to the right and left of the central court.

The weather was heavy, and not the faintest breath of air was stirring; the smoke of the conflagration and musketry weighed upon the combatants like a leaden dome; the whole front, each window of which spat flame, was covered with a sheet of smoke; no one could make out either who sent or who received death.

Pitou, Billot, and the Marseillais, marched in advance, and, amidst the vapor, penetrated into the corridor.

They found before them a wall of bayonets.

The Swiss.

Then it was that the Swiss began their retreat; a heroic one, in which, step by step, stair by stair, leaving a file on each step, the battalion fell slowly back.

When evening came, fourscore corpses were to be counted on the staircase.

All at once, through the rooms and lobbies of the chateau, was heard to ring the cry:

"The King orders the Swiss to cease firing."

This was at two o'clock in the afternoon.

Let us tell what had happened at the Assembly, and what had led to the order to cease firing proclaimed at the Tuileries; an order which owned the double advantage of lessening the exasperation of the victor and covering with honor the vanquished.

At the moment when the door of the Feuillants was shut behind the Queen, and when, through its opening, she had caught a glimpse of iron bars, bayonets and pikes menacing Charny, she had uttered a scream, and had extended her arms towards the door; but, drawn away towards the hall by those accompanying her, at the same time as by that maternal instinct which told her before anything else, to follow her child, she entered, behind the King, to the Assembly.

There, a great joy was in store for her,

She had perceived her son seated on the president's desk.

The man who had carried it was triumphantly waving his red cap over the young prince's head, while gleefully shouting:

"I have saved the son of my master; Long live the Dauphin!"

But, her child being in safety, a sudden return of the Queen's heart reminded her of Charny.

"Gentlemen," said she, "one of my bravest officers, one of my most devoted servitors is at the door, in danger of death; I ask help for him."

Five or six deputies hastened away at the sound of her voice.

The King, the Queen, the royal family and those who had accompanied them stepped towards the seats intended for ministers, and took places there.

The Assembly had received them standing, not on account of the etiquette due to crowned heads, but on account of respect due to misfortune.

Before sitting down, the King made a sign that he wished to speak.

All was silence.

"I am come here," said he, "to prevent a great crime; I thought I could be nowhere in more safety than among you."

"Sire," responded Vergniaud, who presided, "you may rely on the firmness of the National Assembly, its members have sworn to die defending the rights of the people and the constitutional authorities."

The King sat down.

Just then, a fearful rattle of musketry broke out almost at the door of the Manege.

The National Guards, mixed up with the insurgents, were firing, from the lawn of the Feuillants, on the Swiss officers and soldiers who had been the escort to the royal family.

An officer of the National Guard, doubtlessly frightened out of his wits, rushed in in terror and, not stopping till he reached the bar, cried:

"The Swiss! the Swiss! they are driving us back!"

For an instant, the Assembly believed that the Swiss victorious, had quelled the insurrection, and were marching upon the Manege, to retake their King—for, at this time, we must say, Louis the Sixteenth was rather the King of the Swiss than the King of the French.

The whole assemblage rose with one spontaneous, unanimous movement; and representatives of the people, spectators in the gallery, National Guards, secretaries, every one, raising his hand, said:

"Come what come may, we swear to live and die free!"

The King and the royal family had nothing to do with this oath; hence, they remained seated.

This vow, uttered by three thousand tongues, swept like a blast of the storm over their heads.

This error did not last long, but this minute of enthusiasm was grand.

A quarter of an hour afterwards, another cry arose:

"The chateau is destroyed, the insurgents are marching on the Assembly to kill the King!"

Thereupon, these same men, who, in hatred of royalty had just sworn to die free, rose with the same quickness and spontaneity to vow to defend the King to death.

At this very moment, in the name of the Assembly, Captain Durler of the Swiss was being summoned to lay down his arms.

"I serve Louis the Sixteenth, and not the Assembly," returned he, "where is the royal order?"

The messengers of the Assembly had no written order.

"I received my command from the King," went on Durler; "to him only will I restore it."

He was brought almost by force to the Assembly.

He entered black with powder, red with blood.

"Sire." said he. "I have been told to lay down my arms; is such your order?"

"Yes," answered Louis; "give your arms to the National Guards; I do not want brave men like you to perish."

Durler bowed his head, heaved a sigh, and moved away; but, at the door, he stopped and said he would not obey except on a written order.

Then, the King took a sheet of paper, and wrote:

"The King orders the Swiss to lay down their arms, and retire to the barracks."

This was what was being called out in the chambers, passage-ways and on the staircases of the Tuileries.

As this order had restored tolerable tranquillity to the Assembly, the president rang his bell.

"Let us deliberate," said he.

But a representative rose and called notice on the fact that an article of the Constitution forbade debating in the royal presence.

"It is true," said Louis the Sixteenth; "but where can you put me?"

"Sire," replied the president, "we have to offer you the reporters' box of the paper the 'Logography,' which is empty, that journal having ceased to appear."

"It is well, we are ready to proceed thither," said the King.

"Ushers, conduct the King to the box of the Logography."

The ushers hastened to obey.

The King, Queen, royal family, retook, to leave the hall, the same road they had used to enter it, and were soon in the corridor.

"What is that on the floor? it seems to be blood," said Marie Antoinette.

The ushers made no answer.

If the spots were really blood, they were perhaps ignorant from what they came.

The spots, strange thing! were larger and more frequent, proportionately to the party's approach to the box.

To spare the Queen this sight, the King doubled his pace and, opening the box himself, said:

"Enter, madame."

The Queen hurried in; but, as she set her foot over the threshold, she uttered a shriek of horror and, with hands over her eyes, drew herself back.

The presence of the bloody drops was explained; a body had been laid in the box.

It was this body—which the Queen, in her precipitation, had almost stumbled over—that had made her utter a cry and draw back.

"Why, it is the body of that poor Count de Charny?" exclaimed the King in the same tone in which he had said: "Why, that is the head of poor Monsieur Mandat!"

It was, indeed, the count's body, which the deputies had taken from the hands of the butchers, and which they had ordered to be placed in the box of the Logography, not foreseeing that, ten minutes afterwards, the royal family was to be there installed.

The corpse was carried away, and the royal family entered the box.

The floor was about to be washed for the planks were soaked with blood; but the Queen made a sign of opposition, and walked on the first.

No one noticed that she snapped the lacing of her shoes, and dabbled her shuddering feet with that still warm blood.

"Oh!" murmured she, "Charny! Charny! why does not my blood flow out here till the last drop, to mingle eternally with thine!"

Three o'clock of the afternoon rang out.

CHAPTER V.

FROM THREE TO SIX OF THE AFTERNOON.

WE left the chateau at the moment when as the central vestibule was forced in, and the Swiss were being pushed back step by step to the royal apartments, a voice resounded in the rooms and passage-ways, crying:

"Order for the Swiss to lay down their arms!"

This book is probably the last we shall write on this dreadful period; proportionately to the progress of our story do we quit the ground over which we travel never to return. It is this which authorizes us to lay, in all its details, this momentous day before our readers' eyes; we should, therefore, take the more heed to proceed without any bias, hatred, or partiality.

The reader has entered into the Cour Royal with the Marseillais; he has followed Billot through flame and smoke; and he has seen him mount, with Pitou, a bloody spectre rising from among the dead, each step of the staircase at the landing-place of which we left them.

From that moment, the Tuileries was taken

Who was the gloomy spirit that had overseen this victory?

The wrath of the people, it may be answered.

Yes, beyond a doubt; but who directed this passion?

The man whom we have barely named, that Prussian officer who rode on a small black horse beside the giant Santerre and his colossal Flemish horse—the Alsatian, Westermann.

Who was this man who, like the lightning, was only to be seen amid tempests?

One of those whom God keeps hidden in the arsenal of His ire, and only draws forth from obscurity when He has need of them, at the hour when He strikes!

He was WESTERMANN.

The Man of the Wane.

In truth, he appeared when royalty was declining never again to rise.

Who discovered him?

Who divined him?

Who was the intermediary between him and heaven?

Who felt that to the brewer, a giant hewn out of the material granite of flesh, would be lent a soul for that struggle in which the man-Titans were to overthrow the King-god?

Who perfected Geryon with Prometheus?

Who completed Santerre with Westermanne?

Danton.

Where did the fearful tribune go to seek this vanquisher.

In a cell, a sewer, a jail : Saint Lazare.

Westermann was accused—bear it well in mind, *accused*, not convicted—of having forged *billets de caisse*, and kept in durance by a kind of punishment in advance.

Danton had need, for the work of the tenth of August, of a man who would not give way, because, in receding, he would mount the pillory.

Danton surveyed the mysterious prisoner ; at the hour of the day at which he had need of him, he broke chains and bars with his powerful hands, and bade the prisoner :

"Come !"

Revolution consists not only, as we have said, in setting above that which is below, but, besides, in giving captives liberty and in imprisoning free men ; not simply free men, but the most powerful of earth, the greatest, princes, kings !

Doubtlessly, it was in his dependence on what was going to happen that Danton appeared so torpid during the feverish shadows which preceded the bloody dawn of the tenth of August.

He had sown the whirlwind on the eve ; he had nothing further to attend to, certain as he was of reaping the tempest.

The wind was Westermann.

The tempest, Santerre, the gigantic impersonation of the people.

Santerre was hardly to be seen on this day.

Westermann did everything, was everywhere.

It was Westermann who directed the movement of the junction of the Faubourgs Saint Marceau and Saint Antoine at the Pont Neuf.

It was he again who, mounted on his small black horse, appeared at the head of the army, under the wicket of the Carrousel.

It was still he who, as if he was ordering the opening of the door to a regiment taking up its station there, knocked with his sword pommel on the gate of the Tuileries.

We have seen how that gate was opened, how the Swiss had heroically done their duty, how they had beaten a retreat without fleeing, how they had been destroyed without having been vanquished ; we have followed them step by step up the stairs, which they covered with their dead ; let us go with them step by step through the Tuileries, which they were also to strew with corpses.

When the intelligence was made known that the King was going to leave the chateau, gentlemen who had come to die with their sovereign collected in the Hall of the Queen's Guards, in order to settle whether, the King no longer being there to die with them as he had solemnly pledged, they ought to die without him.

Whereupon, they decided, inasmuch as the King had gone to the Assembly, to go thither themselves and join him.

They rallied all the Swiss they could find, a score or so of National Guards and, to the number of five hundred, descended into the garden.

The way was closed by a door of iron bars called the Grate of the Queen ; they tried to blow open the lock, but it resisted.

The strongest began prying at it with a bar, and managed to wrench it off.

The opening gave passage to the troop, but only one by one.

They were some eighty yards from the battalions posted as the grating of Pont Royal.

Two Swiss soldiers were the first to go through the narrow gap ; both fell dead before having gone two steps.

All the others had to step over their bodies.

The band received many gunshots ; but, as the Swiss, from their bright uniforms, offered the easiest aim, it was on them that the bullets were showered in preference ; for two gentlemen killed and one wounded, sixty or seventy Swiss fell.

The two slain gentlemen were de Carteja and de Clerment d'Amboise, the wounded one was Viomesnil.

While marching towards the National Assembly, they had to pass a guardhouse by the bank of the water, under the trees.

The guard came out, firing on the Swiss, of whom eight or ten more fell.

The rest of the column—which, in some eighty steps had lost a man for each step—turned towards the steps of the Feuillants.

Choiseul saw them from a distance, and, sword in hand, running with them under the fire of the Pont Royal and Pont Tournant, tried to rally them.

"On to the National Assembly!" cried he.

Believing himself followed by the four hundred men remaining to him, he rushed into the corridors and up the steps leading to the hall of sessions.

At the top step, he came upon Merlin.

"What are you doing here, with drawn sword?" said the deputy.

De Choiseul looked about him.

He was alone.

"Put up your sword, and go find the King," said Merlin; "I am the only one who has seen you, and that is the same as if no one had seen you."

What had become of the troop which Choiseul fancied was following him?

Cannon shot and musketry had made it turn around wildly as a whirlwind dry leaves, and had pursued it to the Lawn of the Orangery.

Over this lawn the fugitives had hurried to the Square of Louis Quinzieme, and proceeded towards the Garde Meuble to gain the boulevards or the Champs Elysees.

Viomesnil, eight or ten gentlemen and five Swiss took refuge in the mansion of the Venetian Ambassador, on the Rue Saint Florentine, the door of which they had found open.

They were saved.

The remnant of the column tried to reach the Champs Elysees.

Two cannons, loaded with grape-shot, were fired from the base of the Statue of Louis Fifteenth, and shattered the band into three fragments.

One fled down the boulevard and encountered the gendarmerie, which was coming up with the Capucines battalion.

The fugitives fancied themselves saved.

Villiers, once an aid major in the gendarmerie himself, ran up to one of the horsemen with open arms, crying:

"Help, friends!"

The trooper drew a pistol from his holsters and blew out his brains.

On seeing this, thirty Swiss, with a nobleman who had been formerly a royal page, rushed into the building of the Navy Department.

There, they were asked what business they had there.

The thirty Swiss thought they had better surrender and, seeing eight sans-culottes appear, they laid down their muskets, shouting:

"The nation forever!"

"Ha, traitors!" cried the rioters, "you surrender because you see the game is up with you? You cry: 'The nation forever!' because you think that's going to clear you? No, we give no quarter!"

And, at the same time, two Swiss fell, one pierced with a pike, the other by a gunshot.

Instantly their heads were hacked off, and stuck on the points of pikes.

The Swiss, furious at the death of their comrades, picked up their guns and fired all at once.

Seven out of the eight patriots fell dead or wounded.

The Swiss then sprang for the main gateway to save themselves, but found themselves facing a cannon's mouth.

They recoiled.

The gun advanced.

They had grouped themselves in a corner of the courtyard.

The gun was turned with its muzzle on them, and fired!

Twenty-three fell out of twenty-eight.

Fortunately, at almost the same time, while the smoke blinded those who had fired, a door opened behind the five Swiss still remaining and the ex-page of the King.

The whole six sprang through the opening, and the door closed.

The patriots had not seen this trap which had robbed them of the half-dozen survivors; they thought they had killed all, and departed, dragging away their piece with cheers of triumph.

The second fragment was composed of about thirty soldiers and gentlemen;

it was commanded by Forestier de Saint Venant.

Surrounded on all sides at the opening of the Champs Elysees, their leader was bent on making their assailants purchase their lives dearly ; at the head of his thirty men, he, sword in hand, they with bayonets, charged three times a whole battallion massed at the foot of the statue.

In these three charges he lost half his force : fifteen men.

With the fifteen others, he endeavored to cut his way through and reach the Champs Elysees.

A volley killed eight of his men ; the seven others scattered and were pursued and cut down by the gendarmes.

Saint Venant had nearly found shelter in the Cafe des Ambassadeurs, when a gendarme started his horse at a gallop, leaped the ditch separating the sidewalk from the highway and, with a pistol shot, broke the loins of the hapless commander.

The third portion, composed of sixty men, had reached the Champs Elysees, and were hastening to Courbevoie with that instinct which leads pigeons to wing their way to the dovecote, and sheep to the fold ; the barracks were at Courbevoie.

Surrounded by the horse-gendarmes and the mob, they were being brought back to the city hall, where they hoped to be in safety ; two or three thousand furious rioters, assembled on the Place de Greve, tore them from their escort, and massacred them.

One young gentleman, the Chevalier Charles d'Auticamp, was fleeing from the chateau by way of the Rue de l'Echelle, a pistol in each hand.

Two men tried to stop him.

He shot both.

The populace seized him and dragged him to the Greve to there solemnly execute him.

But, luckily, it had been omitted to search him ; a knife was remaining to him, when he had flung away his brace of empty pistols ; he opened it in his pocket, waiting for the moment to make use of it.

When he reached the square of the city hall, the sixty Swiss who had been dragged there, were being slaughtered ; this act took off the attention of those guarding him.

He stabbed the two captors nearest him, glided through the throng like a snake, and disappeared.

The hundred men who had conducted the King to the National Assembly, and who, taking refuge at the Feuillants, had been disarmed ; the five hundred whose story we have told ; a few isolated fugitives, like Charles d'Auticamp, whom we have seen escape death so happily, were the only ones who had quitted the chateau.

The remainder were slain in the passage-ways, on the staircases and landing-places, or had their throats cut in the rooms, even in the chapel.

Nine hundred corpses of Swiss and noblemen were strewn within the Tuileries !

CHAPTER VI.

FROM SIX TO NINE O'CLOCK IN THE EVENING.

THE people had surged into the chateau as one rushes into a wild beast's lair, betraying their feelings by their cries :

" Death to the wolf ! the she-wolf ! and the cub !"

If they had encountered the King, the Queen and the Dauphin, they would certainly, without hesitating, believing they executed justice, have struck off the three heads at one blow.

Let all acknowledge that this death would have been happiest for them !

In the absence of those whom they hunted with their shouts, whom they sought for in cupboards, behind tapestries, under couches, the vanquishers revenged themselves on things as well as persons ; they killed and shattered with the same impassive ferocity ; those walls, within which had been decreed the Massacres of Saint Bartholomew's and of the Champ de Mars, called for terrible repayment.

It will be seen, we do not gloss over

the people; we show them, on the contrary, cruel and bloody as they were.

However, let us hasten to say, the victors came from the palace with red hands, but *empty* ones * !

Peltier (who cannot be accused of partially in favor of the patriots) tells how a wine-seller, named Mallet, brought to the Assembly one hundred and seventy-three Louis in gold found on a priest killed at the chateau; that twenty-five sans-culottes brought there a chest full of the royal plate; that one combatant flung a cross of the order of Saint Louis on the president's desk; that another laid on it the watch of a Swiss; another, a roll of assignats; still another, a bag of crownpieces, another again diamonds; a last one, a casket belonging to the Queen, and containing fifteen hundred louis.

"And," ironically adds the historian, without suspecting that he pays these men a magnificent eulogy, "the Assembly expresses its regret that it does not know the names of the modest citizens who came faithfully to place in its bosom all the treasures stolen from the King."

We are not flatterers of the mob, not at all; we know it to be the most ungrateful, most capricious, most inconstant of all masters; we therefore tell of its crimes as we do of its virtues.

On this day, it was cruel; it reddened its hands with delight; gentlemen were flung living out of windows; Swiss lay dead or dying, with cut throats on the staircases; hearts were plucked from breasts and squeezed between both hands like sponges; heads were cut off and carried on pike-heads; on this day, the mob—believing itself dishonored had one stolen a watch or a cross of Saint Louis—gave itself up to all the dreadful joys of vengeance and cruelty.

Nevertheless, amid all this slaughter of the living and profanation of the dead, at times, like the lion, "preying not on defenceless carcases," it granted mercy.

Mesdames de Tarente, de la Rocheaymon, de Ginestons and Mademoiselle

Pauline de Tourzel had remained in the Tuileries, left behind by the Queen; they were in Marie Antoinette's very room. The chateau being taken, they heard the shrieks of the dying, the threats of the victors, and steps approaching them, hurried and well exciting terror and no hope of pity.

Madame de Tarente went and opened the door.

"Enter; we are only women," said she.

The mob entered, with smoking guns, and blood-streaming swords in their hands.

The women fell upon their knees.

The butchers had their weapons already lifted against them, calling them the counselors of Madame Veto, the Austrian's confidants, when a long-bearded man, an envoy of Petion's, shouted from the threshold:

"Spare the women! do not dishonor the nation!"

And mercy was shown them.

Madame Campan, whom her royal mistress had bade "wait for me; I I will return or else I will send for you to come and meet me—heaven knows where!" Madame Campan, we repeat, was waiting in her room for the return of the Queen or the coming of her messenger.

She relates herself that she had completely lost her wits amid the horrible tumult, and that, not seeing her sister (hidden behind some curtain or crept beneath some article of furniture), she believed she might find her in a room on a lower floor, and rapidly descended thither; but in that chamber, she only could see two waiting-maids belonging to her, and a gigantic man who was the Queen's footman.

On seeing this man, Madame Campan, bewildered as she was, felt how imminent danger was over him, much more than for herself.

"Flee!" cried she, "hasten! the footmen are already far away! Flee while it is yet time!"

But he, trying to rise, fell back, answering plaintively:

"Alas! I cannot, I am dead with fright."

As he thus replied, a troop of drunken, furious, blood-bedabbled men appeared on the threshold, threw themselves on the serving-man, and hacked him to bits.

Madame Campan and the two maids took to flight by way of a secret staircase.

Part of the butchers, seeing the three escape, set off in their pursuit, and presently caught up to them.

The two chambermaids, falling on their knees, pushed away the sword blades with their bare hands, while supplicating the murderers.

Madame Campan, arrested in her course at the head of the stairs, had felt a hand clutch at her clothes to seize her; she saw, like a lightning flash, a sword blade gleam over her head; she was in that short instant which divides life from eternity and which, short though it be, contains a world of recollections, when, at the foot of the steps, a voice called in a tone of command:

"What are you doing up there?"

"Ha! what's the matter?" replied the man.

"No woman-killing, d'you hear!" resumed the voice from below.

Madame Campan was kneeling, the weapon had already impended over her neck, she had already undergone all the agonizing expectation one could have felt.

"Rise! the nation pardons you!" said her executioner.

What, during this time, was the ruler of the nation doing in the box of the Logography.

The King was hungry, and asked for his dinner.

Bread, wine, a chicken, some cold meat and fruit had been brought to him.

Like all the princes of the House of Bourbon, like the fourth Henry and the fourteenth Louis, this sovereign was a great eater; behind the emotions of his mind, rarely betrayed by the soft, unimpressionable muscles of his countenance, incessantly watched those two great requirements of the body: sleep and hunger.

We have seen him obliged to sleep in the chateau, and see him obliged to eat in the Assembly.

The King broke his bread and carved the fowl as at a hearty meal after a chase, without in the least minding what eyes were regarding him.

These eyes were two burning ones, which could not weep: the Queen's.

She had refused everything; despair fed her.

It seemed to her that, with feet in Charny's precious blood, she could there remain eternally, living like a flower on a grave, without other nourishment than that she received from the dead.

She had suffered much on the return from Varennes; much underwent during her captivity at the Tuileries; much suffered in that day and night just passing; but perhaps had less suffered had she not seen her husband eat.

The situation of affairs, nevertheless, was grave enough to deprive of appetite any other man than Louis XVI.

The Assembly, where the King had come to ask for shelter, stood in need of being protected itself; it did not dissimulate its weakness.

In the morning, it had wished to prevent Suleau's murder, and had not been able to do so.

At two o'clock, it had tried to prevent the massacre of the Swiss, and found it had not the power.

Now, it was itself threatened by an exasperated throng which roared:

"Forfeiture!"

A commission assembled.

Vergniaud was one of it; he gave the presidency to Guadet, in order that the power might not leave the hands of the Girondists.

The deliberation of the commission was short; it went on in some sort under the resonant echo of the musketry and cannonading.

It was Vergniaud who took up a pen and drew up the act for provisionally suspending royalty.

He returned to the Assembly, downcast and moody, trying to hide neither his sadness nor his prostration; for this was the last pledge he gave the King of his respect for royalty; the last token to the guest of his respect for hospitality.

"Gentlemen," said he, "I come, in

the name of the extraordinary commission, to present to you a very stringent measure; but I have only to remind you of the grief which fills you to have you see of how much importance it is to the salvation of the country, and to adopt it instantly.

"The National Assembly, considering that the dangers of the country have attained their height ; that the evils of which the nation groaned are principally derived from the distrust inspired by the conduct of the head of the executive power, in a war undertaken in his name against the Constitution and national independence ; that this distrust has provoked from all parts of the state the wish to have the authority confided in Louis the Sixteenth revoked ;

"Considering, nevertheless, that the legislative body does not desire to aggrandize by any usurpation whatever, and that it can only reconcile its oath to the Constitution, and its steadfast desire to save liberty by making an appeal to the sovereignty of the people,

"Resolve the following :

"The French people are invited to form a National Convention.

"The head of the executive power is provisionally suspended from his functions. A resolution will be offered in the regular session for the appointment of a governor for the prince royal.

"The payment of the civil list shall be suspended.

"The King and royal family will dwell within the enclosure of the legislative body until quiet shall have been re-established in Paris.

"The department will prepare the Luxembourg for their residence under the guard of citizens."

The King listened to this resolution with his usual lack of emotion.

Bending over from the box of the Logography, and addressing Vergniaud, when the latter was returning to take his place of president, he said:

"What you are doing is not very constitutional, do you not know that ?"

"True, sire," returned Vergniaud, "still it is the sole means of saving your life. If we do not allow the forfeiture, they will take the *head !*"

His hearer made a movement of his lips and shoulders which signified :

"It is very likely."

And he resumed his seat.

At this moment, the clock placed over his head struck the hour.

He counted each stroke.

When the last one had died away, he said :

"Nine o'clock."

The decree of the Assembly said the King and royal family were to dwell within the enclosure of the legislative body until quiet should have been restored in Paris.

At nine o'clock, the inspectors of the hall came for the King and Queen to conduct them to the provisionary lodging prepared for them.

The King waved them back with his hand as a sign that he wanted them to wait for an instant.

Indeed something was going on which was not without interest to him.

A ministry was being appointed.

The Ministers of War, of the Home Department, of the Treasury were nominated : they were the ministers dismissed by the King, Roland, Claviere, and Servan.

There remained the Ministers of Justice, the Navy and for Foreign Affairs.

Danton received the appointment for the first ; Monge, for the Navy ; Lebrun, for Foreign Affairs.

When the last one was settled upon, the King said :

"Let us go."

Rising. he went out the first.

The Queen followed him ; she had taken nothing since her leaving the Tuileries, not even a glass of water.

Madame Elizabeth, the Dauphin, Madame Royale, the Princess de Lamballe and Madame de Tourzel was their retinue.

The apartment prepared for the King was situated on the upper floor of the old Monastery of the Feuillants ; it was inhabited by Camus, the Keeper of the Rolls, and had four rooms.

In the first, which properly speaking was but an antechamber, such servants of the King as remained faithful to him stopped.

They were the Prince de Poix, Baron d'Aubier, Saint Pardon, Goguelat, Chamille and Hue.

The King took the second chamber for himself.

The third was offered to the Queen; it was the only one that was papered.

On entering it Marie Antoinette threw herself on the bed, biting into the pillow, a prey to a grief beside which the torture of a victim on the rack would be as nothing.

Her two children remained with her.

The fourth room, cramped as it was, remained for Madame Elizabeth, the Princess de Lamballe and Madame de Tourzel, who settled themselves there as comfortably as they could.

The Queen lacked everything: money, for her purse and watch had been taken during the tumult at the door of the Assembly; linen, for our readers will easily understand she had brought nothing from the Tuileries.

She borrowed twenty-five louis from Madame Campan's sister, and sent for some linen at the residence of the British Ambassador.

In the evening the Assembly had the day's decrees proclaimed by torchlight in the streets of Paris.

CHAPTER VII.

FROM NINE TILL MIDNIGHT.

THESE torches, at the moment when they passed before the Carrousel, through the Rue Saint Honore and over the quais, illumined a mournful sight!

The bodily struggle was finished, but the contest still went on in hearts, for hate and desperation survived the fight.

Contemporary recitals, the royalist legends, dwell long, and tenderly shower pity—as we are ready to do ourselves —on the august heads from the brows of which that dreadful day had been plucked the crown; they have shown the courage, discipline, devotion of the

Swiss and gentlemen. They have counted the drops of blood shed for the defenders of the throne; but have not reckoned the corpses of the people, the tears of mothers, sisters and widows.

Let us say a word.

For God—who, in His wisdom, not only allows but, moreover, directs the events of earth—blood is blood, tears are tears.

The number of dead was much more considerable among the men of the people, than among the Swiss and noblemen.

Let us see what is said by the author of "The History of the Revolution of the tenth of August," that same Peltier, royalist though he was:

"The day of the tenth of August cost to humanity in the neighborhood of seven hundred soldiers and twenty-five officers, twenty royalist National Guards, five hundred federals, three commanders in the National Guards, forty gendarmes, more than two hundred domestics of the royal household, two hundred men killed for thieving, * the nine citizens massacred at the Feuillants, and fully *three thousand* men of the people, killed on the Carrousel, in the garden of the Tuileries, or on the Square of Louis the Fifteenth; total, nearly four thousand six hundred men!"

This is easy to be conceived.

Our readers know what were the precautions taken to fortify the Tuileries; the Swiss had generally fired from behind strong walls, the assailants, on the other hand, had had only their breasts to receive the shots.

Three thousand five hundred insurgents, without including the two hundred thieves shot, had perished!

Which supposes as many wounded, for the historian above quoted only speaks of the dead.

Many of this number—let us put it as half — were married men, poor fathers of families, whom intolerable misery had pushed into the rioting to fight with the first weapon their hand had chanced to fall upon, or even without weapons, and who, going to seek

* This popular justice had been since renewed, with respect to plunderers, in 1839 and 1848.

death, had left in their hovels famished children, despairing wives.

This death they had found either on the Carrousel, where the struggle had broken out, or in the apartments of the chateau, where it had been continued, or in the garden of the Tuileries, where it had died away.

From three o'clock in the afternoon till nine in the evening, every soldier wearing an uniform had been hastily picked up and flung into the graveyard of Madeleine Church.

As for the bodies of the mob, that was another thing ; into tumbrels they had been piled and drawn away to their respective quartiers ; almost all were from either the Faubourg Saint Antoine or the Faubourg Saint Marceau.

There—particularly on the Squares of the Bastile and of the Arsenal, on the Places Maubert and Pantheon—they had been laid side by side.

Every time that one of these death-carts, rolling heavily and leaving a track of blood after it, entered one or the other faubourg, the throng of mothers, wives, sisters, children, surrounded it with a fearful sinking of the heart ;* then, as recognitions began to be made between the living and the dead, screams, threats, sobs arose ; they were awful maledictions, which rising like a flock of nocturnal birds of evil augury, flapped their wings in the obscurity, and plaintively winged their way towards the Tuileries.

They sailed, like flocks of crows over battle fields, over the King, Queen, the court, over the Austrian circle surrounding it, over those nobles who advised the Queen.

Some swore future vengeance—and they were given the second of September and the twenty-first of January ; others caught up a pike, a sword, a gun, and, intoxicated with the blood they had drank through their eyes, rushed into the city to kill.

Kill—whom ?

Those remaining of the Swiss, of the nobles, of that court !

To kill the King and Queen, had they met them ! If it were said :

" But, in killing the King and Queen, you make orphans, in killing the nobles you make wives widows, sisters brotherless !"

Wives, sisters and children would have answered :

" But we, too, are orphans ! we are mourning sisters ! we are widows !"

With bosom full of sobs, they went to the Assembly, to the Abbaye Prison, hammering at the doors and screaming : " Vengeance ! vengeance !"

A terrible spectacle was that of the bloody, smoky Tuileries, deserted by all save dead bodies and by three or four knots of guards who were watching that, under pretence of recognizing their dead kinsfolk and friends, the nocturnal visitors did not come to pillage that royal residence with unhinged doors and shattered casements.

There was a post on every vestibule and at the foot of each flight of stairs.

The post of the Clock Pavilion, by the main staircase, was commanded by a young captain of the National Guard in whom the view of all this disaster inspired great pity—if one could judge by the expression of his countenance at each cart-load of corpses carried away in some sort under his supervision—but on whose material needs the fearful events which had transpired seemed to have no more influence than on the King ; for, at about eleven o'clock of the evening, he was occupied in satisfying an ungodly appetite at the expense of a four-pound loaf which he held under his left arm, while his right hand, grasping a knife, without cessation cut off broad slices which he introduced into a mouth that opened proportionately to the size of the edible it was destined to receive.

Leaning against one of the pillars of the vestibule, he was watching that silent procession of mothers, wives and daughters, like shadows, made visible by torches placed from spot to spot, who came to ask of the extinguished crater for the remains of those dearest to them.

Suddenly, at the sight of a half-veiled form, the young captain started.

" My lady the Countess de Charny !" muttered he.

* Michelet, the true, the only historian of the people.

The figure passed without hearing and without stopping.

The young captain beckoned his lieutenant to him.

The latter came to him.

"Desire," said he, "yonder is a poor lady of Monsieur Gilbert's acquaintance, who no doubt comes looking after her husband among the dead; I must follow her, in case she has need of help and attention. I leave you the command of the post; watch for me, too!"

"The deuce! your lady has the air of a regular aristocrat!" rejoined his lieutenant, whom the captain had called by his surname Desire to which belonged the second name of Maniquet.

"So she is an aristocrat," returned his superior; "she is a countess."

"Go; I will watch."

The Countess de Charny had already turned the first corner of the staircase, when the captain, leaving his force, commenced to follow her at the respectful distance of a score of yards.

This latter was not wrong.

It was really her husband that poor Andrée sought; only, she was seeking for him not with the anxious tremor of uncertainty, but with the conviction of despair.

When, on awakening in the midst of his joy and happiness, at the echo of the events in Paris, Charny, pale but resolved, had said to his wife:

"Dear Andrée, the King of France runs risk of his life, and has need of all his defenders. What shall I do?"

Andrée had replied:

"Go where duty calls you, Olivier, and die for the King, if you must."

"But you?" Charny had asked.

"Do not be uneasy about me," Andrée had returned. "As I have lived with you, heaven can but allow me to die with you."

Thus was all agreed upon between these noble hearts; not a word further had been exchanged; they had ordered post horses, had set out and, five hours afterwards, had alighted at the little mansion in the Rue Coq Heron.

On the same evening, Charny, as we have seen—as Gilbert, counting on his influence, was going to send him his note desiring him to come to Paris—

Charny, dressed as a navy officer, had presented himself to the Queen.

Since that hour, we know, he had not quitted her.

Andrée had remained alone with her maids, praying; she had for an instant the idea of imitating her husband's devotion, and of going and resuming her position by the Queen, as her husband went to ask again his place beside the King; but she had not the courage.

The day of the ninth was spent for her in anguish, but without bringing to her any positive ill.

On the morning of the tenth, at about nine o'clock, she had heard the first cannon shots.

It was useless to say that every echo of the warlike thunder made her quiver to the farthest fibre of her heart.

At about two o'clock, the musketry died away.

Were the people vanquished or vanquishers?

She questioned.

The people had won.

What had become of Charny in the fearful struggle? She knew that he must have played a large part in it.

She questioned further.

She was informed that almost all the Swiss had been killed, but that almost all the noblemen were safe.

She waited.

Charny might enter under some disguise; he might have need of instant flight.

She had the horses harnessed and tackled to the carriage.

Horses and vehicle awaited the master; for Andrée well knew that, be the danger what it might, the master would not go without her.

She ordered the doors and gates to be unfastened, that nothing could impede Charny's flight, and awaited.

Hours elapsed.

"If he is hidden anywhere." mused Andrée, "he cannot stir abroad till dusk—let us wait for night!"

Night came but no Charny.

In August, night comes on late.

At ten o'clock only, did Andrée lose all hope.

She drew a veil over her face, and went out.

All along her way, she met groups of females wringing their hands, and bands of men shouting:

" Vengeance."

She passed through both.

The grief of one, the anger of the others was her safeguard; besides, it was men they wanted on this evening and not women.

Everywhere, were weeping women on this night.

Andrée reached the Carrousel; she heard the crying of the decrees of the National Assembly.

All she comprehended was that the King and the Queen were under the ward of the Assembly.

She saw two or three tumbrels roll away and inquired what were their loads.

She was answered that it was bodies picked up on the Square of the Carrousel and in the Cour Royale.

The dead only were as yet removed.

Andrée thought that it was on neither of those places that Charny should be sought, but at the door of the King or of the Queen.

She crossed the Cour Royale, went up the main stairway.

This was the moment when Pitou who, in his rank as captain, commanded the post of the staircase, saw her, recognized her and followed her.

———

CHAPTER VIII.

THE WIDOW.

It is impossible to form an idea of the state of devastation presented by the Tuileries.

Blood trickled from every room and leaped in little rills from step to step of the stairs; several corpses still lay in the apartments.

Andrée did as the other searchers did; she took a torch and went to examine each body.

While looking she drew nearer to the royal apartments.

Pitou still followed her.

There, as in the other room, she sought fruitlessly. For an instant she was indecisive, not knowing where to go.

Pitou noticed her embarrassment and said, stepping up to her:

" Alas, I can guess what your ladyship seeks."

The countess turned.

" Has your ladyship any need of me ?"

" M. Pitou !" exclaimed she.

" At your ladyship's service."

" Oh, yes, yes, I have great need of you !"

Going to him and taking both his hands, she asked:

" Do you know what has become of the Count de Charny ?"

" No, my lady," answered Pitou; " but I can help you to find him."

" There is one," went on the countess," who can tell us whether he is living or dead, and, in either case, where we can find him."

" Who is that, my lady the countess ?" inquired Pitou.

" The Queen," murmured Andrée.

" Do you know where the Queen is ?" said Pitou.

" I think at the Assembly, and I have still the hope that M. de Charny is with her."

" Oh, yes," exclaimed Pitou, snatching at this hope, not on his account, but for the widow; " do you want to go to the Assembly ?"

" They will refuse me admission."

" I will have the doors open to you."

" Come, then ?"

The speaker flung far from her her torch, at the risk of setting fire to the floor and, hence, to the Tuileries; but what was the palace to such deep despair ? so deep that it had no tears !

Andrée knew the interior of the chateau from having lived in it. She took a secret staircase which led to the main vestibule, so that, without passing through all the bloody apartments, Pitou found himself at the post of the Clock.

Maniquet was keeping good guard.

" Well, your countess ?" queried he.

" She hopes to find her husband at the Assembly; we are going there."

Then, in a lower tone, he added:

" As we are likely to find him there,

but dead, send me to the door of the Feuillants, four stout lads on whom I may rely to defend an aristocrat's body as well as though it were a patriot's."

"All right; go with your countess; you shall have the men."

Andrée had remained standing by the garden gate, where a sentinel had been put.

As it was Pitou who had posted the sentinel, he, naturally, let Pitou pass.

The garden of the Tuileries was lighted by lamps which had been lit in different spots, and particularly on the pedestals of statues.

As it was almost as warm as in the daytime, and as the night breeze barely rustled the leaves on the trees, the flame of the lamps rose nearly motionless, like lances of fire, and cast out a strong light, not only into the parts of the garden uncovered and cultivated as low beds, but on the trees and the copses stretched out here and there.

But Andrée was so convinced that only at the Assembly would she receive news of her husband, that she walked out without turning to either right or left.

Thus they reached the Feuillants.

The royal family had been gone an hour from the Assembly, and, as we have seen, had settled themselves in the temporary apartments prepared for them.

To reach the royal family, there were two obstacles to overcome : first, that of the outside sentries, next, that of the gentlemen watching within.

Pitou, captain in the National Guard, commanding the post at the Tuileries, had the password and, consequently, the possibility of conducting Andrée to the gentlemen's antechamber.

Then she could reach the Queen.

We know how was situated the royal apartments; we have spoken of the Queen's despair and have told how, on entering the little green-papered room, she had flung herself on the bed, biting into her pillow with sobs and tears.

Certainly, the loser of a throne, of freedom, of life peradventure, lost enough for no one to think her sorrow unfounded, and for no one to seek, beneath that deep abasement, a more poignant grief to draw tears from her eyes, from her bosom sobs !

By the feeling of respect which this affliction inspired, for the first few moments, the Queen had been left alone.

She heard the door of her room, which opened into the King's, open and shut, but did not turn ; she heard steps approach her bed and yet she remained shrouded in her pillow.

But, suddenly, she started as if a viper had stung her.

A well known voice had uttered the single word :

"Madame !"

"Andrée !" ejaculated Marie Antoinette, rising on her elbow ; "what do you want?"

"I want to ask you what God asked Cain, when he said : 'Cain, Cain, where is your brother?'"

"With this difference," said the Queen, "Cain had slain his brother, while I—I—oh ! I would have given not my life alone, but ten existences, had I them, to save *that one* !"

Her hearer started back ; a cold sweat burst out on her forehead, and her teeth chattered.

"So, he has been killed?" gasped she, making a mighty effort.

The Queen looked at her.

"Do you fancy it is my crown that I weep over?" she said.

Then showing her bloody feet, she went on :

"Do you fancy that, if this blood were mine, I would have thus laved my feet with it?"

Andrée grew from pale to a livid hue.

"Do you know where is his body?" she resumed.

"I will guide you," rejoined the Queen.

"I will wait for you on the staircase, madame," said the countess.

She went out.

Pitou was waiting at the door.

"Monsieur Pitou," said she, "one of my friends is going to lead me to where is Monsieur de Charny's body ; she is one of the Queen's ladies—may she come with me?"

"You know that, if she goes out," responded Pitou, "it is on condition that I bring her back?"

"She will return," said Andrée.

"Very well."

Turning to the sentinel, Pitou said:
"Comrade, one of the Queen's women is going to come out to help us find the body of a brave officer whose widow this lady is. I will answer for this woman body for body, head for head."

"It is well, captain," answered the sentinel.

At the same time, the antechamber door opened, and the Queen appeared, her face veiled.

They descended the stairs, the Queen, first, Andrée and Pitou following her.

After a session of twenty-seven hours, the Assembly had left the hall.

This immense space, wherein so many events and so much tumult had been pressed in those hours, was silent, empty and gloomy as a sepulchre.

"A light!" exclaimed the Queen.

Pitou picked up an extinguished torch, lit it at a lantern and handed it to the Queen, who moved on again.

On passing through the entrance, Marie Antoinette waved the torch towards the door.

"That's where he fell," she said.

The countess did not reply.

One might have fancied her a spectre following its invocator.

On reaching the corridor, the Queen lowered her torch to the floor.

"Behold his blood," she said.

The countess remained mute.

The Queen walked straight to a sort of closet facing the box of the Logography, pulled open the door of this closet and, flooding the interior with light, said:
"Here is his body!"

Still speechless, Charny's widow entered the closet, sat down on the floor and, by an effort, drew Olivier's head upon her lap.

"Thank you, madame," said she, "this is all I have to ask of you."

"But I have one thing to ask of you," said the Queen.

"Speak."

"Do you forgive me?"

There was an instant's silence, as if Andrée wavered.

"Yes," answered she at last; "for, to-morrow, I shall be with him!"

The Queen drew from her bosom a pair of gold scissors, which she had there hidden as one conceals a dagger, in order to have a weapon for oneself in extreme danger.

"And you—" faltered she, almost supplicating, holding out the scissors to Andrée.

The latter took them, cut off a lock of hair from Charny's head, and returned the hair and scissors to the Queen.

She seized her hand and kissed it.

The widow uttered a cry and snatched away her hand, as though Marie Antoinette's lips had been a red hot iron.

"Ah," murmured the Queen flinging a final look upon the body, "who can tell which of us he will love henceforward!"

"Oh, my well-beloved Olivier!" sighed Andrée on her part, "I trust you at least know now that it I who loves you the best!"

Marie Antoinette had already turned back on her way to her room, leaving the widowed countess in the closet with her husband's remains, upon which fell, through a narrow grated window, a pale moonbeam.

Pitou, without knowing who she was, conducted the Queen back and saw her enter her room; then, rid of his responsibility towards the sentinel, he went out on the lawn to see whether the four men he had asked from Desire Maniquet, had come.

They were waiting.

"Come!" said Pitou.

They entered.

Pitou, showing the way with the torch which he had taken from the Queen's hand, led them to the closet where the bereaved countess still gazed, by the sickly moonlight, on her husband's bloodless but still handsome face.

The light of the torch made her raise her eyes.

"What do you want?" the countess demanded of Pitou and his men, as if she dreaded that these strangers came to deprive her of that loved body.

"My lady," returned Pitou, "we come to seek the Count de Charny's body, to carry it to the Rue Coq Heron."

" Will you swear that it is for that ?" demanded Andrée.

Pitou held out his hand over the body with a dignity of which he might have been thought incapable.

" I swear it, madame !" said he.

" Then, I thank you," resumed Andrée, " and will pray heaven, to my last moments. to spare you and yours from the sorrows with which it has laden me——"

The four men took up the body, laid it on their muskets, and Pitou, with naked sword, took the head of the mournful procession.

The widow walked beside the body, holding its cold and already stiffened hand.

When at the Rue Coq Heron, the body was laid on the Countess Andrée's bed.

" Receive," said she to the four men, " the blessings of a woman who, to-morrow, will be praying from above for you."

" Monsieur Pitou," she added to the young man, " I owe you more than I can ever repay you ; may I ask of you a last service ?"

" Order, my lady," said Pitou.

" At eight o'clock to-morrow morning, arrange it so that Doctor Gilbert may be here."

Pitou bowed and went out.

As he went he turned his head and saw Andrée kneeling before the bed as at an altar.

At the moment when he crossed the threshold, three o'clock rang from Saint Eustache's clock.

CHAPTER IX.

WHAT ANDREE WANTED OF GILBERT.

At eight o'clock precisely on the following day, Gilbert knocked at the door of the residence in the Rue Coq Heron.

On hearing the request which Pitou had made in the Countess de Charny's name, the astonished Gilbert had made him relate in all their details the evening's occurrences.

Then he had reflected a long time.

At length, when he went out in the morning, he had called Pitou, had begged him to go for his son Sebastian at the Abbe Berardier's school, and bring him to the Rue Coq Heron.

When there, Pitou was to wait at the door for Doctor Gilbert's coming out.

Doubtlessly, the old porter had been forewarned of the doctor's coming ; for, having recognized him, he ushered him into the drawing-room, which preceded the bed-chamber.

The countess, dressed in black, was waiting.

It was easy to be seen that she had neither eaten nor slept all night ; her face was pallid, her eyes dry.

Never had the lineaments of her face, which denoted will carried to stubbornness, been so firmly set.

It would have been difficult to tell what determination that diamond heart had taken ; but it was visible that it had taken one.

Gilbert, the acute observer, the philosophical physician, noticed this at the first glance.

He bowed.

" Monsieur Gilbert, I have entreated you to come," began the lady.

" And you see, my lady," responded Gilbert, " that I am punctual to your invitation."

" I have asked for you, and no one else, because I wanted him to whom I make my request to be without a right to refuse me."

" You are right, my lady, not perhaps in what you are going to ask, but in what you say ; you have a right to exact everything of me, even my life."

His hearer smiled bitterly.

" Your life, sir, is one of those existences so valuable to mankind, that I would be the first to pray God to make it long and happy, very far from having the thought of shortening it. But acknowledge that, as much as yours is placed under a fortunate influence, so much are there others which seem blasted by a fatal star."

Gilbert was silent.

" Mine, for instance," went on the widow after a pause, " what say you of mine, sir ?"

As Gilbert cast down his eyes without replying, she resumed :

"Let me recal it to you in a few words. Rest at ease, there will be no one to reproach !"

Gilbert made a sign as much as to say :

"Speak !"

"I was born poor; my father was ruined before my birth. My childhood was sad and lonely; you have known my father, and know better than anybody the degree of his affection for me.

"Two men—one of whom must remain to me unknown, the other, a stranger—had over my life a fatal and mysterious influence to which my will was nothing; one disposed of my mind, the other of my body.

"I found myself a mother, without suspecting I had ceased to be a virgin.

"I lost, by that mournful event, the love of the only being who ever cared for me, my brother's.

"I hugged to myself the idea of becoming a mother and being loved by my child; my child was taken from me an hour after its birth.

"I was a wife without having a husband, a mother without a child !

"A queen's friendship consoled me.

"One day, chance set me in the same vehicle as a brave and handsome young man; chance willed it that I, who had never loved anything, should love him.

"He loved the Queen.

"I became entrusted with that passion. I think you have loved without having been loved, M. Gilbert—you may, therefore, understand what I suffered.

"This was not enough.

"One day, it happened that the Queen said :

"'Andrée, save my life ! save more than my life—my honor !'

"I was doomed, while remaining estranged, to become the wife of the man, whom I had loved for three years.

"I became his wife

"For five years I was beside that man, a flame within, ice without, a statue with a burning heart !

"Physician, tell me ! know you what my heart must have suffered ?

"One day, at last, a day of unspeakable bliss, my devotion, silence and self-denial affected this man. For seven years I had been loving him without having let him suspect it by even a look, when he came to fling himself at my feet, crying:

"'I know everything—I love you !'

"Heaven, wishing to reward me, granted that, at the same time that I found my husband, I should recover my child !

"A year passsed like a day, an hour, a minute; that year was my whole life.

"Four days ago the thunderbolt fell at my feet.

"His honor bade him hasten to Paris, and die there. I made him no remonstrance, shed not one tear, but went off with him.

"Hardly had we arrived than he left me.

"I found him dead last night ! He is in yonder room.

"Do you believe that it would be too ambitious for me, after such a life, to wish to sleep in the same grave as he ?

"Do you believe what I make you is a request you can refuse me ?

"Monsieur Gilbert, you are a cunning leech, a learned chemist ; Monsieur Gilbert, you have done me great wrongs, you have much to expiate. Well, give me a sure, speedy poison, and I not only will pardon you but will die with heart full of gratefulness to you !"

"My lady," replied Gilbert, "your life, as you have said, has been a dreadful trial, and gloriously have you stood the test ! you have borne it like a martyr, nobly, holily !'

The countess made a slight movement of the head which signified :

"I am waiting."

"Now, you say to your destroyer: 'You have given me a bitter life—give me a sweet death !' You have a right to speak thus, and have a right to add : 'You will do what I say, for you have no right to refuse anything I may ask of you——' "

"So, sir ?"

"Do you still want the poison, my lady ?"

" I entreat you to give me it, my friend."

" Is life so burdensome to you that it is impossible to support it ?"

" Death is the greatest favor that man can give me, the greatest benefit heaven can confer !"

" In ten minutes, my lady," returned Gilbert, " you shall have what you ask."

He bowed and drew back a step.

The countess held out her hand.

"Ah," said she, " in one instant you have done me more good than in all your life you have done me evil! Be blessed, Gilbert!"

Gilbert went out.

At the door, he found Pitou and Sebastian, who were waiting in a hackney-coach.

" Sebastian," said he, drawing from his bosom a small vial which he wore hanging by a gold chain, containing an opal liquid, " Sebastian, you will give this to the Countess de Charny."

" How long am I to stay with her, father ?"

" As long as you like."

" Where will I find you again ?"

" I will wait for you here ?"

The young man took the vial, and went in.

He came out, about a quarter of an hour afterwards.

Gilbert flung a rapid glance on him. He brought back the vial untouched.

" What said she ?" inquired Gilbert.

" She said ' Oh, not by your hand, my child !' "

" What did she ?"

" She is weeping."

" She is saved, then ?" said Gilbert. " Come, my son."

He embraced Sebastian more tenderly perhaps than he had ever done before.

Gilbert reckoned without Marat.

A week afterwards he learnt that the Countess de Charny had just been arrested and locked up in the Abbaye Prison.

CHAPTER X.

THE TEMPLE.

But, before following Andrée de Taverney-Charny into the prison where she had been sent as a person " suspected," let us follow the Queen into that where she had been immured as a criminal.

We have stated the antagonism of the Assembly and the commune.

The Assembly, as always happens to constitutional bodies, had not moved at the same pace as individuals ; it had flung forward the people on the tenth of August, and had then dropped behindhand.

The wards of the city had formed the famous council of the commune, and it was this formation that really had made the tenth of August, advocated by the Assembly.

The evidence of this is that, against the commune, the King had fled to seek shelter in the Assembly.

A refuge had been given to the King, whom the commune would not have been sorry to have surprised in the Tuileries, smothered between two beds, strangled in a close room, along with the Queen and the Dauphin—the she-wolf and cub—as folks said.

The Assembly had thwarted this design, the success of which, infamous though it would have been, would have, perchance, been a great piece of good fortune.

Therefore, the Assembly—by protecting the royal family and the court —was royalist; the Assembly — decreeing that the King should dwell in the Luxembourg, a palace, in other words—was royalist.

It is true there were in royalism, as in everything else, gradations; what was royalism in the eyes of the commune, or even of the Assembly, was revolutionary to other eyes.

La Fayette, exiled as a " royalist" in France, was going to be imprisoned as a " revolutionist " by the Emperor of Austria.

The commune began by accusing the Assembly of attachment to royalty ; while every now and anon, Robespierre, from the hole where he was perdu, thrust out his small, flat, pointed and venomous head, hissing some calumny.

Robespierre was just about saying, at this juncture, that a powerful party, the Girondists, had offered the throne to the Duke of Brunswick.

The Girondists, bear it in mind !

The very first voice to cry : "To arms !" the first arm offered to defend France !

Now, the "revolutionary commune" to reach the dictatorship, had to disagree with everything the "royalist Assembly" did.

The latter body had granted the King the Luxembourg as residence.

The commune declared that it could not answer for the King if he remained there; for the cellars of that place, the commune assured, communicated with the catacombs.

The Assembly did not want to collide with the commune about such a trifle; it let it choose the royal residence.

The commune selected the Temple. Let us see if the spot was not capitally chosen !

The Temple was not like the Luxembourg, a palace of which the cellars communicated with the catacombs, its walls with the plain, forming an acute angle with the Tuileries and the city hall ; not so, it was a prison within eyeshot and reach of the commune ; this latter had but to extend its hand to open or shut its doors, it was an old solitary donjon, with the moat dug out again ; an ancient round-house, strong and gloomy.

Philip the Fair, royalty that is to say, crushed in it the Middle Ages, which revolted against him ; now royalty entered there to be borne down by Modern Times.

How comes it, that that old tower should have remained there, in that populous quarter, as black and lugubrious as an owl in the sunlight ?

It was there that the commune decided that the King and his family should dwell.

Was there design when there was assigned for abode to this sovereign this place of sanctuary, where formerly bankrupts came to wear "the green cap," as said the law of the Middle Ages ?

No, it was chance, fatality, we would say Providence, but that would be too harsh.

On the evening of the thirteenth, the King, the Queen, Mesdames Elizabeth, de Lamballe, de Tourzel, with Chemilly, royal valet-de-chambre, and Hue, the Dauphin's valet, were transferred to the Temple.

The commune was in such haste to get the King into his new dwelling, that the tower was not ready.

The royal family was, consequently, introduced into that portion of the building where had formerly dwelt the Count d'Artois, when he came to Paris, and which was termed "the palace."

All Paris seemed overjoyed.

Three thousand five hundred citizens were dead, true enough ; but the King, the friend of the foreigners, the great enemy of the Revolution, the ally of the nobles and the priests, was a prisoner !

All the houses looking on the Temple were illuminated.

There were lamps even on the tower.

When Louis XVI. alighted from the coach, he found Santerre on horseback a couple of yards from the doorway.

Two city officers were waiting for the King, their hats on their heads.

"Enter, sir," they said.

The King stepped in and naturally deceived as to his future dwelling, asked to visit the apartments of the palace.

The municipals exchanged a smile, and, without telling that such a visit would be useless, forasmuch as it was the donjon he was to inhabit, they showed him through the Temple, room by room.

The King settled upon which should be his apartments, and the municipals let him enjoy that error which was soon to turn to bitterness.

At ten o'clock, supper was served up.

During the meal, Manuel kept standing beside the King; it was no longer a servant prompt to obey, but a jailor, an overseer, a master !

Suppose two contradictory orders one given by Louis, one by Manuel; the latter would be the one obeyed.

Here really commenced the captivity.

From the evening of the thirteenth forward, Louis the Sixteenth, vanquished at the summit of royalty, glided from the lofty apex and swiftly proceeded down the opposite slope of the mountain at the foot of which the scaffold awaited him.

It took him eighteen years to reach that towering height, and there uphold himself; five months and eight days were enough for him to be precipitated from it !

Let us see with what rapidity he was pushed !

At ten o'clock in the " palace" dining room ; at eleven, in the drawing-room.

The King still *was*, or at all events believed himself *to be*. He was ignorant of what was going out.

At eleven o'clock, one of the commissaries came to give the valets, Hue and Chemilly, the order to take the little linen there was and follow him.

" Where are we to follow you ?" inquired the servants.

" To the night residence of *your* masters," answered the commissaries ; " the palace is only for them during day."

The King, his wife and his son were only superiors to their servants.

At the palace door, was a municipal who walked on before them with a lantern.

They followed him.

By the lantern's faint glimmer, and thanks to the fading illumination, Hue endeavored to scrutinize the King's future abode ; he could only see before him the gloomy donjon, rising in the air like a granite giant on whose brow shone a fiery crown.

" Goodness ! are you leading us to that tower ?" inquired the valet stopping.

" Just so," returned the guide. " The days of rich living are past ! you shall see how the murderers of the people are lodged."

So saying, the lantern-bearer set foot upon the first step of a winding staircase.

The servants were going to stop at the first landing-place, but the guide kept on his way.

At the second . floor he stopped mounting, turned into an entry to the right of the stairs, and opened a room situated on the right of the entry.

A single window let light into this room ; three or four chairs, a table and a wretched bed formed all the furniture.

" Which of you is the King's domestic ?' inquired the municipal.

" I am his valet-de-chambre," said Chemilly.

" Valet-de-chambre or domestic, it amounts to the same thing."

Then, pointing to the bed, he added : " There, your master lies there."

The lantern-bearer flung from a chair a counterpane and a pair of sheets, lit with his lantern a couple of candles on the mantel-piece, and left the two servants alone.

He went to prepare the Queen's apartment, situated on the first floor.

Hue and Chemilly were stupefied.

They had still in their eyes the splendors of royal habitations ; it was no longer even a prison that the King was cast into, but he was thrust into a kennel !

Majesty of the scenery was lacking to misfortune.

They examined the place.

The bed was in an alcove without curtains.

They began cleaning up the room as best they could.

As one was sweeping and the other dusting, the King entered.

" Oh, sire, what a shame !" cried they with the same voice.

The King—was it strength of mind, or carelessness?—was unmoved. He flung a look around him, saying nothing.

As the wall was scratched over with designs, and as some of these were not exactly seemly to a nice eye, he rubbed them out.

" I do not want," said he, " to leave such sights before my daughter's eyes."

His bed having been made, the King laid down and went to sleep as tranquilly as if he were still in the Tuileries —more tranquilly, perhaps !

Certainly, the King would have been the happiest man in his domains if, at this juncture, he had been given thirty thousand a-year, a country house with a forge, a library of books of travels, a chapel wherein to hear mass, a chaplain to say it, and a park of some ten acres, where he might live beyond any intrigue, surrounded by the Queen, the Dauphin and Madame Royale—or, in sweeter words, by his wife and children.

Not so with the Queen.

If she, the proud lioness, did not roar at seeing her cage, it was because so cruel a pang wrung her bosom, making her insensible to all surrounding her.

Her apartments were composed of four rooms; an ante-chamber, where stopped the Princess de Lamballe, a room for the Queen, a closet given to Madame de Tourzel, and a second room where were to dwell Madame Elizabeth and the two children.

All these were a trifle better than the King's residence.

Besides, as if Manuel was ashamed of the kind of meanness displayed towards the King, he announced that the architect of the commune, Citizen Palloy—the same who had been charged with the demolition of the Bastile—would come to make arrangements with the royal captive to render his future habitation as commodious as possible.

Now, while the Countess de Charny has laid in the grave the remains of her dearly-loved husband; while Manuel instals the King and his family in the Temple ; while the carpenter builds the guillotine on the Square of the Carrousel, the field of victory to be turned into a place of execution—let us glance into the city hall, into which we have twice or thrice already entered, and let us note the power which succeeds that of the Baillys and La Fayettes, and which, by substituting itself for the National Assembly, was ready to assume the dictatorship.

Let us observe the men, they will give us an explanation of the acts.

On the evening of the tenth, when all was over, of course; when the cannonading was hushed, and the rattle of musketry extinguished ; when there was nobody to murder, a band of drunken, ragged bullies carried, into the midst of the council of the commune, the blinking owl, the prophet of the populace, the *diviner*, Marat.

He let all this be done ; he had no longer anything to fear ; the victory was decided and the field open to the wolves, vultures and ravens.

They hailed him as the " vanquisher of the tenth of August !" when they had caught him just when he put his head through the opening of his cellar !

They had garlanded him with laurels ; he, like Cæsar, had kept the crown upon his head.

The citizen sans culottes came and flung, as we have said, their god Marat into the midst of the commune.

Thus was the limping Vulcan cast in to the council of the gods.

At seeing Vulcan, the gods laughed ; at seeing Marat, many laughed ; others were filled with disgust ; some shuddered.

The latter were in the right.

Although Marat formed no part of the commune, although he had not been appointed a member to it, and had only been brought there, he remained.

There was arranged for him, expressly for him, a reporter's box ; with the exception that, in lieu of the reporter being under the hand of the commune, like the Logography under the Assembly, it was the commune that was under the claw, the paw of Marat.

In the same way as in the fine drama of our dear, great friend Victor Hugo, Angelo is over Padua, but feels Venice to be over him, so was the commune above the Assembly, yet felt Marat to be above it.

Look how Marat was obeyed by this towering commune which the Assembly obeyed !

Here is one of its first resolutions :

" Henceforward, the presses of poisonous royalists shall be confiscated and adjudged to patriot printers."

On the morning of the day when was formed this resolution, Marat executed it : he went to the royal printing house, had a press carried to his house, with bags of such type as suited him.

Was he not the foremost of patriot printers ?

The Assembly was frightened by the massacres of the tenth ; it had been powerless to prevent them ; murdered men had fallen in its yards, at its door, on its corridors.

Danton had said :

"When the action of justice commences, then should cease popular vengeance. I take before the Assembly the pledge to protect anybody within its pale ; I will march at their head, I will answer for them."

This had been said before Marat was at the commune. From that moment, Danton said nothing more.

Confronting the snake, the lion skulked away, trying to transform himself into a fox.

Lacroix, once an officer, the athletic deputy, one of Danton's hundred arms, mounted the speaker's stand, and demanded that a courtmartial should be appointed by the commander of the National Guard, by Santerre—the man in whom the royalists themselves allowed a compassionate heart beat under his rough shell ; this courtmartial to try the Swiss, officers and men.

The idea of Lacroix, or rather of Danton, was as follows :

This courtmartial would pick out the men who had fought, who were the brave men ; now, brave men respect bravery.

Besides, for the very reason that they were brave vanquishers, were they repugnant to condemn the vanquished.

Have we not seen these victors, though drunk with blood and smoking with carnage, spare women ?

A courtmartial to be chosen from among the Breton or Marseillais federalists would have been the salvation of the prisoners ; and the proof of this being an act of clemency was that the commune rejected it.

Marat preferred massacre.

It was the shortest way.

He cried out "for heads, more heads, and heads again !"

His demand, instead of decreasing, was always growing ; it was fifty thousand heads first, next, a hundred thousand, then, two hundred thousand ; at the end, he demanded two hundred and seventy-three thousand !

Why this queer amount, this strange sum ?

He would have been at a loss to tell why himself.

He demanded massacre, that was all; and massacre was organized.

Danton no longer entered the commune ; his labors as minister absorbed him, it was said.

What did the commune do ?

It sent deputations to the Assembly.

On the sixteenth, three deputations succeeded one another at the bar of the house.

On the seventeenth, a new deputation presented itself.

"The people," it said, "are weary of not being avenged. Beware that it does not do justice ! At midnight to-night, the alarum shall be rung. There must be a criminal tribunal at the Tuileries, a judge from each ward. Louis the Sixteenth and Antoinette wanted blood ; they shall see that of their satellites flow !"

This audacity and hinted threat made two men spring to their feet : the Jacobin Choudieu, Thuriot the Dantonist.

"Those who come here to demand butchery," said Choudieu, "are no friends of the people, but its inciters. An inquisition is wanted—I shall resist it till death !"

"You mean to disgrace the Revolution !" cried Thuriot ; "the Revolution, is not alone France's but mankind's too !"

After petitions came threats.

The appointees of the sections entered next and said :

"If, before two or three o'clock, the foreman of the jury is not nominated, and if the jurors are not ready for action, the greatest misfortune will stalk through Paris."

At this final menace, the Assembly, was forced to yield ; it voted the formation of an extraordinary tribunal.

On the seventeenth, the demand had been made.

On the nineteenth, the tribunal was in order.

On the twentieth, the tribunal went to work, and condemned a royalist to death.

On the evening of the twenty first the sentenced man of the eve before was executed, by torchlight, on the Square of the Carrousel.

The effect of this first execution was fearful; so overpowering that the executioner himself could not resist it.

At the moment when he was showing, to the people, the head of this first victim, who was to lead so long a line, he gave a groan, his head sank and he fell backwards.

His assistants lifted him.

He was dead!

CHAPTER XI.

THE BLOODY REVOLUTION.

THE Revolution of 1789—that of the Neckars, Sieyes, and Baillys—had terminated in 1790; that of the Barnaves, Mirabeaus and La Fayettes had had its end in '92; the great revolution, the the bloody revolution, the Revolution of the Dantons, Marats and Robespierres, was commencing.

Although linking the names of the three last characters together we do not mean to confound them into one appreciation; on the contrary, they represented, to our eyes, in their quite distinct individuality, the three faces of the three years to pass.

Danton is embodied in '92; Marat, in '93; Robespierre, in '94.

Events run on fast; let us look at them; let us examine the means through which the National Assembly and the commune clashed together.

We have fallen almost entirely into history; all the main characters of our book, with a few exceptions, have already been swallowed up in the revolutionary tempest.

What has become of the brothers Charny, George, Isidore and Oliver?

Dead.

What of the Queen and Andrée?

Imprisoned.

What of La Fayette?

Fled.

On August the seventeenth, La Fayette, by an address, had called upon his army to march upon Paris, re-establish the constitution, counteract the tenth of August and restore the King.

La Fayette, the loyal man, had lost his wits like the others; what he intended to do was directly leading the Prussians and Austrians on to Paris.

The army repelled this instinctively as, eight months later, it repelled Dumouriez.

History would have joined the names of these two men—we mean, would have linked them—if La Fayette detested by the Queen, had not had the good fortune to have been arrested by the Austrians and sent to Olmutz; captivity made his act be forgotten.

On the eighteenth, La Fayette crossed the border.

On the twenty-first, the enemies of France, allies of the royalty against whom was made the tenth of August and was going to be made the second of September; these Austrians, whom Marie Antoinette called to her aid during that clear night when the moon shooting through the window panes upon the royal couch, poured light upon her blended with hope, these Austrians, we repeat, were investing Longwy.

After four-and-twenty hours bombardment, Longwy surrendered.

On the eve of its surrender, at the other end of France, La Vendee rose; the taking of the ecclesiastical oath was the pretext of this uprising.

To face these events, the Assembly appointed Dumouriez to the command of the Army of the East, and decreed La Fayette to be arrested.

It also resolved that the instant the town of Longwy should have returned into the power of the French, all the buildings—with the exception of the national ones—should be destroyed, razed to the ground; it formed a law which banished from its territory all priests who had not taken the oath; it authorized domiciliary visits; confiscated and put up at sale the property of emigres.

During this time, what was the commune doing?

We have told who was its mouthpiece : Marat.

The commune was setting the guillotine to work on the Square of the Carrousel. It was given one head per day, very little; but, in a pamphlet which appeared at the end of August, the members of the tribunal explained the enormous task which it had had imposed on itself to obtain that result, far from satisfying though it was.

It is true this pamphlet was signed : "Fouquier Tinville!"

Let us see what the commune is dreaming; it will not be long before we shall see the realization of its dream.

It was on the evening of the twenty-third that it gave out its prospectus.

Followed by a mob picked up out of the gutters of the faubourgs and the markets, a deputation from the commune presented itself, about midnight, at the National Assembly.

What did it want?

It demanded that the Orleans prisoners should be sent to Paris to receive their punishment.

But these prisoners had never been tried.

That made no difference; that was a formality which the commune could dispense with.

Besides, the holiday of the tenth of August came to its aid.

Its artist, Sergent, was the overseer of it; he had already planned the "procession of the country in danger," and the reader knows how he had succeeded in it.

This time, Sergent surpassed himself.

The object was to fill with mourning, vengeance and murder-thirsting grief, the minds of all those who had lost on the tenth of August any one dear to them.

Fronting the guillotine, which was on the Square of the Carrousel, he had erected, in the centre of the great fountain of the Tuileries, a gigantic pyramid covered with black serge; on each side were the massacres of which the royalists were accused; the Massacres of Nancy, of Nimes, of Montauban, of the Champ de Mars.

The guillotine said : "I kill!"

The pyramid said : "Kill!"

It was on the evening of Sunday, August the twenty-seventh—five days after the outbreak of La Vendee, caused by the priests; four days after the rendition of Longwy, of which General Clerfayt was taking possession in the name of King Louis XVI.—that the expiatory procession set out on its march, in order to take advantage of the mystic majesty which shadows fling upon all things.

First, through clouds of perfumes burning along the whole road they went over, came the widows and orphans of the tenth of August in white, a black ribbon around the waist, carrying, in an ark constructed on the model of the ancient one, that petition dictated by Madame Roland, written on the altar of the country by Mademoiselle de Keralio, the bloody leaves of which had been found scattered on the Champ de Mars, and which, since July the seventeenth, 1791, had been calling for a republic.

Next came a very large black sarcophagus, an allusion to those carts which had taken up their loads on the night of the tenth of August in the heart of the Tuileries, and which rolled towards the faubourgs, groaning under the weight of dead bodies.

Then, banners of grief and vengeance, calling death for death.

Then, a colossal statue of Law, armed with a sword as long as itself.

This was followed by the judges of the tribunals, at the head of whom was the revolutionary tribunal of the tenth of August, the same that excused itself for chopping off only one head a day.

The commune, bloody mother of that bloody tribunal, came, leading in its ranks a statue of Liberty, of the same size as the former of Law; lastly, the Assembly, carrying the civic crowns, which perhaps consoled the dead, but were so insufficient to the living!

All this moved majestically, to Chesnier's gloomy chants and Gossec's sad music.

A part of the night was spent in the accomplishment of this expiatory ceremony, a funereal rejoicing of the mob, during which the people, shaking their fists at the empty Tuileries, menaced those prisons, the fortresses which had been given to the King and the royalists in exchange for their palaces and castles.

Finally, the last lamps having died out and the last torches being smothered in smoke, the multitude broke up.

The two statues of Law and Liberty remained alone to watch over the sarcophagus; but, as no one guarded them, either through mean plunder or deep design of insult, during the night, the two effigies were stripped of their garments, so that, the following day, the two poor goddesses were in a shameful condition.

On seeing this, the people gave a yell of rage, accused the royalists, ran to the Assembly crying for vengeance, took away the statues, dressed them up again, and by way of reparation, drew them to the Square of Louis the Fifteenth.

Later, the scaffold followed them there, and gave them, on the twenty-first of January, fearful satisfaction of the outrage done them on August the twenty-eighth!

On this same day of the twenty-eighth, the Assembly passed the law on domiciliary visits.

Rumors began to spread among the people about the junction of the Prussian and Austrian armies, and the taking of Longwy by General Clerfayt.

The enemy of France, called by the King, the nobles and the priests, was marching on Paris, and, supposing nothing checked him, would be there in six days march.

Then, what would befal this Paris, boiling like a crater, whose heaving for three years had shaken the world?

What Bouille's letter had said—that insolent jest which so much laughter had caused and which was to become reality—not one stone of it should lay upon another!

More than this.

As a fact, there was a general judgment spoken of, terrible and inexorable, which after having destroyed Paris. was to destroy the Parisians.

In what way, by whom was this sentence to be carried out?

The writings of the day tell us; the commune's bloody hand is visible in this legend which, instead of relating the past, related the future.

Why, besides, should not this legend be believed?

Here follows what was to be read on a letter, found in the Tuileries on the tenth of August, and which we have read ourselves at the Archives, where it still is:

"Courts will follow the armies; emigres will draw up as they come, in the camp of the King of Prussia, the prosecutions against the Jacobins, and prepare the gibbets for them."

When the Austrian and Prussian armies should have arrived at Paris, the prisoners would be picked out, the sentence read, and there would be nothing more to do than put it in execution.

To confirm what the letter said, in the official war bulletin the following was printed:

"The Austrian cavalry, in the outskirts of Sarrelouis, have taken away the mayors and republicans whose patriotism is well known.

"The hulans, having captured some municipal officers, have cut off their ears and nailed them to their foreheads."

If such acts were committed in the inoffensive country, what would they do in the revolutionary city?

This was no secret.

The following programme was marked out, debated at every crossing, spreading from each centre to the extremities:

A grand throne would be reared for the allied sovereigns in sight of the heap of ruins which Paris would be; the whole captive population would be driven, dragged to the foot of his throne; as at the judgment of the Last

Day, there would be a setting apart of the good and the bad; the good—the royalists, nobles and priests, in other words—would be passed over to the right hand, and France would be given up to them for them to do what ever they liked; the bad—the revolutionary —would be pushed to the left, where they would find the guillotine, that instrument invented by the revolution, and by which revolution should perish.

Revolution, the same as France; not only France — for that would be nothing; people are made to be holocausts for ideas—not only France, but the thought of the country!

Why had France been the first to shout that word, liberty?

She had believed she did a great act, a holy one, an enlightening of eyes, a giving life to souls, when she said:

"Freedom for France! for Europe! for the world!"

She had thought it a great act to emancipate the earth, and it seems that she was wrong! that heaven was bent on showing her her error! that Providence was against her! that, while thinking herself innocent, she was guilty and infamous! that when she fancied she was performing a noble task, she was committing a crime!

She was to be tried, sentenced, beheaded, all amidst the scoffs of the universe, which, though for its salvation she died, would applaud at her death!

But, to face a foreign foe, this poor people had perhaps some self support?

Those whom the country had worshipped, enriched, paid, would defend it?

No.

Its King conspired with its enemy, and, from the Temple where he is confined, continues to correspond with Prussians and Austrians; its nobility marched against it, organized under its princes; its priests made the peasants revolt.

In their prisons, the incarcerated royalists clapped their hands at the defeats of France; the Prussians at Longwy had made a cheer of gladness arise at the Temple, in the Abbaye.

Hence, Danton, the man for extreme measures, entered the Assembly with a growl.

The Minister of Justice believed justice powerless, and came to ask for power to be given him; and then justice could stride forward in its might.

He mounted the tribune, shook his leonine mane, and stretched out that strong hand which, August the tenth, had dashed in the gates of the Tuileries.

"There must be a national convulsion to make despots recoil," began he. "So far we have but played at war; this wretched game must be cast aside. The people must uprise and hurl themselves upon their foes to exterminate them with a single blow; at the same time, they must *enchain all conspirators*, must *remove them* from doing harm!"

Danton demanded a levy in mass, visits to every house, night-searches with the death penalty against whoever fettered the operations of the provisionary government.

He obtained everything he wanted.

Had he asked more, he would have had it.

"Never," says Michelet, "never had a people been so close to death. When Holland, with the Fourteenth Louis hammering at her gates, had no means of safety save to over-flood herself and drown, she was in less danger; she had Europe on her side. When Athens beheld Xerxes' throne on the rock of Salamis, when she spurned the earth and took to the wave, having water alone for native-land, she was in less danger; she was powerful on her fleet, organized in the hand of great Themistocles, and, more fortunate than France, she had no treachery in her bosom."

France was divided, dissolved, betrayed, bought and sold!

France was Iphigenia under Calchas' knife.

The ring of kings waited for her death only to blow upon their sails the wind of despotism; she uplifted her arms to the gods and they were deaf!

But, when she felt death's chilly hand touch her, with a violent contraction, she gathered herself up, and, a volcano of life, she poured out from her eyes that flame which was, for half a century, to flash over the world.

True it is that, to tarnish this sun, there is a speck, a patch of blood upon it.

The splash from the second of September.

We shall presently see who shed this blood and whether the blot should be imputed to France; but, previously, let us borrow, to close this chapter, two pages more from Michelet.

We feel ourselves lacking power beside this giant, and, like Danton, call strength to our aid.

They are here.

" Paris had the look of a stronghold, like Lille or Strasburg. Everywhere there were passwords, patrols, military precautions, premature, truth to say, for the foe was still distant fifty or sixty leagues. The feeling of deep, admirable union was most visible, and really affecting; all spoke and prayed for the country; each was a recruiting officer, going from dwelling to dwelling, offering to him who would go an uniform, weapons, whatever he had; everybody was speaking, preaching, singing patriotic songs.

" Who was not author at this singular period? who did not print, or distribute? who was not actor in this great drama?

" The most simple scenes, in which everybody figured, were enacted in all places, on public squares, at the enroling offices, at the recording offices where names were put down; all around, were songs, cheers, tears of enthusiasm or of farewell; and, above all such voices, all these godspeeds, a mighty voice resounded in every heart, an unspeaking voice, hence so much the deeper—the very voice of France, eloquent in all its symbols, pathetic in the most tragical: the holy, tearful banner, of the country's danger, hanging from the windows of the city hall, an immense sheet floating on the wind, and seeming to wave the popular legions to march speedily from the Pyrenees to the Escaut, from the Seine to the Rhine!

" To learn what was this moment of sacrifice, one should see, in cottages and houses, the pangs of wives, the rending hearts of mothers, on this day of parting; one should see the old woman, with dried-up eyes and broken heart, pack up in haste the scanty wardrobe her child had to carry away, the savings, the hard-earned coppers now given to her son, on this day of uttermost sorrows.

" To give their offspring to this war which opened with so little brightness, to immolate them to this extreme, hopeless task, was far beyond what the greater part could bring themselves to ; they yielded to these griefs, or rather, by a natural reaction, they fell into fits of fury ; they cared for nothing ; no terror whatever could affect such a state of mind. What terror could daunt those wishing for death?

" We are told how one day probably in August or September—a band of these infuriated females met Danton in the street, 'slanged' him as they would the war itself, reproached him for the Revolution, for all the bloodshed, for the death of their children, cursed him, and prayed heaven every ill should fall back upon his head.

" He showed no astonishment, but, although he knew of their nails being ready to claw his face, he turned around abruptly, looked at the speakers, and was seized with pity.

" Danton had much heart.

" He mounted on a post and, to console them, began to rail back at them in their own style of speech; his first words were violent, coarse and broad. They were quite abashed; his fury, real or simulated, distanced their rage.

" This wonderful orator, instinctive yet calculating, had for popular basis, a strong, sensual temperament, formed for physical passions, wherein flesh and blood predominated. Danton was especially a *man*; he had in him something of the dog and the lion, much of the bull, also. His mask frightened a looker-on; the singular uncomeliness of an uneven countenance lent to his abrupt speech which went by fits and starts, a kind of wild spur. The masses, fond of brute force, felt before him what is ever experienced of dread and sympathy from every powerful being, and, beneath that violent, furious mask, in that manly breast, was, also, felt to be a heart, which made one fact be divined : that this fearful man, who only spoke in vaunts and threats, was also a brave man.

"The women gathered around him saw all this confusedly, and let him harangue them, lord over them, master them ; he might lead them wherever he pleased ; he explained to them rudely what use was woman, love, generation ; that one does not give birth to children for oneself, but for the country, and, thus far having gone, he rose suddenly, speaking no longer to any one but (so it seemed) for himself alone.

"His whole heart, so it is said, flowed out from his breast in words of violent affection for France, and down that strange face—rough with small-pox pitting, like the rugged sides of Etna or Vesuvius—began to trickle large drops —tears.

"The women could no longer govern themselves ; they wept for France, instead of bewailing their children, and went away sobbing, their faces hid in their aprons."

Oh, great historian, Michelet, where are you ?

At Nervi !

Oh, great poet, Hugo, where are you ?

At Jersey !

CHAPTER XII.

THE EVE OF SEPTEMBER THE SECOND.

"WHEN the country is in danger," Danton had said, on the twenty-eighth of August, at the National Assembly, "everything belongs to the country."

On the twenty-ninth, at four o'clock in the afternoon, the city drums were beaten.

Everybody knew what that was for ; the domiciliary visits were to begin.

As by the stroke of a magic wand, at the first tap of the drumsticks, Paris changed its aspect ; from being populous, it became unpeopled.

Open shops were closed, each street was stopped up and occupied by platoons sixty strong.

The barriers, giving communication with the country, were guarded, as was the river.

At one o'clock in the morning, the visits commenced at every house.

The commissioners of the sections knocked at the street door in the name of the law, and the door opened.

They knocked at every room, still in the name of the law, and every room was opened to them. They forced in the doors of such places as were not occupied.

Two thousand guns were seized, and three thousand persons were arrested.

Terror was wanted ; it was obtained.

There was born from this proceeding something of which no one had thought, or to which too much thought had been given, perhaps.

These enterings of houses had thrown open to the poor the dwellings of the rich ; the armed men who followed the magistrates had been allowed to throw an amazed look into the silken and gilded retreats of those magnificent mansions where still lived their residents, or whose owners were absent.

Thence, not a greed for pillage, but a redoublement of hatred.

So far from plunder were they, that Beaumarchais, who was then in prison, tells how, in his splendid gardens of the Boulevard Saint Antoine, a woman picked a rose, for which she came near being flung into the water.

Remark that all this happened at the time when the commune was decreeing that "brokers in silver should be punished with the death penalty."

Here was the commune substituting itself for the Assembly ; it decreed the death penalty.

It gave Chaumette the right to open prison and add to the number of prisoners ; it arrogated the right of pardoning. At length, it ordered that at the gate of every place of confinement should be posted a list of the prisoners it enclosed ; this was an appeal to hate and revenge ; enemies had the number down of the cell where was immured the object of their spite.

The Assembly saw what an abyss it was being drawn into. In spite of itself, it would have to dip its fingers in blood.

Who drew it into this?

The commune, its foe.

There was wanted only an occasion for the struggle to break out between the two powers.

This opportunity was given by a fresh exploit of the commune.

On the twenty-ninth of August, the day of the visits, the commune, for an article in a paper, bade Girey Dupre appear at its bar; he was one of the boldest Girondists, because one of the youngest.

Girey Dupre took refuge in the Minister of War's, not having time to reach the Assembly.

Huguenin, the president of the commune, had the place surrounded to tear from it by main force the Girondist journalist.

Now, the Gironde was still in the majority in the Assembly; insulted in one of its members, it fired up and, in turn, called President Huguenin to its bar.

The president did not reply to the summons.

On the thirtieth, the Assembly issued a decree which broke up the commune.

A fact, which proves the horror there was in those days for theft, had strongly helped the decree issued by the Assembly.

A member of the commune, or an individual claiming to be a member, had had the wardrobe entered, and had taken from it a small silver cannon, a gift of the city to Louis Fourteenth when a child.

Cambon, who had been appointed keeper of the public wealth, having information of this robbery, had summoned this accused man to the bar; the accused did not deny the act nor excuse it, but he merely said that this precious article running the risk of being stolen, he had thought it to be safer in his house than anywhere else.

This tyranny of the commune weighed heavily, and was cumbersome to many.

Louvet, a man for bold, initiatory movements, was president of the section of the Rue des Lombards; he declared through his section that the general council of the commune was guilty of usurpation.

Feeling itself supported, the Assembly thereupon decreed that the president of the commune, Huguenin, who would not come willingly to its bar, should be brought there by force and that, in twenty-four hours, a new commune should be elected by the wards of the city.

This decree was issued at five o'clock on the evening of the thirtieth of August.

Let us count the hours, for, henceforward, we are proceeding to the Massacre of the second of September, and every minute see appear, taking a step, the bloody goddess with threatening arms, wildly tossing locks and flashing eye, Terror!

However, the Assembly, from a remnant of fear for its redoubtable enemy, declared, while dissolving the body, that the commune had deserved well of the country; which was not exactly logical.

"*Ornandum, tollendum!*" said Cicero of Octavius.

The commune acted like Octavius

It would let itself be crowned, but would not let itself be driven away.

Two hours after the decree had been issued, Tallien (the dwarf scribe who loudly boasted being Danton's man), the secretary of the commune, proposed for the Thernes Section to march against the Lombards Section.

Here was really civil war, no longer a people against a king, tillers of the soil against aristocrats, cottages against castles, houses against palaces, but city wards against one another, pikes against pikes, citizens against citizens.

At the same time, Marat and Robespierre, the latter as a member of the commune, the former as a kind of looker-on, lifted up their voices.

Marat cried out for the massacre of the National Assembly; that was nothing, folks were growing used to hear him broach such designs.

But Robespierre, the prudent, careful Robespierre, the vague denouncer, demanded that arms should be taken up and that not only should they defend, but attack.

Robespierre must have been well aware of the commune being very strong for him to venture to speak out thus!

It was very strong, in fact, for, that same night, its secretary Tallien went to the Assembly with three thousand pikemen.

"The commune," he said, "and the commune alone, has elevated the members of the Assembly to the level of representatives of a free people, the commune issued the decree against plotting priests and arrested these men, on whom none dared to lay hand; the commune," he finally concluded, "will have purged in a few days the free soil of their presence!"

Hence, it was between the night of the thirtieth and the morning of the thirty-first, before the Assembly itself, which had dissolved it, that the commune spoke the first word of massacre.

Who spoke this opening word?

Who, so to say, waved the blank sheet on which was to be printed the red programme?

We see who it was, Tallien, the man who made the ninth Thermidor.

The Assembly uprose, we must do it that justice.

Manuel, the procureur of the commune, saw that they were going too far; he had Tallien arrested, and forced Huguenin to make reparation to the Assembly.

And yet this Manuel—who arrested Tallien and made Huguenin beg pardon for contempt—knew well what was going to happen, for this pedant, with small mind but honest heart, did the following act.

He had, in the Abbaye Prison, a personal enemy: Beaumarchais.

Beaumarchais, a great sprinkler-about of gall, had profusely drenched Manuel; now, it came into Manuel's head that, if Beaumarchais was murdered with the rest, his murder would be attributed to a mean spite of his. He ran to the Abbaye and called for Beaumarchais.

The latter, on seeing him, was about to excuse himself and give explanations to his literary victim.

"It is nothing now concerning literature, papers or criticism. Yonder is the open door; save yourself to-day, if you do not want your throat cut to-morrow!"

The author of Figaro did not want the words repeated; he slipped through the door and escaped.

Suppose he had hissed the playwright Collot d'Herbois, instead of having criticised the author Manuel—Beaumarchais would have been dead!

The thirty-first of August dawned, the great day which was to decide between the Assembly and the commune, between moderation and extreme.

The commune was bent on remaining in office at any price.

The Assembly had dismissed itself in favor of a new Assembly.

Naturally, the commune wanted to rush forward, all the more from the state of things favoring an onward move.

The people, without knowing what was intended, were eager to do something.

Let loose on the twentieth of June, and on the tenth of August, they felt a vague thirst for blood and destruction.

It must be acknowledged that, on one side, Marat; and Hebert, on the other, were firing their mind!

Robespierre, wishing to regain his much shaken popularity—France had wished war, Robespierre had advised peace—had become a newsmonger; one who by the absurdity of his news, outstripped the most absurd.

A powerful party, he said, offered the throne to the Duke of Brunswick.

What were at this moment the powerful parties.

Three: the Assembly, the commune, the Jacobins; and the commune and the Jacobins might be considered as one.

It could be neither of them, for Robespierre was a member of the club and of the city government; he would not have exposed himself.

This powerful party, therefore, was the Gironde.

We have said that Robespierre sur

passed in absurdity the most absurd novelists; what was more absurd indeed than to accuse the Gironde, which had declared war on Prussia and Austria, of offering the throne to the enemy?

And who were the men accused of this?

The Vergniauds, Rolands, Clavieres, Servans, Gensonnes, Guadets, Barbarouxes, in other words the warmest patriots, and at the same time the most honorable men in France!

But there are moments when a man like Robespierre says anything, and worse, there are times when the people believe anything.

This was the last day of August.

The physician whose finger was laid on the pulse of France, must have felt on this day the pulsations increase every moment.

At five o'clock on the afternoon of the thirtieth, the Assembly had dissolved the commune, as before stated; the decree ordained that in twenty-four hours, the sections should appoint a new council general.

Therefore by five in the afternoon of the thirty-first, the decree should have been carried out.

But Marat's vociferations, Hebert's menaces, Robespierre's calumnies, made the commune press with such a weight on Paris, that the sections did not dare to vote. They gave as pretext for their disobedience that the decree had not been officially notified to them.

About noon of the closing day of August, the Assembly was informed that its previous evening's decree would not be complied with. Force had therefore to be called in, and who could tell whether force would keep the Assembly.

The commune had Santerre through his brother-in-law Panis.

Panis, it will, be recollected, was that Robespierrean fanatic who had proposed to Rebecqui and Barbaroux the appointing of a dictator, and who had made them understand that this dictator ought to be the Incorruptible. Santerre was the faubourgs; the faubourgs had the irresistible might of the ocean.

The faubourgs had broken the gate of the Tuileries; they might easily beat down the doors of the Assembly.

Besides, the Assembly feared, if it armed itself against the commune, not only it would be shunned by the extreme patriots, by those who wanted revolution at any price, but, moreover —which was far worse—feared it would be sustained in spite of itself by the moderate royalists.

Then it would be completely lost!

Towards six o'clock, the rumor ran over its benches that there was rioting around the Abbaye.

One Montmorin had just been acquitted.

The people thought he was the minister who had signed the passports with which Louis the Sixteenth had tried to flee; they rushed in a mob on the prison, crying out loudly for the traitor's death.

The greatest difficulty was had in making the error be understood; all night long there was fearful tumult in the streets of Paris.

It was clear that, next day, the slightest incident coming to help on this ferment would assume colossal proportions.

This incident—which we will endeavor to relate because it concerns a hero of this romance whom we have long lost sight of—occurred in the prisons of the Chatelet.

CHAPTER XIII.

IN WHICH BEAUSIRE IS MET AGAIN.

SINCE the tenth of August, a special tribunal had been instituted to try the thefts which had been committed at the Tuileries.

The people, as Peltier tells us, shot on the spot some two or three hundred thieves caught in the act; but, outside of that, there were quite as many more, as may be easily understood, who momentarily at least, had managed to conceal their doings.

Among the number of these honorable gentry was to be found our old acquaintance, Beausire, ex-exempt in his Majesty's service.

Our readers who remember the antecedents of Oliva's lover and young Toussaint's father, will not be astonished to find him among those who had to render an account, not to the nation, but to the courts, of the share they had in the sacking of the Tuileries.

M. de Beausire, truth to say, had entered the chateau after everybody; he was too sensible a man to commit the folly of entering the first, or as one of the first, that place which he had so much difficulty to enter anyhow.

It was not Beausire's political opinions which led him into the royal dwelling, either to weep over the downfall of royalty, or to applaud the people's triumph. No; M. de Beausire came there as a mere looker-on, soaring above those human weaknesses termed opinions, and having only one design, that of seeing if those who lost a throne had not lost, at the same time, some more portable valuable, one easier to put in a place of safety.

But, to save appearances, M. de Beausire wore a red cap, was armed with an enormous sabre, and had splashed his shirt and stained his hands in the blood of the first dead man he had encountered; so that this wolf skulking after the conquering army, this vulture flapping his wings after the battle to the field, might, by a superficial look, be mistaken for a victor.

It was for a conqueror, indeed, that the majority took him who heard him shout: " Death to the aristocrats !" and who saw him search under beds, open cupboards, and even the drawers of bureaux, in order to make sure that no aristocrats were there hidden.

However, at the same time as he thus conducted himself, for M. de Beausire's misfortune, there was one man who did not shout, or look under beds, or open closets, but who, entering under fire though unarmed, with the conquerors, though having conquered no one, was walking, with his hands behind his back, as if he were strolling in a public garden on a holiday, cold and calm under his seedy black coat, only lifting up his voice from time to time to say : " Don't forget, citizens ; no woman-killing, and no touching jewels !"

To those whom he saw killing men and throwing furniture out of the windows, this man seemed to have nothing to say.

He had remarked at the first glance that M. de Beausire was not one of these last named.

So, at half-past nine o'clock, Pitou—who, as we already know, had obtained as a post of honor the guard of the Clock vestibule—saw stalking towards him, from the interior of the chateau, a kind of huge, lugubrious giant who, with politeness, but also with firmness, as if he had been ordered to put order to the chaos and show justice in vengeance, said to him :

" Captain, you will see come down a man, wearing a red cap and swinging a sword, to be known from his swaggering airs ; you will stop him and have him searched by your men ; he has stolen a casket of diamonds."

" Yes, M. Maillard," answered Pitou, touching his hat with his hand.

" Aha !" said the ex-usher, " do you know me, my friend ?"

" I should think I did know you !" returned Pitou ; " don't you remember me, Monsieur Maillard ? We took the Bastile together ?"

" Very likely !" said Maillard.

" And, on the fifth and sixth of October, we were at Versailles together."

" I was there, then, indeed."

" Of course ! you were escorting ladies and you had a duel at the gate of the Tuileries with a watchman who would not let you pass."

" Well, are you going to do what I said ?" said Maillard.

" That and everything, M. Maillard ; anything you order ! Ah, you are a patriot !"

" So I trust," went on Maillard ; " and that is why we ought not to allow the name we have a right to own be dishonored. Hush ! here's our man."

In fact, at this juncture, M. de Beausire came down the staircase, brandishing his huge blade, and yelling :

" The nation forever !"

Pitou made a sign to Tellier and Maniquet, who, without affectation, placed themselves before the door, and he went to wait for M. de Beausire on the last step of the staircase.

The latter had noticed these evolutions and, no doubt, they made him uneasy, for he stopped and, as if he had forgotten something, he made a half-turn to retrace his steps.

"I beg your pardon, citizen, this is the way to go out," said Pitou.

"Ah! is it?"

"And, as there is an order to evacuate the Tuileries, go out if you please."

Beausire turned again and continued to descend the stairs.

When on the last step, he touched his red cap and, affecting the military style, asked:

"Come, comrade, am I to go or not?"

"You are to go; but first." said Pitou, "you must submit to a little formality."

"Ahem! And what's that, sir captain?"

"You must be searched, citizen."

"Searched?"

"Yes."

"Search a patriot, a conqueror, a man who has been exterminating aristocrats?"

"So runs the order; so, comrade—as comrade you are to be," went on Pitou, "put back your big spit in its case—it is useless, now that the aristocrats are killed—and let yourself be searched willingly or, if you don't, I shall be compelled to employ force."

"Force?" echoed M. de Beausire. "You speak in this way, my fine captain, because you've got twenty men at your back; but were we alone——"

"Were we alone, citizen," interrupted Pitou, "here's what I would do; just this way, I would take your wrist in my right hand; I would tear your sword away with my left hand, and I would break it under my foot, as being no more worthy of being touched by an honest man's hands after having been touched by a thief's!"

Pitou, putting into practice the acts spoken of, twisted the counterfeit patriot's hand with his right hand, pulled from it the sword, and, snapping the blade under his foot, flung the hilt far from him.

"A thief!" exclaimed red cap, "a thief—I, M. de Beausire!"

"My friends," said Pitou pushing the ex-exempt into the midst of his men, "search M. de Beausire!"

"Well, search away," said the man, yielding himself like a victim, "search away."

The speaker's permission was not required for the examination to begin; but to the high amazement of Pitou and especially of Maillard, search as they might, turn pockets inside out, ferret in the most secret places, nothing more could be found on the ex-exempt than a pack of cards of which the spots were hardly discernible, so old were they, and the sum of eleven sous.

Pitou glanced at Maillard.

The latter gave a nod, which was as much as to say:

"I cannot make it out."

"Try it over again," said Pitou, one of whose principal qualities, it will be called to mind, was patience.

They began again; but the second search was no more fruitful than the first; the same pack of cards and the same eleven sous to be met with.

Beausire was triumphant.

"Well," observed he, "is a sword still dishonored by having touched my hand?"

"No, sir," returned Pitou, "and the proof that I do not think it is, is that, if you are not satisfied with the excuses I address you, one of my men will lend you his, and I will give you any other satisfaction you may like."

"Thank you, young man," said M. de Beausire, drawing himself up to his full height, "you have acted pursuant to orders, and an old soldier like myself knows orders are sacred. Now, I must tell you Madame de Beausire must be uneasy about my long absence, and, if I am allowed to retire——"

"Go, sir," said Ptiou, "you are free!"

Beausire gave an elegant salute and disappeared.

Pitou looked around him for Maillard.

He was not to be seen.

"Have you seen M. Maillard?" he inquired.

"I fancied I saw him go upstairs," responded one of the men of Haramont.

"So you did," said Pitou, "for here he is coming down."

Maillard, indeed, was descending the staircase, and, thanks to his long legs taking two steps at a time, he was presently in the vestibule.

"Well, have you found anything?" he asked.

"No," replied Pitou.

"Then, I have been luckier than you, for I have found the casket."

"So we were wrong?"

"Nay, we were right."

Maillard, opening the box, showed some gold articles of jewelry, which were all deprived of the precious stones which had been mounted in them.

"Why, what does this mean?" exclaimed Pitou.

"That the rascal suspected the search, and dug out the diamonds, and, finding the mounting would be rather bothersome, he threw the box into the closet where I have found it."

"Good! what of the diamonds?" queried Pitou.

"Well, he has found some way of giving us the slip with them."

"The villain!"

"Has he been gone long?" inquired Maillard.

"As you came down stairs, he was across the central court by the gate."

"Which way went he?"

"Toward the quais."

"Good bye, captain!"

"Are you going, M. Maillard?"

"I want to have my mind clear," returned the ex-usher.

With that, opening his long legs like a compass, he set off in chase of Beausire.

Pitou dwelt some time pondering over what had happened, and he was still under the weight of this pre-occupation when he fancied he recognized the Countess de Charny, and went through the events which we have narrated in our own place, not deeming it fit to complicate them with an incident which, so we believe, ought to have a place elsewhere.

CHAPTER XIV.

THE EMETIC.

SWIFT as was his step, Maillard could not catch up to Beausire, who had for him three favorable circumstances; firstly, ten minutes' start; next, the darkness; then, the fact of numerous persons crossing the Court of the Carrousel, among whom Beausire had disappeared.

But, having reached the water-line of the Tuileries, the ex-usher of the Chatelet did none the less continue to walk on; he lived, as before mentioned, in the Faubourg Saint Antoine, and it was in his way thither, or very nearly so, to follow the water-front as far as the Square of the Greve.

A thick press of people hurried over the Neuf and Money-changers' Bridges; there was to be an exposure of bodies on the Square of the Palace of Justice, and everybody went in the hope, or rather with the fear, of finding a brother, parent or friend.

Maillard followed the throng.

At the corner of the Rue de la Barillerie and the Palace Square, he had a friend who was a druggist; at that period, they styled such apothecaries.

Maillard entered his friend's shop, took a seat and conversed on the day's doings, while surgeons were buying of the apothecary linen for bandages, plaster, salves, lint, in short, all things needful for the cure of wounded men—for, among the lifeless bodies, was to be discovered from time to time by a scream, a groan, or rattling breath, that some unfortunate being still lived, and this sufferer would be on the instant drawn out from the midst of the corpses, and carried to the Hospital.

There was hence, great ado in the establishment of the worthy apothecary; but Maillard was not a whit in the way; on such days, a patriot of the stamp of Maillard would be received with pleasure, for such a one was as balm in the city and its suburbs.

He had been there for quarter of an hour, with his long legs curled up under him and his whole person drawn in to take as little room as possible, when there entered a woman of thirty-seven or thirty-eight years of age, who, under the livery of most abject misery, preserved a certain remnant of former wealth, and a bearing betraying her aristocracy, if not inborn, at all events well studied.

But what especially struck Maillard was the strange resemblance between this woman and the Queen; he would have uttered an exclamation of amazement, if he had not over himself all the command of which we are aware.

She held by the hand a little boy of eight or nine; she approached the counter with a kind of bashfulness, concealing as best she could the wretchedness of her attire, which rendered still more visible the attention which in her distress, she paid to her face and hands.

For some time she was unable to make herself heard on account of the crowd; but finally, addressing the master of the shop, she said:

"Sir, I want an emetic for my husband, who is sick."

"What kind of a purgative do you want, citizeness?" inquired the shop-keeper.

"Whatever you please, sir, provided it don't come to more than eleven sous."

This peculiar amount struck Maillard.

Eleven sous was precisely the sum which had been found, it will be remembered, in M. de Beausire's pockets.

"Why must it not cost more than eleven sous?" inquired the apothecary.

"Because that is all the money my husband had to give me."

"Make a mixture of tamarinds and senna, and give it to the citizeness," said the apothecary to his boy.

The latter busied himself with this order, while his master waited on other customers.

But Maillard, who had nothing else to do, had concentrated his entire attention on the emetic-asking woman with eleven sous.

"Here's your medecine, citizeness," said the boy.

"Come, Toussaint," said the woman with a drawling tone which seemed habitual to her, "give me the eleven sous, my child."

"Here they are," said the little fellow. "Come, mamma Oliva," said he, laying his hand on the counter; "come quick, papa is waiting."

He tried to drag away his mother crying:

"Come, come, mamma Oliva, come."

"Beg pardon, citizeness," said the apothecary's boy, "here are only nine sous."

"What! only nine?" exclaimed the woman.

"That's so—count 'em yourself," returned the boy.

She reckoned them over; there was indeed only nine sous.

"What have you done with the other two pennies, naughty boy?" said she.

"I don't know nothing about it," replied the child. "Come, mamma Oliva?"

"You ought to know, for you wanted to carry the money and I let you have it."

"I guess I lost it," said the child. "Come, ma."

"You've a fine boy there, citizeness," broke in Maillard, "he appears full of intelligence, but care should be taken that he does not turn out a thief."

"Thief!" echoed the woman to whom the little fellow had given the name of "Mamma Oliva;" "why so, sir?"

"Because he has not lost the two sous, but has hidden them in his shoe."

"I?" cried the boy. "What a lie!"

"In the left shoe, citizeness," went on Maillard, "the left."

Oliva, notwithstanding Master Toussaint's outcries, removed the shoe from his left foot, and, sure enough, found the missing coppers in it.

She gave the two sous to the apothecary's boy, and dragged away her son, threatening him with punishment which would have appeared dreadful to the bystanders if the threat of it had not been accompanied with fondlings which in all likelihood denoted that maternal weakness would gain the upperhand.

This event, of very little importance in itself, would most certainly have passed unperceived among the graver surroundings it had, if the likeness of this woman with Marie Antoinette had not singularly haunted Maillard's mind.

The result of his thinking was that he stepped up to his friend the apothecary and, taking advantage of a momentary lull, asked him:

" Did you remark?"

" What?"

" The resemblance of that citizeness who has just gone out——"

" With the Queen?" said the apothecary laughing.

" Yes, did you notice it as well as I?"

" Long ago."

" What do you mean?"

" Why, it's an historical resemblance."

" I do not understand."

" Don't you recollect the famous Queen's Necklace?"

" An usher at the Chatelet could never have forgotten such a story."

" If so, you should remember a certain Nicole Legay, alias Oliva."

" By heaven, that's true! The same who played the part of the Queen towards the Cardinal de Rohan?"

" And who lived with a sort of swashbuckler suspected of no end of evil doings, an ex-exempt, a gambler, police spy named Beausire."

" Eh?" ejaculated Maillard, jumping as if a snake had stung him.

" Named Beausire," repeated the man of drugs.

" And it's this Beausire she calls her husband?' inquired Maillard.

" Yes."

" And it is for him that she comes for medicine?"

" The rascal has got one of his lies stuck in his throat."

" An emetic—a purging drug?" continued Maillard, like a man on the track of an important secret, who did not want to be turned aside from his idea.

" Yes."

" I've got my man, I have him!" cried Maillard, striking his forehead.

" What man?"

" The eleven sous man!"

" Who's that?"

" Beausire!"

" You've got him?"

" Yes. If I know where he lives, though."

" I know that much, if you do not know it."

" Good! Where does he live?"

" Number six in the Rue de la Juiverie."

" Near by?"

" A step or two."

" Well, I am no longer astonished."

" At what?"

" That young Toussaint should have stolen, or tried to steal, the two sous from his mother."

" Why are you no longer astonished?"

" He is Beausire's son, is he not?"

" His living portrait."

" A good dog shows his blood! Come, dear friend," continued Maillard, " hand on your heart, how long will it take your medicine to operate?"

" Seriously?"

" Most seriously."

" Not before two hours."

" Not before?"

" Fully that."

" That is all I want; I will have plenty of time."

" So you feel interested in M. de Beausire."

" So great an interest that fearing he may not be properly cared for, I am going to get for him——"

" What?"

" Two *Guard*-ians. Good bye, friend."

Leaving the apothecary's shop with a silent laugh, the only one which ever creased his woebegone countenance, Maillard turned back on his way to the Tuileries.

Pitou was absent.

The reader will remember that he had followed, through the garden, in Andrée's steps, the Count de Charny's path, but, in his absence, Maillard found Tellier and Maniquet guarding the post.

They recognized him.

"Is this you, Monsieur Maillard," said Maniquet; "well, did you over take your man?"

"No, but I am on his track," responded Maillard.

"That's good news," said Maniquet; "for, although nothing was found on him, I will wager that he had the diamonds!"

"Bet, citizen," said Maillard; "bet and you will win."

"Good!" exclaimed Maniquet, "are we going to recover them?"

"I hope so, at any rate, if you will help me."

"In what, Citizen Maillard? We are at your orders?"

Maillard beckoned the lieutenant and subordinate to come to him.

"Pick me out from your company two sure men."

"For bravery?"

"For honesty."

"Take any two you like."

Turning to the men, Desire called out:

"Two men!"

A dozen sprang up.

"Come here, Boulanger," said Maniquet.

One of the men stepped up.

"And now you, Molicar."

A second came and took his place beside the first.

"Anything more do you want, Monsieur Maillard?" inquired Tellier.

"No, this will do. Come, my brave fellows!"

The two Haramont federals followed Maillard.

The latter led them to the Rue de la Juiverie, and stopped before the door of No. 6.

"This is it," said he; "let us go upstairs."

The two men entered with him the alley, next went up the stairs and finally arrived on the fourth floor.

There they were guided by the crying of Master Toussaint, not yet recovered from the correction—not maternal—which Monsieur de Beausire, seeing the graveness of the offence, had deemed it his duty to inflict; for he had added several cuffs from his hard hand to the somewhat more gentle taps which, much against her heart, Mademoiselle Oliva had distributed to her darling.

Maillard tried to open the door.

The bolt was shot inside.

He knocked.

"Who's there!"

This challenge was in Mademoisele Oliva's drawling tones.

"In the name of the law, open!" rejoined Maillard.

There was a snatch of conversation in a low voice, the result of which was that young Toussaint became quiet, fancying that it was on account of the two sous which he had tried to steal from his mother that the law was a-foot, while Beausire, believing the knock to be in connection with the domiciliary visits, far from assured though he was, endeavored to calm Oliva's alarm.

At last, Madame de Beausire made up her mind, and, at the moment when Maillard was going to knock for the second time, the door opened.

The three men entered, to the high terror of Mademoiselle Oliva and Master Toussaint, who ran to hide under an old straw-bottomed chair.

Beausire was a-bed, and, on his night table, lit up by a wretched candle smoking in an iron stick, Maillard saw with satisfaction the bottle, empty.

The medicine was taken; the effect might be expected.

During their coming, Maillard had related to Molicar and Boulanger what had happened at the druggist's; so that when they arrived in M. de Beausire's chamber, they were fully informed of affairs.

Hence, after having seen them instal themselves, one on each side of the sick man's bed, Maillard said:

"Citizens, Monsieur de Beausire is just like that princess in the Arabian Nights' who never spoke without being forced to do so, but who, every time she opened her mouth, let a diamond drop! Do not therefore let a word fall from Monsieur de Beausire without examining it. I will wait for you at the municipality; when this gentleman has nothing more to say to you, you will take him to the Chatelet, where you will state that Citizen Maillard advises great care to be taken of him, and you will come to meet me at the city hall with what he shall have imparted to you."

The two National Guards nodded in token of obedience, and stood at ease on either side of Monsieur de Beausire's couch.

The apothecary was not in error; at the end of two hours, his compound operated.

The effect lasted for all of an hour, and never was there effect more satisfactory!

At about three o'clock in the morning, Maillard saw the two men come to him.

They brought from M. de Beausire a hundred thousand francs in diamonds of the purest water.

Maillard, in his name and those of the two men from Haramont, deposited the stones on the desk of the procureur of the commune, who handed over to them a certificate stating that Citizens Maillard, Molicar and Boulanger had deserved well of the country.

CHAPTER XV.

THE FIRST OF SEPTEMBER.

THE conclusion of the tragi-comic event we have just recounted is as follows:

M. de Beausire, confined in the Prison of the Chatelet, had been handed over to the jury charged to specially look into the crimes of theft committed on the tenth of August and the subsequent days.

He could not deny; the act was too clearly established.

Therefore, the accused was compelled to humbly confess his fault and to implore the clemency of the tribunal.

The court had ordered a reference to the antecedents of M. de Beausire; and, far from softened by the information which the inquiry had brought to light, it had condemned the ex-exempt to five years in the galleys and public branding.

M. de Beausire had vainly alleged that he had only been driven into robbery by honorable promptings—in hope of ensuring a peaceful future to his wife and son; nothing could alleviate the sentence; and as, in its position as a special court, it was without appeal, the day but one following the judgment, the sentence would be executed.

Alas! that it had been carried out on the instant.

Fatality would have it that, on the eve of the day on which he would be branded, there was cast into his prison one of his former comrades.

Recognition took place between them, and they were speedily on their former standing.

The new prisoner, he said, was connected with a perfectly organized plot, which was to have its outbreak on the Square of the Greve or of the Palace.

The conspirators were to assemble in great number, under pretext of seeing the first public exposure of criminals (this took place, at this epoch, indifferently on the Greve or before the Palace of Justice) and to shouts of "Long live the King! Hurrah for the Prussians! Down with the nation!" would storm the city hall, call to their help the National Guards, two thirds of whom were royalists or at least constitutionalists, support the abolition of the commune, dissolved on the thirtieth of August by the Assembly, and, in short, complete the royalist counter-revolution.

Unfortunately, this lately-arrested acquaintance of M. de Beausire was the one who ought to give the signal.

Now, as the other conspirators, ignorant of his incarceration, would gather on the square, on the day of the first culprit being exposed, and, as there would not be anybody there to start the cry of "Long live the King and the Prussians, and down with the nation!" the uprising would not take place.

This was all the deeper to be regretted, added the friend, as never was there plot better settled and promising a more certain result.

The arrest of Beausire's friend had, moreover, the more deplorable result from its being certain, in the height of the uproar, that the criminal could not fail to be delivered, to flee, and to escape thus the double penalty of the brand and the galleys.

M. de Beausire, although not boasting a very steadfast opinion, had always inclined to royalty; he, therefore, began by bitterly regretting for the King's sake, and next for his own, that the outbreak was not to take place.

Suddenly, he struck his forehead; his mind had been illuminated by a sudden idea.

"But," said he to his comrade, "this first exposure is going to be mine."

"Beyond a doubt; which, I repeat to you, is why this is a greater loss."

"And you were saying your arrest is unknown?"

"Completely."

"So, the conspirators will come together all the same as if you were free?"

"Just the same."

"So that if anybody gives the signal, the whole thing will burst out?"

"Yes. But who is going to give it, when I am in the jug and cannot communicate with the outside?"

"I!" ejaculated Beausire, in the tone of Medea in Corneille's tragedy.

"You?"

"I, of course! I will be there, won't I, for it is I who will be exposed. Well, I will cry out: 'Long live the King! The Prussians forever! Down with the nation!' That's no hard matter, I should say."

Beausire's friend stood agape as if wonderstricken.

"I have always said you were a man of genius!" cried he.

Beausire bowed.

"If you do that," proceeded the royalist prisoner, "you will not only be delivered, not only be pardoned, but, over and above that, I swear to you that I will proclaim that to you is due the success of the conspiracy, and you may before hand vaunt of receiving a handsome reward!"

"It is not for reward that I act," returned Beausire with the most disinterested air in the world.

"Of course not." chimed in the

friend; "but, never mind, when the reward comes, I will advise you not to refuse."

"If you advise me not to refuse," said Beausire, "I——"

"I shall do more, I will beg you, and, if needs must, will order!" went on his friend majestically.

"So be it," said Beausire.

"Well," resumed the friend, "tomorrow, we will breakfast together—the governor of the prison will not refuse two old comrades that last favor—and we will drink a good bottle of wine to the success of the conspiracy!"

Beausire had a little doubt on the governor's yielding to the morrow's breakfast; but, whether he had a farewell banquet with his friend or not, he was determined to keep the promise he had given.

To his great satisfaction, authorization of the feast was given by the governor.

The two friends breakfasted together; it was not one bottle that was emptied, but two, three, four!

After the fourth, M. de Beausire was a red hot royalist.

Luckily, he was sought for to be led to the Place de Greve before the fifth bottle was opened.

He mounted the cart as a triumphal car, looking down scornfully on that mob which he was going to treat to such a great surprise.

On the post by Notre Dame Bridge, a woman and a little boy were waiting for his passing.

Beausire recognized poor Oliva, in tears, and young Toussaint, who, seeing his father in the hands of gendarmes, cried out:

"Serves the old man right! why did he beat me?"

Beausire sent to them a lofty smile, and he would have added to it a wave of the hand, which must have been of extreme majesty, if his arms had not been pinioned behind his back.

The square of the City Hall was packed with people.

It was known that the culprit was being punished for a theft committed at the Tuileries; it was known, through the accounts of the trial, what were the circumstances attending and following the act, and there was no pity for the sentenced man.

Therefore, when the cart stopped at the pillory, the guard had the greatest possible difficulty to keep back the people.

Beausire surveyed all this movement, tumult, and densely packed crowd, with an air which meant:

"You are going to see something presently."

When he appeared upon the pillory, there was universal clamor; but, when the moment of execution approached, when the executioner had unbuttoned the culprit's sleeve, bared his shoulder, and was stooping to take the red-hot brand from the furnace, there happened what ever occurs, before the overpowering majesty of justice, all were hushed.

Beausire took advantage of this instant and, collecting all his strength, in a full sonorous, resounding voice, he shouted:

"Long live the King! The Prussians forever! Down with the nation!"

Whatever result M. de Beausire may have expected, that which came surpassed the utmost of his hopes; there rose, not shouts, but roars and yells.

The whole throng sent up an immense growl and swept upon the pillory.

This time the guard was powerless to protect M. de Beausire; their ranks were broken, the scaffold was stormed, the executioner flung off the platform, the culprit torn, heaven knows how, from the stake and tossed into that devouring, seething cauldron, the mob.

He would have been trampled to death, torn piece-meal, cut to bits, had there not fortunately sprang a man, wearing the city scarf, from the city hall steps, where he had been looking on the punishment.

This man was the procureur of the commune, Manuel.

There was in him a great humane feeling which he was at times compelled to shut up in his heart, but which escaped in times like the present.

We have not the least design in the world of glorifying Manuel, one of the best abused men of the Revolution; we have the intention simply to tell the truth.

We will let Michelet firstly relate the fact.

" On the first of September, a frightful scene took place on the Place de Greve. A thief, who was going to be branded, and who was doubtlessly in liquor, shouted ' Long live the King! The Prussians forever. Down with the nation!' He was instantly pulled from the pillory and came near being torn to pieces; Manuel, the procureur of the commune, rushing to him, snatched him from the hands of the mob, and saved him in the city hall; but he himself was in extreme peril; he had to promise that a popular jury should try the criminal. This jury pronounced for death; authority held this sentence to be just and valid; it was carried out, the man perished the next day."

To resume.

Manuel contrived to reach Beausire with the utmost difficulty, stretched out his hand over him and, in a strong voice, cried:

" In the name of the law, I claim this man!"

The mob hesitated to obey.

Manuel unclasped his scarf and waved it over the throng, shouting:

" This way, all good citizens!"

A score or so of men ran to him and gathered around him.

Beausire was taken from the hands of the mob; he was half dead.

Manuel had him carried into the city hall; but presently that building was seriously menaced, so high ran exasperation.

Manuel appeared on the balcony.

"This man is guilty," said he, " but of a crime for which he has not been tried. Appoint a jury from among you; that jury will collect in one of the rooms of the hall and decide on the culprit's fate. The sentence, be it what it may, shall be executed, but let there be a sentence."

Is it not curious that it should be on the eve of the prison massacres that one of the men accused of them should speak, in peril of his life, such language?

There are anomalies in politics ; explain them who can.

This pledge appeased the multitude.

A quarter of an hour afterwards, the popular jury was announced to Manuel ; it was composed of twenty-one members, who appeared on the balcony.

"Are these men truly your delegates ?" inquired Manuel of the assemblage.

For answer, the crowd clapped hands.

"'Tis well," said Manuel ; "since we have the judges, justice shall be done."

As he had promised, he installed the jury in one of the rooms of the city hall.

Beausire, more dead than alive, appeared before this improvised tribunal ; he tried to defend himself; but his second crime was as patent as the first ; only, in the eyes of the people, it was still more serious.

To cry : "Long live the King !" when the King, deemed a traitor, was prisoner in the Temple ; to cry : "The Prussians forever !" when the Prussians had just taken Longwy and were scarce sixty leagues from Paris; to cry : "Down with the nation !" when the nation was writhing in its death throes ; this was a fearful crime, one that deserved an equally fearful punishment !

Hence, the jury determined that the guilty man not only should undergo capital punishment, but, besides, to attach to his name the shame which the law had removed by substituting the guillotine for the gibbet, he should be hanged, and hanged on that very spot where had been committed the crime.

Consequently, on the scaffold which the pillory formed, the executioner was ordered to raise a gallows.

The sight of this work going on and the certainty that the prisoner, being watched, could not escape, completed the calming of the multitude.

Such was the event which, as we have said at the conclusion of a foregoing chapter, gave the Assembly much to do.

The day following was a Sunday, an aggravating circumstance ; the Assembly was well aware that everything was tending to massacre.

The commune was bent on maintaining itself at any cost.

Massacre, which is the same thing as terror, was for that purpose one of the surest means.

The Assembly receded from its previous decision ; it recalled its decree.

Thereupon, one of its members rose.

"It is not enough to rescind your decree," said he; "a couple of days ago, on issuing it, you declared that the commune had 'deserved well of the country ;' the eulogium is too vague ; for some day you may say that the commune has deserved well of the country, but that, nevertheless, such or such a member of the commune is not comprised in the laudation ; therefore, such or such a member may be prosecuted. Therefore, it must not be said, 'the commune,' but 'the representatives of the commune.'"

The Assembly voted that "the representatives of the commune" had deserved well of their country.

At the same time as the Assembly passed this resolution, Robespierre was delivering to the commune a lengthy discourse, in which he said that the Assembly having by infamous acts made the general council lose public confidence, the general council ought to retire and employ the sole means which remained of saving the people, to wit : "to restore power to the people."

As ever he was, Robespierre was vague and doubtful, but terrible.

"Restore power to the people."

What signified this phrase ?

Was it to subscribe to the Assembly's decree, and accept the re-election ?

Not probable.

Was it to lay down the legal power and, so doing, to declare by its own self that the commune, after having made the tenth of August, regarded itself as powerless before the continuance of the great revolutionary work, and charged the people to achieve it ?

Now, the uncurbed people, with heart swollen with vengeance, to be charged with continuing the work of August the tenth, was the massacre of the men who had fought against them on that day, and who, since then, had been confined in the various prisons of Paris.

Thus stood affairs on the evening of the first of September, when everybody felt a storm to be making the atmosphere heavy, and the lightnings and thunder to be impending over all heads.

––––

CHAPTER XVI.

DURING THE NIGHT OF THE FIRST AND THE MORNING OF THE SECOND OF SEPTEMBER.

THIS was the state of affairs when, at nine o'clock on the evening of September the first, Gilbert's "officiator"—the name "servant' had been abolished as having an anti-republican smack—entered the doctor's room, saying :

"Citizen Gilbert, the cab is at the door."

Gilbert pulled down his hat over his eyes, buttoned up his coat to the throat, and got ready to go out ; but on the threshold of the apartment stood a man wrapped up in a cloak, whose forehead was shaded by a broad-brimmed hat.

Gilbert recoiled a step ; in darkness and at such a time, everybody is a foe.

"It is I, Gilbert," said a gentle voice.

"Cagliostro !" ejaculated the doctor

"Good, here you are forgetting that I am no longer Cagliostro, but call myself Baron Zanoni. It is true that to you, dear Gilbert, I change neither name nor heart, and am ever—I hope so at least—Joseph Balsamo."

"Yes, and the proof of that is that I was going to see you," said Gilbert.

"I suspected it," said Cagliostro, "and that's why I come here ; for you may easily guess that, in such days, I do not do what Robespierre does: go to the country."

"So I did not fear not meeting you, and I am very glad to see you. Come in, I beg you, come in !"

"Well, here I am. Tell me, what do you want ?" inquired Cagliostro, following Gilbert into the most retired chamber of the doctor's apartments.

"Take a chair, master."

Cagliostro sat down.

"Do you know what is happening ?" began Gilbert.

"You mean what is going to happen," returned Cagliostro, " for, just at present, nothing is going on."

"Yes, you are right ; but something terrible is brewing, is there not ?"

"Terrible, indeed. At times, what is terrible becomes necessary."

"Master," said Gilbert, " when you utter such words with your unfaltering coolness, you make me shudder."

"Can I help it ? I am but an echo—the echo of fate !"

Gilbert bowed his head.

"Do you remember, Gilbert, what I told you that day, the sixth of October, when I saw you at Bellevue and foretold the death of the Marquis de Favras ?"

Gilbert started.

He, so strong before men, and even events, felt himself before this mysterious personage to be weak as a child.

"I told you," proceeded Cagliostro, "that, if the King had in his poor brain an atom of the feeling of self preservation, which I hoped he had not, he would flee."

"Well," returned Gilbert, "he did flee."

"Yes : but I mean, while he had time ; when he did try to flee—you know it !—it was too late ! I added, you have not forgotten, that, if the King or the Queen or the nobles resisted, we would have revolution."

"Yes, you were right there again ; the revolution is made," said Gilbert with a sigh.

"Not completely," returned Cagliostro ; " but it shall be made, as you will see, my dear Gilbert. Do you remember further that I spoke to you of an instrument which one of my friends, Doctor Guillotin, had invented ? Have you ever passed by the Square of the Carrousel, yonder, in front of the Tuileries ? Well, that instrument is at work there—it is the same I showed to the Queen at the Chateau de Taverney, in a glass—you remember ; you were then a little boy, no higher than that, and already in love with Mademoiselle Nicole, and—why, her husband, that dear M. de Beausire, has just been condemned to be hanged."

"Yes, it is at work," observed Gilbert, "and works too slowly, it appears, for they add to it swords, pikes and knives."

"Hearken," said Cagliostro, "you must acknowledge one fact; to wit, that we have to do with persons dreadfully dull-witted! The aristocrats, the court, the King and the Queen, were given all sorts of warnings, yet nothing would they gain from them. The Bastile was taken—nothing was done; there was made the fifth and the sixth of October; and the twentieth of June; and the tenth of August—all without avail. The King was flung into the Temple, and aristocrats shut up at the Abbaye, La Force and Bicetre—no use! The King at the Temple rejoices over the capture of Longwy by the Prussians; the aristocrats at the Abbaye shout: 'Long live the King and the Prussians.' They quaff champagne in the faces of the poor who are glad to get water to drink; they eat truffle pasties before the poor people, hungry for bread! This heedlessness is even in King William of Prussia, to whom would be written:

"'Beware! If you pass Longwy; if you take a step farther towards the heart of France, it will be the royal death-warrant!'

"He would reply:

"'However frightful the situation of the royal family may be, the armies must not retrograde. I wish with all my soul to arrive in time to save the King of France; but, before everything, my duty is to save Europe!'

"He is marching on Verdun; this must end."

"End in what?" exclaimed Gilbert.

"End with the King, Queen, and the aristocrats."

"Would you murder the King and the Queen?"

"Oh, no! that would be a great folly. They must be tried, sentenced, publicly executed, as was done to Charles the First; but, at all events, they must be speedily got rid of, doctor, and the sooner the better."

"And who decides on this? Come," cried Gilbert; "is it of the intelligence, honesty, conscience of this people that you speak? when you had Mirabeau for mind, La Fayette for loyalty, Vergniaud for justice, if you had come to say to me, in the name of those three men: 'kill is the word!' I should have started as now I do; but I should have doubted. Come, now, in whose name say you this? In the name of a Hebert, a seller of countermarks; of a Collot d'Herbois, a hissed playwright; of a sickly-minded Marat—whose physician is obliged to bleed him every time he cries for fifty thousand, a hundred thousand, two hundred thousand heads! Let me, dear master, scorn such commonplace-men, to whom must be given swift, visible changes, fearful crises; these sorry dramaturgists, these powerless rhetoricians, who are fond of sudden destruction, who fancy themselves skilled magicians when, simple mortals, they have ruined the work of God; who think it great, fine, brilliant, to stop that life stream which feeds the world, to exterminate by a word, nod or wink, to make disappear by a breath the living obstacle which nature has taken twenty, thirty, forty, fifty years to create! These men, dear master, are wretches! and you cannot be with such men."

"My dear Gilbert," said Cagliostro, "you are wrong again; you style these beings men—you do them too much honor; they are only instruments."

"Instruments of destruction!"

"Ay, but for the benefit of an idea. That idea, Gilbert, is the freeing of the people; liberty; republicanism—not French—heaven preserve me from such a selfish idea!—but the universal republic, the brotherhood of the world! No, these men have not genius, nor loyalty, nor conscience; but they have what is stronger, more inexorable, more irresistible than that—they have instinct."

"The instinct of Attila!"

"Precisely, you have said it; of Attila, who called himself the Scourge of God, and who came, with the barbarian blood of Huns, Swedes, Alains, to temper Roman civilization, corrupted for four hundred years by the reigns of

Neroes, Vespasians and Heliogabaluses."

"But," cried Gilbert, let us resume. What would you gain by massacre?"

"'Tis a very simple thing; we compromise the Assembly, the commune, the people, all Paris. Paris must be dipped in blood, you must understand, for Paris—the brain of France, the mind of Europe, the spirit of the Old World—feeling that there can no longer be possible pardon for it, will rise as one man, push before it France, and hurl the foe from the sacred soil of the country."

"But you are not a Frenchman," observed Gilbert; "what matters all this to you?"

Cagliostro smiled.

"Can it be that you, Gilbert, you of superior intelligence and of powerful character, can you say to a man: 'Do not meddle with the affairs of France, for you are no Frenchman!' Are not the affairs of France, Gilbert, those of the world? Is France working for herself alone, poor selfish thing? Did Jesus die for the Jews alone? By what right do you say to an apostle: 'You are not of Nazareth?' Hearken, hearken, Gilbert, I have discussed all these things with a genius stronger than mine or thine; with a man or devil called Althotas; one day he gave me a calculation of the blood which must be shed before the sun shall rise on the freedom of the world. Well, this man's reasonings have not shaken my conviction; I have moved onward, do move onward, will move onward, overthrowing everything I may meet in my way, and saying in a calm voice, with a serene smile:

"'Woe to the obstacle! I am the future!'

"Now, you want to ask me for somebody's pardon? I grant you that pardon before you speak. Tell me the name of the person you would save."

"I wish to save a woman whom neither you nor I, master, can allow to die."

"Do you wish to save the Countess de Charny?"

"I wish to save Sebastian's mother."

"You know it is Danton who, as Minister of Justice, keeps the keys of prisons."

"Yes, but I also know that you can bid Danton open such or such a door."

Cagliostro rose, approached the secretary, drew upon a small square slip of paper a cabalistic sign, and said, as he presented the paper to Gilbert:

"There, my son, go find Danton, and ask him for what you like."

Gilbert rose.

"But, afterwards, what do you intend doing?" Cagliostro asked him.

"After what?"

"After days have passed, when the King's turn shall have come."

"I intend," said Gilbert, "to get myself nominated, if I can, Member of Convention, and to oppose with all my power the King's death."

"Yes, I understand that," remarked Cagliostro. "Do according to your conscience, Gilbert; but promise me one thing."

"What is it?"

"There was a time when you promised without any condition, Gilbert."

"In those days, you never told me a people were to be bettered by assassination, or a nation by murder."

"Have it your own way. Well, promise me, Gilbert, that, when the King shall have been tried and executed, you will follow the advice I will give you."

Gilbert held out his hand.

"Any advice coming from you, master, will be precious," he said.

"Will it be followed?" demanded Cagliostro.

"I swear it shall, if it does not affect my conscience."

"Gilbert, you are unjust," said Cagliostro; "I have given you much—have I ever exacted aught of you?"

"Oh, never," replied Gilbert; "and now again, you have given me a life which is dearer to me than my own."

"Go," said Cagliostro, "and may the genius of France, of whom you are one of the noblest sons, guide you!"

Cagliostro went out.

Gilbert followed him.

His cab still was waiting.

The doctor got in and ordered his being set down at the Ministry of Justice. It was there that Danton was.

Danton, as Minister of Justice, had a specious pretext not to appear at the commune.

Besides, what need had he of appearing there ?

Were not Marat and Robespierre there ?

Robespierre would not let himself be outstripped by Marat ; harnessed to murder, they travelled at the same pace.

Moreover, Tallien had his eyes on them.

Two things did Danton expect: supposing he went with the commune, a triumvirate with Marat and Robespierre ; supposing the Assembly decided for him, a dictatorship as Minister of Justice.

He did not want Robespierre and Marat ; but the Assembly did not want him.

When Gilbert was announced to him, he was with his wife at his feet.

The massacre was so known beforehand, that she was imploring him not to let it take place.

The poor woman was ready to die of grief when it did break out.

Danton could not make her understand the fact, very clear, however ; that he could do nothing against the commune's decisions without a dictatorial authorization from the Assembly ; with the Assembly, there was some chance of victory ; without it, there was certain defeat.

"Die, die, if it must be!" screamed the poor woman ; "but let not the massacre take place !"

"A man like me does not die uselessly," responded Danton. "I am willing to die, but let my death be useful to the country !"

Doctor Gilbert was announced.

"I will not go out," said Madame Danton, "until you have promised to prevent this abominable crime."

"Stay, then," said Danton.

The wife fell back a couple of steps, and let her husband go to meet the doctor, whom he knew by sight and reputation.

"Ah, doctor," said he, "you arrive seasonably ; if I had known your ad-

dress, really, I would have sent for you."

Gilbert bowed to the speaker, and, seeing his wife behind him in tears, he bowed to her.

"Here is my wife, the wife of Citizen Danton, the Minister of Justice ; who fancies that I alone am sufficiently strong to prevent Messieurs Marat and Robespierre, supported by the whole commune, doing what they are bent on doing ; that is, killing, exterminating."

Gilbert glanced at Madame Danton, who was weeping, with clasped hands.

"Madame," said Gilbert, "will you allow me to kiss your merciful hands ?"

"Here is reinforcement coming," said Danton.

"Oh, tell him sir," cried the poor woman, "that, if he allows this, it will be a blood-spot on his whole life !"

"Not that only," said Gilbert ; "if this stain would remain on the brow of a single man, and if this stain should only cling to his name, this man would devote himself, believing himself useless to himself, necessary to his country, he would fling his honor into the gulf, as Decius threw his body ! What matters, in circumstances like the present, the life, reputation, honor of a citizen ? But it would be a blot upon France.

"Citizen," said Danton, "when Vesuvius is in eruption, name to me the man able to dam its flood ; when the tide rises, tell me the arm powerful enough to push back the ocean."

"When one bears the name of Danton, he does not ask where is such a man, but says : ' Behold him !' Such an arm is not looked for, but he acts !"

"Why, you are all out of your senses !" cried Danton. "Must I tell you what I do not tell myself, say ? Well, I have the will, the genius, and, if the Assembly were willing, I should have the power ! But do you know what is going to happen ? What happened to Mirabeau : his genius could not overcome his evil reputation. I am not the gusty Marat, to inspire terror in the Assembly ; I am not the incorruptible Robespierre, to inspire confidence in myself ; the Assembly will refuse me the means of saving the state, I will reap the penalty of my evil reputation; it will adjourn, will put off and put off; it will be whispered that I am a man without morality, a man to whom could not be given, even for three days, an absolute, entire, arbitrary power; it will appoint some commission of honest folk, and, meanwhile, the massacre will have taken place, and, as you say, the blood of thousands, the crime of three or four drunken men will draw over the scenes of the revolution a red screen which will hide its sublime heights! No," he added, " no, it will not be France that will be accused— but me; I shall turn aside from her the world's malediction, and have it descend on my head!"

" I—my children?" cried his wife.

" You," repeated Danton, " you will die; and will not be accused of being my accomplice, inasmuch as my crime will have killed you. As for my children, they are boys; they will one day be men, and rest easy, they will have their father's heart and will bear the name of Danton with haughty head, or else will be faint-hearted and will renounce me. So much the better! such weak ones would not be of my race, and I, in that case, renounce them beforehand."

" But, at least, you are going to ask this authority of the Assembly?"

" Do you think I have not expected this? I have sent for Thuriot, for Tallien; wife, see if they are not outside; if so, send in Thuriot."

Madame Danton went out quickly.

" I am going to tempt fortune before you, Monsieur Gilbert," said Danton; " you shall be my witness before posterity for the efforts I shall have made."

The door opened.

" Here is Citizen Thuriot, my friend," announced Madame Danton.

" Come here," said Danton, holding out his broad hand to him who filled by his side the part which an aid-de-camp holds to a general. " You spoke a fine thing the other day from the tribune: ' The French Revolution is not for us but for the world, and we have to give account of it to the whole of humanity!' Well, to keep this revolu-

tion pure and unsullied we are going to attempt a last effort."

" Speak," said Thuriot.

" To-morrow, at the opening of the session, before any discussion shall have arisen, you will bring forward the following motion: that the number of the members of the council general of the commune shall be raised to three hundred; so that, while not removing the former members created on the tenth of August, they shall be annihilated by the new ones. We will constitute on a fixed basis the representation of Paris; we will aggrandize the commune, yet shall neutralize it; we will augment it in number, but shall modify it in spirit. If this proposition does not pass, if you cannot make my intention be understood, come to an understanding, then, with Lacroix; tell him to step boldly into the struggle; let him propose to punish with death those who, directly or indirectly, refuse to execute or fetter in any way whatever may be the orders given and the measures taken by the executive power. If this resolution passes, it is the dictatorship; the executive power is the same as I; I will enter, claim it and, if there is hesitaton to give me it, I shall take it!"

" What will you do then?" inquired Gilbert.

" Then I will snatch up a flag," replied Danton; " instead of the bloody, hideous demon of massacre, whom I will spurn back into the darkness, I will invoke only the noble, serene spirit of battle, who strikes fearlessly and without anger, who looks peacefully at death; I will demand of all these bands if it was to cut the throats of unarmed men that they united; I will declare infamous whoever menaces prisoners! Peradventure, *many* will approve massacre; but the ones who would massacre are far from numerous. I will profit by the military spirit which reigns in Paris; I will enwrap the small number of murderers in the great mass of volunteers really soldiers, who wait but for the order to start, and I will launch them on the frontier— on the foe! the unclean element domineered over by the generous element!"

"Do this, do this?" exclaimed Gilbert, "and you will do a great, mighty, magnificent act!"

"It is the easiest thing in the world," returned Danton, shrugging his shoulders with a singular medley of power, doubt and recklessness; "let me only be aided, and you shall see!"

Madame Danton kissed her husband's hands.

"You will be aided, Danton," said she. "Who would not be of your opinion to hear you speak thus?"

"Unfortunately, I cannot speak thus," said Danton; "for were I to expose all by thus speaking out, by me would commence the massacre."

"Well, might it not be as well that that should happen," said Madame Danton quickly.

"Woman who speaks like a woman! I being dead, what would become of that sanguinary fool Marat and the mistaken utopist Robespierre? No, I must not, am not willing to die yet; what I should do is prevent this butchery, if I can, and, if it breaks out despite me, to clear France of the misdeed by taking it all upon me. I will stride on all the same to my goal; but I will stride on all the more terribly. Call in Tallien."

Tallien entered.

"Tallien," said Danton, "to-morrow, the commune may write for me to come to the municipality; you are the secretary of the commune; arrange things so that the letter cannot arrive, and so that I can prove that it never came."

"The devil! and how am I going to do that?" said Tallien.

"That's your look-out. I tell you what I want, what I will, what must be; it is for you to find the means. Come, M. Gilbert, have you not something to ask of me?"

Opening the door of a small closet, he let Gilbert go in, and followed him.

"Come, in what may I be useful to you?" asked Danton.

Gilbert produced from his pocket the paper which Cagliostro had given him, and handed it to Danton.

"Ah, come you from *him?*" said the latter. "Well, what do you wish?"

"The release of a woman confined in the Abbaye."

"Her name?"

"The Countess de Charny."

Danton drew some paper to him, and wrote the order of release.

"There," said he; "have you no others you want saved? Speak! I would like to save all the unfortunate persons!"

Gilbert bowed.

"I have what I want," replied he.

"Go, Monsieur Gilbert; and, if ever you have need of me, come to me directly, man to man, without any agents; I shall be too happy to do anything for you."

As he ushered him out, he muttered: "Oh, that I had only for four-and-twenty hours your reputation of an honorable man, M. Gilbert!"

He closed the door behind the doctor, whilst sighing and wiping away the sweat streaming from his forehead.

Bearer of the precious paper which gave to him Andrée's life, Gilbert hastened to the Abbaye Prison.

Although it was close upon midnight, threatening groups were still gathered around the prison.

Gilbert passed through them, and knocked at the door.

The gloomy opening beneath the dark vault yawned.

Gilbert passed into it, shuddering; the low vault was not that of a prison, but of a tomb.

He presented his order to the governor.

The order set at liberty instantly the person whom Doctor Gilbert should designate.

Gilbert said the Countess de Charny, and the governor ordered a turnkey to conduct Citizen Gilbert to the prisoner's cell.

Gilbert followed the turnkey, mounting behind him three flights of stairs, and entering a cell lighted by a lamp.

A woman in black, pale as marble under her mourning, was seated near the table, on which burned the lamp, reading a small book bound in shagreen and adorned with a silver cross.

The brands of a fire smouldered in a chimneyplace beside her.

Notwithstanding the creak of the opening door, she did not lift up her eyes; notwithstanding the sound made by Gilbert approaching, she never raised her eyes; she appeared absorbed in her reading, or rather in her musing, for Gilbert remained two or three minutes before her without seeing her turn over a leaf.

The turnkey had pulled the door to behind Gilbert, and was standing outside.

"My lady the countess——" at last began Gilbert.

Andrée raised her eyes, looking for an instant without seeing; the veil of her mind was still between her eyes and the man standing before her; it faded away gradually.

"You, Monsieur Gilbert?" said Andrée. "What do you want?"

"My lady," responded Gilbert, "there are ominous mutterings afloat about what will happen to-morrow in the prisons."

"Yes," said the widow, "it appears we are going to be murdered; but you know, Monsieur Gilbert, I am ready to die."

Gilbert bowed.

"I am come for you, my lady," said he.

"Come for me?" reiterated Andrée in surprise; "to conduct me whither?"

"Wherever you please, my lady; you are free."

He presented to her the order of release signed by Danton.

She read the order, but, instead of returning it to the doctor, kept it in her hand.

"I ought to have suspected this, doctor," said she, trying to smile; something which her face seemed to have lost the art of doing.

"Suspected what, my lady?"

"That you would come to prevent me dying."

"Madame, there is one existence in the world which is more precious than ever would have been my parents', if heaven had granted me a father or a mother to love: that is yours!"

"Yes, and that is why, once already, you broke your pledge.'

"I did not break it, my lady; I did send you the poison."

"By my son!"

"I did not tell you by whom I should send it."

"So you have thought of me, Monsieur Gilbert? so you have entered for me the lion's den? so you have come forth with the talisman which opens doors?"

"I told you, my lady, that so long as I live, you cannot die."

"Nevertheless, Monsieur Gilbert, this time," said the countess with a nearer approach to a smile than before, "I think I have death!"

"I declare to you, my lady, that, if I must employ force to tear you from here, you shall not die."

Andrée, instead of answering, tore up the order of release, and flung the pieces into the fire.

"Try it!" said she.

Gilbert uttered a cry.

"Monsieur Gilbert," said Charny's widow, "I have given up the idea of suicide, but I have not renounced that of death."

"Oh, my lady, my lady!" exclaimed Gilbert.

"Monsieur Gilbert, I *will* die!"

Gilbert let a groan escape him.

"All that I ask of you is that you will endeavor to recover my body, to save me, dead, from the outrages which he, living, did not escape. Monsieur de Charny, rests in the tombs of his Chateau de Boursonnes; it is there that I have spent the only happy days of my life; I wish to rest by him."

"Oh, my lady! in heaven's name, I implore you."

"And, I, sir, in the name of my misfortune, pray you."

"'Tis well, my lady; you have spoken, I shall try to obey your ladyship in all points. I retire, but I am not vanquished."

"Do not forget my last wish, sir," said the countess.

"If I do not save you despite yourself, my lady," returned Gilbert, "it shall be accomplished."

Bowing again to Andrée, Gilbert withdrew.

The door closed behind him with that mournful clang peculiar to prison doors.

CHAPTER XVII.

THE DAY OF THE SECOND OF SEPTEMBER.

WHAT Danton had foreseen came to pass.

At the opening of the session, Thuriot made to the Assembly the motion which the Minister of Justice had formed the previous evening.

The Assembly did not understand; instead of voting at nine o'clock in the morning, it debated, dawdled over it, and voted at one o'clock in the afternoon.

Too late!

These four hours delayed by a century the liberty of Europe.

Tallien was sharper.

Charged by the commune to give the *order* for the Minister of Justice to come to the municipality, he wrote:

" M. LE MINISTRE,
    " SIR :
    " On receipt of the present, you will come to the city hall."

He, however, made a mistake in the direction!

Instead of addressing it: " To the Minister of Justice," he wrote: " To the Minister of War."

Danton was expected.

It was Servan who came, quite puzzled, to ask what was wanted of him.

The error (?) was discovered, but the deed was done.

We have said that the Assembly, by voting at one o'clock, had voted too late; the commune, which was not in the habit of dwelling on things, had profited by the time.

What did the commune want?

Massacre and the dictatorship.

Let us see how it went about it.

As Danton had said, men to massacre were more scarce than was believed.

On the night of the first of September, while Gilbert tried fruitlessly to remove the Countess de Charny from the Abbaye, Marat had let slip his barking dogs into the clubs and sections; bark as they did, they had produced little effect in the clubs, and, out of eight-and-forty wards, only two, the Section Poissoniere and that of the Luxembourg, had voted for massacre.

As for the dictatorship, the commune felt that it could not seize on that save by help of the three names : Marat, Robespierre, Danton.

That is why it sent Danton the order for him to come to it.

We have seen that Danton had foreseen the game; he had not received the letter, and, consequently, would not come.

If he had received it, if Tallien's error (?) had not caused the missive to be taken to the wrong minister, perhaps the Minister of Justice would not have ventured to disobey.

In his absence, the commune was forced to make up its mind.

It decided to form a committee of superintendence ; however, this body could not be selected except from the commune.

Nevertheless, by hook or crook, Marat had to be drawn into this committee of massacre—which is the true title belonging to it !

But how ?

Marat was not a member of the commune.

Panis undertook to smoothe the difficulty.

Through his god Robespierre and his brother-in-law Santerre, Panis weighed with such heaviness on the municipality (our readers will easily understand that Panis, ex-proctor, of harsh, shifting mind, poor little author of a few ridiculous verses, could not of himself have any influence) ; he weighed so heavily, we repeat, that he was authorized to choose three members to complete the superintending committee.

Panis did not dare to exercise alone this strange power.

He joined to him three of his colleagues : Sergent, Duplain, Jourdeuil.

These, on their part, subjoined five persons to them : Deforgues, Lenfant, Guermeur, Leclerc and Durfort.

The original act bears the four signatures of Panis, Sergent, Duplain and Jourdeuil ; but, in the margin, is to be found another name flourished over by one of the four signatures, flourished over in a queer, confused way, but which flourish it is clear belongs to Panis's name.

This name is Marat's ; MARAT, who had no right to belong to this committee, not being a member of the commune.

(*Vide* Michelet, the only historian who has shed light upon the bloody gloom of September. See, also, at the office of the prefect of Police of Paris the act of which we speak, and which our learned friend, Monsieur Labat, keeper of records, will find pleasure in showing it to the curious as he has shown it to us.)

With this name, murder found itself enthroned !

Let us see it sway its sceptre in the awful unfolding of its might.

We have said that the commune had not acted like the Assembly, that it did not trifle with time.

At ten o'clock, the committee of superintendence was formed and had given its first order ; this was to have transferred from the mayor's office, where the committee was in session (the mayor's office was then where our police head-quarters is to-day) twenty-four prisoners to the Abbaye.

Of this number, eight or nine were priests, in other words, nearly a third wore the most hated and execrated dress there was, the garb of those men who had stirred up civil war in La Vendee and the South, the clerical attire.

They were to be taken out of their prisons by the Marseilles federals, four cabs were called, there were six put into each vehicle, and they were ready to start.

The signal of departure was to be given by the third cannon-shot of alarm.

The intention of the commune is plain enough.

This slow, funereal train would feed the wrath of the mob ; it was probable that either on the way or at the gate of the Abbaye, the cabs would be stopped and the prisoners slaughtered ; then, there would be nothing more than to let the massacre follow its course ; commenced on the way or at the gate of the prison, it would easily step across the threshold.

It was at the moment when the cabs were to leave the mayor's that Danton took it into his head to enter the Assembly.

Thuriot's proposition had become useless ; it was too late, as before stated, to apply to the commune the motion just taken.

There remained the office of dictator.

Danton ascended the speaker's stand ; unfortunately, he was alone ; Roland was too honorable a man to accompany his colleague !

They looked about for Roland—he was not there.

Force was seen, but morality was asked vainly for.

Manuel went to announce to the commune Verdun's danger ; he had proposed that, that very evening, the enrolled citizens should come to camp on the Champ de Mars, so that they might start at break of day to march on the enemy.

Manuel's proposition was warmly welcomed.

Another member had proposed, " on account of the urgency of danger," that the alarm gun should be fired, the tocsin rung, the long roll beaten.

This second motion, put to the ayes and noes, had been received like the former.

It was an awful, thrilling, murderous measure, in such circumstances : the drum, the bell, the cannon, have exciting reverberations, awakening vibrations in the calmest heart ; the deeper effect they ought to have on hearts so high wrought up.

All this was calculated.

At the first gun, M. de Beausire was to be hanged.

Let us state, with all the grief attached to the loss of so interesting a character, that, at the opening report M. de Beausire was indeed hanged.

At the third gun, the vehicles before mentioned were to start from the prefecture de police.

Now the guns were fired every ten minutes; those who had gone to see M. de Beausire executed would therefore have time to arrive to see the prisoners pass and to take a hand in the butchery.

Danton had been given information of everything that happened in the commune by Tallien.

He knew of Verdun's peril; of the decision to camp on the Champ de Mars; of the alarm gun to be fired, of the long roll to be beaten.

To give Lacroix the cue—Lacroix, it will be remembered, was to ask for the dictatorship—he took the pretext of the country's danger, and moved the voting on a resolution that: "Whoever refused to serve with his person, or render his arms, should be punished with death."

In order that none should mistake his intentions, or confound his projects with those of the commune, he said:

"The alarm which is to ring is not a signal of alarm, but *the charge on the country's foes!* To overcome them, gentlemen, we must have boldness, more boldness, and still more boldness, and France is saved!"

A thunder-peal of applause greeted his words.

Thereupon, Lacroix rose and demanded in his turn; "that death should be the punishment of those who, directly or indirectly, refused to carry out, or fettered in any way whatsoever, the orders given and measures taken by the executive power."

The Assembly comprehended perfectly well, this time, that the dictatorship was what they were called upon to vote; it approved in appearance, but appointed a committee of Girondists to draw up the decree.

The Girondists, unfortunately, like Roland, were men too nice to have confidence in Danton.

The discussion was dragged along till six o'clock in the afternoon.

Danton was impatient; he meant good and was being forced to permit evil!

He had whispered to Thuriot, and had gone out.

What had he whispered?

The place where he was to be met in case the Assembly entrusted with him the power.

Where was his place of meeting him?

At the Champ de Mars, among the volunteers.

What was his intention, in case the power was confided in him!

To make himself be recognized by that mass of men armed for war, not massacre; to enter Paris with them and sweep, as in an immense net, the cut-throats to the border?

He waited until five o'clock in the afternoon; no one came.

What was, meanwhile, happening to those persons who were to be conducted to the Abbaye?

Let us follow them; they progress slowly, and we may easily overtake them.

At first, the vehicles in which they were protected them; the instinct of the danger which they ran made each squeeze himself into the corners of the cabs, showing themselves as little as possible at the windows; but their guards denounced them themselves.

The people's anger did not rise quick enough; they spurred it with words.

"Here are the traitors!" they called out to the passers-by who looked on. "Here are the accomplices of the Prussians! here are those who will surrender our towns, kill our wives and children, if you leave them behind you when you march to the border!"

Nevertheless, all this was without result, so rare, as Danton had said, were that class who would massacre.

Rage, shouts, threats were obtained; but there was an end of it.

The train went along the water front, over the Pont Neuf and through the Rue Dauphine.

They had not been able to tire out the prisoners' patience; nor to urge the hand of the mob to murder.

They were nearing the Abbaye, being at the Bussy Crossing: it was time to do something.

If the prisoners entered the prison, if they were killed inside, it would be evident that it was by a reflected order of the commune that they fell, and not by the spontaneous indignation of the people.

Fortune came to the aid of such wicked designs and bloody plans.

At the Bussy Crossing was erected one of those theatres where were enlisted volunteers.

There was a jam, a blocking up of the road, the vehicles were forced to stop.

The occasion was a capital one; if that was missed, they deserved never to have another one.

A man forced through the escort, which allowed it, he jumped upon the steps of the first cab, sword in hand, and plunged it several times at random into the vehicle, drawing the blade out red with blood.

One of the prisoners had a cane; with it, he tried to parry the thrusts; he happened to touch one of the men of the escort with the stick in the face.

"Ha, wretches!" shouted he, "we were protecting you, and you strike us! Here, comrades!"

Some twenty men, who were only waiting for this appeal, darted out of the crowd, armed with pikes and knives affixed to long poles, they darted their lances into the doorways and there began to be heard groans and screams of pain, and began to be seen blood of the victims flow out of the bottom of the vehicles, leaving a trail along the street.

Blood calls for blood.

The massacre was commenced; it was to last four days.

The prisoners packed in the Abbaye had, early in the morning, guessed by the countenances of their keepers and the meaning sentences exchanged between them, that something evil was in preparation.

An order from the commune had, in all the prisons, on this day, advanced meal-times.

What meant this change in the habits of the jail?

Nothing good, certainly.

The prisoners, therefore, waited in anxiety.

As four o'clock drew nigh, the distant mutterings of the mob began to grow audible, surging like the first waves of the rising tide, against the base of the prison walls; some, from grated windows which overlooked the Rue Saint Marguerite, caught sight of the cabs; next, yells of rage and agony penetrated the prison through every crevice, and the cry: "Here are the murderers!" spread through the lobbies, echoing in cells and even in the deepest dungeons.

"The Swiss, the Swiss!"

There were a hundred and fifty Swiss in the Abbaye; it had taken many pains to shield them from the mob on the tenth of August.

The commune knew the hatred of the people for the red uniform.

It was, hence, an excellent way to warm up the butchers, by commencing the massacre by the Swiss.

It took nearly two hours to kill these hundred and fifty unfortunate beings.

The last having fallen — this was Major Reading, whose name we believe we have mentioned before—the priests were called.

The priests replied they were willing to die, but wanted to confess.

This wish was granted them; they were given two hours' respite.

How were these two hours employed?

In forming a tribunal.

Who formed it?

Who presided at it?

Maillard.

CHAPTER XVIII.

MAILLARD.

THE man of the fourteenth July, fifth and sixth October, twentieth June and tenth of August, was to be also the man of the second of September.

The once usher at the Chatelet wanted to apply a form, a solemn aspect, an appearance of legality to the massacre;

he wanted the aristocrats to be killed, but killed legally, on a decree issued by the people, whom he regarded as the only infallible judge, and who alone also had the right to acquit.

Before Maillard had set up his tribunal, nearly two hundred persons had been already slaughtered.

One alone had been saved: the Abbé Sicard.

Two other persons, climbing through a window, favored by the tumult, had jumped into the very midst of the section committee in session at the Abbaye; they were Parisot the journalist and La Chapelle the steward of the royal household.

The members of the committee had made the fugitives sit down behind them, and had thus saved them; but the fault must not remain on them that these should have avoided death; it was not their fault.

We have said that one of the curious documents to be seen in the police archives was Marat's nomination to the committee of superintendence; another, no less curious, is the Abbaye register, still splashed with the blood which spirted even on the members of the tribunal.

Ask to see this record, whoever is in search of emotion-giving recollections, and you will every instant see on the margins, below one or the other of the two following notes (written in a large, fair, clear, perfectly legible hand, completely free from agitation, nervousness, fear or remorse), the name of MAILLARD, we repeat, at the foot of the following lines:

"Killed by judgment of the people."
"Acquitted by the people."
The last is repeated forty-three times.

Hence, Maillard saved at the Abbaye the lives of that number.

While he enters into his duties, at about nine or ten in the evening, let us follow two men who leave the Jacobins and proceed towards the Rue Sainte Anne.

It was the high priest and the novice, the master and the disciple: Saint Just and Robespierre.

Saint Just, who appeared to us on the night of the reception of three new Masons at the Rue Platrière lodge; Saint Just, with changing, wan complexion, too white for a man's color, too pale for a woman's, with stiff neckcloth, pupil of a cold, dry, harsh master, yet colder, sterner, harsher than his master!

There was still some emotion in political combats for the latter; passion, passion.

For the pupil, what passed was but a game of chess on a large scale, the stake life.

Whoever played against him should be wary, for he was inflexible, and would grant no grace to the loser.

Doubtlessly, Robespierre had his reasons for not returning this evening to Duplay's house.

In the morning, he had said he would probably go to the country.

Saint Just's little room in furnished lodgings seemed to him, perhaps, for that night between the second and third of September, safer than his own.

They entered it at about eleven o'clock.

It is useless to ask of what this couple were speaking; they spoke of massacre; one, however, spoke with the sensibility of a Rousseauan philosopher; the other with the dryness of a mathematician of the Condillac school.

Robespierre, like the crocodile of the fable, shed tears at times over those he condemned.

On entering his room, Saint Just laid his hat on a chair, took off his cravat, and hung up his coat.

"What are you going to do?" asked Robespierre.

Saint Just stared at him in so astonished a manner that Robespierre repeated:

"I ask you what you are going to do?"

"Lie down, of course," responded the young man, we might even say the still unknown youth.

"Why lie down?"

"Why, for what the bed is made for, to sleep."

"What, can you think of sleeping through such a night?" exclaimed Robespierre.

" Why not ?"

" When thousands of victims fall or are going to fall, when this night will be the last for so many men breathing an hour ago, and who will have ceased to live to-morrow morning—you think of sleeping."

Saint Just dwelt for an instant thoughtful.

As though, during that moment's silence, he had fished up from the depths of his heart some fresh conviction, he said :

" True, I know it ; but I know as well that it is a necessary evil inasmuch as you have authorized it. Suppose the yellow fever, a plague, the black death, an earthquake, and there would die as many—more men than are going to perish, with no benefit at all to society ; while, from the death of our enemies, will result security for us. I therefore advise you to go home and take to your bed as I do, and try to sleep as I am going to sleep."

Saying these words, the cold, impassive politician stretched himself on his bed.

" Good bye till to-morrow !" said he.

And he fell asleep.

His slumber was as long, as calm, as peaceful as if nothing unusual was transpiring in Paris ; he had sunk to rest at half past eleven in the evening and awoke about six in the morning.

Saint Just saw a shadow fall between the light and him ; he turned to the window and saw Robespierre.

He thought that, having departed the night before, Robespierre had already returned.

" What brings you here so early ?" he asked.

" Nothing," replied Robespierre, " I did not go out."

" Not go out ?"

" No."

" Nor lain down ?"

" No."

" Nor slept ?"

" No."

" Where did you pass the night ?"

" Standing here, my forehead pressed against the glass, and listening to the sounds in the street."

Robespierre did not tell an untruth ;

either from doubt, through fear, or by remorse, he had not slept a second.

There had been no difference in sleep for Saint Just between this and other nights.

There was, on the other bank of the Seine, in the courtyard of the Abbaye, a man who had slept no more than Robespierre.

This man was leaning against the corner of the last wicket opening on the courtyard, and was almost invisible in the shadows.

A strange sight was that presented by the interior, transformed into a tribunal.

Around a large table covered with straight and curved swords, and pistols, and illumined by two brass lamps whose light was necessary in broad daylight, twelve men were seated.

By their coarse features, robust forms, the red caps on their heads, the jackets they wore, they were to be known as men of the working class.

A thirteenth among them, in threadbare black coat, white waistcoat, short breeches, solemn and lugubrious face, bare head, presided over them.

He, the only one, perhaps, who knew how to read and write, had before him a book, paper, quills and ink.

These men were the judges of the Abbaye, fearful ones, giving decisions without appeal, which were on the instant carried out by some fifty executioners armed with swords, knives and pikes, who were in readiness in the blood-streaming courtyard.

Their president was Maillard the usher.

Had he come there of himself?

Had he been sent by Danton, who might want to do at the other prisons—the Carmes, Chatelet, La Force—what was done at the Abbaye—save a few persons.

None knew.

On the fourth of September, Maillard disappeared ; he was never seen more, nor was there further speech of him, it is the same as if he had been drowned, engulfed in that blood.

Since ten o'clock in the evening, he had been superintending the court.

He had come there, had arranged the

table, had produced his book, had, at random among the nearest at hand, picked but twelve judges; then he had sat down in the middle of the table: six of his appointees had sat on his left and the massacre had continued, but this time with a kind of regularity.

The name on the book would be read off; the turnkeys would go for the prisoners; Maillard would tell the story of the causes of confinement; the president would consult his colleagues with a glance; if the prisoner was doomed Maillard would say:

" To La Force !"

Whereupon, the outer door would be flung open, and the condemned person would fall under the strokes of the butchers.

If, on the other hand, the black spectre would rise, lay his hand on his head, and say.

" Let him be released !"

And the prisoner would go unscathed.

When Maillard had presented himself at the prison gate, a man had stepped out from the wall and come to meet him.

On the first words exclaimed between them, Maillard had recognized this person, and had—in token, not perchance of submission, but of condescension—bowed his tall form before him.

When he had bidden him enter the prison and his table being fixed and the tribunal ready, he had said:

" Stand you yonder and, when the person you are interested in appears, make me a sign."

The man went and leaned up in a corner, and, since then, he had waited there, mute and motionless.

This man was Gilbert.

He had sworn to Andrée that he would not let her die, and was there to keep his oath.

From four to six in the morning, the executioners and judges had taken a little repose; at six, they breakfasted.

During the three hours of sleep and meantime, the tumbrels sent by the commune had come and removed the dead.

As there was three inches of blood clotted in the yard, as feet slipped on it, and as it would have taken too long to wash it, a hundred bundles of straw had been brought, and strewn over the pavements, by which had been covered the clothing of the victims, and especially the uniform of Swiss.

Clothes and straw soaked up the blood.

While judges and butchers slept, the prisoners were awake, aroused by terror.

However, when the cries died away, and the calling of the names ceased, they recovered some hope; perhaps there was only a certain number of the condemned pointed out to the cutthroats; perhaps the massacre was limited to the Swiss and King's guard.

This hope was of short duration.

At about half after six of the morning, the shouts and the call recommenced.

A jailer came down and told Maillard that the prisoners were ready to die, but asked to hear mass.

Maillard shrugged his shoulders; nevertheless, he allowed the request.

He was, besides, occupied in listening to the congratulations which were addressed to him, in the name of the commune, by an envoy of that body, a thin man, with gentle physiognomy, in puce-colored coat and small perriwig.

This man was Billaud Varennes.

" Brave citizens !" said he to the butchers, " you are purging society of great criminals! The municipality hardly knows how to reward you. No doubt, the spoils of the dead ought to belong to you; but it would look like a theft. As indemnity of that loss, I am charged to offer to each of you twenty-four livres which are to be paid down forthwith."

In fact, the speaker on the instant distributed to the cut throats the wages of their shameful work.

What explained this liberality from the commune was the following incident.

During the evening of the second of September, some of those killing—the minority, the greater part being of the lesser shopkeepers of the neighborhood—some were without shoes or stockings; therefore, they covetously remarked the dead men's shoes. The result was that they asked the section for permission to transfer the aristocrats' shoes to their feet. The commune consented.

Thenceforward, Maillard found that it was thought asking could be dispensed with, and, consequently, no longer were only shoes and stockings taken, but anything that it was thought suitable.

Maillard believed this spoilt the massacre, and he made the commune note it.

Thence Varennes' embassy, and the strict silence with which it was listened to.

During this time, the prisoners heard mass, said by Lenfant, the King's preacher, and served by the Abbé de Rastignac, a religious writer.

They were two old, white-headed men, with venerable faces, whose words, preaching from a rude pulpit, faith and resignation, had a great influence over the doomed ones.

As they were all kneeling, receiving Abbé Lenfant's benediction, the call began again.

The first word uttered was the consoler's name.

He made a sign, finished his prayer, and followed those who had come for him.

The second priest remained and continued his exhortation.

He was called in his turn, and followed those calling him.

The prisoners were left to themselves, when a conversation arose between them gloomy, strange and awful.

They discussed the way of receiving death, and on the chances of a shorter or longer torture.

Some were for stretching out the head, for it to fall at the first stroke; others, for throwing up their arms for death to enter their breasts from all sides; others, lastly, meant to keep their hands behind their backs in order to oppose no resistance.

A young man stepped forward, saying:

"I am going to learn which is the best."

He went up into a little turret, a grated window of which looked on the court of massacre, and, from it, studied death.

Then he returned to say:

"Those die quickest who have the fortune to be stabbed in the breast."

At this juncture, followed by a sigh, was heard the words:

"Oh, my God, I am going to thee!"

A man had fallen on the pavement, and was blood-bedewing the slabs.

He was Chantereine, colonel of the King's constitutional guard.

He had stabbed himself thrice in the breast.

The prisoners inherited his knife; but they struck with hesitation, and only one managed to kill himself.

There were three females there; two frightened girls pressing to the sides of two old men, and a woman in mourning, calmly praying as she knelt, and smiling in her prayer.

The two girls were Mesdemoiselles de Cazotte and de Sombreuil; the old men, their fathers.

The young woman in mourning was the Countess de Charny.

Montmorin was called.

He was, it may be remembered, the former minister who had given the passports by aid of which the King had endeavored to flee; this so unpopular personage had already had a young man of the same name nearly killed on that account.

De Montmorin had not listened to the exhortations of the priests; he had remained in his cell, furious and desperate, calling his enemies, shouting for weapons, shaking his prison cross-bars, and shivering an oaken table, the boards of which were two inches thick.

He had to be dragged by force to the tribunal; he entered pale, with flaming eyes and threatening fists.

"To La Force!" said Maillard.

The ex-minister took the phrase to mean what it appeared to mean: a transfer to the Prison of La Force.

"President," said he to Maillard, "since you are so styled, I hope you will have me taken in a carriage, so as to spare me the insults of your assassins."

"Call a coach for his lordship, the Count de Montmorin," said Maillard with exquisite politeness. " Have the kindness to sit down while waiting for the coach, sir count," added he to Montmorin.

The latter sat down grumbling.

Five minutes afterwards the carriage was announced to be waiting.

Some one had understood the mistake and gave the reply.

The fatal door—that opening on death—was flung open, and Montmorin stepped through it.

He had not taken three steps ere he fell, struck by a score of pikes.

Next came other prisoners whose unknown names have remained steeped in oblivion.

Amid all these obscure names, one name shines out like a flame ; that of Jacques Cazotte ; the illuminati, who, ten years before the Revolution, had foretold to each the fate awaiting them; the author of the " Diable Amoureux," " Olivier," and the " Mille et une fadaises ;" a man of wild imagination, ecstatic soul, ardent heart, who had embraced with fury the cause of the counter-revolution, and who, in letters addressed to his friend Pouteau, employed on the administration of the civil list, had expressed opinions which at the times we are writing of, were punished with death·

His daughter had served him as secretary for these letters ; and, her father being arrested, Elizabeth Cazotte had come to claim her share of his confinement.

If the royalist opinion was allowed to anybody, certainly it was to this old man of seventy-five, whose feet had taken root in the monarchy of Louis the Fourteenth, and who, to lull the Duke of Burgundy to slumber, had composed the two ballads since popular of " Tout au beau milieu des Ardennes (Deep in the depths of dark Ardennes)" and " Commere, il faut chauffer le lit ! (Gossip, you must well warm the bed)."

But such were reasonings to give philosophers, and not to the executioners of the Abbaye ; hence Cazotte was condemned beforehand.

On perceiving the white-headed old man, with flaming eyes and handsome, inspired countenance, Gilbert left his nook and made a step to go to him.

Maillard noted this movement.

Cazotte advanced, leaning on his daughter ; but the latter had felt that they were before judges.

She left her father and, with clasped hands, came to pray to that bloody tribunal with such sweet words that Maillard's assistants began to waver ; the poor girl saw that, under those rough envelopes there were hearts, but that they had to be sought for ; she implored, with compassion for her guide.

These men, who knew not what were tears, wept now !

Maillard drew the back of his hand over his dry, stern eyes which, for twenty hours, without closing once, had contemplated the massacre.

He stretched out his arm and, laying his hand on Cazotte's head, said :

" They are released !"

The girl knew not what to think.

" Have no fear," said Gilbert ; " your father is safe, mademoiselle !"

Two of the judges rose and accompanied Cazotte as far as the street, for fear that some fatal error would restore to death the victim snatched from him.

Cazotte—for this time at least—was saved.

Hours elapsed ; the massacre continued.

Benches had been brought into the courtyard for spectators ; the wives and children of the murderers had a right to see their husbands and fathers at work ; besides, conscientious actors, it was not enough for such men to be paid, but they wanted to be applauded in the bargain.

Towards five o'clock in the evening, Sombreuil was called.

He was like Cazotte, a well known royalist, and it was all the more difficult to save him from every one knowing that governor of the invalides on the fourteenth of July, he had fired on the people. His sons were in the foreign army ; one of them had so borne himself at the Siege of Longwy, that he had been decorated by the King of Prussia.

Sombreuil appeared, noble and resigned also, carrying loftily his snowy head, whose long locks fell down on his uniform; he also was leaning on his daughter.

This time, Maillard did not dare order the prisoners' release; however, making an effort over himself, he said:

"Innocent or guilty, I think it will be unworthy of the people to dip their hands in this old man's blood."

Sombreuil's daughter heard this noble sentence, which must have its weight in heaven's balances; she drew her father towards the door of life, crying:

"Saved, saved!"

No sentence had been delivered, either to condemn or absolve.

Two or three of the cut-throats thrust their heads in the wicket door to ask what was to be done.

The tribunal remained speechless.

"Do what you like," said one member.

"Well, let the girl drink to the health of the nation!" cried the butchers.

It was then that a man, red with blood, his sleeves tucked up, with ferocious visage, held out to Mademoiselle de Sombreuil a glass, some say full of blood, others containing merely wine. She cried "The nation forever," dipped her lips in the liquor, whatever it was, and her father was saved.

Two hours had gone by.

Then Maillard's voice, as passionless in invoking the living as the voice of Minos in summoning the dead, uttered these words:

"Citizeness Andrée de Taverney, Countess de Charny!"

On this name, Gilbert felt his limbs fail him, and his heart sink.

A life, more important to him than his own, was to be debated and tried, sentenced or saved.

"Citizens," said Maillard to the members of the fearful tribunal, "she who is to appear before you is a poor woman who was devoted in former days to the Austrian, but whom the Austrian, ungrateful like the Queen, has paid for devotion with ingratitude; she has lost all to that friendship: her fortune and her husband; you will see her enter, in mourning, and what does that mourning make her? not the aristocrat, but the prisoner of the Temple! Citizens, I ask of you this woman's life."

The members of the tribunal gave a nod of assent.

One alone said:

"We must see her."

"Then, look," returned Maillard.

The door opened and they beheld, in the depths of the corridor, a woman all in black, her forehead covered with a thick veil, coming forward unattended, with a steady step.

One would have declared her to be an apparition from that unknown bourne, from whence, as says Hamlet, "no traveler returns."

On seeing her, the judges shuddered.

She reached the table, and lifted her veil.

Never did a paler beauty appear to man's eye! she was a goddess in marble.

All eyes were fastened on her.

Gilbert was breathless.

She addressed Maillard, in a voice both firm and gentle.

"Citizen," said she, "are you the president?"

"Yes, citizeness," rejoined Maillard, astonished that he, the questioner, should be interrogated.

"I am the Countess de Charny, wife of the Count de Charny, killed on the infamous day of the tenth of August; an aristocrat, a friend of the Queen; I have deserved death and come to meet it."

The judges uttered an exclamation of surprise.

Gilbert turned pale, and drew himself back as far as possible in his corner, endeavoring to shun Andrée's look.

"Citizens," said Maillard, who saw Gilbert's fright, "this woman is mad; her husband's death has made her lose her reason; let us pity her and give her life. The people's justice never punishes the mad."

He rose and would have laid his hand on her head, as he did to all those he proclaimed innocent; but she thrust aside Maillard's hand.

"I have all my senses," said she; "and, if you want to pardon any one, do so to somebody who asks for it and deserves it, but not to me, who does not deserve and who rejects it."

Maillard turned to Gilbert, and saw that the latter had clasped his hands.

"This woman is mad," said he again; "she is released."

And he signed a member of the tribunal to push her out through the door of life.

"Innocent—let her pass!" cried this man.

All made way before Andrée; swords, pikes, axes lowered before this statue of Mourning.

But, after having gone some ten steps, while, leaning on the window, Gilbert watched her departing through the bars, she stopped.

"Long live the King!" said she; "long live the Queen! Shame on the tenth of August!"

Gilbert sprang into the courtyard.

He had seen a sword flash; but, swift as a thunderbolt, the whole blade had disappeared in Andrée's bosom!

He came in time to receive her in his arms.

She turned on him her glazing eyes, and recognized him.

"I told you right when I said I would die in spite of you," murmured she. "Love Sebastian for us both!" she continued in a voice barely intelligible. "Near him! beside my Olivier," she added, still more faintly, "beside my husband for eternity?"

She expired.

Gilbert took her in his arms and lifted her up.

Fifty naked, blood-reddened arms threatened him at once.

But Maillard appeared behind him and said, stretching out his hand over his head:

"Let Citizen Gilbert pass, carrying the body of a poor madwoman killed by mistake."

All parted, and Gilbert, bearing the countess's corpse, strode through the midst of the murderers without one dreaming of barring his way, so sovereign was Maillard's word over the multitude.

———

CHAPTER XIX.

WHAT HAD TRANSPIRED IN THE TEMPLE DURING THE MASSACRE.

THE commune—while organizing massacre, of which we have endeavored to give a specimen, while wishing to subjugate the Assembly and overbear by terror—greatly feared that something evil would happen to the Temple prisoners.

In truth, in the way affairs stood, Longwy taken, Verdun invested, the enemy but fifty leagues from Paris, the King and the royal family were valuable hostages who would guarantee life to the deepest compromised.

Commissioners were, therefore, sent to the Temple.

Five hundred armed men would have been insufficient to guard this prison, which they would perhaps of themselves have opened to the mob.

A commissioner hit upon a surer method than all the pikes and bayonets of Paris; it was to surround the Temple with a tricolored band bearing the ensuing inscription:

"Citizens; you who, to vengeance, know how to ally love of order, respect this barrier; it is necessary to our guard and responsibility!"

Strange period, when oaken door were shattered, when iron bars were snapped asunder, and when people knelt before a ribbon!

The people went down on their knees to this tricolored ribbon of the Temple, and kissed it; not one overstepped it.

The King and the Queen were ignorant, on the second of September, of what was going on in Paris; there was, around the Temple, greater fermentation than usual; but they began to grow accustomed to these fits of fever.

The King ordinarily dined at two o'clock; at that hour he dined as usual, and, after the meal, went down into the garden, as usual again, with the Queen, Mesdames Elizabeth and Royale, and the little dauphin.

During their walk, the outside clamor increased.

One of the officers following the

King leant over to one of his colleagues, and whispered in his ear, though not so low that Clery did not hear him:

"We were wrong to consent to their walking out after dinner."

It was about three o'clock, just at the moment when the prisoners transferred from the commune to the Abbaye were begining to be slaughtered.

The King had, as valets-de-chambre, only Clery and Hue.

Poor Thierry—whom we saw, on the tenth of August, lending the Queen his room for her to confer with Rœderer— was at the Abbaye and was to be killed on the third.

It appeared that the second officer's opinion was just the same as the other's, with respect to its being wrong to have let the royal party go out; for both of them gave it the order to return on the instant.

They were obeyed.

But hardly had they been collected in the Queen's chamber, than two other officers, who were not on duty at the tower, entered, and one of them, an ex-capuchin named Mathieu, advanced towards the King, saying:

"Do you not know, sir, what is happening? The country is in the greatest danger."

"How would you have me learn anything here, sir?" returned the King; "I am in close confinement."

"Well, then, I will inform you of what you do not know; the enemy has entered Champagne, and the King of Prussia marches on Chalons.

The Queen could not suppress a start of gladness.

The municipal noticed this movement, fleeting as it was.

"Oh, yes," said he, addressing the Queen, "yes, we know that we, our wives and children are to perish; but you answer for all: you shall die before us, and the people shall be revenged!"

"Come what heaven pleases," said the King; "I have done everything for the people, and have nothing to reproach myself with."

The same municipal, turning to Hue who was standing by the door, said:

"As for you, the commune charges me to place you under arrest."

"Who, under arrest?" exclaimed the King.

"Your valet?"

"Who?"

"Him!"

The officer pointed to Hue.

"Monsieur Hue!" said the King; "of what is he accused?"

"That does not concern me; but he is to be taken from hence, and seals put upon his papers."

As he went out, the ex-capuchin said to Clery:

"Take care how you act for you will get the same dish served up to you, if you don't toe the mark."

At eleven o'clock on the following morning (the third of September) the King was with his family in his wife's apartment; an officer gave Clery the order for him to come up into the King's chamber.

Manuel and several other members of the commune were there.

All their faces expressed high uneasiness. Manuel was not bloodthirsty and there was a moderate party even in the commune.

"What does the King think of the removal of his servant?" inquired Manuel.

"His Majesty is very uneasy," answered Clery.

"No harm will befal him," returned Manuel; "but I am charged to inform the King that he cannot come back, and that the council will replace him. You may inform the King of this measure."

"I would rather not do so, sir," responded Clery; "be so kind, therefore, as to spare me from announcing to my master news that will displease him."

Manuel reflected for an instant, when he said:

"Be it so; I will go down to the Queen's room."

He did, indeed, descend, and found the King.

The latter received the news given him by the proctor of the commune with a calm air; then, with the same impassive countenance he had worn on the twentieth of June and the tenth of August and which he was to wear on the scaffold, he said :

" 'Tis well, sir ; I thank you, I shall be served by my son's valet (Clery was the Dauphin's attendant), and, if the commune opposes that, will wait upon myself. I am resolved," added he, with a slight shake of the head.

" Have you any request to make ?"

" We are wanting in linen," said the King, "a great privation to us. Do you think that you can obtain from the commune permission to be furnished according to our needs ?"

" I will mention it to the council," replied Manuel.

Seeing that the King had nothing further to say, he withdrew.

At one o'clock, the King expressed his wish to take a walk.

During the walks, there was almost always some signs of sympathy encountered, made from a window of an attic or through some blind ; and that was a consolation.

The municipals refused to let the royal family go out.

At two o'clock, they went to table.

About the middle of dinner, there arose a sound of drums, and an increase of the shouting—all approaching the Temple.

The royal family rose from table, and gathered in the Queen's room.

The sound drew nearer.

What caused it ?

There was massacre going on at La Force as at the Abbaye ; not under a Maillard's presidency, but under a Hebert's ; hence the slaughter was more fearful.

Yet, the prisoners had a better chance to escape : there were less political captives at La Force than at the Abbaye ; the assassins were less numerous, the lookers-on less blood-thirsty ; but, instead of its being Maillard domineering over the massacre, as at the Abbaye, here Hebert was oversway-ed by the massacre.

Forty-two persons were saved at the Abbaye ; only six at La Force.

Among the prisoners at the latter place was the poor little Princess de Lamballe.

We have seen her pass through the foregoing works of " The Queen's Necklace," " Six Years Later," and the "Countess de Charny," as the devoted shadow of the Queen.

Her death was earnestly desired. She was called " the Austrian's counselor." She was her confidant, her intimate friend, something more—'twas said—but in no way her adviser. The darling granddaughter of the Duke of Savoy with her finely chiselled mouth, her fixed smile, was capable of loving, as she proved ; but to counsel, and counsel a masculine, stubborn, domineering woman, such as the Queen was, never !

The Queen had loved her as she had loved Mesdames de Guemene, de Marsan, de Polignac, but, fickle, inconstant in all her sentiments, she had perhaps made her suffer as much as friend as she had made Charny suffer as lover ; however, as we have seen, the lover grew weary ; the friend, on the contrary, had remained faithful.

Both perished for her whom they had loved.

Our readers will recal that evening in the Pavilion of Flora, to which we conducted them. The Princess de Lamballe received in her apartments those whom the Queen could not see in her own. Suleau and Barnave at the Tuileries ; Mirabeau at Saint Cloud.

Some-time afterwards, the princess had retired to England ; she might have remained there and lived long in peace ; the good gentle creature, knowing the Tuileries to be threatened, returned to ask again her place near the Queen.

On the tenth of August, she had been separated from her friend ; taken to the Temple first with the Queen, she had, almost immediately, been transferred to La Force.

There, she had felt herself crushed under the burden of her devotion ; she had been willing to die beside the Queen, with the Queen ; under her eyes, death would have appeared to her sweet : away from the Queen, she had no longer the courage to die.

She was not a woman of Andrée's stamp ; she was wild with terror.

She was not ignorant of all the

hatred in agitation against her. Shut up in one of the lofty chambers of the prison with Madame de Navarre, she had, on the night of the second, seen Madame de Touzel go away; it was as if she been told:

"You remain to die."

So, she was swooning every minute on her bed, covering her face with the bedclothes at every gust of clamor that came up to her like a fearful child, and when she returned to herself after each fainting fit, she would sigh:

"Oh, heavens, I hoped I would be dead! If one could die as one faints! 'Twould be neither so painful nor so hard."

Murder was everywhere; in the court, at the door, in the lower rooms: the scent of blood crept up to her like a vapor from the grave.

At eight o'clock in the morning, the door of her chamber opened.

So great was her terror this time that she neither swooned nor hid her face.

She turned her head and saw two National Guards.

"Come, get up," said one of them brutally to the Princess; "you've got to go to the Abbaye."

"Oh, gentlemen," said she, "it is impossible for me to leave the bed; I am so weak that I cannot walk. If you call me to kill me," she added in a hardly intelligible voice, "you can kill me here as well as anywhere else."

One of the men stooped down to her ear while the other spied at the door.

"Obey, my lady," said he; "we want to save your highness."

"Then retire, till I dress," said the prisoner.

The two men went out, and Madame de Navarre helped her to dress or rather dressed her.

In ten minutes, the two men returned.

The princess was ready, but she could not walk; she trembled all over. She took the arm of the National Guard who had spoken to her, and, leaning on it, went down the stairs.

On reaching the wicket, she found herself facing the tribunal of blood presided over by Hebert.

On seeing these men with tucked-up sleeves, who were constituted judges, and the red-handed men who were executioners, she fainted.

Three times questioned, she swooned each time.

"I tell you they want to save you!" repeated the man who had already spoken to her.

This pledge restored the poor woman a little strength.

"What do you want of me, gentlemen?" she murmured.

"Who are you?" demanded Hebert.

"Marie Louise of Savoy Carugnan, Princess de Lamballe."

"Your quality?"

"Superintendent of the Queen's household."

"Have you knowledge of the plots of the tenth of August?"

"I did not know that there were any; but, if so, I was completely ignorant of them."

"Swear liberty, equality, hatred of the King, the Queen and royalty."

"I will willingly swear the two first; but I cannot swear to the rest, which is not in my heart."

"Swear!" whispered the National Guard, "or you are dead!"

The princess stretched out her hands, and reeled instinctively towards the door.

"Swear!" said her protector

Then, as if, in her terror of death, she feared that she might utter a shameful oath, she clapped her hand to her mouth to repress the words which might escape despite her.

Several moans passed through her fingers.

"She has sworn!" shouted the National Guard accompanying her; and he added:

"Go out quickly by that door before you; as you go, shout: 'The nation forever!' and you are saved."

As she went out, she was taken in the arms of an assassin who was waiting for her; this assassin was "big Nicholas," the same who had cut off the heads of the two body-guards at Versailles. This time, he had promised to save the princess.

He dragged her away towards something shapeless, blood-dripping, while saying to her :

"Call out : 'The nation forever !' why don't you ?"

No doubt she was going to cry out ; unfortunately, she opened her eyes and beheld herself in front of a pile of corpses, while walking on which a man with his hob-nailed shoes made the blood gush out, like a man pressing grapes.

She saw this disgusting sight, turned away, and could only gasp :

"Fie ! how horrid !"

This exclamation was extinguished.

A hundred thousand francs, it is said, had been given by her father-in-law, Penthievre, to save her.

She was being pushed into the narrow passage leading from the Rue Saint Antoine to the prison, called the Priests' Blind Alley, when a wretch, Charlot, a perriwig-maker, who had enlisted as a drummer in the volunteers, pushed through the hedge formed around her, and knocked off her bonnet with his pike.

Did he only mean to do this simple act, or was it his intention to strike her in the face ?

Blood flowed.

Blood calls for blood.

A man flung a club at the princess, striking her behind the head ; she stumbled and fell on one knee.

There was no means to save her, now ; from all sides, swords were thrust, pikes darted.

She did not emit even a scream ; she had died, in reality, when she spoke her last words.

Hardly had she expired—although she may have still breathed—than there was a rush for her ; in an instant, all her clothes were torn off.

An obscene prompting had swayed all on her death and led to this stripping ; there was a low desire to behold that peerless form which the women of Lesbos would have worshipped.

Nude as she had been born, she was lifted up before all eyes upon a post and there was exposed from eight o'clock till midday.

Finally, they grew tired of the scandalous story they told over this corpse.

A man stepped up and cut off her head.

That long, flexible neck like a swan's offered little resistance !

The miscreant who committed this crime, more hideous on a corpse than on a living being, was named Grison.

History is the most inexorable of goddesses ; she plucks a feather from her wing, dips it in blood, writes a name, and that name is given to the execration of posterity.

This man was guillotined, hereafter, as head of a band of thieves.

A second named Rodi, cut open the princess's bosom, and tore out the heart.

A third, named Mamin, hacked off another part of the body.

It was on the account of her love for the Queen that this poor thing was mutilated.

How they must have hated the Queen !

They stuck on pikes the three severed fragments of the body, and marched off towards the Temple.

An immense throng followed the three assassins ; but, apart from several boys and drunken men who insulted, the whole train kept an awful silence.

A wigmaker's shop was on the road ; it was entered.

The man carrying the head laid it on a table.

"Frizzle me that head," said he ; "she is going to see her mistress at the Temple."

The barber curled the princess's magnificent hair ; and off they started again for the Temple, this time with loud cheers.

This was the outcry the royal family heard.

The party arrived ; for it had the abominable idea of showing the Queen this head, heart and body of the princess.

They presented themselves at the Temple.

The tricolored ribbon barred their passage.

These men, assassins, murderers, dared not step over a ribbon !

They demanded that a deputation of six ruffians, three of whom should bear the fragments aforesaid, should enter the Temple and parade through it, to display these bloody relics to the Queen.

The request was *so* reasonable, that it was granted without discussion.

The King was seated and apparently playing back-gammon with the Queen.

In thus being close together under pretext of playing, the prisoners at least could exchange a few words unheard by the officers.

Suddenly, the King saw one of the latter shut the door and, springing to the window, quickly pull the blinds.

This was one named Danjou, formerly a seminarist, a large man, who was styled on account of his stature Abbe Six-foot.

" What is it ?" inquired the King.

This man, taking advantage of the Queen having her back turned, waved with his hand for the King not to question.

The shouts, yells, threats and insults came to the room notwithstanding the closed door and blinds.

The King comprehended that something unwonted was to occur, and laid his arm on the Queen's shoulder for her to remain in her place.

At this moment, there came a knock at the door, and, in spite of himself, Danjou was obliged to open it.

It was the officers on guard and the municipals.

" Gentlemen, is my family in safety ?" inquired the King.

" Yes." replied a man dressed as a National Guardsman, wearing double epaulets ; " but there is a rumor that there is nobody in the tower, that you have all escaped. Show yourself at the window to belie it."

The King, unaware of what had happened, saw no reason he should not obey.

He took a step towards the window ; but Danjou stopped him.

" Do not do so, sir !" said he. " The people," added he, turning to the officers of the National Guard, " ought to show more confidence in their magistrates."

" Well," said the man in epaulets, " that is not it ; they want you to come

to the window to see the Princess de Lamballe's head and heart, which they have brought to show you how the people treat their tyrants. I advise you, therefore, to appear, if you do not want them to bring them here."

The Queen screamed and fell swooning into the arms of Mesdames Elizabeth and Royale.

" Sir," said the King, " you might have spared the Queen this painful blow. See what you have done," added he, pointing to the group of the three women.

The man shrugged his shoulders, and went out singing the " Carmagnole."

At six o'clock, Petion's secretary came in to give to the King two thousand five hundred francs.

Seeing the Queen standing motionless, he fancied that it was from respect for him that she thus was not seated, and he had the goodness to beg her to be seated.

" My mother thus stood," says Madame Royale in her Memoirs, " because, since those dreadful words, she had been fixed in that posture, seeing not what happened in the room."

Terror had changed her to a statue.

CHAPTER XX.

VALMY.

AND now, for the present, let us remove our eyes from those frightful scenes of massacre, and follow to the valleys of Argonne, one of the characters of our work on whom rests, at this juncture, the weighty destinies of France.

Dumouriez.

He had, we have seen, on leaving the cabinet, resumed his employment of active general and, on La Fayette's flight, had received the appointment of commander of the Army of the East.

This appointment was a kind of miracle of intuitiveness on the part of those in power.

Dumouriez was, indeed, detested by some, scorned by others ; but luckier than Danton had been on the second of

September, he was unanimously recognized as the only man who could save France.

The Girondists, who appointed him, hated Dumouriez; they had put him into the ministry, he had driven them out; and yet they went to seek him in the Army of the North and made him general-in-chief.

The Jacobins hated and scorned Dumouriez; they, however, felt that this man's great ambition was glory, and that he would win or die.

Robespierre, not daring to sustain him on account of his hurtful reputation, got Couthon to support him.

Danton neither hated nor despised Dumouriez; he was one of those of sturdy temper who judge things from on high and little care for reputations, ready as they are to make use of vices themselves, if they will give the expected results.

Still, Danton, knowing the party that might gain by Dumouriez, distrusted his stability; he sent two men to him: Fabre d'Eglantine, his mind, Westermann, his arm.

All the strength of France was put into the hands of him whom they styled an intriguer.

Old Luckner, a stupid German, whose incapacity had been proven at the opening of the campaign, was sent to Chalons to raise recruits.

Dillon, brave soldier and distinguished gentleman, though outranking Dumouriez, received an order to obey him.

Kellermann also was put under this man's orders, to whom despairing France handed her sword, saying:

"You are the only one who can defend me; do so!"

Kellermann grumbled, swore, but obeyed; only, he obeyed poorly, and the cannon's thunder had to make him what he was, a son devoted to his country.

Now, how came the allied sovereigns, whose march was marked out in stages to Paris, to stop all at once, after the taking of Longwy and the surrender of Verdun?

A spectre had arisen between them and Paris; Beaurepaire's ghost.

Beaurepaire, once officer in the Rifles, had formed and commanded the Maine-et-Loire Battalion.

When they learnt that the foe had set foot on French soil, he and his men raced over France from the West to the East.

They met on their way a patriot deputy who was returning home.

"What shall I say of you to your families?" he asked.

"*That we are dead!*" a voice made answer.

No Spartan starting for Thermopylæ could have given a better reply.

The enemy, we repeat, had arrived before Verdun, on the thirtieth of August, 1792; next day, the place was summoned to surrender.

Beaurepaire and his men, supported by Marceau, wanted to fight on till death.

The council of defence, composed of town officers and the head townsmen, ordered him to surrender.

Beaurepaire smiled scornfully.

"I have sworn to die rather than to surrender," said he. "Survive for your shame and dishonor, if you will; I will keep faithful to my oath. This is my last word. I die."

And he blew out his brains.

This spectre was as great and more frightful than the giant Adamastor.

Thereupon, the allied sovereigns, who fancied, from what the fled nobles had said, that France would cower away before them, saw quite another sight.

They beheld this French soil, so thickly settled, changed as by the stroke of a magic wand; all went to the West.

The armed peasant alone stood in the furrow; those owning guns had taken them; those with scythes, them; those with only pitchforks, them.

Again, the weather helped the French; a steady rain drenched men, softened the ground, spoiled the roads. This rain fell equally on French and Prussians, but all were helping the former, all against the latter.

The peasant, who had for the enemy only his gun, scythe, or fork, had, for his countrymen, the wine hidden in the woodpile, the cask of beer buried in a corner of his cellar, and dry straw, the soldier's bed.

Nevertheless, there were faults on faults, Dumouriez foremost in making them; and, in his Memoirs, he tells of his own as well as of his lieutenants'.

He had written to the National Assembly:

"The defiles of Argonne are the Thermopylæ of France; but, more fortunate than Leonidas, I shall not die there."

Yet he had poorly guarded these defiles, one of which was taken, and he was compelled to retreat.

Two of his subordinates were lost; he was nearly lost himself, with only fifteen thousand men, so demoralized that twice they took to flight before fifteen hundred Prussian hussars!

But he never despaired; he kept his hopes and spirits, writing to the ministers:

"I answer for all."

In fact, though pursued, turned, cut off, he made a junction with Beurnonville's ten thousand and Kellermann's fifteen thousand men; he rallied his lost generals, and, by September the nineteenth, was at Sainte Menehould camp, with seventy-six thousand men, when the Prussians had not seventy thousand.

This army often murmured, being sometimes two or three days without bread.

"My friends," said Dumouriez, coming to mingle with them, "the famous Marshal Saxe writes in a book on war that at least once a week the troops should be deprived of their bread ration to make them, in case of necessity, less sensible to that privation; we are just so situated, and you are luckier than the Prussians you see yonder, who are often four days without bread, and are eating their dead horses. You have lard, rice and farina; make cakes; liberty will season them!"

There was something worse: the scum of Paris, the off-scourings of the second of September, who had been pushed into the armies after the massacre.

These wretches had swaggered in, roaring the Ça ira, crying they would not allow any epaulets, crosses of Saint Louis, or embroidered coats, would tear off decorations and plumes, and would soon set things to rights.

Thus they came to camp, and were astonished to find everybody giving them the cold shoulder, not deigning to listen to their threats; the general, however, announced a review for the next day.

The next day, the new comers found themselves, by an unexpected evolution, caught between a numerous body of cavalry, threatening to cut them down, and a mass of artillery, ready to blow them to shreds.

Thereupon, Dumouriez stepped up to these men, who formed seven battalions.

"You fellows," said he, "for I will call you neither citizens, soldiers nor my sons—you see before you this artillery, behind you this cavalry; I have you 'twixt steel and fire! You are disgraced by your crimes; I will not allow here any murderers and cut throats. I will have you cut to pieces at the first sign of mutiny! If you reform and behave yourselves in this brave army in which you have the honor of being admitted, you will find in me a kind father. I know that there are among you some scoundrels charged to incite you into crimes; drive them away yourselves, or denounce them to me. I will render you responsible for one another."

And not only did these men bow their heads and become good soldiers, not only did they repel the worst of them, but they moreover, cut into pieces the wretch Charlot who had struck the Princess de Lamballe and borne her head on a pike.

Thus stood affairs when Kellermann was expected, without whom nothing could be risked.

On the nineteenth, Dumouriez received intelligence that he was two leagues on the left from him.

Dumouriez immediately sent word for him to occupy next day the camp between Dampierre, and the Élize, behind the Auve.

The plans were clearly marked out. At the same time as he despatched these instructions to Kellermann, Dumouriez saw the Prussian army roll upon the Lune Mountains; so that the enemy slipped in between him and Paris, being consequently nearer that city than he.

In all likelihood, the Prussians were seeking battle.

Dumouriez, therefore, sent Kellermann to take his fighting ground on the Heights of Valmy and Gizaucourt.

Kellermann confounded the first and second orders; he stopped on Valmy Heights.

A great fault or wonderful skill.

Placed where he was, Kellermann could not return save by passing his whole army over a narrow bridge; he could not fall back on Dumouriez' right, but by crossing a marsh, which would swallow him up; he could not retreat by his left for there was a deep valley in which he would be crushed.

No retreat was possible.

Is this what the old Alsatian soldier wanted?

If so, he had wonderfully succeeded.

It was a splendid place to win or die!

Brunswick beheld this with astonishment.

"Those posted yonder," said he to the King of Prussia, "are determined not to draw back!"

But the Prussian army had been led to believe that Dumouriez was cut off, and had been assured that the army of tailors, beggars and shopkeepers, as the emigres styled it, would disperse at the first shot.

The French had neglected to occupy Gizaucourt Heights with General Chazot—who had been stationed along the Chalons Highway—heights from which the enemy would have been taken on the flank; the Prussians profited by this carelessness, and took that position, by which act they out flanked Kellermann's corps.

The day broke with a dense fog; but that little mattered; the Prussians knew where the French army was; on Valmy Heights, and could not be elsewhere.

Sixty cannons were fired at once, at random, but being shot at masses, taking aim was of little account.

The first shots were a great hardship for that enthusiastic army to support, which was admirably fitted for attacking, but was restless under the curb.

Chance—not skill, it was easy to be seen—was against the French.

The Prussians shelled a train and two caissons caught fire and blew up.

The teamsters jumped down off their horses to run from the explosion.

Kellermann spurred up his horse to the spot still in confusion, where struggled fog and smoke.

Suddenly, he and his horse rolled on the ground.

A bullet had gone through the animal, but the rider was unhurt; he sprang upon another horse and rallied some breaking companies.

It was eleven o'clock; the fog began to lift.

Kellermann caught sight of the Prussians forming in three columns to storm Valmy Heights; he formed his soldiers also in three columns and said, riding up and down the line:

"Soldiers, no firing; wait for the enemy and receive him on the bayonet!"

Then, waving his hat on the point of his sword, he cried:

"The nation forever! let us conquer for her!"

On the instant, his whole army did likewise; each soldier flourished his hat on his bayonet, shouting:

"The nation forever!"

The fog lifted and the smoke blew away and Brunswick saw through his glass, a strange, extraordinary unheard-of sight: thirty thousand men with bare heads, brandishing their weapons, only replying to their enemies' shots by the cry:

"The nation forever!"

Brunswick shook his head; had he been alone, the Prussian army would not have taken another step; but the King was there, who wanted battle and he had to obey him.

The Prussians steadily mounted under the eyes of the King and the duke; they crossed the space between them with the firmness of an army of Frederick; every man seemed bound to his comrade by an iron ring.

Suddenly, in the centre the immense

serpent glittered ; but its coils straightened again.

Five minutes afterwards, it was again shining, but became dull once more.

Twenty of Dumouriez' guns had taken the column in the flank and showered on it, an iron rain ; the head could not ascend, checked as it was every instant by the body being torn by grapeshot.

Brunswick saw the day was lost, and was ordering the recal to be sounded.

The King ordered the charge to be beaten, took the head of his men and led his docile, valiant infantry through the double fire of Kellermann and Dumouriez; he met the French lines.

Something luminous seemed to be around the young army : faith !

"I have never seen such fanatics since the religious wars !" said Brunswick.

They were fanatics, fanatics of freedom.

The heroes of '92, they opened that grand conquest of war which was to end by the conquest of minds.

On the twentieth of September, Dumouriez saved France.

On the following day, the National Convention emancipated Europe by proclaiming the Republic.

CHAPTER XXI.

THE TWENTY-FIRST OF SEPTEMBER.

At noon on the twenty-first of September—before the news of Dumouriez' victory saving France was known in Paris—the doors of the hall of the Manege opened to admit, slowly and solemnly, each throwing on the others questioning looks, the seven hundred and forty-nine members composing the new Assembly.

Out of that number, two hundred had belonged to the old Assembly.

The National Convention had been elected under the effects of the September news; it would have been fancied, at first blush, a reactionary congress. More than that: many noblemen had been elected ; a very democratic thought had called in servants to vote; some had appointed masters.

There were, besides, among the new deputies, tradesmen, physicians, lawyers, professors, priests who had taken the oath, literary men, editors, etc.

The spirit of this mass was wavering and shifting, five hundred representatives, at least, were neither Girondists nor Jacobins ; events were to determine what place they should occupy in the Assembly.

But all were unanimous in a two-fold hatred against the September doings, and against the Parisian deputation, almost entirely from the commune, which had caused those fearful deeds.

The blood spilt seemed to have flowed through the hall, separating the hundred Jacobins from the rest of the Assembly.

The centre itself, as though to avoid the ruddy brook, leaned to the right.

The Mountain (so were the Jacobins styled from their having the upper seats) presented a formidable aspect.

As we have said, it was in the inferior ranks, picked out of the commune ; above the commune, that famous committee of superintendence which had made the massacre ; then, like a three-headed hydra, at the apex of the triangle, were three fearful, deeply characteristic faces.

First, Robespierre's cold, emotionless one, its parchment skin as if glued to his narrow brow ; with winking eyes, hidden under spectacles ; his open hands on his knees, like to those Egyptian figures cut in porphory,the hardest of all marbles ; a sphynx which alone seemed to know the key to the revolutionary enigma, but of which none dared to ask it.

Beside him, Danton's contorted countenance, with mouth awry, his mobile mask, impressed with unutterable ugliness, his fabulous body, half man, half bull ; almost sympathized with for all that, for it was felt that what made this flesh quiver, his lava-like words pour out, was the beating of a profoundly patriotic heart, and that his large hand, obeying his slightest wish, would be stretched out with the same readiness to fell a standing foe or raise a fallen one.

Next, behind these so different visages, appeared another, not a man's—human beings could not have such a degree of repulsiveness—but a monster's, a chimera's, an ominous, ridiculous vision.

Marat's!

Marat, with his brazen face suffused with bile and blood; with impudent eyes; his broad mouth, ever ready to send forth or rather to spit out insult; his twisted nose, drinking in, by its open nostrils, that breath of popularity which, for him, was generated in the sewer and fumed up from the gutter; Marat, "got up" like the humblest of his admirers, his head bound up in a rag, with clouted shoes, without buckles,often without strings; his trousers of coarse cloth, spattered, or rather soaked with mud; his shirt open over his chest, thin yet broad relatively to his size; his greasy, narrow neckerchief, showing the hideous tendons of his neck, which, unsuiting one another made his head lean to the left; his dry, flabby hands, always threatening, clenching, and in the intervals of their threats, tugging at his coarse hair.

All this form, giant's trunk on dwarf's legs, was hideous to see; the first movement of whoever saw him was to turn aloof; but the eye would not leave him so speedily that it could not read on it all: "Second of September!" and then the eye would remain rivetted and blasted as before another Medusa's head.

These were the three men whom the Girondists accused of aspiring to the dictatorship.

They, on their part, accused the Girondists of wishing federalism.

Two other men who are bound, by different interests and opinions, to the narrative we have undertaken, were seated on opposite sides of this Assembly : Billot and Gilbert.

The latter was on the extreme right, between Lanjuinais and Kersaint; Billot on the extreme left, between Couthon and Thuriot.

The members of the former Legislative Assembly escorted the convention; they came to solemnly abdicate, and hand over the power into their successors' hands.

Francois de Neufchatel, the last president of the dissolved Assembly, mounted the tribune and said :

"Representatives of the nation, the Legislative Assembly has ceased its functions; it places government in your hands.

"The aim of your effort should be to give the French freedom, laws and peace : freedom, without which, the French cannot live; laws, the more firmly to implant freedom ; peace : the only design of war.

"Freedom, the laws, peace, three words graven by the Grecians on the doors of the Temple of Delphos ; you must impress them on the whole soil of France !"

The Legislative Assembly had lasted a year.

It had seen immense fearful events transpire : the twentieth of June, the tenth of August, the second and third of September !

It left to France war with the two Northern powers, civil war in La Vendee, a debt of two billion, two hundred million of assignats—and the victory of Valmy, to arrive that evening but still unknown.

Petion was appointed president by acclamation.

Condorcet, Brissot, Rabaut Saint Etienne,Vergniaud, Camus and Lasource were made secretaries ; five Girondists in the six.

The whole Convention, aside from perhaps thirty or forty members, wanted a republic; the Girondists however, had decided, in a meeting at Madame Roland's, that they would not allow discussion on the change of government save at their time and place, that is when they should have gained the executive commissions and the commission on the constitution.

But, on the twentieth of September, the very day of the Valmy battle, other combatants contested an action quite as decisive.

Saint Just, Lequinio, Panis, Billaud Varennes, Collot d'Herbois and several other members of the future Assembly, were dining at the Palais Royal; they resolved that next day, the word Republic should be hurled at their antagonists.

"If they take it up," remarked Saint Just, "they are lost, for we will have been the first to have uttered it; if they avoid it, they are lost again, for by opposing this passion of the people, they will be submerged by the unpopularity which we will heap upon their heads."

Collot d'Herbois took the making of the motion on himself.

Therefore, hardly had Francois de Neufchatel transferred the powers of the Old Assembly to the New, than d'Herbois rose for the floor.

It was granted him.

He mounted the speakers-stand; the watchword had been given to the impatient.

"Citizens representatives," began he, "I propose that the first act of the Assembly now in congress shall be the abolition of royalty."

On these words great uproar rose from the hall and the galleries.

Two opposers at once rose, well known republicans: Barrere and Quinelle. They moved that the will of the people should be awaited.

"The will of the people? why so?" broke in an humble village curate; "why debate when all are agreed? Kings are, in the mental order, what monsters are in the physical grade; courts are the studios of crimes; the history of kings is the martyrology of nations!"

There was inquiry as to who was the man who had given this short but energetic story of royalty. Few knew his name: Gregoire.

The Girondists felt the blow dealt at them: they saw they were going to be the Jacobins' towline.

"Let the decree be drawn up this session!" cried from his seat Ducos, Vergniaud's friend and pupil. "The decree has no need of consideration; after the light which the tenth of August has outpoured, the deliberation on your resolve of abolition of royalty would be the chronicle of Louis the Sixteenth's crimes!"

Thus was the balance restored; the Mountain had demanded the abolition of royalty; but the Girondists demanded the establishment of the Republic.

This was not resolved; but was passed by acclamation.

Not only was the future leaped into to avoid the past, but the unknown was begged in preference to the known.

The proclamation of the Republic answered an urgent popular need: it was the consecration of the long struggle the people had maintained since the communes: the absolution for the Jacquerie, the Maillotins, the Fronde, the Revolution; the crowning of the mob to the detriment of royalty.

So much more freely did each citizen breathe, that one would have thought each breast relieved of the weight of a throne.

Such hours of illusion are short, but blissful; it was fancied a republic had been proclaimed, it was consecrating a revolution.

The true republicans, the purest, at least—who wanted the Republic free from crime, those who were next day to beard the triumvirate of Danton, Marat and Robespiere,—the Girondists, were at the summit of delight.

The Republic was their dearest wish, thanks to them, under the ruins of twenty centuries, was to be found the type of human government. France had been an Athens under Francis the First and Louis the Fourteenth; it was going to be a Sparta with them!

A splendid dream.

They assembled to a banquet that evening at Minister Roland's.

There was Vergniaud, Guadet, Louvet, Petion, Boyer Fonfrede, Barbaroux, Gensonne, Grangeneuve, Condorcet, guests who were, before a year was over, to meet at a feast much more solemn than this! but, at this time all turned their backs on the morrow, closed their eyes to the future, voluntarily threw a veil before the unknown they were launching upon, where was heard the roaring of the whirlpool which, like the Maelstrom of Scandinavian fables, was to draw down, if not the bark, at all events the pilot and crew.

The minds of all were in their infancy, just taking a form, an aspect, a body;

the young Republic leaped forth helmed and speared like " feather'd Mercury," what more could be asked ?

During the two hours' solemnity, there was an exchange of lofty thoughts behind which was the utmost devotion, these men spoke of their lives as of a thing no longer theirs, but the nation's. They reserved honor, that was all ; at need, they would abandon renown.

In the roaming fancy of youthful hope, there were some who saw open before them such azure, boundless skies as one sees in dreams ; these were the young and ardent, who had entered into the most enervating of all strifes, the warfare of the rostrum : they were Barbaroux, Rebecqui, Ducos, Boyer Fonfrede.

There were others who stopped, halting in the middle of the road, girding up their loins for the course yet to be accomplished : they were those who had been bowed by the hard days' work of the Legislative ; the Guadets, Gensonnes, Grangeneuves, Vergniauds.

There were still others, who felt they had reached their goal, fully aware popularity had cast them off ; resting under the growing shade of the republican tree, they melancholy pondered whether it was worth while to rise, gather up their strength afresh and take up once more the pilgrim's staff to stumble over the first pebble, the Rolands, the Petions.

But, to the eyes of all these men, who was the future leader ?

Who was the principal author, who would be the future moderator of the young Republic?

Vergniaud.

At the close of the dinner, he filled his glass and rose.

" Friends, a toast," said he.

They all stood like him.

" To the everdurance of the Republic !"

They all repeated after him.

He was going to drink, but Madame Roland said :

" Hold !"

She drew from her bosom a new-blown rose, just bloomed like the new era opening ; she plucked off its leaves and, as did an Athenian damsel to Pericles' goblet, she scattered them within Vergniaud's glass.

The latter smiled sadly, emptied his glass and, stooping to Barbaroux's ear, said :

" Alas ! I fear me this great soul is deceived ! Not rose leaves but cypress sprigs should be steeped in our wine this night. While drinking to a republic whose feet are stained by September's blood, heaven knows whether we do not drink to our death ! But, never mind !" added he, glancing upward, " were this wine my blood, I would quaff it to freedom and equality !"

" The Republic forever !" chorussed the guests.

At very nearly the moment when Vergniaud gave his toast, and the feasters answered to it by the shout of " The Republic forever !" trumpets flourished before the Temple, and all were hushed into deep stillness.

Then, in their rooms, where the windows were open, the royal couple might hear a crier proclaim, in a steady, ringing, sonorous, voice, the abolition of royalty and the formation of the Republic.

———

CHAPTER XXII.

THE LEGEND OF THE MARTYR KING.

THE reader will see with what impartiality we have, albeit under the guise of romance, placed so far under his eyes what there is fearful, cruel, good, praiseworthy, great, sanguinary, low and mean, in the men and events springing from them.

The men we speak of are dead ; the events alone, immortalized by history, never dying still exist.

We would not fear to invoke from the grave all its tenants to ask them have not we told their story—if not as it was (who can boast of having known such mysteries) at least as we have seen it.

We would say to Mirabeau.

" Arise !"

To Louis the Sixteenth :

" Martyr, arise !"

We would say:

"Arise, all ye who were called Favras, la Fayette, Bailly, Fournier the American, Jourdan the Cut-throat, Maillard, Theroigne de Mericourt, Barnave, Bouille, Gamain, Petion, Manuel, Danton, Robespierre, Marat, Vergniaud, Dumouriez, Marie Antoinette, Madame Campan, Barbaroux, Roland, Madame Roland, King, Queen, workman orators. generals, murderers, arise! tell me if I have not represented you to my generation aright, to my people, the women especially, to mothers of our sons, to whom truthfully should be taught history."

We would say to events, standing still on either side of the road we have traveled over:

"Great luminous day of the fourteenth July; darksome, lowering nights of October the fifth and sixth; bloody storm of the Champ de Mars where the powder flash mingled with the lightning's bolt, and the cannon's roar with the thunder roll, prophetic invasion of the twentieth June, fearful victory of the tenth of August, hateful remembrance of the second and third of September, have I spoken of you aright? have I truly depicted you? have I wittingly lied? have I endeavoren to spare or defame you?"

Men would answer, as would events:

"You have searched for the truth without hate or passion; you have believed what you have said; you have remained faithful to all the glories of the past, insensible to all the glare of the present, trusting to the promise of the future; be absolved."

As we have done, not as a self-appointed judge, but as an impartial chronicler, so will we do to the end; which is fast approaching.

We are gliding down the steep, and there are few stoppages from the twenty-first of September (date of the death of royalty) to the twenty-first of January, day of the King's death.

We have heard the Republic proclaimed beneath the windows of the royal prison, and that calls us to the Temple.

Let us, therefore enter the gloomy building which confines a king become

a man, a Queen still a Queen, a virgin to be a martyr, and two poor children innocent through age, if not by birth.

The King was at the Temple—how came he there? was it meant beforehand that he should fill the shameful prison?

No.

Petion had at first had the idea of transporting him to the centre of France, giving him Chambord, and treating him as an idiot monarch.

Suppose that all the European sovereigns would impose silence on their ministers and generals and manifestos, and merely look on what was happening in France, without intention to meddle with the French internal policy, this forfeiture of the throne, this existence limited to a handsome palace in a fine climate, in that spot styled the garden of France, was not so cruel a punishment for the man who was not simply expiating his faults, but those of the Fifteenth and Fourteenth Louis.

La Vendee had just revolted: it was objected that there might be some sudden dash made for the King.

This reason appeared sufficient; Chambord was given up.

The Legislative Assembly were for the Luxembourg, a no less suitable place than Chambord for a dethroned monarch. The plausible pretext was made that the cellars of Mary de Medicis' Florentine palace opened on the catacombs.

So the commune settled on the Temple.

By this was understood, not the Tower Temple, but the Palace of the Temple, the ancient commandry of the Order of Knights Templars, one of the pleasure houses of the Count d'Artois.

When Petion installed the royal family in the palace, as the King had settled about his household, a denunciation came to the commune, and Manuel was sent to finally change the municipal determination, and substitute the donjon for the castle.

Manuel arrived, examined the place destined for the abode of Louis the Sixteenth and his wife, and came down in shame.

The donjon was hardly habitable, being only occupied by a kind of porter, offering insufficient room, with narrow rooms, infested with vermin.

There was in this more of that fatality weighing on dying races than of infamous premeditation on the part of its judges.

The National Assembly had not haggled over the expense of the royal table. The King ate a great deal : which is no reproach that we make him, for it is the Bourbon temperament to be hearty eaters ; but the King ate unseasonably.

He ate, and with much gusto, while there was slaughter going on at the Tuileries.

Not only in his prosecution did the judges reproach him for this meal so out-of-place, but, moreover, which is more serious, implacable history has recorded it in its archives.

The National Assembly had resolved five hundred thousand livres for the expenses of the royal table.

During the four months that the King remained at the Temple, his outlay was forty thousand livres — ten thousand francs a month—three hundred and thirty three francs a day—in assignats, it is true, but, at this period, paper money had hardly declined six or eight per cent.

Louis had at the Temple three servants and thirteen waiters on the table.

His dinner was composed every day of four services, six roasts, four salads, three stews of fruit, three dishes of fruit, a decanter of Bordeaux, another of Malvoisie and a third of Madeira.

He alone, with his son, drank wine ; the Queen and the princesses only water.

Materially, the King had nothing to complain of.

But what he essentially wanted was exercise, the sun and air.

Accustomed to hunts at Compeigne and Rambouillet, in the parks of Versailles and the Grand Trianon, Louis found himself reduced—not to a garden, or even a promenade—but to a bare, dry ground, with four beds of withered sod, a few dying trees, leafless from the autumnal wind.

Here, every day at two o'clock, the King and his family walked ; or rather, the King and his family were led, like animals, on a walk.

It was something unknown, cruel, ferocious ; but less so than the dungeons of the Inquisition at Madrid, the lead mines of Venice, the cells of Spielburg.

Remark, we no more excuse the commune than we do crowned heads ; we only say the Temple was but a reprisal, though a fatal and ill-devised one ; for, of a sentence, was made a persecution ; of a guilty man, a martyr.

Now, what were the aspects of the various characters whom we have undertaken to follow through the principal phases of their lives?

The King, with his purblind eyes, fat cheeks, hanging lips, heavy, unwieldy walk, seemed a well-to-do farmer, struck by some piece of bad luck ; his melancholy was that of an agriculturist whose barns the lightning had fired, or whose wheat-fields the storm had levelled.

The Queen looked, as ever, rigid, haughty, dreadfully provoking ; Marie Antoinette had inspired love in the days of her greatness ; in the hour of her fall, she gave rise to devotion, but not to pity : pity is born of sympathy, and the Queen was not at all sympathetic.

Madame Elizabeth — in her white robe, token of the purity of her mind and body ; with her light hair, still finer since she had been forced to leave it unpowdered ; with a blue ribbon round her waist—Madame Elizabeth seemed the guardian angel of the family.

Madame Royale, notwithstanding the charm of her age, excited little interest ; Austrian like her mother, entirely a Maria Theresa and a Marie Antoinette, she had already in her look the scorn and pride of royal races and birds of prey

The little Dauphin with his golden hair and fair but sickly complexion, was interesting ; he had nevertheless, a stern, cold blue eye, of an expression betimes beyond his age ; he understood everything, carried out adroitly such plans as his mother gave him in a look, and had all the ins and outs of infantile acuteness which sometimes draws tears from the eyes of the executioners themselves. He had affected even Chaumette, the poor boy! Chaumette, that fox with pointed snout, that weasel in spectacles.

"I can give him education," said the ex-lawyer's-clerk to Hue, "but he must be removed from his family, to make him forget his rank."

The commune was both cruel and imprudent; cruel in surrounding the royal family with evil treatment, vexations and even insults; imprudent in showing it weak, crushed, imprisoned.

Every day it sent fresh keepers to the Temple under the name of municipals; they entered incarnate enemies of the King, they came out enemies of Marie Antoinette, but almost all pitied the King and his children, and glorified Madame Elizabeth.

Indeed, what saw they at the Temple, instead of the wolf, she-wolf and cub?

A common family, the mother a little fiery, sort of Elmira who would not suffer the hem of her dress to be touched—but no tyrant—not a trace!

How did the family spend the day? Let us state how.

But let us first glance over the prison; we will presently return to those it enclosed.

The King was in the little tower which was close to the large tower, without inner communication; it formed a parallelogram flanked by two pepper-boxes: in one of these turrets was a small staircase running from the first floor to a gallery on the roof; in the other were rooms corresponding to each floor of the tower. The body of the building had four floors.

The first was composed of an antechamber, an eating-room and a closet; the second was about the same; the largest room being the sleeping-chamber of the Queen and the Dauphin, the second, separated from that by a small, dark ante-chamber, was occupied by Mesdames Royale and Elizabeth.

The King had the third floor, which had the same number of rooms; he slept in the largest; the closet served him as his study; beside it was a kitchen, preceded by a little box which, before they had been separated from the King, had been occupied by Chemilly and Hue, but on which, since Hue's removal, had been put seats.

The fourth floor was nailed up; the ground-floor was full of sculleries and kitchens of which no use was made.

Now, how did the royal family live in this contracted space?

We will tell.

The King rose usually at six in the morning; he shaved himself; Clery dressed him and dressed his hair; so soon as this was done, he would pass into his reading-room, the library of the archives of the Order of Malta, containing fifteen or sixteen hundred volumes.

One day, the King, in looking for some book, pointed out to Hue the works of Voltaire and Rousseau.

"There," said he in a low voice, "there are the two men who have ruined France."

On entering, Louis would kneel and pray for five minutes or so, then read or write till nine o'clock; meanwhile, Clery would clear up the King's room, prepare breakfast, and go down to the Queen.

The King would amuse himself translating either Virgil or Horace's odes; to continue the Dauphin's education, he had taken up Latin again himself.

This study was very cramped; the door was always open; the municipal stood by the bedroom door, seeing what the King was about.

The Queen would not open her door until Clery's coming, in order that, the door being shut, the municipal should not enter her rooms.

Clery then, would dress the young prince's hair, help the Queen dress, and pass into the next room to render Madame Royale and Madame Elizabeth the same service. This moment of dressing, brief yet valuable, was that when Clery could inform the Queen and the princesses of whatever he had learned; a sign indicated he had news to impart; the Queen or one of the princesses would converse with the watcher, and Clery would take advantage of the latter's attention being diverted to empty his budget.

At nine o'clock, the Queen, her four children and Madame Elizabeth would go up to the King's room, where breakfast was served; during the dessert, Clery would clear up the rooms of the Queen and princesses; a man named Tison, and his wife, had been added to Clery under pretence of helping him in his work, but really to spy the royal family and even the municipals.

The husband, formerly clerk at the barriers, was a harsh, wicked old man, incapable of any humane feeling; the wife—only a woman from her love for her daughter—carried this love to such a point, that, separated from her daughter, she denounced the Queen in hope of seeing her child again.*

At ten o'clock, the King descended to the Queen's room, and there spent the day; almost exclusively occupied in teaching the Dauphin, making him repeat passages from Racine or Corneille, giving him a lesson in geography and teaching him to draw maps. France, since three years before, had been divided into departments, and, it was particularly on the charts of that country that the King exercised his son.

The Queen, on her part, attended to Madame Royale's education, interrupted often to fall into deep, gloomy reveries; when this happened, her daughter, leaving her to that unknown grief unblessed with tears, would go away on tiptoe and motion her brother to keep silent; the Queen would dwell shorter or longer in her musing, till a tear would roll down her cheek, falling on her hand yellowing to the tone of ivory, and then the poor prisoner, free for an instant in the boundless domain of mind—the far-extending field of remembrances, would start abruptly from her dream and, glancing about her, would be again, with bowed head and broken heart, in her prison.

At noon, the three ladies went into Madame Elizabeth's room to change their morning attire.

* See the "Chevalier of Maison Rouge" which follows "Andree de Taverney."

At one o'clock, weather permitting, the royal family were brought down into the garden: four officers and a colonel of the legion of the National Guard accompanied, or rather watched over them.

As there were at the Temple a number of workmen employed in destroying houses and building new walls, the captives could only use a portion of the "Chestnut Alley."

Clery was out in these promenades; he would give the young prince exercise by playing with him at quoits or football.

At two o'clock, they returned to the tower.

Clery brought up dinner; and, at this hour every day, Santerre came to the Temple with a couple of aides, carefully visiting the royal dwellings.

Sometimes the King spoke to him; the Queen never—she had forgotten the twentieth of June and what she owed to this man.

After meals, they went down to the first floor, where the King played piquet or backgammon with the Queen or his sister.

Clery dined.

At four, the King took his nap on a *causeuse* or in an armchair; the deepest silence then reigned; the princesses took up a book or their work, and all were motionless, even to the Dauphin.

Louis, without any transition, passed from wakefulness into slumber; physical requirements were tyrannical in him.

The King slept thus regularly an hour and a half or two hours. On his waking, conversation opened anew; Clery was called—he was never far away—and gave the Dauphin his writing lesson; this done, he took the boy into Madame Elizabeth's room and played at ball and battledore and shuttlecock.

Night come, the whole family gathered around the table; the Queen read aloud something suitable to amuse or instruct children; Madame Elizabeth succeeded the Queen, when she was tired. This reading lasted until eight o'clock; then the young prince took supper in Madame Elizabeth's room;

the family were in the same room, while the King took down a file of the *Mercure de France* which he had found in the library, and gave his children rebuses and charades to guess.

After the Dauphin's supper, the Queen would hear her son say his prayers.

Clery would put the Dauphin to bed, and one of the princesses would wait till he was asleep.

At this hour every night, a newsboy passing would cry out the news; Clery would listen and transmit the information to the King.

At nine, the King would take supper in his room.

Clery would take in supper to whoever watched by the Dauphin's bedside.

His meal over, the King would enter the Queen's room, give her and his sister a wave of the hand as a farewell, kiss his children, return to his study, and read there till midnight.

The princesses would shut themselves up in their rooms; one officer would remain in the little entry separating the rooms; the other followed the King.

Clery would then draw his bed up next to the King's; but, before lying down, the latter would wait till the new officer had come up, in order to see who he was and whether he had ever seen him before.

These officers were relieved at eleven in the morning, five in the afternoon and at midnight.

This unchanging life lasted as long as the King remained in the little tower, till September the thirtieth.

Clearly it was sad, and all the more worthy of commiseration from its being worthily supported; the most hostile relented at the sight; they came to watch the abominable tyrant who had ruined France, massacred the French, called in the foreigner; on a queen who had adjoined Messaline's depravity to the Second Catherine's dissoluteness—they found a man in grey clothes, whom they confounded with his servant, who ate heartily, drank deeply, slept quietly, played cards or backgammon, taught his son Latin and geography, and gave his children puzzles to guess, and a woman, proud and disdainful undoubtedly, but calm, self-possessed, resigned, still handsome, teaching her daughter tambour-work, and her son to pray, speaking softly to servants, and styling a valet: "my friend."

At the first blush was hate; each of these men coming with feelings of vengeance and animosity, began by giving free course to those sentiments; gradually he relented; starting from home in the morning threatening, with lofty head, he would return sad and with bowed head; his wife would be waiting for him.

"Here you are?" she would exclaim.

"Yes," he would laconically reply.

"Well, have you seen the tyrant?"

"I did see him."

"Has he a very ferocious look?"

"He seems like a retired tradesman living on his income."

"What's he doing? is he mad? is he cursing the Republic?"

"He spends his time studying with his children, teaching them foreign tongues, playing at cards with his sister, giving his children puzzles to guess."

"Hasn't the wretch any remorse?"

"I have seen him eat, and he eats like a man whose mind is at ease; I've seen him sleep and I'll wager he don't have the nightmare."

The woman would fall to thinking herself.

"But," she would say, "so he isn't as cruel and guilty as folks say?"

"Guilty, I don't know anything about that; cruel, I will answer he is none of that; unfortunate, I'm sure he is!"

"Poor man!" the wife would sigh.

So things came to pass: the lower the commune debased its captive, and the clearer it showed that he was only a man like another man, the deeper men felt pity for him they discovered to be their fellow-man.

This softening sometimes was directly manifested, to the King himself, to the Dauphin, to Clery.

One day, a stone-cutter was busy in making holes in the antechamber walls to there set some enormous bolts.

While the workman was eating his dinner, the Dauphin amused himself in play with his tools; the King took from the boy's hands the mallet and chisel and showed him (for he was a skilful locksmith) how they should be used.

The mason, from the corner where he was seated, eating his bread and cheese, looked on in astonishment at what passed.

He had not risen before the King and the Dauphin, but he rose to the man and son, and, approaching, his jaws still at work, but hat in hand, he said to the King:

"When you leave this tower, you may say you helped work at your own prison."

"Ah!" answered the King, "when and how am I to leave it?"

The Dauphin began crying; the workman wiped away a tear: the King dropped the mallet and chisel and, entering his room, walked up and down it.

Another day, an officer came up stairs to guard as usual the Queen's door, he was a coarsely dressed faubourgian, but well behaved.

Clery was alone in the room writing. The man watched him with deep attention.

In a little while, Clery, called elsewhere by his service, rose and was going to go out, but the man, while crossing his musket before him, said in a low, timid, almost trembling voice:

"You cannot pass here."

"Why so?" queried Clery.

"Because my order is to keep sight of you."

"Of me?" said Clery. "Surely, you must be wrong."

"Are you not the King?"

"Don't you know the King by sight?"

"I have never seen him, sir; and, if I must say so, I would rather not see, if I've got to see him here."

"Speak low," said Clery; and, pointing to a door, he added:

"I will enter that room and you will see the King; he is seated by a table reading."

Clery went in and told the King what had occurred; upon which the King rose and walked from one room to the other, in order to give the man a good sight at him.

So, suspecting that it was to oblige him that the King had done this, the faubourgian said to Clery:

"How good the King is, sir! I cannot believe he has done us all the evil they say he has."

Another man posted at the end of the alley which served as promenade to the royal family, one day, motioned to the illustrious captives that he had something to transmit to them.

At the first turn in the promenade, no one showed any symptoms of having noticed him; but, at the second, Madame Elizabeth approached him to see if he would speak.

Unfortunately, through either fear or respect, the young man, who was of superior appearance, remained speechless; tears rolled from his eyes, and he with his finger denoted a heap of rubbish where, probably, a letter was concealed.

Clery under the guise of looking for some pebbles for the little prince in the pile, began looking over the mass; but the municipals, doubtlessly divining what he was seeking for, ordered him to give over his search, and forbade him, under pain of being parted from the King, ever speaking to the sentinels.

However, all those who approached the Temple prisoners did not show similar sentiments of pity and respect; in many, hatred and revenge was so deeply implanted that the sight of the royal misfortunes supported with human virtues could not remove them from them, and ofttimes the King and Queen had to bear with coarse remarks, insults even.

One day, the municipal on service by the King was one named James, a professor of English; this man clung to the King like his shadow, never quitting him.

The King entered his study.

The officer followed at his heels and sat down by him.

"Sir," said the King with his habitual gentleness, "your foregoers were in the habit of leaving me alone in this place because, the door remaining always open, I could not escape their watch."

"Those before me," replied James, "had their own way of doing things, and I've got mine."

"Remark, if you please, sir," resumed the King, "that the room is so small that two cannot remain in it."

"Then, let's go into a larger one," rejoined the officer brutally.

The King rose without saying anything and entered his bedroom, into which the English teacher followed him and continued to hang about him till relieved.

One morning, the King mistook the man on guard for the same he had had on the previous evening (we have stated there was a relieving guard at midnight).

He stepped up to him and, with an air of interest, said:

"I regret, sir, that they should have forgotten to relieve you."

"What do you mean?" asked the fellow rudely.

"I mean you must be tired."

"Sir," returned this man, who was named Meunier, "I come here to watch over what you do, and not to have you meddling with what I do."

Then, pulling his hat on the more firmly, and stepping up to the King, he added:

"No one, and you last of all, has a right to meddle with my business."

Once, the Queen ventured to speak to a municipal.

"What quartier do you live in, sir?" she inquired of one of the men watching her eat her dinner.

"The country!" replied he proudly.

"But is not the country France?" resumed the Queen.

"Saving the part occupied by the enemy you have called here."

Some of the commissaries never spoke to any of the royal family without adding some foul epithet or broad oath.

One day, Turlot, a municipal, said to Clery, loud enough for the King not to lose a word of what was said:

"If the executioner does not guillotine this confounded set, I'll do the job myself!"

On going out for the walk, the royal family had to pass before a great number of sentinels, many of whom were even stationed inside the little tower. When the officers passed, the sentries presented arms; but when the King came, they would all ground arms, or turn their backs on them.

It was the same with the outer guards at the foot of the tower; when the King went by, they with affectation put on their caps and sat down.

The insulters went farther still.

One day, a sentinel, not satisfied with saluting his superiors and not the King, wrote on the inside of the prison gate:

"The guillotine is permanent, and is waiting for the tyrant Louis the Sixteenth."

This was a novel idea, which obtained great success; therefore, the author had imitators; soon, all the walls of the Temple, and particularly that of the stairs which the royal family had to go up and down, were covered with figures and inscriptions in the following style:

"Madame Veto will dance (with a sketch of a slip noose and rope)."

"We will have to put the fat fellow on short allowance."

"Down with the red ribbon! it will do to strangle the cubs with!"

Many words, like a legend under an engraving, explained some menacing design.

One of these latter represented a man on a gallows; underneath was:

"Louis taking an air bath."

But the most inveterate tormentors were two attendants at the Temple: one, Simon the shoemaker; the other, the sapper, Rocher.

Simon was everything; not only cobbler but municipal; not only municipal, but one of the six commissioners charged to inspect the work going on at the Temple.

By this triple title, he never left the tower.

This man, whose severities over the royal child have made notorious, was insult personified; every time he appeared before the captives, it was to outrage them anew.

If the valet asked anything of him for the King he would say:

"Let Capet ask for all he wants at once: I can't be running up and down all day for him."

Rocher was a counterpart to him: he was not a bad man, however; on the tenth of August, he had caught up the Dauphin in his arms at the doors of the National Assembly, and had set him down on the president's desk.

Rocher, from a saddler as he was, became an officer in Santerre's army, next doorkeeper to the Temple tower; he was usually dressed as a sapper, with long beard and moustachios, a bearskin hat, a broad, short sword by his side and, around his body, a belt from which hung a bunch of keys.

He had been placed there by Manuel rather to watch over the King and Queen to prevent any harm coming to them than for him to harm them himself; he was like a boy to whom might be given to guard a cage of birds, which he had been told not to let anybody torment, yet who for distraction plucked out their feathers himself.

When the King asked to go out Rocher would present himself at his door, but would not open till he had made the King wait some time, jingling the keys; then, he would noisily shoot back the bolts; flinging open the door, he would hurriedly descend and place himself by the last wicket, a pipe in his mouth; as each member of the royal family passed, but particularly the females, he would puff smoke into their faces.

These mean, cowardly acts had for witnesses the National Guards who, instead of opposing such annoyances, often drew up benches and sat down like people to see a play.

This encouraged Rocher, who was saying everywhere:

"Marie Antoinette is mighty stiff on her high horse, but yonder wicket brings her down a peg; it's so low that they have to stoop before me."

Then he would add:

"Every day, the whole pack, one after another, catches a whiff from my pipe. The sister the other day asked our commissioners: 'Why Rocher smokes all the time?' Says they:

"'Apparently, because he likes it.'"

There are, in all great expiations, besides the torture inflicted on the sufferers some man who makes them drink the chalice to the dregs. But, when the victim has undergone his doom, when his life is taken, such men poetise the torture, sanctify the death!

These are the true characters for legends; so they belong of right to the long and gloomy popular tales.

But, however unfortunate were the captives, they had an immense consolation: they were together.

The commune resolved to separate the King from his family.

On the twenty-sixth of September, five days after the proclaiming of the Republic, Clery learnt, through a municipal, that the room intended for the King in the large tower was nearly ready.

Clery transmitted this sorrowful intelligence to his master; but the latter, with his usual courage, said:

"Endeavor to learn beforehand the day of this painful separation, and inform me."

Unfortunately, Clery could find out nothing.

At ten o'clock on the morning of the twenty-ninth, six municipals entered the Queen's room as the whole family were together; they came, bearers of a decree of the commune, to take from the captives paper, ink, pens, pencils. Search was made not only in the rooms, but on the persons.

"Whenever you need anything," said the spokesman, Charbonnier, "your valet de-chambre will come down and write your demands on a register which will be in the council chamber."

The King and Queen made no remark; they turned their pockets inside out, and gave all they had about them; the princesses and domestics followed their example.

It was then only that Clery, by a few words dropped by a municipal, learned that Louis the Sixteenth was the same evening to be transferred to the main tower; he told Madame Elizabeth, who transmitted it to the King.

Nothing new transpired until evening. At every sound, whenever a door opened, the prisoners' hearts bounded, and their hands would join in an anxious clasp.

The King remained later than usual in the Queen's room.

At length, the door opened; the six municipals who had come in in the morning entered again with a new decree of the commune which they read to Louis the Sixteenth; it was the official order for his transfer to the main tower.

This time, the royal impassibility failed him.

Whither were tending these new steps along the gloomy way?

The mysterious and unknown world was being journeyed into, and with tears and tremors.

The parting was long and painful. The King was forced to follow the officers.

Never had the door, closing behind him, appeared to send out so funereal a sound.

In such haste were they to impose on the prisoners this fresh pain, that the apartments into which was conducted Louis the Sixteenth were not yet finished; there was only a bed and two chairs; the painting and the glue in the joining, quite fresh, gave the rooms an insupportable odor.

The King went to bed without complaining.

Clery passed the night on a chair beside him.

Clery rose and dressed Louis, as was his custom; then he was about to go to the little tower to attend to the Dauphin; this was opposed, and one of the municipals, Veron, said:

"You will have no communication with the other prisoners; the King is not to see his children any more."

This time, Clery had not the courage to impart the news to his master.

At nine o'clock, Louis the Sixteenth, unaware of the strict decision, asked to visit his family.

"We have no order to allow you to do so," said the commissioners.

The King persisted, but they would give him no other answer and retired.

The King remained alone with Clery.

Half an hour afterwards, two municipals entered, followed by a boy, who brought for the King some bread and a glass of lemonade.

"Gentlemen," said the King, "am I not to dine with my family?"

"Our orders come from the commune," returned one of them.

"But, if I cannot go down, may not my valet descend? He is needed by my son, and, I hope, nothing prevents him serving me."

The King spoke so simply and with so little animosity, that these men, astonished, knew not what to say; his tone, manner, resigned sorrow, were so far from what they expected that it dazzled them.

They merely answered that it did not depend on them, and quitted the room.

Clery had remained motionless by the door, gazing on his master with deep painfulness.

The King broke in two the bread brought to him, and, offering him half, said:

"Poor Clery, it seems your breakfast is forgotten. Take half of this; the other half will be enough for me."

Clery refused; but, the King insisting, he took the bread.

At ten o'clock, a municipal brought in the workmen who were fixing up the apartment; this municipal approached the King, in compassion, and said:

"Sir, I have just seen your family breakfast, and may tell you that they are all well."

The King felt his heart relieved.

"I thank you," said he, "and beg you to give, in exchange, news of me to my family, and inform all I am well. Now, sir, may I not have some books which I left in the Queen's room? If I may, be so kind as to send for them."

The officer was willing; but he did not know how to read. Finally, he confessed his embarrassment to Clery, begging him to accompany him to pick out himself the books the King desired.

Clery was too glad to accept: it was a means of giving the Queen news of her husband.

Louis gave him a look, which contained a world of recommendations.

Clery found the Queen in her room with Madame Elizabeth and her children.

The ladies wept; the little Dauphin was crying, too—but tears dry quickly in the eyes of children.

On seeing Clery, the three females rose, questioning him with looks, not voice.

The little Dauphin ran to him, saying:

"My good Clery."

Unfortunately, Clery could only speak a few reserved words; two municipals who accompanied him were in the chamber.

"Oh, sir," said the Queen, addressing them directly, " may we not stay with the King, if only for a few minutes !"

The other captives did not speak, but wrung their hands.

The officers looked on without replying : their stillness drew tears and sorrowful exclamations from the bosoms of the ladies.

"Well, they may dine together to-day."

"But to-morrow?" inquired the Queen.

"Madame," answered the municipal, " our conduct is subordinate to the decrees of the commune ; to-morrow we will do what the commune orders. Do you not think so, citizen ?" the speaker asked his companion.

He nodded in token of agreement.

The Queen and the princesses, who were anxiously awaiting this sign, uttered a cry of joy.

Marie Antoinette took up both her children in her arms, pressing them against her heart; Madame Elizabeth, with upraised hands, thanked heaven.

The favor so unexpected, which they earned by sobs and tears, had nearly the aspect of a grief.

One of the municipals could not restrain his tears, and Simon, who was present, growled :

"I think these women are going to make me weep !"

Then, to the Queen, he said :

"You didn't weep thus when you murdered the people on the tenth of August !"

"Ah, sir," said the Queen, "the people are much mistaken in our feelings ! Were we known better, the people would, like yonder gentleman, weep for us."

Clery took the books the King asked for, and hastened to announce the grant to his master; but the municipals had almost outstripped him—it is so happy for one to be good !

The dinner was served up in the King's room, where all the family was united ; it seemed a feast ; much seemed to have been obtained by gaining a day !

Everything had been gained, indeed, for nothing more was heard of the commune's decree, and the King continued, as in the past, to see his family in the daytime and take meals with it.

CHAPTER XXIII.

IN WHICH GAMAIN REAPPEARS.

On the morning of the same day when the preceding incidents occurred at the Temple, a man wearing a short-skirted coat and red cap, leaning on a crutch which helped him walk, presented himself at the office of the Home Department.

Roland was an easy man for one to have access to; but, however accessible he was, he was, nevertheless—as if he had been a minister of a monarchy, instead of being a republican minister—forced to have ushers in his ante-chamber.

The man with crutch and red cap was therefore obliged to stop in the outer room, before the usher who stopped up the way, saying :

"What do you want, citizen?"

"I want to speak to the citizen minister," replied red cap.

(Since a fortnight, the title of "citizen" and "citizeness" had been substituted for "monsieur" and "madame.")

Ushers were still ushers—that is, very impertinent personages; we are speaking of ministers' ushers; were we speaking of ushers of the wand, instead of ushers of the chain, we would apply another epithet!

The usher answered in a lofty tone:

"My friend, learn one thing: this is not the way to speak with the citizen minister."

"How is one to speak with him, citizen usher?" inquired red cap.

"One has to have a letter of audience to see him."

"I thought what you say was under the tyrant's reign, but that, under the Republic, in times when all men are equal, folks were less aristocratic."

This reflection set the usher thinking.

"It's not very amusing," proceeded red cap, "not very amusing, look you, for one to come from Versailles to render a minister a service, and not be received by him."

"Did you come to render Citizen Roland a service?"

"A little!"

"What sort of a service do you mean?"

"I come to reveal a conspiracy to him."

"Pooh! we are over head and ears in conspiracies."

"Are you?"

"Is that what you came from Versailles to do?"

"Yes."

"Well, you had better go back to Versailles."

"Very well; I shall do so; but your minister will repent not having received me."

"Can't help it—it's the rule. Write to him and call again with a letter for an audience; then, all will go well."

"Is that your last word?"

"The last."

"It seems to be harder to enter Citizen Roland's rooms than it was to see his Majesty Louis the Sixteenth!"

"How do you know?"

"I say it's so."

"What say you?"

"I say there was a time when I entered the Tuileries just when I liked."

"You?"

"I; and I did not have to give my name either."

"What is your name? Are you King Frederick William or the Emperor Francis?"

"No, I'm not a tyrant or a slave trader, or an aristocrat; I am simply Nicolas Claude Gamain, master over the master, hence, master over all."

"Master in what?"

"In lockmaking! Don't you know Nicolas Claude Gamain, once teacher of lockmaking to Capet?"

"How now! you, citizen, the—"

"I'm Gamain."

"The ex-King's locksmith?"

"His master in the art, do you understand, citizen!"

"That's what I mean."

"In flesh and blood, myself."

The usher looked at his fellows questioningly, and they replied with an affirmative nod.

"That's another thing," then said the usher.

"What do you mean?"

"I mean you will write your name on a slip of paper, and I will take in the name to the citizen minister."

"Write? it's easy to say write! but it was not my great accomplishment before those scoundrels poisoned me; but, now, it is still worse! See how arsenic has affected me!"

Gamain showed his twisted limbs, his spine deviated, and his hand drawn up like a claw.

"What! was it they who thus ruined you, my poor man?"

"Themselves! and that's what I am going to denounce to the citizen minister, along with something else. As they say that wretch Capet's prosecution is being arranged, what I have to say must not be lost to the nation, in the present state of affairs."

"Well, sit down yonder, and wait, citizen; I will send in your name to the citizen minister."

The usher wrote on a piece of paper:

" Claude Nicholas Gamain, formerly the King's master lockmaker, asks of the citizen minister an immediate audience for an important revelation."

Whereupon, he handed the writing to one of his fellows whose special business it was to introduce visitors.

Five minutes afterwards, this man returned saying:

" Follow me, citizen."

Gamain made an effort which wrung from him a cry of pain, rose and dragged himself after the usher.

The latter conducted Gamain, not to the closet of the official minister, Citizen Roland, but to the closet of the real minister, Citizeness Roland.

This was a very simple little room, papered in green, lighted by a single window, in the recess of which, seated at a small table, Madame Roland was at work.

Roland was standing by the fire-place.

The usher announced Citizen Nicolas Claude Gamain ; and Gamain appeared on the threshold.

The locksmith had never been, even in the days of his best health and best fortune, of very prepossessing look ; but the ailment he suffered with (nothing else than articulary rheumatism) while contorting his limbs and disfiguring his face, had added nothing, the reader will understand, to the comeliness of his features.

The result was that, when the usher had closed the door behind him, never did honest man—and, it must be said, none better than Roland deserved such an appellation—never did honest man, we repeat, find himself confronting a rogue with baser, and more repulsive physiognomy.

The minister's first feeling was one of deep repugnance. He scanned Gamain from head to foot and, seeing that he trembled on his crutch, a sentiment of compassion for the suffering of a fellow being—supposing that Gamain was a fellow being with Roland—made the first words of the minister to the locksmith be :

" Take a seat, citizen ; you appear ill :

" I should think I was ill !" said Gamain, sitting down ; " and I have been ill ever since the Austrian poisoned me."

On these words, an expression of deep disgust passed over the minister's countenance, and he exchanged a glance with his wife, who was concealed partly in the recess of the window.

" And was it to denounce this poisoning that you came ?" inquired Roland.

" To denounce that to you and something more."

" Do you bring any proof of your denunciation ?"

" As for proof, you have only to come with me to the Tuileries, and the safe shall be shown to you."

" What safe ?'

" The safe where that tyrant hides his treasure. Oh, when, after the work was done, the Austrian said to me in her oily voice ; ' You are warm, Gamain, drink this glass of wine—it will do you good !' I ought to have suspected that the wine was poisoned."

" Poisoned ?"

" Yes. And I knew, too," went on Gamain with an expression of gloomy hatred, " that men who help kings to hide treasures never live long."

Roland approached his wife, and questioned her with a look.

" There is something at the bottom of all this," said she ; " I remember now this man's name ; he was the locksmith who taught the King."

" How about this safe ?"

" Well, ask him about it."

" My friend, what is this safe ?"

" What is it ?" rejoined Gamain. " I can tell you enough about that ! It's an iron chest built into the wall, with a puzzle-lock, and Citizen Capet hides his gold and papers in it."

" How do you know of the existence of it ?"

" Why, he sent for me and a fellow workman to come to Versailles to fix a lock which he had made and which wouldn't work."

" But this safe must have been opened, broken, pillaged on the tenth of August."

" There's no danger of that," replied Gamain.

" No danger ?"

"Not a bit, I defy anybody in the world, except the King and I, finding it and, especially, opening it."

"Sure?"

"I am sure and certain! As it was when he left the Tuileries, so is it to-day."

"When was it you helped King Louis to fashion this concealment?"

"I cannot tell you exactly; but it was three or four months before his departure for Varennes."

"How did the whole thing happen? let me hear, excuse me, my friend; the tale appears to me so extraordinary that, before starting with you in search of this safe, I would like to ask you for some details."

"Oh, it's easy to give you the whole story, citizen minister. Capet sent for me to come to Versailles. My wife didn't want me to go—poor woman, she had a sort of forewarning; she said: 'The King is in a bad way—you had better not get mixed up with his doings.' 'But,' says I, 'as he sends for me about something in the craft, and as he is my pupil, I'll have to go.' 'Good!' says she, 'there's politics in it; he's got something else to do just now besides making locks.'"

"Be brief, my friend. In spite of your wife's opinion, you did go?"

"Yes, and I would have done better to have listened to my wife; I wouldn't be as I am now. But the poisoners shall pay me!"

"Go on."

"Well, to return to the safe——"

"Yes, friend, and try not to ramble from it. All my time is the Republic's, and I have no leisure."

"Then, he showed me a lock, one of the sort that open on either side, but it wouldn't work; he had made it himself, which proves that, if he could have made it all right, he would not have sent for me—the traitor!"

"He showed you a lock," interposed the minister, bent on keeping Gamain in the right track.

"And he asked me: 'Why won't it go, Gamain?' Says I: 'Sire, I will have to look at the lock.' Says he: 'That's right.' Then, I examined the lock, and says I: 'Do you know why it won't go?' 'No,' said he "else I should not have asked you.' 'Well, sire (they called the brigand "sire" in those days), it won't work because—' Now, pay attention to my reasoning; for not being so learned in making locks as the King, maybe you will not understand me. By the bye, I remember now: it was not a double-sided lock, but a chest-lock."

"It's all one to me, my friend," observed Roland; "as you say, I am not so versed as the King in the mysteries of lockmaking, and I do not know the difference between the two locks."

"I will explain you the difference in a trice——"

"'Tis useless. You were saying——"

"I was going to tell the King why his lock would not work. Shall I tell you why?"

"If you like," responded Roland, who began to believe that it was best to let Gamain run on in his prolixity.

"Well, it would not work because the beard of the key was so close to the main ward that the ward only would turn easily half its circle, but, so far having gone, as it was not filed sloping, it could not move any farther: that's the way! now, you understand, don't you? the sweep of the ward being six lines, and the second peg five lines from its starting point, and the slope being but a quarter, of course it catches—you understand?"

"Quite well," returned Roland, who understood not a word.

"'So it is,' said the King (they still gave the infamous tyrant that title!) 'well, Gamain, do what I did not know how to do, master.'"

"Well?"

"Well, I set to work, while Capet talked with my boy, whom I have always suspected of being an aristocrat in disguise; in ten minutes' time all was finished. Then I came down with the iron door to which belonged the lock, and said: 'Here it is, sire!' 'Very well, Gamain,' said he, 'come with me.' He went before. I followed him: he led me first to his bedchamber, then into a dark entry which led from his alcove to the Dauphin's room; there it was so dark that we had to have a lighted candle.

"Take this candle, Gamain, and light me.' Then he took out a panel of the wainscotting behind which there was a hole of some two feet square, and, re-marking my astonishment, he said: 'I have made this hiding-place for my money; now, you see, Gamain, this opening is to be closed with this iron door.' 'That will not take long,' I an-swered him, 'for here are the hinges and bolt.' I lifted up the door, and had on-ly to push it for it to fit in nicely, then the panel was put up, and good bye to safe, door and lock !"

"So you think, friend," said Roland, "that this safe was only intended for a strong box, and that the King went to all this trouble to hide money ?"

"Stay, that's a trick; he fancied him-self very clever, did the tyrant! but I am no less clever than he. I will tell you what passed. 'Here, Gamain,' said he, 'help me count the money I mean to hide in this place.' And so we counted two millions in double louis, which we put up in four leathern bags; but, while we were counting, I saw from the corner of my eye the valet carrying papers after papers, and says I to my-self: 'The safe is for papers; the money is only a blind !' "

"What do you say about this, Made-leine ?" inquired Roland of his wife, as he bent towards her in order that Gam-ain should not hear him.

"I say that this revelation is of the utmost importance, and there's not an instant to be lost."

Roland rang a bell.

The usher appeared.

"Have you a carriage ready in the courtyard ?" he asked.

"Yes, citizen."

"Call it to the door."

Gamain rose.

"Ah," said he in annoyance, "it seems you have had enough of me ?"

"Why so ?" asked Roland.

"From your calling your carriage. So ministers still have coaches under the Republic?"

"My friend," replied Roland, "min-isters should have coaches in all times:

a vehicle is not a luxury for a minister, but economy."

"Economy ?"

"It saves time, the dearest and most precious commodity in the world."

"So I am to call again ?"

"What for ?"

"To lead you to the safe wherein is the treasure."

"Useless."

"Why useless ?"

"Because I have called the carriage to go."

"Go whither ?"

"To the Tuileries."

"Are we going ?"

"Immediately."

"I'm glad to hear it."

"But, by the bye——" said Roland.

"What ?" asked Gamain.

"The key ?"

"What key ?"

"That to the safe. It is not likely Louis left the key in the door."

"Not he, certainly, for fat Capet is not so stupid as he looks to be."

"Then, you will have to take your tools."

"Wherefore ?"

"To open the safe."

Gamain produced from his pocket a quite new key.

"What do you call this ?" he in-quired.

"A key."

"The key to the safe, which I have made from remembrance; I well studied it, suspecting that, some day——"

"This fellow is a great rogue !" whis-pered Madame Roland to her husband.

"What do you think ?" inquired the latter in some hesitation.

"I think we in our position, have not the right to refuse any information for-tune may make us to reach the know-ledge of the truth."

"Here it is !" Gamain was saying as he brandished the key.

"Do you believe," asked Roland with disgust which it was impossible for him to conceal, "do you believe that this key, made from recollection, after eighteen months, will open the iron safe ?"

"At the first turn, I'll wager," repli-ed Gamain. "It's not to fail in such things that one is master of the master."

"The citizen minister's carriage is waiting," said the usher.

"Am I to go with you?" inquired Madame Roland.

"Certainly! if there are papers it's to you I want to trust them; are you not better than the most honest man I know of?"

Then turning to Gamain, Roland said: "Come, my friend."

Gamain followed him, growling between his gums:

"Ah, I was right in saying, I would pay you up for *that*, Monsieur Capet."

That? what did he mean by *that?* The good the King had done him.

CHAPTER XXIV.

THE RETREAT OF THE PRUSSIANS.

WHILE Citizen Roland's carriage rolls towards the Tuileries, while Gamain discloses the safe hidden in the wall; while pursuant to the promise, the key forged from recollection opens with wonderful ease the iron safe, while the safe surrenders the fatal deposit confided to it, which—notwithstanding the absence of the papers entrusted to Madame Campan by the King himself— were to have so cruel an influence over the destiny of the Temple prisoners; while Roland carries away those documents to read them one by one, seeking uselessly among them all a trace of the so much denounced venality of Danton—let us see what the ex-Minister of Justice was doing.

We say the ex-Minister of Justice, because, once the Convention was installed, Danton had in haste handed in his resignation.

He had mounted the speakers-stand, and said:

"Before expressing my opinion on the first decree the convention forms, let me be allowed to resign to it the duties which were delegated to me by the Legislative Assembly. I received them amid the cannon's roar; now the armies have joined, the representatives are being joined. I am merely one sent by the people in which capacity I speak."

To the words "the armies have joined," Danton might have added: "And the Prussians are beaten," for he uttered those words on the twenty-first of September, while, on the twentieth, had taken place the Battle of Valmy; but Danton was ignorant of this.

He simply said:

"Let us disperse those vain phantoms of dictatorship by which the people are alarmed; let us declare there shall be no form of government save that accepted by them. Till to-day, the people have had to be excited, and aroused against the tyrant; now, let the laws be as dreadful against those who violate them, as the people were in destroying tyranny! let all the guilty be punished! Let us be done with any exaggeration; let us proclaim that all property shall be eternally maintained."

Danton, with his usual acuteness, answered in a few words to the two great fears of France.

France feared for her liberty and her property; and, strange thing! who feared especially for property?

Why, the new proprietors, those who had bought estates only the day before, who still owed, perhaps, for three-quarters of their purchase!

They had become conservatives, much more than the nobles, the former aristocrats and land-owners; the latter preferred their life to their immense domains, for they had abandoned their possessions to save their lives; while the peasants, the gainers by the national property, landholders from yesterday, preferred their patch of land to their life, watching over it gun in hand, and, for nothing in the world, willing to leave it.

Danton had understood this; he had seen that it was right to encourage not only those just become landowners yesterday, but such as were going to buy property to-morrow; for the great idea of Revolution was:

"All the French must own something; property does not make man the better, but the worthier, by giving him the consciousness of his independence."

Therefore, the spirit of Revolution was summed up in Danton's words :

"Abolition of dictatorship; preservation of all property ; in other words—point of starting : man has the right of governing himself; design : man has the right of preserving the fruit of his free labor."

Who said this ?

The man of the twentieth of June, and tenth of August, and second of September—that giant of the Cape of Storms, who became a pilot, and dropped into the sea those two anchors of national safety : freedom, property.

The Gironde did not understand ; it, in its honesty, had an unconquerable repugnance to the—the—well, easy Danton ; it had been seen that he had refused the dictatorship at the very juncture when he asked for it so as to prevent massacre.

A Girondist rose, and, instead of applauding the man of genius who had thus quieted the two great fears of France, he cried out to Danton :

"Whoever tries to preserve property injures it ; to touch it, even to steady it, is to overthrow it. Property is anterior to any law."

The Convention passed the following motions :

"There can be no constitution till the people adopt it."

"The safety of persons and property is under the nation's guard."

This was the thing, and yet not quite it.

Nothing is worse in politics than "very nearly so."

Danton's resignation had been accepted.

But, surely, the man, who had believed himself strong enough to take upon himself the second of September, the terror of Paris, the hatred of the country, the world's execration, must have been a very powerful man !

In fact, he held, at the same time, the guiding strings of war, police and diplomacy ; Dumouriez, and, consequently, the army, was in his hands.

The news of the victory at Valmy had reached Paris and caused great de-light; it had flown thither on eagle's wings, and it was regarded as much more decisive than it was really.

Hence, from the utmost fear, France passed to extreme boldness ; the clubs dreamed but of war and battle.

"Why, if the King of Prussia was beaten, why was not he a prisoner, bound and pinioned, or at least thrown back to the other bank of the Rhine ?"

This was said aloud.

But, in an undertone, ran the answer, as follows :

"It's very simple; Dumouriez has betrayed ! he sold himself to the Prussians."

Dumouriez was receiving already the reward for a great deed—ingratitude.

The King of Prussia did not in the least think himself beaten ; he had attacked Valmy Heights, and had not taken them, that was all ; each army had kept its camp ; the French—who, from the opening of the campaign, had constantly been retreating, pursued by panics, defeats and reverses—had this time stood their ground, nothing more or less.

As for the loss in men, that was pretty nearly equal on both sides.

Such was the need of the French for a great victory that this could not be told to Paris, France, and Europe ; but Dumouriez informed Danton of it through Westermann.

So far were the Prussians from being beaten and in retreat that, two weeks after Valmy, they were still motionless in their camps.

Dumouriez had written to learn whether, in case of the King of Prussia opening negociations, he ought to treat.

This inquiry received two replies : one from the ministry, haughty and official, dictated by the enthusiasm of victory ; the other, calm and wise, but from Danton alone.

The former missive ran thus :

"The Republic will not treat so long as the foe has not evacuated the territory."

Danton's said :

"Provided the Prussians evacuate the territory, treat at whatever the cost."

To treat was not so easy an act, in

the King of Prussia's present mind; about the same time that at Paris arrived the news of Valmy, at Valmy came the intelligence of the abolition of royalty and the proclamation of the Republic.

The King of Prussia was furious.

The consequences of this invasion, undertaken with design to save the King of France, but which so far had had no other result than the tenth of August, second and twenty-first of September : to wit, the King's captivity, the massacre of the nobility and the abolition of royalty — these consequences had made Frederic William fall into fits of gloomy fury : he wanted to fight come what might, and had (September the twenty-ninth) given the order for a stubborn battle.

This was far, anybody can see, from abandoning the land of the Republic.

On the twenty-ninth, in place of an action, there was a council.

Dumouriez, however, was prepared on all points.

Brunswick, very insolent in his speech, was very prudent as to deeds; he was more of an Englishman than of a German ; he had married a sister of the Queen of England ; this made his inspirations flow as much from London as Berlin.

If England decided to fight, he would fight with both hands : with one for Prussia, the other for England ; if, the English, his masters, did not draw the sword, he was ready to put up his.

Now, on the twenty-ninth, Brunswick produced at the council letters, from Great Britain and Holland, which refused to join the coalition.

Besides, Custine, marching along the Rhine, was threatening Coblentz; and, if Coblentz fell, the gate to return to Prussia would be closed to Frederic William.

Then, there was something more serious than all this !

By chance, the King of Prussia had a mistress, the Countess of Lichtenau.

She had followed the army, like a great many—like Gœthe who was dreaming, in an army wagon of his Prussian Majesty, over the first scenes of *Faust*—she was thinking of a military pleasure-trip to Paris, which city she wanted to see.

Meanwhile, she had stopped at Spa.

There, she had learnt of the Valmy action and of the dangers her royal lover had run. She feared greatly two things, did the beautiful countess : the Frenchmen's bullets, the Frenchwomen's smiles ; she wrote letters after letters, and the postscript of them, the summing up of the thoughts of the writer was the word "return !"

The King of Prussia, sooth to say, was only held by the shame of abandoning Louis of France. Many considerations swayed him ; but the two foremost were his mistress's tears and the peril of Coblentz.

He none the less insisted that Louis the Sixteenth should have freedom.

Danton hastened to transmit to him, through Westerman, all the decrees of the commune which showed the prisoners " to be surrounded by good treatment."

This satisfied the King of Prussia— who was not hard to please !

His friends assure us that, ere retiring, he made Danton and Dumouriez give their word to save the King's life: nothing proves this assertion.

On September the twenty-ninth, the Prussian army began its retreat, and moved a league ; next day, another league.

The French army escorted it as though to do it the honors of the country.

Everytime the French wanted to attack, strike at the rearguard, in short enrage the boar and make it stand at bay, Danton's men drew them back.

That the Prussians should leave France, was all Danton's wish.

On the twenty-second of October, this patriotic desire was accomplished.

On the seventh of November, the Girondists brought on the prosecution of the King.

On the sixth, the day before, had thundered the cannon of Jemapes.

Something similar had occurred six weeks before : when, on the twentieth of September, Dumouriez had won Valmy, and on the twenty-first, the Republic had been proclaimed.

Each victory had in some sort its coronation, and forced France to take a step farther in revolution.

This time, it was a fearful step!

The unknown goal was being neared, towards which for three years travelers had gone blindfold; as it happens in nature, while advancing, the shape of objects was distinguished after having only seen the masses.

Now, what was seen in the horizon? A scaffold!

At its foot a king!

In this material period, when the infernal instinct of hatred, vengeance and destruction gained the upper hand of the elevated ideas of some superior minds; when a man like Danton—one who took upon himself the bloody September days—was accused of being "the leader of the *indulgents*," it was difficult for the idea to prevail over the act; what the men of the Convention did not understand—or what only certain among them did divine, some clearly, others instinctively—was that the prosecution should have been on royalty, not the king.

Royalty was a gloomy abstraction, a menacing mystery of which nobody wanted any more; an idol gilded without—a whited sepulchre—full of dust and worms within.

But the King was another thing; he was a man; one of little account in the days of his prosperity, but whom misfortune had purified, captivity had enlarged; and, even to the Queen, the gilding of adversity had been so bright that—whether from a new feeling, or from repentance—the prisoner of the Temple had come, if not to love (that poor broken heart had lost all it had contained of love, like a shattered vase loses all its contents, drop by drop), at least to venerate and worship, in the religious sense of the word, this monarch, prince, this man whose vulgar appetites had so often made the blood mount to her cheeks.

One day, the King entered the Queen's apartments, and found her surveying the chamber of the sick Dauphin.

He stopped on the threshold, let his head fall on his breast, then, with a sigh, he said:

"Oh, madame, what an act for a Queen of France! If they at Vienna saw what you are doing here! Who would have dreamt that, by uniting yourself to my fate, I would drag you down so low!"

"Do you esteem it as nothing," rejoined Marie Antoinette, "the glory of being the wife of the best and most persecuted of men?"

What the Queen said she never believed to have been overheard by an humble valet who had followed the King, and who treasured up the words, which, like black pearls, were kept to form a diadem, no longer on a royal brow, but on the head of a doomed man.

Another day, it was Madame Elizabeth whom Louis saw cutting, for lack of scissors, with her teeth the ribbon which belonged to the Queen's dress.

"Poor sister!" observed he, "what a contrast with that pretty little house at Montreuil where you wanted for nothing!"

"Can I regret anything, brother," responded the maiden, "when I share your misfortunes?"

And all this was known, and spread about, and was embroidered in golden arabesques over the martyr's gloomy legend.

Royalty struck by death, but the guarded king living, had in it a great and mighty thought; so great and mighty, that it never entered the heads of but a few men, who—so unpopular was it—hardly dared express it.

"A people have need of being saved, but none to be avenged!" said Danton at the Cordeliers.

"Certainly, the King must be tried," said Gregoire to the Convention, "but he has earned so much scorn that there is no room for hate."

Paine wrote:

"I would have the prosecution drawn up, not against Louis the Sixteenth, but against the band of kings. Of such, we have but one in our power; he will put us in the track of the general conspiracy. Louis the Sixteenth is most useful to show to all the necessity of revolutions."

Therefore, lofty minds, like Thomas Paine's, and great hearts, like Danton's and Gregoire's, were in agreement on this point: that they should be made, not the King's prosecution, but the prosecution of kings, as witness in which case, Louis was to be called in.

Republican France, the majority, should proceed in its name and in that of the people submissive to royalty, the minority; France would be in session, then, no longer like an earthly judge, but as a divine arbitrator; she would rule in superior spheres, and her words would no longer rise to the throne like a splash of mud and blood, but would fall upon crowned heads like the thunderbolt.

Suppose this public prosecution, supported by proofs, to commence with the Second Catherine, murderess of her husband and executioner of Poland; suppose the details of such monstrous lives to be laid bare in full light as was the Princess de Lamballe's corpse; imagine the Northern Pasiphae enchained to the pillory of public opinion—and say what would the result be over people of such a proceeding.

However, what good may have arisen from it, yet remains to be done.

CHAPTER XXV.

THE PROSECUTION.

THE papers from the iron safe, revealed by Gamain (to whom the convention granted a life annuity of twelve hundred livres for that praiseworthy deed, and who died bent double and racked by rheumatism, after having a thousand times regretted death by the guillotine, to which he had helped send his royal pupil); these papers, from which had been removed those we saw Louis XVI. give Madame Campan, to the great disappointment of the Rolands, contained nothing against Danton and Dumouriez; they especially compromised the King and priesthood; they displayed that mean, narrow, shallow mind of the ungrateful Louis, who only hated those who had wished to save him: Neckar, La Fayette, Mirabeau.

There was nothing against the Gironde.

The debate on the prosecution commenced on the thirteenth of November.

Who opened this weighty discussion?

Who made himself the swordbearer of the Mountain?

Who soared above this moody congress like the exterminating angel?

A young man, a boy rather of twenty-four, sent before the proper age to the convention; one whom we have seen several times appear in this work.

He was a native of Nievre, one of the roughest districts of France; he owned that bitter, aspic sap which makes dangerous men, if not great ones.

He was the son of an old soldier whom thirty years' service had raised to the cross of Saint Louis, ennobled, consequently, to the rank of knight; he was born sad, heavy, grave; his family had a little property in the Aisne Department, at Blerancourt, near Noyou, and dwelt in a modest cottage, far from being of the golden medium of the Latin poet.

Sent to Rheims to study law, he made poor studies and wretched verses, a licentious poem in the style of Rolando Furioso and the Pucelle; published without success in 1789, this poem was republished with no more success in 1792.

He had hastened to leave the provinces, and came to Camille Desmoulins, the brilliant journalist, who held in his hands the future reputation of unknown poets.

The latter, a lad full of spirit, wit, airiness, saw one day enter to him a student, full of pathos and pretension, of slow, measured speech, his words falling one by one like drops of water wearing rocks, and from a woman's mouth; as for the rest of his face, there were steady, stern, blue eyes, heavily capped by black brows, a complexion white, yet rather sickly than pure—his stay at Rheims may have given him the scrofulous malady which kings have the pretention to cure—a chin lost amid the folds of an unwieldy neckcloth swathing his neck, when everybody else let their cravats stream loose as though to give the headsman every facility to untie it; a rigid bust, automaton-like; as ridiculous as a machine as he was to become awful as a spectre; all this surmounted by so low a forehead, that the hair came down to his eyes.

Camille Desmoulins saw this strange figure walk into his sanctum one day : he was sovereignly repugnant to him.

The young man read his verses to him and told him among other thoughts, that the world was empty since the Romans had gone.

The verses appeared poor to Camille, as the thought appeared false ; he laughed at the poet and at the philosopher ; the poet-philosopher returned to the solitude of Blerancourt, " Like Tarquin," says Michelet, the great portrait-painter of these kind of men, " beheading poppies with a switch, in some Desmoulins, in others Danton."

His occasion came as it ever does to certain men.

His village, Blerancourt, was threatened by the loss of a market by which it lived ; without knowing Robespierre, the young man wrote to him, to beg him to support the local petition he transmitted to him, offering to give, to be sold for the profit of the nation, his humble property, all he possessed.

What made Desmoulins laugh set Robespierre thinking ; he called to him the young fanatic, studied him, recognized him to be of that stamp of men with whom revolutions are made, and, through his credit at the Jacobins, got him appointed member of the convention, although he was not of the requisite age.

Jean de Bry, president of the electoral body, protested, and sent for the baptismal register of the new candidate, the latter was, indeed, but three months over his twenty-fourth year ; but before Robespierre's influence this vain remonstrance disappeared.

It was into this young man's abode that Robespierre entered on the night of September second ; it was this young man who slumbered while Robespierre

could not sleep—for this young man was Saint Just.

" Saint Just," said Camille Desmoulins to him one day, " do you know what Danton says of you ?"

" No."

" He says you carry your head like a ball on a pole."

A smile curled the young man's feminine mouth.

" Well," said he, " I will make him carry his like a Saint Denis !"

And he kept his word.

Saint Just slowly descended from the summit of the mountain, slowly ascended the speakers stand, and slowly asked, we mean *ordered*, death.

An atrocious speech was that made by this handsome young man.

" There must be no long trying the King," said he ; " he must be *killed*.

" Must be killed, for there are no laws by which to try him, for he has destroyed them.

" Must be killed as a tyrant : citizens alone are tried. To try the tyrant, he would have to be made citizen again.

" Must be killed as a guilty man caught redhanded in the deed ; royalty is, at any rate, an eternal crime ; a king is unnatural : between people and king, there is no natural connection."

Thus he spoke for an hour, without warming in his theme, or becoming animated, with a rhetorician's voice and pedant's gesticulations, and at the end of every sentence, returned those words falling with singular weight, exerting over his audience a shock like that of the guillotine's chopper :

" Must be killed !"

This speech had a fearful sensation ; not one of the judges listening to it was not pierced to his heart with a chill as of steel !

Robespierre, himself, was alarmed to see his pupil plant so far beyond the republican outposts the bloody flag of revolution.

Thenceforward, not only was the indictment of Louis the Sixteenth settled upon, but he was, moreover, condemned.

To try to save the doomed one, was to earn death.

Danton had the idea, but not the

courage: he had had enough love of country to bear the name of murderer but not enough stoicism to accept that of traitor.

On the eleventh of December, the prosecution opened.

Three days previously, a municipal had gone to the Temple, at the head of a commune deputation, and had taken from the prisoners knives, razors, scissors, in short, all such cutting and pointed instruments as culprits are generally deprived of.

Madame Clery had come, accompanied by a female friend, to see her husband; as usual, the valet had been called down into the council hall; there Clery had conversed with his wife, who affected to speak of family matters in a loud tone, while her friend said in an undertone:

"Next Thursday, the King will be taken to the Convention. The trial is going to commence. The King may have a defender; this you may rely on."

The King had forbidden Clery hiding anything from him; bad as was the news, the faithful servant resolved to impart it to his master.

Consequently, while undressing him that night, he repeated to him the above words, adding that, during the trial, the commune intended to separate him from his family.

Four days, therefore, remained for Louis to converse with his wife.

He thanked Clery for his faithfulness in keeping his word.

"Continue," he said, "endeavor to discover something about what is wanted of me; do not fear to afflict me. I have agreed with my family for us not to appear in the secret, in order not to injure you."

But the closer the day approached on which was to open the case, the more distrustful because the watchers.

Clery therefore had no other intelligence for the prisoners than that contained in a paper which had been smuggled to him: this sheet published the decree ordering, on the eleventh of December, Louis the Sixteenth to appear at the bar of the convention.

At five o'clock in the morning of the eleventh December, the long roll was beaten all over Paris; the gates of the Temple were opened, and cavalry and artillery were let into its yards.

If the royal family had been in ignorance of what was going to transpire, this sound would have excited much alarm; all pretended, however, not to know the cause and asked questions of the commissaries, who refused to reply.

At nine o'clock, the King and Dauphin went to breakfast in the princesses' room: another hour to be spent together, although under the eyes of the municipals; at the end of that time, they had to part, and, as they were forbidden to say anything, each kept their thoughts confined.

The Dauphin, indeed, knew nothing: his youth had shielded him from the knowledge. He insisted on playing ninepins; much as he had on his mind, his father consented to amuse the boy.

The Dauphin lost every game, three times being unable to get more than sixteen.

"What a number!" he exclaimed; "I believe sixteen brings bad luck."

The King said nothing, but the number struck him to be a mournful presage.

At eleven o'clock, while he was giving the Dauphin his reading lesson, two officers entered, announcing that they came after young Louis to take him to his mother.

The King wanted to know the reason of this removal.

The officers merely answered that they were carrying out the orders of the council of the commune.

The King embraced his son, and charged Clery to take him to his mother.

Clery obeyed and returned.

"Where have you left my son?" inquired his master.

"In the Queen's arms, sire," returned Clery.

One of the officers re-appeared.

"Sir," said he to Louis XVI., "Citizen Chambon, Mayor of Paris (Petion's successor), is at the council, and is coming here."

"What does he want of me?" inquired Louis.

"I do not know," rejoined the municipal.

He went out, leaving the King alone. The latter walked up and down his room a while, and then sat down in an armchair at the head of his bed.

The principal retired with Clery into the neighboring room, where he said to the valet:

"I dare not go in to the prisoner for fear he will question me."

Meanwhile, there was such a stillness in the other room, that the officer grew uneasy; he entered softly and found Louis, with head on his hands deeply immersed in thought.

At the noise of the door creaking on its hinges, the latter lifted his head and asked:

"What do you want?"

"I fear," replied the municipal, "that you are not at ease."

"I am obliged to you," replied the prisoner; "no, I am not at ease: the fashion in which my son was snatched from me has pained me deeply."

The officer withdrew.

The mayor appeared at one o'clock only.

He was accompanied by the new procureur of the commune Chaumette, the recording secretary Coulombeau, many officers, and Santerre, who was accompanied himself by his aid-de-camps.

"What do you want, sir?" he asked, addressing the mayor.

"I come for you, sir," responded the latter, "by virtue of a decree of the Convention which the secretary-recorder will read."

In fact, the secretary-recorder unfolded a paper and read:

"Decree of the National Convention which ordains that Louis Capet——"

On this word the hearer interrupted the reader.

"Capet is not my name," he said, "but the name of one of my ancestors."

Then, as the secretary was about to continue his reading, the King said:

"It is useless, sir; I have read the decree in a paper."

And, turning to the commissioners, he added:

"I would have wished my son could have been left to me during the two hours I have spent in waiting for you:

of two cruel hours, that would have made two sweet ones. However, such treatment is but a continuation of that I have endured for four months. I will follow you, not to obey the Convention, but because my enemies have power on their side."

"Then, come," said Chambon.

"I only ask time to slip on an overcoat over my coat. Clery, my overcoat!"

The valet handed his master the article of clothing asked for.

Chambon walked out first.

The prisoner followed.

At the foot of the stairs, he looked with emotion on the guns and pikes, and especially on the blue-uniformed troopers, of whose formation he was unaware, then, he flung a final look on the tower, and they moved away.

It rained.

The King was put into a carriage, and went with calm countenance.

While passing the Gates Saint Martin and Saint Denis, he inquired which of the two it was proposed to be pulled down.

On the threshold of the Manege, Santerre laid his hand on his shoulder and conducted him to the bar, to the same place and same chair where he had sworn to the Constitution.

All the deputies had remained seated at the moment of the King's entry: one alone, when he passed before him, rose and bowed.

He turned in amazement and recognized Gilbert.

"Good day, Monsieur Gilbert," said he. "Do you not know Monsieur Gilbert?" he added to Santerre; "He was in former days my physician; you will not think him wrong in having bowed to me."

The examination commenced.

Here, the gilding of misfortune began to be worn away under publicity; not only did the royal prisoner reply poorly to the questions put to him, but as hesitatingly, with as much stammering, denial and haggling about his life as a village lawyer might display while arguing about a five-acre farm.

Broad daylight was no time for such a man.

The interrogation lasted till five o'clock.

At that hour, Louis XVI. was conducted to the conference hall, where he waited for his carriage.

The mayor stepped up to him.

" Are you hungry, sir?" he inquired ; " is there anything you would like?"

" I thank you," responded the King shaking his head.

But almost instantly, seeing a grenadier draw a loaf of bread from his knapsack, and give half to Chaumette, procureur of the commune, he approached the latter and asked him :

" Will you be so kind as to give me a bit of your bread, sir?"

But as he had spoken quite low, Chaumette did not believe his ears.

" Speak louder, sir," said he.

" Oh, I cannot raise my voice for that," was the answer, given with a sad smile ; " I begged a bit of bread."

" Willingly," returned Chaumette.

And, holding out his half-loaf he said : " There, cut ! It's a Spartan meal ; had I a root, I would give you half."

They descended to the courtyard.

On seeing Louis, the mob broke into the chant of the Marseillais, laying stress on the lines :

> " Tremble, tyrant ! with your allies,
> Whom all hate with one accord.
> Tremble ! for your murd'rous projects
> Are fated soon to gain reward."

Louis turned slightly pale, and stepped into the vehicle.

There, he began to eat, but only the crust of his bread ; he did not know what to do with the crumb, and, seeing him turn it in his hands, the substitute of the commune's procureur took it from him and flung it out of the window.

" That's wrong," observed the prisoner, " to thus throw away bread, especially when flour is so scarce."

" And how do you know anything about breadstuffs?" queried Chaumette ; " you have never known what it was to want bread."

" I know flour must be scarce from this bit of bread which was given me having so much grit in it."

" My grandmother," resumed Chaumette, " always used to be telling me : ' Little boy, never waste bread, for you may come to want it.' "

" Monsieur Chaumette," returned his hearer, " your grandmother was, it appears to me, a woman of much sense."

There was a silence.

Chaumette was mute, leaning back in the carriage.

" What ails you, sir? you are turning pale !" exclaimed the King.

" Indeed, I don't feel quite myself," rejoined Chaumette.

" Perhaps it is the rolling of the carriage ?" remarked the King.

" Perhaps so, indeed."

" Have you ever went to sea ?"

" I went through the war with La Motte Picquet."

" La Motte Picquet !" repeated Louis, " he was a brave man !"

And he fell into silence.

Of what was he thinking?

Of his fine navy, victorious in the Indies ; of his port of Cherbourg, won from the ocean, of his splendid admiral's uniform, red and gold, so different from that he wore at this moment ; of those cannons bellowing with delight at his coming ; of his days of prosperity ?

Far from this was poor Louis the Sixteenth, cramped up in the wretched, slow going cab, which cleaved before him the masses of people who flocked to see him, waves of an infectious, surging sea whose source was the gutters of Paris ; blinking his eyes in the daylight, with long beard of a sickly tint, with his thinned cheeks hanging on his neck in folds, clad in a grey coat, with dark overcoat, and muttering, with that automatical memory of children and the Bourbons :

" Ah, here is such-and-such a street, and yonder is street so-and-so."

On reaching the Rue d'Orleans, he said :

" Ah, here's the Rue d'Orleans."

" Say the Rue Egalite," some one prompted him.

" Ah, yes," said he, " on account of———"

He did not finish, but relapsed into silence, and from the Rue de l'Egalite to the Temple, uttered not another word.

CHAPTER XXVI.

THE LEGEND OF THE MARTYR KING.

THE prisoner's first care, on return-ing was to ask to be taken to his family, but he was answered that there was no order for that given.

Louis comprehended that, like all such as are being tried for life, he was to be kept from outer communication.

"At least, let my family know of my return," he said.

Then, without minding the four muni-cipals who surrounded him, he began his usual reading.

He had still one hope : namely, that at supper-time his family would come to him.

He waited vainly : no one appeared.

"I suppose," said he, " that my son will pass the night with me, for here are his things ?"

Alas, no longer, even with respect to his son, had the prisoner the certainty he affected to have.

He received no more reply to this saying than he had got to his others.

"Come, let us to bed," said the King.

Clery undressed him as usual.

"Oh, Clery," muttered he, "I was far from expecting such questions as were addressed me."

In fact, almost all the questions put to the royal captive had their source from the iron safe, and Louis, unaware of Gamain's treachery, did not suppose that depositary had been discovered.

However he went to bed and, hardly having done so, he fell asleep with tranquility of which he had already given such proofs, and which, under certain circumstances, might be deem-ed lethargy.

It was not so with the other prisoners ; this absolute privacy was for them dreadfully significative : it was the seclu-sion of those condemned.

As the Dauphin's bed and clothes were in his father's rooms, the Queen had to let her son sleep in her own bed and all night long looked on his slumber, standing by his pillow.

So deep was her grief, so like a statue was the posture of this mother as be side her child's grave, that Madame Elizabeth and Madame Royale resolved to pass the night on chairs beside the Queen ; but the officers intervened and forced the two to leave the room.

On the following day, for the first time, the Queen implored her keepers.

She begged two favors : to see her husband and to be allowed to have the papers, to be posted on the affairs of the day.

These two requests were taken to the council.

One, that for the newspapers, was re-fused completely ; the other was partly granted.

The Queen was never again to see her husband, nor the sister her brother, but the children might see their father, on condition they should nevermore see their mother or aunt.

This ultimatum was brought to the King.

He reflected for an instant ; and then, with his customary resignation, said :

" Whatever happiness I might feel at seeing my children, I renounce. The great affair in which I am busy prevents me, besides, giving them the time they have need of. The children shall re-main with their mother."

On this reply, the Dauphin's bed was put up in the mother's room, who did not leave her children until she went to be sentenced by the Revolutionary Tri-bunal, as her royal consort went to be condemned by the Convention.

There had to be means found of com municating notwithstanding the seclu sion.

It was still Clery who took upon himself this task, with the aid of a ser-vant of the princesses, named Turgy.

Turgy and Clery would meet as they went and came on service ; but the watchfulness of the municipals rendered conversation difficult between them.

The only words they could exchange were limited generally to :

" The King is well."

" The Queen, princesses and the chil-dren are well."

One day, however, Turgy gave Clery a note.

Madame Elizabeth slipped this into

my hand as I handed her a napkin," said he to his fellow.

Clery ran to convey the paper to his master.

It was marked with prickings by pins, for the princesses had long been without either ink, pens or paper; it ran thus:

"We are well, brother. Write in return."

The King answered; for, since the opening of the prosecution, writing materials had been allowed him.

Holding out his answer open to Clery, he said:

"Read it, my dear Clery, and you will see that this note contains nothing to compromise you."

Clery respectfully refused to do so, and repulsed the royal hands.

Ten minutes afterwards, Turgy had the reply.

On the same day, the latter, on passing by Clery's room, through the door of his room, which stood a-jar, tossed in to his bed a spool of thread; this enclosed a second note from Madame Elizabeth.

This was a method agreed-upon.

Clery wound the thread around a missive of his master and hid it in the cupboard.

There Turgy found it and put back the reply in the same spot.

This proceeding was repeated many times; however, every time his valet gave him some fresh proof of faithfulness and cunning in this course, the King would say, shaking his head:

"Take heed, my friend, this is exposing yourself."

This mode was, in truth, too precarious; Clery puzzled his wits about some other.

The commissaries gave their prisoners candles in thread-bound packets.

Clery carefully saved the thread and, when a sufficient quantity was obtained, he announced to the King that he had a means of making his correspondence easier; this was by lowering his thread to Madame Elizabeth, whose bedroom was below his and a window of whose room corresponded with that of a little corridor contiguous to Clery's chamber. She, in the nightime, could hang her letters on this thread, and in the same way receive the King's.

A projection was under the windows, which prevented the letters falling into the yard.

Besides, in this way, could be lowered writing materials; which did away with pin-point scratches.

The prisoners were thus enabled to have news every day, the princesses of the King, the latter of his son and the princesses.

Louis' position was much injured since he had been before the convention.

Two things were generally believed; either that—following the example of Charles the First, whose history he so well knew—Louis would refuse to answer the Convention; or that, if he did answer, he would do so haughtily and proudly, in the name of royalry, not like an accused man at a petty trial but like a knight who accepted the defiance, and picked up the gauntlet.

Unfortunately for himself, the Sixteenth Louis had not a nature royal enough to take either one or the other of these two courses.

He answered timidly, awkwardly, as we have said; and, aware that, from so many proofs appearing to have fallen into his enemies' hands, he was fettered, poor Louis concluded by asking for counsel.

After tumultuous debate which followed the prisoner's departure the counsel was granted.

Next day, four members of the Convention, appointed commissioners for that purpose, went to ask the accused whom he chose for his lawyer.

" Monsieur Turgot," he replied.

The commissioners withdrew and Turgot was informed of the honor the royal criminal did him.

This man—one of great worth, formerly a member of the Constitutionalists one of those who had taken the active part in the formation of the Constitution—this man, we repeat, was afraid !

He dastardly refused, turning pale before his century, to blush with shame before posterity !

But the day following that on which the King had been examined, the president of the Convention received the foling letter:

" CITIZEN PRESIDENT :

" I am ignorant whether the Convention will give Louis the Sixteenth a counsel to defend him, and leave him the choice of one ; in this event, I wish Louis the Sixteenth to know that, if he select me for this function, I am ready to take its duties upon me. I do not ask you to inform the Convention of my offer ; for I am far from believing myself so important a personage as to have that body busy themselves about me, but I was twice called in to the council of him who was my master in the days when to be his servant was a position which was everybody's ambition ; I owe him the same service when it is something which many will deem dangerous.

" Did I know of any other possible method of imparting to him my desire, I should not have taken the liberty of addressing you.

" I thought that, in the place you occupy, you had more than anybody else, the way of transmitting to him this intention.

" MALESHERBES."

Two other requests arrived at the same time ; one from a lawyer of Troyes, Sourdat.

" I am," said he boldly, " ready to defend Louis the Sixteenth from the feeling which I have of his innocence."

The other, from Olympe de Gouges, the strange southern improvisatrice, who dictated her comedies, because, some said, she did not know how to write.

Olympe de Gouges had made herself a woman's lawyer ; she wanted women to have the same rights as men, to be allowed to form deputations, debate on laws, declare for war or peace ; and she supported her pretention with the sentence :

" Why should not women mount the rostrum ; they go up on the scaffold bravely !"

She did, indeed, mount the scaffold nobly, poor creature ; although, when her doom was given, she became a woman again, weak, and, wishing to take advantage of the law, declared she was with child.

The tribunal sent to her an examining committee who would not accept her claim.

Before the scaffold, she became once more a man, and died as a woman like her should die.

As for Malesherbes, he was the same Lamoignon de Malesherbes, who had been minister with Turgot, and had fallen with him.

We have spoken of him elsewhere, as a small man of between seventy and seventy-two, born naturally awkward and ungraceful, somewhat stout, vulgar, with "a real face for an apothecary," says Michelet, and one from whom should be the last expected a heroism of antiquity.

Before the Convention, he never would call his client anything but " sire "

" What makes you bold to speak thus before us ?" a conventionalist asked him.

" The scorn of death," Malesherbes unaffectedly responded.

And he did in truth much scorn that death to which he walked chatting with his companions in the hurdle, and which he received as though it were merely— according to Guillotin—feeling a *slight coolness* on the neck.

The keeper-of-the-keys at Monceaux —to which place were carried the bodies of the executed—brings forward a singular proof of this scorn of death ; in the fob of the breeches of the headless trunk, he found Malesherbes' watch, which had run down at two o'clock. According to his habit, the condemned man had wound it up at noon, the hour when he set out for the scaffold.

The royal client, not having Turgot, took, hence, Malesherbes and Tronchet ; they, pushed for time, joined to them the lawyer Deseze.

On the fourteenth of December, it was announced to Louis that he had permission to confer with his defenders, and that, on the same day, he would receive a visit from Malesherbes.

The latter's devotion had affected him, albeit his temperament made him little accessible to such emotions.

On seeing him come with the utmost simplicity, an old man of three-score and ten, the King's heart swelled, and his arms—royal arms which were seldom unfolded—opened, and, in tears, he said :

"My dear Monsieur de Malesherbes, come to my breast. I know how stand affairs," continued he ; "I expect death, and am prepared for it. As you see me at this moment—and I am calm, am I not?—so shall I walk to the scaffold !"

On the sixteenth, a deputation presented itself at the Temple; it was composed of four members of the Convention : Valaze, Cochon, Grandpre and Duprat.

Twenty-one deputies were selected to examine the royal indictment; these four formed part of the commission.

They brought to the royal defendant his act of accusation and documents relative to his case.

The whole day passed in verifying these papers.

Each was read by the secretary ; after the reading, Valaze would ask :

"Do you know ?"

The King would reply yes or no, and that would be settled.

A few days from this, the same four returned and read to the prisoner fifty-one new documents, which were signed like the preceding.

In all, a hundred and fifty-eight, of which copies were left.

At this time, the King was afflicted with a fluxion.

He recollected Gilbert's bow to him when he entered the Convention ; he asked the commune to let his former physician, Gilbert, pay him a visit, but it refused.

"Let Capet drink only ice-water," said one of its members, "and he will have no fluxions."

It was on the twenty-sixth that the royal captive was, for the second time, to appear at the bar of the Convention.

His beard had grown—an uncomely, ill planted beard—Louis asked for razors ; some were allowed him, but on condition that he should only use them before four municipals !

At eleven o'clock on the evening of the twenty-fifth, he began writing out his will.

(This work is so well known, that, touching and Christian as it is, we will not copy it here.)

Two last testaments have often attracted our attention : that of Louis the Sixteenth, who faced the Republic and yet only saw royalty ; that of the Duke of Orleans, who confronted royalty though only seeing the Republic.

We will merely quote one sentence from the will of Louis XVI. because it will help us to shed light on a question of "point of view."

Every one sees, not only the reality of an object, but according to the point of view from whence he looks.

"I conclude," wrote Louis the Sixteenth, "by declaring before God, in whose presence I am to appear, that I cannot reproach myself with any of those crimes advanced against me."

Now, how came Louis the Sixteenth to say the above, to which he owes, peradventure, the reputation of an honest man which posterity grants him ; although, he was forsworn in all his oaths, fleeing to the foreigner, leaving a protest against his oaths ; although he had discussed, formed notes upon, and appreciated the plans of La Fayette and Mirabeau calling enemies to the heart of France ; although ready to appear, as he himself said, before heaven, consequently believing in heaven's justice and its reward for good and evil actions—how could he say what he did ?

The very construction of the phrase explains how.

Louis XIV. did not say :

"The crimes put forward against me are *false*."

But—which is not at all the same thing :

"I do not reproach myself with any of the crimes advanced against me."

Louis XVI., ready to step upon the scaffold, was still the Duke of Vauguyon's pupil !

To say "The crimes put forward

against me are false," was to deny those crimes, and Louis could not deny them; to say that he reproached himself of none, was, strictly speaking, saying " Such crimes may exist, but I do not reproach myself with them."

And why did he not reproach himself with them?

Because he was looking from the point of view of royalty; because,— thanks to the medium in which they are reared, to that elevation of legitimacy, that infallibility of divine right, kings do not see crimes, and particularly political ones, in the same light as other men.

Thus, for Louis XI., his revolt against his sire was no crime ; " but war for the public good."

For Charles the IX. the Massacre of Saint Bartholomew was not a crime, but " a measure advised by the public safety."

To the eyes of the Fourteenth Louis, the Revocation of the Edict of Nantes was not a crime ; but simply " a state reason."

This same Malesherbes, who now defended the King, in other days, being minister, had tried to have the Protestants given some privileges.

He found in Louis Sixteenth obstinate resistance.

" No," the latter had replied to him, " no, the proscription of the Protestants is a *State law*, a law of Louis the Fourteenth ; do not let us remove ancient landmarks."

" Sire," Malesherbes rejoined, " politics never run counter with justice !"

" But," ejaculated his hearer, like one who did not understand, " where, in the Revocation of the Edict of Nantes, was a blow dealt at justice ? That revocation was for the safety of the State, was it not ?"

So, for the Sixteenth Louis, this persecution of Protestants by an old devotee and a hateful Jesuit, the atrocious measure which set blood flowing in rivulets down the steeps of the vales of the Cavennes ; which kindled the pyres of Nimes, d'Albi, and of Beziers, was not a crime, no, but, on the contrary, a state reason.

Then there was another thing which

had to be viewed from the royal point of view ; to wit, that a King, born almost always of a *foreign* princess from whom he sucked half his blood was almost always foreign to his people ; he governed them, that was all ; and, besides, how did he govern them ? By his ministers !

Not only were the people not worthy of being his parent, of being allied to him ; but was not worthy of being directly governed by him ; while, on the other hand, foreign sovereigns were the parents and King of the ruler, who had no relations in his kingdom and who corresponded directly with them without any ministerial medium.

Bourbons of Spain, Naples, Italy, mount back to the same source : Henry the Fourth ; they were cousins.

The Emperor of Austria was a brother-in-law, the Princes of Savoy were allied to Louis Sixteenth, Saxon by his mother's side.

Now, the people having reached the point of wishing to impose on their ruler conditions which the latter did not believe it his interest to follow, to whom did Louis appeal against his rebellious subjects.

To his cousins, brother-in-law, relations ; for him the Spaniards and Austrians were not enemies of France ; because they were the friends and kinsmen of the *King*, and the King, in the royal point of view, was France.

What came these monarchs to defend ?

The holy, inassailable, almost divine cause of royalty.

That's why Louis the Sixteenth could not reproach himself of any of the crimes advanced against him :

Royal egotism had nursed popular selfishness ; and the people who had so far pushed their hatred of royalty as to abolish God, because from Him it was said sprang royalty, had doubtlessly their *State reason*, in their point of view, when they made the fourteenth of July, fifth and sixth of October, twentieth of June and tenth of August.

We do not say the second of September ; nor will we, for we repeat it was not the people who made that day, but the commune.

CHAPTER XXVII.

THE PROSECUTION.

THE day of the twenty-sixth arrived and found the royal captive prepared for everything, even death.

He had made his will the previous evening ; he feared, none knew why, being assassinated next day going to the Convention.

The Queen had been forewarned that, for the second time, her husband went to the Convention.

The movement of the troops and the drumming, would have alarmed her exceedingly had not Clery found means of informing her of the cause.

At ten o'clock in the morning, Louis started, under guard of Chambon and Santerre.

On reaching the Convention, he was made to wait an hour : the people were avenging themselves for five hundred years' delay in the ante-chambers of the Louvre, Tuileries and Versailles.

A debate had taken place at which the prisoner could not be present ; a key handed by him (on the twelfth) to Clery, had been seized in the valet's hands : the idea had been thought of to try this key in the iron safe, and it had opened it.

This key had been shown to Louis the Sixteenth.

" I do not recognize it," he had replied.

In every likelihood, he had fashioned that key himself.

It was in such little things that he completely was lacking in greatness.

The discussion being concluded, the president announced to the Convention that the prisoner and his lawyers were ready to appear at the bar.

The King entered, accompanied by Malesherbes, Tronchet and Deseze.

" Louis," said the president, " the Convention has decided that you may be heard to day."

" My counsel will read my defence to you," rejoined the royal defendant. There was deep silence.

All the Assembly comprehended that it might easily leave a few hours to this ruler from whom royalty was torn,

to this man who was to be deprived of life.

Perhaps, too, this congress, several members of which had given evidence of so superior a mind, expected to see a mighty discussion begin ; ready to lie in its bloody grave, already draped in its shroud, perchance royalty would uprise suddenly, clad in the majesty of the dying, and speak some words such as history registers, and centuries repeat.

Not so : Deseze's speech was a true lawyer's discourse.

Nevertheless, a fine cause to defend was this heir's to so many monarchs, whom fate led before the people, not only in expiation of his own misdeeds, but, over and above them, in expiation of the crimes and faults of his whole race.

It seems to us that on this occasion that, had we the honor of being Deseze, we would not have spoken in Deseze's name.

The speech should have been of Saint Louis and Henry the Fourth : these two great leaders of a race should have cleansed the Sixteenth Louis of the weakness of Louis the Thirteenth, the prodigalities of Louis the Fourteenth, the debauchery of Louis the Fifteenth !

It was not so, we repeat.

Deseze was an arguer where he should have been affecting, yet he seemed bent not on being concise, but on being poetical, he aimed at the heart, not the mind.

But, perhaps, when this commonplace production came to an end, Louis would take up the speech, and, since he had consented to defend himself, would do so, like a king, right royally, worthily, grandly, nobly.

"Gentlemen," began he, "my grounds of defence have been made clear to you ; I shall not renew them, as I speak to you it may be for the last time. I declare to you that my conscience reproaches me in nothing, and that my defenders speak only the truth.

" I have never feared that my conduct should be publicly examined ; but my heart is affected at having found in the act of arraignment the imputation of having wished to shed the blood of the people, and especially at having the misfortunes of the tenth of August attributed to me.

"I acknowledge that the multiplied proofs which I have given in all times of my love for the people, and the manner in which I have borne myself, appear to me to be evidence that I little have feared to expose myself to spare its blood, and to a shield for me against such an imputation."

Can you, reader, understand how the successor of three-score crowned heads, the descendant of Saint Louis, Henry the Fourth and Louis the Fourteenth, could only find the above to respond to his accusers?

The more unjust the accusation was in your point of view, sire, the more indignation should have made you eloquent. You should have left something to after ages, if only a curse on your executioners!

Therefore, the Convention inquired in astonishment:

"Have you nothing else to add to your defence?"

"No," rejoined the King.

"You may retire."

Louis withdrew.

He was conducted into one of the halls adjoining the main one.

At five o'clock in the afternoon, he returned to the Temple.

An hour afterward, his three defenders entered his room as he left table.

He asked them to take some refreshments.

Deseze alone accepted.

While he was eating, the prisoner said to Malesherbes:

"Well, you see now, that from the very first, I was not mistaken, and that my sentence was settled upon before even I was heard."

"Sire," rejoined Malesherbes, "on leaving the Assembly, I was surrounded by a crowd of good citizens who assured me that you should not perish, or not until they and their friends should have died."

"Do you know any of them, sir?" the King quickly inquired.

"I do not know them personally; but, certainly, I would recognize them."

"Well," said Louis, "endeavor to see some of them and tell them that I would never pardon myself if there is a single drop of blood spilt on my account. I did not wish any bloodshed when it might have preserved my throne and my life; I have all the stronger reason at present from sacrificing anybody."

Malesherbes went away early with the intention of obeying the order given him.

The first day of January, 1793, arrived.

Kept most rigorously secluded, Louis the Sixteenth had but one servant about him.

He was sadly brooding over this isolation one day, when Clery came up to his bed.

"Sire," said the valet in a low voice, "I beg permission to present to you my most earnest wishes for the end of your misfortunes."

"I thank you, Clery," said his master, holding out his hand.

At the moment when Clery was helping his master to dress, municipals entered.

Louis scrutinized them one after another, and seeing one whose face denoted a little compassion, he approached him.

"Oh, sir," said he, "render me a great service."

"What is it?" inquired the man.

"Go, I beg you on my behalf, and learn news of my family, and give it my good wishes for the coming year."

"I will go," returned the municipal, visibly affected.

"Thank you," said the prisoner. "I hope heaven will repay you for what you do for me!"

"But," observed one of the officers to Clery, "why don't the prisoner ask to see his family? Now that the questioning is over, I am sure that there will not be any difficulty."

"To whom is such a request to be put?" asked Clery.

"To the Convention."

An instant after, the municipal who had been in the Queen's apartments, returned.

"Sir," said he, "your family thanks

you for your kind wishes, and sends you the same."

His hearers smiled mournfully.

"What a New Year's Day!" muttered he.

In the evening, Clery informed his master of what the municipal had re marked, on the possibility of his seeing his family.

The King reflected for an instant, and appeared to hesitate.

"No," said he at length, "in a few days they will not refuse me that consolation; we must wait."

The Catholic religion has fearful macerations which it imposes on its followers!

It was on the sixteenth that was to be pronounced the sentence.

Malesherbes remained long with his client during the morning; about noon, he went out, saying that he would return to give an account of the call by name as soon as that should be terminated.

The voting was to be on three frightfully simple questions:

First: Is Louis guilty?

Second: Shall there be an appeal from the judgment of the Convention to the decision of the people?

Third: What shall be the penalty?

For the future to see clearly that— if the vote was not without *hate*—it was at least devoid of *fear*, the vote had to be public.

A Girondist named Birotteau demanded that everybody should mount the speaker's stand, and say aloud his sentence.

A Jacobin, Leonard Bourdon, went still farther; he had it decreed that the votes should be signed.

Lastly, a man of the right-hand side, Rouyer, demanded that the rolls should mention the absentees on the commissions, and that all others should be censured, and their names sent to the departments.

Thereupon commenced that great, noteworthy session which was to last seventy-two hours.

The hall presented a singular aspect little in harmony with what was going on.

The work in action was sad, gloomy and funereal: the appearance of the hall gave no idea of the drama.

The back seats had been transformed into boxes where the handsomest ladies of Paris, in their winter dress, covered with velvet and furs, ate oranges and ices.

The men came to bow to them and speak with them, returned to their seats, exchanged signs: one would have thought it an Italian playhouse.

The part of the Jacobins was to be specially remarked for its display.

It was among them that the millionaires were seated: the Duke of Orleans, Lepelletier de Saint Fargeau, Herault de Sechelles, Anacharsis Clootz, the Marquis of Chateauneuf.

All these gentlemen had reserved seats for their ladies, who came in all over tricolored rosettes and ribbons, with tickets or letters to the ushers, who played the part of the box-openers.

The high galleries opened to the people were never empty during the three days; there was drinking going on there as in wineshops, eating as in restaurants, speech-making as in the clubs.

To the first question: "Is Louis guilty?" six hundred and eighty three voices responded:

"Yes."

On the second question: "shall the decision of the convention be submitted to the confirmation of the people?" two hundred and eighty-one voted for the appeal to the people; four hundred and eighty-three *contra*.

Then came the third question, weighty and final:

"What shall be the penalty?"

When this stage was reached, it was eight o'clock in the third day's evening, a January day, oppressive, chilly and rainy; all were weary, vexed, impatient; human strength, among the actors as well as among the spectators, yielded under forty-five hours' permament session.

Each deputy mounted in turn to the stand, and uttered one of the four dooms: imprisonment, exile, death with some imprisonment or appeal to the people, and death.

All tokens of approval or disapproval had been forbidden, and still, whenever the popular galleries heard anything except the word : "Death !" they murmured.

Once, however, this word was heard and followed with growls, hoots and hisses.

This was when Philippe Egalite ascended the speakers-stand, and said :

"Solely intent upon my duty, convinced that all who have attempted or do attempt to gain the sovereignty of the people deserve death, I vote for death."

In the height of this terrible act, one deputy, a sick man named Duchatel, was carried into the convention. He came to vote for banishment, a vote which was admitted from its tending to indulgence.

It was Vergniaud, the president of the tenth of August, who was again president on the nineteenth of January; after having proclaimed the forfeiture of the throne, he was to proclaim death.

"Citizens," said he, "you are performing a great act of justice. I trust that humanity will lead all to keep the utmost order ; when justice shall have spoken, humanity may be heard in its turn."

He read the result of the balloting.

Out of the seven hundred and twenty-one voters, three hundred and thirty-four had voted for banishment or imprisonment, and three hundred and eighty-seven for death — some immediately, others with a respite.

Therefore, there were for death fifty-three more than for banishment.

When was taken from these fifty-three the forty-six who had voted for death with adjournment, there remained in all, for immediate death, a majority of seven.

"Citizens," said Vergniaud, with a tone of deepest pain, "I declare, in the name of the convention, that the penalty which it pronounces against Louis Capet is death."

It was in the evening of Saturday the nineteenth that death was voted, but it was not till Sunday the twentieth, at three in the morning, that Vergniaud gave out the decree.

Meanwhile, Louis XVI., deprived of all outer communication, yet knew that his fate was being determined, and alone, far from wife and children— whom he had refused to see in the aim of mortifying his spirit, as a sinning monk mortifies his flesh—he, with apparent indifference, left his life and death in his Creator's hands.

On Sunday morning (January the twentieth), at six o'clock, Malesherbes entered the royal apartments.

Louis XVI. had already risen ; his back was turned to a lamp on the mantlepiece, his elbow leaned on a table ; while his face was buried in his hands

The sound made by his counsel entering drew him from his reverie.

"Well," he inquired on seeing who it was.

Malesherbes did not dare reply ; but the prisoner could see, by the expression of his face, that all was over.

"Death !" exclaimed Louis ; "I was sure of it. Monsieur de Malesherbes," said he, "since two days I have been searching whether in the course of my reign, I have deserved of any of my subjects the slightest reproach; well, I swear to you in all the sincerity of my heart, as a man who is going to appear before my Maker, that I have always meant the happiness of my people, and have never formed a single wish contrary to it."

All this passed before Clery, who could not help weeping.

His master had pity on his grief; he took Malesherbes into his closet, and was there shut up an hour with him; then he came out, shook hands with his defender, and begged him to return that evening.

"That good old gentleman has greatly affected me," he observed to Clery on entering his chamber. "But what ails you ?"

This inquiry was prompted by a trembling which had overtaken Clery since Malesherbes, whom he had received in the ante-chamber, had told him that the King was condemned to death.

Thereupon, Clery, endeavoring to

dissemble as much as possible his agitation, prepared his master's shaving materials.

The King—while Clery was holding the basin before him—all at once turned pale, his lips were bloodless.

Clery, fearing that he was ill, put down the basin and got ready to help him, but his master said :

" Courage !"—and went on shaving in tranquility.

Towards two o'clock, the executive council came to inform the prisoner of the sentence.

At the head were Garat, the Minister of Justice, Lebrun, Minister of Foreign Affairs, Grouvelle, secretary of the council, the president and procureur-general-syndic of the department, the mayor and the procureur of the commune, the president and public accuser of the criminal tribunal.

Santerre stepped out.

" Announce the executive council," he said to Clery.

The latter was about to obey, but his master, who had heard the noise, saved him the trouble : the door opened and he appeared in the corridor.

Then, Garat, wearing his hat, said :

" Louis, the National Convention has charged the provisionary executive council to inform you of the resolutions of the fifteenth, sixteenth, seventeenth, nineteenth and twentieth of January ; the secretary of the council will read them."

Upon which, Grouvelle unfolded a paper, and read in a faltering voice :

" ARTICLE I.

" The National Convention declares Louis Capet, last King of the French, to be guilty of conspiracy against the nation's freedom, and of attempts against the general safety of the State.

" ARTICLE II.

" The National Convention resolves that Louis Capet shall suffer death.

" ARTICLE III.

" The National Convention declares *nul* Louis Capet's act brought to the bar by his counsel, and appeals to the people for the judgment against him rendered by the National Convention.

" ARTICLE IV.

" The provisionary executive council will notify the present decree to Louis Capet, and will take the necessary measures of police and safety to ensure the execution within twenty-four hours, counting from his notification, and will report to the Convention immediately after he shall have been executed."

Throughout the reading, the hearer's face had remained perfectly calm, save when his features had expressed two quite distinct feelings ; on the words : " guilty of conspiracy," a scornful smile had ran over his lips ; and at those : " shall suffer death," a look had been thrown upward, which seemed to lift the condemned King to heaven.

The reading being concluded, the King took a step towards Grouvelle, took the decree from his hands, folded it up, put it in his portfolio, and drew from it another paper which he presented to Minister Garat, saying :

" Monsieur the Minister of Justice, I beg you to speedily transmit this to the National Convention."

Seeing that the minister appeared to hesitate, he continued :

" I will read it to you."

Whereupon he read the ensuing in a voice which greatly contrasted with Grouvelle's :

" I ask a three days' delay to prepare myself ; I ask for that purpose the authorization to freely see the person whom I will indicate to the commissioners of the commune, and that this person shall be sheltered from any fear and uneasiness for the charitable act he will have done me.

" I ask to be rid of the perpetual watchfulness the council general has established since several days.

" I ask, in that interval, to be enabled to see my family whenever I please, without witnesses ; I would like the National Convention to settle immediately on the fate of my family, and either allow it to retire free or be tried at once.

"I recommend to the benevolence of the nation all the persons attached to me; there are many who have lost all their fortune in my employ, and, losing that, will be in want; among the pensioners, there are many old men, women and children, who had only that on which to live.

"Done at the Temple Tower.

"LOUIS.

"20th January, 1793."

Garat took the letter.

"Sir," said he, "it shall be given to the Convention without delay."

The King opened again his portfolio, and took from it a little slip of paper.

"If the Convention grants my request as to the person I desire," said he, "here is his address."

The paper bore this direction in Madame Elizabeth's handwriting:

"Edgeworth de Firmont,
"483 Rue du Bac."

Having nothing more to say or hear, the King took a step back as in the days when, giving an audience, he meant by that movement that the audience was over.

The ministers and those accompanying them went out.

"Clery," said the King to his valet, "ask for my dinner."

Clery went into the dining-room to obey the order; there he found two municipals who read to him a decree that the prisoner should not have either knives or forks. One knife only had been allowed to Clery for him to cut his master's food in presence of two commissaries.

The King broke his bread with his fingers and cut up his meat with his spoon; contrary to his custom, he ate but little, his meal lasting but a few minutes.

At six o'clock, the Minister of Justice was introduced.

The prisoner rose to receive him.

"Sir," said Garat, "I carried your letter to the Convention, and it has charged me to notify you the following reply:

"'Louis is free to call upon the minister for whatever he wants, and to see his family without witnesses.

"'The nation, always free and just, will take care of his family's fate.

"'Just indemnity will be granted to the creditors of his house.

"'The National Convention has passed an order for the respite.'"

His hearer nodded and the minister retired.

"Citizen minister," the officers on service asked of Garat, "may Louis see his family?"

"But in private," replied Garat.

"Impossible! by decree of the commune, we are not to lose sight of him day or night!"

This was, indeed, a puzzling matter; however, it was settled by the decision that the prisoner should receive his family in the dining-room, so that they might see through the glass but the door should be shut so that they could not hear.

During this time, Clery had been told to "see if the Minister of Justice is still here, and call him back."

In an instant, the minister entered.

"Sir," said Louis to him, "I forgot to ask you if Monsieur Edgeworth de Firmont had been found at home, and when I am to see him."

"I brought him with me," returned Garat: "he is in the council hall, and is coming up."

In fact, at the moment when the minister uttered those words, Edgeworth de Firmont appeared in the doorway.

CHAPTER XXXIII.

THE TWENTY-FIRST OF JANUARY.

EDGEWORTH DE FIRMONT was Madame Elizabeth's confessor; nearly six weeks before, on the King's asking (foreseeing the condemnation which had befallen him) his sister for opinion on the priest who should accompany him in his last moments, and she had advised her brother to settle upon the Abbe de Firmont.

This worthy ecclesiastic, of English origin, had escaped the September massacres, and retired to Choisy-le-Roi under the name of Essex.

Madame Elizabeth, having sent him information at Choisy, hoped that, at the time of the condemnation, he would be at Paris.

She was not wrong.

Abbe Edgeworth had accepted the mission with resigned delight.

On the twenty-first of December, 1792, he wrote to one of his friends in England :

" My unfortunate master has looked upon me as the one to prepare him for death, if so far goes the iniquity of his people. I am, myself, ready to die, for I am convinced that popular fury will not let me survive by an hour the horrible scene ; but I am resigned, my life is nothing ; and if, through losing it, I can save his whom God had enthroned for the good or evil of many, I shall willingly make the sacrifice, and will not have died in vain."

Such was the man who was not again to leave Louis XVI., until the latter left earth.

The King led him into the closet and there shut himself up with him.

At eight in the evening, he came out of his closet, and said to the commissioners :

" Gentlemen, have the goodness to take me to my family."

" That cannot be," replied one of the officers ; " but it can be brought to you, if you like."

" So be it," returned the King, " provided I can see my family freely and unwitnessed, let it be in my room."

" Not in your room," observed the same municipal, " but in the dining-room ; we have settled how it should be with the Minister of Justice."

" Still," remonstrated the prisoner, " did you not hear that the decree of the convention permits me to see my family without witnesses ?"

" True ; you shall be to yourselves : the door shall be closed ; but we can watch you through the window panes."

" 'Tis well ; do so."

The municipals went out and the King passed into the dining room.

Clery followed him there, where he pulled the table one side, and drew up the chairs so as to give more space.

" Clery," said Louis, " bring in a little water and a glass, in case the Queen should be thirsty."

There was on the table one of those pitchers of ice-water with which a member of the commune had reproached the King.

Clery therefore, brought only a glass.

" Fetch some water," said Louis ; " if the Queen drinks ice-water, to which she is not accustomed, it might do her harm. And, stay, Clery ; beg at the same time, Monsieur de Firmont not to leave my closet ; I fear that the sight of him may have too great an impression on my family."

At half past eight, the door opened.

The Queen came first, holding her son by the hand ; Mesdames Royale and Elizabeth followed her.

The King held out his arms.

Clery went out and closed the door.

For several minutes, there was a deep stillness, unbroken save by sobs ; then the Queen tried to drag away her husband into his room.

" No," said Louis, resisting her, " I cannot see you but here."

The Queen and royal family had learnt that the sentence had been delivered, but knew nothing of the details of the case : the prisoner related these to them, excusing the men who had tried him and making his wife remark that neither Petion nor Manuel had voted for death.

The Queen burst into sobs every time she tried to speak.

The poor prisoner had some reward : in his last hour, he was adored by all surrounding around him, even by the Queen.

As our readers have seen in the romantic portion of this work, the Queen had easily let herself be drawn to the picturesque side of life; she had that lively imagination which, much more than character, make women imprudent; Marie Antoinette was imprudent all her life, in her friendships as in her amours.

Her captivity saved her in the moral point of view, for she fell back into the pure holy affection of family, from which the passions of her youth fled, and—not knowing how to do anything save passionately—she had come to deeply love in misfortune that King, that husband, of whom, in the sunny days of happiness, she had only seen the coarse, vulgar sides; Varennes and the tenth of August, had shown Louis the Sixteenth to her as a man without resolution, wavering, slow to act, almost cowardly; at the Temple, she began to see that not only had the woman ill judged her husband, but the Queen the King; at the Temple, she saw him calm, patient under outrages, firm yet gentle; all she had of worldly roughness was worn away, melted and joined the torrent of her good sentiments.

In the same way as she had too much disdained, so did she love too well.

"Alas," said Louis to Firmont, "ought I be loved so well, so tenderly!"

Hence, in this last interview, the Queen let herself be borne away by a feeling which resembled remorse. She had wished to take her husband into his room in order to be for an instant quite alone with him; when she saw that could not be, she drew him away into the recess of a window.

There she would have doubtlessly fallen on her knees and, amid tears and sobs, have craved his pardon.

He understood all, for he prevented her, and, drawing his will from his pocket, said:

"Read this, my well beloved wife."

With his finger he pointed to the following paragraph, which the Queen read in an undertone:

"I beg my wife to forgive me for all the hardships she has undergone for me, and the grievances which I may have given her in the course of our union, as she may be sure that *I have nothing against her*, though SHE may have SOMETHING TO REPROACH HERSELF WITH."

Marie Antoinette took the royal hands and kissed them; there was a merciful pardon in the phrase: "she may be sure that I have nothing against her;" an extremely great delicacy in the words: "though she may have something to reproach herself with."

So that royal Magdalen died at peace; her love for her husband, late in the day as it sprung up, won for her divine and human mercy, and her pardon was granted, not low and mysteriously like an indulgence of which the King was himself ashamed, but loudly and openly.

Who would venture to reproach in any way her who was going down to posterity, doubly crowned with the martyr's glory and her husband's forgiveness?

She felt none would venture this; she felt that, from that moment, she was strong before history; but she became only the weaker before him whom she loved so late, well aware that she had not loved him enough. It was no longer words that flowed from the unfortunate woman's bosom, but sobs and half-smothered groans; she said that she wanted to die with her husband, and that, if this was refused her, she would starve herself.

The municipals—who gazed upon this painful scene through the glazed door—could not contain themselves; they at first turned aloof their eyes, and then, although seeing no longer, as they still heard sobs, they became men, and burst into tears.

The farewell lasted until seven o'clock.

At last, at a quarter past ten, the King rose, his wife, sister and children clinging to him. The whole group moved together, uttering moans, sobs, exclamations, among which might be distinguished such ends of sentences as the following:

"Are we not to meet again?"

"Yes, yes. Be of good cheer!"

"To-morrow—to-morrow morning at eight o'clock?"

"I promise."

"Why not at seven?" inquired the Queen.

"Well, well, be it at seven," returned her husband; "but now, farewell, farewell!"

He uttered the final word in so expressive a voice that one could divine that he feared his courage was failing him.

Madame Royale could support this no longer; she gave a sigh, and sank upon the floor in a fainting fit.

Madame Elizabeth and Clery lifted her up.

The King felt that it was his duty to be strong; he tore himself from the arms of the Queen and the Dauphin, and entered his room, crying:

"Farewell!"

He closed the door behind him.

The Queen, in bewilderment, crept close up to the door, not daring to ask admittance, but weeping and sobbing and striking the panels with her hands.

The King had the courage not to come out.

The municipals, then, asked the Queen to retire to her room, renewing the already given assurance that she could see her husband next day at seven o'clock.

Clery wished to carry the still swooned Madame Royale to the Queen's room, but, on the second step, the officers stopped him and forced him to go back.

The King had rejoined his confessor in the turret chamber, and made him relate in what manner he had been led to the Temple.

Did this narrative enter his mind, or did the words confusedly hum in his ears, extinguished by his own thoughts? None can tell.

Forewarned by Malesherbes, who had made an appointment with him at the residence of Madame de Senozan, that the King might have need of him if he should be condemned to death, Abbe Edgeworth, at the risk of the danger he incurred, had returned to Paris; fearing what had been the sentence rendered that Sunday morning, he waited in the Rue du Bar.

At four o'clock in the evening, a stranger had presented himself to him, and had handed him a note conceived in the following terms:

"The executive council, having something of the utmost importance to communicate to Citizen Edgeworth de Firmont, invites him to come to its place of meeting."

The stranger had an order to accompany the priest.

A cab was waiting at the door.

The abbe got into it with the stranger.

The vehicle stopped at the Tuilleries.

The ministers were in conference.

At the abbe's entrance, they rose.

"Are you the Abbe Edgeworth de Firmont?" inquired Garat.

"Yes," returned the abbe.

"Well," continued the Minister of Justice; "Louis Capet having informed us of his desire to have you by him in his last moments, we have sent for you to learn whether you consent to render him the service he claims of you."

"Since the King has set his choice upon me," returned the priest, "it is my duty to obey him."

"In that case," proceeded the minister, "you will come with me to the Temple."

He took away the abbe in his carriage.

We have seen how the latter, after having gone through the usual formalities, had reached Louis XVI.; how the latter had been called away by his family, and how he had returned to the Abbe Edgeworth, of whom he asked what the reader has just read.

When the account was given, the King said:

"Sir, let us forget everything now, to think of the great business of my salvation."

"Sire," rejoined the abbe, "I am ready to do my best, and I trust that heaven will accord me a little merit; but would you not think it a great consolation to hear mass and receive the communion?"

"Beyond a doubt," answered the prisoner, "and rest assured that I would feel all the worth of such a favor: but how can you obtain all this?'

"That concerns me, sire, and I am bent on proving to your Majesty that I am worthy of the honor which he has done me in selecting me for his sustainer. Let your Majesty give me free will, and I will answer for everything."

"Proceed, then, sir," said Louis the Sixteenth. "Go," added he, shaking his head; "but you cannot succeed."

Abbe Edgeworth bowed and went out, asking to be taken to the council chamber.

"He who is going to die to-morrow," said Edgeworth to the commissioners, "desires, before dying, to hear mass and to confess."

The municipals stared at one another in astonishment; they had not even had the idea that such a request could ever be put to them.

"And where the deuce," exclaimed they, "is a priest and church ornaments to be found at this hour?"

"The priest is already found," replied Abbe Edgeworth, "since you see me here; as for the ornaments, the nearest place of worship will furnish them: you have merely to send for them."

The officers hesitated.

"But suppose this is a trap?" observed one of them.

"What mean you?" exclaimed the abbe.

"Suppose, under cloak of the prisoner receiving the communion, you poison him."

Abbe Edgeworth looked fixedly at him who had put forward this doubt.

"Let me tell you," went on the municipal, "that history furnishes plenty of examples in that line, and it behoves us to be circumspect."

"Sir," said the abbe, "I was so minutely searched on entering here, that you ought to be well aware that I have no poison about me; if, therefore, I have any to-morrow, it is from you that I should have received it, inasmuch as nothing can come to me save through your hands."

The absent members were called in, and there was a deliberation.

The request was granted on two conditions: first, that the abbe should draw up a petition which he should sign with his name: second, that the ceremony should be ended before seven o'clock at the latest the next day, the prisoner having to be conducted, at eight o'clock precisely, to his place of execution.

The abbe wrote out his request and left it on the desk; then he hastened back to the King, to whom he brought the grateful intelligence that this wish was granted.

It was ten o'clock.

Abbe Edgeworth remained shut up with the King until midnight.

Then, said the King:

"Monsieur l'Abbe, I am tired; I want to sleep; I have need of strength to-morrow."

Then, he called:

"Clery!"

Clery entered, undressed his master, and was about to unloose his hair, but, with a smile, Louis said:

"It is not worth the trouble."

Upon which, he went to bed, and said, as Clery drew the curtains:

"Wake me at five."

Hardly was his head on the pillow, than the prisoner fell asleep, so overpowering in this man were bodily needs.

Edgeworth threw himself on Clery's bed, who spent the night on a chair.

Clery's slumber was full of agitation and fits of waking: so he did not miss hearing five o'clock ring.

He rose instantly and commenced to make a fire.

At the sound he could not help making, his master was aroused.

"Well, Clery, has five o'clock yet rung?" inquired he.

"Sire," returned the valet, "It has rung out from many steeples, but the clock has not struck."

He came to the bed.

"I have slept soundly," observed Louis, "I had need of it; yesterday had dreadfully worn me out. Where is Monsieur de Firmont?"

"On my bed, sire."

"On your bed! Why where did you pass the night?"

"On this chair."

"I'm sorry. You were wrong to have done so."

"Oh, sire," responded Clery, "could I think of myself in such a moment."

"Ah, poor Clery!" ejaculated the doomed King.

He held out his hand which the valet kissed.

For the last time, the faithful servant dressed the King, in a brown coat, grey breeches, grey silk stockings.

Then Clery dressed his hair.

Meanwhile, Louis removed from his watch a seal, put it in his vest pocket, and laid his watch on the mantel-piece; then taking a ring from his finger he put it in the same pocket with the seal.

When Clery handed him his coat, he drew out his pocket-book, eye-glass, and snuff box, which he laid on the mantle-piece, along with his purse.

All these preparations took place before the municipals, who had entered the prisoner's room so soon as they saw the light.

The half hour after five rang out.

"Clery," said the King, "go wake up Monsieur de Firmont."

The latter was already awake and up; he heard the order given to Clery, and entered.

The King nodded to him to step into his closet.

Then Clery hastened to arrange the altar—which was the bureau of the room covered with a sheet. The sacerdotal ornaments had been procured, as Abbe Edgeworth had said, in the first church they had applied to; this was the capuchin church in the Marais, near the Soubise Mansion.

The altar being ready, Clery went to his master.

"Can you serve the mass?" the latter asked him.

"I hope so," replied Clery; "but I do not know the responses by heart."

Louis gave him a prayer-book which he opened at the *Introit*.

Edgeworth was already in Clery's room, where he put on his dress.

Fronting the altar, the valet had placed an armchair, and a thick cushion before it; but the King bade him re move it, and went himself for a smaller one, stuffed with horse-hair, which he usually used to kneel upon during his devotions.

When the priest entered, the municipals—who, no doubt, feared being sul-lied by the contact of a churchman—withdrew into the ante-chamber.

It was six o'clock, when the mass commenced.

After mass, the King received the communion, and Abbe Edgeworth, leaving him to his prayers, went into the neighboring room to put off his sacerdotal attire.

The King took advantage of this space to thank Clery, and bid him fare-well; then he returned to his closet.

Firmont there rejoined him.

Clery sat down on his bed to weep.

At seven o'clock, his master called him.

Louis led him into the recess of a window, and said to him:

"You will give this seal to my son, and this ring to my wife. Tell them that I do not part with them without emotion! This little packet encloses the hair of all my family—you will hand this also to the Queen."

"But are they not to see you again, sire?" inquired Clery.

The King paused for an instant, then he proceeded:

"No, decidedly, no! I know I pro-mised to see them this morning; but I wish to spare them the pain of so cruel a seperation. Clery, if you see them again, you will tell them how much it cost me to go without bidding them good-bye—"

He wiped away his tears.

"Clery," he concluded with his most sorrowful tone, "you will bid them good-bye for me, will you not?"

He went into his closet.

The watchers had seen the prisoner hand to Clery the different objects we have mentioned.

One of them claimed them, but ano-ther proposed that Clery should keep them till the council decided on their fate.

This course prevailed.

A quarter of an hour afterwards, Louis came again from his closet.

Clery was in waiting.

"Clery," he said, "ask if I may have a pair of scissors."

And he entered.

"May the King have scissors?" in-quired Clery of the commissioners.

" What for ?"

" I do not know ; ask him yourself."

One of the officers entered the closet. The prisoner was on his knees before Abbe Edgeworth.

"You ask for scissors," said he ; " what do you want to do ?"

" They are for Clery to cut my hair," replied the King.

The officer went down to the council chamber.

There was a half-hour's deliberation, the result of which was that scissors were refused.

The municipal came up to say :

" The council will not allow them."

" I will not touch them," said Louis ; " and Clery shall cut my hair in your presence. Try again, sir, I entreat you."

The officer went down once more to the council, repeated the royal request, but the council persisted in its refusal.

A municipal, approaching Clery, said to him :

" I think it's time for you to get ready to accompany your master to the scaffold."

" Heaven forbid !" exclaimed Clery, trembling.

" Why, no," said another, " Jack Ketch will do all the work."

The day began to break.

The long roll was beaten in all the districts of Paris.

This sound and the awakening noise penetrated the tower, and chilled the blood in the veins of Clery and the Ab-be Edgeworth.

But Louis, calmer than they, listened for an instant, and then observed with out emotion :

" It is probably the National Guard being assembled."

A little while afterwards, detach-ments of cavalry entered the Temple Court ; the horses were to be heard neighing and officers speaking.

Louis listened to this, and said with the same calmness :

" Apparently they are approaching."

From seven to eight o'clock in the morning, at different times and under various pretexts, there was knocking at the closet door, and every time Edge-

worth dreaded it was the last one ; but, every time, the King rose without any emotion whatever, went to the door, quietly answered to the persons who interrupted him, and returned to sit down beside his confessor.

Edgeworth did not see who were the people who thus came, but he over-heard some of their words. Once he heard one of these interruptors say to the prisoner :

"Oho ! it was very fine fun to be King, but you are not to be King much longer !"

Louis returned with the same tran-quil face ; only, he said :

"See how these men treat me, father ! But this is what makes suffer-ing !"

There was another knock, and again Louis went to the door ; this time, he returned, saying :

" These men see daggers and poison everywhere—they do not know me. To kill myself would be a weakness ; they fancy I do not know how to die."

At last, at nine o'clock, the sounds increased, and the doors opened noisily.

Santerre entered, accompanied by seven or eight municipals and ten gen-darmes, whom he arranged in two lines. On this movement, without waiting till the closet door was knocked at, the prisoner went out.

" Do you come for me ?" he inquired.

" Yes, sir."

" I ask a minute."

He went again into the closet, shut-ting the door.

" This time, all is over," said he, kneeling before the Abbe Edgeworth. " Give me your last blessing, father, and pray heaven to sustain me to the end."

The blessing being given, the prisoner rose, and, opening the closet door, he advanced towards the municipals and gendarmes, who were in the middle of his bedroom.

All wore their hats.

" Give me my hat, Clery," said Louis

Clery hastened to obey the order.

" Is there among you," inquired the prisoner, " any member of the com-mune ? You are one, I believe ?"

This he addressed to a municipal named Jacques Roux, a priest who had taken the oath.

"What do you want of me?" asked the latter.

Louis drew his will out of his pocket.

"I beg you to take this paper to the Queen—my wife."

"We are not here to take your orders, but to take you to the scaffold," replied Jacques Roux.

The King received this reply meekly, and with the same humility, turning towards another municipal named Gobeau, asked:

"And will you refuse to take it, also?"

As Gobeau appeared to waver, he went on:

"It is my will; you may read it: there are some things in it which I would like the commune to know."

The officer took the paper.

Then, seeing that Clery—who, like Charles the First's valet, fearing his master might tremble with cold, and have it mistaken for fear—seeing that Clery was holding out to him not only the hat he had asked for, but a cloak, he said:

"No, Clery; give me only my hat."

Clery gave him his hat, and his master took advantage of this occasion to shake his faithful servant's hand a last time.

Then, in that tone of command which he had so rarely used in his life, he said:

"Let us go, gentlemen!"

These were the last words he spoke in his room.

On the stairs, he met the keeper of the tower, Mathay, (whom, a couple of nights before, he had found seated by his fire and had peremptorily ordered to get up).

"Mathay," said he, "I was a little hasty with you night before last: do not bear any ill will against me."

Mathay turned his back on him without reply.

The prisoner crossed the first courtyard a-foot, and, in crossing it, turned two or three times to bid farewell to his single love, his wife; his sole friendship, his sister; his only joy, his children.

At the entrance to the courtyard, was a green cab; two gendarmes were holding the door open; on the approach of the condemned man, one of them jumped in, and sat on the front seat; the King entered next and beckoned Edgeworth to sit beside him in the back; the other gendarme took his place beside the first, and shut the door.

Two rumors were current.

The first, that one of these two gendarmes was a disguised priest; the second that the two had received an order to take the King's life at the slightest attempt made to rescue him.

Neither of these two assertions have any solid basis.

At a quarter after nine, the train started.

A word more on the Queen, Madame Elizabeth and the two children:

After the evening's interview with her husband, painful yet pleasing at the same time, the Queen had barely enough strength to throw herself, dressed, on her bed; and during the long winter's night, Madame Elizabeth and her daughter had heard her moan with cold and anguish.

At a quarter past six, the Queen's door was opened, and search was made for a prayer-book.

From this moment, the family prepared, believing—after the promise which the King had given the previous evening—that they would be called down stairs; but time passed.

The Queen and the princess, still standing, listened to the different sounds which had not affected Louis, but which made the priest and the valet start; they heard the sound of doors opened and shut; and the shouts of the mob hailing the prisoner's appearance, and then, the increasing din of horses and cannon.

Thereupon, Marie Antoinette fell upon a chair, murmuring:

"He has gone!"

Her sister-in-law and her daughter knelt down by her.

Thus were all the hopes flown one by one: at first had been hoped imprisonment or banishment; next, a respite;

lastly, nothing more was to be dreamt of save some rescue on the way, and that was to vanish !

The vehicle had gone quite a distance in the mean time, and had reached the boulevard.

The streets were almost deserted, the shops were half closed ; no one was in doorways or up at windows.

A decree of the commune had forbidden citizens taking any part in the armed escort, or showing themselves at windows on the line of march.

A lowering, misty sky barely let one see a forest of pikes among which shone a few bayonets ; before the vehicle rode troopers, and before them marched a multitude of drummers.

The prisoner would have conversed with his confessor, but such was the din that they could not hear.

The abbe lent him his prayer-book : he read.

At the Porte Saint Denis, he lifted his head, fancying he heard some peculiar shout.

Indeed, a dozen young men rushed down the Rue Beauregard, broke through the press, sword in hand, shouting :

" This way all who would save the King !"

Three thousand was the number sworn to obey this appeal made by the Baron de Batz, an adventurous conspirator ; he bravely gave the signal, but, out of the three thousand, only a few responded.

The Baron de Batz and his forlorn hope of royalty, seeing there was no chance, took advantage of the confusion caused by their attempt, and saved themselves in the network of streets around the Porte Saint Denis.

It was this incident which distracted the royal captive from his prayers, but it was of so little importance that the cab did not even have to stop.

When it did stop, at the end of two hours' time, it had reached the end of its journey.

When the King felt the movement cease, he bent over to his priest's ear, and said :

" We are arrived, sir, if I am not mistaken."

The other kept silent.

At this moment, one of the three brothers Samson, executioners of Paris, came to open the door.

Then Louis, laying his hand on the abbe's knee, said in a master's tone :

" Sirs, I recommend this gentleman to you. Take care after my death that no harm comes to him."

During this time, the two other executioners had approached.

" Yes, yes," said one of them, " we shall take care of him ; leave him to us."

Louis alighted.

The executioners' assistants surrounded him and were going to remove his coat ; but he scornfully repulsed them, and took off his clothes himself.

For an instant, the prisoner was alone in a ring he had made, throwing down his hat, taking off his coat and unfastening his neckerchief ; but then the executioners approached him again.

One of them held a rope in his hand.

" What do you want ?" inquired Louis.

" To pinion you," replied the one holding the rope.

" I will never consent to that," cried the King, " give up the idea. Do what you are commanded ; but you shall not bind me—no, never !"

The executioners raised their voices.

A hand-to-hand struggle was about, in everybody's eyes, to deprive the victim of the merit of six weeks' calmness, courage and resignation, when one of the Samsons, moved by compassion, but still compelled to perform his duty, stepped up and said in a respectful voice :

" *Sire*, with this handkerchief."

The prisoner glanced at his confessor.

The latter made an effort to speak.

" Sire," said he, " 'twill be but a trial the more."

The King looked upward with a deep expression of pain.

Then, turning to the executioners, while holding out his hands, he said :

" Do what you will ; I will drain the chalice to the dregs."

The steps of the scaffold were high and slippery ; he mounted them, sustained by the priest.

For an instant, the latter, feeling the weight pressing upon his arms, feared some weakness in the last moment ; but, on reaching the top step, the King sprang from his confessor's hands and hastened to the other end of the platform.

He was very high in color, and had never appeared so animated.

The drums beat, but he imposed silence on the drummers with a look.

Then, in a strong voice, he spoke the following :

" I die innocent of all the crimes imputed to me, I forgive the authors of my death, and I pray heaven that the blood you are about to shed will never fall upon France !"

"Strike up drums!" exclaimed a voice which was long believed to have been Santerre's, but which was that of de Beaufranchet, Count of Oyat, natural son of Louis Fifteenth and Morphise the Courtezan—the natural uncle of the condemned.

The drums beat.

Louis XVI. stamped his foot.

" Be silent !" thundered he ; " I have more to say."

But the drums continued their roll.

" Do your duties !" roared the pikemen surrounding the scaffold to the executioners.

The latter sprang on their man, who was slowly returning towards the knife, flinging a glance at the chisel-edged blade of which, a year before, he himself had furnished the design.

Then his eyes wandered back on the priest, who was praying on his knees at the edge of the scaffold.

There was a confused movement behind the two uprights of the guillotine ; the prisoner's head appeared in the opening, a flash descended, a dull chop was heard, and then there gushed out a jet of blood.

One of the headsmen, picking up the head, showed it to the people, sprinkling the sides of the scaffold with the royal blood.

On seeing this, the pikemen shouted with joy, and rushed forward to dip in the blood, some their pikes, others swords, others—those that had them— their handkerchiefs, to the cry of,

" The Republic forever !"

But, for the first time, this great cry, which had so often excited the people with gladness, died away without echo.

The Republic had on its brow one of those fated spots never to be effaced ! it had, as hereafter said a great diplomatist, committed more than a crime —a fault.

There fell upon Paris a feeling of stupefaction ; in some, this went to desperation : a woman leaped into the Seine ; a wigmaker cut his throat ; a bookseller became mad ; an old officer died outright under his deep impression.

Finally, at the opening of the session of the Convention, a letter was read by the president.

It was from a man who begged that the body of Louis the Sixteenth should be given to him, that he might bury it beside his father's.

The body and head were separated ; let us see what became of them.

We do not believe anything can speak clearer than the very report of the burial.

" *Report of the Burial of Louis Capet.*

"On the twenty-first of January, 1793, year II of the French Republic, we, the undersigned, administrators of the Department of Paris, charged with the power by the general council of the department in virtue of the decrees of the provisional executive council of the French Republic, proceeded, at nine o'clock in the morning, to the abode of Citizen Ricave, Curate of Saint Madeleine's Church.

" Having found him at home, we asked him if he had provided for the execution of the measures which he had been recommended to take the previous evening by the executive council and the country for the burial of Louis Capet.

" He replied to us that he had carried out all that he had been ordered by the department and executive council, and that everything was in readiness.

" From thence (accompanied by Citizens Renard and Damoreau, both vicars of the Parish Saint Madeleine, charged by the citizen curate with proceedings for the burial of Louis Capet), we proceeded to the burying-ground of the said parish, situated in the Rue d'Anjou Saint Honore, where we saw the fulfilment of the orders by us delivered the night before to the citizen curate, in virtue of the commission we received from the general council of the department.

"In our presence, there was brought into the cemetery by a detachment of the foot-gendarmes the corpse of Louis Capet, which was entire in every respect, the head being apart from the trunk; we remarked that the hair on the back of the head had been cut, and that the corpse was without cravat, coat and shoes ; it was dressed in shirt, vest, grey cloth breeches, a pair of grey silk stockings.

"Thus attired, it was placed in a coffin, which was lowered into the grave, which was filled up instantly. And all this was performed in a manner conforming with the orders issued by the provisionary executive council of the Republic; and we have signed with Citizens Ricave, Renard and Damoreau, curate and vicars of Saint Madeleine.

"Leblanc, ⎱ administrators of
"Dubois, ⎰ the department,
"Damoreau,
"Ricave,
"Renard."

So died (January the twenty-first, 1793) and was buried King Louis the Sixteenth.

He was aged thirty-nine years, five months and three days; he had reigned eighteen years; he had been prisoner five months and eight days.

His last wish was not accomplished, for his blood fell not alone on France, but, besides, on the whole of Europe !

CHAPTER XXIX.

COUNSEL FROM CAGLIOSTRO.

Upon the evening of this noteworthy day—while pikemen roamed through the unpeopled though lighted streets of Paris, rendered still more mournful from their very brightness, waving at

the end of their weapons shreds of handkerchiefs and shirts soaked with red, and yelling : " The tyrant is dead ! behold the tyrant's blood !"—two men were in the room on the first floor of a house in the Rue Saint Honore, in equal silence, but very different attitudes.

One, dressed in black, was seated before a table, his head supported by his hands, and plunged into deep thought or profound grief.

The other, dressed like a country squire, was striding up and down, with dull eye, wrinkled brow and folded arms ; however, every time that, in his walk diagonally cutting the chamber, this latter passed by the table, he would fling upon the other a side-long, questioning look.

How long had this couple been here ? We cannot tell.

At last the countryman, appeared to be weary of the stillness, and, stopping before the man in the black coat whose head was upon his hands, he said, fixing his eyes upon him :

" So, Citizen Gilbert, do you call me a cut-throat because I voted for the King's death ?"

The other man lifted up his head, shook his melancholy brow, and, holding out his hand to the speaker, replied :

" Nay, Billot, you are no more deserving of such a term than I am of that of aristocrat ; you voted according to your conscience, as I did according to mine ; only, I voted for life, you, for death. Now, 'tis a fearful thing this depriving a man of that which no human power can restore !"

" Hence, to your mind," exclaimed Billot, " despotism is inviolable, freedom is a revolt, and there is no justice on earth save for kings, tyrants, in other words ? Then, what remains to the people ? The right of serving and obeying ? And is it you, Monsieur Gilbert, the pupil of Jean Jacques Rousseau, the citizen of the United States, who speaks thus ?"

" I say nothing like this, Billot, for it would be impiety against mankind."

" I," resumed Billot, " I speak to you, Monsieur Gilbert, with the straightforwardness of my coarse, good sense, and I would not have you to reply to me with all the cunning of your mind. Do you admit that a nation which believes itself oppressed has the right of casting off its church, of abasing or even doing away with its throne, to fight and to free itself?"

"To be sure."

"Then has it not the right to consolidate the results of its victory?"

"Yes, Billot, it has such a right, uncontestably; but nothing can be cemented by violence, by murder. Do you forget it is written: 'thou shalt not kill!'"

"But the King is not a man like me!" exclaimed Billot; "the King is my enemy. I can remember, when my poor mother read me the Bible, I can remember what Samuel told the Israelites who asked him for a king."

"So do I remember that, Billot; and still, Samuel anointed Saul, but did not kill him."

"Oh, I know that if I go to cope with you in learning, I will be overthrown. So I say to you simply: 'Had we the right to take the Bastille?'"

"Yes."

"Had we the right, when the King endeavored to deprive the people of their freedom of speech, to hold the Tennis-court Meeting?"

"Yes."

"Had we the right, when the King tried to overawe the National Assembly by the banquet of the body-guards and by a gathering of troops at Versailles, to go for the King at Versailles and bring him back to Paris?"

"Yes."

"Had we the right, when the King attempted to flee and pass over to the enemy, to arrest him at Varennes?"

"Yes."

"Had we the right—when, after the Constitution of 1791 had been sworn to, we saw our ruler parley with the self-exiled nobles and conspire with foreigners—to make the twentieth of June?"

"Yes."

"When he refused his sanctions to the laws emanating from the people's will, had we the right to make the tenth of August, namely, take the Tuileries and deprive him of the throne?"

"Yes."

"Had we the right, when, confined in the Temple, our prisoner continued to be a living conspirator against freedom, to take him before the National Convention and try him?"

"You had the right."

"If we had the right to try him, we had that to doom him."

"By exile, banishment, perpetual confinement to anything and everything, excepting death."

"Why not to death?"

"Because, guilty in the result, he was not in intention. You judge him looking from the people's stand, my dear Billot; he acted as one born in the purple. Was he a tyrant, as you style him? Not so. Was he an oppressor of the people! Nay. An accomplice of the aristocracy? No. An enemy of freedom? No."

"Then did you judge him from a royal standard."

"No, for had I done so, I should have acquitted him."

"Did you not acquit him by voting against death?"

"For life—yes, but with imprisonment for life. Billot, believe me, I judge him more partially than I should have wished. One of the people, or rather, son of the people, the balance I pressed in my hands leaned on the side of the people. You looked on him from a distance, Billot, and saw him not as I did: unfitted for the regal station to which he was born, pulled to one side by the Assembly; harassed in one quarter by an ambitious Queen; in another, by a restless, humbled nobility; and by an implacable clergy; by a selfish set of self-outlaws; still again by his brothers, who went through the world seeking in his name enemies to the Revolution.

"You say, Billot, the King was not a man like you; but your enemy. Now, that enemy was down, and such are not killed. A murder in cold blood is not an execution but an immolation. You have given royalty martyrdom, to justice something like vengeance.—

Beware! in doing too much, you have not done enough.

"Charles the First lost his head, and the Second Charles became King. James the Second was banished, and his sons died in exile. Human nature is pathetic, Billot, and we have alienated from us for fifty years, perhaps for a hundred, that immense portion of a population who test revolutions by the heart. Believe me, friend, republicans should most deplore the blood of Louis the Sixteenth, for that blood will fall upon them, and cost them the republic."

"There is some truth in what you say, Gilbert!" broke in a voice from the door of entrance.

The two men started and turned with the same movement; then, in the one voice, they exclaimed:

"Cagliostro!"

"Certainly, yes," replied that person, "But there is also truth in what Billot said."

"Alas!" said Gilbert, "here lies the misfortune; we plead the cause from an opposite side, and each, seeing as each does, may say: 'I am right!'"

"Yes, but you must also acknowledge you are wrong," said Cagliostro.

"Your opinion, master," said Gilbert.

"Yes," said Billot.

"You just now tried the accused," said Cagliostro, "I will try the judgment. Had you condemned the King, you would have been right. You sentenced the man, and you were wrong!"

"I do not understand," remarked Billot.

"Proceed; I see," said Gilbert.

"Louis should have been killed," continued Cagliostro, "as he was at Versailles and the Tuileries, unknown to the people, behind his screen of courtiers and wall of Swiss; he should have been killed on the seventh of October or the eleventh of August; he was a tyrant on those days! But, after having left him five months at the Temple, in communication with all, eating, sleeping under every one's eyes, a fellow for the masses, the workingman and petty shopkeeper; elevated, by this apparent abasement to the dignity of a man; in short, to treat him like a man should have been the course—that is to say, banish or imprison him."

"I did not understand you," said Billot to Gilbert, "but I understand Citizen Cagliostro."

"Of course, during those five months of captivity, he exhibited all there could be in the way of innocence, to affect and make respected; he showed himself to be a kind husband, good father, good man. The blockheads! I fancied them less of dolts than this, Gilbert! They changed him, re-made him; as the sculptor brings forth the statue from the marble block by dint of blows and cuts, so was carved out of this heavy nature—the prosaic being, vulgar, submerged in sensual habits, rigidly devout, not in the manner of an elevated mind, but like a parish serving-man—a figure of courage, patience, and resignation; lo! they set this work upon misfortune's pedestal; lo! they so elevated this poor King, so added to him, so holy made him, that it came to pass that his wife loved him! Ah, my dear Gilbert," continued Cagliostro, "who would even have thought, on the fourteenth of July, fifth or sixth of October, or the tenth of August, that Marie Antoinette would ever love her husband!"

"Oh, had I only guessed this!" muttered Billot.

"Why, what would you have done, Billot?" inquired Gilbert.

"What done? I would have slain him on one of those days, as it was easy for me to have done."

These words were uttered with such an accent of patriotism, that Gilbert forgave them, and Cagliostro admired them.

"Ay," said the latter after an instant's pause, "but you did not do so. You, Billot, voted for death; you, Gilbert, for life. Now, hearken to a last piece of counsel. You, Gilbert, only got yourself appointed to the Convention to fulfil a duty; you, Billot, to accomplish a vengeance; duty and vengeance are both accomplished; you have no further need here: go!"

They looked at the speaker.

"I am right," resumed Cagliostro;

"you are neither men of parties, but men of instinct. Now, the King being dead, the parties will come together, and, once they are facing one another, the parties will begin to destroy. Which will be the first to fall? I do not say I know, but they will fall, one after another; therefore, to morrow, Gilbert, a crime will be made of your indulgence, and the day after that, it may be before, a crime will be made of your severity, Billot. Believe me, in the mortal struggle which is preparing between hate, fear, vengeance, fanaticism, very few will remain unspotted; some will be sullied with the mire, others with blood. Go, my friends, go!"

"But France?" ejaculated Gilbert.

"Yes, France!" echoed Billot.

"France, materially, is saved," returned Cagliostro; "the enemy without is beaten, the minor enemy dead. Dangerous as may be for the future the scaffold of January, it is, incontestably, a mighty power for the present; the power of revolutions without backward steps. The death of Louis the Sixteenth devotes France to the revenge of thrones, but endows the Republic with the convulsive, desperate strength of death-doomed nations. Look at Athens in ancient times, Holland in our days. Transactions, negotiations, indecisions have ceased from this morning forth; the Revolution brandishes an axe in one hand, the tri-colored flag in the other. Go at ease: before she lays down that blade, aristocracy will be headless; before she lays aside the red-white-and-blue, Europe will be vanquished. Go, my friends, go!"

"Oh!" said Gilbert, "heaven is my witness that, if the future you foretell be true, I do not regret France; but whither shall we go?"

"Ungrateful man!" exclaimed Cagliostro, "have you forgotten your second country, America? its oceans, lakes, its unprofaned forests, its prairies widespreading as seas? Have you, who need repose, no need of the repose of nature, after the fearful agitations of society?"

"Do you follow me, Billot?" inquired Gilbert, rising.

"Will you forgive me?" asked Billot taking a step towards his friend.

They rushed into one another's arms.

"'Tis well, we will go," said Gilbert.

"When?" inquired Cagliostro.

"In—in a week."

Cagliostro shook his head.

"You will start this evening," said he.

"This evening?"

"This very night."

"Why?"

"Because I go away to-morrow."

"Where?"

"You shall learn one day, friends."

"How are we to go?"

"The 'Franklin' sets sail within thirty-six hours for America."

"But passports?"

"Here."

"My son?"

Cagliostro went and opened the door.

"Come in, Sebastian," said he; "your father calls you."

The young man entered.

Billot heaved a deep sigh.

"We only want a post-carriage," said Gilbert.

"Mine is already at the door," responded Cagliostro.

Gilbert went to a secretary where was locked up the common treasury: a thousand louis, and beckoned Billot to take his share.

"Have we enough?" said Billot.

"We have more than will buy a whole county in the New World."

Billot looked around him with embarrassment.

"What are you seeking, my friend?" inquired Gilbert.

"I am looking," replied Billot, "looking for something which would be useless to me if I did find it, for I do not know how to write."

Gilbert smiled and took out some paper, ink, and pen.

"Dictate," said he.

"I want to send Pitou good-bye," said Billot.

"I will write it out for you," said Gilbert.

He wrote for a moment.

When he had finished, Billot asked him:

"What have you written?"

Gilbert read :

"MY DEAR PITOU :
" Billot, Sebastian and I are about leaving France, and we all three affectionately bid you farewell.
" We thought that, as you are at the head of Billot's farm, you want for nothing.
" Some day, in all likelihood, we will write for you to join us.
   " Your friend,
     " GILBERT."

" Is that all ," inquired Billot.

" There is a postscript," replied Gilbert.
" What is it ?"
Gilbert looked the farmer in the face, and read :

" Billot entrusts Catherine to you."

Billot uttered a grateful exclamation, and squeezed his friend's hand.
Ten minutes afterwards, the postchaise which carried far from Paris Gilbert, Sebastian and Billot, rolled over the Road to Havre.

EPILOGUE.

CHAPTER I.

WHAT ANGE PITOU AND CATHERINE BIL-
LOT WERE DOING ON THE FIFTEENTH
OF FEBRUARY, 1794.

A little more than one year after the execution of Louis the Sixteenth, and the departure of Gilbert, Billot and Sebastian, on a fine, crisp morning in the terrible winter of 1794, three or four hundred persons, the sixth part, very nearly, of the population of Villers Cotterets, were waiting on the castle square and in the yard of the mayor's office, the coming forth of two young betrothed : whom our former acquaintance, M. de Longpre, was uniting in wedlock.

The young couple was Ange Pitou and Catherine Billot.

Alas! many a serious event had to transpire to bring the Viscount de Charny's mistress, little Isidore's mother, to become Madame Ange Pitou.

These events everybody was relating and commenting upon each in his own fashion ; but, tell them and criticise them as they pleased, there was not one of the relations circulating around which was not to the greater glory of Ange Pitou and the wise choice of Catherine Billot.

Only the more interesting the future man and wife was, the more they were compassionated.

Perhaps they were far happier than any of the individuals male or female composing the crowd ; but so a crowd is, it always compassionates or envies,

This day, it was turned to pity, and it pitied.

The events foreseen by Cagliostro on the evening of January the twenty-first, had moved with rapid stride, leaving after them a long, ineffacable stain of blood.

On the first of February, 1793, the National Convention had issued a decree ordering the creation of the sum of eight hundred millions of assignats ; which brought the total amount issued in that currency to the sum of three billions one hundred million.

On the twenty-eighth of March, 1793, the Convention, on Treilhard's motion, had issued a decree which banished forever the self-exiled nobles, declaring them civilly dead, and confiscating their property, to the profit of the Republic.

On the seventh of November, the Convention had issued a decree which charged the committee of public instruction to present a plan tending to substitute a civic, reasonable worship for that of the Catholic religion.

We will not speak here of the death and proscription of the Girondists, nor of the execution of the Duke d'Orleans, of the Queen, of Bailly, Danton, Camille Desmoulins, and many others, such events having their reverberation even in Villers Cotterets, but not their influence over the persons whom it remains for us to dwell upon.

The result of the confiscation of property was that, Billot and Gilbert being considered as emigres, their possessions had been confiscated and put up at sale.

It was the same with the estate of the Count de Charny, slain on the tenth of

August, and of his countess, massacred on the second of September.

In consequence of this decree, Catharine had been put out of the farm at Pisseleu, regarded as national property.

Pitou had a great mind to claim it in Catharine's name; but Pitou had become a " moderate," and was a little " suspected," and wise persons gave him the advice not to oppose in word or action the orders of the nation.

Pitou and Catharine had retired to Haramont.

The young woman had at first the notion of going to live, as in former days, in Pere Clovis's hut; but, when she had presented herself at the door, the ex-huntsman of the Duke of Orleans had laid his finger on his mouth in token of silence, and had shaken his head in token of impossibility.

This impossibility arose from the place being already tenanted.

The law against such of the priests as had not taken the oath had been vigorously put in action, and, as the reader will understand, the Abbe Fortier, not being willing to take the oath, had been banished, or, rather, was banished.

But he had not deemed it seasonable to try to cross the frontier, and his banishment consisted in leaving his dwelling at Villers Cotterets, where he had left Mademoiselle Alexandrine to watch over his goods, and in going to ask of Pere Clovis a shelter which the latter had eagerly given him.

Pere Clovis's hut, it will be recollected, was simply a cave dug in the earth, wherein one person was rather ill at ease; it would have been, therefore, rather difficult to add to the Abbe Fortier Catharine Billot and little Isidore.

The reader will also remember the intolerant conduct of the Abbe Fortier on the death of Mother Billot.

Catharine was not good Christian enough to pardon the abbe for his refusal to bury her mother, and, had she been good Christian enough, the Abbe Fortier was too steadfast a Catholic to forgive her.

Therefore, the idea of being in Pere Clovis's palace had to be given up.

There remained the dwelling of Aunt Angelica at Pleux, and Pitou's little cottage at Haramont.

Aunt Angelica's house was not even to be dreamt of; proportionately to the progress of the Revolution, she had become more and more tart and crabbed, which seemed incredible, and thinner and thinner, which appeared impossible.

This change in her mind and body came from Villers Cotterets having had its churches shut up, waiting until a reasonable public worship should be invented by the committee of instruction.

Now, the churches being closed, the letting of chairs which had been Aunt Angelica's principal revenue fell to nothing.

It was this drying up of her resources which made the old maid thinner and more acerbated than ever.

Let us add that she had so often heard the relation of the Taking of the Bastile by Billot and Ange Pitou, she had so often seen, at the period of the great doings at Paris, the farmer and her nephew set out suddenly for Paris, that she never doubted but that the French Revolution was led by Ange Pitou and Billot, and that Citizens Danton, Marat and Robespierre and others were merely secondary agents to those principal leaders.

Mademoiselle Alexandrine, as a matter of course, encouraged her in the ideas, however erroneous, to which Billot's regicidal vote had given all the hateful exaltation of fanaticism.

So Catharine was not to think of going to Aunt Angelica.

There remained Pitou's little cottage at Haramont.

But how could two, and even three, inhabit that little place without giving rise to the worst talk?

This was still more impossible than to live in Pere Clovis's hut.

Pitou had therefore made up his mind to ask hospitality of his friend, Desire Maniquet; hospitality which the worthy Haramonter granted him, and which Pitou repaid by all sorts of work.

But all this did not give poor Catharine a position.

Pitou had for her all the attention of a friend, all the affection of a brother; but Catharine was clearly aware that it was neither as friend nor as brother that Pitou loved her.

Little Isidore, poor child, felt something of this as well, and not having the joy of knowing his father, he loved Pitou as he would have loved the Count de Charny, better perhaps; for, it must be said, Pitou was the worshipper of the mother, the slave of the boy. It seemed that he, like a cunning strategist, comprehended that there was but one way of entering Catharine's heart: through Isidore.

But let us hasten to state, no calculation of this species tarnished the purity of honest Pitou's feelings.

Pitou had grown up what we saw him, the simple, devoted lad of this book's first chapters, and, if any change had taken place in him, it was that, on attaining his majority, Pitou had become perhaps more devoted and candid than ever.

All these qualities touched Catharine.

She felt that Pitou loved her ardently, even to worshipping her, almost to fanaticism, and at times she would say she would she could repay such a great love, so complete a devotion by some feeling more tender than friendship.

Thus, it came to pass that, little by little, Catharine—feeling herself, apart from Pitou, perfectly isolated in the world; plainly seeing that, if she should die, her poor boy would be alone, apart from Pitou again, Catharine had reached the point of giving Pitou the single recompense which was in her power: all her friendship and her person.

Alas! her love, that bright, sweet-scented blossom of youth, was now in heaven!

Nearly six months had gone by during which Catharine, not yet settled in her thought, kept it in a corner of her mind, rather than in the depths of her heart.

During that half year, Pitou, although greeted every day with a sweeter smile, and dismissed every evening with a more affectionate pressure of the hand, had never had even the idea that there was taking place, in Catharine's sentiments, such a return in his favor.

But, as it was not in the hope of a reward that Pitou had devoted himself and loved; Pitou, though ignorant of Catharine's dwelling upon him, was only the deeper devoted to her, and only the more enamored of her.

This would have thus gone on till the death of two—had Pitou reached the age of Philemon and Catharine that of Baucis—without the faintest alteration in the heart-workings of the captain of the National Guard of Haramont.

Therefore, Catharine had to speak first, as do all women.

One evening, instead of holding out her hand to him, she presented her forehead.

Pitou fancied this to arise from Catharine's absent mind; he was too honorable a man to profit by it.

He drew back a step.

But Catharine had not released his hand; she drew him to her, no longer presenting her forehead to him, but her cheek.

Still Pitou hesitated.

Which seeing, little Isidore began crying:

"Why won't you kiss mamma Catharine, papa Pitou?"

Pitou muttered some unintelligible words, while turning pale as if he were going to die.

And he pressed his cold, bloodless and quivering lips on Catharine's cheek.

Taking up her boy, then Catharine put him in Pitou's arms.

"I give you the child, Pitou; will you take the mother with him?" said she.

Pitou's head swam, he closed his eyes, and while pressing the boy on his breast, he fell upon a seat, exclaiming with that delicacy of the heart which the heart alone can appreciate:

"Oh, Monsieur Isidore! dear Monsieur Isidore, how I love you!"

Isidore called Pitou "papa Pitou," but the young man called the son of the Viscount de Charny "Monsieur Isidore."

Then as he felt that it was especially through love for her child that Billot's daughter had come to love him, he said what we have recorded, not:

"Oh, how I love you, Mademoiselle Catharine !"

This point settled, that Pitou loved Isidore better thar he did Catharine, marriage was spoken of.

Pitou said to the young woman:

"I shall not press you, Mademoiselle Catharine ; take all the leisure you like ; but, if you mean to make me quite happy, do not take too long !"

Catharine took a month.

At the end of three weeks, Pitou, in full uniform, went respectfully to pay a visit to Aunt Angelica, with the intention of imparting to her the intelligence of his near at-hand union with Mademoiselle Catharine Billot.

The old maid saw her nephew coming from a distance, and hastened to fasten her door.

But the young man continued none the less to step up to the inhospitable door, at which he rapped gently.

"Who's there?" challenged the old maid in her roughest voice.

"I, your nephew, Aunt Angelica."

"Go on your way, Septembrist!" said the old maid.

"Aunt," continued Pitou, "I come to announce to you a bit of news which cannot fail to be pleasing to you, in asmuch as it tends to my happiness ! '

"What is your piece of news, you Jacobin?"

"Open the door to me, and I will tell it to you."

"Say it through the door ; I will not open my house to a sans-culotte like you."

"Is that all you have to say, aunt of mine ?"

"It's my last word."

"Well, my dear little aunt, I am going to get married."

The door flew open as by enchantment.

"With whom, wretch?" inquired his affectionate relation.

"With Mademoiselle Catharine Billot," replied Pitou.

"Oh, the wretch ! the fool ! the jolterhead !" cried Aunt Angelica, "he is going to marry a—avaunt, wretch, I curse you!"

With a gesture full of labored greatness, the speaker stretched out her yellow, withered hands against her nephew.

"Aunt," said Pitou, "you must know well that I am too used to your maledictions for this one to affect me more than the others. Now, I owed you the politeness of announcing my marriage ; I have announced it, the polite act is performed ; I wish you good bye, Aunt Angelica."

Upon which, the young man, bringing his hand militarily to his three-cornered hat, saluted his kind relation, and resumed his way through Pleux Lane.

CHAPTER II.

OF THE EFFECT ON AUNT ANGELICA FROM HEF NEPHEW'S MARRIAGE WITH CATHARINE BILLOT.

PITOU had gone to inform of his future marriage M. de Longpre, who dwelt in the Rue de l'Ormet.

This gentleman, less prejudiced against the Billot family than the old maid, congratulated the young man on the good act he was performing.

Pitou was in wonderment while he listened, not comprehending how, whilst making his own happiness, he should be doing at the same time a good act.

Pitou, a pure republican, was more than ever grateful to the republic, from its having suppressed the publishing of bans and such ceremonies, by the act of suppressing marriages in churches.

It was therefore agreed between Pitou and M. de Longpre that, on the following Saturday, Catharine Billot and Ange Pitou should be united at the mayor's office.

It was on the ensuing day, Sunday, that was to take place, by adjudication, the sale of the farm of Piselue and the Castle of Boursonne.

The farm was estimated at the cost of four hundred thousand francs, and the castle at six hundred thousand francs in assignats.

The paper money was commencing to

sink frightfully : the louis of gold was worth nine hundred and twenty francs in paper.

But nobody had gold.

Pitou went back on a run to announce the good news to Catharine. He had allowed himself to advance by two days the period fixed for the wedding, and he had great fear that this anticipation would not suit his intended.

But the latter did not appear to be in the least offended, and the young man was in heaven.

Only, Catharine exacted that Pitou should pay a second visit to his aunt, to announce to her the precise day of the nuptials, and to invite her to attend the ceremony.

This was the only kinsfolk Pitou had, and, albeit she was no wonderfully affectionate one, Pitou should perform all the prescribed duties.

Consequently on Friday morning, Pitou set out for Villers Cotterets, with the design of making a second visit to his aunt.

Nine o'clock struck as he arrived in sight of the house.

This time, no Aunt Angelica was on the threshold, and, as though she had expected Pitou, the door was closed.

The young man fancied she had gone out, and was delighted at the lucky chance.

His visit was made, and a very tender and respectful note would replace the speech he had been reckoning he would have to make.

But, as Pitou was a very conscientious lad, he knocked at the door, tightly closed as it was, and no one replying to his knocks, he called out.

At the double noise Pitou made with fist and voice, a neighbor appeared.

"Ha, Mother Fagot," inquired Pitou, "do you know whether my aunt has gone out?"

"Hasn't she answered?" counter-queried Mother Fagot.

"No, you see ; no doubt, she's not at home."

The woman shook her head.

"I should have seen her go out," she remarked ; "my door opens on hers, and it's very seldom when she get up in the morning, that she don't come into our place to get a little warm ashes in her shoes ; with which, poor dear soul, she keeps herself warm all day—ain't that so, neighbor Farolet?"

This interpollation was addressed to a fresh actor who, in turn opening his door at the noise, came to have a hand, or rather a voice, in the conversation.

"What were you saying, Madame Fagot?"

"I said Aunt Angelica had not gone out. Did you see her go out?"

"No, and I'm sure she's still at home, inasmuch as, if she were up and out, her shutters would be open."

"True, so they would," agreed Pitou. "Goodness, can there have happened anything ill to my poor aunt?"

"It's very likely," said Mother Fagot.

"It is more than likely, it's probable," observed Farolet sententiously.

"'Pon my word, she was not so very kind to me," said Pitou ; "but, never mind than, I would not like any misfortune to have befallen her. How can we find out?"

"Pooh !" broke in a third neighbor, "that's no difficult matter ; you've only to send for Rigolet, the locksmith."

"If you want him to open the door," said Pitou, "that would be lost labor ; I have the knack of opening the lock with my knife."

"Well, open it, my boy," said Monsieur Farolet; "we are here to prove that you did not open it with any evil intention."

Pitou drew out his jack-knife.

In the presence of some dozen persons, attracted by the occurrence, he stepped up to the door, and, with a dexterity which proved that more than once he had used this method to enter the domicile of his youth he slipped a blade of it into the keyhole, and turned his knife.

The door opened.

The room was in the deepest obscurity.

But, the door having been widely opened, the dawn struggled into it gradually—the sad, greyish light of a winter's morning—and, by this light, faint though it was, might be distinguished on the bed the form of the old maid.

Pitou twice called out:

"Aunt Angelica!"

But the couched form remained unmoving, and without a word.

Pitou stepped up to the body which he touched.

"Oh," exclaimed he, "she is cold, and stiff!"

The windows was flung open.

Aunt Angelica was dead.

"This is dreadful!" said Pitou.

"No great loss to you," observed Farolet; "the woman never thought much of you, my boy."

"It's possible," said Pitou; "but I was fond of her."

Tears, large and running fast, fell down the worthy fellow's cheeks.

"Oh, my poor Aunt Angelica!" said he.

He fell on his knees beside the bed.

"Say, Monsieur Pitou," said Mother Fagot, "if you have need of anything, we are ready to help you. A neighbor is a neighbor, you know!"

"Thank you, Mother Fagot. Is your boy at hand?"

"Yes. Here, Fagotin!" called the good woman.

A boy of fourteen made his appearance on the threshold of the door.

"Here I am, mother," he said.

"Well," said Pitou, "beg your lad to run to Haramont, and tell Catharine that she is not to be uneasy, but that I found Aunt Angelica dead, poor aunt!"

Pitou wiped away some fresh tears.

"And that that is what is keeping me at Villers Cotterets," added he.

"You hear, Fagotin?" said Mother Fagot.

"Yes."

"Well, make yourself scarce."

"Go through the Rue de Soissons," remarked the sententious Farolet, "and warn Monsieur Raynal that there's a case of sudden death to be looked into at Aunt Angelica's."

"Do you hear?"

"Yes, mother," replied the boy.

With what, taking to his heels, he darted off in the direction of the Rue de Soissons, which formed a continuation of Pleux Lane.

The crowd had been increased; there were all of a hundred persons now before the door; each expressing his or her opinion on the old maid's death, some leaning to the idea of apoplexy, others for a rupture of the vessels of the heart, while others again were decided it was consumption at the last stage.

All were muttering:

"If Pitou is not a dull fellow, he will find a nice pile on the top shelf of a cupboard, in a pot of butter, or in a bed or in an old rag."

While all this was going on, Doctor Raynal arrived, preceded by the receiver general.

The question was of what had the old maid d ed.

Doctor Raynal entered, went up to the bed, examined the body, and declared, to the high amazement of the beholders, that Aunt Angelica had died simply of cold and, in every likelihood, of starvation.

Pitou's tears redoubled on this declaration.

"Oh, poor aunt, poor aunt!" groaned he; "there was I thinking her rich! I am a wretch for having abandoned her! Oh, if I had only known it! It cannot be, Monsieur Raynal, cannot be!"

"Look in the cupboard, and find me a scrap of food; hunt over the house and fetch me a stick. I have always foretold that the old starve-mouse would die off in this way."

Search was made.

There was not a crumb of bread in the cupboard, nor was there a splinter of fire-wood in the place.

"Oh, had I but known this!" exclaimed Pitou; "I would have brought from the forest enough wood to keep her warm; I would have poached to keep her in provisions. It's your fault," continued the poor youth, accusing those around him, "your fault; why did you not tell me she was poor?"

"We did not tell you she was poor, Monsieur Pitou," responded Farolet, "for the very simple reason that everybody believed her sick."

Doctor Raynal had drawn the sheet over the dead woman's head and was proceeding towards the door.

Pitou ran to him.

"Are you going, Doctor Raynal!" inquired he.

"What would you have me do here, my boy?"

"Is she really dead?"

The doctor nodded.

"Oh, good heaven!" cried Pitou; "and dead with cold, and hunger!"

M. Raynal beckoned the young man, and the latter obeyed.

"Lad," said he to him, "I none the less advise you to search high and low—you understand?"

"But Monsieur Raynal, since she died of want, cold and hunger——"

"Misers have been known," returned Doctor Raynal, "to have drawn their last breath, lying on their treasure."

Then laying a finger on his lips he said:

"Hush!"

And went out.

CHAPTER III.

AUNT ANGELICA'S ARMCHAIR.

PITOU would have perchance reflected most deeply on what Doctor Raynal had first said, if he had not seen in the distance Catharine, running with her son in her arms.

Since his neighbors had learnt that, according to all probability, the young man's relation had perished by cold and starvation, their eagerness to pay her the last duties had become a little less great.

Catharine, therefore, came wonderfully seasonably.

She declared that, looking upon herself as Pitou's wife, it was she who should attend to the dead woman, which she did with all the respect which, eighteen months before, she had, poor creature, paid to her mother.

Pitou, during this time, went to order everything requisite for the burial, which had to be put off two days, the fact of sudden death compelling the body to remain above ground for eight-and-forty hours.

He had only to arrange with the mayor, coffinmaker and gravedigger, religious ceremonies being suppressed with respect to interments as well as to marriages.

"My friend," said Catharine to Pitou, as he took up his hat to go to M. de Longpre's office, "after the accident just happened will it not be better to put off our wedding for a day or two?"

"It's just as you like to say, Mademoiselle Catharine," returned Pitou.

"Will not folks find it singular if, on the very same day as that you bury your aunt, you should accomplish so important an act as your marriage?"

"Very important to me, in truth," said Pitou, "forasmuch as it is for my happiness."

"Well, my friend, go consult M. de Longpre, and, whatsoever he advises you to do, do."

"Very well, Mademoiselle Catharine."

"And then this marrying on the edge of the grave might bring us misfortune——"

"From the moment when I shall be your husband," said Pitou, "I defy bad luck to look at me."

"Defer it till Monday, dear Pitou," said Catharine, holding out her hand. "You see that I am trying to make your wishes fit the requirements of the case as much as possible."

"But, two days, Mademoiselle Catharine, that's a long while!"

"What!" exclaimed the young woman, "when one has waited five years——"

"A great many things may happen in forty-eight hours," said Pitou.

"It cannot happen that I should love you less, my dear Pitou, and, as that is, as you assert, the only thing that you have to fear——"

"The only one! oh, yes, the only one, Mademoiselle Catharine."

"Well, in that case—Isidore."

"Mamma," answered the boy.

"Say to papa Pitou: 'Don't be afraid, papa Pitou; mamma loves you dearly, and will love you always.'"

And the little child repeated this in his weak, sweet voice.

On this assurance, Pitou made no further remonstrance against going to M. de Longpre's.

Pitou returned at the end of an hour's time; he regulated everything, burial and marriage, paying all in advance.

With what was left of his money, he had purchased a little wood and provisions for two days.

It was time for the wood to come.

In that wretched house, which the wind entered from every side, death by freezing was nothing out of the way.

On his return, Pitou found Catharine half frozen.

The marriage, according to the young woman's desire, had been postponed until Monday.

The two days and nights elapsed without the two young people being separate for an instant. They spent the two nights, watching by the bedside of the dead woman.

Notwithstanding the roaring fire which Pitou had taken care to kindle in the chimney-place, the sharp, biting air penetrated, and Pitou acknowledged that, if his aunt had not died of hunger, it was not a bit improbable that cold had taken her away.

The time came to remove the body.

The transportation was not to be a long one: Aunt Angelica's house almost adjoined the cemetery.

The whole of the population of Pleux Lane and part of the town followed the defunct to her last home.

In the country parts of France women follow the dead: Pitou and Catharine led the mourners.

The ceremony being terminated, Pitou thanked the assistants in the name of the dead woman and of himself; and after having sprinkled holy water over the old maid's grave, every one, as is customary, filed before Pitou.

Remaining alone with Catherine, Pitou turned towards where he had left her.

She was gone.

He found her on her knees, with little Isidore, on a grave at each of the four corners of which rose a cypress tree.

This grave was Mother Billot's.

The four cypresses had been dug up by Pitou in the forest, and transplanted there.

He did not like to disturb Catharine in such a pious occupation; but, thinking how cold Catharine would be when her prayer should have been finished, he ran on to his house with the intention of making an enormous fire.

Unfortunately, one thing opposed him realizing this good intention : since morning, his stock of firewood had been exhausted.

Pitou scratched his head.

The rest of his money, it will be called to mind, had gone toward provisions and the wood.

Pitou looked about him, seeking some article of furniture which he might sacrifice under the temporary pressure.

There was his aunt's bed, cupboard, and armchair.

The former articles, without having great value, were, nevertheless, not beyond service ; but it was a long while since anybody, except its owner, had ever ventured to sit in the rickety armchair, so out of joint was it.

The chair was therefore doomed.

Pitou proceeded like the revolutionary tribunal : hardly was the armchair doomed, than it was to be executed.

Pitou pressed his knee on the cushion, black with age, caught with both hands one of the arms and pulled to him.

At the third tug, it gave way.

The chair, as though it underwent some pain at this dismemberment, gave vent to a plaintive groan.

Had Pitou been superstitious, he might have believed the soul of the former owner was enclosed in her armchair.

But Pitou had only one superstition in the world ; to wit, his love for Catharine.

The chair was condemned to warm Catharine, and if it had shed as much blood and uttered as many complaints as the enchanted trees in Tasso's wood, the armchair would have been broken to bits.

Pitou therefore, grasped the second

arm with as vigorous a grip as he had caught the first and, with a similar effort to his previous one, he tore it from its connection, which was dreadfully dislocated,

The chair emitted the same strange sound, somewhat metallic.

Pitou remained pitiless.

He lifted up by the leg the mutilated mass, swung it around his head, and, to make short work of it, brought it down with all his might against the floor.

This time the armchair split in two and, to Master Pitou's high amazement, through the yawning gap vomited, not a flood of blood, but masses of gold coin.

The reader will instantly remember how, when Aunt Angelica used to save up eight louis in silver, she used to change that amount for a louis of gold, and introduce that louis in the armchair.

Pitou stood aghast, ready to drop with surprise, bewildered with astonishment.

His first thought was to run for Catharine and little Isidore, bring them both there and display to them the treasure which he had discovered.

But a fearful reflection checked him.

Would Catharine, learning he was rich, still be willing to wed him?

He shook his head.

"No, no," said he, "she will refuse."

He remained for an instant motionless, pondering and thoughtful.

Then a smile ran over his countenance.

Beyond a doubt, he had found some way to rid himself of the embarrassment into which he had been thrown by this sudden accession to such unexpected wealth.

He picked up the louis that had fallen out, finished the cutting up of the chair with his knife, seeking in the most remote corners and pulling apart the horsehair stuffing.

All was packed with gold.

There was quite enough to fill the earthenware pot wherein Aunt Angelica had cooked that famous chanticleer which had brought to pass, between the aunt and the nephew, the terrible scene which in its time and place we have related.

Pitou counted the louis.

He found fifteen hundred and fifty!

Pitou was therefore worth thirty-seven thousand two hundred livres.

Now, as the gold louis was worth at this epoch nine hundred francs-livres in assignats, Pitou was worth one million three hundred and twenty-six thousand livres!

And at what a moment had this colossal fortune come to him?

When he was obliged, having no more money to buy wood, to break up, to warm Catharine, the furniture.

How lucky it was that Pitou had been so poor, the weather so cold, and the arm chair so old!

Who knows, had it not been for this concomitance of events fatal in appearance, what would have become of the so precious armchair?

Pitou began by stuffing his pockets with louis; then, after having eagerly shaken every fragment of the chair, he shivered the larger pieces, built a fire, managed with great trouble to strike fire, and with a nervous hand, lit the pile.

It was time he did so!

Catharine and little Isidore entered, blue and shivering with cold.

Pitou pressed the child to his breast, kissed Catharine's benumbed hands and ran out, crying:

"I have an indispensable act to do; warm yourselves and wait for me."

"Where is papa Pitou going?" inquired Isidore.

"I do not know," replied his mother; "but, surely, when he runs so fast, it is to do something, not for himself, but for you or me."

Catherine might have said:

"For you *and* me."

CHAPTER IV.

WHAT PITOU DID WITH THE LOUIS FOUND IN THE ARMCHAIR.

THE reader has not forgotten that it was on the following day that was to commence at public auction the sale of Billot's farm and the chateau of the Count de Charny.

It will also be recalled that the farm was estimated at the sum of four hundred thousand francs, and the castle at six hundred thousand, in assignats.

When the day dawned, Mayor Longpre bought, for an unknown bidder, the two lots for the sum of three hundred and fifty louis d'ors, in other words, for a million, two hundred and forty-two thousand francs in assignats.

He paid down on the nail.

This took place on Sunday, the eve of the day on which was to take place the wedding of Pitou and Catharine.

The latter, early on this Sunday, had set out for Haramont, either to procure some little ornament which the simplest female will do on her marriage eve, or because she did not want to stay in the town, while there was being sold that fine farm wherein had passed her youth, where she had been so happy, had suffered so much !

At eleven o'clock on the following day, the whole crowd gathered before the door of the mayor's office, were bewailing and so deeply praising Pitou for having married a girl so completely poverty-stricken—who, over and above that, had a child, which, missing its chance of being one day better off than she, was now much worse off !

Meanwhile, M. de Longpre asked, as usual, of Pitou :

" Citizen Pierre Ange Pitou, do you take for your wife the Citizeness Anne Catharine Billot ?

And of Catharine Billot :

" Citizeness Anne Catharine Billot, do you take for your husband the Citizen Pierre Ange Pitou ?"

Both had answered.

" Yes."

When both had answered with the " yes," Pitou in a voice full of emotion, Catharine in one of serenity ; when

M. de Longpre had proclaimed, in the name of the law, that the two young people were united in wedlock, he beckoned little Isidore to come to him.

The boy put up on the mayor's desk, came to him.

" My child," said Mayor Longpre, " here are papers which you will hand to your mamma Catharine, when your papa Pitou shall have taken you home."

" Yes, sir," the boy had replied.

And he grasped the two papers in his little hand.

All was over.

However, to the high surprise of the bystanders, Pitou drew from his pocket five louis in gold and, handing them to the mayor, said :

" For the poor, Monsieur le Maire."

Catharine smiled.

" Are we so rich ?" she inquired.

" One is always rich when one is happy, Catharine," rejoined Pitou ; " and you have just made me the richest man in the world."

With that, he offered her his arm, on which his wife tenderly leant.

On going forth, they found that crowd of which we have spoken at the door of the mayor's office.

It greeted the young couple by unanimous cheers.

Pitou thanked his friends and gave any amount of handshaking.

Catharine smiled to her friends, and nodded times beyond count.

Meanwhile, Pitou had turned to the right.

" Whither go you, friend ?" inquired Catharine.

Indeed, if Pitou was returning to Haramont, he ought to take the left hand course by the park.

If he meant to return to Aunt Angelica's house, he should have followed the right, by way of the Castle Square.

Where was he going by descending towards the Fountain Square ?

This is what Catharine asked him.

" Come, my dearly beloved," said Pitou ; " I am going to lead you to visit a place which you will be very well pleased to see again."

She let him conduct her.

" Where are they going ?" inquired such as were watching them go.

Pitou crossed the Place de la Fontaine without stopping on it, took the Rue de l'Ormet, and, on reaching the end of that street, turned up the little lane where six years previously, he had met Catharine on her donkey, on that day when, driven from home by Aunt Angelica, he knew not of whom to beg shelter.

"I hope we are not going to Pisseleu?" inquired Catharine.

"Come on, Catharine," returned Pitou.

The young woman uttered a sigh, followed the little lane, and entered the plain.

At the end of ten minutes' walk, they had arrived on the little bridge at which Pitou had found her fainted on the night of Isidore's departure for Paris.

There, Catharine stopped.

"Pitou," said she, "I can go no farther."

"Oh, Mademoiselle Catharine," appealed Pitou, "as far as the hollow willow-tree only!"

This was the tree wherein Pitou had come to seek Isidore's letters.

Catharine gave another sigh, and continued her road.

On reaching the tree, she said:

"Let us return, I implore you!"

But the young man laying his hand upon his wife's arm, said:

"A few steps farther, Mademoiselle Catharine; I only will beg that."

"Ah, Pitou?" murmured Catharine in so painful a tone of reproach, that the young man stopped in his turn.

"Oh, mademoiselle," said he, "I was fancying this would make you quite happy!"

"Did you think to make me happy, Pitou, by making me see again a farm where I was brought up, which had belonged to my parents, which ought to belong to me, and which, sold yesterday, belongs now to some stranger whose name I do not even know."

"Mademoiselle Catharine, fifty yards farther; I will only ask that."

A score of steps, indeed, turning the corner of a wall, unmasked the main gateway of the farm.

There were grouped all the former farmhands, ploughboys, stableboys, dairymaids, women of the farm, Pere Clovis at the head.

Each held a bouquet in his or her hand.

"Ah, I understand," said Catharine, "before the new owner arrives, you wanted to bring me a last time here, so that all the old servants could bid me farewell. Thank you, Pitou!"

Leaving her husband's arm and little Isidore's hand, she went up to the assemblage, the people forming which surrounded her and dragged her into the great hall of the farmhouse.

Pitou took up little Isidore in his arms—the child still held in hand the two papers—and followed his wife.

The latter was seated in the middle of the main hall, pressing her head between her hands, as when one awakes from a dream.

"In heaven's name, Pitou," exclaimed she, her eyes showing surprise and her voice feverish, "what are they saying to me? My friend, I do not understand what they are saying."

"Perhaps the papers which our son will give you will teach you something, dear Catharine," said Pitou.

He pushed Isidore towards his mother.

Catharine took the two papers from the child's little hand.

"Read," said Pitou.

The young woman opened one of the papers at random, and read:

"This certifies that the Chateau of Boursonne and the grounds dependant upon it were bought from and paid for to me, the undersigned, yesterday on account of Jacques Philippe Isidore, minor son of Mademoiselle Catharine Billot, and that, consequently, to this child the said Chateau of Boursonne, and the said grounds in dependence on it, belong by right:

"*Signed:*
"De Longpre,"
"Mayor of Villers Cotterets."

"What does this mean, Pitou?" inquired the reader. "You ought to see that I cannot understand one word of all this!"

"Read the other paper," said Pitou.

Catharine unfolding the second sheet, read as follows :

"This certifies that the Farm of Pisseleu and its appurtenances were bought from and paid for to me yesterday, on account of Citizeness Anne Catharine Billot, and that, consequently, to her belongs by right the Farm of Pisseleu and all its appurtenances.

"*Signed :*
"DE LONGPRE.
"Mayor of Villers Cotterets.

"In heaven's name!" cried Catharine, "tell me what this means, or I shall go mad!"

"This means," returned Pitou, "that —thanks to fifteen hundred and fifty louis in gold which I found day before yesterday in my Aunt Angelica's old armchair, which I had to break up to warm you on your return from the funeral — the grounds and castle of Boursonne will not go out of the Charny family, nor the Farm of Pisseleu and its land out of the Billot family."

Thereupon, Pitou gave his wife a full account of what we have related to the reader.

"Oh!" said Catharine, "and did you have the courage to burn up that old armchair, dear Pitou ; when you had so many louis to go and buy wood with them?"

"Catharine," replied the young man, "you were coming home ; you would have been forced to wait, before warming yourselves, until the wood could have been bought and brought, and you would have been cold while waiting."

Catharine opened her arms.

Pitou lifted up little Isidore to them.

"You, too! you, too, dear Pitou!" said Catharine.

With the same clasp, she embraced her son and her husband.

"To think," muttered Pitou, choking with joy, and at the same time shedding a last tear to the old maid, "to think that she should have died of cold and hunger! Poor Aunt Angelica!"

"'Pon my word," observed a stout wagoner to a fresh, rosy-cheeked dairymaid, as he pointed to Pitou and Catharine, "yonder pair do not seem to me to be fated to die of any such death!"

THE END.

www.ingramcontent.com/pod-product-compliance
Lightning Source LLC
Chambersburg PA
CBHW060427030726
47495CB00003B/769

* 9 7 8 1 4 1 0 1 0 0 6 0 3 *